**It's the season to let miracles ~~and~~
marriage wa~~...~~**

Christmas
Village

A fabulous collection brought to you
by Caroline Anderson, Sarah Morgan,
Josie Metcalfe & Jennifer Taylor

Christmas in the Village

Caroline Anderson
Sarah Morgan
Josie Metcalfe
Jennifer Taylor

Mills & Boon, an imprint of Harlequin (UK) Limited, Eton House, 18-24 Paradise Road, Richmond, Surrey TW9 1SR

CHRISTMAS IN THE VILLAGE
© Harlequin Enterprises II B.V./S.à.r.l. 2011

Christmas Eve Baby © Caroline Anderson 2007
The Italian's New-Year Marriage Wish © Sarah Morgan 2007
The Doctor's Bride By Sunrise © Josie Metcalfe 2007
The Surgeon's Fatherhood Surprise © Jennifer Taylor 2008

ISBN: 978 0 263 89668 8

024-1211

Harlequin (UK) policy is to use papers that are natural, renewable and recyclable products and made from wood grown in sustainable forests. The logging and manufacturing processes conform to the legal environmental regulations of the country of origin.

Printed and bound in Spain
by Blackprint CPI, Barcelona

Christmas Eve Baby

CAROLINE ANDERSON

Caroline Anderson has the mind of a butterfly. She's been a nurse, a secretary, a teacher, run her own soft-furnishing business and now she's settled on writing. She says, "I was looking for that elusive something. I finally realised it was variety and now I have it in abundance. Every book brings new horizons and new friends and in between books I have learned to be a juggler. My teacher husband John and I have two beautiful and talented daughters, Sarah and Hannah, umpteen pets and several acres of Suffolk that nature tries to reclaim every time we turn our backs!" Caroline also writes for the Mills & Boon® Cherish™ and the Mills & Boon® Medical series.

CHAPTER ONE

Early May

'LUCY.'

'Ben!' She spun around, her heart tripping and a smile she couldn't hold breaking out at the sound of his voice. 'I didn't think you'd come.'

Hoped, yes, stupidly much, even though she'd known it was an outside chance, but here he was, the answer to a maiden's prayers—well, hers, at least—and her knees had turned to mush.

'Oh, you know me, ever the sucker,' he replied with that lazy, sexy grin that unravelled her insides. 'I had my arm twisted by one of my patients, and it would have been churlish to refuse. Besides, if I remember rightly, the food's amazing.'

So, he hadn't come to see her, then, but what had she expected? Two years was a long time, and so very much had happened. Too much.

Stifling the strangely crushing disappointment, she looked away from those piercing eyes the colour of a summer sky and glanced behind her at the barbeque. 'It certainly smells fabulous. I wonder when we can get stuck in? I haven't eaten since breakfast, and that was before seven.'

'Sounds as if your day's been like mine,' he murmured, and she realised he'd moved closer. Much closer, so that she could not only hear his voice more clearly, but smell the clean, fresh scent of his skin. He never wore aftershave, but he didn't need to, not to enhance him, because the combination of soap and freshly laundered clothes, underscored by warm, healthy man, was a potent combination.

She felt herself sway a little towards him and wrenched herself back upright. 'Sorry—my heels are sinking into the grass,' she said, not untruthfully, but it gave her an excuse to shift her position and move a fraction away from him. Just far enough so she couldn't smell that intoxicating blend of citrus and musk.

'So—how are you?' he asked, his voice still soft, and even though she knew it was silly, that it didn't matter how nice he was to her, her heart opened up to his gentle enquiry.

'Oh—you know.'

His smile was wry. 'No, I don't, or I wouldn't be asking. How's general practice working out?'

She tried to inject some enthusiasm into her voice. 'It's fine. Great. I was on call last night and I had a surgery this morning, so I'm a bit tired today, but it's OK. I'm really getting into it.'

'Pity.'

She tipped her head and looked up at him curiously. 'Why?'

'My registrar's leaving—decided for some reason to throw away a promising career in favour of maternity. I don't suppose I can tempt you back to A and E?'

Oh, she was tempted. So tempted. To work alongside him again—well, opposite him, to be exact, their heads and hands synchronised, fighting together to save a patient against all odds, their eyes meeting from time to time, his crinkling with that gorgeous, knee-melting smile—but there were too many reasons why not, and one of them was insurmountable, at least for now if not for ever.

She shook her head regretfully and tried to smile. 'Sorry, Ben. Anyway, I still get to do emergency medicine, and we've got a really busy minor injuries unit.'

'What, sprains and jellyfish stings with the odd heart attack thrown in for good measure?' he teased. 'That isn't emergency medicine, Lucy.'

'We do more than that, and it's enough drama for me,' she said, ignoring the little bit of her that was yelling *liar!* at the top of its voice. 'And anyway, we've been thinking about expanding. We're already too busy in our minor injuries unit, so why not expand and make it a state-of-the-art MIU? Still walking wounded, but a bit more sophisticated than what we've got. Maybe have a dedicated space for one of the community physios instead of her just sharing the nurses' room, and ideally get our own X-ray—I don't know. And while we're at it, expand our minor surgery. We'll have to talk to the trust—see if we can convince them it's a good idea. We could take some of the heat off St Piran, especially in the summer with all the tourists.'

She was babbling, trying to ignore the bit of her that was screaming *Yes, take me back!* but he was listening as if she wasn't talking utter rubbish, and he nodded slowly.

'Sounds as if you've given it a lot of thought, and it certainly makes sense. Our A and E's running flat out, and if you've got good minor surgical facilities as well, that's all to the good. You'd need that for all the stitching of wounds in the MIU, and you could maybe take on some more complex minor surgery. I'm sure they do loads of things in the day surgery unit that don't really need a GA. If the simpler things could be done out in the community under local anaesthetic, it would shorten the waiting list, but the X-ray idea's brilliant. People often sit for hours just to be told they've got a sprain. If you could filter some of those out, maybe put casts on undisplaced fractures or reduce the odd dislocation, it could really take the heat off us. I like it. I like it a lot. I'm all for people being seen quicker and closer to home, and I'd be happy to help in any way I could.'

'I may well take you up on that in your new capacity as head honcho of A and E,' she said with a smile, her heart giddy at the idea of working with him again in any capacity at all. 'All I have to do is convince the bean counters.'

He grinned. 'I wish you luck,' he said drily. 'Whatever, I'm more than happy to advise you, if you want, and if you need any help with leaning on anyone in the primary care trust or the hospital trust for funding, give me a shout. I won't guarantee I've got any influence, but you're welcome to what little I have.' He hesitated for a moment, then added softly, 'I see your father's here. How is he, Lucy?'

Oh, lord. Her father. She shook her head slowly. 'I'm not sure, really. Sometimes he seems fine. Other times he's moody and preoccupied, as if he's still sad inside. I just get the feeling he hasn't let go. Hasn't grieved properly. I mean, it's been nearly two years, Ben, but he still doesn't talk about Mum. Not naturally, in conversation. And I want to talk about her. She was my mother, I loved her. I don't want to forget her.' She looked round, spotting her father at the barbeque, turning sausages and talking to Kate.

Kate was the backbone of the practice, his practice manager and her mother's friend. His friend first, from way back when, but nothing more than that. Sometimes she wondered if Kate would have liked it to be more, but she didn't think there was any chance of that. Not on her father's side, at least. Not unless he could move on.

'I didn't know if he'd be here. Do you think he'll object to my presence?'

'No,' she said quickly, although she wasn't sure. 'Don't be silly. It's a fundraiser, you have every right to be here. Besides, you haven't done anything wrong, and you don't have to talk to him.'

'No, I suppose not. I just didn't want to make him uncomfortable.'

She shrugged. 'It's his problem, not yours. Anyway, he's got other things to think about, and so's Kate Althorp, our practice manager. That's her, next to him—dark hair, in the pale pink top.'

'Yes, I've met her in the past. Nice woman.'

'She is. She practically runs this thing every year. Did you know her husband James was our lifeboat coxswain? She lost him, and Dad lost his father and brother, in the storm in '98.'

His brow creased into a frown. 'I didn't know that. I wasn't living here at the time, and the names didn't mean anything to me. I just remember there was a group of schoolchildren studying the rockpools and they were cut off by the tide, and some of the rescuers died.'

Lucy pointed across the harbour to the headland jutting out, crowned by the lighthouse and the church. 'It was over there.'

He was looking at the headland, his brow furrowed. 'What

on earth were the kids doing out there anyway? Weren't they supervised?'

'Oh, yes, but the teacher's watch had stopped and they didn't realise the tide was coming in until it was too late. Add in the huge sea, and you get a disaster.'

'Absolutely. I'm sorry, I didn't realise any of them were connected to you. I just remember one of them was a local doctor.'

She nodded. 'My uncle. They were trying to rescue the children from the bottom of the cliff over there, and it all went wrong. Phil—my uncle—had abseiled down the rocks and got most of them up, but the storm had got really wild by then and he was swept off the cliff by a huge wave and suffered severe head injuries. My grandfather had a heart attack and died on the clifftop just after they brought Phil's body up.'

Ben's eyes searched hers, his expression sombre. 'That must have been horrendous for you all.'

She nodded. 'Especially my father. Apart from Mum and my brothers and me, they were his entire family. He'd lost his mother a couple of years before, and his brother wasn't married. And his father was only sixty-eight.'

'And Kate's husband?'

'James? He was swept off the rocks. They sent out the inshore lifeboat to pick up the kids on the rocks at the end of the promontory, but James had a broken rib so he wasn't on the lifeboat, so he went down out onto the rocks to help a girl who was too scared to move. They threw him a line and a life-jacket, and he got it on her and tied her to the line, but the same wave that killed my uncle swept several of them out to sea and his body was never recovered.'

Ben made a sympathetic noise. 'How awful for Kate.'

'I'm sure it was, but she seems to have dealt with it pretty philosophically. As she said, the sea was going to get him one way or another. At least he died a hero.'

Ben nodded. 'It must have left a huge hole in the community.'

'Oh, yes, but my father never talks about that night. It's as if it never happened. He's always like that. Anything bad that happens, anything personal, he just shuts down.'

'I'm surprised he comes to this event.'

Lucy gave a rueful laugh. 'Oh, I don't think Kate gives him a choice. They've been friends for ever, and she pretty much organises this event every year. He just does what he's told. And anyway, it's for a good cause. The lifeboat's been part of Penhally for generations, and there's nobody who hasn't lost someone close to them or someone they knew well at some time in the past—sorry, I'm going on a bit, but I'm quite passionate about it.'

'Don't apologise. I'm all for passion. The world would be a much duller place without it.' He grinned and added, 'You can get passionate with me any time you like.'

Innocent words, said to lighten the mood, but there was something in his eyes that was nothing about lifeboats and all about passion of another sort entirely, and she felt her heart skitter. Crazy. She hadn't seen him for nearly two years, and their brief relationship had been cut off abruptly, but if it hadn't…

'Mr Carter! You came!'

He turned to the grey-haired woman with a cast on her arm and smiled and shook her other hand. 'I said I would.'

'Lots of people say that. Most of them aren't here. And you're with our lovely Dr Lucy. How are you, dear? Keeping well, I hope? I haven't seen you for a while.'

'No, you've defected and moved to Wadebridge, Mrs

Lunney,' Lucy said, grateful for the distraction. 'You look well on it—well, apart from your arm. I take it that's how you met Mr Carter.'

She smiled. 'Yes—and I'm getting married again because of it! All my neighbour and I had ever done was say hello over the fence for the past six months, but when I broke my arm Henry was just there for me, doing all sorts of little jobs without me asking, and then—well, let's just say he was very persuasive! And we're getting married next month, when I've got this cast off.'

Lucy hugged her gently. 'That's wonderful. I'm really pleased for you. Congratulations. I hope you'll both be very happy.'

'Thank you, dear. Now, you two enjoy yourselves. I'd better get back to Henry—he's a bit out of his depth here, and they'll be giving him a bit of a grilling, checking him out. You know what they're like! I'd better rescue him.'

Ben chuckled. 'You do that—and congratulations. I'm glad something good came out of your broken arm. Now,' he said softly as she walked away, 'Mrs Lunney's typical of the sort of cases we don't need to see at St. Piran. Simple, undisplaced fracture, and she had to come all that way and sit and wait for an hour and a half before she was seen and given pain relief. Crazy. You could have had her sorted out and on her way by the time she arrived at St. Piran.'

'Don't. I'm working on it, Ben, and Dad's very keen.' Partly because he didn't want anyone who didn't have to go there being sent to St Piran. Since her mother…

He lifted his head and cocked an eyebrow towards the food. 'Looks like we're on,' he said, and she fell into step beside him, dragging her mind back to the present.

'Thank goodness for that. I'm going to fade away in a minute! That piece of toast was much too long ago.'

They joined the queue, many of them known to her, either as patients or old friends of her family, and several of the villagers recognised Ben from their trips to the A and E department, so as the queue moved steadily towards the food they were kept busy chatting.

She picked up two plates and handed one to Ben, and then they were there in front of the massive oildrum barbeque, and her heart sank. She'd hoped her father might have moved on to do something else, but he was still there beside Kate, turning sausages and piling up steaks and burgers, and he lifted his head and paused, a sausage speared on a long fork hovering in mid-air.

Ben met his eyes and inclined his head the merest fraction in acknowledgement.

'Dr Tremayne, Mrs Althorp,' he said, and Lucy felt her pulse shift up a notch. It was inevitable that they'd end up running into each other, but now, watching as they eyed each other in silence like stags at bay, she conceded that maybe Ben had been right about not being here.

For an awful, breathless moment she thought her father was going to make a scene, but then he handed the fork to Kate, muttered something to her and walked off.

'He's just remembered something he had to do,' Kate said apologetically, but she couldn't look them in the eye and Ben shook his head and turned to Lucy with a strained smile and handed her the plate.

'I'm sorry, I appear to have lost my appetite. Enjoy the rest of the party.'

And he turned on his heel and strode away through the

crowd, heading for the gate that led out of the car park. Lucy turned back to Kate, her eyes wide with distress.

'Why is Dad like this? Why can't he just get over it?' she said helplessly.

'I don't know. I'm sorry, Lucy. Can I get you anything?'

She looked across the crowded car park. Ben had turned the corner, gone through the gate into Harbour Road, but she could still catch him…

'No. Sorry, got to go!' she said, turning back for a moment to dump the plates back on the pile. Ignoring the damage to her high heels, she sprinted across the car park and through the gate into the road and followed him. He was just reversing his sleek BMW convertible out of a space, and she ran over to the car and wrenched open the passenger door.

'Ben, wait!'

'What for?' he asked, his eyes bleak. 'I shouldn't have come, Lucy, it was stupid of me. I'm out of here.'

'Me, too,' she pointed out, sliding in beside him and shutting the door. 'After all, we have to eat, and we're all dressed up with nowhere to go. It seems a bit of a waste.'

'I don't know. I don't think I'll be very good company.'

'I'll risk it,' she said, holding her breath. 'We could always get fish and chips.'

For a moment he just sat there, the engine idling, and then he gave a ragged laugh and cut the engine. 'Go on, then. Go and buy them. Here—take this. I'll wait here.' He handed her a twenty-pound note, and she ran over the road to the chippy. It was deserted, because everyone was at the barbeque, so she was served quickly. She put the change into the Penhally Bay Independent Lifeboat Association collecting tin on the counter and ran back to Ben.

He was staring sightlessly out to sea, his eyes fixed on the horizon, and she slid into the seat beside him and gave him a smile. 'I gave your change to the PBILA,' she told him, and he gave a crooked smile.

'How appropriate. Right, where to?'

'Somewhere quiet?'

He grinned. 'I know just the place.' Starting the engine again, he nosed out into the crowd, drove slowly down Harbour Road and then, as they left the crowds behind, he dropped the clutch and shot up out of the village along the coast road with a glorious, throaty roar. The sun was low over the sea, but it was behind them and once past the caravan park he hit the accelerator, the car hugging the curves and dips of the road as if it were on rails.

She gathered her long, tumbled curls in one hand and turned to him, raising her voice to be heard over the roar of the engine and the rush of air. 'So where are we going?' she yelled.

'There's a viewpoint along here, and we can catch the sunset. It's my favourite place,' he said, his eyes fixed on the road, and she nodded.

'Good.'

And at least no one from Penhally Bay would be there. They were all safely at the barbeque. She settled back in the seat, and waited for the sick feeling in her stomach to settle.

'That was fabulous.'

He crumpled up the paper and wiped his hands on it. 'It was—and probably no more unhealthy than a barbeque, even if it was the most expensive fish and chips I've ever had,' he added pointedly.

'I'm sorry,' she said feeling a flicker of guilt, but he just grinned.

'Don't be. Fancy a stroll?'

'In these shoes?' She laughed.

'You'd be all right in bare feet on the sand.'

'But I have to get there, and I won't get down those steps in these heels.'

'I'll carry you,' he said.

'Don't be ridiculous,' she told him, but she took her shoes off anyway and started to pick her way over the stones to the edge of the car park, wincing and yelping under her breath.

'Idiot,' he said mildly, and, scooping her into his arms and trying not to think too much about the feel of her warm, firm body against his chest, he carried her down the steps and set her on her feet on the sand. 'There,' he said, and he heeled off his shoes, stripped off his socks and rolled his trouser legs up to the knee. 'Last one in the water's a sissy,' he said, and sprinted towards the sea.

She couldn't resist it. He'd known she wouldn't be able to, and he let her catch him, grabbing her hand at the last moment and running with her into the surf.

Just ankle deep, and so early in the year that was enough, but it brought colour to her cheeks and laughter to her brown eyes, and then the laughter faded and she lifted her hand and rested it against his cheek.

'Ben, I'm so sorry about my father…'

He turned his head and kissed her palm gently. 'Don't be. It's my fault. I suspected he'd be there and I should have stayed away.'

'But he was so rude to you.'

'I can cope with it. It's my own fault, but I hoped you'd

be there, and you were, so let's forget about your father and just enjoy being together. Come on, let's walk for a bit.'

It was like something out of a film set. They were strolling beside the water, their hands still linked, and it was wonderful—romantic, peaceful, with the sun's last rays gilding the rippling surface of the sea. But he was unsettled, churned up inside by his encounter with Nick Tremayne and going over it all again and again, as if it would change the past.

Stupid. It was over—finished. He put it out of his mind and turned to Lucy. The sun was about to slip below the horizon, a pale gold orb hovering just above the surface of the sea, the sky shot through with pink and gold, and he put his hands on her shoulders and turned her, easing her against him so her back was warm against his chest, and he held her there motionless as together they watched it flare, then sink into the sea and disappear.

'I never get tired of watching it set,' she said softly. 'I can see it from my sitting-room window at this time of year, and I love it. I can quite see why people worship the sun.'

She turned slowly and lifted her head, her eyes gazing up at him. They were beautiful, the softest brown, warm and generous. Windows on her soul. Such a cliché, but so, so true, and for the first time that day Ben felt she was really letting him in. He felt his pulse pick up, felt the slow, heavy beat of his heart against his ribs, the first stirrings of need.

'Have I told you how lovely you look today?' he said a little unevenly.

She let her breath out in a little rush that could have been a laugh but might just have been a sigh. 'No. No, you haven't.'

'Remiss of me. You look fabulous.' He ran his eyes over her, over the soft gauzy dress that was cut on the cross and clung gently to those slender curves. It was sea-blue, not one colour but many, flowing into each other, and with the surf lapping at her ankles, she could have risen from the water.

'You look like a siren,' he said gruffly, and then without stopping to think, he leant forward, just a fraction, and lowered his mouth to hover over hers. 'Luring me onto the rocks,' he added, his words a sigh.

And then he touched his lips to hers.

For a moment, she just stood there, her eyes staring up into his, and then her lids fluttered down and she shut out everything except the feel of his lips and the sound of the sea and the warmth of his hands on her shoulders, urging her closer.

She didn't need urging. She was ready for this—had been ready for it for ever—and with a tiny cry, muffled by his lips, she leant into him and slipped her arms around his waist, resting her palms against the strong, broad columns of muscle that bracketed his spine.

He shifted, just a fraction, but it brought their bodies into intimate alignment, and heat flared in her everywhere they touched. She felt the hot, urgent sweep of his tongue against her lips and she parted them for him, welcoming him in, her own tongue reaching out to his in greeting.

He groaned, his fingers tunnelling through her hair, and steadying her head with his broad, strong hands, he plundered her mouth, his body rocking against hers, taut and urgent and, oh, so welcome. She heard herself whimper, felt him harden, felt his chest heave in response, and she thought, We can't do this. Not here. But she couldn't stop, couldn't drag herself out of his arms, couldn't walk away…

'Lucy.'

He'd lifted his head, resting his forehead against hers, his breath sawing in and out rapidly. 'What the hell are we doing?' he rasped softly.

What we should have done years ago, she thought. She lifted her hand and cradled his jaw. 'Your place or mine?' she murmured, knowing it was stupid, knowing it was the last thing she ought to be doing but unable to stop herself.

He lifted his head and stared down into her eyes, his own smouldering with a heat so intense she thought she'd burn up.

Then the ghost of a smile flickered over his taut features. 'Mine,' he said gruffly. 'It's not in Penhally. And it's closer. Come on.'

And freeing her, he slid his hand down her arm, threaded his fingers through hers and led her back to the steps, pausing only to hand her his shoes before scooping her up and carrying her up the steps and across the stones to his car.

'Ouch,' he muttered, limping, and she laughed breathlessly.

'That'll teach you to behave like a caveman,' she teased, and he dumped her over the door into her seat, vaulted past her and slid down behind the wheel.

'I'll give you caveman,' he growled, and she felt a delicious shiver of anticipation.

'Want your shoes?'

'No. The only thing I want is you,' he said tautly, gunning the engine and shooting backwards out of the space, then hitting the coast road in a spray of granite chips while she grappled for her seat belt and wondered if it had been quite wise to wake this sleeping tiger...

'Lucy?'

She opened her eyes and stared up at him, reaching up a hand to rub it lightly over the stubble on his jaw. That siren's smile hovered on her lips, rosy and swollen from his kisses, and he wanted to kiss her all over again. 'Well, if it isn't my very own caveman,' she said softly.

He laughed, then bent his head and touched his lips to hers, tasting her smile. 'Good morning,' he murmured, his mouth still on hers, and he felt her lips curve again.

'Absolutely,' she replied, and opened her mouth to his, drawing him in, her arms sliding round him and cradling him closer. He felt the heat flare between them, felt her pelvis rock, felt the soft, moist heat of her against his thigh as she parted her legs to the urging of his knee.

Hell. He hadn't been going to do this again. He'd been going to talk to her, to tell her all the reasons why this was such a lousy idea, but her body was hot and naked against his, her soft, welcoming flesh too much for him to resist. He'd wanted her for years, ever since they'd worked together, and if it hadn't been for her mother's death…

Damn.

He shifted, pulling away, but she followed him, her hands holding him to her, rolling after him and taking over, her body hot and sweet and so, so lovely, and as she lowered herself and took him inside her, he lost rational thought.

He groaned her name, arching up as she rocked against him, taking him deeper, and then, grasping her hips, he drove into her again and again, feeling her passion build, feeling the tension spiral in her until her breathing grew ragged and she sobbed his name. He felt her body contract around him, felt the incredible power of her climax, and followed her headlong over the edge.

It was her phone that woke them, ringing from somewhere downstairs in the depths of her handbag.

'I'll let it ring,' she said, but then it rang again, and again, and finally she got up. ran downstairs naked and answered it.

He followed her slowly, pulling on his dressing-gown and going into the kitchen to put on the kettle, the shirt he'd worn the previous day flung over his shoulder.

'Dad, I'm fine. No, I'm not at home,' she was saying as he threaded her arms one at a time into the shirt. 'I'm twenty-nine years old, for heaven's sake! I don't need your permission to leave my house on my day off!'

She rolled her eyes at Ben, and he smiled faintly and turned back to the kettle, listening by default to her side of the conversation as he made them tea.

'Yes, I'm sorry, too. Yes, I think you do. Yes, I'll tell him if I speak to him. OK. I'll see you on Tuesday, after the bank holiday.'

He heard her cut the connection, heard the soft sound of her bare feet on the floor and turned with a smile. 'You looked a little underdressed,' he said, glad now that he'd covered her because she looked sexier in his shirt than he could have imagined in his wildest fantasies.

'Thanks.' She threw him a fleeting smile and pulled the shirt closed, buttoning it and running her hands round the neck and lifting her hair out in a soft, gleaming tumble of curls that made him want to gather them in his hand and tug her gently back to his arms. Or bed. Whatever. Closer, anyway.

He turned back, poured the tea and handed her a mug instead. 'What did your father want?'

'To apologise for being rude to you yesterday. He said he owed you an apology, too. He asked me to tell you if I saw you.'

Ben grunted. Nick Tremayne probably did owe him an apology after yesterday, and if he hadn't just spent the night with the man's daughter Ben might have been less forgiving. As it was, he just felt sick at heart and deeply sorry for everything that had happened, even though it hadn't been his fault.

He wondered if Lucy really believed that he wasn't to blame, or if somewhere deep inside there was a bit of her that wasn't quite sure. He must have been crazy to bring her back here last night and complicate things like this...

'Ben?'

He glanced up at her, his face sombre, and she felt her heart sink.

'This isn't going to work, is it?'

'Us?' He shook his head and sighed softly. 'No.'

She felt tears sting her eyes and blinked them away. She wasn't going to cry. She wasn't. 'Too much baggage.'

He didn't reply. There was nothing more to add.

So that she didn't have to go home in the same dress everyone had seen her in the day before, he lent her a pair of denim cut-offs that were loose on her waist and snug on her hips, and the shirt she was already wearing, and drove her home. He pulled up outside her front door. Gathering her things together, she paused, her hand on the car door.

'Thank you for last night, it was wonderful,' she said, and, leaning over, she kissed him goodbye.

It seemed horribly, unbearably final.

CHAPTER TWO

Mid-November

'RIGHT, Lucy and Dragan, don't forget I've booked you both off this afternoon for the MIU meeting with the St Piran consultant. He's coming about two-thirty,' Kate said.

'Pointless,' Nick said flatly. 'I don't know why you've booked him in with Lucy. Can't you reschedule it for when I'm around? She won't be in a position to implement the changes and we've got more than enough to think about at the moment. We won't need all the extra hassle while we've got a locum in. I think we should forget it for now.'

'No,' Marco interjected. 'The community needs more than we can offer, Nick, and we do need to do this as soon as we can. We've talked it over endlessly.'

'So why Lucy? Why not us? It's our practice.'

'Because she's the most appropriate person,' Kate pointed out calmly. 'Apart from the fact that you've shown no interest in being involved in this up to now, emergency medicine is her area of responsibility in the practice, and this was all her idea. It's only a feasibility study, Nick,' she went on, 'planning for the future. Someone's got to do it, so why not her? Besides,' she added before Lucy could interrupt and point out that she was still, actually, in the room, if they'd all finished talking about her, 'they've worked together before, so it makes sense.'

They had? When? Or more importantly…

Nick's brow pleated into a scowl. 'Who is it?' he asked, yet again before Lucy could speak.

'Oh—didn't I mention that?' Kate said guilelessly. 'It's Ben Carter.'

'Ben?' Lucy said, her heart lurching against her ribs. Oh, no. Not Ben! Not when she still hadn't told him…

Her father's frown deepened. 'Carter!' he growled. 'Why the hell is *he* coming?'

'Because he, like Lucy, is the most appropriate person for the job—and he volunteered.'

Really? Why on earth would he do that, seeing that the last time she had spoken to him it had been to agree that they shouldn't see each other again because of the situation between him and her father?

Nick was emphatic. 'No. Not Carter. I don't want him in my practice.'

'Our practice,' Marco pointed out mildly. 'And anyway, it's irrelevant what you or I or anybody else want. If we're going to do this, we need an expert, and he's the best.'

'Rubbish, the man's incompetent.'

'Dad, no! You cannot go around saying things like that about him.'

'Why not, if it's the truth?'

'Because it isn't! The inquiry exonerated him absolutely.'

'It was a whitewash. Utter whitewash, and if you weren't so hoodwinked by the man you'd realise it.'

'Nick, that's not fair,' Kate said gently. 'He's very well regarded.'

He stood up and banged his mug down on the draining-board. 'Think what you like, he's the last person we need here,' he said stubbornly. 'It doesn't matter what any of you say, you'll never convince me otherwise. Ben Carter's bad news, and I don't want anything to do with him.'

He spat Ben's name as if it were poison, and Lucy's heart sank. Was he ever going to be able to see this clearly? Because if not…

'Nick, you're getting this totally out of proportion,' Kate said firmly. 'Anyway, you don't have to have anything to do with him. You're busy with your antenatal stuff, Marco's concentrating on the paeds, this is all Lucy and Dragan. Mostly Lucy. And if they're all happy about it, I really don't see why it's such an issue. It's not as if he's going to be having any involvement in the running of the unit.'

Nick opened his mouth to reply, but Marco cut him off.

'She's right. Move on, Nick. Let it go.'

He shut his mouth, opened it again, and then turned abruptly and stalked towards the door. 'Fine. Don't any of you mind me, I'm just the senior partner,' he snapped, and slammed the door shut behind him.

Lucy winced, Marco shrugged, Dragan shook his head and frowned and Kate smiled briskly at everyone and headed for the kettle. 'Right. That's that settled. Coffee, anyone?'

Lucy couldn't believe it was Ben.

Of all the people to be coming, why did it have to be him?

Although she had to see him some time, and preferably soon. Unless she just wasn't going to…

No. That wasn't an option. She just wanted time to think it through, to work out the words, to find a way of introducing the subject.

Ridiculous. She'd had months to talk to him, months to think up the words. She was just a coward—a coward with a patient who was staring at her a little oddly, waiting.

'Right, Mrs Jones, I'm sure you'll be all right. I'm confident that as I first thought it's just a little bit of fluid on your lungs from your heart problem, so I'm juggling your pills a little and we'll see if you improve. Here's your new prescription, but in the meantime the injection I've just given you should start to shift it soon, and the extra frusemide should do the trick in the long term.' She clipped her bag shut with a little snap, and picked it up. 'If I don't hear anything from you, I'll come back and see you next week to make sure it's cleared up, but if you're at all worried, you call me, OK? No being stoic.'

Edith Jones nodded. Recently widowed, she was struggling to cope with her new independence, and Lucy worried about her. Her heart condition had been fine until her husband's sudden and traumatic decline, and since then she'd been neglecting herself. Not any more, though. Lucy simply wouldn't let her. Edith was still a little breathless, but even in the short time since Lucy had given her the diuretic injection, she'd noticed an improvement.

'I'll be fine, Doctor,' Edith said with a smile. 'Thank you so much for coming.'

'My pleasure. You stay there, I'll let myself out.'

'No, that's all right, I'll see you to the door. I have to get up to go to the toilet anyway. That's one of the problems with your medicine!'

Good. More evidence of the drugs working, but just to be on the safe side, Lucy warned, 'Don't forget to keep drinking. I don't want you thinking you can keep the fluid off your lungs by dehydrating yourself. That's not how it works. Cut down on your salt intake, and have lots of water and fruit juice, and not too much of that mega-strong tea you like to drink, or you'll be getting problems with your waterworks to make life even more interesting! And don't forget—if you aren't entirely convinced it's working, ring me.'

'I will, Doctor. Thank you.'

She waved goodbye, got into her car and drove the short distance back to the surgery. It was ten past two, and Ben would be arriving in twenty minutes. Just time for a bite of lunch and a little hyperventilation before she had to see him again…

He was early.

He hadn't meant to be, but the morning had gone badly and he hadn't stopped for lunch in case the roads were busy, then they'd been clear and he'd found himself at the practice at five past two. So he was sitting in his car and killing time, staring out over the harbour and wondering whether he should go in and what kind of reception he would get from Nick Tremayne.

Hopefully better than the reception he'd got in May when he'd come to the barbeque here. Still, Nick had agreed to their meeting, so presumably Lucy had finally talked him round. Not that he expected miracles. A chilly silence would be more like it, but even that might be better than outright hostility.

A vessel caught his eye, a little fishing smack coming into the harbour, running in on the waves. The sea beyond the harbour mouth was wild and stormy today, the water the colour of gunmetal. It looked cold and uninviting, and he was glad he didn't make his living from it.

He turned his head and studied the cars in the car park, wondering which one of them was Lucy's. The silver Volvo? No. That was most likely to be Nick's. The little Nissan? Possibly. Not the sleek black Maserati that crouched menacingly in the corner of the car park, he'd stake his life on it. That, he'd hazard a guess, was Marco Avanti's.

He was just psyching himself up to get out of the car and go inside when a VW turned into the car park and drove into one of the spaces marked 'Doctor'.

Lucy. His pulse picked up, and he took a slow, steadying breath to calm himself. After all, the last time he'd seen her had been in early May, and they'd both made it clear it wasn't going anywhere. He was sure they could be adult about this—even if it had taken weeks to get her out of his mind again.

Longer still to get her out of his dreams, but he'd done it, finally, by working double shifts and staying up half the night trawling the internet in the name of research. And he was over her. He was.

So why was his heart racing and his body thrumming? Crazy. He shouldn't be here. He should have let someone else do it—one of the other A and E guys…

She was getting out of the car, opening the door, and in the rear-view mirror he could see her legs emerging, and then her…body?

He was on his feet and moving towards her before he had time to realise he'd moved, before he'd thought what he was going to say, before he'd done anything but react. And then, having got there, all he could do was stare.

'Ah, Mr Carter, welcome!'

He realised Kate Althorp was beside them, talking to him, and over the roaring in his ears he tried to make sense of it. She was holding out her hand, and he sucked in a lungful of air, pulled himself together and shook it, the firm, no-nonsense grip curiously grounding. 'Ben, please—and it's good to see you again, Mrs Althorp. Thank you for setting this up.'

'Call me Kate—and it's my pleasure. Lucy, I've put tea and biscuits out in my office for you, so you won't be disturbed. Dragan Lovak's had to go out on a call—he'll be joining you later. But since we're here now, why don't we have a quick guided tour before the clinics start, and then I'll leave you both to it?'

And he was led inside, Lucy bringing up the rear, her image imprinted on his retinas for life. He followed the practice manager through the entrance to Reception, smiling blankly at the ladies behind the counter, nodding at the patients in the waiting room, vaguely registering the children playing in the corner with the brightly coloured toys. He saw the stairs straight ahead, easy-rising, and the consulting rooms to the right, on each side of the short corridor that led to the lift.

'It's a big lift,' Kate was saying as the doors opened and they stepped in. 'Designed for buggies and wheelchairs and so on, but not big enough for stretchers, although we don't have any call for them really. If people collapse and have to go to hospital in an ambulance, they've probably been in to see one of the doctors, and as most of the consulting rooms are downstairs anyway, that's more than likely where they'll be. If not, the paramedics usually manage to get them down in the lift without difficulty. The trouble is the building wasn't designed to be a surgery, so it's been adapted to make the best use of what we have.'

'How long has the practice been here?'

'Two years. After Phil died there wasn't a practice here in Penhally Bay until two years ago. A neighbouring practice closed and they lost the last of the local doctors, and Marco Avanti and Nick set up the practice here where it is now to fill the gap.'

The lift doors opened again and he found himself at the end of a corridor the same as the one downstairs, with rooms to left and right. 'We've got the nurses' room and a treatment room up here, and our MIU, such as it is. I'll let Lucy show you that, she'll know more about it than me.'

'What about a waiting area?' he asked, forcing himself to concentrate on something other than Lucy. She was going through a door marked 'Private', closing it firmly behind her. Damn.

'We have a couple of chairs out here but we don't tend to use them except in the summer when it's busier,' Kate was saying. 'Usually they call the patients up one at a time from downstairs. Our staffroom and shower and loo are up here, too, as well as another public toilet and the stores, and this is my office.'

She opened the door and ushered him in. 'Have a seat,' she said. 'Lucy won't be a moment. I'll put the kettle on.'

He didn't sit. He crossed the room, standing by the window, looking out. It was a pleasant room, and from the window he could see across the boatyard to the lifeboat station and beyond it the sea.

He didn't notice, though, not really. Didn't take it in, couldn't have described the colour of the walls or the furniture, because there was only one thing he'd really seen, only one thing he'd been aware of since Lucy had got out of her car.

The door opened and she came in, and with a smile to them both Kate excused herself and went out, closing the door softly behind her, leaving them to it.

Lucy met his eyes, but only with a huge effort, and he could see the emotions racing through their wary, soft brown depths. God only knows what his own expression was, but he held her gaze for a long moment before she coloured and looked away.

'Um—can I make you some tea?' she offered, and he gave a short, disbelieving cough of laughter.

'Don't you think there's something we should talk about first?' he suggested, and she hesitated, her hand on the kettle, catching her lip between those neat, even teeth and nibbling it unconsciously.

'I intend to,' she began, and he laughed and propped his hips on the edge of the desk, his hands each side gripping the thick, solid wood as if his life depended on it.

'When, exactly? Assuming, as I am, perhaps a little rashly, that unless that's a beachball you've got up your jumper it has something to do with me?'

She put the kettle down with a little thump and turned towards him, her eyes flashing fire. 'Rashly? *Rashly?* Is that what you think of me? That I'd sleep with you and then go and fall into bed with another man?'

He shrugged, ignoring the crazy, irrational flicker of hope that it was, indeed, his child. 'I don't know. I would hope not, but I don't know anything about your private life. Not any more,' he added with a tinge of regret.

'Well, you should know enough about me to know that isn't the way I do things.'

'So how do you do things, Lucy?' he asked, trying to stop

the anger from creeping into his voice. 'Like your father? You don't like it, so you just pretend it hasn't happened?'

'And what was I supposed to do?' she asked, her eyes flashing sparks again. 'We weren't seeing each other. We'd agreed.'

'But this, surely, changes things? Or should have. Unless you just weren't going to tell me? It must have made it simpler for you.'

She turned away again, but not before he saw her eyes fill, and guilt gnawed at him. 'Simpler?' she said. 'That's not how I'd describe it.'

'So why not tell me, then?' he said, his voice softening. 'Why, in all these months, didn't you tell me that I'm going to be a father?'

'I was going to,' she said, her voice little more than a whisper. 'But after everything—I didn't know how to. It's just all so difficult…'

'But it *is* mine.'

She nodded, her hair falling over her face and obscuring it from him. 'Yes. Yes, it's yours.'

His heart soared, and for a ridiculous moment he felt like punching the air, but then he pulled himself together. Plenty of time for that later, once he'd got all the facts. Down to the nitty-gritty, he thought, and asked the question that came to the top of the heap.

'Does your father know it's mine?'

She shook her head, and he winced. 'So—when's it due?'

'The end of January.'

'So you're—'

'Thirty weeks. And two days.'

He nodded. That made sense, but there was another question that needed answering. 'You told me you were on the Pill.'

She bent her head. 'I was, but because it was only to regulate my periods I probably hadn't been as punctual all the time as I should have been. I used to take it in the morning, but I didn't remember till the Tuesday, by then it was too late.' Because she'd been crying since the moment she'd closed her front door behind her on Sunday morning and retreated into the sanctuary of her little home, wearing his shirt day and night until she'd had to take it off to shower and dress to come to work after the bank holiday, and then she'd found the pills...

'So why not take the morning-after pill just to be safe?'

Why not, indeed? She shook her head. 'I didn't have any, and by the time I was able to get them from the pharmacy it would have been too late. And anyway, I thought I was safe,' she told him, and wondered, as she'd wondered over and over again, if there'd been a little bit of her that had secretly wanted to have his baby. And when her periods had continued for the next two months, she'd put it out of her mind.

Not for long, though. Eventually it had dawned on her that things were different, that the lighter-than-usual periods had been due to the hormones, and she'd kept it a secret as long as she could. Eventually, though, the changes to her body had become obvious, and her father had been shocked and then bossily supportive.

And he hadn't asked about the father, not once she'd told him that he was out of her life for good and she didn't want to think about him any more. Not that she had wanted Ben out of her life, but he was, to her sorrow and regret, and she didn't want to think about him any more. She'd been sick of crying herself to sleep, missing him endlessly, wishing he could be with her and share this amazing and fantastic thing that was happening to her body.

Her stomach rumbled, and she gave the biscuits a disinterested glance. OK, she could eat them, but she really, really wanted something healthy, and if Dragan was held up...

'Have you had lunch?' she said suddenly.

'*Lunch?*' he said, his tone disbelieving. 'No. I got held up in Resus. There wasn't time.'

'Fancy coming back to my house and having something to eat? Dragan can ring when he's on his way back and we can meet him here. Only I'm starving, and I'm trying to eat properly, and biscuits and cakes and rubbish like that just won't cut the mustard.'

'Sounds good,' he said, not in the least bit hungry but desperate to be away from there and somewhere private while he assimilated this stunning bit of news.

She opened the door, grabbed her coat out of the staffroom as they passed it and led him down the stairs. 'Kate, we're going to get some lunch. Can you get Dragan to ring me when he's back?'

'Sure,' Kate said, and if Lucy hadn't thought she was being paranoid, she would have sworn Kate gave her and Ben a curiously speculative look.

No. She couldn't have guessed. It had been months since she'd seen them together.

Six months, one week and two days, to be exact. And Kate, before she'd become practice manager, had been a midwife.

Damn.

They walked to her flat, along Harbour Road and up Bridge Street, the road that ran alongside the river and up out of the old town towards St Piran, the road he'd come in on. It was over a gift shop, in a steep little terrace typical of Cornish coastal towns and villages, and he wondered how she'd manage when she'd had the baby.

Not here, was the answer, especially when she led him through a door into a narrow little hallway and up the precipitous stairs to her flat. 'Make yourself at home, I'll find some food,' she said, a little breathless after her climb, and left him in the small living room. If he got close to the window he could see the sea, but apart from that it had no real charm. It was homely, though, and comfortable, and he wandered round it, picking up things and putting them down, measuring her life.

A book on pregnancy, a mother-and-baby magazine, a book of names, lying in a neat pile on the end of an old leather trunk in front of the sofa. More books in a bookcase, a cosy fleece blanket draped over the arm of the sofa, some flowers in a vase lending a little cheer.

He could see her through the kitchen door, pottering about and making sandwiches, and he went and propped himself in the doorway and watched her.

'I'd offer to help, but the room's too small for three of us,' he murmured, and she gave him a slightly nervous smile.

Why nervous? he wondered, and then realised that of course she was nervous. She had no idea what his attitude would be, whether he'd be pleased or angry, if he'd want to be involved in his child's life—any of it.

When he'd worked it out himself, he'd tell her. The only thing he did know, absolutely with total certainty, was that if, as she had said, this baby was his, he was going to be a part of its life for ever.

And that was non-negotiable.

* * *

What on earth was she supposed to say to him?

She had no idea, and didn't know how it could be so hard. When they'd worked together, he'd been so easy to talk to, such a good friend, and they'd never had any tension between them. Well, that was a lie, but not this sort of tension.

The other sort, yes—the sort that had got her in this mess.

No. Not a mess. Her baby wasn't a mess, and she wasn't ever going to think of it as one.

She put the sandwiches on plates, put the plates on a tray with their two cups of tea and carried them through to her little living room. 'Sit down, Ben, you're cluttering the place up,' she said softly, and with a rueful little huff of laughter he sat, angled slightly towards her so he could study her.

Which he did, with that disconcertingly piercing gaze, the entire time she was eating her sandwich.

'We could get married,' he said out of the blue, and she choked on a crumb and started to cough. He took the plate and rubbed her back, but she flapped him away, standing up and going into the kitchen to get a glass of water.

And when she turned he was right behind her, so close that she brushed against him, her bump making firm and intimate contact with his body. For a moment he froze, and then his eyes dropped and he lifted a hand and then glanced back up at her, as if he was asking her permission.

She swallowed slowly and nodded, and he laid his hand oh, so tenderly over the taut curve that was his child. Something fierce and primitive flickered in his eyes, and then he closed them, and as the baby shifted and stretched she watched a muscle jump in his jaw.

His hand moved, the softest caress, and he opened his eyes, lifted his head and met her eyes.

'I felt it move,' he said, and there was wonder in his voice, and joy, and pride.

And for the first time she felt the tension ease and some of the dread fade away.

'It'll be all right, Lucy. Don't worry. I'll look after you.'

'We aren't getting married, Ben.'

'Don't close your mind to it,' he said softly.

'It's too soon.'

'Of course it is—but it's one of our options.'

Ours?

She would have moved away from him, but he had her pinned up against the sink and in the narrow kitchen there was nowhere to go. So she turned her back to him, but it didn't help because he simply moved up closer, sliding his arms around her, resting both hands on her tummy and drawing her gently back into his warm embrace. 'Don't be scared.'

'I'm not scared,' she lied. 'I just don't like you turning up out of the blue and telling me what to do.'

'Out of the blue? I hardly abandoned you, Lucy. The last conversation we had, you told me it wasn't going to work. Too much baggage.'

'And you agreed.'

'So I did,' he said thoughtfully. 'But that was then, and this is now, and things are different. The baggage certainly is. I can't let you face your father alone.'

'And you really think you being there, telling him you're the baby's father, will help?'

He sighed and moved away at last, giving her room to

breathe, to re-establish her personal space and gather her composure around her like a security blanket.

'Come on,' he said. 'You haven't finished your sandwich. Come and sit down and put your feet up and tell me what you were planning.'

She laughed wryly. 'I didn't have any plans,' she confessed, feeling suddenly lost again. 'I was just winging it, getting through a day at a time. And Dad hasn't really asked very much about the baby's father. Just how could I have been so silly and that I'd have his support. He wants me to move back in with him, but I don't want to.'

'Lucy, you can't stay here,' he said, his voice appalled, and she felt her mouth tighten.

'Why not? Don't come in here and start insulting my home, Ben.'

'I'm not insulting your home, sweetheart, but look at it. It's tiny, and it's up a steep hill and a narrow flight of stairs, with no parking outside—where do you keep your car? The surgery? That'll be handy in the pouring rain when you've got a screaming baby and all your shopping.'

She bit her lip, knowing he was right and yet not wanting to admit it. Of course the flat wasn't suitable for a baby, and she'd been meaning to find somewhere else, but anything rented was usually in holiday lets in the summer, and she couldn't afford those rates, not unless she went back to work, and buying somewhere in the village on a part-time salary probably wasn't an option either.

'I don't suppose he's any nearer to accepting that I wasn't to blame for your mother's death?' he suggested, and Lucy shook her head.

'I don't think so. He wasn't very pleased this morning when Kate announced that it was you coming.'

A frown pleated his brow. 'Really? But it was decided weeks ago. Kate said everyone was fine with it. I assumed he must know.'

She met his eyes, and realisation dawned. 'She's worked it out,' she said slowly. 'She knows you're the father. Well, at least, she knows I don't have a life outside Penhally, because she can see the surgery car park from her house up behind it, and she'll know my car's always there unless I'm out on a call or visiting friends, and she can see my window here—that's her house over there,' she said, pointing out to him the pretty little cottage tucked against the hillside above the surgery. 'So there's nothing I can do without her knowing, and if I had a man, believe me, Penhally would be talking about it. And the last man I was seen with was you, and of course she knows we'd worked together, that we were friends.'

'I don't know how you can stay in this place,' he said gruffly, and sighed. 'You reckon she knows?'

'I think so. She gave us a look as we left the surgery.'

'A look?'

'Yeah—one of those knowing ones.'

He grinned a little crookedly. 'Ah. Right. And do you think she'll tell your father?'

Lucy felt a little bubble of hysterical laughter rising in her chest. 'I wish. Maybe that way he'd calm down before I had to talk to him about it.'

'You really think it'll be that bad?'

She stared at him blankly. 'You don't have any idea, do you? Because you haven't seen him since Mum died, apart from the lifeboat barbeque. Ben, he—' She broke off, not knowing quite how to put it, but he did it for her, his voice soft and sad.

'Hates me? I know. I've already worked that out. And I can see why.'

'But it wasn't your fault!' she said, searching his face and finding regret and maybe a little doubt. 'Ben, it wasn't. The inquiry exonerated you absolutely. Mum died because she didn't tell anyone how sick she was until it was too late. I wasn't there, Dad was too busy setting up the practice with Marco, and she downplayed it just too long.'

'Lucy, she died because when she arrived in the A and E department she didn't check herself in straight away, so nobody flagged her up as urgent, nobody kept an eye on her, nobody realised she was there until they found her collapsed in the corner. There'd been a massive RTA, there were ambulances streaming in, we were on the verge of meltdown— I don't have to explain it to you. You know the kind of mayhem I'm talking about, you've seen it all too often. I was trapped in Resus, the walking wounded were way down the list. Too far. And the other people waiting just thought she was asleep, instead of which she'd all but OD'd on painkillers and by the time we got to her it was too late.'

'They said her appendix had ruptured. She must have been in so much pain. I knew she'd been feeling rough but I had no idea how rough. It must have been agony.'

'Yes. Hence the painkillers. She'd obviously had a hell of a cocktail. We found codeine and paracetamol and ibuprofen and aspirin in her bag. The codeine must have knocked her out, but it was the aspirin that killed her. By the time she arrived at the hospital, she was too woozy to talk to anyone. The CCTV footage shows her stumbling to a chair in the corner and sitting down, and because she didn't check in or tell anyone how bad she felt, she was overlooked until it was too late. You know how aspirin works—it's an anticoagulant, like warfarin, and it stops the platelets clumping to arrest a bleed in the normal way. And with the rupture in her abdomen, she just bled out before we could get to it. If your father hadn't phoned her mobile, she wouldn't have been found until she was dead. It was only because the phone kept ringing and she was ignoring it that the alarm was raised. And we did everything we could at that point, but it just wasn't enough, and everything we touched was breaking down and starting another bleed. And I can tell you how sorry I am for ever, but it won't bring her back.'

She shook her head and squeezed her eyes shut to close out the images, but they wouldn't be banished, and she knew her father had seen it because they'd called him immediately to ask if he knew why she might be there, and he'd arrived while they had been in Resus, fighting for her life, and had insisted on going in. It must have been hideous for him, but it didn't change the facts. 'It wasn't your fault,' she told Ben yet again.

'I was in charge. I know I wasn't a consultant then, but I was the most senior person in the department that day, and so the responsibility rested with me.'

'You're not God.'

'No. So I needed to be more careful, because I don't just know everything, but things are different now that I'm a consultant and actually have some say. It couldn't happen now. All patients are intercepted on their way into the department by the triage nurse, people waiting are checked at regular intervals, and I insist on being constantly alerted to what's happening in my department. I can't let it happen again.'

'Ben, you didn't let it happen. You weren't negligent.'

'Maybe not. But I can see where your father's coming from, and I wouldn't want a man I thought was responsible for the death of my wife, no matter how indirectly, being the father of my grandchild.'

'Well, he's going to have to get over it,' she said firmly, 'because you are the father—unless we just aren't going to tell him?'

'That's not an option, Lucy,' he said, shaking his head. 'This baby may not have been planned, but it's mine, and I fully intend to be involved in its life. And I can't do that in secret. I can't, and I won't, so, come what may, your father has to know.'

But how? She had no idea, but at least now Ben was in the picture. One down, one to go, she thought.

But then he went on, 'I know you'll say it's too soon, and you're probably right, but I intend to look after you and my baby for the rest of your lives, so get used to the idea.'

She sat up straighter, absently massaging the bump. 'Out of a misplaced sense of duty? No, Ben. It has to be more than that. I agree, I can't stay here, but I'm not moving in with you any more than I'm moving in with my father. I don't want to be someone's duty. I'm sick of duty. I want love for my baby. And for me. Nothing else.'

'It will be love.'

'It will. From me, for a start. But we're part of a package, the baby and I, and we're both equally important, and I'm not going to do anything hasty. You and I haven't seen each other for months, and that was a one-off. You weren't even ready to carry on seeing me because things were too difficult. Well, if they were difficult before, they're much worse now, and I'm not going to do anything until I'm sure the time is right.'

'Right with who?'

'With me—with you—with my father.'

His jaw tensed, the muscle working, and he turned away. 'OK. So—you need accommodation. Somewhere we can have some privacy so I can share my baby with you without causing any of you unnecessary grief—is that what you're suggesting? That we duck around, grabbing a few minutes together every now and then when your father and the rest of Penhally Bay aren't looking? No. It's my baby, Lucy, and I'm damned if I'm going to be ashamed of it. Your father can just learn to deal with it, and the rest of this flaming community can just learn to mind their own business.'

She stared at him, then with a choked laugh she turned away, picked up the tray and stood.

'If you imagine for a moment that's going to happen, Ben Carter, you're in cloud cuckoo land,' she said, and, taking the tray through to the kitchen, she dumped it down and brushed off her hands. 'We'd better get back to the surgery.'

'I thought Dragan was going to phone you.'

'So did I, but he's obviously been held up. There's a lot we can achieve without him, so let's get on with it.' And without waiting for him to reply, she picked up her coat, slid her arms into it and headed for the door.

CHAPTER THREE

THERE was no sign of Nick, thank goodness. Ben had been in suspense, waiting for him to appear, but he noticed the silver Volvo was gone, so maybe he could relax for now. Not for ever. He knew that, but if they were going to have a confrontation, he'd rather it wasn't in a crowded surgery in front of half of Penhally Bay's insatiably curious residents.

There was no sign of Dragan Lovak either, and Ben wondered if Kate had sent him off on a wild-goose chase or told him that they'd gone for lunch and to take his time. If Lucy was right, that wasn't beyond the realms of possibility.

Whatever, Lovak wasn't there to keep them on the straight and narrow, and he had to force his attention back to the Penhally Bay surgery's MIU and away from the smooth, firm protrusion that was his child.

'Have you had a scan?' he asked abruptly, and Lucy stopped talking and turned and looked at him in frustration.

'You haven't heard a word I've said, have you?'

He opened his mouth to deny it, then shook his head. 'Sorry. I'm finding it a bit hard to focus.'

She sighed and reached out a hand, but then thought better of it and withdrew it. 'Look—are you busy tonight? I've got a surgery from five to six-thirty, but I'm not doing anything later. If you're free, perhaps we could talk then? Deal with some of your questions?'

He nodded, a little shocked at how eager he was to have that conversation—a conversation about a child that until a very short while ago he hadn't even known existed. 'Of course.'

'And for now,' she said, her voice gently mocking, 'do you think you could keep your eyes on my face and concentrate on what I'm saying about our minor injuries unit?'

'Sure.'

He nodded, swallowed and tried to smile, but it was a feeble effort and he just wanted to fast-forward to the evening and get the hell out of there.

'Come and see what we have,' she said, and led him into the room in question. It was about twice the size of a consulting room, on the upper floor, and not ideal. He forced himself to concentrate.

'It needs to be bigger and it could do with being on the ground floor,' he told her without preamble.

'We know that. We're looking at funding for expansion.'

He nodded.

'In the meantime, this is what we have and what we do. There's a room next door where we do minor surgery, but it really is minor and very non-invasive—skin lesions, ingrowing toenails and the like. It's more of a treatment room, it's not a proper theatre, although of course we use sterile techniques, but I don't think we can realistically create a dedicated theatre environment either in there or anywhere else in a general practice setting. It simply isn't called for, but it's adequate for what we do surgery-wise. And this room is where we do all our minor injury stuff that we handle at present.'

'Such as?'

'Oh, all sorts. If I tell you the areas that we can currently cover and where I feel the holes are in our provision, maybe you can give me some advice on what we'd need both short and long term to improve that?'

'Sure.'

'Good. Right. Well, in the summer, we get tourists, of course, who as well as coming for medical treatment come to the MIU with things like stings, sprains, cuts and fractures. You'd be surprised how many people travel without a first-aid kit.'

He chuckled. 'No, I wouldn't. We get them all the time.'

'Of course you do. I forgot,' she said, smiling at him and dragging his mind away from medicine and onto something entirely more interesting.

'Then all year round but particularly in the warmer months we have surfers with all their associated injuries—scrapes on rocks, collisions with their own surfboards and with others, the odd weaver fish and all the other touristy things, and we get anyone who needs more than the basic first aid the lifeguards give on the beach, but our baseline local population is farmers and fishermen and their families, so we have a lot of work-related injuries. I've lost count of the number of tetanus shots I've given in the last year. We do a lot of needlework, obviously—cuts and tears, many of them dirty, so we have a certain amount of debriding to do. Some have to come to you because they're too extensive and need plastics or specialist hand surgery, for example. And we have fractures, lots of simple undisplaced fractures and dislocations that with X-ray we could deal with here if we had plaster facilities. They'd still need the care of the orthopaedic team for anything more complex, of course, but there are so many little things we could sort here locally.'

He nodded. 'I agree. The medical emergencies are still going to have to come through us, but from the point of view of straightforward physical injury you could take a lot off us.'

He looked around the room, noting the two couches, the chairs and trolleys and screens, the bench along the side with pretty much the same equipment you would find in a practice nurse's room or one of the cubicles in his A and E department, but for the most part that was all that would be necessary.

'What about resuscitation equipment?'

'Standard GP stuff for an isolated rural practice. We've got a defib and oxygen and a nebuliser, of course, and 12-lead ECG and heart monitor…'

She rattled off a list of things they had and things they wanted, leaving nothing out that he felt would be in any way useful or necessary, and he was impressed.

'You've done your homework,' he said softly, and she stopped and stared at him, giving an exasperated sigh.

'Did you really think we'd get you over here to talk this through if we hadn't? I want this to work, Ben. We need it. We're too far from St Piran. Some of the injuries we see—if we had better facilities so we could just treat them here, at least initially… That journey must be horrendous if you've got a fracture. It's not so much the distance as the roads—so narrow, so twisty, and lots of them are rough. The main road's better, but reaching it—well, it doesn't bear thinking about, not with something like a spinal injury or a nasty compound fracture. We have to fly some of our surfers out just for that reason, because they'd have to come to you, but for the others—well, it's just crazy that we can't do it. There's certainly the demand.'

'I'm sure. You know, if you weren't about to be taking maternity leave, it would make sense for you to come and spend some time in the department. Catch up on your X-ray, diagnostic and plastering skills.'

'I could do that anyway—well, not the X-ray, not until the baby's born, but the rest. I'm going to be coming back to work—I can't afford to stop— And don't say it!' she ordered, cutting him off before he could do more than open his mouth.

So he shut it again, shrugged his shoulders and smiled wryly. 'So where are you going to site the X-ray machine?' he asked. 'Bearing in mind that the room needs screening on all six sides?'

'Out on the end of the sea wall?' she suggested, eyes twinkling, and he chuckled.

'Nice one. Not very practical, though. Do you have a spare room?'

She laughed wryly. 'Not so as you'd notice. In an ideal world, as Kate says, it would all be on the ground floor, but down in the old town like this it's difficult. The sides of the cove are so steep, so all the houses are small and on top of one another. The only way around it would be to build it up out of the town, and that's not where it's needed.'

'Unless you sited it up near the church, halfway between the old town and the beach. Handier for the tourists and all the people staying in the caravan park, and no harder for the people you serve who don't live right in the centre and have to come by car anyway.'

'Except that when we tried to sound them out we couldn't get planning permission and, anyway, any site up there which they'd allow development on would have such stunning sea views it would be worth shedloads and we couldn't afford it, so it's academic. This is what we have, Ben. And there's room to extend at the back—behind the stairwell there's an area of garden which isn't used for anything except sneaking out in breaks and having a quiet sit down out of earshot of the locals. And we're so busy that that isn't really an option in the summer, and in the winter—well, frankly it's not very appealing, so really it's dead space.'

'Can I see?'

'Sure.'

She led him downstairs, snagging her coat from the staff-room on the way, and they went out the front and round the side, between the boatyard and chandlery and the end of the surgery building. 'Here,' she said, pointing to an area that was behind the waiting room and stairs.

He nodded approval, running his eyes over it and measuring it by guesswork. 'It's ideal. It's big enough to make a proper treatment area for suspected fractures and house the X-ray facilities, and you could put further accommodation on top—a plaster room, for instance, and somewhere for people to rest under observation. And you'd still have the existing room upstairs which you could use for other injuries, cuts and such like, jellyfish stings, weaver fish—you name it. Or you could relocate one of the consulting rooms currently downstairs upstairs to that area and use more of the downstairs space for those things, so you've got all your injuries together. And weren't you talking about physio? That probably needs to be downstairs…'

She started to laugh, and he broke off and scrubbed a hand through his hair ruefully. 'OK, so it's not big enough for all that, and it's robbing Peter to pay Paul, but I don't see what else you can do. If you want to do this properly, you'll have to compromise. And you'll have to sell it to the people who'll be compromised.'

'Except my father doesn't want me involved, because I'm going to be on maternity leave. He thinks he should be doing it, but it's not his area of expertise, and I really wanted to oversee it, to make sure it works,' she said softly, the smile fading from her eyes and leaving a deep sadness in its place.

And Ben felt guilty—hugely, massively guilty—because all he'd done by taking Lucy back to his house and making love to her had been to cause her even more grief to add to the emotional minefield that was her life. 'It'll work, Lucy. I'm sure it will—and by the time you come back to work it'll be ready for you to commission.'

'I'm sure you're right,' she said, but she didn't sound it.

She shivered, and he frowned and turned up her coat collar, tugging it closer round her. 'You're cold. Come on, let's go back inside and jot some of this down, do a few doodles…'

'I've done some. I'll show you. And we can have tea.'

The universal panacea. He smiled. 'That would be good. Come on.'

She led him back inside, shivering again and realising that she'd let herself get chilled. It wasn't cold—in fact, it was incredibly mild overall—but the wind was blustery today and cut right through her.

'Kate, is it OK to use your room still?' she asked, leaning over the counter and smiling a greeting at the receptionist, Sue.

Kate put her hand over the receiver and nodded. 'Sure. Go on up. Oh, and Dragan's on his way in—he's bringing Melinda. She's been bitten by a dog. That's why he's been held up. He asked if you could see her. I think she needs suturing.'

'Oh. Right. Can't Dad see her, or Marco?'

'No. Your father's gone over to the house to meet the agent, and Marco's got a clinic, so if you wouldn't mind fitting her in?'

'No, sure. Send them up. I'll use the treatment room upstairs,' she said, and felt the tension draining out of her at the news that her father had gone out and wasn't about to pop out of the woodwork at any moment and cause a scene.

She headed for the stairs, still thinking about her father and not really conscious of the extra effort it took to mount them now that she was pregnant, but evidently Ben noticed because as she arrived at the door of the staffroom he asked, 'How long are you planning to work?'

His voice had a firm edge to it and she looked up at him questioningly.

'Today? Till six-thirty.'

'In your pregnancy.'

'Oh.' So he was doing the proprietorial father bit, was he? 'Till I have the baby,' she said defiantly, and then, before he could argue, qualified it with, 'Well, as long as I can, really. I'll cut out house calls soon, especially if the weather gets bad, and I've already stopped doing night calls. That's one of the advantages of being a pregnant woman in a practice of three single men—they're so busy fussing over me and taking work off me I have to fight them for every last patient!'

His mouth twitched, and he gave a soft laugh. 'And I bet you do.'

'Absolutely. I don't need to be pandered to,' she told him firmly. 'I'm pregnant, Ben, not sick.' She filled the kettle and switched it on, made them two mugs of tea and picked them up. 'Can you get the doors, please?' she said, and he dutifully led her through into Kate's room and shut the door behind them.

She plonked the mugs down on Kate's desk, took the plans of the surgery from the drawer in the filing cabinet and smoothed them out, then laid her tracing-paper alterations over the top. 'Right, this is what I'd thought could be done,' she said, and launched into her explanation.

He couldn't fault it.

She knew just what she wanted and, apart from a very few suggestions, there was nothing she'd planned he wouldn't have been more than happy with in their situation.

He told her so, pointed out the few changes he'd make, and they did some little scribbles on the tracing paper, then she sat back and rubbed her tummy and winced.

'Braxton Hicks?' he guessed, and she nodded.

'Yes. It's beginning to drive me mad. Every time I sit still for any length of time I get them, over and over again. I swear I don't need any more practise contractions. My uterus is going to be so toned up by the time I give birth it's ridiculous.'

'I suppose you're sure of your dates?' he said, and then immediately regretted it because she glared at him as if he'd lost his mind.

'As there was only the one occasion,' she snapped, 'it would be hard to miscalculate.'

'Three, if I remember correctly,' he murmured.

'Three?'

'Occasions,' he said, and she coloured and turned away with a little sound of frustration.

'That's irrelevant.'

'Not to me,' he said. Her colour deepened and she stood up and walked over to the window, rubbing her back. He got up and followed her, standing by her side and drawing her against him, putting the heel of his hand into the small of her back and massaging it firmly while he held her steady against his chest.

Silly girl. She needed him, and he wasn't going to let her get away with this independent nonsense a minute longer.

For a moment she stood stiffly, then with a ragged little sigh she leant into him, dropped her head forward and gave herself up to the comfort of his touch. It just felt so good to have him hold her, and she'd missed that so much, having someone to hug her and hold her. Her mother had always hugged her, and her father used to, but her mother was gone and her father had shut down and now there was no one.

Except Ben, and his hand was moving slowly, rhythmically round on her back, easing out the kinks in her muscles and soothing the tension. And she would have stood there for ever, but she heard footsteps outside and a tap on the door, and she stepped away from Ben just as Dragan put his head round the door and smiled.

'Hi. Sorry I'm late. I've got Melinda here—Kate said you'd look at her?'

'Sure. Hi, Melinda,' she said, greeting the young vet who was fast becoming a treasured part of their community. 'I gather you've been bitten?'

'Yes—stupid,' she said, her slight Italian accent at odds with the gorgeous golden blonde of her hair. She tossed it back over her shoulder out of the way and it slid forward again, obviously irritating her. 'It was my own fault. The dog was injured—we found her on the road near the pub. We'd been for lunch to the Smugglers' and we were on the way down when we saw her. She was in pain, she didn't know me—it was just one of those things.'

'Is she OK?'

'She is now,' Dragan said drily. 'We had to follow her, of course, and catch her, and then take her to the surgery and put her in a cage to rest. I had to drag Melinda here.'

'I could have cleaned it up myself—'

'It's bleeding much too fast. You need serious attention, the right antibiotics—'

'You think I don't have antibiotics suitable for dog bites?' she said mildly, but she held out her left arm to Lucy, her right hand holding down a blood-soaked swab on the inside of her forearm. 'He's right. It is bleeding heavily. I think she's nicked one of the vessels.'

'Let's go into the treatment room and have a look. Oh, by the way, sorry, Dragan Lovak, Melinda Fortesque, Ben Carter,' she said economically, getting the introductions over and ushering her into the treatment room where they did their minor surgery. 'Let's have a look at it,' she suggested. Easing off the pad of gauze, she winced at the bloody mess and pressed the pad quickly back in place over the briskly bleeding vein.

'Ouch.' Ben leant over her shoulder. 'May I take a closer look in a moment?'

'Of course,' Melinda said.

'Nasty bite. We need to clean it thoroughly,' Lucy said as Ben joined her at the basin and started scrubbing.

'That vein needs suturing,' he murmured. 'Are you happy to do that or do you want me to have a go? Assuming it's something we can tackle here?'

She shrugged uncertainly. 'Well, I can have a go,' she said.

'Have you got any fine suture material?'

'I believe so. I don't suppose, since you're here…? We might as well take advantage of the head honcho—you're bound to be better than me, your skills are more up to date than mine.'

He chuckled. 'I doubt if that's true, but if you're happy for me to do it to save sending her to St Piran?'

'Of course I am. It's not my arm, of course, but I'm sure Melinda doesn't want to go to St Piran either.'

'No, I don't,' she said promptly from behind them. 'I have to get back to the dog, and I don't care which of you does it so long as one of you does.'

'Right, let's take a look at it before we make any rash promises,' Ben said. Snapping on gloves, he settled down on a stool next to the couch and studied the wound, blotting it frequently with a gauze swab to keep the field clear of blood. 'Looks sore.'

'It is sore. Some local wouldn't hurt before you go poking it.'

He chuckled and met her eyes with a smile that made Lucy feel instantly, absurdly jealous. Dragan, too, unless she was much mistaken, and she wondered what the situation was between them. Something, otherwise he would have done this himself, but what?

Lovers? Friends? Two strangers in a strange land? Dragan was Croatian, and he'd been living in England since his teens. He didn't talk about his past, but there were shadows in his eyes, and as for Melinda, although Lucy knew little about her past there was an air of quiet dignity about her that hinted at breeding. Yet even so, she was open and friendly and down-to-earth, and anyone more lacking in airs and graces she could hardly imagine.

She looked up at Dragan to say something, and found him watching her, his brooding eyes thoughtful. Then his eyes dropped to Ben, and back to her, and she thought, Good grief, is it so obvious? Do I have a sign on my bump that says, *Child of Ben Carter* on it?

Or was she just reading something that didn't exist into his expression?

'Lucy, can we put a cuff on the arm to cut off this blood supply? And can I have some saline to irrigate this, please?' Ben asked, and she stopped worrying about Dragan and what he was thinking and concentrated on doing her job—or rather helping Ben do his, which she had to admit he was doing beautifully.

He numbed the area and sutured the vessel so neatly Lucy could only watch in awe, then he cleaned the wound thoroughly and released the cuff to check his suturing had worked. 'Good,' he murmured, and trimmed away the little flaps of skin that had lost their blood supply and drew the edges of the wound together with Steristrips. The whole thing had only taken him a few minutes.

'There,' he said, flexing his shoulders and nodding in satisfaction. 'That should sort you out. I can't suture the skin because of the high risk of infection, but the tape should hold it together well enough. Keep it dry, though—and I think you should have a broad-spectrum antibiotic. They've discovered bugs in dog bites that they didn't know infected humans, so I like to provide a broader cover than a simple penicillin type. Lucy, could I have a sterile non-adherent dressing, please?'

'Sure.' She handed him the pack, found the tape and helped him dress the wound.

'OK,' he said, sitting back with a smile. 'Hopefully it'll heal fast, but I'm afraid you might end up with a scar.'

Melinda shrugged and smiled. 'It won't be the first—occupational hazard. Thank you, Ben. Now I can get back to my patient.'

'How's your tetanus?' Lucy asked, and she laughed.

'Well and truly up to date. I got bitten last year. You'd think I'd learn but apparently not.'

Ben chuckled. 'Right, Lucy had better give you your prescription—and you'll need painkillers. Something with codeine, probably, and a non-steroidal. And look out for reddening, fever, swelling, shivering and anything else unusual in the next week. OK?'

'OK. And thank you so much. Right, now I *must* get back to this dog.'

'You should get someone else to do it,' Dragan said, frowning, but she brushed his suggestion aside.

'No. She's frightened, that's all. She's only young, and she was hurt. She's not vicious. I'll get a nurse to help me, we'll be fine.'

He muttered something unintelligible and foreign under his breath. 'I should be here, we're meant to be having a meeting, but you haven't got your car,' he said to Melinda, and Lucy shook her head and handed over the prescription.

'Don't worry, Dragan, you give her a lift back. We've talked it all through and, anyway, I've got a surgery starting in a few minutes. We'll catch up tomorrow and I'll fill you in, and we'll schedule another meeting in a week or two.'

He nodded and, shaking Ben's hand and thanking him, he ushered Melinda out, leaving them alone.

She was about to offer him more tea when Ben glanced at

his watch. 'Right, I suppose I ought to shoot off. I'll pick you up tonight—from here? Six-thirty?'

She shook her head. The last thing she wanted was him picking her up from the surgery when her father was likely to be lurking around. 'I'll meet you somewhere at seven. Your house?'

He nodded. 'Fine. Do you still know the way?'

Know it? She'd almost worn out the road, toing and froing, desperate to see him and yet unable to bring herself to ring the bell and tell him she'd made a mistake about them not being together. And then she'd found out she was pregnant, and she had been wearing out the road for another reason, trying to screw up the courage to tell him that.

'Yes, I know the way,' she said. 'I'll see you there. And make it eight. That'll give me time to get home and eat something.'

'No. I'll feed you.'

'Seven-thirty, then,' she agreed, because for some perverse reason she wanted to go home after her surgery, shower and change into something—well, something else. Something pretty. Something that didn't make her feel like a heffalump.

She walked him back down to Reception, sent him on his way and went into her consulting room, watching him through the window as he got into his BMW and drove away.

It was nearly five. The lights were on in the village, twinkling all around the harbour and giving it a cosy feel, and she could imagine how it must be to enter the harbour mouth and see the lights of home ahead of you.

Safe. Reassuring.

And unaccountably she thought of Ben. Her eyes tracked to his car, following the lights out of the village, along

Harbour Road, up Bridge Street and past her front door, out of sight.

Two and a half hours, she told herself, and felt a little shiver of something she hadn't felt for a very long time.

'Kate?'

The knock on the door came again, and Kate opened it to find Nick standing there, hands rammed deep into his pockets, a brooding look on his face. She frowned in concern.

'Nick—hi. What can I do for you?'

'Oh, I was just— I've been clearing the last of the things out of the house. It seems so odd—end of an era. The agent's expecting a good turn-out at the auction, but I've told him to lower the reserve. He was putting a high one on with a view to marketing it in the spring if it doesn't go, but I told him no. I just want it gone.'

'And you're feeling lost.'

'Not at all. Has to be done,' he said briskly.

But Kate knew him better than he knew himself, she sometimes thought, and she knew just how hard he'd be finding this. His mother's family home, the place he'd been born and raised in, the house his father had been living in at his death. The sale had been a long time coming, but he'd got there in the end. Maybe he'd always imagined retiring there with Annabel in the future, but of course that wouldn't happen now, and the pointlessness of owning it had gradually come home to him.

Poor Nick. He'd lost so much. 'I'm sure the sale will be a great success,' she said just as briskly. 'Some Londoner who wants to divide their time—someone with a family who'll come down and spend quality time together, bring it to life again. Just what it needs, and you'll be able to take a nice long holiday on the proceeds. Got time for coffee?'

'I suppose so. Thanks—yes, coffee would be lovely.'

He followed her through to the kitchen and propped himself up against the island unit, watching her while she made their drinks. 'Where's Jem?' he asked.

'In bed—Nick, it's nearly ten.'

'Is it?' He sounded startled, and checked his watch disbelievingly. 'So it is. I'm sorry—want me to go?'

'No, you're fine,' she said. 'Let's go and sit down.'

She handed him his coffee and led him through to the sitting room. He sat beside her on the sofa, propping his feet on the box that served as a coffee-table and resting his head back with a sigh. 'I'm bushed,' he confessed.

'Of course you are. Clearing the house was always going to be hard. You should have asked for help.'

'No.'

Nothing else, just the one word. Then he sat up straighter and looked down into his coffee. 'Do you know where Lucy is?'

'At home in bed, I imagine, if she's got any sense.'

'Her car's not at the surgery. It's always there.'

'Perhaps she's out meeting friends. Maybe they've gone out for a meal or something. She sometimes goes out with Chloe and Lauren.'

'But if she's not—if she's in trouble…'

'Nick, she's fine.'

'I'm going to ring her.'

'No. Let me do it. If you really insist, let me do it. She won't bite my head off.'

She put her coffee down, got up and went into the kitchen.

Quite unnecessarily, because it was a cordless phone, but she wanted Nick out of earshot. 'Lucy, your father's worried,' she said when Lucy answered. 'He noticed your car wasn't there. I said you'd probably gone out for a meal with friends.'

There was a heartbeat of silence, then Lucy said, 'Um— yes, I have.'

'I thought so,' Kate said, reading between the lines. 'You enjoy yourself—and don't worry about him.'

There was another tiny hesitation, then Lucy said softly, 'Kate, keep him off my case.'

'Sure. I'll see you tomorrow.'

'Thanks.'

Kate hung up and went back into the sitting room.

'Well?'

'She's out for dinner with friends—I told you she would be.'

'She never goes out without telling me. I wonder if she's with the father?' Very likely, Kate thought, knowing that Lauren was out with Martin, Alison's little one wasn't well, and Chloe was on call, but kept it firmly to herself as he went on, 'If I knew who it was who'd left her to give birth and bring up her child alone, I'd hang him out to dry. How she got herself in this mess—'

'Oh, Nick, leave the girl alone. She's a mature, independent professional woman. She's perfectly capable of fighting her own battles.'

'Is she?'

'Yes, of course she is.'

'So how did she end up like this? And how's she going to manage? For God's sake, I was only eighteen when Annabel got pregnant. We managed. And it was twins! And then we had Edward far too soon afterwards, but still we coped. We

stuck together, we made a family—for all the good it's done,'
he added despairingly. 'Lucy's pregnant and alone, Jack's got
some bee in his bonnet about cosmetic surgery, he's been running around London with one tarty little it-girl after another
and won't speak to me, and Edward can't hack it in the army.
So why the hell did we bother? Sometimes I think it's a good
thing Annabel isn't around to see it.'

'Oh, Nick.' Kate sat back with a sigh. 'You really are
down in the dumps, aren't you? You and Annabel did a fantastic job bringing up your children. You gave them every
chance you could, they've all ended up qualified doctors and
they're all doing well. You should be proud of them. What
more could you want?'

'To know my daughter's marrying the father of her child?
A man worthy of her? To know my sons aren't going off the
rails—although if either of them would talk to me it would
be an improvement—'

'And when did you last try and talk to them?'

He went silent.

'I thought so. Give them space, Nick, contact them—send
them a text, tell them you're thinking of them. Tell them
about the house. Anything. Tell them you love them. Just
don't nag.'

He snorted, and she took his mug out of his hand and stood
up. 'Come on, it's time you went home. I need to go to bed
and so do you. You look exhausted. It'll all feel better in the
morning.'

'Will it?'

His face was bleak, and she realised he was thinking about
Annabel, about going home alone to an empty house. She
knew all about that. Oh, she had Jeremiah, and she adored

every hair on his precious little head, but her bed was still cold and lonely at night.

'Goodnight, Nick,' she said firmly, and shut the door on him.

CHAPTER FOUR

'WAS that Kate?'

Lucy nodded and sighed, pushing her hair back off her face and running her fingers through it absently. 'I'm sorry. Apparently my father was worried. He must have seen that my car wasn't there and my lights were off. I expect he panicked. He's such a worrywart.'

She looked troubled, and Ben just wanted to hug her, but he didn't want to push it. Instead he tried the gentle voice of reason. 'I can understand his concern. He's lost a lot of people in his family. That would make him overprotective even if you weren't pregnant and alone. And if he didn't know you were going out.'

'Oh, I know, but I just feel stifled—as if I have to log a flight plan every time I go to the supermarket! That's why I won't live with him, although in some ways it might be easier because I could just let him fuss me and give up fighting, but he'd drive me mad in a week.'

That made him smile. He could imagine her frustration but, like her father, he didn't want her living alone. Not now. Not with the baby so close. He settled back on the sofa and looked across at her curled up at the other end, her slender legs tucked up beneath her, the blatant fecundity of that smooth, round curve bringing out his paternal instinct in spades. 'So—if you aren't staying in your flat, and you don't want to live with your father, and you won't let me bully you into living with me—where do you want to live?' he asked, trying hard to keep his voice casual. 'If you could choose anywhere, regardless of anything.'

Her expression was wistful. 'Really? Total fantasy? My grandparents' house,' she said, surprising him. 'It was my grandmother's family home for ages—the farmhouse, originally, although her brother died without a family and so she inherited it, and they sold off the farm and kept the house. It's gorgeous. It's a bit rundown now. I went over there with Dad the other day and it was looking so tired. That's where he was this afternoon, clearing it out after the tenant left. He was elderly and he's left it in a bit of a state, and it needs so much work if it's going to be let again that Dad's finally decided to get rid of it. It's being auctioned this week.'

'Really?' His attention sat up and took notice of that, because his own house, dull and safe and just a stop-gap until he found somewhere with a bit more character, had been sold. That was why he was asking her, because now would be a perfect time to tailor his choice of new house to something that would fit her dreams. He'd lost the house he had been after, but he'd already accepted an excellent cash offer on his own house. The contracts had been exchanged, it was just a matter of settling the moving date—and that might just put him in a very good position...

'I feel ridiculously sad about it going out of the family,' Lucy was saying, her voice echoing her feelings, 'and I think he does, too, but there's no point in him keeping it, and I can't afford it, and there's no way my two bachelor brothers would bother with it. It's not a huge house, only four proper bedrooms and a bit of an attic, and it needs serious updating, but it's got fabulous sea views, lovely garden—I adore it. So that's my fantasy. Silly really.'

He felt a ripple of excitement. 'Not at all. It sounds lovely. What's it called?'

'Tregorran House.'

He made a mental note, but it wasn't necessary. 'Have you got internet access?' Lucy was asking, and he nodded.

'Yes—why?'

'It's on the agent's website,' she told him, and within minutes he had it all. The details, the date of the auction, the guide price, the viewing arrangements and the location.

'It looks pretty.'

'Oh, it's very tired and rundown,' she pointed out. 'Not that it matters. I won't go again. The only good thing is the council has rejected any suggestion of developing the site, so I know it'll stay as a home for some lucky family. Just not mine.'

She turned away from the computer, and he clicked the little heart that made it a favourite place so he could find it again when he next logged on, and shut it down.

She was back on the sofa, looking a little uncomfortable and very tired. He went over to her, hunkered down next to her and took her feet in his hands, lifting them onto his thigh and rubbing them gently.

'Oh, that's lovely,' she sighed, and he shifted so he was kneeling and her feet were in his lap, and she closed her eyes and sighed again. She was looking so tired. Lovely, but so, so tired. Worn down by the worry of all this, of not knowing what to do about her father and her accommodation, and he wanted so much to help her, to ease that burden, and yet he'd caused it.

Ben's hands slowed and stopped, and he realised she was asleep. Very carefully and gently he lifted her legs up and swung them round onto the sofa, and she made a little noise and snuggled down. He took off his sweater and tucked it around her, then sat down by her feet and watched her while she slept. The baby was moving, her bump shifting and wriggling, and he watched it, fascinated, for what seemed like hours.

And then suddenly her eyes flew open, screwed up then she wailed and struggled to her feet.

'What is it?' he asked, panicking, and she grabbed her calf and muttered something pithy under her breath about idiots.

'Cramp!' she yelled when he asked her again. 'Can't you see I've got a cramp?'

'So sit down and give me your leg,' he ordered, stifling the urge to laugh at his reaction. He pushed her carefully back onto the sofa and took the leg out of her hands, bending her foot up, stretching out the muscle and massaging it firmly until it softened under his hands and she groaned with relief.

'Sorry,' she said meekly, but he didn't care about what she'd said, what she'd called him, because he'd been holding her leg up in the air and trying really, really hard not to notice that under the pretty, clingy little jersey dress she'd put on for the evening she was wearing the most outrageous lacy knickers.

He dropped her leg as if it was red hot and moved away. 'OK now?'

She nodded and hauled her skirt down, but it was too late for that, the damage was done. She yawned, sighed and made to get up, and he sat down next to her and reached out a hand, resting it gently on her knee.

'Stay.'

'Stay, as in good dog?'

He smiled and shook his head. 'Stay with me. You're tired, you shouldn't be driving when you're tired.'

'And sleeping with you is any more sensible?'

'Why not? It's not as if I'm going to get you pregnant.'

She laughed and stood up, moving away from him. 'Why on earth do you want me to stay, Ben? I'm fat, I'm waddling…'

He thought of the knickers. 'No. You're pregnant. You're not fat, and you're not waddling.'

'Humph.'

'Well, not much,' he said, trying to suppress a smile. 'And you're still the most beautiful woman I've ever seen.'

'You're such a liar.'

'No. You are—beautiful and funny and warm and intelligent and sexy as hell.'

'Sexy?' she said, as if he was mad.

The knickers popped into his head again. 'Yes. Sexy,' he said firmly. 'Desirable. Gorgeous.'

'I'm pregnant,' she said sceptically.

'Yes. And still sexy as hell.'

She rolled her eyes. 'Oh, I get it. You're one of those men with a thing about pregnant women…'

'Only when they're carrying my child.'

Her jaw dropped fractionally, and she shut it and turned her head slightly. He could almost hear the cogs turning.

'Lucy?'

She looked back, soft colour touching her cheeks. 'Ben, I— This is a really lousy idea.'

'Why? I'm not walking away. I fully intend to be there for you and the baby for ever. Why not start now? You don't even have to sleep with me. I've got a spare room.'

She laughed a little oddly. 'Bit late for that.'

He wanted to go to her, scoop her into his arms and carry her up to bed, but he forced himself to be still, to wait there for her to make the first move.

But she didn't. She stood there, her lip caught between her teeth, her eyes wary. 'Ben, what if—'

'What if—what?' And then he realised. She was afraid that when she took her clothes off he'd change his mind, find her unattractive. Crazy, silly woman. Not a chance. 'Please?' he said softly. 'I just want to hold you.'

And that must have been enough, because her eyes filled with tears and she nodded, and then she was in his arms and he was carrying her up the stairs, laughing and protesting that he'd put his back out if he wasn't careful. Once he'd put her down on the edge of the bed he sat beside her and stroked the hair back from her face.

'Do you want a T-shirt to sleep in?' he asked, knowing she'd be shy, and she nodded. He pulled a long one out of his drawer and handed it to her. 'There's a new toothbrush and some toothpaste and clean towels and stuff in the bathroom. You go first,' he said, and shooed her in that direction, then turned back the quilt, stripped off his clothes, went into the *en suite* shower room and cleaned his teeth, then ran downstairs and brought up the tealight holder from the dining table and lit the candles.

He turned out the light, contemplated stripping off his jersey boxers and thought better of it, then got into bed.

He heard the loo flush, the water running, the door open,

the light click off, and then she was there, hovering in the doorway, her face troubled in the candlelight. He held his arm out to her in invitation.

'Come and have a cuddle,' he said gently, and after another moment's hesitation she slipped into bed beside him.

'Oh! It's chilly,' she murmured, and he tucked her up against him so that the firm bulge of her tummy was snuggled against his abdomen and her legs were tangled with his, and gradually, as all he did was hold her, he felt the tension ease out of her and her body relaxed against him.

God, it felt good to have her in his arms. He could feel the baby kicking, and he wondered how on earth she could rest while it fidgeted about like that. Then he got to wondering whether it was a boy or a girl, and if he cared, and he decided he didn't, just so long as everything was all right.

And then he heard a soft snore, and with a wry chuckle he shifted slightly so her head was on his shoulder and not his arm. Tucking the quilt around her shoulders to keep out the draughts, he closed his eyes and lay there and thought about the future.

He didn't know what it would bring, but one thing he was sure of—he and Lucy would be together, with their child, come hell or high water.

It was still dark when she woke up.

Dark, and warm, and deep inside her pillow she could hear a heart beating. Hers?

She shifted her legs, and found they wouldn't move because they were tangled in—legs? Hard, muscular legs, hairy legs, long and lean and definitively masculine.

And her arm was draped across a lean, firm abdomen, her hand resting on a deep chest that rose and fell steadily.

Ben. Safe and solid and apparently not in the least interested in her if last night was anything to go by.

She lifted her head a fraction and tried to ease away, but the arm around her back tightened and eased her back again. 'Don't go.'

'I need the loo,' she said, and he sighed and released her.

The candles had gone out, and she couldn't see where she was going. She heard the bed creak, felt the mattress shift, and the bedside light came on. 'OK?'

'Fine. Thanks.'

'Want a drink?'

'Oh. Water?'

'Want tea? It's nearly six. I have to get up soon.'

'Tea would be great,' she said, and then hurried to the bathroom as the baby shifted against her bladder and reminded her of why she'd woken up. And she sat there on the loo, looking down at this huge blimp that was her body now, and thought, He didn't want me. He just held me all night, and he didn't want me—not once he'd seen me like a beached whale in a T-shirt.

And she felt a stupid, stupid urge to cry. After all, she hadn't wanted to sleep with him, hadn't wanted him to initiate anything, and she'd been really tired.

Now, though, she was perversely disappointed, and she flushed the loo and had a quick wash and cleaned her teeth and wondered if she had time to get dressed again before he got back to the bedroom with the tea.

The answer was no. He was in bed, a mug on each bedside table, and he had his hands locked behind his head so she could see the broad expanse of his chest, lightly scattered with soft, dark hair, his arms powerful and strong. She knew they were strong. They'd lifted her last night as if she weighed nothing, and she remembered that the last time he'd carried her, back in May, it had been because he had wanted her.

Not last night, though.

Damn. And now she had the embarrassing morning-after thing to get through.

'You look better. You looked shattered last night.'

Oh, the compliments were flying today. 'I was,' she said, sliding into bed beside him and wondering how quickly she could drink her tea and get out of this humiliating situation.

'What time do you have to be at work?'

'Eight-thirty.'

'It's only ten to six. I don't have to leave till seven.'

It could have been a simple statement of fact, but there was something in his voice, something warm and gentle and coaxing, and she risked a glance at him and saw he was looking at her with a question in his eyes.

She swallowed, and put her tea down untouched. 'Ben—'

'Come here.'

So she lay down, and rested her head on his chest, and his arm closed around her back, his free hand lifting her chin gently and tilting her head back so he could see into her eyes. 'I want to make love to you, Lucy,' he said softly, and she felt her eyes fill with tears.

'Really?'

He gave a strangled laugh. 'Really. Really, really really— if it's what you want?'

'Oh, yes, please,' she whispered, and with a ragged sigh he rolled towards her, his mouth meeting hers hungrily. His hand ran down her body, his fingers splayed over her hip, her abdomen, up over her ribs, under the T-shirt and cupped her breast with a groan. He pushed the T-shirt impatiently out of the way, then stared down at her, swallowing hard.

'Your nipples are darker than they were. Like chocolate.'

And lowering his head, he took one into his mouth, rolling the other between finger and thumb, just gently, as if he knew how sensitive they'd be, and then his mouth moved on, feathering kisses over the baby, murmuring 'Good morning' on the way past, so she could feel the puff of his breath and hear the smile in his voice, and then he lifted his head.

'I hope you don't wear these outrageous knickers for your antenatal checks,' he murmured, and, slipping a finger under the elastic, he eased them down, tapping her bottom so she'd lift it and he could slide them free.

'Better,' he said, bending his head and kissing her tummy once again. And then his mouth travelled lower, the devastating accuracy of his caress robbing her limbs of control and stealing her breath.

'Ben!' she screamed, and he shifted, stripping the little scrap of lace away from her feet, ripping off his boxers, rolling to his side and taking her with him, leaving her in no doubt about his need of her.

He was so gentle, so careful, but his touch drove her crazy, his hand never leaving her, taking her over the edge in a blinding climax that left her shaken to her core.

Dimly, she was aware of his body stiffening, the ragged cry, the long, slow shudder of his release, and then his hand, trembling, cupping her face, cradling her head as he leant forward and kissed her long and slow before folding her against his still pounding heart.

She felt the baby move, felt his hand splay over it in a gentle caress, and the tears welled in her eyes.

'Are you OK?'

She nodded, squeezing her lids tightly shut, but his fingers caught her chin and lifted it. 'Look at me,' he murmured, and she made herself open her eyes and meet his, so blue, so gentle, yet still smouldering with the last embers of passion.

'You're beautiful,' he whispered. 'So beautiful. I wish I didn't have to go to work.'

'Don't worry. I have to go to work, too.'

'I know.'

He leant forward and kissed her again, softly, lingeringly, then with a sigh he rolled away, threw back the quilt and stood up, walking unselfconsciously into the *en suite* shower room and turning on the water.

He left the door open, and she sat up in bed and drank her now tepid tea. She watched Ben through the steamy glass of the cubicle door and wondered how she could ever reconcile her father to the fact that the man he was convinced had caused the death of his wife was the man she loved.

Because, she realised, she did love him. She'd loved him for years, ever since they'd worked together, and if her mother hadn't died, they might well have been together since that time.

But now it was all the most awful mess, and she had no idea where they could go from here.

'I'll see you later,' he said, shrugging into his jacket and picking up his briefcase. 'What time do you finish work?'

'Six—but, Ben, I don't know…'

'Don't know?'

'If it's a good idea.'

He stared at her, then rammed a hand through his hair,

rumpling the still damp strands and muttering something inaudible under his breath.

'Look, I'll call you,' he said after a moment. 'You drive carefully.'

'You, too.'

He gave her a fleeting smile, hesitated and came back to where she was perched on the third step and pressed a quick, hard kiss on her lips. 'Love you,' he said, and went out, leaving her open-mouthed and speechless.

'He didn't mean it,' she told the empty hall when she could speak. 'He was just saying it. Figure of speech. Nothing more. Don't read anything into it.'

But she couldn't help the crazy, irrational joy that filled her heart. She tucked it away, a warm, cosy glow to keep her going for the rest of the day…

'Morning, Lucy. Good time last night?'

She fought down a blush and smiled at her father. 'Morning, Dad. Yes, thanks.' Good? Try amazing. Incredible.

Love you.

Oh, more than amazing.

'So how did it go with Carter?'

'Car— Oh, the meeting? Fine. Very useful. Dragan couldn't make it but I'm going to fill him in later. How was the house?' she added, hoping to distract him.

'Fine. All done. So, er, where did you say you spent the night?'

Sly old fox. 'I didn't,' she said to make the point, 'but it was late by the time we'd finished dinner and I was falling asleep, so I stayed over,' she said, crossing her fingers under the edge of the desk. To her relief, Kate passed the door and stopped.

'Morning, Lucy. Nick, I wonder if I could have a word? There's a letter here from the PCT that really needs your urgent attention.'

'Oh. Sure.' He turned away.

Lucy met Kate's eyes gratefully over his shoulder and mouthed, 'Thank you.'

Kate just smiled and escorted him away, and Lucy closed the door with a sigh of relief. It dawned on her that if Kate knew the baby was Ben's and was on her side, she could make life a great deal easier. But, then, she'd thought yesterday that Dragan knew, too. And Marco? The smouldering, passionate Italian? He knew about love, although his own marriage was up the creek. Would he see the love for Ben in her eyes and know?

Which only left the reception and nursing staff and her father. And if they talked—

Her phone rang, and she lifted the receiver, banishing the little flutter of panic. 'Hello?'

'Your first patient's here, Lucy, and Toby Penhaligan's just come in—he thinks he's broken his arm. Are you free to see him?'

'Sure. I'll do that first. I'll come out,' she said.

Toby was a local fisherman, a good-looking young man in his twenties, and it wasn't the first time she'd treated him or another member of his family. He was standing in Reception, still in his oilskins and cradling one arm in the other hand. 'Hi, Doc. Sorry about this. Stupid of me—caught my toe on something and went down on deck. I thought I was OK, but I've got no strength in my arm at all and Dad reckons I've broken it.'

'Let's have a look,' she said, and led him up to the MIU.

'Toby, can you get your oilies off? Don't want to go cutting your jacket if we can avoid it, do we?' she said.

He shrugged the good arm out of the jacket and with her help he gritted his teeth and eased the coat down over his hand. By the time she'd sat him down his face was colourless and he was grim-lipped and silent. There was nothing obvious about the arm, now she could see it, and his hand was warm with good capillary refill, but he was cradling the forearm ultra-cautiously in his other hand and she'd bet her life the radius was broken, and probably the ulna as well.

'Can you squeeze my fingers?' she asked, and he tried, but he wouldn't have crumpled a tissue with that much pressure.

'Right. Can you feel your fingers?'

'Can feel the whole darned thing,' he said in disgust. 'It hurts like a proper cow. Dad's right, isn't he? It's broken.'

'I'm afraid it almost certainly is. I'll put a splint on it just to get you to hospital a bit more comfortably, but you'll have to go to St Piran and get a cast on it.'

'Pity you can't do that here.'

'It is, and we're working on it, but it'll be a while yet, Toby. Sorry.' She smiled apologetically at him, wrapped his arm in wadding and taped it to a flat support. 'There. That should stop it moving around too much until you get to St Piran. Rest it on a pillow or a cushion on your lap for the journey. And when you get there, if you see Mr Carter, can you ask him to give me a ring and let me know how it is?'

'Sure. Thanks, Doc. It'll be a while yet. Dad's got the fish to unload and if he doesn't get it away soon he'll miss the market.'

'Well, don't leave it too long. Can't you get someone else to give you a lift?'

He shook his head. 'They've all got things to do—boats

to clean down, nets to repair. Nobody's got time to run about after me. I could take the bus.'

'Not with a fracture. You could call an ambulance.'

'What, and waste their time? No, Doc, it was my own fault. I'll wait for my dad.' He stood up. 'I'll give Mr Carter your message,' he said, opening the door, and typically her father was just outside.

'What message?' he asked, stepping through the door after Toby had gone out and scowling.

'What?' she asked, pretending ignorance.

'For Ben Carter.'

'Oh. About Toby's fracture. I think it's exactly the sort of thing we could treat here—I wanted his opinion. It's really difficult for Toby to get to St Piran. He won't call an ambulance because of the waste of resources, and his father can't leave till they've unloaded the fish and got them away. And they've been out all night and they're exhausted. X-ray and plaster facilities here would improve things so much for people like him.' She smiled at him and kissed his cheek. 'And now, if you'll excuse me, I've got a full surgery and I'm already running late.'

He grunted, gave her a fleeting hug—the first for how long?—and opened the door for her. She gave a quick sigh of relief, went back down to her consulting room and carried on with her work.

CHAPTER FIVE

'LUCY?'

'Ben—hi. I take it you've seen Toby Penhaligan?' Her voice was light, as if she was pleased to hear from him. He hadn't been sure how she'd react once she'd had time to think about last night, but at least she wasn't cool and distant, and he felt a surge of something he couldn't quite analyse. Relief? No, more than that…

'Yes. He had a simple undisplaced fracture of both radius and ulna. Were you worried about him, or thinking you could have treated him there with the right facilities?'

'Oh, the latter. I thought he seemed just the sort of case I was talking about, and it was so frustrating that I had to send him to you.'

'Absolutely. You know he did it yesterday, don't you? But they were out all night and couldn't get back until they'd hauled in the lines.'

'And his father couldn't bring him to you till the fish were unloaded and away, or they would have lost their money for the catch. It's a tough life for our fishermen, and I wouldn't want to be doing it in those rough seas, I'm not good on the water,' she said, and then went on with a slightly self-conscious laugh, 'That's by the by. I wanted to know—so I can use it in an argument with the powers that be—what time he arrived, when he was seen and how long it took, so I can compare it to what would have happened if I could have put a cast on it when I saw him at eight forty-five this morning.'

Of course she did. All business. Ben forced himself to stop thinking about the sound of her voice and concentrate on her words. 'Let me check the notes. Right, he arrived at the department at ten-fifty, was seen by the triage nurse and sent to wait until eleven twenty-five, then he was seen by one of the doctors, X-rayed and then a cast put on it at twelve-ten. He was discharged from the department at twelve forty-two. I got the staff to log it because I knew you'd want to know.'

He could hear the smile in her voice. 'You're a regular sweetheart,' she said, then went on in a more businesslike tone, 'So he had a wait for the doctor, a wait for X-ray, a wait for the doctor to confirm the diagnosis and a wait for the cast. And it took one hour fifty-two minutes.'

'Yup. Which is pretty good for here. And then there's the travelling time and parking—say another hour to an hour and a half.'

'Three hours, then, on a good day, not to mention the added discomfort of the journey.'

'And you could have done it in—what? Forty-five minutes?'

'Something like that,' she agreed. 'So he would have been out of here and on his way home by nine-thirty, instead of one-thirty—four hours earlier—and his father wouldn't have been taken away from his work. And, of course, if one of the nurses was trained to take X-rays, it would cut down the time I or one of the other doctors would be tied up as well. That's fantastic. Thank you so much for all that information.'

'My pleasure. I wasn't sure if I'd catch you, actually,' he added, trying to sound casual. 'I thought you might have gone home for lunch.'

'No, Kate nipped out and bought us all sandwiches from the bakery. I'm just eating them now.'

'Are you alone?'

'Yes. I'm in my consulting room.'

'So—about tonight,' he murmured, trying very hard not to think about what they'd done that morning and how very, very much he wanted to do it again. 'How about supper?'

There was a slight pause, and his heart sank. She's going to say no, he thought, but then she said, 'That would be lovely, but can we make it early? I'm really tired. I could do with getting back for an early night.'

His heart, on the way up, sank again, but he told himself not to be selfish. She was pregnant. She needed her rest. 'Good idea,' the doctor and father in him said. 'So are you coming to me, or shall I bring something to you, or are we ready to go public?'

She laughed softly. 'You think coming to me isn't going public? Dream on, Ben. This is Penhally.'

Of course. 'So—where, then?'

'Yours?'

'Sure,' he said, disappointed that he didn't get to take her out and spoil her, but glad that he'd be seeing her anyway. 'Want me to pick you up, or would you rather drive yourself?'

'I'll drive. Shall I come over as soon as I've finished?'

'Good idea. Anything you particularly fancy?'

'Fish,' she said promptly. 'Sea bass. There are some in the fridge here, courtesy of the Penhaligans. Shall I bring two?'

'That would be good. And I'll make you something irresistible for pudding.'

She chuckled, and the sound did amazing things to his nerve endings. 'Chocolate,' she ordered, and he laughed.

'How did I guess?' There was a tap on his door and his specialist registrar stuck her head round it. Ben lifted a hand to keep her there. 'Lucy, I'm sorry, I have to go now, but I'll see you later,' he said, and replaced the phone on its cradle. 'Jo, thanks for coming by. I've got an appointment at two-thirty. It's only a few minutes away—fifteen at the most. Can you hold the fort?'

'Sure. It's pretty quiet at the moment.'

'Don't say that,' he warned, and glanced at his watch. Five to two. Just time to catch up on some paperwork before he had to leave.

So this was it. Tregorran House, Lucy's grandmother's family home and the house of her dreams. Ben walked slowly up to the open back door and called out, and a young man in a suit appeared and strode towards him, hand outstretched.

'Mr Carter? Come on in.'

He shook hands and went into what seemed to be a lean-to scullery or boot room, and through to the dirty and desperately dated kitchen. 'Sorry about the back door, the front door won't open,' the agent was saying. 'They're never used in this part of the world, and the key seems to have gone missing. It's a shame because it's a lovely way in and out, you get to see the views from there. Come on through and have a look around.'

It was smaller than he'd expected. Low ceilings, but here and there were old oak beams that hinted at a concealed structure crying out to be revealed. There was a huge granite inglenook in the kitchen, an ancient and filthy cream Aga fitting easily into the space once occupied by the range, and smaller, more functional granite fireplaces in the two living rooms that bracketed the front door. The rooms weren't huge, but they were cosy, overlooking the garden, and he could imagine them with fires crackling in the grates.

Upstairs the fireplaces were boarded over, but he'd bet his bottom dollar there were pretty little cast-iron grates behind the boards, or there had been in the past.

But the outstanding thing about the whole property, once you got over the poor state of the decor and the fact that it clearly needed a serious cash injection, was the view. All the principal rooms faced west, looking down the coast towards the Atlantic Ocean, and the sunsets Lucy loved would be spectacular.

'Does it go down to the beach?' he asked, and the agent shook his head.

'No. The plot's quite small, just the half acre of garden the house sits in, but there isn't really a beach here anyway, just a pile of rocks. You can get to the beach about half a mile away over the fields, though. They're owned by the neighbouring farmer. It's a lovely little cove and there's quite a good road to it, too. It's very pretty, and the path's well maintained—it's part of the Cornish Coastal Path—but, no, it hasn't got beach access. Otherwise the guide price would be a great deal higher. There's nothing the London buyers like more than their own private beach. And, of course, because the planners have ruled out any development of the site other than extension of the existing house within the realms of permitted development, that's also going to keep the price a bit more accessible. That said, we've had quite a keen interest in the property,' he added, as if he was worried he'd put Ben off. Or was it agent-speak for 'This is highly sought after and you'd be foolish to miss it'?

Maybe.

Whatever, it was irrelevant to Ben. The house was awful at the moment, dingy and rundown and outdated, but it had the potential to be a lovely cosy family home, and it was Lucy's dream. If he could get it for her without bankrupting himself into the hereafter, he'd do it.

'I'm sorry to rush you, but I've got another viewing to get to. Could I leave you to go around the outside on your own?' the agent asked, and Ben nodded.

'Of course. I've seen all I need to.' More than enough to make up his mind.

He spent a few minutes looking around the outside, checking out the structure and exploring the rundown and tangled garden that Lucy obviously remembered through rose-tinted specs, and then he headed back to the hospital.

To his relief Jo had coped without him, and it was still quiet, so he shut himself away in his office and rang his solicitor.

'What's the procedure for buying a house at auction?' he asked. 'Because I want you to do it for me. Friday, two o'clock, Tregorran House. And I don't want to take any chances.'

'Ah, Lucy. Got time for a chat?'

'Dragan—hi. I've been meaning to catch up with you.' She sat back in her chair and stretched out the kinks in her neck. 'How's Melinda?'

'Oh, fine. Thank you both so much for sorting her arm out.'

'Pleasure—well, hardly, but you know what I mean,' she said with a laugh. 'I'm sorry you missed our meeting. How's the dog?'

He smiled. 'Really sweet. She's got a broken leg and a

huge laceration on her side, but nobody's come forward yet to report her missing. Melinda's set the leg and she's looking after her for now.'

'No more biting?'

He shook his head and smiled again. 'No. She's a sweetheart. She was just scared. Anyway, this meeting...'

'Yes—really useful. Ben thinks we could do it. If we could build on out the back as we'd discussed, then he thinks it'll be fine. Maybe reorganise upstairs a bit and have downstairs as a fracture clinic, essentially.' She ran through the key points of their discussion. Dragan nodded at intervals, and then she sat back and stretched again and sighed.

'You OK?'

'Oh, Dragan, I'm so tired. Just the thought of another six or eight weeks before I can give up is enough to send me to sleep!'

He frowned in concern. 'Lucy, you shouldn't be overdoing it. You should be resting now. We can manage.'

'You're sounding like my father,' she pointed out, and he gave an embarrassed laugh and sat back.

'OK, it's not my job, but I care about you. We all do.'

She flapped her hand at him, touched but still not having any of it. 'I'm fine. I think we ought to have a meeting. Kate was talking about setting something up with the local NHS trust architect and Ben here on site, but Dad's so anti.'

'Don't worry about him, Lucy. He wants what's best for the patients.'

'He's just so blinkered,' she said, thinking not only of the forthcoming meeting but also of the news she yet had to give her father—news that couldn't possibly make the situation any easier.

'I take it he doesn't know?'

She jerked her head up and met his eyes, her mouth already opening to deny everything, and saw the gentle understanding in Dragan's eyes. She swallowed and looked away. 'No. He doesn't know.'

'That will be hard.'

'It will be impossible,' she said softly, 'but it has to be done.' She sucked in a breath and straightened up. 'Right, I have to get on. I've got a clinic in a minute. If you let Kate know when you're free for this meeting, she'll try and organise it.'

'I'll do that,' he said, and got to his feet, then hesitated. 'Lucy, if there's anything I can do…?'

He left it hanging, and with a fleeting smile he went out. He was so kind and thoughtful. So was Marco. The two of them fussed over her like a couple of clucky old hens. It was only her father she had a problem with.

And she was going to have to deal with it.

Ben cooked the sea bass beautifully.

Outside, on a charcoal barbeque with the lid shut, in the bleak and windy garden, and then brought them into the house with the skin lightly charred and the inside meltingly tender. He'd prepared a green salad and hot jacket potatoes, and then he produced the wickedest hot chocolate sauce pudding she'd ever seen in her life.

'It's a fabulously easy recipe—my mother taught it to me,' he said with a grin, and put a big dollop of it on a plate and handed it to her. 'Here, you need this,' he said, and gave her a dish of clotted cream.

'Define need,' she said wryly, and he chuckled.

'You have to have some treats. Anyway, it's probably full of vitamin D.'

'You don't have to talk me into it,' she said, plopping a generous spoonful onto the top of the chocolate goo and then tasting it.

'Mmm,' she said, and then didn't talk any more for a few gorgeous, tastebud-melting minutes. Conversation would have been sacrilege.

'Good?' he asked when she'd all but scraped the glaze off the plate, and she laughed and pushed the plate away and arched back, giving her stomach room.

'Fabulous,' she said emphatically. 'Assuming I don't just burst. Thank you.'

'My pleasure. Coffee?'

'Mmm—thanks. Can I help wash up?'

'No—the dishwasher'll do it all. You can go and sit down in the sitting room and put your feet up.'

'Is that an order?' she asked, and he tipped his head on one side and studied her closely.

'That's a loaded question,' he retorted after a moment, a grin tugging at one corner of his mouth. 'I don't think I'll answer it.'

Chuckling to herself, she went into the sitting room and curled up on the sofa, not because he'd told her to but because she wanted to anyway. She'd had a busy day, starting with Tony Penhaligan and ending with an overrunning surgery, and she'd hardly had a minute to herself in between. So she was more than happy to sit down, and after a moment she stretched her legs out, rested her head back and closed her eyes.

There was a gorgeous smell of fresh coffee drifting from the kitchen, and she sniffed it appreciatively. It would set off the chocolate pud to perfection. She heard him come in, heard him set the tray down and felt the end of the sofa dip under his weight.

'White, no sugar,' she murmured, and he chuckled and rubbed her feet affectionately before pouring the coffee.

'Here—sit up and open your eyes,' he said, and she did as she was told, watching him over the rim of the mug as she sipped it.

'Thank you for cooking for me,' she said, wriggling her toes under his thigh.

He smiled. 'My pleasure. Thank you for the sea bass.'

'I'll pass it on to the Penhaligans. Good day?'

His eyes flicked away, his attention turning to his coffee. 'Yes. Very good. Busy. How about you?'

'Oh, busy, too. I phoned you during the afternoon to try and set up a time for this next meeting with the architect, but they said you were out of the department.'

'Mmm—I had a meeting,' he said, but he didn't elaborate. Not that he had to tell her everything about his life, of course he didn't, and if he started poking about in her life she'd be less than impressed, but somehow she felt excluded, and she didn't like it. She wanted, she realised with some surprise, to be entitled to know who he'd met with and why. Probably someone on the hospital management committee, the chief exec or something, nothing interesting at all—but it would have been nice if he'd told her, or if she'd had the right to ask.

Which was just plain silly. They hardly knew each other. Just because they had an unfortunate tendency to end up in bed every time they met, it didn't mean they were part of each other's lives!

And then he said, 'Stay with me tonight,' and she felt an overwhelming urge to do just that. To go to bed with him, to curl up in his arms and sleep, just as she had last night. She hadn't slept so well in ages, but she couldn't let herself be lured into it so readily. It would be all to easy to let it become a habit, and until her father knew...

'I can't,' she said, with genuine regret, and he sighed and smiled ruefully.

'I knew you'd say that.'

'It's just...'

'Difficult? I know. Lucy, if you want me there when you tell him—'

'No!' she said quickly, sitting up so fast she nearly slopped her coffee. 'No,' she said again, more calmly this time. 'I just need to find the right moment.'

He nodded, then looked down at her feet, giving them undue attention. 'I do love you, you know. I wasn't just saying it this morning.'

She put the coffee down, very carefully, on the table that was conveniently in reach, and stared at him. 'You do? But you hardly know me.'

'Rubbish. You haven't changed. We spent six months together when you were on your A and E rotation.'

'And you had a girlfriend!'

'Not for all of it. I ended it because she wasn't what I wanted. I hadn't known that until I met someone who was, and then it gradually dawned on me that I was with the wrong woman. And because I wanted to be sure, I gave us time, because I felt that this could really be it—the once-in-a-lifetime thing. Then you got to the end of your rotation, and shortly after that—'

He broke off and looked away again, and she finished for him, 'My mother died, and it all went horribly wrong.'

He nodded, and for a moment neither of them spoke, then she said softly, 'Ben, what if I've changed? What if I'm not the woman you think I am? What if time's altered your perception of me and I can't live up to your mental image?' She swallowed, facing her fears head on. 'And what if you don't live up to mine?'

He glanced over, a quick frown pleating his brow, and he searched her face. 'So we'll take it slowly,' he suggested at last. 'Give ourselves time to get to know the people we are now. But to do that, we need to spend time together, so we have to find a way to do that.'

She nodded, knowing he was right. Marriage was for life, as the saying went, not just for Christmas, and she wasn't sure if they knew each other well enough yet for such a huge commitment. But if everything was right between them by then, she'd much rather they were married when the baby was born, old-fashioned though it might be. Some things, she thought, were meant to be old-fashioned. And if they were to get to know each other, they had to spend time together, despite her father complicating the issue.

'This weekend?' she suggested. 'I'm off from Friday after my morning surgery until Monday morning.'

'Sure. That would be good. I'm on call tomorrow night, but I've got the afternoon off on Friday. I've got things to do but we could meet up when I'm done. I'll book us a table somewhere for dinner on Friday night—perhaps in Padstow—and then we can come back here and chill for a couple of days. Go for a walk, toast crumpets, whatever—what do you think?'

She nodded again, even the thought enough to make her

feel more relaxed. 'Sounds blissful,' she said with a smile. 'And now I really ought to go home so I don't fall asleep at the wheel.'

Or succumb to the seductive charm of those gorgeous blue eyes...

He helped her up, held her coat for her, tucked it around her to keep her warm and kissed her lingeringly before waving her off, then went back inside.

What if I can't live up to your mental image? And what if you don't live up to mine?

He felt a tense knot of something strangely like fear in his chest. Please, God, by the weekend he'd have something good to tell her. Something that hopefully would help a little with the mental image she had of him?

Oh, hell. What if it didn't? What if it was just nostalgia for the house and not a real urge to live there? And what if he didn't get the house after all? What if, despite all his preparation, despite getting the money sorted, pinning his purchaser down to a date, getting his solicitor to bid for him over the phone and sort out the paperwork—what if, despite all that, he was quite simply outbid at the auction? If the price just went up and up and up until it was out of his reach?

Lucy stared out of her consulting-room window across the car park to the sea beyond the harbour wall, her emotions torn.

He loved her. He'd said it as if he really meant it, not in a moment of passion, not as a passing farewell like before, but quietly, thoughtfully.

And she so, so wanted to believe him, but there was a bit of her that was afraid he was talking himself into it because of the baby. Because he wanted to create the image of the perfect family, and that was the first step, the cornerstone.

Maybe he genuinely believed he did love her, but she was too scared to believe it.

Her phone rang, and it was Hazel, the head receptionist, to tell her that her first patient had arrived. Even the thought exhausted her. She'd been busy yesterday, and no doubt today would be the same. She hoped not, because otherwise she'd be too tired by tomorrow to enjoy her long weekend with Ben. But putting it off any longer wouldn't make it go away.

As she'd expected, the day was hellish, and she fell into bed exhausted at eight o'clock. She heard the phone ring in the sitting room, but she'd forgotten to bring it into her bedroom because she wasn't on call, and by the time she'd decided she ought to get up, it had stopped ringing.

Oh, well, if it was important they'd ring again, she thought, but whoever it was didn't. She could dial 1471 and check, she thought, or see if there was a message.

She fell asleep again, then had to get up in the night because the baby was wriggling around on her bladder, and on her way back to bed she checked the answering-machine and found a message from Ben.

Damn. She should have got out of bed and taken the call, and really wished she had. She played the message, sitting in bed with the phone, listening to his voice and wishing she was with him.

She played it again. 'You aren't there, or maybe you're having an early night. It's not important. I just wanted to talk to you. It seems odd not seeing you two nights running. Take care. I'll see you tomorrow.' Then a pause, then, 'Love you.'

She looked at her bedside clock. Two-thirty in the morning—too late, or too early, to ring. Except he was on call—so either he was working or he would be asleep. Either way, she couldn't really disturb him, and he wouldn't ring again.

She sent a text to his mobile.

'Thanks for message. Early night. Looking forward to w/e. Lucy.' And then, for good measure, 'X'. She nearly put 'Love you' like he had, but it seemed too massively important to risk getting it wrong, and when she did tell him, if she ever did, she wanted to see his face.

Suddenly the afternoon seemed much, much too far away…

Ben didn't want to be at the auction.

He wasn't sure if Nick Tremayne would be there, but he didn't want to risk it. He didn't know how the man would feel about him buying the house, but frankly he didn't care. This wasn't about Nick, it was about Lucy, and if he'd thought enough of the place to hold on to it for several years, then once he and his daughter had sorted out this glitch in their relationship, Ben was sure that keeping the house in the family could only be good for all of them.

But Lucy was his primary concern, and he had so much riding on it he felt sick.

He'd booked the time off, but now he wished he hadn't. He couldn't go home and sit there, though, just waiting for the phone to ring, so he drove to the house. Well, almost. He didn't want to push his luck, tempt fate, whatever. So he sat in the car, just down the lane, and rang his solicitor.

He got his secretary, and asked her to get him to ring as soon as there was any news.

'I'll call you on another line,' she promised, 'while Simon's bidding—that way he can talk to you at the same time, give you a chance to decide how you want to play it.'

He felt the tension ratchet up a notch. 'OK. I'll keep the phone free,' he promised, and plugged in the charger. He wasn't going to lose the house because of something stupid like a flat battery.

There was a woman up on the headland, leaning into the wind, her clothes plastered against her body and her hair streaming out behind like a figurehead on an old sailing ship. Except—this figurehead was pregnant. *Lucy?* Yes, Lucy— standing there, keeping vigil, saying goodbye while the house was sold out from under her.

Well, hardly, because she didn't live there, but emotionally it must feel like that, he realised, and he felt the tension ratchet up yet again. He *had* to get it.

The phone rang, startling him, and he grabbed it.

'Ben—it's Simon. We're on. I've got the auctioneer on hands-free so you can listen in and talk to me at the same time.'

'Great.'

Except it wasn't great, it was terrifying, and he realised that even in the grip of a major accident, when the hospital instituted its MAJAX plan, he'd never felt quite this scared that things would go wrong.

He could hear the bidding, hear the figures rising perilously close to his maximum. He'd still got the budget for the work in hand, but it needed that. He couldn't use it all, but he could dip into it if he had to—

'Ben?'

'Another five thousand—in ones,' he instructed, and listened as the price climbed slowly up, long pauses now between the bids.

'The other bidder's only gone up five hundred—he must be close to his limit,' Simon said.

'Call his bluff. Go up five thousand more, in one jump,' Ben said, his heart pounding. 'See if you can knock him out.'

There was a long, long silence, then he heard the auctioneer say, 'Going once… Going twice…' and the sound of the hammer coming down. But who—?

'Congratulations!' Simon said. 'You've got yourself a house.'

Somehow Ben ended the call. He wasn't sure what he'd said, what he'd agreed to do. It didn't matter. He'd call Simon back later. For now there was a woman standing on the headland, and she needed his attention.

He drove up to the house—his house, or it would be soon—and turned in the gate. Her car was there, pulled up by the door, and he blocked her in just in case he missed her somehow.

He didn't. She was still there, standing staring out to sea, and he went down the track by the side of the garden, across the field and walked up behind her.

'Lucy?'

She turned slowly, and he could see the tears on her cheeks, dried by the wind.

'It's gone,' she said woodenly. 'The house. It's gone. The sale was at two.'

'I know.'

She hugged herself, her hands wrapping around her slender arms and hanging on, and he stood between her and the biting wind and cupped her face in his hands.

'I've got something for you,' he said softly. 'Come back to the house with me.'

Her brow furrowed. 'The house?'

'Mmm.'

She turned, and he put his arm round her and led her carefully back over the field. At the gateway to the house he stopped and scooped her into his arms.

'What are you doing?' she asked, startled.

'It's tradition,' he said, 'except it should be the front door, but I can't do that because I haven't got the keys and anyway the front door key's missing.'

She stared at him blankly. 'Tradition?'

'To carry your woman over the threshold.' He took a deep breath and walked through the gateway. 'Welcome to your new home, Lucy.'

She stared at him for an age, then hope flickered in her eyes. 'My new…?'

'I bought the house—for you,' he told her gently, and she burst into tears.

CHAPTER SIX

She couldn't believe it.

He'd put her down carefully on her feet, on the driveway of the house, and he was looking down at her expectantly.

No, not expectantly, exactly, but as if he wasn't quite sure what reception his news was getting, and needed—desperately needed—to know.

'Oh, Ben,' she said, flinging her arms around him and hugging him, then letting him go and looking up at him searchingly while she hunted for a tissue.

'Here,' he said, and handed her one with a smile, and she blew her nose, scrubbed away the still welling tears, and stared up at him again.

'I can't believe— How on earth did you afford it? It must have gone for a fortune. You're crazy!'

'Only a tiny fortune,' he said with a wry, slightly uncertain smile. 'I'd sold my house—never did like it—and I'd been looking for somewhere older, somewhere with character. Then you told me about this, and—well, there I was, in a position to do something about it, and I thought— Hell, I don't know what I thought, but if the chance was there to give you the house of your dreams, somewhere you'd be safe and happy, I didn't want to risk not doing it. And if you really didn't want it after all, I thought I could always stick it back on the market.'

'You really bought it for me?'

His mouth quirked into a smile again. 'Well, I was kind of hoping you'd let me share it, but—yes, I bought it for you. You and the baby.' His face shadowed. 'But it's quite isolated—apart from the farmhouse over there, you can't see another house, and it's nearly a mile to the village, if you can call it that. It seems like a pretty tiny community. If it was just nostalgia—'

'No!' she said hastily, hurrying to correct him. 'No, Ben, it wasn't just nostalgia. I *love* this house. I've always loved it. I just can't believe—' She broke off, not knowing how to continue, what to say, still utterly overwhelmed by what he'd done.

And the way he'd presented it, too, not as some kind of grand gesture, not a '*ta-da!*' but humbly, as if he'd done it to make her happy and not to score Brownie points.

'It's a shame we can't go inside, but I won't get the keys for ages.'

She dangled them under his nose. 'I got them off Dad. Said I wanted to have a last look around.' She held them out to him. 'Well, go on, then,' she said, but he shook his head.

'It's not mine yet,' he reminded her, and it was as if the mention of her father's name had taken all the colour out of the day. But he was still smiling, his eyes searching her face for clues, and suddenly she wanted to look around it with him, to tell him about her grandmother, to show him the house from her memories.

'I can take you in,' she pointed out, waggling the keys. 'I have the vendor's permission to be here.'

And taking him by the hand, she led him to the back door, opened it and then stopped him when he would have lifted her. 'No,' she said. 'Not yet. Not until we're…' She caught herself, then went on, 'Not until it's properly yours.'

What had she been going to say?

Not until we're—what?

Married?

One step at a time, he warned himself, cutting off his hopes before they got totally out of sync with reality.

He stopped worrying about it and followed her into the house, watching her face as she went from room to room, telling him stories.

'Oh, it looks so dirty and shabby, but I can remember my grandfather's coat hanging here, and my grandmother's elderly jacket that she used for the garden. Tweed, good and thick, utterly hideous, but it kept her warm. And the dogs always slept here, next to the Aga,' she said, moving through to the kitchen. 'Grannie was always baking—apple pies, cakes, wholemeal bread that was so wonderful I still haven't found anything to match it. And there was often a casserole in the bottom oven, or a baked egg custard made with milk from the house cow and eggs from the chickens that used to scratch about outside.'

'Do you want chickens?' he asked, fascinated by the emotions flitting over her face.

She laughed. 'Maybe. There was a cockerel who used to crow outside my bedroom window at some revolting hour of the morning, but I never minded because it meant I was here, and I loved it so much. Yes, chickens would be fun, but not the house cow. Too much like hard work! I remember being kicked off the milking stool by her when I was nine, and my mother wouldn't let me milk her again. Said it was too dangerous. Anyway, we can get milk from the Trevellyans down the road.'

We?

They went through to the rooms at the front, the one she'd said had been the dining room and the one with the lovely fireplace that was just crying out for a big old dog grate with fragrant apple logs burning in the hearth.

'We used to toast crumpets here by the fire,' she told him. 'And we'd butter them, and it would drip through and onto our fingers and the dogs would sneak up and lick the backs of our hands where the butter had run round. They used to get yelled at and shooed out.'

'Collies?'

'Mostly. There was a Jack Russell at one time, but he was ancient. He was allowed in here by the fire, and sometimes even on my lap. Grannie was so upset when he died.'

They went upstairs, to the rooms overlooking the sea, and she took him into the smallest one over the front door. 'This was mine. Jack and Ed shared the room at the back, and Grannie and Grandpa were in the big bedroom next door that way, and my parents were in that room.'

'Jack and Ed?'

'My brothers.' She stroked her fingers reverently over the window-sill, wide enough to sit on, and told him about how she'd sat there by the open window in the summer, after the cockerel had woken her, and waited for the dawn. 'Sometimes I saw a fox sneak past the chicken house, and once I saw one run off with a chicken in his mouth. Grannie was livid.'

She laughed, the sound like a waterfall, and he felt the tight knot of tension that had been there for days start to ease. It was going to be all right. He knew it was.

They just had that one last hurdle to get over…

'Did you know about this?'

The door crashed back against the wall, and the baby inside her stiffened, startled by the sudden noise. Lucy cradled it automatically, soothing it with her hands, and met her father's eyes with as much composure as she could muster.

She didn't pretend not to know what he was talking about. He was brandishing a letter from the estate agent, and his face was stiff with fury.

'Yes, I knew,' she said. 'Not until afterwards, though.'

'And you didn't think fit to tell me? My own daughter, and you didn't tell me that *that man* had bought my house?'

'Your mother's house,' she pointed out, and he growled under his breath and slapped the paperwork down on her desk.

'Don't split hairs, Lucy! How did you know?'

'I was there,' she told him, lifting her chin. 'At the house— saying goodbye. Ben turned up. He told me then—right after the auction. He'd bid over the phone.'

'Coward.'

'Not at all,' she said, frustrated. 'He'd been at work. He didn't have time to drive all the way to the auction house.'

'God! He only did it to spite me.'

'Don't be ridiculous, Dad. It's a lovely house. He's been looking for something for ages.'

Tell him! her conscience urged, but she bottled out in the face of his already considerable anger. Not because she was afraid of him, because she knew perfectly well how much he loved her and that he would never lift a finger to her, but because now wasn't the time. She had a surgery starting in a minute, and so did he.

And she wanted time to talk it through with him, to explain her feelings, to discuss her mother's death a little more rationally. But right now, she knew, he simply wouldn't listen.

'Well, I wanted to let it go,' he said at last. 'And maybe it's for the best. At least now I know I'll never have to go into the house again.'

And he strode out, leaving her sitting there in the ringing silence.

So much for her blissful, relaxing weekend. They'd had a wonderful time. Ben had taken her down to Padstow, to a café, one of her favourite places, where the food was fresh and unpretentious and the atmosphere lively. It wasn't romantic, but it was fun, and she'd accidentally squirted Ben with prawn juice and they'd laughed till she'd thought they'd die from lack of oxygen.

Then they'd gone back to his house and he'd made love to her on the sofa in front of the fire, and then again in the morning, lying in bed lazily until midday while he'd waited on her and indulged her every whim.

Breakfast in bed—*pain au chocolat*, gallons of delicately flavoured tea with just a touch of milk, fresh fruit sliced into a bowl and fed to her with his fingers—and then she'd sucked the juice off them, and his eyes had darkened and he'd put the bowl down, moved the tray and kissed the juice from her lips.

It had taken a very long time, Lucy remembered with a fleeting smile. In the afternoon they'd gone to the supermarket and bought crumpets, and rump steak and shoestring fries for dinner with loads of salad, and he'd cooked the chocolate pudding again.

They'd got up earlier on Sunday and gone for a lovely walk on the coastal path by Tregorran House, and then they'd gone back inside and talked about what he was going to do to the house. She'd stayed over that night as well, and had only got home this morning in time for surgery.

And now her father was baying for Ben's blood, and she didn't know what to do for the best.

She shut the door, sank down at her desk and let her hands drift down to cradle her baby. It had been such a lovely weekend, and by the end of it she'd managed to convince herself that everything would be all right.

Ben had been so good to her, and they'd had so much fun. She knew she loved him, and she was beginning to think that, yes, he really did love her, and they'd get married and live happily ever after in Tregorran House and everything would be great.

Stupid. She'd let herself get carried away on a big fluffy cloud, and now she was down to earth again with a bang.

Eight and a half weeks to go, she thought. Eight and a half weeks to convince her father that Ben was all right and he hadn't done anything wrong, and reconcile them to the point that he would give her away to Ben with his blessing, so they could get married before the baby came.

Not a chance.

If only things were more normal and they were married. So the baby could be born in wedlock.

Grief, what an old-fashioned saying. Wedlock. Like prison.

Only with Ben, she knew, it wouldn't be. It would be wonderful. But there was still the problem of her father, and getting both him and Ben at the wedding might be more than she could manage.

So could she marry Ben without her father there? She swallowed hard, blinking back tears. Without her father's knowledge?

No. She couldn't do that. It would be bad enough not having her mother there. For her father not to be there either—no. She couldn't even contemplate it.

And anyway, they were light years from that, and before she could worry about it, she had a surgery to get through, and a whole batch of visits, including one to Edith Jones. She'd tried to ring her first thing but hadn't got any reply. There could have been lots of reasons for that, not least that Edith couldn't move that fast any longer.

On the other hand—no, don't borrow trouble, she told herself, and worked her way steadily through her patients, putting Edith and Ben and her father firmly out of her mind for now.

Doris Trefussis, the practice cleaner and general all-round good egg, stuck her head round the door after her last patient had left. 'Want a cuppa, my bird?' she asked, giving Lucy a smile that still twinkled even though she was beginning to show her age. She was supposedly fifty-nine, but by all accounts she'd been fifty-nine for years. Thin, wiry and always smiling, Lucy didn't know what they'd do without her.

'No, I'm fine, Doris, thank you. I've got to go out on my visits. I'm a bit worried about Edith Jones—she's not answering her phone.'

'Saw her yesterday out in her garden—she looked all right,' Doris said. 'Can't you have a little drink first?'

Lucy smiled but still shook her head. 'No. You can make me one when I get back. And if you've got a minute, you couldn't slip round to the bakery and pick up a sandwich, could you? Wholemeal bread, something healthy without too much mayo?'

'Of course, dear. I'll get one with a nice bit of chicken in it—easily digestible. And a little apple turnover—I know you love them.'

'You spoil me,' she said, giving Doris the money and wondering how huge she was going to be by the time everyone, including Ben, had finished feeding her up. 'Right, I'm off to Mrs Jones. I'll see you later. Bless you.'

She drove to Edith's first, a little bungalow high up above the old town, in a development characterised by its lack of any architectural merit but a comfortable, friendly community for all that. Edith and her husband had lived there all their married lives, and Lucy sincerely hoped Edith could continue to live there for ever. She'd certainly have support from her neighbours. She'd known most of them for years and years.

She pulled up on the road outside and looked around, seeing nothing out of the way. Nothing to indicate that there was a problem, certainly. Getting her bag out of the car, she went up to the front door and rang the bell, listening carefully.

Odd. The television wasn't on. It always was. Perhaps she'd gone away—spent the weekend with one of her children and not got back yet, perhaps? Except Doris had seen her yesterday, out in the garden. She rang the bell again, and bent down and peered through the letter box.

'Mrs Jones?' she called. 'Edith? It's Dr Lucy. Are you all right?'

Silence, and then, just as she let the flap go, she heard a faint cry. She pushed it open again. 'Edith? Are you there?'

'In the kitchen—key under the pot,' Edith called weakly.

Pot? Which pot? There were hundreds, in all shapes and

sizes, clustered around the front door. She checked under all the obvious ones, then went round to the back door and tried there, and to her relief there it was under the first pot she lifted—a shiny silver key. She opened the door and went straight into the kitchen, and found Edith lying awkwardly on the floor, propped up against the kitchen cupboards where she'd hauled herself.

'Edith!' she exclaimed softly, crouching down beside her a little awkwardly and touching her cheek in a gesture of reassurance.

'Oh, Dr Lucy, I'm so glad to see you. I knew you were coming—it's the only thing that's kept me going. I heard the phone ring and ring, and I just couldn't get to it. I was so hoping you'd come—not just think I was out.'

Lucy felt a huge wave of relief that she hadn't, in fact done that. She knew many doctors would have, but people in this tight-knit community didn't let each other down, and if Edith hadn't been going to be there, she would have told her.

'Don't move. Let me check you over. You just stay there. Let me get you a pillow for your head and something to tuck behind your back.' She ran into the bedroom, came back with a pair of pillows and the quilt off the bed and, after checking that Edith wasn't experiencing any back pain, she slid the pillows into place and then ran her hands gently over all her limbs.

'Oh!' Edith cried when Lucy touched her left leg. 'Oh, that's so sore. I think I landed on my knee—I must have tripped over the cat, I think.'

Possibly. There was no sign of a cat, but Lucy was much more worried about Edith. The knee was hugely swollen, a dark purple bruise fanning out from the centre of her kneecap, and she wouldn't have been surprised to learn it was a starburst fracture. 'Any idea how long ago you fell, my love?' she asked gently, her eyes still scanning over the damaged leg.

'Hours.'

Hmm. Edith was breathless, obviously in pain, and Lucy knew the first step was to get her over to St Piran and get her checked out. 'I'm going to call an ambulance and get them to take you to the hospital to get this knee looked at,' she said, and it was a measure of how serious the pain was that Edith, stubborn and independent as she was, didn't argue.

Once she'd called the ambulance service, Lucy tucked the quilt around her and gave her pain relief, hooked her up to the portable oxygen and sat back to wait, holding Edith's hand. It didn't take long. Paramedic Maggie Pascoe, a familiar face not only to Lucy from her time in the emergency department at St Piran but also to Edith, as she was a local girl, came running up the path to the door, and Lucy quickly let her in.

'You're lucky, we were just parked up the road having our lunch,' she said with a smile. 'Hello, Edith—what have you done to yourself, you silly thing?'

'Oh, I know—so stupid. I just fell. And I think I've wet myself,' Edith added in distress, as Lucy handed over to Maggie.

'Don't worry, my love, we'll soon sort you out,' Maggie said with a smile, and they quickly loaded her onto the trolley and trundled her down the hall. The path from the door was mercifully flat and straight, and Lucy had given her enough pain relief to make the journey bearable.

'My cat!' she called, just as they were about to close the doors. 'Don't forget my cat! Sarah Pearce will feed it—number 12. She knows about the key.'

'I'll tell her—don't worry.'

Lucy watched them go, closed up the house, put the key back under the pot and went round to see Sarah Pearce, filling her in quickly, then she got back into her car out of the wind and phoned Ben.

'Lucy, hi. Are you all right?'

'I'm fine. I'm sending a patient to you—Edith Jones. She's had a heavy fall in the kitchen and hit her knee on the corner of a cupboard, by the look of it. Might have a starburst fracture, but she's also wet herself. It might be nothing, but she has congestive heart failure and occasional irregularities of her heart rhythm. Might be worth checking it out to make sure she didn't have a little stroke or TIA. No other symptoms apart from breathlessness. She's on her way.'

'OK, I'll look out for her. Thanks. Um—I had a call from your father.'

She felt a chill run over her. 'About the house?'

'Mmm. He's not pleased.'

'No, I know. He came in this morning and had a go—then he ended by saying it was just as well, he wanted a clean break with the house and at least he'd never have to go in it again.'

She felt a sob welling in her chest, and clamped her lips together to stop it coming out, but Ben must have heard something, because his voice was concerned. 'Lucy, don't,' he said softly. 'Oh, my love, I'm so sorry. I thought I was helping you. I didn't want to make it worse.'

'No, you haven't,' she said quickly. 'It's just me. It's hormones. I'm just feeling sentimental and I want everything to be perfect and it isn't. Ignore me. Look out for Edith. I'll speak to you later.'

'OK. Take care. Love you.'

She opened her mouth, shut it again, then said, 'You, too. I'll see you later.'

You, too, what?

You, too, take care? Or, I love you, too?

Ben stared at the phone, put the receiver down softly and stood there for a second. How long could this go on? How long could Nick continue to persecute his daughter because of his stiff-necked reluctance to accept the facts?

He paused beside Resus. The room was empty, but in his mind's eye he could see Annabel lying there, blood everywhere, and Nick's agonised face as he realised that his wife's life was slipping away and there was nothing anyone could do to save her.

He'd struggled and fought to get to her, had needed to be restrained from sticking his hands into her abdomen to hold the bleeding vessels. No wonder the man was scarred by the events of that day. Anyone would be.

But it seemed that the person who was suffering most and who had had the least to do with it was Lucy, and that tore him apart.

CHAPTER SEVEN

EDITH had split her kneecap cleanly in two. It wasn't a starburst fracture, just a vertical break that needed to be held together so the strain put on it by bending her knee didn't pull the two sides apart. So it could have been worse, but nevertheless it was a very painful injury, and she'd be immobilised for some time.

And, as Lucy had thought, there was a possibility that she'd had a minor stroke.

Ben watched as Edith was wheeled away for her CT scan. The orthopaedic team would sort her knee out, and it was over to them now to play their part in her recovery. His job was done, and he phoned Lucy and told her what had happened.

'Oh, dear,' she said sadly. 'I hope it doesn't mean she can't cope on her own. I do so want her to be able to get back to her bungalow. She's lived there all her married life, since she and her husband bought it in 1967 when it was first built. He died earlier in the year, and she's lost without him. She'll be devastated if she has to move.'

'Poor woman, she's got enough on her plate. She was worried about her cat, by the way.'

'Dealt with. Her neighbour's looking after it for now. I expect she'll be in to see her soon. Ben, I'm glad you've phoned,

Kate's had another word with me about this meeting. She said the trust architect can make Thursday at four. Any chance you could do that?'

And no doubt Nick would be there this time. 'Yes, that'll be fine,' he agreed. He'd worry about Nick as and when he had to. 'What do you want for supper?'

'On Thursday?'

'Tonight,' he said, smiling. 'How about chicken?'

'Just had a chicken sandwich and an apple turnover. I ought to have something light and less full of fat. I'm going to be a barrel otherwise.'

'I've got news for you,' he said with a chuckle. 'Leave it to me, I'll sort it. I'll see you later. Are you staying the night at mine?'

'No,' she said, a little trace of regret in her voice. 'I should be at home.'

It didn't matter. She needed her rest, and there'd be plenty of time for them to be together in the future. 'OK. I'll see you later. Take care.'

He put the phone down and went back to work, whistling softly under his breath. Jo, his registrar, gave him an old-fashioned look. 'You look happy,' she said, almost accusingly, and he gave a slightly embarrassed laugh.

'There's no law against it, is there? And life's good.'

Or it would be if Nick Tremayne could only move on. One thing was for sure—Thursday was going to be interesting.

'So who's going to be here for this meeting this afternoon?' Nick asked.

'The trust architect, someone from the finance department, you, Marco, Lucy, Dragan and Ben Carter,' Kate said.

'Him again!'

Oh, here we go, Lucy thought, closing her eyes and letting her father and Kate Althorp argue it out.

'Why is it that everything that's mine, everything I hold dear, that man has to interfere with?'

If you only knew the half of it, Lucy thought, and opened her eyes to find Marco and Dragan both watching her thoughtfully. Oh, damn. Double damn, in fact. And then Kate looked at her, concern in her eyes, and she thought, Make that triple damn. With a cherry on top.

'I've got to get back to work,' she said, hoisting herself out of her chair and heading for the staffroom door, losing her mug on the draining-board on the way.

She shut herself in her consulting room for a moment, gathering her composure around her like a cloak. This afternoon's meeting was going to be a doozy, she thought, and she was dreading it.

She got through her morning surgery, went out on her visits, grabbed a sandwich, courtesy of Doris Trefussis, and declined the apple turnover in favour of a Cornish fairing brought in by Hazel Furse, the dumpy little head receptionist, who, as well as baking the best biscuits in the county, knew nearly as many people as Doris and ruled the appointments book with a will of iron.

Luckily she was also blessed with a great deal of common sense and, unlike a lot of receptionists Lucy had heard about, she didn't see her role as protecting the doctors from nagging patients who ought to wait their turn. So when Hazel popped in and said that a farmer, old Charlie Tew, was in Reception and urgently needed an appointment and could Lucy fit him in, she didn't hesitate.

She didn't have a surgery at the time, and was just about to see Chloe MacKinnon, the midwife, for an antenatal check, but something in Hazel's voice alerted her.

She went out into Reception and found him sitting there looking uncomfortable but not so bad that he would ring alarm bells. Not unless you took a really close look. She took him through to her consulting room and sat him down, her eyes making a quick inventory. Pale skin, clammy, sweating. 'What's the problem, Mr Tew?' she asked. 'You don't look very comfortable.'

'I pulled something,' he said bluntly. 'Heifer got stuck in the ditch and I couldn't get the tractor close enough, so we pulled 'er out with ropes. And I got this pain, Doc—right 'ere.' He pointed to the centre of his abdomen. 'It's like backache, only...'

He might have got a hernia. That was the most likely thing, or a ruptured psoas muscle, although that would tend to be at the side. The rectus abdominus muscle? Or...?

'Could you just slip your trousers down for me and pop onto the couch?' she asked, and he shuffled out of them and lay down cautiously, exposing a large, hairy abdomen encased in the biggest underpants she'd ever seen. She eased them down and pressed gently, then went very still.

Damn. She was right. The skin of his lower abdomen and legs was pale and mottled, and in the centre of his abdomen was a large, pulsating mass, beating in time with his heart. An abdominal aortic aneurism, she was sure, and if it was, there was no time to mess around. Left for very long, it would rupture. If it hadn't already, the blood enclosed in the space behind the peritoneum.

'I'm afraid you're going to have to go to hospital and have

an operation, Mr Tew,' she said gently. 'Stay there. I don't want you to get up, you just relax and keep still while I call an ambulance to take you to St Piran.'

'What, now? Only I've got a lot to do today. This heifer's put me right back. I could go in drekly, Doc.'

She smiled, knowing that the Cornish version of 'directly' was nothing of the sort.

'No, I think you need it a little sooner than directly,' she told him with a reassuring pat to his shoulder.

'Hernia, is it?'

'I don't think so. I think you might have a bulge in the wall of one of your blood vessels. And if you have, you'll need an operation now.' If you even get there, she added mentally. 'I'll call them straight away. Is there anyone with you?'

'No, I drove myself.'

She winced inwardly, knowing that if he'd had a collision and hit the steering-wheel or seat belt it would have been enough to finish him off.

'Stay there,' she warned again. Covering him with a blanket, she went out to Reception. 'Can you call an ambulance, Hazel, please? Mr Tew's got an aortic aneurism, I think. Urgent transfer—blue lights and all that. Cheers. I'll call the hospital and warn them. Oh, and could you ask Marco or Dragan if they're free to pop in? I know my father's got an antenatal class going.'

'Sure. Oh, there's your father now.'

'Thanks. Dad, old Mr Tew's here.' She filled him in quickly, then added, 'He's your patient. Do you want to examine him?'

He shook his head. 'No. I trust your judgement, Lucy, and if you're right he doesn't need any more poking about. I'll call the ambulance—fill them in. Hello, Mr Tew,' he said, sticking his head round the door. 'Gather you've been over-doing it. I'll see you in a minute, just going to call you some transport. Lucy, you might want to get a line in,' he added softly. 'Large-bore cannula. Two, if you can. And give him oxygen.'

'I was just about to. Thanks. Right, Mr Tew, I'm going to give you a little oxygen for now, and I'm just going to put a little needle in your arm, all ready for the hospital. It'll save time later.' She slipped it in easily, grateful for her time in A and E, then repeated the procedure in the other hand. 'There—one to let things in, one to let things out,' she said with a grin. 'Now, how about your wife? I think I'd better give her a call—can she get to the hospital?'

He frowned and studied her closely, as if the seriousness of it was suddenly dawning on him. 'How bad is it, Doc?' he asked. 'Is it going to finish me off?'

'I hope not,' she said honestly, not wanting to worry him but owing him the truth. 'But it is a major operation, and I think if I was your wife I'd finish you off anyway if you didn't let me know.'

His weather-beaten old face twisted into what could have been a smile, and he gave a dry chuckle. 'Well, we don't want that, do we, my bird? Best give her a call, then.'

Hazel came bustling in with a little tap on the door. 'Now, Charlie, I've phoned Grace and she's going straight to the hospital,' she told him, getting there ahead of them. 'The boy's going to take her, and she'll have some pyjamas for you and your wash things.'

'Good idea,' he said, and Lucy wondered if he really had the slightest clue how much danger he was in, and hoped, most sincerely, that he didn't. There was a difference between knowing that something was serious and realising it could kill you at any second.

She saw the flashing lights coming down Harbour Road, and for the second time that week Maggie Pascoe came to the rescue.

'Taxi!' she said with a bright smile, leaving her partner Mike to wheel the trolley in and going over to Mr Tew to pat his hand. 'Hello, Charlie, my love. What's this I hear about you pulling heifers out of ditches, you silly old goat? You should be leaving that to the young 'uns and issuing instructions on the sidelines. Should have thought that was right up your street.'

Charlie chuckled, and Lucy realised they must know each other well. Not that that surprised her. Nearly everyone knew everyone, and if they didn't, they knew someone who did.

'I s'pose you're old enough to have your driver's licence,' Charlie said drily, and Maggie rolled her eyes.

'Oh, no, I just stole the ambulance for a bit of fun—felt like a joy-ride. Anyway, I don't have to drive it, I get to sit in the back and tell you off all the way to the hospital. Right, you stay there, my love, we'll slide you across. Lucy, let go of that, you aren't pulling anything!' she said, and Lucy let go of the sheet and watched as Maggie and Mike pulled him easily, sheet and all, across the Pat-slide and onto the trolley.

In moments he was tucked up in a blanket, strapped down and away, and again Lucy rang Ben and warned him. 'I'm sending you a patient with a query abdominal aortic aneurism. No known history, but he's not the complaining sort so he may have had a bit of a bulge for ages. Whatever, it's a large midline pulsatile mass, and I don't like the look of him at all. I don't know if you'll still be there or if you'll be on your way here, but he needs to go straight to Theatre.'

'Are you certain?'

'As I can be.'

'That's good enough for me,' he said. 'I'll tell them to expect him and get a theatre slot primed. And I'll see you in an hour for this wretched meeting. Should I wear my stab vest?'

She laughed a little uneasily. 'I'm sure that won't be necessary. It'll be highly civilised. I'll make sure we've got plenty of Hazel's Cornish fairings to keep us going. We can always throw them at each other if it hots up.'

'Oh, no, that would be such a waste. I've heard about those biscuits of hers, even from this distance. She feeds them to the paramedics, apparently.'

'Well, don't get too excited. If Dad's found them, there may not be any left.'

He chuckled, said goodbye and hung up, and she buzzed through to Chloe. 'I'm sorry, I got held up with a patient. Do you want me today or not?'

'Yes, when you're ready. I've just seen my last patient, so come on up. Don't forget your urine sample.'

'As if,' she mocked, and went via the loo. 'Here—hot off the press,' she said, handing it over.

Chloe tested it and nodded. 'It's fine. Good. And your blood pressure's nice and low. I haven't seen you for days, though. I get the feeling you're doing too much. How are you feeling generally?'

Tired? Stressed? Worried sick that her father and her lover were about to kill each other in less than an hour? 'I'm fine, too,' she said, but her smile couldn't have been convincing, because Chloe gave a sceptical grunt.

'You look exhausted. You must be overdoing it. Maybe you should stop work sooner.'

'I can't—' she began, but Chloe just tutted and pointed at the scales.

'You haven't gained anything. That's the second week in a row. I think you should have another scan. They were a bit worried about your placenta with the last one, weren't they? Thought it was a bit low down?'

'Not very low. They were talking about another scan at thirty-four weeks to check it, but they were pretty sure I wouldn't need a C-section.'

'And what are you? Thirty-two weeks on Saturday? I think you should have it now.'

She sighed, then thought of Ben and how much he'd like to be there. 'OK,' she agreed. 'I'll give them a call.'

'No, *I'll* give them a call—make sure it happens. You take care of that little one, Lucy.'

'I will.'

'I'll book you in for the scan tomorrow morning.'

'Tomorrow!'

'Yes. Tomorrow—morning. Get Hazel to reschedule your patients. And get Ben to feed you over the weekend.'

She looked up, startled, into Chloe's wide and seemingly innocent green eyes. 'Why should Ben feed me?'

'Oh, Lucy, come on. You've been seen together. People talk. All my patients are commenting this morning—Dr Lucy's boyfriend is gorgeous, isn't he? Have you seen him? Beautiful car. Do you think Dr Lucy and her lovely Mr Carter will get married before the baby's born?'

'What? That's crazy!'

'They saw you at the barbeque, Lucy. Nobody's seen you with anyone since, and they certainly didn't before. You don't date any more than I do. And you've been seen with him again recently. And they all know that he's bought Tregorran House. It's gone through the village like wildfire, and it's obvious to everyone but your father why he's done it.'

She stared into Chloe's gentle, caring eyes another second, then looked away hastily, her eyes prickling with tears. 'I hadn't realised gossip was that rife.'

'Oh, Lucy, this is Penhally. And it's only because everybody loves you and wants a happy ending for you.'

She swallowed hard. 'I wish.'

Chloe squeezed her arm. 'Come on. You'll get there. Fancy coming round to mine this evening and letting me feed you?'

She opened her mouth, shut it, then said, 'I ought to talk to Ben. My father doesn't know yet but, judging by the sound of it, it won't be long.'

'OK. But make him feed you properly, and get an early night. And go straight to the hospital tomorrow—in fact, sit there, I'll book you in now.'

She rang the hospital while Lucy sat obediently, and thought about her friend's revelations. Did the whole world *really* know about Ben? Or did it just seem like it?

'Right. Eight-thirty. So you can stay at Ben's, and you won't have such a long drive in the morning.'

'I can organise my own life,' she grumbled gently, but Chloe just laughed and opened the door for her.

'Of course you can. I'll get them to call me with the results. Don't forget to eat.'

'Stop nagging,' Lucy said, and went into the staffroom. It

was empty, but the coffee-tables had been moved to the centre, the chairs were grouped around them and there were clean mugs set out on the side next to a tin of Hazel's fairings.

Eat, Chloe had said, so she ate. She had one, then another, and then there was a tap on the door and Ben came in.

'Hi!' she said, overjoyed to see him, and he shut the door and pulled her into his arms.

'How's my favourite girl today?' he murmured, smiling down at her and nuzzling her nose with his.

She sighed and rested her head on his chest. 'In trouble. I've just had a lecture from my midwife. Apparently I need to eat more.'

'Well, I keep telling you that. Are there any of Hazel's biscuits around?'

'Yes, in that tin—and I've had two, before you start. And I've got to have a scan tomorrow morning—eight-thirty. Can I stay with you tonight?'

He paused, his hands on the tin, and turned back to her. 'Of course you can.'

'Do you want—?'

'Can I—?'

They spoke together, and Ben laughed and said, 'You first.'

'I was going to ask if you want to come.'

'And I was going to ask if I could.'

'That's a yes, then.'

'If you don't mind.'

'I'd love you to be there.'

He tipped his head on one side and studied her thoughtfully. 'Funny time for a scan.'

'My placenta was a little low at the eighteen-week scan, so they wanted to check at thirty-four.'

His brows clamped together. 'Low? How low?'

'Nothing to worry about. It's just a routine check.'

'But you're not even quite thirty-two weeks,' he said, holding her at arm's length and searching her eyes. 'So why now? Two weeks early? Is this because you're not gaining enough? It's that bad?'

She sighed and confessed. 'I haven't put any weight on for two weeks.'

'Then I'm definitely going to be there,' he said firmly. 'Now, about these fairings,' he said, opening the tin and holding one out to her.

'Ben, I've had two.'

'That's not enough. Come on, open wide.'

She was laughing up at him, pushing him away and fighting over the biscuit when the door opened and her father walked in and stopped dead in the doorway.

Oh, rats. Of all the timing...

Ben dropped his hands, stepped away from her and met his ice-cold eyes. 'Dr Tremayne.'

'Carter,' he said, but she could tell the word nearly choked him. Even the sound of Ben's name had been like a curse for years. He hated him. Blamed him for her mother's death, and hated him, and no amount of reasoning would get him to see sense.

This afternoon, clearly, wasn't going to be the time. His taut, still firm jaw was clenched, the dark eyes unyielding as he stared at Ben for an endless, breathless moment.

Please, don't let him be rude, Lucy prayed. Don't let him start anything. Not here, not with everyone due here in moments.

God was obviously otherwise engaged.

'Bit early, aren't you?' Nick said softly, but there was a deadly edge to his voice that made Lucy's heart beat faster.

Ben shrugged. 'Not really. I didn't want to be late. I consider this expansion to be very important for the local community, and since I'm part of it I take my contribution very seriously—'

Her father's snort cut him off and his mouth tightened. 'Really? I can see just how seriously you were taking it.'

'Dad!' she cut in, trying to avert a scene. 'Come on. This isn't the time or the place.'

His eyes flicked back to her. 'No—and I would have thought you could have found yourself something more useful to do than fighting over the biscuits,' he growled, and she felt her temper start to fray.

'Actually, he was trying to get me to look after myself,' she pointed out, but her father just snorted again.

'It'll be a cold day in hell when a member of the Tremayne family needs advice on their health from Ben Carter,' he said, his voice harsh. 'And I would have thought you'd have greater loyalty to your mother than to be playing the fool with the man who—'

'Leave my mother out of this,' she snapped. 'You know perfectly well that Ben wasn't at fault.'

'Do I?' He looked Ben up and down with eyes that blazed with anger and pain, and a lesser man would have flinched.

Ben just calmly returned his stare. 'Dr Tremayne, this was settled two years ago—'

'You expect me to believe that report? You know damn well the inquiry was rigged.'

Lucy gasped, and there was a muted sound of reproach from Kate. Behind him, she could see the practice manager with the trust architect and finance executive in tow, the other GPs clustered on the landing behind them.

How much had they all heard? She didn't know. Anything would be too much. A muscle twitched in Ben's jaw, but apart from that and the dull run of colour on his cheekbones there was no other reaction from him.

'I'll pretend I didn't hear that,' he said, and made to turn away, but Nick's voice stopped him in his tracks.

'What—the truth?' her father went on doggedly, but Ben had had enough.

He turned back, eyes blazing with anger, and said, his voice deathly quiet, 'Dr Tremayne, I'm not here because I want to be, but because I believe in this project. I was asked to contribute, and if you don't want me here, all you have to do is say the word and I'll leave. Believe me, I have plenty to do.'

They glared at each other, then Nick took a deep breath and let it out. 'We're in the same boat, then. I'm only here because I want what's best for my practice and my community. You, I keep being told, are the best. So stay, and we'll get this damned meeting over, and then we can all go and get on with our lives. But stay away from my daughter, Carter. There are some nasty rumours flying around, and I hope they're just that. If I ever hear you've laid so much as a finger on her—'

'You'll what?' Lucy cut in, furious with him and on the verge of tears. 'He's a friend of mine. I can't help it if you don't like that, but I'm twenty-nine, for heaven's sake! You don't get to dictate my friendships, so just get over it and let's move on. Everybody's waiting.'

Kate gave Nick a none-too-gentle shove in the ribs, and

he took a step forward. Ben moved back out of his way and the cameo broke up, everyone busily settling themselves down and not knowing quite where to look.

Except Ben. He sat opposite her while Kate made the tea and handed it round, his eyes fixed on her, and every time she looked up he was there, the look in his eyes reassuring.

'Right, shall I introduce everybody?' Kate said, and gradually the awkward silence eased. She and Ben both put in their contributions on the proposed plans, she talked the architect through it on paper, Dragan and Marco chipped in with their take on it—only Nick was silent, speaking when he was spoken to but otherwise just watching, his eyes never leaving Ben's face.

He knows, she thought with sudden certainty. Or thinks he does. He certainly suspects.

'What do you think, Lucy?'

Think? Think about what? She dragged her mind back to the discussion, apologised and asked Marco to repeat what he'd said.

'We were talking about the advisability of delaying the implementation of the new MIU until after you return from maternity leave,' Kate said.

'Um—no,' she said, wondering if she would be returning from maternity leave or if she'd even have a job to come back to once her father knew the truth. 'I think you should go ahead, at least with the planning stage. That'll take some time, won't it?'

'Indeed,' the architect said. 'I need to examine the outside of the building before it's dark, and see where you're proposing to put this extension.'

'Right behind you, down there,' Kate said, getting up and

pointing through the window. 'Dragan, would you like to show him? To save Lucy going down?'

'I can do it,' she said, and got to her feet at the same time as Ben and her father. 'No, really, I can do it. Ben—your comments might be useful,' she said, and they trooped out, leaving Kate and the other members of the practice to discuss financing it with the bean counter, while her father glowered after them in brooding silence.

'You OK?' Ben asked softly, and she nodded.

'This would be the link through if we went two-storey,' she pointed out to the architect as they stood on the landing. 'At the moment it's staff cloakroom and showering facilities, but there's a big lobby area that could be taken to make a way through.'

She showed him around, then they went downstairs and out into the garden.

'Hmm.' The architect was studying the land behind, the steep granite escarpment behind the practice which ended in an outcrop of rock right where they wanted to build. 'You want to put it here?'

'It's dead space, and it links in well,' she explained.

The architect frowned. 'I don't know. I think it could be very expensive. The rock would have to be cut away and there isn't room round the side to bring in heavy gear to do it. Is there anywhere else? At the front, for instance?'

She struggled to pay attention. 'Not really. We need all the car parking space we can get our hands on, so we can't take that, and there isn't enough room at the side.'

'Pity.' The architect looked up at the building to the side of them. 'What's this?'

'A boatyard—repairs, engineering works and sail loft, and

a chandlery. Don't worry, we've already considered it. The practice manager is co-owner, but there isn't any possibility of taking part of the land, even if we could afford to buy it from them. They're already overcrowded.'

'Hmm. How about going out over the top of the car parking area?' he suggested as they walked back round to the front. 'It would be expensive, but not as expensive as buying the land next door or shifting the rock. Planning might be a bit of an issue. I'll have to think about that one and come back to you on it.'

He glanced at his watch. 'Right, I need to get a move on. Let's go and break the news to the others, and we'll have to reconvene after I've had a think. Can I borrow your plans? I'll get them copied and have them sent back to you tomorrow.'

'Of course,' she agreed, and they went back upstairs.

'Ah, you're back. More tea?' Kate offered, but the two men from the trust shook their heads.

'We need to get away. If we could just take these?'

They were folding the plans, shuffling paper into briefcases, putting on their coats, and Lucy sneaked a quick glance at her father. He was talking to Kate and the finance man, ignoring Ben, and as she looked away she caught Dragan's eye.

He raised an enquiring brow, and she smiled reassuringly. He nodded, apparently satisfied, and, glancing at his watch, he stood up. 'If you'll all excuse me, I have a visit to make.'

'Really?' she said as he walked past her. 'I didn't think you were on call this evening.'

He smiled a little awkwardly. 'I'm not, but there's a certain dog who seems to be expecting me to go and play games with her. And I may well be offered supper, so I don't have to cook. As I have no food, that would be good.'

'Ah.' She smiled. 'Well, give Melinda my love,' she said, and watched in fascination as his neck darkened slightly. Poor Dragan, it was mean to tease him. He was such a serious, thoughtful man so much of the time, and on the few occasions she'd seen him with Melinda he'd looked genuinely happy.

'I will,' he said, then paused and looked at Ben, standing beside her. 'Look after her, OK? She's looking tired. She's doing too much.'

No! Don't tell Ben to look after me in front of my father, she thought frantically, but Nick was busy talking and Ben just smiled.

'Leave her to me,' he said softly. 'I'll take care of her.'

'Good. Someone needs to.' And he nodded to the others and left. The men from the trust followed, then Marco and, rather than have to talk any more to her father, she propelled Ben towards the door, grabbing his coat on the way.

'In a hurry to get rid of me?' he murmured as they went downstairs.

'Not at all. I'm in a hurry to get you away from my father before you kill each other. Ben, I think he knows.'

He stopped dead on the bottom stair. 'Really?'

'Really. Come on. We'll talk about it this evening. I've got a surgery starting in a minute.'

'I've rescheduled you,' Hazel said, overhearing. 'Chloe told me to, so I've put your patients in with your father and Marco, and you've got tomorrow off.'

She opened her mouth to argue, then changed her mind. She felt sorry for Marco, but her father deserved it. She smiled at Hazel. 'Thank you.'

'Pleasure. Oh, and Charlie's wife called. He's out of

Theatre and he's in ITU. Apparently they got him there just in time, so well done.'

'Good,' she said, then added more softly, 'At least that's one thing I've done right today.'

'You've done nothing wrong today,' Ben said gruffly.

'My father wouldn't agree. I'm so angry with him.'

'Don't be. He's just hurting.'

'Ben, it's slander!'

He just smiled wryly and gave her a slow, lazy wink. 'Relax. I'll see you soon at my place. I'll go via the supermarket and get you something jumping with vitamins and calories.'

She let her smile out at last. 'You're a star,' she said softly. 'I'll see you later.'

He went out, crossing the car park briskly and getting into his car just as her father came up beside her. 'I want to talk to you,' he said firmly, and taking her elbow he propelled her into her consulting room and shut the door.

'About Carter,' he began, but she was watching Ben through the window, turning the car and lifting his hand in farewell, and she thought of the dignity with which he'd handled the whole awful, embarrassing situation and she wanted to kill her father.

She turned back to him, her whole body trembling with reaction, and shook her head. 'You had no right to say those things to him. No right at all! It's just lies, and you're flinging them around willy-nilly in front of everybody. It would serve you right if he took you to court, and it's just rubbish, Dad! You know why she died.'

'And so do you—and if you're blinded by his lies, then you're not the daughter your mother and I thought you were. There are some ugly rumours flying around, Lucy. I don't want to believe what I'm hearing, and I don't. Just don't give me any reason to doubt you, because the last thing I want to hear is that that bastard has fathered my grandchild.'

She stared at him, her eyes filling with tears, and then looked across the car park. Ben had pulled out into Harbour Road, but she could follow him—

'Lucy! Lucy, come back here.'

'No,' she said, turning back to look her father in the eye. 'No, this time you've gone too far. The only bastard in all of this is you—oh, and your grandchild, and I'm just about to do something about that.'

She scooped up her bag, ran upstairs for her coat and then ran down, fighting back the tears. Her father was still standing in the door of her consulting room, his jaw set, and without sparing him a second glance she went out to her car, got in it and drove off after Ben.

CHAPTER EIGHT

BEN was gutted.

Gutted for Lucy, and furious with her father. If Lucy didn't manage to silence him soon, then he was going to, because this couldn't be allowed to go on. Tremayne could think what the hell he liked about him, but he wasn't going to go spreading it around the county like that. How he hadn't hit him he had no idea.

He called the solicitor on the way to the supermarket, not really expecting him to be at work still, but to his surprise Simon answered.

'Hi. You're working late. It's Ben Carter—I just wondered if there was any news.'

'Oh, hi, Ben. It's all done,' Simon said, to his surprise. 'Actually, I was just going to call you on my way out of the office. I've had confirmation in writing that the purchaser's quite happy for you to continue to live in your present house and rent it from him until the end of February, if necessary, so as you instructed I've gone ahead and completed on both houses today. The Orchard Way house is sold, and Tregorran House is yours. Congratulations. The paperwork's all in the post, and the keys of Tregorran House are with the agent.'

'Amazing,' he said, stunned. 'God, you're efficient! Thank you, Simon. You're a star.'

'My pleasure. If there's anything else I can do, just ask.'

Like getting a restraining order on Nick Tremayne? 'I'll bear it in mind,' he said, biting his tongue, and cut the connection, his mind whirling.

Hell's teeth, he'd done it. He'd got Lucy's house.

He threw back his head and laughed in relief. There'd been a few moments in the past week when he'd wondered if Nick would try and block the sale, or at least throw up something he could to stall it, but apparently not. He was evidently as pleased to get rid of it as Ben was to have acquired it.

Now all he had to do was tell Lucy. He couldn't wait to see her face.

He wasn't there.

Of course he wasn't. He was going via the supermarket, and he might be ages. And she should have gone via her house and picked up some things, if she was staying here tonight.

She shut her eyes, dropped her head back against the headrest and sighed. She'd got herself so psyched up, convinced herself she'd be able to do this, but now he wasn't here, she was losing her nerve. What if he—?

Stop it, she told herself. Deal with it later.

For now she'd ring him, get him to pick her up some knickers and deodorant at the shop. She fished in her bag for her phone and called him.

'Could you buy me some knickers for tomorrow?' she asked, and he gave a strangled laugh.

'What kind? Not those tiny scraps of string.'

She couldn't help the smile. He loved the tiny scraps of string. 'No, something a bit more—'

'Stop there. Just a bit more will do.'

'Not granny knickers,' she pleaded, but he just laughed.

'Don't panic. What else?'

She gave him a list, and he grunted. 'Right. I was about done. Give me ten minutes and I'll be on my way.'

She shut her eyes and leaned back and waited, trying to be calm, trying not to think negatively, and finally she saw the sweep of his headlights against her closed lids, and heard his car pull up beside hers and stop.

Then her door opened, and Ben reached in and hugged her. 'Come on, out you get, we're celebrating.'

'Celebrating?' she said, wondering what on earth they had to celebrate when her father had been so unreasonable—unless, of course, he'd turned into a mind reader—but he was grinning from ear to ear and taking off her seat belt, all but hauling her out. 'Celebrating what?' she asked as he scooped up the carrier bags from the passenger seat and shoved his car door shut with his knee.

'Aha! Come inside.'

'Celebrating what?' she repeated, trailing him in, and he put the shopping down, picked her up in his arms and whirled her round, laughing.

'The house—it's ours. We've got it—completed.' He put her down very gently on her feet, cradled her face in his hands and kissed her tenderly. 'You've got your house, my darling. As of today we are the official owners of Tregorran House. We can get the keys tomorrow.'

She was confused. 'But—what about this house? Didn't you have to sell it first—move out of it?'

'Not yet. The new owner's renting it to me until the end of February, to give us time to sort the other one out before we move in.' He stopped talking and searched her face, his eyes concerned. 'You will move in with me, won't you? Live with me? In the house? Even if we have separate rooms—'

'No.' She put her fingers on his lips. 'Not separate rooms. I want us together, in the room my grandparents had. When I was little and the cockerel woke me, I used to get into bed with Grannie in the morning and snuggle up, and it was lovely. I've always loved that room.'

She felt her eyes fill, and blinked the tears away so she could see his dear, wonderful face. 'Oh, Ben, thank you,' she said, and then the tears won and she closed her eyes and let them slip down her cheeks.

'Hey, you aren't supposed to cry,' he said softly, and she laughed and hugged him, bubbling over with joy.

'Sorry. Just happy. Ignore me.'

'No. I'm going to make you a cup of tea, and sit you down with your feet up, and then I'm going to cook you supper.'

'I want vegetables.'

'You're getting vegetables. Roasted root vegetables, steamed cauliflower and broccoli, and roast lamb.'

'Roast lamb?'

'Don't you like it?'

'I love it,' she admitted. 'I just never cook it for myself. I don't think I've had roast lamb since Mum died—' She broke off, the emotions of the day suddenly overwhelming her, and Ben muttered something under his breath, wrapped her in his arms and cradled her against his heart.

'Oh, sweetheart, I'm so sorry.'

'What for?' she asked, choked.

'That you haven't got your mother now,' he said, going right to the heart of it. 'She ought to be here for you when you're having your first baby, and I'm so sad for you that she can't be.'

'She'll never see my children,' she said, finally voicing one of the huge regrets that had plagued her since her mother's death. She gave a hiccuping sob, and he held her tighter, rubbing her back gently and cuddling her while she wept. 'Oh, sorry, I'm being so silly,' she said, scrubbing the tears away with the palms of her hands.

'No, you're not. You're sad, and you're tired, and you've had another fight with your father.'

'Oh, I know. He's a nightmare. I don't know what to do with him. I want to tell him about the baby—I'm desperate to talk to him, for him to come to terms with you being its father, but I just don't see it happening. He's so awful to you—it's just not like him, and it's as if I've lost him, too.'

'He's just angry that she died, and a little lost without her, I guess. He needs someone to lash out at, and I'm convenient. I can cope with it, Lucy.'

'But the things he was saying, about the inquiry—'

'Are just rubbish. I know that, he knows that—we all know that. Your mother died because of a whole series of events. She was as much to blame as anyone else. If she'd been a bit more forthright about her condition and told your father how ill she was, or if she'd come to us sooner, it would have been quite different. But she left it too late, and she didn't check in, and nobody spotted her. It was the whole chain of events that led to her death, and what caused it ultimately was the number of painkillers she'd taken.'

'And he feels guilty that he didn't spot anything, that she

could have been feeling that bad and he just didn't notice.' She shook her head. 'If only I'd been at home at the time, but I was away on a course the day she was taken really ill, and I hadn't been home for ages. I was still living in the hospital after finishing my A and E rotation—it was only days after I'd finished, if you remember. If only I'd still been there, she would have asked for me, and I could have done something…'

Her voice was tortured, and he wanted to weep for her. There was nothing she could have done. Nothing anyone could have done—including him. He hadn't caused Annabel's death. He knew that. Deep down, he knew it, but there was still a sick feeling inside him whenever he thought about the waste of her life, and today's row with her husband had brought it all back in spades. As it was, he just felt sick at heart and deeply sorry for everything that had happened, even though it hadn't been his fault.

He wondered if Lucy really believed that he wasn't to blame or, if despite all her defence of him, somewhere deep inside there was a bit of her that wasn't quite sure. And in any case, her father still clearly blamed him for everything that had gone so horribly wrong the day Annabel had died.

How were they ever going to sort it out if Nick wouldn't even discuss it?

'You mustn't blame yourself,' he told her gently. 'There's no way you were at fault. You weren't even there.'

'No. Nobody was. She gave so much of herself to us all, and when she needed us, none of us were there for her. I think she felt she didn't matter, that we were all too busy to be disturbed for something as trivial as her illness, and we must have let her think that. Four doctors in the family, Ben, and we didn't even realise she was sick. We're all to blame in that, and Dad's busy trying to lay the blame at someone else's door. I feel as if I've lost them both.'

She straightened up and gave him a wan smile that twisted his heart. 'Did you say something about tea?'

'I did,' he said, and gave her a gentle push towards the sofa. 'Go on, sit down, put your feet up and have a rest. I'll bring it through in a minute. I just want to put the supper in the oven. It won't take long, it's only a fillet.'

'Oh, gorgeous.' She gave him a weary smile. 'Thanks, Ben,' she said softly, and he swallowed the lump in his throat. 'Any time.'

He went into the kitchen, took his feelings for Nick out on the unsuspecting vegetables, shoved the meat in the oven once it was hot, poured the tea and took it through.

At first he thought she was asleep, but then he saw the tears trickling down her face, and he put the tea down with a sigh, sat next to her and pulled her gently into his arms. 'Oh, Lucy.'

It felt so good to let him hold her. She rested against him for a moment, then tilted her head back and looked searchingly into his eyes. All she could see was love and concern and a fathoms-deep kindness that went all the way to the bottom of his heart. She loved him so much, and if he loved her, too, as much as his eyes said he did, then maybe…

She gathered up her courage. 'Ben, when you found out about the baby two weeks ago, and we were talking about it, at my flat—you said some things.'

He groaned and closed his eyes. 'Oh, hell. I said all sorts of things, but if any of them are upsetting you, for God's sake tell me—'

'No. Not at all. I just wondered—you said we shouldn't

rule certain things out, and I wondered if you still felt that way. You see— Oh, I don't know how to say this, but I just feel... Ben, will you marry me?'

His eyes flew open. 'Marry?' He stared at her for an endless moment, and then his eyes filled and he looked away and gave a short cough of laughter. 'Oh, hell, now *I'm* going to cry,' he said, and dragged her further into his arms. 'Of course I'll marry you, you stupid woman. I'd love to marry you. Nothing would make me happier.'

His lips found hers, and he rained soft, desperate kisses all over her mouth, her jaw, her eyes, back to her lips, then with a last, lingering, tender kiss, he lifted his head. 'Of course I'll marry you,' he repeated. 'I'd be honoured.'

She smiled, a pretty watery event, she thought, but he was hardly going to be able to criticise her for that. She lifted her hand and gently smoothed the tears from his cheeks, then kissed him once more. 'You don't have to go that far,' she said a little unsteadily, 'but I'm so glad you said yes, because if you'd said no...'

'Not a chance,' he said, his laugh ragged and cut off short. His arm tightened around her, and he tucked her in against his side and leant forward, passing her her tea then going back for his. 'When did you have in mind? Soon, I would think?'

She shrugged diffidently, still trying to absorb the fact that it was really going to happen. 'Before the baby comes?'

'And what about your father?'

'Oh, lord.' She sighed, considering the ramifications. 'What about my father? I'll ask him. I'll have to, and if I'm honest, I'd love to have him there, but I don't know if he'll come, and I really don't think it matters any more. It's not him I'm marrying, it's you, and I'm not going to let him spoil it.'

'Good. And I'll do everything I can to make you happy. You know that.'

'You already do, Ben.' She rested her head against his chest, sipped her tea and sighed. 'We ought to celebrate with champagne,' she said, 'what with getting the house and getting married, but I probably shouldn't drink.'

'No, and I don't need to. I've got all I need right here.'

'What, a cup of tea?' she teased, and he chuckled and hugged her.

'Absolutely. So, tomorrow, after your scan, I think we should go and get a ring, and then sort out a venue. Register office or church?'

She thought of the pretty little church up on the headland, next to the coastguard lookout station and the lighthouse— the church where her mother, grandfather and uncle were all buried. It would seem so right...

'The church—St Mark's, in Penhally Bay, up on the headland,' she told him. 'If we can. I don't know. I'm not sure of the rules.'

'We'll find out. And if we can't do that, maybe we can be married in the register office and have a blessing in the church later.'

'Mmm. Ben?'

'Mmm?'

'I hate to be practical, but is the supper OK?'

He jackknifed to his feet and ran to the kitchen, yanking down the oven door and letting out a cloud of smoke and steam.

'It's OK,' he yelled. 'Just.'

She got slowly to her feet and went through, to find him examining the vegetables. One or two were a little singed around the edges, but the rest were fine and the meat looked perfect.

'Gosh, it smells fantastic. I'm really hungry. What about the cauliflower and broccoli?'

'Two minutes, while I make the gravy. Sit.'

'Yes, sir,' she said, but she sat anyway and watched him while he dished up, and then she ate everything he put on her plate.

'More?'

She laughed and shook her head. 'No, I'm full. No room now with the bump in the way, but Chloe would be proud of you for getting so many calories into me.'

'I'll give you ice cream later,' he said, and shooed her back into the sitting room while he cleared up.

She went quite willingly. Chloe's news about her weight had worried her, and she realised she probably had been over-doing things. Well, not any more. She needed to give her baby the best possible chance, and if that meant Ben loading the dishwasher alone, so be it.

So she sat, and switched on the television, and after a while Ben came and joined her, and when her eyes started to droop, he carried her up to bed, snuggled her spoon-like against his chest and fell asleep with his hand curved protectively over the baby and the reassuring beat of his heart against her back...

'There—everything looks fine. There's not an awful lot of fluid—maybe you need to drink more. But the position of the placenta isn't a worry, it's moved up enough that it's away from the cervix.'

Ben stared, transfixed, at the screen. He could hear Jan

Warren, the obstetrician, talking, but all he could see was his baby, arms and legs waving, heart beating nice and steadily.

'Would you like to know what sex it is?'

'No,' they said in unison, and he laughed awkwardly. 'Well, it's not really my call.'

'I don't care, so long as everything's all right,' Lucy said.

'Well, it all looks absolutely fine. The baby's a good size, everything seems perfectly normal—there, how about that for a photo?'

Jan clicked a button, and seconds later handed them a grainy, black and white image of their child. Ben felt his eyes prickle and blinked hard, and Lucy handed it to him. 'Here— put it in your wallet,' she said, and he nodded, but he didn't put it away.

Not yet. He wanted to look at it a little longer, while Lucy— in respectable knickers!—was wiped clean of the ultrasound gel and helped up to her feet.

'I need a pee,' she said bluntly, and the obstetrician smiled.

'Go on, then. I'll see you in a couple of weeks.'

'Fine,' she said, and all but ran out of the door. Jan gave Ben a searching look as he gave the photo one last lingering stare and put it away.

'Can I take it you have a vested interest in this baby, Ben?' she asked, and he laughed softly.

'I don't think it's going to be a secret for long,' he admitted. 'We're getting married as soon as we can.'

Her face broke into a smile. 'Well, congratulations.'

'Thanks. Is the baby really OK? She's not been looking after herself.'

'Babies are very good at doing that for themselves, unless the conditions are really unfavourable, and yours is fine.'

'Good. Thanks, Jan.' He felt his shoulders drop and, shaking her hand, he headed out into the corridor to wait for Lucy. She wasn't long, and he put his arm around her shoulders and hugged her. 'OK?'

'Fine. Relieved—in every sense of the word.'

He chuckled and they fell into step side by side.

'Where are we going next?' she asked.

'My office, to phone the vicar? How do you feel about coming down to A and E to see everyone and give them the news?'

'The news?' she said, looking up him and sounding puzzled. 'What news?'

'That we're getting married?'

'Oh! Yes, of course,' she agreed. 'I thought you meant that the baby was OK.'

'No. They don't know about it, or at least not from anything I've said, so if you'd rather not?'

She took a deep breath. 'No. No, I'd like them to know. I want everyone to know that you're the father. I'm proud of the fact, and I love you, and I've got nothing to hide. Anyway, it would be nice to see them again.'

And slipping her hand into his, she walked beside him into A and E. It was the first time she'd been there since her mother had died, and as they passed Resus, she looked in and paused.

'Oh, Lucy, I'm sorry,' he said, immediately picking up on her feelings, but she just smiled at him.

'Don't be. It's fine. It's just a room, and she's hardly the first or the last. And I know you did everything you possibly could.'

'Do you really believe that?' he asked quietly, and she looked up at him and saw doubt in his eyes.

'Oh, Ben, of course I believe it!' she exclaimed, resting a hand over his heart. 'I know you did everything. Don't for a moment tar me with the same brush as my father.'

'I don't.'

'Good.' She looked back at Resus and sighed. 'I just wish my father hadn't seen it.'

'No. That was awful. Nobody should see someone they love in those circumstances. It's hard enough when you're detached.'

'I know. I remember.' She dragged in a breath and smiled up at him. 'Shall we get this over, then? Tell them you're getting married and break the hearts of all the women in the department who fancy they're in love with you?'

'Idiot,' he said, laughing. Putting his arm around her shoulder, he led her away from Resus to the work desk in the central area.

'Ah, Jo,' he said, greeting a young woman who was bent over some notes. 'Jo, this is Lucy. Lucy, my registrar, Jo. Um, we've got some news,' he told her, and she looked at Lucy's bump pointedly and her eyes twinkled.

'You don't say,' she teased.

He chuckled. 'Actually, the news is I'd like you to cover for me for the rest of the day. I've got some arranging to do— we're getting married.'

'Oh, Ben, that's fabulous!' she said, throwing her arms round his neck and hugging him. 'Hey, guys! Guess what! Ben's getting married!'

They must have come out of the woodwork, Lucy thought, because in the next few seconds the place was swarming with people, many of whom remembered her, and she was hugged and kissed and the baby exclaimed over, and finally they got away into Ben's office and shut the door.

'Phew!' she said, and Ben laughed apologetically and hugged her.

'You OK?'

'I'm fine. They're lovely. Right, can we ring the vicar now?'

An hour later they were sitting in his office at the vicarage in Penhally, and to her relief Mr Kenner was being more than helpful.

'I'd be delighted to marry you both,' he said fervently, taking Lucy's hand and squeezing it. 'I've been worried about you. Ever since your mother died, there's been such an air of sadness about you and your father, and it's wonderful to see you so happy. And I imagine you want to move this on quite swiftly?'

She laughed at the irony. 'I think that would be good. I know it sounds old-fashioned, but I really want my baby—*our* baby—to be born in wedlock. Do they still use that dreadful expression?'

He chuckled and let go of her hand. 'I think you've summed it up very well—and some things are meant to be old-fashioned,' he added, unwittingly echoing her own thoughts. 'Ben, I take it you're quite happy with this marriage?'

'More than happy,' he said, and any doubt she'd had vanished into thin air at the conviction in his voice. His arm slid around her shoulders and squeezed, and she leant against him with a smile.

'Excellent. Right, the procedure is this. The banns have to be read out in church on three consecutive Sundays before the wedding—so as it's a Friday, if we start this weekend, you should be able to get married in just over a fortnight. So two weeks on Monday would be the earliest, in law.'

'Can we do it then?'

He hesitated, then smiled. 'Of course. It's usually my day off, but under the circumstances, and since I can't think of a single thing I'd rather be doing than joining you two in marriage, I'd be delighted to do it then. Do you have a time in mind?'

'No. Well—I don't know who's going to be there. Um—can we make it twelve? Ben, what do you think? Then people from the practice can be there, and we can go to the Smugglers' for lunch perhaps.'

He met her eyes. People from the practice? She could see him thinking it, wondering if her father would come. And in truth she had no idea, but she had to ask him.

'I think if twelve would be all right with Mr Kenner, it would be fine.' His eyes flicked back to the vicar, and he nodded.

'Twelve it is, then. Right, we have some paperwork to attend to next.'

So that was it. They were getting married, and once the banns were read out on Sunday, the whole village would know.

She had to see her father, but not now. Not in the middle of surgery, or while he was trying to get out on his visits, or when he had a clinic. And they had something else to do first, something she'd much rather do, and she couldn't wait another minute…

'You know, with a really good scrub and a coat of paint, it would be fine.'

He stared at her in astonishment, and realised she was serious. Absolutely serious, and so he looked again at the house, and realised with an equal degree of astonishment that she was right. It was dirty, it was dated and things like the curtains and wallpaper and lampshades made it all seem much more dreadful than it was.

But a coat of paint, some new carpets and curtains and a few pictures on the walls and it could be transformed.

'I had a survey done before the auction, and the wiring and plumbing are both sound,' he said slowly. 'The Aga's awful—'

'No!' she protested. 'Ben, I *love* the Aga!'

'What—that one? Solid fuel and probably temperamental as hell?'

She weakened. 'Well, maybe not that one.'

'So, a new Aga and a new bathroom suite, and we could probably manage for a while. And that way we could be in by Christmas. Even in time for the wedding.'

Her eyes widened, and her mouth made a round O before the tears welled up and she shut her mouth, clamping down on her lips to hold back the tears. It didn't work, and he laughed softly and wiped them away.

'Silly old you.'

'I just— If we could be in here before the baby—it would be so fantastic.'

'I'll give it my best shot. They owe me some leave. I'll take a bit now, and you can have some as well, to put your feet up—'

'What, while you're here painting the house? I don't think so! I'll be painting, too.'

'No, you won't,' he said firmly, meaning it. 'I don't need to be worrying about you inhaling fumes and wobbling about on ladders. You can sleep in in the mornings, and if you're very good you can bring me over a picnic at lunchtime and we can eat it together and I'll let you tell me I'm wonderful, and then you can go off and choose carpets and things for an hour before you go back to lie on my sofa and watch daytime TV.'

She wrinkled her nose, and he wanted to kiss it. 'I hate daytime TV,' she said, and he laughed.

'So spend the time planning the wedding,' he suggested, and she sighed.

'Oh, Ben. Do you think he'll come?'

He took her hand in his and rubbed the back of it absently. 'I don't know. Whatever happens, I'll be there, come hell or high water. But you have to talk to him, Lucy, or I will, because he needs to know, and he needs to come to terms with my role in your mother's death, because if I have anything to do with it, your father's going to be there at our wedding, and he's going to give you to me with his blessing. Now, come on, let's get out of here and find some lunch, and we probably need to start planning this wedding.'

He pulled her into his arms, gave her a quick hug and steered her towards the door.

CHAPTER NINE

THEY went to the Smugglers' Inn for a late lunch, up on the cliff near the church, and talked to the landlord, Tony, about booking a room for the day of the wedding.

'Just a small lunch party,' Lucy said, being deliberately vague.

'How many?' Tony asked, and she looked at Ben helplessly and shrugged.

'I don't know. Twenty, at the most?'

'Probably,' Ben agreed. 'I don't know. We need to make a definitive list yet, but would it be possible in principle?'

'Oh, yes. Mondays aren't busy. Want to see our buffet menu? It's very popular for weddings.'

She felt herself colouring. 'Is that your usual party fare?' she asked, refusing to answer the question in his eyes, but he just smiled and handed her the menu.

'Just have a look through,' he said, and pushed himself away from the bar. 'Now, let me get you a drink and you can sit down and browse through that and draw up your list over lunch. Are you ready to order?'

'Mmm—scampi and chips,' she said without hesitation. 'I love it here.'

'And for you, sir?'

'I'll have the same. And something non-alcoholic, times two. Lucy?'

'Oh—apple juice, please, Tony. Thanks.'

'Make that two.'

Tony set them on the bar. 'Here you go—look, there's a table by the fire. Go and warm yourselves and I'll bring the food over to you.'

'So—who's coming?' Ben asked softly once they were settled, pulling a notepad out of his pocket and flipping to a clean page.

She looked up at him, doubts flooding her. 'I don't know. My father, if I can persuade him. Jack, my twin, but I haven't spoken to him for ages and I know he's really busy, so he may not be able to get here on a weekday. Ed's in Africa, so he can't come. Marco and Dragan, although someone will have to be at work, I suppose. Kate, of course, and Chloe, my midwife, and Lauren, the physio, and Alison—she's a practice nurse and we've worked together a lot on the minor surgery. Melinda—the vet, you remember her, you stitched her arm. Vicky, the hairdresser—she'll do my hair, too, if I ask her. Gosh, I don't know. Mike and Fran Trevellyan? Mike's family bought the land from my grandmother's family donkey's years ago, and they live just up the road from Tregorran House. They'll be our closest neighbours, and I've known Mike since my childhood. I used to think he was gorgeous—he was my hero, and he put up with us trailing around after him with amazing patience. They've got a farm shop, and he runs the farmer's market here every Saturday. Fran's a teacher—so she may not be able to make it because she'll be at school, I expect. And, of course, Hazel and Sue and Doris from the surgery. How many's that?'

'Fifteen, if everyone comes. If your father and Jack and either Marco or Dragan and Fran can't make it, eleven.'

'What about you?'

'My parents—they're only in Tavistock, so that's not a problem. They're both working, but I'm sure they'll take the time off. My brother, Rob, and his wife, Polly? They're in London, so I expect they'll come down and stay with my parents for the weekend. Rob can be my best man. Jo, my registrar? A couple of other work colleagues. We can always have a big party later on, after the baby's born and we're settled in. Maybe a big christening in the summer.'

By which time, she thought, her father might have mellowed a little, Ed might be back from Africa and if she gave him enough notice, even Jack might manage to be there.

'Good idea,' she said with a smile. She picked up the notepad. 'That's somewhere between twenty and twenty-five, including us. Good guess. What about this menu?'

'What, the party food?' he teased, handing her the wedding buffet menu Tony had given them to look at, and she laughed awkwardly.

'I don't want to put it around the village until I've spoken to my father,' she said.

Tony came over at that moment and put their meals down and said in a low voice, 'I think you should know you were seen coming out of the Vicarage earlier, and the people of this village have always been good at adding two and two. If you're hoping to keep it a secret, you're in the wrong place, my friends. You've been well and truly rumbled.'

They exchanged rueful looks, and then the significance of it hit Lucy.

'Oh, Ben, I'm going to have to talk to my father now, before anybody else does.'

He put out a hand and stopped her. 'No. Eat your lunch, and we'll go together in a minute. Tony, lunch for twenty-five max from this menu will be lovely. Thank you.'

He handed it back to the landlord, who nodded, patted Lucy on the shoulder and said, 'Don't worry. We'll look after you. Everyone's delighted.'

Everyone except her father. And she still had to find out quite how undelighted he was.

He wouldn't even talk to her.

'I haven't got time to see you,' he said curtly when she went into his consulting room anyway, leaving Ben outside. 'Besides, I thought you said everything that was necessary last night. You've made it clear where your affections lie, so I suggest you get on with it.'

'Oh, Dad, please,' she said, her eyes filling. She blinked the tears away furiously, knowing they would only irritate him, and tried again. 'I love him. I know you think he was responsible—'

'No. I *know* he was responsible, and I'm having nothing more to do with either of you. You've made your bed, Lucy. Go and lie in it.'

She recoiled in shock, hardly able to believe how much he'd changed from the busy but caring parent he had been in her childhood. When had he turned into this man she didn't even know? She tried again. 'Dad, please. I want you to come to the wedding. I need you there. I can't get married without either of you—'

'That's your choice. And you've made it. You're marrying

a man who hasn't even got the guts to come with you and talk to me. Well, he's welcome to you. You deserve each other. Now I have a surgery, patients waiting, and I don't need this. Please go.'

She stood there for a moment longer, unbearably torn, but he ignored her pointedly, and in the end she stumbled through the door into Ben's arms. She hadn't let him come in with her, hoping it would help to soften her father, but it hadn't. It had made it worse.

'I'm going to talk to him,' Ben said, his voice shaking with anger, but she stopped him.

'No. Just get me out of here. I've had enough.'

He took her out to the car, opened the door for her, helped her in and closed the door, then disappeared. She looked round over her shoulder and saw him going back inside.

Oh, no! He was going to cause a scene...

He came back out again, opened his door and slid behind the wheel, then started the engine. 'I just told Kate you're taking next week off. She's arranging cover.' He shot her a quick glance, his eyes troubled. 'Are you all right?'

She couldn't hold it in any longer. Pressing her hand to her mouth, she shook her head, then burst into tears.

He swore, softly but comprehensively, and drove her home, then held her until she'd finally cried herself out. Then he made her a hot drink, tucked her up in bed and left her to sleep.

She didn't think she'd be able to, but she was exhausted by emotion, devastated by her father's rejection, and sleep promised oblivion. She closed her eyes, snuggled down on Ben's pillow, inhaling the scent of him, and finally dropped off to sleep.

* * *

'I can't believe it! She actually had the gall to ask me to go to her wedding!'

Kate sighed and closed the door of her office. Nick was pacing like a caged lion, the emotions chasing one after the other across his tortured face, and she didn't know what to say to him. She never did these days, and certainly not about this. Not about Annabel's death, but Ben didn't deserve this, and Lucy certainly didn't, and she couldn't just let it go.

'Why are you punishing your daughter because you feel guilty for letting Annabel down?' she asked softly, hitting right at the heart of it, and he stopped pacing and glared at her.

'I what?'

'You heard me. Annabel's death was nothing to do with Ben, and you know it. And you really can't go around accusing him of rigging the inquiry in public—unless you want to end up in court,' she added, getting into her stride. 'You've got to get a grip, Nick. She's been in love with Ben for years, since before Annabel died, and he's in love with her. This has been a long time coming, and with the baby on the way, it's not a moment too soon. I can't let you ruin her day for her, or her marriage, or her joy at becoming a mother. Just think about this, Nick. What would Annabel have had to say about your behaviour?'

And with that she walked out, shaking with anger and a whole range of other emotions she really didn't want to confront, and left him to think about it. Maybe when he'd cooled off and the dust had settled he'd change his mind, but she really didn't think he would.

The chances of him going to Lucy's wedding were slim to none, and Kate's heart ached for her.

* * *

Ben had to go to work on Sunday. He was on call, and he couldn't get out of it, but he hated leaving Lucy.

It was as if all the light had gone out of her, and he was furious with her father and worried sick about her. She'd even talked about calling off the wedding, but he'd managed to convince her it was silly. The wedding wasn't about her father, it was about their love and commitment for each other, and he was damned if Nick was going to screw up something so important because of his foolish and stiff-necked refusal to recognise the truth.

And then he ended up having to call him, because they had three people, a couple and a man on his own, presenting with similar symptoms of violent stomach cramps, acute nausea and vomiting and profuse diarrhoea, all within three hours of each other, and although the couple were from Exeter and the man from Birmingham, they had one thing in common— they'd all been staying at Trevallyn House in Penhally.

Damn. Ben didn't want to speak to him, and he was sure it was mutual, but he cut straight to the point. 'Dr Tremayne, I'm phoning from St Piran. It's Ben Carter—there's an outbreak of vomiting and diarrhoea that may be connected to Trevallyn House in Harbour Road in Penhally. It's run by—'

'Beatrice Trevallyn. I know. What are the symptoms?'

'Acute abdominal cramps, profuse diarrhoea—in one of the patients it's bloody and mucoid—vomiting, headache, pyrexia of 38.5°C. The first patient in is a man from Birmingham who stayed there last night, the other couple have been there since Friday and were on their way home. They became ill just after they started their journey. There are no other links that we can establish between them apart from Trevallyn House.'

'Right. I'll check it out. Have you notified Public Health?'

'No, I'm just about to. I suspect it's salmonella, and Public Health will want to inspect the premises. I'm just alerting you as it's likely you'll be called by anyone local who may be suffering from it. If it's not restricted to that one source, we need to know so we can set up an isolation unit.'

'Fine. I'll get on it now.'

And Nick hung up without another word. Ben shrugged. It suited him. The last thing he could envisage with the man was small talk!

He went back to the patients, isolated together in one bay, and concentrated on getting fluids into them and monitoring their symptoms. They were all too ill to travel home, and until they got the results of the stool samples from the Public Health lab, they needed to be barrier nursed in isolation. The last thing they needed in the hospital was an outbreak of winter vomiting virus, and the symptoms were similar.

He set up IV fluid replacement, checked them all again to make sure there was no further deterioration, and then he was vomited on.

Great.

He went and showered very, very thoroughly. He didn't need to take home anything nasty to a pregnant woman who already had quite enough on her plate.

'Call for you, Ben,' the charge nurse said through the door. 'It's Nick Tremayne.'

'Take a message,' he yelled, and towelled himself roughly dry, pulled on a clean set of scrubs and went back out. 'What did he want?'

'Mrs Trevallyn is sick, and her son, Davey, is in a state of collapse—he's got learning difficulties as well, by the way.

He's sending them in. He says there are no other residents, nobody else has been there in the last seventy-two hours and he hasn't been called out by anyone from outside the guest house.'

'Right. Thanks. Looks localised, then. Anything from Public Health?'

'No. I'll chase them up.'

'Do that—and can we get these three up to a medical ward? All five can be nursed together, and if I'm right, that'll be the end of it, unless it's meat from a local supplier, in which case we could get many more.'

'Look on the bright side, why don't you,' the charge nurse said with a grin, and went to organise the removal of their patients from the unit.

'I'll get a fleet of cleaners in to deal with this lot,' he threw over his shoulder. 'We'll need a serious hosing-down of all this contaminated equipment before we can put it back into use.'

'Good idea.'

And he needed to phone Lucy. He couldn't leave the department until he had the results back and was sure it was only a restricted salmonella outbreak and not something much worse and more widespread.

It was the best and yet the most appalling fortnight of Lucy's life. If it hadn't been for Ben, it would have been intolerable—but if it hadn't been for Ben, it wouldn't have been intolerable, so that was stupid.

After Sunday when he was at work, they spent a lot of time together, both at Tregorran House and in his old house in Orchard Way. She was having only three days off, and refused to take any more despite Ben's persuasion, so she had to make the best of it. And they were lovely days.

She wasn't allowed to do anything, but he couldn't stop her planning, and she ordered a skip and watched him fill it with the horrible carpets and curtains, and made notes for the wedding.

Not that there were many to make.

She needed a dress. She needed flowers—a simple posy would do, nothing much, and as it was Advent the church wouldn't have flowers. Foliage, then—ivy and eucalyptus and variegated laurel from the garden. She could see plenty of things from where she was sitting, and if she had a few white flowers interspersed—roses, perhaps?—that would be enough.

The food was taken care of, and the drinks they'd get from Tony, and she'd spoken to everyone except Jack and Ed. Ed she'd emailed, because it was the easiest way to deal with it, and she'd sent Jack a text.

Needless to say, he hadn't called her back, but he was obviously up to his eyes. He was working hard, throwing himself into his career—although to hear her father on the subject you'd be forgiven for thinking he was never out of nightclubs—and she knew he'd get back to her when he could.

As for the rest—well, there was no 'rest'. That was it, the sum total of the arrangements. The hymns were chosen, the order of service typed up on Ben's computer and printed off on fine card, and there was nothing left to do but wait for Jack to ring and her father to come round.

She wasn't holding her breath.

'You OK?'

She smiled up at Ben. 'I'm fine. How about you?'

'Good. All done. The skip's full, the house is empty, all

ready for the decorators to come in and blitz it, and guess what I found?'

He dangled a big old iron key in front of her, and she exclaimed in delight and reached for it. 'The front door key!'

'Is it? I thought it might be. It was under the mat. Want to try it?'

'Oh, yes. I expect it'll be a bit rusty, but we used to go out into the garden in the summer through the front door. It's got bolts as well—I'll let you do those.'

So he struggled with the bolts and finally freed them, and she put the key in the lock and turned it, and although it was a bit stiff, they heard the lock go, and together they turned the doorknob. A gust of wind caught the door and blew it open, and in front of them, beyond the garden and the field, was the sea, sparkling in the low winter sunlight.

She filled her lungs with the cold, fresh air and laughed. 'Oh, that's gorgeous! Oh, Ben, thank you.'

'What, for finding the key? We could have had another one made.'

'No,' she said, turning to him and cradling his face in her hands. 'For getting me my house.'

He stared down at her in silence for a moment, then he sighed softly and drew her into his arms.

'It's a pleasure,' he murmured. 'Just to see you happy is more than enough reward.'

He let her go, lifting his head, then he said, 'Is that your phone?'

'Oh—yes. I'll get it.' She hurried to her bag and pulled it out, pressing the button just in time. 'Hello?'

'Hi, kiddo.'

'Jack! Oh, Jack, I'm so glad you've got back to me. You got my text?'

'Yes, I got it. That's why I'm ringing you.'

'Tell me you can come,' she pleaded. 'Dad's being really difficult—it's because it's Ben. He's still being really stupid about it and I can't get through to him. I don't think there's a prayer he'll come to the wedding, and Ed's in Africa—Jack, I want you to give me away.'

There was a lengthy silence, and her heart sank. 'Jack?'

'Ah, hell, Lucy. Oh, God, I'm so sorry, kiddo, I can't. Did you hear India died?'

'Yes, of course I did. It was in all the gossip rags. Not that you told me, of course, because you never tell me anything—'

'She's got a child,' he cut in.

'Yes, I saw. But—'

'Lucy, he's mine. His name's Freddie, and—he's my son. I've been granted custody of him, and—oh, sis, I need you. I'm just so out of my depth. I don't know what I'm doing with him.'

She walked back into the kitchen and sat down again at the table they'd set up in there. 'Oh, Jack. I don't believe it. How old is he?'

'Um—little. Nearly three. I'm just— I'm having problems with him adjusting to me. He misses his mother, and he doesn't know who the hell I am, and I really don't think I can leave him right now, and I certainly can't bring him, not all that way. And all the fuss would just confuse him more.'

He wasn't coming. And he was a father! Much more important, she told herself, and set aside her disappointment.

'Oh, Jack, I quite understand. Don't beat yourself up over it. And remember, you're not alone. We're all here for you. You could move back down here, so we can all help you.'

'I can't see Dad helping. He'd say I brought it on myself.'

'No,' she said, but with more conviction than she felt. 'He'll come round.'

'I wish I had your confidence. Oh, Lucy, I just don't know how to deal with Freddie—what to say to him to make it better.'

'Just put yourself in his position, and be there for him, and be kind. And think about what I said, about moving back here. You don't have to do this by yourself.'

He gave a ragged laugh that broke in the middle. 'Just at the moment I don't know if I can do it at all, sis. You know, give me a job I can do—a really messy RTA with lots of re-construction work—and I'm happy as a pig in muck. Give me a little boy with huge blue eyes that watch me warily all day long, and I just fall apart. He needs a mother, and his own was bloody useless but at least she loved him…'

His voice cracked, and Lucy's heart ached for him. For both of them. 'Oh, Jack, you'll cope,' she said gently. 'If I wasn't so pregnant I'd come and see you, but—'

'No, don't be silly. You marry your Ben, and I'll be thinking of you at the time, but I can't get down. I'm so, so sorry.'

'Don't be. You're doing the right thing. Give him a hug from his Aunty Lucy, and you take care. I'll send you both a bit of cake.'

'You do that—and have a really great day. Love you, kiddo.'

'Love you too, big bro.'

She lowered the phone to her lap and looked up at Ben, her heart heavy. 'He can't come. He's got a son—Freddie. He's only just found out, and he's having problems with him and can't leave him. There won't be anybody in my family there, Ben. Not one.'

'Oh, darling…'

He gathered her into his arms and cradled her close, his heart breaking for her. And then the baby kicked him, and he lifted his head and smiled down at her. 'That's not true. I'll be there, and so will the baby. I don't know if it's enough, but we're your family, too, and we'll be there. So you won't be alone.'

Her hands slid down and cradled the baby, and a tear slipped down her cheek, catching on her lip as she smiled. 'No. I won't. You're right. And you're all I need—all I'll ever need.'

Kate knocked briefly on Nick's consulting-room door and walked in.

He was standing at the window, his jaw set, arms folded, and a muscle twitched in his cheek.

'Nick?'

'I'm not going.'

'Why?'

He turned, letting out his breath in an explosive sigh. 'You know why.'

She couldn't let him do this. She couldn't let him miss his own daughter's wedding because when he came to his senses it would be another layer of guilt to add to the countless others.

'You have to go. This isn't about you, it's about Lucy, and it's about her mother.'

'Her *dead* mother.'

'Exactly. Her mother who can't be there for her. Her mother who can't sit just over her left shoulder, sniffing into a handkerchief and being ridiculously proud of her. Lucy's not asking you to give her away, and neither am I. Mike Trevellyan's doing it. She just wants you there, in the congregation, so she's not the only one there from the Tremayne family.'

'He let her die.'

'No. No, he didn't, Nick. He did everything he could, and he was gutted that she died. And he loves Lucy to bits. He'll be a good husband and father. He'll make her happy—which is more than you're doing at the moment. So—are you coming, or not?'

For a moment she thought he'd say no, but then he snatched his coat off the back of the door, shrugged into it and yanked the door open. 'Well, come on, then, we don't want to be late.'

Nick couldn't believe he was doing it.

Going to Lucy's wedding, in the church where his father and brother and Annabel had all been laid to rest.

He nearly turned round and drove back, but Kate wouldn't have let him and, anyway, she was right. He had to be there, for Lucy's mother.

The church car park was full, to his surprise, and he had to go to the Smugglers' Inn. It was only a few yards further, but as they hurried back, he saw Lucy arriving in Mike Trevellyan's wonderful old car. It was done up with ribbons, and it was gleaming, and as Mike helped her out, Nick's footsteps faltered.

He should be doing that. Giving her away. Not some man who was almost a stranger.

He broke into a run, Kate after him, and they reached the church just as the music started and she was walking down the aisle.

'Here,' Kate said, tucking a flower into his buttonhole, and she gave him a little shove.

The vicar was there in his ceremonial robes, Ben standing ramrod straight in front of him, and when he turned to look at Lucy, his eyes met Nick's and held. Then he looked down into Lucy's face and smiled.

* * *

'He's here,' Ben said.

'Who?'

'Your father.'

She turned, searching the crowd, but then she saw him, hesitating at the back of the church, as if he was unsure of his welcome. He smiled at her, a sad, twisted smile, and she held out her hand, but he didn't move.

For an endless moment everyone held their breath, and then she gave up, and turned back to the vicar. Ben's hand caught hers and tightened on it, giving her support, and she clung to him.

Her father was here. He'd said he wouldn't come, but he was here. Mike was hovering beside her, unsure what to do, but she smiled at the vicar and nodded, and he smiled back.

'Dearly beloved,' he began, and Lucy listened and tried to concentrate, but then, when Mr Kenner said, 'Who gives this woman to be married to this man?' there was a ripple through the congregation, and her father's voice rang out.

'I do,' he said, and reaching her side he took her right hand, kissed her cheek and said softly, 'I'm sorry,' and placed her hand in Ben's.

CHAPTER TEN

BEN wasn't sure he could believe it.

After all the agonising and trauma of the past two weeks, he'd come, in the end, and given his daughter away.

And his eyes, as he'd placed her hand in Ben's, had held a challenge that should probably have struck fear into Ben's heart.

It didn't, because it was a challenge he had every intention of meeting. He was going to make Lucy happy if it took his last breath, and he didn't need Nick Tremayne to challenge him to do it.

And Lucy *was* happy.

Her face shone, her eyes were bright, and she'd never looked more beautiful. And when she paused outside the church and walked over to her mother's grave and laid a single white rose from her bouquet in front of the simple headstone, her eyes sparkled with tears, and he was sure his did, too.

He didn't know about Nick. He wasn't looking at him, he had eyes only for Lucy, and as they made their way to the Smugglers' Inn, it seemed as if the whole of Penhally had turned out to shower them with good wishes.

Ben chuckled to himself. They might be the most phenomenal load of old busybodies, but they were there because they loved Lucy, and he couldn't blame them for that.

He recognised several of the faces in the crowd gathered on the clifftop—Toby Penhaligan, the fisherman with the broken arm, Bea Trevallyn from the guesthouse with the salmonella outbreak, fortunately contained to just the five identified, and others such as Mrs Lunney, with her new husband Henry, who'd come all the way from Wadebridge just to cheer them as they came out of the church.

It was touching, and as they walked away, Lucy tucked her hand tighter into the crook of his arm and smiled up at him.

'He came.'

'I know.' But he was worried, and he said softly, 'Lucy, don't expect too much. One step at a time.'

She nodded. 'I know. Early days. But one step, today, is enough for me.'

The pub was packed.

They'd booked a room for up to twenty-five, and it should have been enough, but so many people had come to wish them well, and her father asked the landlord to give them all a drink in celebration.

'Ouch. That'll cost him,' she said with a smile, and Ben chuckled.

'I don't think he'll mind. Come on, we need to stand here and greet everyone.'

As a reception line, it was a strange affair, oddly formal in the rather informal and yet curiously fitting surroundings of the pub.

Her father, Ben's parents—lovely, lovely people who'd

been so sweet to her in the last two weeks—his brother, Rob, just like him in many ways, his sister-in-law, Polly, who she was looking forward to getting to know much, much better, and hovering in the background organising, as ever, was Kate.

Dear Kate, who must have talked her father into coming, because without her Lucy was sure he wouldn't have come.

She greeted her with a heartfelt hug and a whispered, 'Thanks.'

Kate smiled back and mouthed, 'Any time,' and then moved on down the line, followed by all the others.

Neither Marco nor Dragan had come, both electing to hold the fort to make sure Nick had no plausible excuses, she was sure, but apart from Sue who was manning the reception desk and Alison Myers who had a baby clinic, the rest of the staff were there, and Ben's colleagues, and after them, it seemed, came the whole of Penhally, so many of them, come to wish her and Ben well.

And get plastered on the doctor's slate.

There wouldn't be a lot of work done in Penhally that afternoon, she thought, and wondered how many more people were going to hug and kiss her before she could go and sit down…

Nick hated speeches, and this was one he'd never intended to make, so it was short and to the point.

'I've never seen my daughter look so radiant,' he said. 'And her mother, who should have been here, would have been so, so proud of her. And on her behalf, I'd like to wish you every happiness. Ben, take care of her. Love her well. And may you be as happy as we were. Ladies and gentlemen, the bride and groom.'

And he drained his glass, sat down and took a deep, steadying breath. He didn't like Ben, and he didn't intend to spend time in his company, but Lucy apparently loved him, and after all he didn't have to live with the man. And today, on their wedding day, he wasn't going to fight with him.

Nick reached for the bottle of champagne and refilled his glass. He only lived at the bottom of the hill. He could walk home. It was his daughter's wedding day, and everybody was having too much to drink. He was damned if he wasn't going to join them...

'Ben, why are we here?'

'Just humour me,' he said. 'Stay there.'

Lucy paused, her dress caught up in her hand so it didn't trail in the dirt, and Ben disappeared round the side of the house, came back a moment later, scooped her up in his arms and carried her, laughing, round to the other side of the house and in through the front door.

'You're crazy. What are you doing?' she said breathlessly, then realised, and her heart lodged in her throat. He was carrying her over the threshold.

'There,' he said, sliding her carefully to her feet. 'You wouldn't let me do it before we were married, but there's no excuse now. Welcome home, Mrs Carter.'

'Thank you.' She went up on tiptoe and kissed him, still laughing, then looked around and gasped. She hadn't been allowed in the house for days, and she'd spent last night at her flat, getting ready this morning with Chloe and Lauren to help her.

But now...

'It's furnished!' she exclaimed. 'How? When?'

'Today. The removal men had strict instructions, and hopefully they've done everything right. I'm sure they won't have done, and we'll have to move all sorts of stuff, but I wanted to bring my bride home—to our real home.'

'Oh, Ben,' she said, lost for words. Taking him by the hand, she went from room to room. 'Oh, it's lovely. Oh! The nursery! Oh, Ben, you've had it painted in just the right colours.'

'*I* painted it,' he said, following her into the room she'd used as a child. 'I wanted to do it myself. For the baby.'

'Oh, Ben,' she said again, and then she couldn't talk any more. She just threw herself into his arms and hugged him so hard she thought she could hear his ribs creak.

'Is it OK? Do you like it?'

But she could only nod, because the tears were clogging her throat and she just couldn't believe how much he'd achieved in so short a time.

'I take it that's a yes,' he said with a laugh, and hugged her back, rather more gently. 'Come on, you haven't see our bedroom yet.'

And he led her up the corridor and opened the door. A beautiful old French sleigh bed took pride of place opposite the window, positioned just where she'd be able to sit up in bed and look at the sea. It was made up with fresh, crisp white linen, the duvet a cloud of goosedown, and piled with pillows just right for propping herself up to take advantage of the view.

It also looked hugely inviting.

She was tired. It had been a long day and was hard on the heels of a night when she hadn't slept a wink.

'How do you fancy trying it out?' he asked, drawing her back against him. 'I missed you last night, and I didn't sleep at all.'

'Neither did I.' She turned in his arms and smiled. 'I think trying it out sounds wonderful. Take me to bed, Mr Carter—please?'

He chuckled. 'Since you ask so nicely,' he said.

They couldn't take any time off.

Because it was so close to Christmas, they both had to go back to work on Tuesday morning, and it was a real effort to drag themselves out of the blissfully comfortable embrace of their new bed.

Ben had to leave earlier than Lucy, and after he'd gone she wandered around the house, touching it, remembering. 'I wonder what you'd make of it, Grannie?' she murmured. 'I hope you're happy that we're here. We'll look after it, and love it, and love each other and our children just as you did. You can rest now.'

Gosh, such sentimental nonsense. She blinked hard and went into the kitchen to make herself another cup of tea before she had to leave. The old Aga was still there, and there was a six-week wait for a new one, but she didn't mind. There was something curiously comforting about the sight of it, and Ben had promised her he'd try and get it going for Christmas. In the meantime there was a rather elderly electric stove standing next to the fridge, but it would do.

She drank her tea, washed up the mug—a novelty, that, not having a dishwasher, she'd got rather used to Ben's—and went to work.

Wow. Christmas Eve.

She'd done her Christmas shopping on Saturday, with Ben, and the presents were wrapped and under the tree in the sitting room—all except for the fire dogs she'd bought him from the salvage yard to put in the big granite fireplace in the sitting room. They'd been hiding in the boot of her car under a blanket until she'd struggled to heave them out that morning after Ben had gone, but they were a bit heavy for her to lift and she'd had to tuck them round the corner of the little stone barn beside the house. Her father had been hard to buy for. What could you give a man who didn't seem to connect with life any more?

Not at any real level. Even after the wedding, he'd still been distant, and any hopes she might have cherished that they were back to normal had been dashed when she'd asked him to join them at the house for Christmas Day, the following Tuesday.

'I'm going to Kate's,' he'd said. 'Sorry. Can't let her down. But I'm sure you'll have a lovely day.'

'Can't you come for some of it? Bring Kate and Jem—come for a drink, or tea, or something.'

'Sorry, Lucy.'

And that had been that. So she'd bought him a bottle of a fine single malt whiskey and a Christmas cake and a pot of Stilton, and put them in a wicker basket, and it was under her desk at the moment waiting for a chance to give it to him. Dull, boring but safe, she thought, and wondered if he'd be disappointed. No more than he was disappointed in her, she was sure.

Oh, well. She didn't have time to worry about it. She had a surgery until ten, and then two minor ops booked in, one the removal of a sebaceous cyst on the back of a man's neck, the other a seborrhoeic keratosis, harmless but irritating and looking troubling like a melanoma to the uninitiated.

She was examining it, reassuring herself about her initial diagnosis, when she noticed Ben's car pull up in the car park.

What was he doing here?

She forced herself to concentrate, and infiltrated the area in the man's armpit with local anaesthetic, listening to his stream of inconsequential chatter and putting in the odd remark from time.

'Oh, I've got a message for you from Mrs Pearce, Mrs Jones's neighbour. She says to tell you Edith's doing really well and hopes to be home in a week or two.'

'Oh, good. I'll go and see her when I'm next at St Piran. Right, is that numb now?'

'Yes—can't feel a thing.'

'OK.' She curetted it off, cauterised the wound and dressed it with antibiotic cream and a non-adherent dressing. 'Right, keep it dry if you can, put the cream on twice a day, leave it uncovered once it stops being sore and in two to three weeks it should be gone. It'll just look and feel like a burn, and that's what it is, really, because I've singed the blood vessels to seal them. OK?'

'What about that thing?' He pointed at the flat brown blob of tissue she'd removed and put in a specimen tube.

'I'll send it for analysis, just to be on the safe side, but I'm absolutely confident that it's harmless.'

'So you're sending it off so I can't sue you?'

She chuckled. 'No, I'm sending it off because I want to know that I've done everything I should have for you. I'm only a doctor, I don't have all the answers. And I don't want to let you down.'

He nodded. 'Fair enough. Thank you very much.'

He left, and she thought about it. Would she send the

sample off just so she didn't get sued if it later turned out to be a melanoma? Or was it belt and braces?

The latter. Being sued would be horrible, but the chances were it would happen in her working lifetime. Being responsible for someone's death because she hadn't taken enough care—that was quite different. It would destroy you, unless you simply didn't have a conscience.

She felt a twinge—nothing much, just another of those wretched Braxton Hicks contractions that she'd been plagued with for ages. Still, she was finished now, and she wasn't due back to work until Thursday. And Ben was here. He must have popped in to see her, but she had to get the sample off.

She was just coming out of her consulting room with the histology sample in her hand when she overheard his voice coming through her father's open consulting-room door.

'Please, come—not for me, but for Lucy. Even if it's just for a drink. She's so disappointed that we won't see you.'

'Well, that's her fault, not mine. She knows where I'll be, and it won't be with you. Just because I was at the wedding doesn't mean I've forgiven you or changed my mind about you. I only went to the wedding for Lucy, and for Annabel. I gave her away because I couldn't break her heart, but I don't have to like it, or you, and if you've got any ideas about cosy little suppers and so forth you can just forget it, because frankly even one minute in your company is one minute too long. You've taken my family home, taken my daughter, taken my wife—'

'No!' Ben cut in, his voice firm, and Lucy sagged against her open door, wondering if this was ever going to stop. 'I didn't take the house, I bought the house at a fair market price at an open auction because I thought it would make your daughter happy, and I didn't take Lucy, she came to me because she loves me and knows I love her and I didn't take your wife, Tremayne. On the contrary, I did everything I could to save her once she came to my attention.'

'That's a lie!' Nick said furiously. 'You gave up on her! I saw you!'

'I know. And you shouldn't have done. But we didn't give up. We stopped, simply because she was already dead. Her pupils were blown, her heart had stopped beating thirty minutes before. She was dead, Nick. She was dead, and if I could have changed that, for you, for her, for Lucy, don't you think I would have done so? But I never, ever gave up on her while there was the slightest chance of saving her.'

'She should have gone to Theatre.'

'There wasn't one free—and there wasn't time. So we did what we could, and we failed. And I'm sorry. But it's not my fault. If you want someone to blame, I suggest you look a little closer to home!'

'Just what the hell are you implying?'

'I'm not implying anything. I'm telling you that if it was anyone's fault she died, it was yours, because you were too busy building your empire to notice that the woman you supposedly loved was so sick she was overdosing on painkillers because she didn't want to trouble you! And that is why she died.'

Lucy gasped, and behind Reception Hazel and Kate stood transfixed.

The door slammed back against the wall and Ben stormed out, his face taut with anger. The noise of the door seemed to free them, and Lucy sagged against the doorframe, utterly shocked at the terrible things that had been said. Kate hurried towards her. 'Lucy—oh, my dear, I'm so sorry. Come and sit down.'

'No. I have to talk to him. He can't...'

She walked through her father's door on legs of jelly, and found him throwing books out of his bookcase, searching through them and discarding them furiously.

'Dad?'

'I'm going to sue him. I'm sorry, I know he's your husband now, but I can't let him get away with that.'

'What if he's right?'

He froze, then glared at her, his eyes suddenly ice cold. 'Get out,' he said flatly. 'If that's what you think, get out, and go home to him. I don't want to see you again!'

'Nick, really, this is ridiculous—' Kate interjected.

'Fine, I'll go,' Lucy sobbed. Turning, she ran back past Kate to her consulting room and grabbed her handbag. The histology bottle was still in her hand, and she gave it to Hazel on the way out. 'Um, could you send that for histology, please? Thank you. And—happy Christmas,' she added, before, blinded by tears, she ran out to the car, climbed awkwardly behind the wheel and drove out.

The roads were slick with rain, and as she drove towards Tregorran House and Ben, the rain turned to sleet and then snow, swirling, blinding snow of the sort they rarely saw in Cornwall. It would be gone in a moment, but for now it was blinding her, mingling with the tears until she couldn't see.

She felt the jolt, felt the car slide, and then judder and tilt alarmingly before coming to rest, the engine still running.

Oh, God, no, she thought. Phone. Where's the phone? Got to call Ben. Bag. Where is it?

In the footwell. Her bag was in the passenger footwell, right over on the far side and she suddenly understood the meaning of the expression heavily pregnant. She was hanging in her seat belt, leaning towards the passenger side, and she just couldn't quite— Got it!

And it was wet. Very wet, and as she watched the water rose further, and the car shifted and settled lower into the ditch. She had to get out, but how?

Turn off the engine, she remembered. Turn off the engine. Creaks, hissing, bubbling—it was like something out of a horror movie. She wasn't even sure where she was, but she couldn't be far from home. A hundred yards? Two hundred?

She pushed the door with all her strength, and it lifted, then dropped back. Ben, she thought, and phoned him, but he was out of range.

Nine nine nine?

Or her father?

No. She wasn't hurt, she was just stuck. She sent Ben a text, and told him where she was, then took her seat belt off, manoeuvred herself round so she was kneeling on the seat with her feet braced on the handbrake and her head by the window, and she heaved the door up and out of the way, pushing it until it held on the stay.

Would it remain there? The car was only tilted, not on its side, so it might stay there long enough for her to scramble out. Especially if she wedged it with something. Something like her handbag, always too full of things but on this occasion usefully so. She jammed it under the bottom of the door, so at least it wouldn't slam on her, and then clambered awkwardly out into the swirling snow.

Why was it snowing? She slipped on the road surface and grabbed the door to save herself, then remembered her bag. It was squashed now, but nothing in there was important.

Except her phone.

Fingers trembling, she pulled it out and saw with horror that it was cracked. She tried to use it, but it didn't work.

As if it could get any worse, she thought a little hysterically, and then she felt another of those annoying contractions, but it wasn't just annoying, it was huge, painful, and very significant.

And then there was a warm, wet, rushing sensation down her legs.

'Oh, no. Ben, please come,' she mouthed silently. 'I can't do this on my own.'

She looked around her frantically, desperately searching for anything she could recognise, and then she spotted the barn, and her heart sank. She was at least half a mile from home, and she couldn't possibly walk that distance. She'd have to get back in the car, she thought, and wait for Ben, but then there was a creak, and a groan of tortured metal, and the car tilted further and slid down into the ditch.

So that took care of that.

It's a good job I took the fire dogs out, she thought, and then wondered how on earth she could worry about something so trivial when she was about to give birth on the roadside in a blizzard!

Another contraction hit her, and she sagged against the car, let it pass and then straightened up. She could get to the barn. It was only a few yards away—fifty at the most. It wouldn't be warm, but at least she'd be out of the snow and sleet, and she could sit down and wait for Ben.

Wherever he was. What if he didn't get the message? What if he didn't come?

She wrote, 'IN THE BARN' on the side of the car in the dirty snow, and hoped someone would come. Anyone.

And soon…

* * *

'"Had crash near home. Please come. L xxxx". Oh, my God.' Ben felt cold all over, sick and scared and useless. He'd been shopping—shopping, of all things!—and she'd had a car accident and been unable to reach him!

He dialled her mobile number, but it went straight to voicemail. She might be calling someone else, he reasoned, so he left a message. 'I'm coming, sweetheart. Stay there. Don't move, and call an ambulance if you need to.'

And then, after a second's hesitation, he phoned the practice. Kate answered, sounding distracted and upset, and he wondered if it was a good idea, but it was better than leaving Lucy without help.

'Kate, it's Ben. I've had a text from Lucy to say she's had a car accident on her way back to the house. Have you heard from her?'

'No, but she was really upset. Ben, she heard the row.'

He swore, then thought for a moment. 'Kate, I'm worried. I can't get her. Her phone might not be working. Can you try and find her? I'm on my way but I might need help. She might have gone into labour—you're a midwife, aren't you?'

'Yes. Don't worry, we'll come. I'll bring a delivery pack just in case. And I'll call the ambulance. You just get to her.'

He drove fast—probably faster than was truly sensible, but not so fast that he was likely to end up in a ditch.

'Lucy!' He pulled up behind her car, ran to the door and yanked it open, but the car was empty, canted over at a crazy angle and filling with water. Hell. He dropped the door and looked round, then spotted the barn. Would she have gone there?

He looked around again, then noticed something on the side of the car. Writing. IN THE BA. Barn? The barn!

He wrote it again, clearing the fresh snow from the letters, and then got back in his car and shot down the road, pulling up outside in a slither of slush and gravel. 'Lucy!' he yelled, and he heard an answering sob.

'Ben! In here—I'm having the baby.'

Dear God. And he had nothing with him—no gloves, no sterile drapes, nothing to protect her from contamination. He ran into the barn and found her huddled against some straw bales, and gathered her, sobbing, into his arms. 'Are you hurt?'

'No—but the baby's coming, Ben. I can feel it—I can feel the head. It can't come now, I'm only thirty-four weeks! It's too early.'

'You'll be fine,' he said, giving her one last squeeze. 'There's an ambulance on the way, and I've called Kate, just in case. You stay there. I'm going to sort these bales out and then have a look at you.'

He stood up, shifted a few bales to make a flat, clean area of fresh straw, then stripped off his coat and laid it on them, scooped her up and set her down in the middle of it. 'We need to get these wet trousers off you,' he said, and peeled them down her legs, taking the tiny lacy knickers that he adored with them.

Hell. She was right. The baby's head was crowning, and there was no time to do anything except catch it.

'I want to push.'

'No. Just wait—if you can. Pant. Wait for Kate, she won't be long.'

'Lucy?'

'What's he doing here?'

'He's your father.'

'He didn't want to see me again.'

'Lucy?' Another bellow from Nick.

'In here,' Ben yelled, thinking that he'd never expected to be pleased to see Nick Tremayne, but, by God, he was. And Kate—dear, sensible Kate, who elbowed them both out of the way, thrust a delivery pack in Nick's hands and told him to unwrap it, sent Ben to hug Lucy up at the other end and took over.

'The cord's around its neck,' Kate said. 'Lucy, I'm just going to put my finger in and free it, then you can push again, darling, all right? Just hang on, just another minute, there's a good girl.'

She wriggled a loop of cord free, worked it over the baby's head, felt again, and then smiled. 'Right, my love. In your own time, when you feel the next contraction, just pant and push gently with your mouth open— That's it, lovely, nice and steady— Well done. Ben, can I have your jumper, please?'

He peeled it off over his head and handed it to her, and with the next contraction she delivered the baby onto the jumper, lifted it and laid it on Lucy's abdomen, tucking the warm fabric round it.

'I need to suck it out,' Kate said, taking the aspirator from Nick and clearing the baby's nose and mouth of mucus while Ben held his breath and prayed.

And then there was an indignant squall, and Lucy sobbed with relief, and he closed his eyes, hugged her close and wondered if he'd ever heard anything more beautiful in all his life.

'Well, I have to say, if you were going to have a baby in a stable at Christmas, you could have had a boy,' Kate murmured, and Lucy gave a fractured little laugh and peered in amazement at the baby.

'It's a girl?'

'Yes—yes, it's a girl,' Kate said gently. 'Congratulations.' She turned. 'Nick, could you go and flag down the ambulance? I can hear it coming.'

He turned and went without a word, but Ben caught a glimpse of his face, taut with emotion, and wished he could unsay the words he'd said that morning. However true.

'I love you,' Ben said, pressing a lingering kiss to his wife's brow, and she looked up at him, her eyes filled with wonder, and smiled.

'I love you, too. Oh, Ben, look at her, she's beautiful.'

She wasn't. She was streaked with blood and mucus, covered in the creamy vernix that protected her skin *in utero*, and her face was screwed up with indignation, and he'd never seen anything so amazing in all his life.

'Ben? Ben, can you get the door?'

Lucy was lying propped up in bed, the baby in her arms, and she didn't know where Ben was. He'd gone downstairs to start cooking their lunch some time ago, and there wasn't a sign of him.

'Ben?'

'I've got it,' he yelled, and she heard the front door creak open, and then silence.

Silence?

'Ben, who is it?' she called, but there was no reply, and she slipped out of bed and padded to the top of the stairs, the baby in her arms.

She could hear voices, but she couldn't hear what they were saying until she reached the end of the landing, and then she saw them. The big front door at the foot of the stairs was closed, and Ben and her father were standing there in front of it, talking in hushed tones.

'I'll quite understand if you want me to go.'

'No. No, I don't want you to go, Nick, but I'm not going to let you upset Lucy.'

'I won't. I promise. But I must see her—and you. I owe you both a massive apology. You were right—I neglected Annabel, and I didn't want to see it, so I made you the scapegoat. And I don't know how you can ever forgive me for that. It was unforgivable—'

'No, it wasn't. You were blinded by grief, and you were lashing out. I don't have that excuse. I was really hard on you—I said dreadful things, and I'm really sorry.'

'True things. I was busy with my empire.'

'No, you were busy setting up a vital community health centre, and you took your eye off the ball. We all do it. And really the fault, if any, was Annabel's for downplaying it too long. It was just one of those terrible things, Nick. I'm just so sorry that I couldn't do anything about it.'

'It wasn't your fault,' her father said, gruffly uttering the words Lucy had given up hoping he would say, and she must have made a noise because they both lifted their heads and looked up at her.

'Hello, Dad,' she said, and his face twisted.

'Hello, Lucy. Happy New Year. I've brought something for the baby.'

He seemed so uncertain, so uncharacteristically unsure and, tucking the baby more securely in her arm, she went carefully down the stairs and into his arms. 'Happy New Year,' she said softly, going up on tiptoe and kissing his cold cheek. 'Here—say hello to your granddaughter.'

He bent and touched her little face with a blunt fingertip, and his mouth compressed. 'She's lovely. May I hold her?'

'Of course. Ben, can you take Dad's coat? Come through to the sitting room, we've got the fire going.'

And she led him through into the room where he'd spent so much time in his own childhood, and there, in a chair by the fire, she settled him down and laid the baby in his arms.

'She's beautiful,' he said gruffly. 'Just like you were. Does she have a name yet?'

Ben came up beside her, one arm around her shoulders, holding her close. 'We thought—if you didn't mind—we'd like to call her Annabel.'

Nick's throat worked, and when he lifted his head, his eyes were filled with tears.

'I think Annabel would be a lovely name for her,' he said. 'A very fitting name. And I'm sure your mother would think so, too.' He cleared his throat. 'So—should we wet the baby's head?' he suggested. 'I brought you a bottle of champagne as a peace offering. Not much of one, but I thought you could always hit me over the head with it—it's nice and heavy.'

Ben laughed, dispersing the tension, and disappeared, coming back moments later with glasses. He opened the bottle with a soft pop and filled them, then lifted his glass.

'To Annabel,' he said, and her father's jaw tensed.

'To Annabel,' he echoed, and pressed a kiss lightly to the baby's forehead. 'Both of them.'

Lucy didn't speak. She just lifted the glass and touched the champagne to her lips. Just a tiny taste, because of her milk. And she thought of her mother, of the terrible bitterness of the last two years now finally laid to rest, and as Ben's arm came around her shoulders again, a tear slid down her cheek.

'To both of them,' she echoed softly.

The Italian's New-Year Marriage Wish

SARAH MORGAN

As a child **Sarah Morgan** dreamed of being a writer and, although she took a few interesting detours on the way, she is now living that dream. With her writing career she has successfully combined business with pleasure and she firmly believes that reading romance is one of the most satisfying and fat-free escapist pleasures available. Her stories are unashamedly optimistic and she is always pleased when she receives letters from readers saying that her books have helped them through hard times.

Sarah lives near London with her husband and two children, who innocently provide an endless supply of authentic dialogue. When she isn't writing or reading Sarah enjoys music, movies and any activity that takes her outdoors.

Readers can find out more about Sarah and her books from her website: www.sarahmorgan.com. She can also be found on Facebook and Twitter.

To Sheila Hodgson, for all the support and encouragement. Thank you.

CHAPTER ONE

'I WANT a divorce, I want a divorce, I want a divorce...'

Amy recited the words in her head as the taxi wound its way along the small country roads that led towards the North Cornish coast. The snow that had fallen overnight had dusted fields, trees and bushes with a wintry layer of white that now glistened and sparkled under the bright early morning sunshine. It promised to be a perfect day—perfect for people who weren't about to end their marriage.

She felt sicker than she'd ever felt in her life and the brief glimpse of the sea in the distance increased the tension in her stomach until it felt as though she'd swallowed a loop of knotted rope. No amount of logical reasoning or deep breathing produced the desired feeling of calm and suddenly Amy wished she hadn't chosen to come in person. But what else could she have done when he'd refused to respond to her letters or phone calls?

He'd left her no choice.

Staring out of the window at the familiar landmarks, she admitted to herself that his protracted silence had surprised her. It was so unlike him. He was Italian after all, and she'd braced herself for an ongoing display of simmering, volcanic passion.

Marco was single-minded and determined. A man who knew what he wanted from life and took it.

Which just went to prove that he clearly hadn't wanted her.

Amy felt her throat close and she swallowed hard, controlling the tears, aware that she was being completely illogical. It wasn't as if she'd *wanted* him to put up a fight. It would have made it so much harder to do what had to be done.

Amy curled her hands tightly over the edge of her seat. She wanted to tell the taxi driver to turn round and take her back to the station but she knew that she couldn't give in to that impulse. If she didn't do this now then she'd only have to do it later and she'd already put it off as long as possible.

It was time to finally end their marriage.

She was so lost in thought that it took a moment for her to realise that the taxi driver was speaking to her. 'I'm sorry? Did you say something?'

The taxi driver glanced in his mirror. 'Just wondering if you live in Penhally.'

Amy managed a polite smile. 'No.' She consciously relaxed her hands. 'Not any more. I used to, before…' *Before her entire life had fallen apart.* 'I lived here for a while.'

'So…' He drove carefully down a road still white with snow. 'I expect you're home to celebrate New Year with your family? Are you staying long?'

No family. No celebrations.

'It's just a short visit,' she said huskily. 'I'm here until this evening. My train is at eight o'clock.'

Which left her just enough time to confront her husband and say, 'I want a divorce.' And then she would never see Penhally again.

'Well, keep an eye on the weather. Can you believe that it snowed again last night? I mean, when did we last have snow like this on the coast? When was it last this cold?' He shook his head. 'Global warming, that's what it is. Our entire climate has gone bonkers. And there are severe storms forecast. Leave plenty of time or you'll find yourself stranded and miss that train.'

Barely listening, Amy glanced out of the window. She'd be leaving Penhally that evening even if it meant walking.

As the taxi turned into the main street, her heart rate doubled, as if her body was instinctively bracing itself for conflict.

She slid down slightly in her seat and then frowned with exasperation and sat up again. *What was she doing?* She was behaving like a fugitive, not a thirty-five-year-old doctor with a responsible career!

But the thought of actually seeing Marco again shredded her self-control, confidence and dignity into tiny pieces. For the past two years she'd dreamed about him, thought about him and cried about him. No matter what she'd been doing, he'd dominated her thoughts, but she'd spared herself the torture of actually bumping into him by taking herself as far away as possible.

Unable to trust herself not to weaken, she hadn't just left the village or the country—she'd left the continent.

'Stop here.' Suddenly anxious that she might bump into Marco before she was ready to see him, she leaned forward. 'Thank you, this is perfect. I can walk from here.' She fumbled in her bag for her purse, paid the taxi driver and slid out of the back of the car, clutching her small bag.

She waited for the taxi to pull away and stood for a moment, staring down the main street of Penhally. It was still too early for the shops to open but Christmas lights twinkled in the windows and decorations glittered and winked. The addition of snow produced a scene that could have been taken straight from a Dickens novel and Amy gave a tiny smile, suddenly feeling more Christmassy than she had over Christmas itself. Memories slid into her head: memories of walking hand in hand with her grandmother, choosing decorations for the Christmas tree; collecting the turkey from the butcher.

She'd always thought that Penhally was a magical place.

Her few happy childhood memories were centred on this Cornish fishing village.

She'd wanted her own children to grow up here.

'Amy? Amy Avanti?'

The voice came from directly behind her and she turned, her palms damp with sweat and her heart pounding frantically against her chest. It was as if she'd been caught shoplifting instead of just returning home unannounced.

'Tony…' She managed a smile even though she was secretly wishing that the landlord of the Smugglers' Inn hadn't chosen this particular moment to walk up the street. 'You're up early.'

'Busy time of year.' The collar of his coat was turned up against the winter chill as he studied her face, a question in his eyes. 'So that's it? I haven't seen you for ages and all you can say is, "You're up early"?'

'Sorry.' Feeling suddenly awkward, Amy huddled deeper into her coat. 'I suppose I don't really know what to say…'

'You always were a woman who listened more than you spoke…' Tony grinned '…which makes a pleasant change. Does Marco know you're home?'

'No.' *She hadn't wanted him forewarned.* Her only hope was to catch him off guard. She was banking on the fact that he'd be so shocked to see her that he wouldn't say much. *Wouldn't make things difficult.* 'It was an impulse thing. We have things to discuss.'

'Well, I heard the Maserati roaring down the street earlier so he's probably already at the surgery. They're busy over there.'

His words brought a disturbingly vivid memory to life. A memory of a hot summer's day two and a half years before when she and Marco had just arrived in Penhally, newly married and full of plans. *Full of hope and optimism.* Marco had taken her for a ride in his beloved Maserati, a car that perfectly matched his testosterone-driven approach to life. He'd driven the car along the coast road, one hand on the wheel, the other laid possessively over the back of her seat, and Amy had been so madly and crazily in love with him that she'd spent the entire trip gazing in disbelief at his profile.

And he'd guessed how she'd felt, of course, because he was a man who knew women and his cool sophistication and greater life experience had just increased her own, deep-seated insecurity.

Why was he with her?

How many times had she asked herself that question? Amy swallowed hard and pushed the thought away. He *wasn't* with her. Not any more. And although it had been her decision, she knew that by leaving she'd simply hastened the inevitable. 'I'm surprised he's driving the Maserati. It always hated cold weather.'

'It still hates cold weather. Last week it died by the side of the road and your husband was gesticulating and letting out a stream of Italian. The entire village was in the bookshop looking up words in the Italian dictionary but we all know that when it comes to his precious car, Marco doesn't always use words that are in the dictionary.' Tony scratched his head. 'I suggested he buy a traditional English car designed to cope with traditional English weather, but he treated that suggestion with the contempt that it probably deserved.'

'I can imagine he wasn't enthusiastic.'

'It's good to see you back, Amy. We were surprised when you went.'

'Yes.' She had no doubt that she'd left the entire village reeling with shock. Marco Avanti just wasn't a man that women left, especially not a plain, ordinary woman like her, who should have been grateful to have attracted the attention of anyone, let alone an Italian heartthrob.

And she hadn't offered an explanation.

How could she? It had all been too personal, too private. *Too devastating.*

'Well, it's good to see you home, even if it's only for a short time. If you hurry, you'll catch Marco before he starts surgery. He's pretty busy. I expect you heard about Lucy? She had her baby early and so now they're a doctor down.'

Were they?

She hadn't had news of Penhally for a year, not since that one, solitary letter she'd received from Kate Althorp, the practice manager, who had once been her friend.

'They must be busy.' Which made it better for her. Marco wouldn't have time to argue or make things difficult. She was going to walk into the surgery, say what needed to be said and then leave before he had time to compose arguments. Hopefully he'd be too wrapped up in the needs of his patients to be particularly bothered about an almost ex-wife.

Amy shivered slightly, her breath leaving clouds in the freezing air. 'I'll see you later, Tony.'

'Make sure you do. Pop into the Smugglers' for a drink before you leave.'

'Yes.' She smiled, knowing that she wouldn't. What was the point of exposing herself to gossip for the sake of one drink when the entire liquid contents of the pub wouldn't be enough to dull the pain of seeing Marco Avanti again?

At the other end of the village in the state-of-the-art GP surgery that served the local community, Marco Avanti lounged in his chair, staring with brooding concentration at the computer screen on his desk. 'Kate?' he called through the open door. 'Didn't you say that the blood results for Lily Baxter had come through?'

'We haven't had time to enter them on the system yet.' Kate walked into the room, carrying a mug of coffee. 'With Lucy going on early maternity leave, we've been concentrating on finding a locum. Being one doctor down over the Christmas period just doesn't work. I found four more grey hairs when I woke up this morning.' She moved a stack of journals and put the coffee on his desk. 'Here, drink this. You're going to need it. It's going to take you until this evening to get through the amount of patients booked in today.'

The pungent, seductive aroma of fresh coffee filled the air and Marco gave an appreciative groan. 'You made that for me? Truly, you're an angel, *amore*.' He curled long, strong fingers around the mug and lifted it, the smell penetrating the clouds of tiredness that threatened to fog his brain. '*Tutto bene*? Everything OK? Tell me the worst. The village has been consumed by an attack of cholera? Plague? Everyone is queuing to see me, no?'

'Don't even joke about it. And as for the queue…' Kate smiled wearily. 'You don't want to know. Just take them one at a time and if you're still here tonight, I'll bring you a sleeping bag.'

'Just make sure the sleeping bag contains a warm, willing woman,' he drawled, and Kate smiled.

'You're incorrigible.' She moved towards the door and Marco put the mug on his desk.

'Did you find time to call the garage about the Maserati?'

'Yes. They're coming in a minute to see to it. Give me the keys and then I won't have to disturb you.'

Grateful that there was one less thing that he had to manage, Marco reached into the pockets of the coat that he'd thrown over the back of the chair and tossed her the keys. 'Here. *Grazie*, Kate. Not only are you *molto belissima*, you are also efficient.'

'It's called time management. If I sort out your car, then you spend more time with patients. It's a solution that works for everyone, so you don't need to waste your Italian charm on me.'

'Why is it a waste?' Enjoying the brief distraction of meaningless banter, Marco leaned back and gave her a slow smile. 'Run away with me, Kate. We could both leave this cold, windy place and live in sin in my beautiful Italy. I own a *palazzo* in Venice, right on the edge of the canal.' He watched as a shadow flickered across her eyes.

Then she noticed his gaze and blushed slightly, smiling quickly as if she didn't want him to know that she was unhappy.

'Maybe I will leave,' she said softly. 'Maybe it is time I did something different. But not with you. I'm not that stupid. My New Year's resolution is never to get involved with a man who is still in love with another woman and you fall into that category.'

Marco felt every muscle in his body tense but carefully controlled his facial expression. 'The only woman I love,' he purred softly, 'is currently parked outside this surgery with an engine problem. *She* is my baby.' He kept his tone neutral but Kate gave a faint smile and shook her head slowly.

'You don't fool me, Marco. Whenever Amy's name is mentioned, you always appear so cool and in control, but I know that you're not. What's happening under that cloak you put between yourself and the world?'

Nothing that he had any intention of sharing.

'You want to know what's under my cloak? This isn't the time or the place, *tesoro*.' How had they suddenly shifted from talking about her problems to talking about his? He teased her gently, swiftly and skilfully manoeuvring the conversation back to safer ground. 'I have surgery starting in less than five minutes and that won't be enough to do justice to your beauty. When I make love to a woman, I need at least twenty-four hours.'

'Stop it or I'll have to throw a bucket of water over you!' Kate gave a reluctant laugh. 'It's bad enough that all the women in the village are in love with you. They're all waiting for your broken heart to heal so that they can pounce.'

'My heart isn't broken.' Marco reached forward and checked something on his computer. 'In fact, all my organs are intact and in perfect working order.'

'Well, don't tell anyone that! There'll be a stampede and we're busy enough here.' Kate's smile faded. 'I wish I was more like you. How do you do it? You and Amy were so in love—'

Taken aback by her frank, personal comment, Marco uttered a sharp expletive in Italian but then noticed the haunting sadness in Kate's eyes. With ruthless determination he pushed aside dark, swirling thoughts of his wife and focused his attention on his colleague. 'Kate…' With an effort, he kept his voice gentle. 'This is not about me, is it? It's about you. About you and Nick. Perhaps you should just tell him that you love him. Be honest.'

'What? I don't…' Flustered and embarrassed, Kate lifted a hand to her chest and shook her head in swift denial. 'What makes you say that? Marco, for goodness' sake…'

'Nick is the senior partner and my colleague,' Marco drawled softly, wondering why relationships were so incredibly complicated. 'You are also my colleague. It is hard to miss the tension between the two of you. Often I am in the middle of it.'

'Nick and I have known each other a long time.'

'Sì, I know that.' Marco sighed. 'You're in love with him. Tell him.'

'Even if you were right, which you're not,' Kate added quickly, her shoulders stiffening, 'you think I should just knock on the door of his consulting room and say, "I love you"?'

'Why not? It's the truth. Speaking as a man, I can tell you that we prefer a direct approach. Feminine games are an exhausting optional extra. If a woman wants to tell me that she loves me…' he shrugged expressively and lounged deeper in his chair '…why would I stop her?'

Kate laughed in disbelief. 'Sorry, but I'm just trying to picture Nick's face if I were to follow your advice.'

Marco watched her for a moment, noting the dark shadows under her eyes. 'Your problem is that you have fallen in love with an Englishman and English men know nothing about love. They are closed up, cold, unemotional. Give them twenty-four hours to make love to a woman and they would spend twenty-three of those hours watching football on the television.' As he'd planned, his words made her smile.

'Perhaps you're right.' She straightened her shoulders, suddenly looking less like a vulnerable woman and more like an efficient practice manager. 'You're a good friend. And for a man, you're very emotionally advanced. It would have been much simpler if I could have fallen for a hot Italian instead of a cold Englishman.'

Marco thought of his own disastrous marriage. 'Hot Italians can get it wrong, too,' he said wearily. *Badly wrong.* 'And Nick isn't really cold, just badly hurt. He carries a lot of guilt. A lot of pain. This has been a bad time in his life.'

A bad time in both their lives.

Given the events of the last few years, it was amazing that he and his partner were still managing to run a GP practice.

Reaching for his coffee, he cleared his mind of the dark thoughts that threatened to cloud the day.

Not now.

He wasn't going to think about that now.

It was the festive period and he had a punishing workload ahead of him.

There was going to be no time to brood or even think.

Which was exactly the way he wanted it.

* * *

Amy paused outside the surgery. The fresh sea air stung her cheeks and from above came the forlorn shriek of a seagull.

She had ten minutes before Marco was due to start seeing patients and she lost her chance to speak to him.

Ten minutes to finally end a marriage.

It would be more than enough time to say what had to be said. And he wouldn't be able to prolong the meeting because he would have patients waiting to see him.

Without giving herself time to change her mind, she pushed open the door and walked into Reception. The sudden warmth hit her and she walked up to the desk and saw Kate Althorp in conversation with the receptionist.

Once, they'd been friends even though the other woman was at least ten years her senior. Had that friendship ended with her sudden departure? Amy had no doubt that everyone in Penhally would have judged her harshly and she could hardly blame them for that. She'd given them no reason not to.

'Do you have an appointment?' Crisp, efficient and obviously busy despite the time of day, Kate glanced up and her eyes widened in recognition. '*Amy!* Oh, my goodness.' Abandoning her conversation, she walked round the desk towards Amy, clearly at a loss to know what to say. 'You're *home*? I thought you were still in Africa with that medical charity!'

'Not any more. Hello, Kate.'

Kate hesitated and then stepped forward and gave her a warm hug. 'It's good to see you, Amy. Really. Does Marco know you're here? Why didn't you call?'

'I was hoping— Marco doesn't know I'm here but I'd like to see him for a moment.' Amy cringed as she listened to herself. She hadn't seen her husband for two years and she was making it sound as though she'd just popped in to ask whether he'd be home in time for dinner.

Doubt flickered across Kate's face as she glanced in the

direction of the consulting rooms. 'He's about to start surgery and we've been incredibly busy because—'

'I know about Lucy and it's just for a moment,' Amy urged, unable to keep the note of desperation out of her voice. If Kate refused to let her see Marco that would mean waiting, and Amy wasn't sure that her courage would survive any sort of wait. She had to do this now. *Right now.* 'Please, Kate.' Unaccustomed to asking for help from another person, she stumbled over the words and the older woman looked at her for a moment, her responsibilities as practice manager clearly conflicting with her desire to help a friend so obviously in need.

After a moment of hesitation, Kate walked back round the desk and reached for the phone, her eyes still on Amy's face. 'I'll phone through to him and tell him that you're—'

'No!' Amy was already walking towards Marco's consulting room. 'I'll just go straight in.' Quickly, before she had time to change her mind.

Her heart pounding rhythmically against her chest, Amy tapped on his door.

'*Sì*, come in.'

The sound of his smooth, confident voice made her stomach lurch and she closed her eyes briefly. Despite his enviable fluency in English, no one could ever have mistaken Marco Avanti for anything other than an Italian and his voice stroked her nerve endings like a caress.

Her palm was damp with nerves as she clutched the doorhandle and turned it.

He was just a man like any other.

She wasn't going to go weak at the knees. She wasn't going to notice anything about him. She was past all that. She was just going to say what needed to be said and then leave.

Ten minutes, she reminded herself. She just had to survive ten minutes and not back down. And then she'd be on the train back to London.

She opened the door and stepped into the room. 'Hello, Marco.' Her heart fluttered like the wings of a captive butterfly as she forced herself to look at him. 'I wanted to have a quick word before you start surgery.'

His dark eyes met hers and heat erupted through her body, swift and deadly as a forest fire. From throat to pelvis she burned, her reaction to him as powerful as ever. Helplessly, she dug her fingers into her palms.

A man like any other? Had she really believed that, even for a moment? Marco was nothing like any other man.

She'd had two years to prepare herself for this moment, so why did the sight of him drive the last of her breath from her body? What was it about him? Yes, he was handsome but other men were handsome and she barely noticed them. Marco was different. Marco was the embodiment of everything it was to be male. He was strong, confident and unashamedly macho and no woman with a pulse could look at him and not want him.

And for a while he'd been hers.

She looked at him now, unable to think of anything but the hungry, all-consuming passion that had devoured them both.

His powerful body was ominously still, but he said nothing. He simply leaned slowly back in his chair and watched her in brooding silence, his long fingers toying with the pen that he'd been using when she'd entered the room.

Desperately unsettled, Amy sensed the slow simmer of emotion that lay beneath his neutral expression.

What wouldn't she have given to possess even a tiny fraction of his cool?

'We need to talk to each other.' She stayed in the doorway, her hands clasped nervously in front of her, a shiver passing through her body as the atmosphere in the room suddenly turned icy cold.

Finally he spoke. 'You have chosen an odd time of day for a reunion.'

'This isn't a reunion. We have things to discuss, you know we do.'

His gaze didn't flicker. 'And I have thirty sick patients to see before lunchtime. You shouldn't need to ask where my priorities lie.'

No, she didn't need to ask. His skill and dedication as a doctor was one of the qualities that had attracted her to him in the first place.

His handsome face was hard and unforgiving and she felt her insides sink with misery.

What had she expected?

He was hardly going to greet her warmly, was he? Not after the way she'd treated him. *Not after the things she'd let him think about her.* 'I didn't have any choice but to come and see you, Marco. You didn't answer my letters.'

'I didn't like the subject matter.' There was no missing the hard edge to his tone. 'Write about something that interests me and I'll consider replying. And now you need to leave because my first patient is waiting.'

'No.' Panic slid through her and she took a little step forward. 'We need to do this. I know you're upset, but—'

'*Upset?*' One dark eyebrow rose in sardonic appraisal. 'Why would you possibly think that?'

Her breathing was rapid. 'Please, don't play games—it isn't going to help either of us. Yes, I left, but it was the right thing to do, Marco. It was the right thing for both of us. I'm sure you can understand that now that some time has passed.'

'I understand that you walked out on our marriage. You think "upset"…' his accent thickened as he lingered on the word. 'You think "upset" is an accurate description of my feelings on this subject?'

Amy felt the colour touch her cheeks. The truth was that she had absolutely no insight into his feelings. She'd never really known what he had truly been feeling at any point in their relationship and she hadn't been around to witness his reaction to her departure. If he had been upset then she assumed that it would have been because she'd exposed him to the gossip of a small community, or possibly because he'd had a life plan and she'd ruined it. Not because he'd loved her, because she knew that had never been the case. How could he have loved her? What had she ever been able to offer a man like Marco Avanti?

Especially not once she'd discovered—

Unable to cope with that particular thought at the moment, Amy lifted her chin and ploughed on. 'I can see that you're angry and I don't blame you, but I didn't come here to argue. We can make this easy or we can make it difficult.'

'And I'm sure you're choosing easy.' The contempt in his tone stung like vinegar on an open wound. 'You chose to walk away rather than sort out a problem. Isn't that what you're good at?'

'Not every problem has a solution, Marco!' Frustrated and realising that if she wasn't careful she risked revealing more than she wanted to reveal, she moved closer to the desk. 'You have every right to be upset, but what we need now is to sort out the future. I just need you to agree to the divorce. Then you'll be free to…' *Marry another woman?* The words stuck in her throat.

'*Accidenti*, am I right in understanding that you have interrupted my morning surgery to *ask me for a divorce*?' He rose to his feet, his temper bubbling to the surface, a dangerous glint in his molten dark eyes. 'It is bad enough that I am expected to diagnose a multitude of potentially serious illnesses in a five-minute consultation, but now my wife decides that that in that same ridiculous time frame we are going to end our relationship. This is your idea of a joke, no?'

She'd forgotten how tall he was, how imposing. He topped six feet two and his shoulders were broad and powerful. Looking at him now, she had to force herself not to retreat to the safety of Reception. 'It's not a joke and if I'm interrupting your surgery, it's your fault. You wouldn't answer my letters. I had no other way of getting in touch with you. And this needn't take long.'

He gripped the edge of the desk and his knuckles whitened. 'Do you really think you can leave without explanation and then walk back in here and end our marriage with a five-minute conversation?' His eyes blazed with anger and his voice rose. *Is that what you think?*

Startled by his unexpected loss of control, Amy flinched. *She hadn't thought he'd cared so much.* Or was he angry because she'd chosen to confront him in his place of work? 'Don't shout—there are patients in Reception. They'll gossip.'

'Gossip? It's a little late to be worrying about gossip.' But he dropped back into his seat, threw her a dark, smouldering glance and then raked both hands through his glossy, dark hair. Several strands immediately flopped back over his forehead and she felt her breath catch.

The yearning to touch him was so powerful that she had to clasp her hands behind her back to prevent herself from reaching out and sliding her hands into his hair.

As if sensing her inner struggle, his gaze caught hers and held for a moment, his eyes darkening in a way that was achingly familiar. The atmosphere in the room shifted dangerously and awareness throbbed between them, drawing them into a tense, silent communication that said far more than words ever could.

Amy felt the instant response of her body. She felt her stomach quiver and her limbs warm.

It was still there, that inexplicable attraction that had

pulled them together with magnetic force from the moment they'd met.

Which meant that she had to get this over with. Quickly. Trying to ignore the insidious curl of feminine awareness deep in her pelvis, Amy gritted her teeth and backed towards the door.

This was why she'd gone so far away. She'd known that only by putting an ocean between them would she be able to resist the unbelievably powerful chemistry that knotted them together.

She had to leave.

Fast.

'Marco—it's all history, now. Let's not make this more painful than it has to be.'

'You're the one who made the whole thing painful, Amy.' His voice was suddenly dangerously quiet, but before he could say any more the door opened and Kate flew in.

'Marco, you have to see little Michelle right now! I've explained to your first patient that they're going to have to wait. I'm sorry.' She threw an apologetic look towards Amy. 'Is there any chance that you can grab a cup of coffee upstairs in the staffroom or something?'

Amy watched as Marco straightened his shoulders and wrenched back control. But his mind obviously wasn't on his work because for the briefest of moments his expression was blank. 'Michelle?' He said the name as if he'd never heard it before and Kate looked momentarily startled, as if detailed explanations were uncommon in their working relationship.

'Yes, Michelle! What's the matter with you?' Then she glanced at Amy and blushed slightly, as if she'd just realised what might be the matter. 'Michelle *Watson*. Carol said that she was off colour last night but she's suddenly gone downhill. She called an ambulance but they said that they'd be twenty minutes because they're stuck behind a gritting lorry. Honestly, Europe can have feet of snow and manage fine, but if we have so much as a dusting the entire country grinds to a halt. I'm tempted to go and organise them myself.'

'Michelle Watson. Of course. Michelle.' Marco uncoiled his lean, powerful body and rose to his feet again but there were lines of strain around his eyes. 'Bring her in.'

'Watson?' Amy remembered that Carol Watson had just delivered when she'd left and she glanced at Marco as Kate hurried out of the room. 'Carol's baby girl?'

'She isn't a baby any more.' His tone was flat and he didn't glance in her direction as if he was trying to get his mind firmly on the job. 'You've been gone two years and I don't have time to brief you on everything that has been happening in the village during your long absence.' He moved across the consulting room. 'You left, Amy. You made your choice.'

'Yes, but—' She broke off, wrestling against an instinctive desire to defend herself. What would he say if she told him the truth? Told him that she'd *had* to leave. *That she'd done it for him.* But she knew that she couldn't. She could never, ever tell him the truth because if he knew the truth then everything would become even more complicated. 'That's right.' She felt horrible. *Just horrible.* There was so much she wanted to say but she couldn't say any of it. 'I left.' Her voice shook but his swift glance was unsympathetic.

'Go and get a cup of coffee. Or just leave. It's what you're good at.'

'I can't leave until we've talked.'

He yanked open a cupboard and removed a pulse oximeter. 'Then you're going to have to wait until I have time to see you,' he growled. 'I think the current waiting time for an appointment with me is a week. Ask the girls at Reception. They just might be able to fit you in.'

CHAPTER TWO

THE door flew open and Kate hurried back into the room with Carol, who was carrying the toddler wrapped in a soft, pink blanket. A sulky-looking teenager followed them, her pretty face half hidden by a thick layer of make-up.

Amy was on the point of leaving the room and then she looked at the toddler and saw at a glance that Kate had been right to interrupt them. The child was fighting for each breath.

'Oh, Dr Avanti.' There was panic in Carol's voice. 'Thank goodness you're here. She's had this cold and I was up in the night with her and then this morning she just seemed so much worse. Her little chest was heaving so I panicked and called the ambulance but they're stuck on the coast road and you always know what to do so I just thought I'd come and take a chance in case—'

'*Calma.* Try and be calm, Carol.' Marco's voice was gentle and reassuring as his gaze rested on the child, his eyes sharp and observant. 'You did the right thing to come.'

Amy stepped forward, her own problems momentarily forgotten. 'Let me help. What do you want me to do, Marco?'

He glanced at her and then gave a brief nod. 'Let's give her some oxygen straight away.'

Amy located the oxygen and mask. 'Do you want me to set up a nebuliser?'

'To begin with I'll give her a beta 2 agonist via a spacer. It is better at this age than a nebuliser.' He turned back to the child and stroked his hand over the child's neck, palpating the neck muscles with gentle fingers. 'Michelle, what have you been doing, *angelo mia*? Are you worrying your poor mother?'

No one would have guessed that only moments earlier he'd been braced for a fight. All the hardness had gone from his tone and there was no trace of the anger that had been simmering inside him. Instead, he was kind and approachable, his smooth, confident movements removing the panic from the situation.

He'd always been amazing with children, Amy thought numbly as she handed him the oxygen mask. They found his strength reassuring and responded to his gentleness. *Strength and gentleness*. A killer combination. When she'd first met him he'd been working as a paediatrician and his skills in that field were very much in evidence as he assessed the little girl.

To someone who didn't know better it might have looked as though he was simply comforting the child and putting her at ease, but Amy watched the movement of his fingers and the direction of his gaze and knew that in that short space of time he'd checked the little girl's respirations, her pulse rate and the degree of wheezing.

Carol cuddled the child and looked at him helplessly. 'She ate a tiny bit of breakfast and then she was sick everywhere. After that she was just too breathless to eat. I've never seen her this bad.'

The teenager slumped against the wall and rolled her eyes. 'For goodness' sake Mum, stop panicking.' She broke off and coughed a few times. 'You make everything into such a drama.'

'Don't you tell me to stop panicking, Lizzie,' Carol snapped angrily. 'You were giving her breakfast! You should have noticed sooner that she wasn't breathing properly!'

'Well, I'm not a bloody doctor, am I?!' The tone was moody and defiant, but Amy saw the worry in the teenager's eyes and remembered that this was Carol's second marriage. Presumably Lizzie was her child from her previous marriage.

Clearly things weren't altogether harmonious in the house-hold.

'She is here now and that is what is important.' Swiftly but calmly, Marco reached for the hand-held pulse oximeter, attached the probe to the child's finger. 'I want her as quiet as possible so that I can examine her properly. You will have a nice cuddle with your mama, Michelle. I'm going to help you with your breathing, *tesoro*.'

Tesoro.

Trying not to remember that he'd called her the same thing in happier times, Amy looked at the pulse oximeter.

'That's a neat device.' It was typical of Marco to have all the latest technology to hand, she mused silently. Oxygen, spacer, pulse oximeter. He may have chosen to move from paediatrics to general practice but he still insisted on having all the latest equipment.

'It's a very fast and reliable method of obtaining a reading.' He glanced at Carol, immediately offering an explanation. 'It tells me how much oxygen is in her blood. I'd like the level to be higher than it is. I'm going to give her something that will help her breathing.'

Carol's face was white and strained. 'Is it her asthma again?'

'*Sì*, it seems that way. She has had a virus and that can sometimes be a trigger.' He connected a face mask to the mouthpiece of a spacer.

'Michelle, I'm going to put this mask over your nose and mouth and I want you to just breathe normally.' He settled the mask gently over the child's face and actuated the inhaler. 'Just breathe for me now. Good girl. We'll start with this and see if this improves things.'

Michelle stared up at him in terror, her breath coming in rapid, rasping gasps.

Equally terrified, Carol rubbed her back gently. 'It's all right, darling. Dr Avanti is going to make you better. He always does, you know he does.'

The little girl clawed at her face, trying to remove the mask, and Marco gently took her hand and squatted down so that he was level with the child. 'Don't pull it off, *cucciola mia.*' His voice was deep and soothing. 'This mask is going to help you breathe and I want you to try and relax and forget it is there. You're going to listen to me instead of thinking of the mask. The mask is doing magic.' Still stroking the child's fingers with his own, he lifted his head and looked at Carol. 'What's her favourite story?'

'Story? I—I don't know…'

'"Sleeping Beauty",' Lizzie muttered, and Amy glanced towards her, surprised.

So she wasn't as indifferent as she seemed, then.

Assessing Michelle and sensing that Marco was going to choose to put a line in, Amy turned away and prepared an IV tray and then reached into the cupboard for hydrocortisone, which she was sure he was going to need.

'Ah, "Sleeping Beauty". That is my favourite, too.' Marco gave a smile that would have captivated the most cynical princess and stroked the little girl's blonde curls away from her face, his eyes flicking to her chest as he watched her breathing. 'So now I will tell you my version of the story. Once upon a time there was a beautiful princess called Michelle who lived in a wonderful castle by the sea— Amy?' His voice lowered. 'Can you get me a 24-gauge needle and fifty milligrams of hydrocortisone? Normally I would try oral medication but if she's vomiting, we'll go straight to IV.'

Their differences momentarily forgotten, Amy handed him the tray that she'd already prepared and he took it from her, still telling the story. 'Princess Michelle was very loved by her mummy and daddy and they decided to give her a big party for her birthday. Everyone was invited.' He was a natural storyteller, his Italian accent curling around the words as he calmed the child. She looked at him, clearly listening as he spoke, and Marco stroked the back of the little girl's hand, searching for a vein. Then he gave a nod and looked at Amy. 'Can you squeeze for me? Michelle, I'm just going to put a little tube into the back of your hand so that I can give you some extra medicine to make you feel better. More magic.'

Amy stared at Michelle's plump, tiny hand and was suddenly relieved that she wasn't the one searching for a vein.

Carol looked the other way, her teeth clamped on her lower lip. 'There isn't another doctor in the world I'd allow to do this,' she muttered, screwing up her face in trepidation. 'It's only because you used to be a kids' doctor and I know you've done it before. Her hands are so small, let alone her veins. I can't even think about it.'

Amy was inclined to agree.

She never could have chosen paediatrics as a speciality.

But Marco's expression didn't flicker and it was obvious that he wasn't concerned. This was where he excelled—where he was most comfortable. 'And Princess Michelle invited all her friends to her party and her big sister Princess Lizzie, who she loved very much.' He lifted his head briefly and flashed a smile at Lizzie, who blushed furiously under his warm, approving gaze.

'Michelle, you might feel a little scratch now.' The movement of his fingers was deliberate and confident as he slid the tiny needle through the child's skin and checked that he was in the vein. The child barely whimpered and Marco picked up the syringe of hydrocortisone, swiftly checked the ampoule and injected it into the child, barely pausing in his rendition of the story. 'And it was the biggest and the best party that anyone had ever been to. Everyone was in pretty dresses and there was dancing and Princess Lizzie met a handsome prince.'

'Not likely in boring old Penhally,' Lizzie muttered, and then started to cough again.

Marco dropped the empty syringe back onto the tray and lifted his gaze to the teenager. 'The prince was in disguise, passing through on his way home to his castle.' His eyes were amused and Amy watched as Lizzie gave a reluctant smile.

It was impossible not to respond to him, Amy thought helplessly. He charmed everyone, whatever their age. And he did it all while managing a potentially serious asthma attack.

Anyone who said that men were incapable of multi-tasking had never seen Marco dealing with an emergency. Perhaps that was one of the advantages of having spent so long in hospital medicine. Or perhaps he was just the sort of man who coped well under pressure.

Carol was still watching him anxiously. 'Will she have to go to hospital? My husband is waiting at the house to tell the ambulance where we are. Lizzie can run back and tell him what's going on.'

'Why me? Use the phone, Mum!' Lizzie's momentary good humour vanished and her tone was impatient. 'It's freezing out there!'

'Why can't you ever just *help*?' Clearly at the end of her tether, Carol snapped, and then pressed her lips together. 'All you ever think about is yourself!'

'Well someone has to because you obviously don't give a damn about me!'

Carol gasped. 'Elizabeth!!'

'Oh, get off my back!' Coughing again, Lizzie turned and

stamped out of the consulting room, slamming the door behind her.

Carol flinched, her face scarlet with embarrassment and anger. 'As if I haven't got enough on my plate,' she said in a shaky voice. 'I'm very sorry about that. I just don't know what's happening to Lizzie. She's undergone a complete personality change over the past few months. She used to be so sweet and loving. And she just adored Michelle. Now it's like living with a hand grenade.'

'She is a teenager,' Amy said quietly, aware that Marco was writing a letter to the hospital and needed to concentrate.

'She explodes at the slightest thing, she's out all hours and I never know where she is. She used to be top of her class and her marks have plummeted.' Carol cuddled Michelle closer. 'And she's been mixing with those awful Lovelace children and everyone knows what *they're* like. I see them on a Saturday night, just hanging around on the streets. I wouldn't be surprised if they're taking drugs…'

Reminded of the complexities of working in a community practice, Amy lifted a hand to her aching head and wondered how Marco managed to stay so relaxed.

He tapped a key on the computer and glanced at Carol. 'Have you spoken to the school about Lizzie?'

'Twice. They just gave me a standard lecture about handling teenage girls.'

The printer whirred into action. 'How bad are her mood swings?'

'Very.'

'I noticed she was coughing.' He took the letter from the printer and signed it. 'How long has she had that?'

'Coughing?' Carol looked a little startled. 'I don't know, really. A while, I think, now you mention it. Just an irritated sort of cough. I even asked her if she was smoking but she just gave me one of her looks and stomped out of the room.'

Marco put the letter in an envelope and handed it to her. 'Lizzie is reaching a difficult age, that's true,' he said softly. 'Not quite a woman but no longer a child. Unsure of who she is. A little rebellion is natural and good.'

'You think that's all it is?' The faith in Carol's eyes surprised Amy. It was quite obvious that the woman was ready to believe anything Marco told her.

'I think we should talk about it properly when there is more time.' He slipped his pen back into his pocket. 'For now your priority is Michelle. She has not improved as much as I would have liked so I want her to go to the hospital. In all probability she will be fine and we could monitor her here, but if we send her home, you will be worried.' He gave an expressive shrug that betrayed his Latin heritage. 'And you have already had enough worry for one day. So, we will send her to the hospital and then they can do the worrying. That will leave you free to give some attention to Lizzie.'

'I don't know what attention to give her,' Carol said flatly. 'It's like communicating with a firework. One minute she's inanimate, the next she's exploding in my face. I find it easier coping with toddlers than teenagers.'

Marco listened and then gave a lopsided smile. 'Being a mother is the hardest job in the world because your skills have to change all the time. You are a good mother and good mothers always find a way—remember that.'

Amy saw the gratitude on Carol's face and turned away for a moment, struggling with a painful lump in her throat. Why couldn't Marco have been careless and unfeeling? Even in a crisis he could see the bigger picture. He didn't just deal with the small child—he also handled the teenager and the worried mother.

She'd needed him to be unskilled and insensitive.

It would have made everything so much easier.

As it was, just ten minutes in his company had confirmed

her biggest dread. That two years of self-enforced absence had made no difference to her feelings. She would love Marco Avanti until she took her dying breath.

Marco picked up the phone and spoke to the paediatrician at the hospital, keeping one eye on Michelle. He was concerned that her breathing didn't seem to be improving as much as he would have liked.

Had he missed something?

Was there something else he should have done?

He didn't usually have reason to question his medical skills but neither was he usually expected to handle an emergency while dealing with the unexpected appearance of his wife. Or was she now an ex-wife? It was obvious that she considered their relationship dead. And so had he. Until she'd walked into the room and asked for a divorce.

Seriously unsettled for the first time in his adult life, he ground his teeth, under no illusions that his concentration had been severely tested by Amy's sudden and unannounced arrival. Given that she clearly had no intention of leaving until she'd said what she'd come to say, he needed to somehow forget that she was there.

Forcing his mind back to Michelle, he ended the phone call and then mentally ran through the algorithm for handling an acute asthma attack in a toddler and assured himself that he'd done everything that should be done.

The child needed to be in hospital. And his wife was watching him, waiting for the right moment to ask him for a divorce.

Why now? Why did she have to pick what must be the busiest week of the year? And not only that, but they were a doctor down. He didn't have the time to argue with her. Their relationship was in its death throes and he didn't have the time to try and save it.

Which had presumably been her intention. Why else would she have picked this particular moment out of all the moments that might have presented themselves over the past two years? Was she hoping that the pressures of work would make him easier on her?

Was she hoping that he'd just sign on the dotted line and sever all ties? Kill everything they'd ever shared?

The door opened and Kate bustled in. 'Carol, your husband redirected the ambulance and he's holding on right now on the phone. I have a paramedic in Reception, wanting to know if they're still needed. Are you planning to send Michelle to the hospital, Dr Avanti?'

Carol looked at Marco. 'You really think she should go in?'

Pushing aside his own problems, Marco gave a decisive nod. 'Definitely. I called the paediatrician and she's expecting Michelle. They'll admit her overnight, monitor her breathing and then assess her in the morning. We might need to change her medication. I'll speak to her once she's had a chance to examine Michelle.'

Carol closed her eyes briefly. 'It's so hard,' she whispered. 'She's so tiny and it's so, so scary. Worry, worry, worry, that's all I seem to do. I just want her to live a normal life and be like any other toddler. What's going to happen when she goes to school?'

'Carol, I know that you're worried but you have to take it one step at a time—isn't that the phrase you English use?' He placed a hand on her shoulder, his touch gentle. 'I will discuss her management with the hospital and you and I will watch her and see how she goes as winter progresses. And if, from time to time, she has a few problems then we will deal with those problems together. We are a team. If you have a worry, you make an appointment to see me and we sort it out. And soon we will find time to talk about your Lizzie.'

Carol's eyes filled and she bit her lip. 'Don't be kind because you'll make me cry.' She pressed a hand to her mouth. 'Sorry. You must think I'm such an idiot.'

'I think you're a loving mother who is tired and worried,' Marco said quietly, his gaze flicking to Michelle. An uneasy feeling stirred inside him. The little girl was pale and her respiratory rate was more rapid than he would have liked. Making a swift decision, he looked at Kate. 'I want to go in the ambulance with her.'

The practice manager didn't manage to hide her dismay. 'You're leaving in the middle of your surgery?'

Aware that Carol was listening, Marco tried humour. 'Not in the middle,' he drawled, reaching for his bag. 'I haven't actually started yet.'

Kate shook her head, despair in her voice. 'Marco, we have patients queuing halfway back to the next county. Dr Tremayne and Dr Lovak are already seeing patients and with Lucy gone—'

'We have a sick child here who needs my care,' Marco reminded her softly, dropping a bronchodilator into his bag.

Kate gave him a desperate look and then sighed. 'Of course. Go with Michelle. That has to be the priority. We'll manage here. Somehow.'

Carol glanced between them, her expression guilty. 'I'm *really* sorry.'

'You have no reason to be sorry,' Marco said swiftly. 'In this practice each patient gets the attention they need when they most need it. The patients will not mind because they know that next time it could be them.'

Judging from the expression on Kate's face she wasn't convinced and Marco thought for a moment, aware that he was leaving her and the receptionists to cope alone with the flak from the patients. His gaze settled on Amy, who stood in the corner of his consulting room, looking awkward and out of place. 'Amy can take the rest of my surgery. That will save Nick and Dragan having to see extra patients.'

Judging from her shocked expression he might as well have suggested that she run naked along the harbour wall.

'I— *Me*?'

'Yes, you. You're a qualified GP.' He added a few more bits to his bag. 'You happen to have arrived when we're in crisis. I'm sure you won't mind helping out.'

'But—'

'What a brilliant idea! That would be fantastic,' Kate enthused, her relief evident as she ushered Carol towards the door, catching the pink blanket before it slid to the floor. 'I'll help Carol and Michelle into the ambulance while you pack what you need, Marco. Join us when you're ready. Then I'll come back and brief you, Amy. You can use Lucy's consulting room.'

Amy's expression was close to panic. 'But I'm not staying—' The door closed behind Kate and Amy flinched and turned to Marco, her hands spread in a silent plea. 'Marco, this is ridiculous. I just need to talk to you for five minutes, that's all.'

'As you can clearly see, I don't have five minutes. I don't have one minute. I can't talk to you until the patients have been seen.' Strengthened by the prospect of a brief respite before the inevitable confrontation, Marco snapped his bag shut with a force that threatened the lock. 'If you want to talk to me, help with surgery. Then perhaps I'll find time to talk to you.'

'But—'

He lifted the bag. 'That's my price for a conversation.'

'We *have* to talk, you know we do.' She wrapped her arms around her waist and then let them drop to her sides and gave a sigh. 'You don't leave me with much choice.'

'About as much choice as you gave me when you walked

away from our relationship.' He glanced out of the window, remembered the snow and reached for his coat. Suddenly he couldn't wait to put distance between them. He was angry with her. *And angry with himself for still caring so much after two years.* He needed space. Needed perspective. He needed to work out what he was going to do. 'It's non-negotiable, Amy. If you want to talk to me, stay and do the surgery. When the patients have been seen, I might find time to listen to you.'

'If you can't find anything, just let me know.' Kate threw open a few more cupboards and waved a hand vaguely. 'Everything you're likely to need should be here. And if you need any inside information on the patients, Nick should be able to help. Press 2 on your phone and you're straight through to him.'

Nick Tremayne, the senior partner. Although he was a good friend of Marco's, Amy had always found him more than a little intimidating.

What would he think of her being there? Just after she'd left Marco, Nick himself had suffered tragedy when his wife, Annabel, had died suddenly.

'How is Nick? I was so shocked when I received your letter telling me the news.'

'Yes.' Kate slipped a pile of blank prescriptions into the printer, her face expressionless. 'We were all shocked. I thought you ought to know, although finding an address for you was a nightmare. Even the medical charity you were working for didn't seem able to guarantee that they could get it to you.'

'I was moving around. It took about six months to catch up with me.' Amy sank into the chair, remembering how awful she'd felt when she'd read the news. 'I wrote to him. Just a card. Is he—is he doing all right?'

Kate reached for a pen from the holder on the desk. 'I suppose so. He just carries on. Doesn't give much away. Lucy's baby will help, I suppose. They've called her Annabel.'

'Oh, that's lovely,' Amy said softly. 'I bumped into Tony earlier. He said the baby was premature?'

'Yes, she was born a few weeks early but she's doing fine by all accounts. Still in Special Care but once they're happy with her feeding, she should be home.'

'And Nick—has he met anyone else?'

The pen that Kate was holding slipped to the floor. 'He dates plenty of people.' She stooped and picked up the pen, her voice slightly muffled. 'But I don't think any of them are serious. Are you ready? I'll send in your first patient.'

Amy slid a hand over the desk and looked at the computer, feeling as though she was on a runaway train. She'd come to talk to Marco and here she was sitting in a consulting room, preparing to take a surgery. What had happened to her ability to say no? 'How many patients?'

'You don't want to know but let's just say that Marco is a very, very popular doctor around here. If Dragan Lovak gets any cancellations, I'll send a few his way.' Kate smiled. 'This is so kind of you, Amy. We really appreciate it. I've been trying unsuccessfully to find locum cover for the past few weeks but no one wants to spend Christmas and New Year in freezing Cornwall at short notice. You're a lifesaver.'

A lifesaver? Amy bit back a hysterical laugh. She didn't feel like a lifesaver. She felt like the one who was drowning. 'I'm not sure how much use I'll be. I won't know any of the patients.' She felt a brief flutter of anxiety. During her time in Africa, her focus had been on tropical diseases. Was she capable of running a busy surgery?

'You're a qualified doctor. That makes you of use.' Kate leaned across and flicked on the computer on her desk. 'Hit this key to get everything up on the computer. You'll be fine.

You've been working in deepest Africa for the past two years so the problems of a little Cornish town should seem like a walk in the park by comparison.'

Suddenly she craved Africa. *Craved distance from Marco.* Amy closed her eyes briefly and tried not to think about what was going to happen when he returned. It was clear that there was no way the conversation was going to be easy. 'Kate, how do I call the patients?'

'There's a buzzer right there.' Kate moved a pile of papers. 'List of hospital consultants in your top drawer, just in case you need to refer anyone.'

Amy watched her go and then reached out and pressed the buzzer before she could change her mind. She squashed down a flicker of anxiety and smiled as her first patient was walking into the room.

'Hello, Mrs…' Amy checked the screen quickly '…Duncan. Dr Avanti has had an emergency trip to the hospital with a child so I'm covering his surgery. How can I help you?'

'I've been feeling rotten for a couple of days. Since Christmas Day, I suppose.' Paula Duncan sank onto the chair and let her handbag slip to the floor. 'I assumed it was the flu or something—there's so much of it around. I wasn't even going to bother making an appointment but this morning my head started hurting and I've had this numbness and tingling around my right eye.'

Amy stood up, her attention caught. 'How long have you had that rash on your nose?'

'I woke up with it. Lovely, isn't it?' Mrs Duncan lifted a hand to her face and gave a weary laugh. 'On top of everything else, I have to look like a clown. I can throw away the dress I bought for the New Year's Eve party, that's for sure. Unless the Penhally Arms decide to turn it into a masked ball.'

Amy examined the rash carefully and remembered seeing

a patient with a similar rash in one of her clinics in Africa. 'It started this morning?'

'Yes. Just when you think life can't get any worse, it gets worse.'

Thinking of her own situation, Amy gave a faint smile. 'I know what you mean.'

'If I wasn't in so much pain I'd be really embarrassed to be seen out but I don't even care any more. I just hope there's something you can do. I have no idea where the rash has come from. I spent Christmas on my own so I can't imagine that I've caught anything.'

Amy washed her hands and sat back down at her desk. 'The rash suggests to me that you have ophthalmic shingles, Mrs Duncan. I'm going to send you up to the hospital to see the ophthalmologist—an eye doctor.'

'Shingles?' The woman stared at her. 'That's like chickenpox, isn't it? And in my eye? Surely that isn't possible.'

'I'm afraid it's entirely possible.' Amy opened the drawer and pulled out the list of consultants that Kate had mentioned. She'd had no idea that she'd be using it so soon. 'It's caused by the same virus.'

'So I *must* have been in contact with someone with chickenpox? But who? I don't even know any small children!'

Amy shook her head. 'It doesn't work like that. There's no evidence that you can catch shingles from chickenpox, although it can occasionally happen the other way round if a person isn't immune. But once you've had chickenpox, the virus lies dormant and then flares up again at some point.'

'Can we let it go on its own? Why do I need to see an eye doctor?'

'The rash on your nose means that it's likely that your eye is affected. The ophthalmologist will give you a full examination and follow-up. But I'm going to give you a prescription that I want you to take.'

'Drugs?'

'Yes. Aciclovir.' Amy selected the drug she wanted on the computer screen and the printer next to her purred softly. 'I don't always prescribe it, but if it's within seventy-two hours of the symptoms starting then there's a good chance that it can lower the risk of you developing post-herpatic pain. Hopefully, in your case, it will help. Take it with you to the consultant in case he wants to give you something different.'

Mrs Duncan tucked the prescription into her bag. 'So I have to go there now?'

'Go straight to the eye ward. I'll call them so that they're expecting you.'

Mrs Duncan rose to her feet. 'Thank you.' She looked stunned. 'I don't know what I was expecting but it wasn't that.'

'If you have any questions you can always come back and talk to me.'

And then Amy realised that she wasn't going to be here. In a few hours she'd be gone. She glanced at her watch and wondered how long Marco was going to be. Was Michelle all right? It felt strange to be back in England, taking a surgery.

She saw a seemingly endless stream of patients and then Nick Tremayne walked into the room.

'Nick.' Flustered, Amy rose to her feet. 'I— It's good to see you.'

'It's good to see you, too.' His gaze was quizzical. 'And surprising.'

'Yes. I— Marco and I had things to talk about and then things became very busy and so I said I'd help out.' She sank back into her chair and he gave a faint smile.

'We're glad you're helping out. How are you?'

'Good,' she lied. 'And you? I hear that Lucy's made you a grandfather! Congratulations. Although I must say you look far too young to be anyone's grandfather.'

'That's what happens when you have your own children young,' Nick said drily. 'So how was Africa?'

'Interesting.' *Miserable.* She hesitated, unsure what to say but knowing that she had to say something about the sudden death of his wife. 'I was so sorry to hear about Annabel, Nick.'

'I was grateful for your card.' He was cool and matter-of-fact, revealing nothing of his emotions. 'So what are your plans, Amy?'

Divorce. 'I'm not sure, yet. Marco and I need to talk.'

Nick nodded. 'Well, if you have any problems with the rest of his surgery, just call through to me or Dragan.'

'Thanks.' Amy watched him leave and moments later Kate appeared with a cup of coffee. 'Is that for me?'

'You've earned it. I can see the floor in the waiting room now, so that's a good sign.'

'Is Marco back?'

'Yes, but he had to go straight out again. Man from the brewery developed chest pains while he was making a delivery at the Penhally Arms. Probably the weight of the alcohol we're all going to drink on New Year's Eve.' Kate put the coffee on the desk. 'Black, no sugar. Is that right?'

Amy glanced at her in surprise. 'Yes. Thank you.'

'Tip from Marco. He said that you're useless in the morning unless you've had your coffee.'

Memories of long, lazy mornings lounging in bed with Marco filled her brain and Amy felt the colour flood into her cheeks. She reached out a hand and buzzed for the next patient. 'Right, well, thanks, Kate. I suppose I'd better get on. Is it always like this?'

Kate laughed. 'No, sometimes it's busy.'

Thinking of the number of patients she'd seen so far, Amy suddenly realised that Marco probably hadn't been playing games when he'd said he didn't have time for conversation.

'Dr Avanti?' A man hesitated in the doorway and Amy smiled, recognising him immediately. *A face from her childhood.*

'Rob! How are you?' She blushed and waved an apologetic hand. 'Sorry. Obviously you're not that great or you wouldn't be spending your morning in the doctor's surgery. How can I help you?' It felt weird, sitting here, talking to someone that she'd known as a child. Rob, a trawlerman, was part of her childhood. How many hours had she spent watching him bring in the boat and haul in the catch?

And how did he see her? As someone who was still a child?

Or as someone who was capable of handling his medical problems?

'My hand is agony.' Without hesitation, he sat down and took off his coat. 'Been like this for a few days. I thought it might settle but it's getting worse and the rash is going up my arm.'

Amy leaned forward and took a closer look at his hand, noticing the inflammation and the discolouration spreading up his arm. Her mind went blank and she knew a moment of panic. *What was it?* 'Have you been bitten? Scratched?' She lifted his hand, noticing that Rob flinched at her touch. 'That's tender?'

'Very.' He frowned thoughtfully down at his hand. 'I don't think I've scratched myself but you know what it's like, handling fish. It's pretty easy to get a cut from a fish spine or the bones. Then there's the broken ends of warps—to be honest, we're too busy to be checking for minor injuries all the time. Aches and pains and cuts are all just part of the job.'

Fish. Of course. Amy studied his hand again, noticing the raised purple margin around the reddened area and the pus. *Erysipeloid.* For a moment she forgot Marco and the real reason that she was sitting in the surgery. She forgot all her own problems in her fascination of practising medicine. 'I think that's probably what has happened, Rob. You must have scratched yourself without knowing and that's allowed an infection to get hold. Bacteria are easily carried into the wound from fish slime and guts.' She ran her fingers gently over his arm, taking a closer look. 'I'll give you some antibiotics. Are you allergic to penicillin?'

'Not to my knowledge. So you've seen this before, then?'

'Actually, no, but I've read about it.' Amy turned back to the computer, hit a few keys and then scrolled down to find the drug she wanted. 'Fishermen are particularly prone to infections of the hands and fingers because of the work they do. This particular infection is called erysipeloid. I'll give you an antibiotic and that should do the trick, but prevention is better than cure, Rob. You should be spraying disinfectant over the surfaces where you work and using a hand wash after handling fish. Something like chlorhexidine gluconate would do the trick.'

Rob pulled down his sleeve. 'It's there, but we don't always use it. When you're hauling in nets and fighting the wind and the waves, it doesn't seem like a high priority.'

Amy signed the prescription. 'Take these, but if it gets worse, come back.'

Rob stood up, his eyes curious. 'Little Amy. I remember you when you were knee high.' His voice gruff, he slipped the prescription into his pocket. 'Every summer you visited your grandmother and stayed in that tiny cottage by the shore. Always on your own, you were. You never joined in with any of the local kids. You used to stand on the harbour wall and watch us bring in the catch. You were all solemn-eyed and serious, as if you were wondering whether to run away to sea.'

Amy stared at him, unable to breathe.

She *had* been wondering whether to run away to sea. Every morning she'd scurried down to the harbour and watched the boats sail away, all the time wishing that she could go with the tide and find an entirely new life. A better life.

Happiness doesn't just land in your lap, Amy, you have to chase it.

Rob frowned. 'You all right? You're a bit white.'

Tripped up by the memories of her grandmother, Amy somehow managed to smile. 'That's right. I loved staying here.'

'She was a good woman, your grandmother. And she was so proud of you.'

Feeling her poise and professionalism unravel like a ball of wool in the paws of a kitten, Amy swallowed. 'She always wanted me to be a doctor.'

'And didn't we know it.' Rob grinned. 'Couldn't walk past her in the village without hearing the latest story about her clever granddaughter.' His smile became nostalgic. 'She's missed is Eleanor. But that young couple you sold the cottage to are very happy. The Dodds. They've got two children now.'

'Good.' Desperate to end the conversation, Amy rose to her feet and walked towards the door. 'Come back to one of the doctors if you have problems with your hand, Rob.'

He didn't move, as if he sensed some of the turmoil inside her. 'She wanted to see you married with children—would have loved to see you together, you and Dr Avanti. It's good that you're back. And it's great for the practice. I know how much they're struggling with Lucy going into labour so suddenly.'

Back? 'I'm not exactly— I mean, that isn't why—' She broke off and gave a weak smile. 'It's lovely to see you, Rob.' There was no point in explaining that she wasn't staying—that she should already have been back at the train station. They'd find out soon enough that her visit had been fleeting and she wouldn't need to give explanations because she wouldn't be here.

Feeling a twinge of guilt that she was going to be leaving Marco to deal with still more gossip, Amy showed Rob out of the consulting room and then returned to her desk and sank onto her chair with her head in her hands, the lump building in her throat as memories swirled around her exhausted mind.

'So—judging from the expression on your face, delivering patient care in Penhally isn't any easier than it was in Africa.' Marco's smooth, accented tones cut through her misery and she jumped and let her hands fall into her lap.

Even though she'd been longing to have the conversation with him, now the moment had arrived she wasn't entirely sure she could cope with it.

CHAPTER THREE

'MARCO. I—I didn't hear you come in.'

'Presumably because you were miles away.' He pushed the door shut with the flat of his hand and strolled into the room, his cool control in direct contrast to her own nervous agitation. 'You look pale. What's the matter?'

That was twice in five minutes she'd been told that she looked pale. Making a mental note to dig out a pot of blusher and use it, Amy gave a humourless laugh. 'I would have thought it was obvious.'

'Not to me. Any woman who finds it that easy to walk away from a marriage can't possibly be daunted by the prospect of spending a few hours wandering down memory lane.'

He had no idea.

And that was her fault, of course, because she hadn't wanted him to know the truth. She'd wanted to spare him a difficult decision. Wanted to spare them both the slow, inevitable destruction of their marriage. So she'd made the decision for both of them and gone for a quick, sudden end. She'd thought it would make it less painful in the long term.

Now she wasn't so sure. *Could the pain have been worse?*

'It wasn't easy for me, Marco.' She didn't want him thinking that and she looked at him, almost hating him for his insensitivity but at the same time relieved, because she knew that his anger made him blind. Anger would prevent him from delving deeper into her reasons for leaving. *And she didn't want him delving.* 'I did what was right for both of us.'

'No, you did what was right for you. I wasn't involved in the decision.' He prowled across the consulting room to the desk where she was seated. 'One minute we were planning a future, the next you decided that you were going to spend the future on your own. There was no discussion. You gave me no choice.'

In a way, that was true, and yet she knew that the decision she'd made had been the right one.

'Do you want to talk about this now?' Strangely enough, even though she was the one who'd pushed, she just didn't feel prepared to say what had to be said. In Africa she'd thought she'd resigned herself to the reality of her life, but one look at Marco had unravelled her resolve.

'That was the reason you came, wasn't it?'

Feeling vulnerable next to his superior height, she rose to her feet and their eyes locked. 'All right, let's have this discussion and then we can both get on with our lives. I ended our marriage, yes, that's true.'

'You left without talking it through with me.'

'I *did* talk to you!'

'When?'

'I told you I was unhappy. We should never have moved back to Penhally. It was a mistake.' She sank back into her chair because her legs just wouldn't hold her any longer. 'I didn't feel the way I thought I was going to feel.'

'You underwent a complete personality transformation!' Anger shimmered in his eyes. 'One moment you were lying in my bed, planning our future, and the next thing you were packing your bag so quickly you almost bruised yourself running through the front door. It didn't make sense.'

It would have made perfect sense if he'd known what she'd discovered.

'I didn't have a personality transformation,' she said stiffly. 'I just changed my mind about what I wanted. People do it every day of their lives and it's sad, but it's just one of those things. The reason you're angry is because you felt that you weren't part of the decision and you always have to be in control.'

'Control?' He lifted an eyebrow in cool appraisal. 'You saw our relationship as a power struggle, *amore*?'

Unsettled by the look in his eyes and the sheer impact of his physical presence, she left her chair and walked to the window, keeping her back to him. 'It's time to be honest about this. We made a mistake, Marco. We never should have married. I mean, it was all far, far too quick! Three months! Three months is nothing!' She fixed her gaze on a point in the distance and recited the words she'd rehearsed so many times. 'How can anyone know each other in three months? Yes, there was chemistry, I'm not denying that. But chemistry alone isn't enough to bind a couple together for a lifetime.'

There was an ominous silence and when he finally spoke his voice was clipped. 'You're describing hormonal teenagers. We were both adults and we knew what we wanted.'

'Adult or not, the chemistry was still there. The relationship was fine, but marriage—that was a stupid impulse.' *A fleeting dream that had been cruelly snatched away.* She could feel his gaze burning a hole between her shoulder blades and this time it took him almost a full minute to reply.

'At least have the courtesy to look at me when you reduce our relationship to nothing but a sordid affair.' There was a dangerous note in his voice and she took a deep breath and turned slowly, struggling to display the calm and neutrality that she knew she needed in order to be convincing.

'Not sordid, Marco,' she said quietly, hoping that her voice was going to hold out. 'It was amazing, we both know that. But it was never going to last. We shouldn't have tried to hold onto it or make it into something that it wasn't. We wanted different things.'

He watched her for a moment, his eyes intent on her face as if her mind were a book and he were leafing through every single page, searching for clues. 'Until we returned to Penhally, I wasn't aware that we wanted different things. We'd made plans for the future. I was going to work with Nick in the practice and you were going to stay at home and have our babies until you decided to return to work. It was the reason we chose the house.'

She inhaled sharply, unable to stifle the reaction. *She couldn't even bear to think about the house.* 'I'm sorry I didn't keep my end of the bargain. I'm sorry I decided that I wanted a career instead of a family.'

He looked at her as if she were a complete stranger and then he muttered something in Italian that she didn't understand and Amy looked at him helplessly.

'If this conversation is going to have any hope of working then you at least have to speak English so that I can understand you.'

'*You* are speaking English and I don't understand you at all! The complexities of this situation appear to transcend the language barrier.' He raked long bronzed fingers through his glossy dark hair. 'You talk about wanting a career, and yet when we first met you talked about nothing but family and children. You were soft, gentle, giving. Then we moved to Penhally and suddenly, whoosh…' He waved a hand expressively. 'You underwent this transformation. Soft, affectionate Amy became hard, distant Amy. And distant Amy suddenly became career Amy. It was as if the woman I was with suddenly reinvented herself. What happened? *What happened to change everything?*'

She stared at him blankly, teetering on the edge of confession. It would have been so easy. So easy to tell him exactly what had happened.

But that would have made things so much more complicated and they were already more complicated than she could comfortably handle.

The truth created a bad taste in her mouth and for a moment she just stood there, trapped by the secrets and lies that she'd used to protect him. 'I suppose it was several things.' With an effort, she kept her tone careless. 'Penhally isn't exactly the centre of the universe. There wasn't enough to keep me occupied. I was bored. I missed medicine. I missed the patients.' It was true, she consoled herself, she *had* missed the patients.

'If that was the case, you should have said so and we could have found you work, if not in Penhally then at another surgery.' Marco turned and paced across the surgery, as if he found the confined space intolerable.

'It's all history now,' Amy murmured. 'Going over it again is going to achieve nothing. It's time to move on, Marco. Let's just have the discussion that we need to have and then I'll leave you in peace.'

'Peace?' He turned, his eyes glinting dangerously, his lean, handsome face taut. 'Is that what you think leaving will give me when you walk out again? Peace? I haven't known a moment's peace since you left.'

He hadn't?

Her heart gave a little lift and then crashed down again as she realised that his feelings made absolutely no difference to what she had to do. And anyway his feelings had more to do with injured pride and inconvenience than anything deeper. Marco Avanti was a man who knew what he wanted out of life and she'd temporarily derailed his plans—that was all.

'I'm sorry,' she said softly, telling the truth for the first time since she'd walked into Penhally. 'Truly I'm sorry for any hurt I've caused.'

He watched her, his eyes sharp on her face. 'But you're still asking me for a divorce?'

For the space of a heartbeat she paused. 'Yes,' she croaked. 'I am. It's the only course of action.'

'*Not* the only course.' He strolled towards her and then stopped. 'I never thought of you as a quitter, Amy, and yet you haven't once mentioned trying again. Instead of abandoning our marriage, you could try and fix it.'

She froze as he dangled temptation in front of her and her heart stumbled in her chest. Like an addict she gazed at him and then she remembered how far she'd come, how much she'd already suffered to get to this point, and shook her head. 'It isn't fixable.'

'You don't know that because you haven't tried. And this time we'd be trying together. Talk to me, Amy, and we can fix it.'

'You can't fix something when the two halves don't match. We want different things. You want a family, Marco. You made that clear on many occasions. Women have been chasing you for years, but you never settled down with any of them because you weren't ready to have children. But then suddenly that changed.'

'It changed when I met you. The first thing I thought when I laid eyes on you was that you were the sexiest woman I'd ever seen.' His voice was a soft, seductive purr. 'You were wearing that little navy suit with a pair of high heels and your legs came close to being the eighth wonder of the world. You were serious and studious and didn't stop asking me questions.'

She felt the colour rush into her cheeks. 'You just happened to be lecturing on an aspect of paediatrics that interested me.'

'Then, when I stopped looking at your legs and your beautiful brown eyes, I realised how intelligent you were and how warm and kind. I knew immediately that you were the woman I wanted to be the mother of my children. I knew it in a moment.'

The mother of his children.

There was a long, tortured silence. Knowing that some response was required, Amy tried to speak but her voice just refused to work. Instead, she stooped, picked up her bag and yanked her coat from the back of the chair. Only once she'd slipped her arms into the sleeves and belted the waist did she find her voice.

'I'm sorry I ruined your plans, but I can't be the mother of your children, so it's time you started searching for another candidate. And now I have to go.' *Before she collapsed in front of him.*

'I thought you wanted to talk to me?'

'It's not— I can't…' Needing fresh air and space, she stumbled over the words. 'You're just too busy. I shouldn't have come, I see that now. I'll leave you to see your patients and I'll write to you again and perhaps this time you'll reply. It's the best thing for both of us.' She moved towards the door but he caught her arm, his strong fingers biting through the wool of her coat as he pulled her inexorably towards him.

'You came all this way to talk.' He held her firmly. 'And we haven't finished. Last time you just walked out and you wouldn't listen to me. You're not doing that again, Amy.'

Why had she ever thought that seeing him face to face was a good idea?

'You still have patients waiting.'

'I'll see my patients. Then I'll buy you lunch at the Smugglers' Inn. We can talk then.'

He couldn't have picked a place more public. 'You want to be the subject of gossip?'

'Gossip doesn't worry me and never will. Kate will make

you a cup of coffee and find you somewhere to sit. Then I'll give you a lift.'

She gave a faint smile. 'The Maserati has learned to cope with snow?'

'She is moody and unpredictable, that's true, but it is just a question of handling her correctly.' His eyes held hers and she wondered briefly whether he was talking about the car or her.

'You don't need to give me a lift. I'll wander around the village for an hour or so and then meet you up there. The walk up the coast road will do me good. But I'm going back to London tonight.'

His eyes narrowed slightly and his expression was unreadable. 'So that means that you have plenty of time for lunch. Twelve-thirty. Be there or this time I'll come looking for you.'

The Smugglers' Inn was perched near the edge of the cliff on the coast road, a short drive out of Penhally.

The Maserati gave a throaty growl as Marco turned into the car park. He turned off the engine and sat for a moment, breathing in the scent of leather. Usually the car calmed him but today he felt nothing, his body too tense after his encounter with Amy.

With a soft curse he locked the car and walked towards the pub, distracted for a moment by the wild crash of the waves on the rocks below. The temperature had dropped and Marco stood for a moment, trying to formulate a plan, but his normally sharp brain refused to co-operate and he suddenly realised that he had no idea what he was going to do or say.

The irony of the situation didn't escape him. Of all the women who'd wanted to settle down with him over the years, he'd finally picked one who was wedded to her career and wasn't interested in having children.

He frowned. Except that she *had* been interested in having children. More than interested. At the time, he'd assumed that her longing for a family stemmed from the disappointing relationship that she'd apparently had with her own mother. Perhaps he'd been wrong about that. Perhaps he'd been wrong about all of it.

It was true that people changed their minds, but still…

He should give her a divorce, he told himself grimly, because that was clearly what she wanted and, anyway, she'd been gone for two years. What was there to salvage?

Anger exploded inside him once again and he took a deep breath of cold, calming air before turning towards the pub. With only a slight hesitation he pushed open the heavy door and walked inside.

Warmth, laughter and the steady buzz of conversation wrapped itself around him and drew him in. Immediately his eyes scanned the bar, searching for Amy.

Would she be there or had she run? Was she now shivering on the station platform, waiting for the train that would take her away from him?

How badly did she want the divorce?

And then he saw her, a slight figure, huddled on her own by the blazing fire, still wearing her coat and scarf as if all the heat in the world wouldn't warm her. She looked out of place and vulnerable. Her dark hair had been smoothed behind one ear and Marco felt something stir inside him as he remembered all the times he'd kissed her slender neck, *the tempting hollow of her throat…*

He dragged his eyes from her neckline, frustrated by the unexpectedly powerful surge of lust that gripped him.

So, people were wrong about some things, he thought bitterly. *Time didn't always heal.* In his case, time hadn't healed at all. Despite everything, Amy still affected him more than any woman he'd ever met.

His jaw clenched and he stood for a moment, feeling the now familiar tension knot inside him. Why? Was it because she was the only woman who had walked away from him? Was this all about his ego?

Was he really that shallow?

And then the lust was replaced by anger and he didn't even try and subdue it because over the past two years he'd learned that anger was the easiest emotion to deal with. Anger was so much better than pain and disillusionment.

Back in control, he strolled across the room and nodded to the man behind the bar. 'Tony. Give me something long and cold that isn't going to dull my senses.'

The landlord's gaze flickered towards Amy, who was still staring blankly into the fire. 'Looks to me as though you might need something stronger.'

'Don't tempt me. I've always found that my diagnostic abilities are better when I'm sober, and I'm on call. Has she ordered?' No point in pretending that his ex-wife hadn't just appeared out of nowhere with no warning. The locals had eyes and he had no doubt that they'd be using them.

Tony reached for a glass and snapped the cap off a couple of bottles. 'Arrived ten minutes ago. Paid for a grapefruit juice, made polite conversation for about three seconds and then slunk into the corner like a wounded animal. Hasn't touched her drink. If you want my opinion, she's not a happy woman. You might want to use your famous doctoring skills to find out what's bothering her.'

Marco's long fingers drummed a steady rhythm on the bar. *He knew exactly what was bothering her.* She wanted a quick and easy divorce and he wasn't playing ball.

The landlord poured the contents of the bottles into the glass. 'Here you go. One doctor-on-duty fruit cocktail. Full of vitamins, totally devoid of alcohol. No charge. If you want to eat, let me know. Cornish pasties came out of the oven five minutes ago and the fish and chips are good, but I'm guessing you don't want to feast on cholesterol in front of your patients.'

Marco gave a faint smile, took the drink and strolled across to the fire. 'Sorry I've kept you waiting.' He put his glass down on the table and shrugged off his coat. 'Our patients haven't quite got the hang of developing ailments that can be seen easily within the allotted time.'

'It doesn't matter.' She looked across at him, the flickering fire sending red lights through her dark hair. Away from the pressure of the surgery he noticed that her face was paler than ever and there were dark shadows under her eyes. And she'd definitely lost weight since he'd last seen her.

He studied her thoughtfully.

For a woman following her chosen path of career over motherhood, she didn't appear either settled or happy.

Was something wrong with her? Something other than the prospect of a divorce? Had she picked up some tropical disease while she'd been working in Africa?

'So...' he lifted his drink '...tell me about your work. Is it hard?' Was that why she was so pale? Did her work explain the weight loss? Had she been ill?

'Sorry?' She glanced at him, her expression blank, as if she hadn't heard him.

'Your work. The thing you care most about, remember, *tesoro*?' It was hard not to keep the irony out of his voice. 'How is this amazing career that was so much more important to you than marriage and children?'

'My career?' She gave a little start, as though she'd forgotten that she even had a career. Then she straightened her shoulders, her gaze returning to the fire. 'Yes. I was running a malaria project.'

'And that was interesting? Fulfilling?' *Why wouldn't she look at him?*

'Yes.'

Marco felt the anger surge again and struggled against the temptation to slide his hand around the back of her neck and force her to meet his gaze. 'Worth sacrificing our marriage for?'

Her breathing quickened and her eyes slid to his. 'Our marriage was something separate.'

'No.' He growled the word and noticed a few heads turn towards them. *Why had he decided to have this discussion in a pub?* 'It wasn't separate, Amy. You ended our marriage because you chose a career over family. It's that simple.'

'There was nothing simple about it. Keep your voice down. People are looking at us, Marco.' She reached for her drink and her hair slid forward, framing her cheek. 'You chose to do this in a public place so can we at least try and keep this civilised?'

'Civilised?' Heat exploded inside him, the flame of his anger fuelled by her unreasonable calm. 'You ripped our marriage to shreds with your bare hands. Forgive me, *amore*, if I don't feel completely civilised. I feel—' He broke off, his fluency in English momentarily stunted by emotion, but before he could find the words to express his feelings she half rose to her feet.

'This conversation is pointless. I shouldn't have come.'

Grimly determined not to let her leave, Marco reached out a hand and caught her arm. 'Sit down. You're the one who wanted this conversation.'

'This isn't conversation, Marco, this is confrontation.' She was breathing quickly. 'You're losing your temper and I simply wanted us to discuss the facts.'

'I'm *not* losing my temper.' He drew in a breath, struggling to keep his tone level. 'I have a question.'

She sank back onto her chair, her beautiful eyes wary. 'What?'

'Do you think about us? About what we had? Have you forgotten what we shared?'

Her swift intake of breath and the brief flash of awareness in her eyes was sufficient answer. 'Marco—'

The phone in his pocket rang and he cursed fluently in Italian and slid it out of his pocket, wishing at that moment that he had chosen a different career path. One that would have permitted him five minutes' free time with the guarantee of no disturbance. He checked the number and sighed. 'That's Kate. She wouldn't ring unless it was important.'

'It's fine. Take the call.'

Frustrated that he'd been interrupted in what had to have been the most important part of the conversation, Marco hit the button and spoke to the practice manager, aware of Amy's eyes on his face.

Never before had he so badly wanted his work to go away.

And then Kate spoke and immediately she had his attention.

By the time he ended the call, Amy was no longer his priority.

She looked at him expectantly. 'Something bad?'

'The Knight boys have gone missing.' He rose to his feet. 'Eddie is only five years old.' He reached for his coat just as the door to the pub flew open and a little boy stood there, breathing hard.

'Dr Avanti! You have to come *now*! Alfie and I went to play on the rocks and Eddie followed because he always tags along and then he slipped and now we can't wake him up and he's bleeding everywhere and—' He broke off, his breath hitching as he spoke. 'We think he's dead, Dr Avanti. *He's dead!*'

CHAPTER FOUR

'*CALMA*. Calm down, Sam.' Marco squeezed the boy's shoulder and squatted down so that he was level with him. 'Tell me where they are. Slowly.'

'We were playing pirates. Mum said we weren't to go near the rocks but we went anyway and Eddie followed and now…' Sam's face crumpled. 'He's dead. There's blood everywhere.'

Marco put an arm around the boy and spoke softly to him.

Amy couldn't hear what he said but it had a positive effect on Sam, who straightened his shoulders and stopped crying, his gaze trusting as he looked up at Marco. 'You mean that? Really?'

Marco nodded and let go of the boy. 'And now I want you to show me where they are.' He rose to his feet and noticed Amy. 'Stay here. Promise me you won't leave until we've finished this conversation.'

'I'm coming with you.'

Already on his way to the door with Sam, Marco frowned at her. 'I can't have a conversation while I'm administering first aid.'

'I'm coming to help you,' she said calmly. 'I'm a doctor, too, remember?'

Marco's jaw tensed. 'I thought you couldn't wait to leave

this place?' His tone was rough and his eyes scanned her briefly. 'You're not dressed to scramble down cliffs.'

'I'm fine. We're wasting time, Marco.'

'Hurry up or they'll have no blood left!' Sam was still in the doorway, his eyes huge and worried. 'I'll show you where they are.'

Marco glanced towards the bar. 'Tony—call the coast-guard and let them know what's happening. If it's serious we might need the helicopter to lift them off the rocks.'

Sam sprinted from the pub to the steep, narrow path that led down to the rocky cove below. 'Come on! Come on!' he urged them.

Amy didn't hear Marco's reply because she was too busy trying to keep her balance on the path. The wind had risen and now whipped her hair across her face, obscuring her vision. She knew just how steep the path was because it had been a favourite of hers as a child. The cove below was rocky and dangerous and held just the right amount of wicked appeal for an adventurous child.

Ahead of her, Marco covered the distance with sure, confident strides, drawing away from her, leaving her only the occasional reassuring glimpse of his broad shoulders.

She couldn't decide whether she was relieved or sorry that their conversation had been interrupted yet again.

It was obvious that Marco was equally frustrated by the interruptions. The question was whether he was frustrated enough to just agree to the divorce and let her walk out of Penhally before nightfall.

Did he believe her claim that she'd chosen a career over marriage and children?

Resisting the temptation to hurry because haste might result in her crashing onto the beach and becoming another casualty, Amy followed more slowly and finally clambered over the huge boulders that guarded the entrance to the cove. In the summer it was a favourite place for tourists who came with their nets and their buckets to explore the rock pools. In winter it was a wild and dangerous place and the sudden drop in the temperature had made the rocky beach particularly deadly.

Jagged rocks glistened black with sea spray and Amy glanced across and saw the boys. One lay still, the other sitting beside him, his face covered in blood.

Sam and Marco were already there and Amy picked her way across the rocks to join them.

'We didn't mean him to die. We didn't mean him to die. Do something, Dr Avanti,' Alfie whispered, his whole body shaking and juddering as he fixed his terrified stare on the inert form of his little brother. 'We didn't know he'd followed us and then I tried to take him back but he slipped and banged his head really hard. And when I tried to get to him, I slipped and hit my head, too. Then he stopped talking. I couldn't get him to answer me.' He started to sob pitifully and Sam started to cry, too. He caught Marco's eyes and took a shuddering breath.

'It will be all right, Alfie,' he said in a wobbly voice. 'We've got to be strong and try and help. What do you want us to do, Dr Avanti?'

Marco was on his knees beside the still body of the little boy. 'Just sit there for a moment, Sam. He isn't dead, Alfie. I can tell you for sure that he isn't dead.'

Amy knelt down beside Marco, wincing slightly as the sharp rocks took a bite out of her knees. 'Is he conscious?'

'No.' Marco was checking the child's scalp, nose and ears, searching for injury. And then the child gave a little moan and his eyes drifted open. 'All right. Well, that's good. He's drowsy. Obviously knocked out, from the boys' description.' His fingers probed gently. 'He's got a nasty haematoma on the back of his skull. I can't be sure that he doesn't have neck injuries.'

'Is he going to die?' Alfie's voice shook and Marco lifted his head and looked at him.

'No. He's not going to die.' His voice was firm and confident. 'You did the right thing to send Sam up to the pub. Good boy. Well done.'

Alfie looked at him, clearly doubtful that he'd done anything worthy of praise, and Amy noticed fresh blood oozing from the cut on his scalp.

'I'll ring the coastguard and then look at Alfie.' Amy started to dig for her phone but Marco shook his head.

'There's no signal on this beach. We can't carry him back up that path without possibly making things worse. Sam.' Marco's gaze slid to the other boy who was huddled next to Alfie, a look of terror in his eyes. 'I want you to go back up to the pub and tell Tony that we need a helicopter. Do you understand me?'

Sam shot to his feet and nodded, his face white and terrified. 'Helicopter. I can do that. I can do that, Dr Avanti.'

'Good boy. Go. And be careful on the rocks. We've had enough casualties here for one day.' Marco turned back to the child. 'Eddie? Can you hear me? He's cold, Amy. Wet from the sea and freezing in this weather. If we're not careful it's going to be hypothermia that is our biggest problem.' He cursed softly. 'I have no equipment. Nothing.'

Next to them, Alfie started to sob again, the tears mingling with the blood that already stained his cheeks. 'He's going to die. I know he's going to die. He chose me a really great Christmas present. I don't want him to die. This is all my fault. We're not supposed to be down on this beach anyway.'

Concerned about the amount of blood on Alfie's head, Amy made a soothing noise and examined his scalp. As she balanced on the slippery rocks, searching for the source of the bleeding, she suddenly developed a new admiration for paramedics. Then she saw blood blossom under her fingers and pulled off her gloves and took the scarf from her neck. 'I'm going to press on this for a minute, Alfie, and that should stop the bleeding. They can have a better look at it at the hospital.'

'I don't want to go to hospital. I want my mum—*Ow!*' Alfie winced. 'That really hurts.'

'You've cut yourself,' Amy murmured. 'I'm just going to put some pressure on it.'

'I don't care about me.' Alfie's eyes were fixed on his brother. 'If we'd stayed in the house it never would have happened. I wish we'd done that. I'm *never* playing on the beach again. I'm just going to stick to computers.' He sobbed and sobbed and Amy tightened the scarf and then slid her arms round him, cuddling him against her.

'It was just an accident, sweetheart,' she said softly. 'Accidents happen. Eddie's going to be all right, I know he is.'

Having examined Eddie as best he could, Marco removed his coat and pulled his jumper over his head. Then he wrapped the boy in the layers, giving him as much protection from the elements as possible. Then he glanced at Alfie and winked at him. 'Do you know how many accidents can happen sitting indoors, playing on the computer?'

Alfie sniffed, still clinging to Amy. 'Now you're kidding me.'

'You can have an accident without ever moving from your chair at home. The ceiling can drop onto your head. You can develop muscle strain and eye strain from too much gaming. Heart disease from lack of exercise. At least you were having fun outdoors.'

'But Eddie wouldn't have been here if it hadn't been for me. I chose the smugglers game. He loves dressing up as a pirate.'

'So—you're a fun brother to have and pirates sounds like a good game,' Marco said easily. 'You'll have to tell me more about it someday soon.' He glanced at Amy and gave a faint smile of approval as he saw her first-aid measures. 'Very inventive.'

'You learn to be inventive in Africa.' She pressed hard on the wound. 'They're not exactly flush with equipment over there.'

Something flickered in his eyes and then he turned his attention back to his little patient.

'Do we have to go to hospital?' Alfie's voice wobbled and he sounded very young. 'Our mum is going to go mad.'

'She'll just be relieved you're safe. Now, sit down here for a moment.' Amy helped him sit down on a flat piece of rock. 'Don't move. It's very slippery and I don't want you to fall again and I want to help Dr Avanti with your brother.'

Shivering without the protection of her scarf, she moved across to Marco and knelt down beside him. 'You must be frozen. You gave all your layers to Eddie.'

'I have more body fat than he does.'

Amy's eyes slid to his powerful, male frame. Not an inch of fat was visible. Just lean muscle under a thin T-shirt that clung to the impressive width of his shoulders. But she knew there was no point in pointing out that he was getting cold. Marco would do everything within his power to save a child. She'd always known that about him.

A hiss and a crash reminded her that the sea in winter was hungry and unforgiving and frighteningly close. 'That was a big wave, Marco.'

'Yes.' Marco's tone was matter-of-fact. 'If the helicopter doesn't arrive in the next few minutes, we might have to move him. I don't want to but it's the lesser of two evils.'

Amy glanced up at the sky, willing it to arrive.

Eddie gave a little whimper and Marco murmured something reassuring and tucked the layers more tightly around the child. 'He's in and out of consciousness. I should have asked Sam to bring blankets down from the pub.'

'The helicopter will be here before Sam gets back,' Amy said optimistically. 'I can give him one of my layers.' She started to take off her coat but he reached out and caught her arm.

'No.' This time his voice was harsh. 'Keep your coat on. You need it.'

'But—'

'Don't argue with me, Amy. You don't exactly have an excess of body fat to keep you warm. Didn't they feed you in Africa?'

She swallowed but was spared the trouble of thinking up an answer by the noise of the approaching helicopter.

'Good.' Marco watched with visible relief as the helicopter appeared in the sky like a giant insect. In a matter of minutes it was overhead and Amy could see the winchman in the doorway of the helicopter.

With precise, accurate flying and slick teamwork, the winchman was lowered onto the rocks next to them.

He unclipped the harness and moved across to them. 'How many casualties, Marco?'

Amy was wondering how they knew each other and then remembered that the RAF winchmen were trained paramedics who often practised their skills alongside local doctors.

'Two. One of them serious. According to his brother, he lost consciousness when he fell. GCS was 13 when we arrived on the scene…' Marco gave a swift, comprehensive summary of the situation and together they prepared Eddie for his transfer to hospital. Finally, strapped to a backboard, the child was winched into the helicopter.

Shivering like a wet puppy, Alfie watched. 'Wow!' His

voice was awed, concern for his little brother momentarily forgotten. 'That's so cool!'

Marco pulled on his jumper. 'It's definitely cool,' he murmured, helping the boy to his feet as the paramedic returned, ready to take his second patient.

'I'm going up there, too? Just wait until they hear about this at school.'

'Maybe he would have been safer on the computer,' Marco murmured, watching as the second child was safely winched into the helicopter. Then he lifted his hand in acknowledgement and the helicopter soared away on the short journey to hospital.

Around them the sea thrashed and boiled like a wild beast, angered that its prey had been snatched from its jaws.

Amy was shivering uncontrollably. 'Let's get moving,' she muttered, and was suddenly enveloped in warmth as Marco wrapped his coat around her.

'Wear this.'

'You can't give me your coat!' Protesting, she tried to shrug her way out of it but he was stronger than her and more determined.

'Put it on.' His voice rough, he fastened the coat as if she were a child and then gave a faint smile. 'It swamps you.'

'Well, you're bigger than me.'

His eyes darkened and she flushed and turned away, picking her way across the rocks back towards the path. She knew that he was bigger than her. She'd always been aware of his physical strength. It was one of the things that drew women to him.

At the top of the path a little crowd was waiting, including the boys' mother, Mary.

'I sent them to play in the garden because they've been on those wretched game machines all holiday and then when I went to call them for lunch, there was no sign of them.' She covered her mouth with her hand but the sobs still came. 'I guessed they'd gone to the beach and that Eddie had followed them. Everyone's saying that he's badly hurt—'

Without hesitation, Marco stepped forward and slid an arm around her shoulders. 'They are boys and they were playing,' he said, his accent thicker than usual. 'Alfie has a cut on his head, but nothing that a few stitches won't sort out. Eddie also banged his head…' He paused. 'From Alfie's description it sounds as though he might have been knocked out when he fell on the rocks. But he was starting to regain consciousness when we got to him and they've taken him to the hospital.'

'I need to get up there right away. I need to call my husband so that we can go to the hospital.' Trying to hold herself together, Mary fumbled in her bag for her phone, her hands shaking so much she dropped the bag twice. 'He's gone to help my brother take down a shed in his garden. It will take him ages to get back with the way the roads are.'

Marco stooped, picked up her bag and handed it to her. 'I'll take you in the Maserati.' He looked at his watch. 'I've got time to drive you and still be back in time for afternoon surgery. Tell your husband you'll meet him up there.'

Mary looked at him, her eyes swimming with tears. 'You'd do that for me?' She bit her lip. 'But there must be other more urgent things you should be doing.'

Marco looked directly at Amy and she knew what he was thinking. *That the thing he should be doing was giving her the conversation she'd demanded.*

So it was up to her, then, to decide. He was giving her the choice. She could insist that he stay and finish the conversation they'd started or she could let him take this frantic mother to her children.

'We can talk later,' she said quietly, slipping off his coat and handing it to him. 'My train doesn't leave until four.'

With only the briefest hesitation Marco reached into his pocket and gave his car keys to Mary. 'Go and sit in the car. I'll be with you in a minute.'

The woman walked across the car park and Amy gave a faint smile. 'Trusting someone else with your precious Maserati, Marco?'

'Only because I need to talk to you without an audience,' he growled, reaching out and removing a smudge of blood from her cheek. 'You're freezing and you need a shower. Go back to the surgery and ask Kate to sort you out with a change of clothes. Wait for me there. We'll talk later.'

'I think our conversation is doomed. We're running out of time.'

'Then stay overnight.'

She stared at him. 'That's out of the question.'

'I thought you wanted to talk? Stay the night, Amy, and then at least we're guaranteed peace and quiet. I'm not on call. You can come out to the house and we can eat, talk and then you can get the first train back tomorrow. I'll drop you at the station myself.'

'That's not—no.' She had to say no. 'I can't.'

'Amy.' His voice was impatient and he glanced towards his car where Mary was now waiting in a state of anxiety. 'We can't tie this up in a matter of minutes. We need time and we need privacy. You're the one who wants to do this. It makes sense. In fact, I can give you the house keys and you can go now and have a shower at home. That's a much better idea. Wait for me there. I'll be home by six and we can talk.'

She hadn't wanted to go to the house. It would just be too painful.

'I don't—'

'Stop arguing and looking for problems.' He dug in his pocket and pulled out his house keys. 'In that car is a woman worrying herself to death about her children and in the hospital are two young children who need their mother. They need my help and you're holding me up.'

Amy swallowed and took the keys from his hand. 'I'll see you later.'

Marco let himself into the house and walked through to the enormous sitting room that faced out to sea.

Amy was standing by the glass, staring out across the crashing waves. She was wearing the same soft wool trousers that she'd been wearing all day but she'd removed the rest of her soaked clothes and helped herself to one of his jumpers. The fact that it swamped her just increased the air of vulnerability that surrounded her.

She didn't turn when he entered the room but he could tell from the sudden increase in tension in her narrow shoulders that she was aware of his presence. 'The view is incredible.' Her voice was almost wistful. 'It was this room that sold me the house.'

Vulnerable, maybe, but still capable of wreaking havoc.

Engulfed by a fresh spurt of anger, Marco dropped his coat over the back of the sofa. 'It's a shame you didn't stay around long enough to live in it.'

She turned, pain in her eyes. 'Don't do this, Marco. This doesn't have to be an argument. Just let it go.'

'Like you did?' He watched her face, searching for some glimpse of the woman he'd married. 'You just let our relationship slip through your fingers. You never once tried to solve whatever problem it was that you suddenly found. You just walked away.'

Anguish flickered across her face and for a moment she looked as though she was going to defend herself. Then her shoulders sagged and she turned back to look out of the window as if she'd lost the will to fight. 'We wanted different things. You married me because you wanted to start a family and at first I thought I wanted that, too.' She broke off and sucked in a breath. 'But I discovered that I didn't. That sort of difference is too big to bridge, Marco.'

He stared at her with mounting incredulity.

She made herself sound both flighty and indecisive and neither adjective fitted what he knew about her. *Nothing she said made sense.*

'So you had a sudden change of heart—why didn't you discuss it with me?'

'There was nothing to discuss. You wanted one thing, I wanted another.'

Marco tried to make sense of her words. She was saying that she didn't want children and yet he'd seen her with children and had been captivated by how gentle and kind she was. Just now with Alfie, she'd been tactile and gentle. He'd seen how much she cared. In fact, he would have said that she was better with children than adults.

'You love children. You couldn't wait to be a mother,' he said hoarsely. 'That's why I married you.'

'Yes.' This time when she turned to face him, her expression was blank. 'I know that's why you married me. And that's why I knew that it would never work. I knew that there was no point in "trying again" or working at our marriage. There was no point in talking it through or having endless discussions that wouldn't have led anywhere. You married me because you wanted to settle down and have a family. You were perfectly clear about that. And I'm telling you right now that that isn't what I want. So ending our marriage is the fairest thing for both of us. You should be with a woman who wants children. That's very important to you and you can't ignore something like that.'

Marco inhaled sharply and laid himself bare. 'For me, you were that woman, Amy. What was I to you?' *She wasn't good at communicating but he'd thought he'd known what she'd felt. He'd felt utterly secure in her love. Arrogance on his part? Maybe.*

'You were—' She broke off and her eyes slid from his. 'You were a wonderful affair that never should have become anything more.'

If he hadn't been so exasperated and confused he would have laughed. 'You're trying to tell me you wanted the sex and no commitment? Do you have any idea how ridiculous that sounds, coming from you? You don't have affairs!' *It was one of the reasons he'd wanted to marry her.*

'How would you know? We were only together for three months before we married. That's not enough time to know someone. You never really knew me, Marco.'

He'd *thought* he'd known her. 'I know you're not the sort of woman to have a casual affair.'

'Maybe I *am* that sort of woman in some circumstances! I'm not the first woman to find you irresistible, Marco. You're an incredibly sexy guy. Intelligent, good company…' She shrugged as if his attractions were so obvious it was point-less naming them. 'I don't suppose there's a woman in the world who would reject you.'

He decided not to point out that *she* was rejecting him. 'So now you're saying that I seduced you?'

'Of course not. I'm just saying that…the physical side took over.'

'Physical? You married me because I'm good in bed? What about the rest of our relationship?' Finding the entire conver-sation completely unfathomable and beginning to wonder whether his English was less fluent than he'd previously believed, Marco ran a hand over the back of his neck and held on to his temper with difficulty. 'As I said before, we weren't teenagers, Amy. Yes, there was strong chemistry but our minds were working, too. We shared a great deal more than an in-credible sex life.'

Colour bloomed in her cheeks and he remembered just how shy she'd been when they'd first met. 'We were friends, yes. But we never should have been more than that.'

'Was our relationship really that shallow? What about all those plans we made, or is my memory playing tricks? The way you're describing our life together...' he spread his hands in a gesture of raw frustration '...I'm beginning to think we're talking about a completely different relationship!'

'Perhaps we just saw it differently.'

'When we met you enjoyed your work, certainly, but your plans for the future were the same as mine. Family. We lay in bed and talked about having children. We agreed that I would work and you would stay at home with them. You thought it was important for a child to be with its mother, to know it was loved. These weren't *my* plans, *tesoro*, they were *our* plans.'

'To begin with, yes. But then I realised that it was never going to work.'

'Answer me one question, Amy. Did you love me?'

She froze and her eyes slid from his. 'No.' Her voice was so faint he could barely hear her. 'Not enough.'

Her answer shocked him so much that for a moment he didn't answer. *She'd loved him.* He *knew* that she'd loved him.

Or had he been deluding himself?

She'd left, hadn't she? She hadn't tried to mend their marriage. The only contact she'd had with him had been in relation to their separation. Were those the actions of a woman in love? No.

Which left him guilty of arrogance.

Just because attracting women had never been a problem in his life, he'd grown complacent.

He watched her for a moment, trying to make sense of it all—*searching again for the Amy he'd married.* 'So when did you first realise that you didn't love me enough?' The words almost stuck in his throat. 'Everything was fine until we moved back to Penhally. You seemed happy enough to begin with.' Scrolling through events in his mind, he watched her, still searching for clues. 'When did you suddenly decide that you wanted career, not family? And why didn't you share your thoughts with me?'

She turned back to the window. 'You were working, Marco—busy setting up the surgery with Nick. You were hardly ever home so it was hard to share anything with you. I was lonely. And I discovered that I missed working. I discovered that my own career was more important to me than I'd thought it was. Our relationship was so intense that for a short time I was totally infatuated with you. Babies—a family—that was all part of the same infatuation. But good, stable marriages aren't based on physical passion.'

Marco frowned. 'So when did you have this sudden change of heart? Not in the first few weeks, that's for sure. You spent your days going to estate agents because we both agreed we wanted a house out of town and preferably right on the cliffs. You dismissed three properties because they didn't have a garden. I still remember the day you rang me at work to tell me about this place. You were so excited! You'd even picked out the room that you thought should be the nursery. Where was the career woman then, Amy? *Where was she?*' He stared at her profile and saw the faint sheen of tears in her eyes.

The tears diluted his anger and he gave a soft curse and turned away from her, guilt tearing through him. '*Mi dispiace.* I'm sorry. Don't cry. Don't do that.' He hated it when women cried, although to be fair to her, she'd never done that to him before. He stared moodily down at the waves crashing onto the rocks, feeling as though his body and mind were under the same steady assault as the coastline. 'If you truly don't love me enough then there is nothing to be done.' This was entirely new territory for him. In the past he'd been the one to tell a woman that a relationship was over—*that he didn't love her enough.*

Only now was he discovering that it wasn't an easy thing to hear.

He glanced towards her and wondered why, if she didn't love him, she looked so utterly, utterly lost and miserable. 'You've changed so much.'

'Perhaps I have. Didn't you always say that women are sometimes difficult to understand? That we think in different ways?'

Marco gave a twisted smile, bitterly amused at his own arrogance. To think that he'd once thought that he understood women. Amy had long since proved that not to be the case. 'So, after two years of thinking in your very different way, you decided to turn up and ask for a divorce.'

'We've been apart for two years.'

'And that's some sort of magic figure? If you were expecting me to smile and sign, you picked the wrong man to marry and divorce.' His mouth tightened. 'Perhaps I should have mentioned this before, but I don't believe in divorce.'

'Surely that depends on the marriage. You don't want to be married to someone who doesn't love you. It's time to get on with our lives, Marco. I can pursue my career. You can find someone else. You can marry someone else who will give you a whole houseful of children.'

Was that what he wanted?

He'd only ever imagined this house full of his and Amy's children. *Did he want children with another woman?*

CHAPTER FIVE

THE phone rang and Marco let out a stream of Italian, clearly incensed at being interrupted yet again. His eyes glittered dangerously and he glared at the phone as if his anger alone should be enough to silence it.

'Answer it, Marco,' Amy said wearily. 'It's probably someone else whose life needs saving.'

He was angry with her. *So angry with her.*

And intellectually he was outmanoeuvring her at every step, pouncing on holes in her argument like the most ruthless trial lawyer. And there were plenty of holes. Her defence was thin and full of inconsistencies, she knew that, but she hadn't expected to be on trial long enough for it to matter. She'd expected a quick conversation and a rapid exit. She hadn't expected him to argue with her.

She hadn't expected him to *care* enough to argue and she certainly hadn't expected him to ask if she'd loved him.

That had been the most difficult lie of all.

And what now? Was he going to let her go?

Was he going to find another woman to share his heart and have his children?

The thought of another woman living in this house, living with Marco, brought a lump to her throat.

She wasn't going to think about that right now.

Grateful for the brief respite offered by the phone, she watched as he strode across the room and lifted the handset, his movements purposeful. He was a man who was focused and didn't waste time, hence the reason he was able to cope with such a punishing workload without crumbling under the pressure.

'Nick? Problems?' He didn't even bother to disguise his impatience at the interruption and Amy winced slightly, wondering what the senior partner in the practice was thinking about her sudden unexpected return. Was he cursing her for distracting his partner when they were so busy?

It was obvious from the conversation that Nick was asking Marco about a patient and Marco sprawled into the nearest chair and gave the information that was needed.

He was never given any peace, Amy thought to herself, listening as he and Nick debated different courses of action. But he never tried to hide from his responsibilities. From the moment he'd decided to set up the surgery in Penhally with Nick, he'd been dedicated to delivering the very best health care to the local population. He was that sort of man.

The sort of man who would be an amazing father.

Feeling slightly sick, Amy tried to subdue the misery that bubbled up inside her. *Not now.* She wasn't going to think about that now. She dare not. Marco was far too astute. She had to make it look as though this was what she wanted.

'Amy?' The conversation concluded, he replaced the phone and looked at her. 'Sorry for the interruption. Since Lucy left it's been crazy. The snow hasn't helped. No one is used to having snow in the village and everyone is slipping on pavements and injuring themselves.' He ran a hand over his face. 'And it's New Year's Eve in a few days' time.'

Amy knew from experience that New Year's Eve was always busy for the local health team and being one doctor down would be a problem. 'You haven't managed to find anyone to cover Lucy?'

'We weren't exactly expecting her to deliver so early. We didn't have time to arrange locum cover. Kate is still working on it.' He leaned his head back against the sofa and closed his eyes. His dark lashes brushed the hard, strong lines of his cheekbones and Amy stared hungrily.

The early morning had always been her favourite time of day, when he had still been asleep and she'd been able to just study his face without having to worry about what she was revealing.

'She told me this afternoon that she may have found someone, but he can't start for another month. Until then it's all hands on deck, except that the ship is sinking. I haven't even asked—how was surgery this morning?' He opened his eyes suddenly and she coloured, embarrassed that he'd caught her looking at him.

'Surgery was interesting.' *Talking about work was good.* 'Along with the usual coughs, colds and sore throats, I saw my first ever case of erysipelas and a case of ophthalmic shingles.'

'I suppose the erysipelas was one of the trawlermen; it usually is. Ophthalmic shingles?' He raised an eyebrow. 'Who was that?'

'A Mrs Duncan?'

'Paula? She's a writer. Detective novels, I think. Lives in that white house on the cliffs. You're sure it was shingles?'

Astonished that he knew so much about his patients, Amy nodded. 'Yes, she had all the symptoms and skin lesions on the side of her nose.'

'Did you refer her to the hospital?'

'Yes.'

'Poor Paula. That's the last thing she needs over the Christmas holidays. Did you give her oral aciclovir? Eight hundred milligrams?'

Amy sighed. 'Marco, if you're so worried about my skills, don't ask me to take your surgery.'

'Sorry.' He gave a faint smile, the first smile that had touched his mouth since she'd walked back into his life that morning. 'I'm not used to delegating. And especially not to my wife.' He studied her for a moment, his dark eyes narrowed and his long legs stretched out in front of him. He looked impossibly sexy and Amy's mouth dried and she turned away from him, her heart thudding hard against her chest.

'Well—it was just the one surgery,' she muttered, feeling his gaze burning a hole between her shoulder blades.

'So what are your plans once you finally catch that train? Are you returning to Africa or are they sending you somewhere else?'

'I don't know. They've asked me to go to Pakistan.'

'But you haven't accepted?'

'Not yet.' She turned, wondering where the conversation was going. 'I wanted to get things sorted out here first.'

Marco held her gaze. 'So you're out of a job. You, who love work above everything else.' It was impossible to miss the sarcasm in his voice and Amy's tongue tied itself in a knot.

'I'm not exactly out of work.' She tried to retrace her steps. 'I'll go where I'm needed.'

'Is that right? In that case I have a proposition for you. You stay in Penhally for a month. Work in the practice. You've probably noticed that we're struggling. Nick, Dragan and I can't keep it going on our own.'

Amy stared at him for a moment, wondering if she'd misheard. 'That's out of the question.'

'Why? You've just said that you'll go where you're needed. You're needed here, Amy.'

'No.'

'You keep telling me how important it is for you to work. We need another doctor in Penhally. Urgently. You're good at what you do and you're capable of just stepping in and getting on with things. You proved that this morning. If you hadn't been here, surgery would have ground to a halt.'

'You don't want your ex-wife working in your practice.'

'My *wife*.' He emphasised the word gently. 'Actually, you're my *wife*, Amy, not my ex-wife. And why is that a problem? If you don't love me then there are no emotions involved, so working together should be easy. It's a good solution.'

Not for her.

Amy stood there in a blind panic, once again trapped by her own words. 'That's a ridiculous suggestion. We can't work together.'

'Why not?'

Because it would be too painful. *Because she wouldn't be able to hide her true feelings.* 'Marco, don't do this.'

'Don't do what? Don't talk sense? We need a doctor, you need a job. You don't love me—fine, we work together as friends and colleagues and at the end of a month I give you that divorce you want. One month, working side by side as we've done today.'

So basically she had to allow herself to be tortured for a month in order to achieve something that she didn't really want anyway.

She almost laughed.

'It would be too…awkward. Marco, how can you even suggest it?'

'We are both mature, professional people. Why would it be awkward? The only possible reason for it to be awkward would be if you still felt something for me. Is that the case, Amy? Do you feel something?'

It was like being in court in front of a deceptively gentle prosecutor determined to dig up the truth. 'I don't— That isn't what I mean.' She stumbled over the words. 'I don't feel anything for you, Marco. I'm sorry if that's hurtful but it's better that I tell the truth.'

'*Are* you telling the truth?' He was watching her closely, his gaze disturbingly intense. 'There's something going on here, Amy. Something that isn't right.'

'You're putting me in an impossible position, that's what isn't right! I can't stay, Marco.'

'Why not?' There was a hard edge to his tone. 'You've said that you never loved me and that our relationship was just a fling. Since when did a bit of hot sex need to get in the way of a sensible business arrangement? Work is all-important to you and I'm offering you work. If emotions aren't involved, there can't be a problem, can there?'

Her emotions *were* involved. But to admit that would be to admit that she was still in love with him and that would lead to complications that she couldn't handle.

Amy waded through her options and found them depressingly limited. It was obvious that if she refused he would take her refusal as an indication that she was in love with him and she just didn't want him knowing that.

Desperate now, she searched for another excuse—*anything*—that might help her extricate herself from the situation. 'I only planned to come for the day. I don't have clothes or anything.'

'All your clothes are still here. Upstairs in the wardrobe where you left them.' His tone was even. 'In case you've forgotten, you didn't take much with you.'

She'd been too upset to even bother with packing.

Amy turned away and walked over the window, her mind racing. Unlike him, she wasn't thinking clearly.

She could walk away, but then she'd just have to come back and go through all this again another time. Or she could stay and work in Penhally and prove that their relationship was truly over.

All she had to do was keep up the act for a month and then he'd give her a divorce.

She stared out to sea, watching the waves rise and fall. It wasn't as if they'd see that much of each other, she reasoned. She'd already seen how much of his life was tied up with the practice. They'd both be working. She wouldn't be spending a lot of time in his company.

How hard would it be?

'You're joining us?' Nick Tremayne stared at Amy across the desk, a serious expression on his face. 'You're going to work as a locum?'

'Just until Dr Donnelly arrives. Kate has confirmed that he can start in a month.' Exhausted after a sleepless night in Marco's spare room, Amy summoned up a smile that she hoped reflected the correct amount of enthusiasm for the situation. 'I took Marco's surgery for a while yesterday morning and I enjoyed it. I'm between jobs at the moment and you're stuck so it seemed a sensible solution.' *Did she sound convincing?*

Probably not, given that she wasn't entirely convinced herself.

But Marco had pushed so relentlessly that she'd found herself trapped between all the lies she'd told.

Nick looked at her, his gaze just a little too probing for her liking. 'I hate to point out the obvious…' he glanced towards Marco '…but you guys haven't seen each other for two years. Much as we need the help professionally, I can't risk the problems of your personal life invading practice business.'

'We're very civilised,' Marco said easily. 'Working together won't be a problem.'

Wouldn't it? Unconvinced, Amy glanced at him, trying to read his mind, but his face gave nothing away. *Was he really as relaxed about the whole thing as he seemed?*

Perhaps Nick was asking himself the same question because he studied his friend and colleague for a moment before turning back to Amy. 'Where are you going to live?'

Amy opened her mouth to reply but Marco was there first. 'In the house, with me. Where else? I'm rattling around with five bedrooms.' His emphasis on the word 'five' could have been a linguistic slip or else a gentle reminder that they'd chosen the house with the intention of filling it with their children. 'Amy missed her train so she stayed last night. We managed to get through the night without killing each other so I don't anticipate a problem.'

He was expecting her to live in the same house as him? No! That hadn't been part of the original plan. She'd been banking on the fact that, apart from the odd bit of professional communication at work, she'd be able to avoid him. Yes, she'd stayed the previous night—shivering in the spare room like an interloper—but she'd assumed that she'd be finding herself alternative accommodation at some point. Already her eyes were gritty and her head ached as a result of a night in his spare bedroom. She'd spent the entire night awake, imagining Marco just next door, probably sprawled naked in the enormous bed that they'd chosen for the main bedroom, and now she discovered that she was going to be staying there every night.

Amy opened her mouth to argue and then caught Nick's searching look and instead smiled weakly. Thanks to Marco's confident announcement she now had no choice but to stay with him. 'That's right,' she said hoarsely. 'I'm staying with him. No problem.'

Nick shrugged. 'Well, if you both think you can handle it. God knows, we need another doctor badly so I'm not likely to put up much of an argument. Welcome back, Amy, and welcome on board.' His tone was brisk. 'Well, this is a good start to the New Year. I was starting to think we might have a nervous breakdown before we found anyone to cover Lucy's maternity leave.'

'How is Lucy?' Amy tried to ignore the heavy feeling of dread that sat in her stomach. 'Is she doing all right?'

'Very well, considering the baby was premature. Annabel is still in Special Care but they're hoping to be back home for New Year.' Nick tapped his fingers on the desk, his expression thoughtful. It was clear that he was already planning, his mind on the practice and the needs of the local population. 'So, Amy, it's pretty obvious that you should just take on Lucy's patients and the antenatal clinic. I seem to remember that obstetrics was always your big love so it makes sense.'

Amy's mouth dried. 'No!' Forgetting all about the sleeping arrangements, she shook her head. 'No. I mean…could I do one of the other clinics?' *Not antenatal. Please, God, not that. Not now.* 'It would be great to do something different. Don't you do the antenatal clinic? I'd hate to take it away from you.' Aware that Marco was looking at her in astonishment, she tried to recover herself but Nick was frowning, too.

'Since Lucy left I've had to cover the minor surgery and I can't do it all. Marco does child health, of course, and Alison Myers, our practice nurse, does a fair few clinics on her own with no help. Dragan has other responsibilities that take him further afield, so he can't take on obstetrics.' Nick narrowed his eyes, studying her face carefully. 'You love obstetrics. Pregnant women were always your special interest. What's the problem? Is it something to do with your stint in Africa? I mean, it's not as if you're going to be expected to deliver the babies or anything. Just deliver the antenatal care. Have you had a drama that we ought to know about?'

'No. Nothing like that.' Her heart was galloping and her palms were damp. 'There's no problem, really,' she lied, her voice barely working. 'I just thought maybe it would be better to have a more permanent doctor doing that particular clinic. For continuity. Women like continuity, don't they?'

She wished Marco would stop looking at her. And now Nick was looking at her, too. And she had a feeling that the older doctor would be asking her questions sooner rather than later.

'Ideally, yes,' Nick said slowly, his gaze intent on her face. 'But in this case I think they'll just be delighted to have a female doctor with expertise in obstetrics. I can't imagine that anyone is going to protest.'

She was protesting. But now they were both staring at her and she knew that she'd already betrayed far too much.

'Well, if you're sure they won't mind—I'll do the clinic, of course.' She gave what she hoped was a casual smile. 'It will be fine.' Fine. Fine. Fine. She was a trained professional. She could deliver whatever medical care was required of her.

She could do antenatal.

She could switch off. Shut down her feelings. Wasn't that what she'd done for the past two years?

'Good.' Nick's eyes lingered on her face for a moment longer and then he turned back to Marco. 'So that's decided, then. I'll tell Kate and she can inform the patients. Good news. Thanks, Amy. A timely arrival on your part if ever there was one. Lucky for us.'

Not lucky, Amy thought miserably, biting her lip so hard that she tasted blood. *Not lucky at all.*

'All right, so what the hell is happening between you and Amy? Is this happy ever after?' Nick hooked his hands behind his head and rocked back on his chair. 'Are the two of you back together?'

Marco lounged in the chair opposite, his expression guarded. 'Are you asking as my friend or my colleague?'

'What difference does it make? It's a simple yes or no answer.'

'We're not back together again…' Marco paused. 'Yet.'

'But you're working on it. It's what you want, obviously.' Nick made an impatient sound. 'What about Amy? The two of you were good together. What the hell is going on? I never really understood why she left in the first place.'

Marco kept his response factual. 'Apparently she wanted a career instead of children.'

'*Amy?*' Nick looked at him in disbelief. 'That doesn't sound right. She was very excited about starting a family. I remember catching her staring at a baby outfit in a shop window one day. She went a deep shade of scarlet but she had that look in her eyes. That look that warns you to go out and buy a people carrier.'

Marco didn't laugh. 'Well, the look has disappeared. It isn't what she wants any more. She doesn't want babies and she doesn't want me.'

'I wonder why not.'

'She doesn't love me enough.' Marco gave what he hoped passed as a casual shrug. 'It happens.'

Nick laughed with genuine amusement. 'But not to you. Women always love you. It's the accent and the dark, brooding eyes. Come on, Marco! What's the matter with you? Amy loves you! Anyone can see that. She isn't a woman who is fickle in her affections! She's a one-man woman and you're that man. You always have been.'

'Apparently not.' Feeling suddenly irritable, Marco rose to his feet. 'Was there anything else we needed to talk about? Because my love life has run its course as a topic of conversation.'

'How's the car? Did you get the Maserati fixed?'

'Yesterday. Kate arranged it.'

The change in Nick's expression was barely perceptible. 'She's a wonderfully efficient practice manager.'

And she was willing to be a great deal more if Nick would only give her some encouragement, Marco thought, wondering if his colleague was truly as obtuse about Kate's feelings as he pretended to be. Or was it much more complicated than that? Was he still churned up and guilty about the death of his wife? Unable to commit to anyone else?

Marco gave a mental shrug and decided not to pursue the subject. He had enough problems of his own in that department and he certainly wasn't in a position to lecture other people on how to run their love lives. 'I've put Amy in Lucy's consulting room. I assume that's all right with you.'

'As long as she's seeing patients I don't care if she's doing it from the toilet,' Nick drawled. Then he leaned forward. 'Any idea why she was so reluctant to run the antenatal clinic?'

'She doesn't really want to be here at all.' Marco gave a grim smile. 'I used some psychological leverage to get us a doctor for a few weeks. She's here under duress, I'm afraid.'

'Well, I guessed that.' Nick frowned and tapped his pen on the desk. 'But I had a feeling that there might be something more going on. She looked...distraught at the thought of doing that clinic. Pale. Ill. Maybe she's just tired.'

Marco felt a flicker of unease. 'Yes, I think something is wrong, too. That's why I want her to stay. Once I find out what it is and help her solve it, I'll let her go. Perhaps the problem is just that she wants to be as far away from me as is humanly possible.'

'It could be that. But she's a woman...' Nick flicked the switch on his computer '...which also means that it's likely to be something a million times more complicated than that. Watch her, Marco. There's something going on. Just don't let your personal life affect the practice.'

Marco tensed and his voice was a low growl. 'I don't need that lecture from you.'

'Good.' Nick gave a cool smile. 'Then I won't give it.'

'He's getting these headaches,' the woman said, pulling the little boy onto her lap. 'Always behind the left eye and he says it's like a drilling pain.'

Amy glanced at the child's notes, checking that there was nothing in his history that she should know about. 'And what's he like when he gets the headache, Sue? Can he still play or does he have to go and lie down?'

'I give him paracetamol syrup and he lies down. Then he's generally up and playing within about an hour and a half. The syrup works really well.'

Amy turned to the child. 'And when you have your bad headache, Harry, do you feel sick?'

'Sometimes I feel a bit churny in my stomach.'

'A bit churny.' Smiling at the description, Amy gave a sympathetic nod. 'Are you actually sick?'

'No, but when it happens at school they give me a bowl, just in case.'

Amy looked at Sue. 'And how long has he been getting headaches?'

'It's hard to say.' Sue bit her lip. 'I mean, children get headaches, don't they, so I didn't really think about it at first. Then it became more frequent and when he gets them he's sobbing and crying and it's quite scary. And I started to think—I mean—you're going to think I'm completely paranoid. A headache is just a headache isn't it? It's just that—' She broke off and glanced at the boy, clearly concerned about saying too much in front of him.

Amy leaned forward and wrote on a piece of paper. Then she leaned forward and gave it to the child. 'Harry, would you be kind enough to take this to the lady behind Reception for me? And then come back here. Thank you, sweetheart. That's really helpful.'

Eager to please, Harry left the room and Amy turned to the mother. 'I sense that there are things that you don't want to say in front of him.'

'Well, I don't want to worry him. And I'm probably just being paranoid but it's hard not to be with my history. I was diagnosed with bowel cancer two years ago and everyone told me that it couldn't possibly be anything serious. And then it was. I've had chemo and operations and—well, it's been really, really hard. And it makes you realise that things go wrong. People say, "Oh, it won't be anything," but that's what they said about me and they were wrong. It *was* something. And when that happens you can't just look at a headache and think headache, can you? I try and do that and all the time I'm thinking brain tumour.'

'You're not alone in that and you have more reason than most to worry, given everything that has happened,' Amy said softly, feeling her heart twist with sympathy. 'You've obviously had a terrible time. I'm so sorry.'

'It's not too bad now, things have gone quiet. But now this.' Sue looked at Amy and her eyes filled. 'I can cope with anything that happens to me but if anything happens to my child—to Harry—that's it, I'm telling you that now. That's it for me. No more. If my baby is ill, then I'll…' Tears poured down her cheeks and Amy reached out and gave her hand a squeeze.

'It is very unlikely that this is anything serious, but I can understand why you're worried, so this is what we're going to do. We're going to take a very, very good look at him and if necessary we'll refer him to the paediatrician for a specialist opinion. Anything we need to do to reassure you.'

'And how long will that take?' Sue reached into her bag for a tissue and blew her nose hard. 'I'm not sleeping at night because I'm so worried.'

The door opened and Harry bounced back into the room. 'She said, "thank you."'

Sue immediately pulled herself together, her smile just a little too bright as she scrunched up the tissue and pushed it up her sleeve. 'Good boy.'

'Yes, thank you, Harry.' Amy smiled and then turned back to Sue. 'Let's start by taking some history. Does anyone in the family suffer from migraines?'

'My mother and my sister. But not for years. I did take Harry to have his eyes tested because I thought it might be that, but the optician said that his eyes are fine. I brought you the report, just in case you wanted to see it.' She rummaged in her bag and pulled out a piece of paper.

Amy glanced at the results and nodded. 'Yes, they're fine. Nothing there that should cause a headache.' She asked a few more questions, recorded the answers carefully and then smiled at the boy. 'Hop on my couch, Harry, and I'll take a look at you.'

She examined the child thoroughly, found nothing that alarmed her but saw the desperate worry in Sue's eyes.

Amy thought for a moment. 'Sue, I can't find anything that would lead me to believe this is anything other than a straightforward headache, but given your history I think it would be reassuring for you to have a second opinion. Dr Avanti is a qualified paediatrician, as you know. I think what we might do, given how worried you are, is to ask him to take a look at Harry.'

'Would he have time?'

Amy looked at the clock. 'Well, it's the end of surgery so let me just pop in and ask him and see how he's fixed.'

She left the room and found Marco in his consulting room, talking on the phone. He waved a hand towards a chair, finished the conversation and then looked at her expectantly. 'Problems?'

'I have Sue Miller in my room.'

'Sue?' His gaze sharpened. 'What's the matter with her? She was diagnosed with colorectal cancer a couple of years ago. I know Lucy did some follow-up with her.'

Amy looked at him curiously. 'Do you know everyone's patients?'

'*Sì*, if they have a history of serious illness, it's my business to know. It's important that all the partners are aware of what is going on.' He shrugged. 'She was discussed in a practice meeting a while ago. She's always a priority patient for us. So, why is she seeing you today?'

'It isn't about her. It's about Harry. He's seven and he's been having headaches.'

Marco gave a slow nod. 'And she thinks this is symptomatic of a brain tumour, no? I'm sure she is very anxious.'

'Exactly. Understandable in the circumstances.'

'Of course. And you've examined him?'

'Yes. I can't find anything, but I can see that she's very worried. I could always refer her to a paediatrician, but that would take time and given that you are a paediatrician, I thought you might look at him for me. Provide instant reassurance.' She frowned. 'Always assuming that there *isn't* anything to worry about.'

'Now who is being paranoid?' Marco said softly, a faint flicker of humour in his eyes. 'Less than one per cent of headaches are caused by a brain tumour. I think you know that statistic.'

'Yes.' Amy gave herself a little shake. 'But try telling that to a thirty-five-year-old woman who developed cancer when she shouldn't have done. I don't think she's a big believer in the relevance of statistics.'

'Point taken. Of course I will see him. Your room or mine?'

His voice was silky smooth and Amy felt the colour flood into her cheeks and cursed herself for reacting so strongly. Why couldn't she be indifferent? Why?

'You may as well come to my room. Harry is playing happily and it might be less unsettling for him.'

Marco picked up his stethoscope and auriscope and followed her out of the room.

'By the way...' He paused outside the door. 'They're having a New Year's Eve party at the Penhally Arms. We're both invited.'

'Thanks, but no.' Amy shook her head. 'I'm here to work, not to party. You go. I'll stay at home and catch up on some paperwork.'

'You need to be there. You're a member of the community now. You need to make a showing.'

'I'm only here for a short time.'

'If you don't go, people will say that we're afraid to be seen together. We need to present a united front. They don't want to think that there's dissent at the surgery.'

Feeling trapped once again, Amy paused with her hand on the door. 'I can't go to a party with you, Marco.'

'Why not?' He looked genuinely puzzled. 'We're friends and colleagues. Why wouldn't you? We can spend a pleasant evening together. What's the problem? Let's go and take a look at Harry.' And he pushed open the door of her consulting room and walked inside, leaving her staring after him with frustration.

CHAPTER SIX

HE ALWAYS seemed to get his own way.

She'd come to Penhally planning to stay for an hour and here she was, working in the surgery, living with him in their old house and now contemplating going to a party with him. It was ridiculous!

Amy watched as he spoke quietly to Sue and then dropped into a crouch next to Harry.

'Hi, there, Harry.' His voice was good-humoured. 'Good Christmas? What did Father Christmas bring?'

'The most *amazing* remote-control car. You should see it, Dr Avanti, it's so cool.'

'You didn't bring it with you?' When Harry shook his head, Marco looked disappointed. 'Shame. Never mind. Next time I see you perhaps you'll have it with you.' He asked Harry a few questions and then did the same of Sue. 'I'm going to take a look at you, Harry. Can you take off your jumper and shirt and sit on that couch, please?'

Marco listened to the child's heart and lungs and then laid him down and examined his abdomen. 'How long have you been at your school, Harry?'

'Oh…' The boy thought for a moment. 'Pretty much my whole life.'

'Since nursery,' Sue muttered, a soft smile on her face as she looked at her child. 'Age four.'

Marco felt the femoral pulse. 'And who lives at home with you?'

'Well, my mum mostly.' Harry wrinkled his nose thoughtfully. 'And my dad comes home in the evenings.'

'Because he's at work all day,' Sue interjected hastily, and Marco smiled.

'Children are very literal. Any brothers or sisters, Harry?'

'Just Beth. She's two. She doesn't say much but she bites a lot. I suppose she's all right.' Harry looked a bit unsure on that point and Sue gave him a quick hug.

'She doesn't mean to bite, sweetheart. She's very little and her teeth are hurting.' She gave Marco an apologetic look. 'Beth is going through a biting phase at the moment. I'm talking to the health visitor about her in clinic next week.'

'Good idea.' Marco picked up the patella hammer and gently rolled up Harry's trouser leg. 'And what's your favourite subject at school?'

'Science.' Harry giggled as his leg jumped. 'Are you going to break my leg?'

'Definitely not.' Marco smiled and tested the reflexes in the child's feet. 'Doctors don't break legs, they fix them. Do you like your school, Harry? Are you happy?'

'Yes. Except for the lunches. The lunches are gross.'

'What do they give you for lunch?'

'Slugs and snails.'

Marco looked interested. 'Cooked or raw?'

Amy smiled. He was so good with children and they just adored him.

Harry was giggling. 'And worms. They call it spaghetti but it's *definitely* worms.'

'In Italy, where I come from...' Marco picked up the

child's T-shirt and handed it to him '…we eat a lot of worms. You can get dressed now.'

'You eat worms?' Harry shuddered and pulled on his clothes. 'Weird.'

'Very weird,' Marco agreed. 'Now, I want you to sit up and play a few games with me.'

'Games? Cool.' Harry sat up cheerfully, his legs dangling over the edge of the trolley, his expression enthusiastic. 'Now what?'

Marco stood in front of him, legs planted firmly apart, supremely confident. 'I want you to touch my finger and then touch your nose—that's good. And now with the other hand. Faster. Oh, you're good at that.'

'It's easy.'

'Now look at me.' Marco held his hand to the right of the boy's head and wiggled his finger. 'Tell me if my finger is moving or still.'

'Moving.'

'And now?'

'Still.'

Marco switched sides, performed a few more tests and then reached for the ophthalmoscope. 'And now I want to look in the back of your eyes. Amy, can you close the curtains for me, please? Look straight ahead at the picture on the wall, Harry. Keep looking at it even if I get in the way.' He examined the back of both eyes and then put the ophthalmoscope down and drew the curtains.

'Can you see my brain with that light?'

Marco smiled. 'Not your brain exactly but the back of your eye tells me things about your brain. Now put your arms up.' He carried on with the examination while Sue watched anxiously and Amy watched with interest. 'Sit on the floor for me, Harry.'

Eager to please, the little boy slid off the couch and sat on the floor. 'This is fun. Now what?'

'Now stand up as fast as you can.'

The boy leapt to his feet. 'I'm the quickest at gym.'

'I can see that.' Marco walked across to him, putting his heel directly in front of his other foot. 'Can you do this? It's like walking on a tightrope.'

'You mean like in the circus?' Harry chuckled and walked, arms outstretched like an acrobat. 'Like this?'

'Perfect. You're good at that. Better than me. So—we're finished. Good boy.' Marco sat down in the chair opposite Sue. 'All right. I don't see anything that worries me. I don't think this is what you're afraid it is, but if you want more definite reassurance I can refer him for an MRI scan.'

Sue pulled a face. 'I was scanned so many times. I wouldn't want him to have that. It's radiation, isn't it?'

'You're talking about CT scans. An MRI scan is different.' Marco's voice was calm and patient. 'There is no radioactivity, no risk to the patient and Harry is old enough to tolerate it with no problem.'

Sue looked at him and her eyes filled. 'You don't think it's…anything? Truly?'

Amy knew she was avoiding saying the word 'cancer' because the little boy was still in the room.

'I don't think so, although medicine is never an exact science, as you are well aware.' Marco's sympathetic smile indicated that he was referring to her own medical history. 'I think Harry might be suffering from migraines. Not an easy diagnosis to make in a child because the pattern of headaches is not always predictable, but what you describe—the drilling pain, the very definite episode, which is relieved by paracetamol, the fact he needs to lie down…' Marco shrugged his shoulders. 'This sounds to me like migraine and there is some family history to support the theory.'

Sue looked at him. 'If he were your child, what would you do?'

Amy felt her stomach flip. *Marco's child.*

His mind clearly in tune with hers, Marco's gaze flickered to hers momentarily and something burned, slow and hot, in the depths of his eyes. Amy swallowed, knowing that he was thinking of the plans they'd made to have a family.

'If he were mine…' Marco dragged his gaze from Amy's and glanced across at the little boy, who was playing happily on the carpet. 'If he were mine, I would watch him for a while, see how he goes. I think you should keep a diary of the headaches so that we can assess exactly how many he is getting, how long they last and whether there are any obvious triggers. Do that for six weeks and then make an appointment with one of us to go through the diary. We can look at the frequency and decide whether to refer him to the paediatricians at the hospital for them to take a closer look.'

'But you don't think—'

'No.' Marco's voice was firm. 'I don't. But we will watch him. And if you decide that you would be happier if he had an MRI scan, you have only to let me know and I will arrange it.'

Sue closed her eyes for a moment and let out a long breath. 'Thank you for that. I'll pass on the scan for the time being. But what could be causing the migraines, do you think?'

'It's hard to say.' Marco watched the child play. 'Often we underestimate children, especially very young children. We imagine that because they are young, they are somehow not aware of what is going on around them, but that is rarely the case. Most children are extremely intuitive and even if they don't pick up on conversations they pick up on atmosphere. Is he a sensitive child, would you say?'

'Very.' Sue looked at her son. 'He's a worrier. And very caring. Even in the playground at school, he's always watching out for other children.'

Marco nodded slowly. 'So—we know that the past two years have been very hard for you personally and also for your family. It would be almost impossible for that not to have had an impact.'

'I suppose so. We've done our best to protect the children, but inevitably some of it filters through.' Sue rose to her feet and managed a smile. 'But things are going better now. I'm hoping this is going to be our lucky year. Will you be in the Penhally Arms on New Year's Eve, Dr Avanti? I hear they're planning quite an evening.'

'*Sì.* Where else would I be on New Year's Eve when the drink is free?' Marco winked at her. 'I'll be there.'

'Then we might see you. Thank you, both of you. Harry…' Sue held out a hand to her son. 'Let's go and write a few more thank-you letters for all those Christmas presents.'

Harry gave an exaggerated shudder but followed his mother out of the room with a wave at Marco.

'Sweet boy,' Amy said quietly, and then realised that Marco was watching her.

'I thought you didn't like children?'

She stiffened. 'I never said I didn't like children. I just said I didn't want any of my own. That's completely different.' Uncomfortable under his scrutiny, she turned away. *She couldn't live like this.* Couldn't be on her guard the whole time. It was exhausting and she was a useless, terrible liar. 'So we'll keep an eye on him, then. Thanks for looking at him. You really think he's all right?'

'Who?' It was as if his mind was somewhere else entirely. Then he sighed. 'Oh, Harry—yes. Amy, his neurological examination was normal, there was no evidence of poor co-ordination, ataxia or nystagmus. His peripheral nervous system was normal. His cardiovascular system was normal. Personally, I wouldn't even scan him, but if Sue carries on worrying, it's worth arranging it.'

'I'll do that. Or I suppose the locum can do it if I've gone.
I'll make sure the notes are detailed. Thank you, Marco.'

He studied her in brooding silence. 'My pleasure.'

The antenatal clinic was held that afternoon and Amy spent
her entire lunch hour wondering whether there was any way
she could get out of it without drawing attention to herself.

Five minutes before it was due to start she was still sitting
in the staffroom when Kate hurried in. 'You haven't forgotten your clinic, Amy?'

If only.

'No.' Amy forced a smile. 'Just having five minutes' rest
before I start.'

'We almost cancelled this particular clinic as it's the week
between Christmas and New Year, but there were so many
patients that in the end I decided that we had to run it. Are
you going to eat that sandwich in front of you or just look at
it?' Kate flicked the switch on the kettle and waited for it to
boil.

'I'm not really hungry.' *It was a shame they hadn't cancelled the clinic.*

'You have a busy afternoon ahead of you. You should eat
lunch.' Kate made her coffee and added some milk. 'Is it
Marco that's made you lose your appetite? What's going on
with the two of you?'

Amy hesitated. Kate was a friend, but she wasn't used to
confiding in people. All her life she'd made her own decisions
and relied on herself. To begin with she'd had no choice, and
then it had become a way of life. 'We're— Well, let's just say
our relationship is still over. We're just working a few things
out.'

'That must be hard.' Kate put her mug on the table and sat
down. 'You're very pale, Amy. Are you ill? Or is it just the
stress of seeing Marco again?'

Could she pretend she was ill?

It would get her out of doing the clinic and it wasn't altogether a lie. The mere thought of spending an afternoon talking to pregnant women was enough to make her ill. But if she said she was ill, Marco would be on to her, trying to find out what was wrong.

'I'm not ill.'

'Then it must be stress. Do you honestly think the two of you are going to be able to work together?' Kate slowly stirred sugar into her coffee. 'I know that Nick's worried about it. He thinks that the history between you is going to make things difficult.'

'It will be fine. Nick has nothing to worry about. Marco and I are not planning to discuss the demise of our marriage at work.'

'No—all the same, it was good of you to stay and help us. I'm guessing that you didn't want to but Marco is very persuasive, as we both know. He has a way of getting a person to say yes to all sorts of things.' Kate's voice was gentle. 'Whatever you say to the contrary, I know this can't be easy for you, Amy. I never really understood what went wrong between the two of you but if you want someone to talk to, you have a friend in me. I just wanted to remind you of that.'

'Thanks. Thanks, Kate.' Unbelievably touched, Amy rose to her feet quickly before she was tempted to blurt out the truth about the current situation. 'Love is complicated, isn't it? And painful.' She had no doubt that Kate knew firsthand how painful love could be. Hadn't she lost her husband in a tragedy at sea that had left her to bring up a child alone?

'Yes. It's both those things.'

'How are things with you? How is Jeremiah?'

'Jem? He's fine. Really good. He's eight now. Unbelievable, really, how time passes.' For a moment, Kate stared blankly into the distance and then she cleared her throat and reached for her coffee, suddenly brisk and efficient. 'I envy you doing the antenatal clinic. At least pregnant women are healthy and cheerful.'

Amy's smile froze. 'Yes.'

'There are days when I miss midwifery.'

'I'd forgotten that you're a trained midwife.' *This was a conversation she didn't want to be having.* 'I'd better get on. I'll see you later, Kate.'

She had a clinic to run. A clinic that she didn't want to take. And she needed to prepare herself.

Amy worked on automatic, barely registering the identity of each patient.

It was as if a part of her mind was shut off.

By four o'clock, she only had one pregnant woman left to go and she poured herself a glass of water and drank deeply, promising herself that she was going to go straight home after the clinic. She was going to go straight home and hide under the duvet.

The door opened and her last patient walked in, a blonde woman in her late twenties, carrying a baby in a car seat.

'I know, I know, you're thinking I'm in the wrong clinic.' The woman laughed and sat down on the chair. 'Can you believe it? This little one is only four months old and I'm pregnant again! It's done wonders for my husband's ego. He thinks he's some sort of stallion. So much for the contraceptive effects of breastfeeding! I didn't believe it at first but I've done the test three times so I don't think there's any doubt. I rang for an appointment and they told me to come along this afternoon. They like you to get checked out as soon as possible these days, don't they?'

'That's right. You did the right thing to come.' Amy's mouth dried. 'Congratulations. Are you pleased?'

'Oh, yes. Well, Geoff, that's my husband, always wanted

a large family so it's not a problem. We hadn't quite planned on having them so close together but it's quite good when they're close in age, isn't it?' The baby started to cry and she bent down, undid the straps and gently lifted the baby from the car seat. 'Oh, now I've woken him up with my loud voice. Are you ready for your milk? Ridiculous, isn't it? Breastfeeding while you're pregnant. I mean, that's one of the things I wanted to talk to you about. Is it OK? I don't want to deprive the new baby of nutrients or anything.'

Amy watched as the woman lifted her jumper and skilfully attached the baby to her breast. The baby greedily clamped its jaws around her nipple and then closed his eyes and started to suck, a blissful expression on his face.

What did it feel like?

'Are you all right, Dr Avanti?' The woman frowned at her. 'You look a bit pale, yourself.'

'I'm fine,' Amy said tonelessly.

'And you're married to the other Dr Avanti. Lucky you. Now, that's a man any woman would want to make babies with.'

The pain inside her was so vicious that it took Amy a moment to find the breath to speak. 'It shouldn't be a problem to continue breastfeeding.' Somehow she forced herself to deliver the facts. 'Your biggest problem is likely to be that you'll feel very tired. Make sure you get plenty of rest and eat well. The taste of the milk might change and the baby might object to that for a while…' With difficulty she got through the consultation, saying what needed to be said and carrying out the tests that needed to be done.

By the time she finally closed the door on her consulting room at the end of clinic she felt emotionally drained. Sliding back into her chair, she felt the hot sting of tears behind her eyes.

Appalled at herself, she took a huge gulping breath and tried to control her emotions, but her misery was just too great to be contained and the tears spilled down her cheeks as the dam broke.

Sobs tore through her body and she put her head in her arms and gave in to it, crying like a child, consumed by the emotion that had been building inside her for so long.

She didn't hear the door open—wasn't aware of anything apart from her own misery until she felt a gentle hand on her shoulder and the sound of her name.

She gave a start and lifted her head to find Nick standing there, a look of concern on his face. 'Amy? What's happened?'

'Nothing.' Mortified, she sat up instantly and rubbed her palms over her cheeks, trying to compose herself. 'Well, this is embarrassing. I'm so sorry. *Really* sorry. I'm just tired or something. It's been a bit of a long week.' Her voice was thickened by crying and she knew that she must look a mess.

'Tired?' He studied her for a moment and then pulled up a chair and sat down next to her. 'No one cries like that just because they're tired. Are you depressed?'

Depressed?

Sodden with misery, Amy just stared at him. Clearly he wasn't going to leave her alone without an explanation and she was worn out with searching for new explanations that would keep people satisfied. 'Honestly, I'm not depressed. I'm sorry, Nick.' She yanked a tissue out of the box on her desk and blew her nose hard. 'That was very unprofessional of me. I can assure you that I was fine in front of the patients. I didn't—'

'Amy.' His tone was gruff as he interrupted her anxious apology. 'At this precise moment I don't give a damn about the patients. I'm not thinking about the patients. It's you that I'm worried about.'

'That's kind of you.' She blew her nose again and then gave him a smile. 'But there's no need to worry. I'm fine. Really.'

'Fine doesn't make you sob your heart out on the desk. Does this have something to do with the antenatal clinic? You really didn't want to run it, did you? And we didn't listen.'

'It's not the antenatal clinic.'

Nick watched her. 'Did you lose a baby, Amy?'

'No!' She shot him an anguished look, the pain twisting inside her. 'No, I didn't.'

'Then what's this about? Tell me.'

Amy teetered on the edge of confession and then suddenly remembered just who Nick was. 'I can't.' The tears threatened to start again and she gritted her teeth. 'I— It wouldn't be fair to you.'

'So it's something to do with your relationship with Marco and you're afraid that telling me would put me in a difficult position. You're also not sure that you trust me not to tell him. He mentioned that you'd changed your mind about having a family. Is this related?'

'Don't ask me. I can't talk to you, Nick.'

'I'm your doctor. You can talk to me and it's confidential.'

She blew her nose again and gave a watery smile. 'You're not my doctor. I've only been back in the country for five minutes. I don't have a doctor.'

'Well, you clearly need one, so from now on I'm officially your doctor. Kate will take care of the paperwork.' There was a faint trace of humour in his eyes. 'I need new patients. In case you hadn't noticed, we're nowhere near busy enough around here. I want to know why you were crying, Amy.'

She looked at him, her reluctance dissolving under the kindness she saw in his eyes. 'I find the antenatal clinic difficult.'

'Yes. I gathered that.' His voice was soft. 'Tell me why, Amy. Tell me why you find it difficult.'

She waited a heartbeat. 'Because I can't have children. I'm infertile.'

Nick was silent for a moment and then he sat back in his chair and gave a slow nod. 'All right. Now things are starting to make more sense. And this, presumably, is why you ended a relationship with a man you love?'

'I had no choice.'

'What about Marco? Didn't you think he deserved to know?'

'Don't judge me, Nick!' Her voice sharp, she rose to her feet and paced across the consulting room. Then she turned and wrapped her arms around her body, rubbing her hands up her arms to try and warm herself. 'I did what had to be done.'

'Can we take this a step at a time? When the two of you first arrived in Penhally, you were planning to start a family, I know. That's why you didn't bother finding a job. You were chasing around looking for suitable houses. You'd only been together for a few months. Given that you were in your early thirties, I wouldn't have expected you to become pregnant immediately. It often doesn't work like that, as you well know.'

'I know.' Should she tell him the truth? 'I went for tests.'

'After three months?'

'It was longer than that. By the time I had the tests, we'd been together for six months. No contraception. No pregnancy.' She started to pace again. 'To begin with I thought what you thought. I said all those things women always say to themselves when they're trying to get pregnant. Six months is nothing. I'm over thirty, it might take a while. And then I bumped into an old friend I was in med school with and she turned out to be an infertility specialist at a clinic in Exeter. I decided I may as well have some tests.'

'You didn't tell Marco?'

'No.' She stopped pacing. 'I wanted to find out for myself.'

'So what did the tests show?'

'Scarring.' Such a simple word for something that had had such a massive impact on her life. 'Mild endometriosis. Not enough to need treatment but quite enough to interfere with my fertility. The doctor said that my Fallopian tubes are completely gummed up.'

Nick listened carefully and then he stirred. 'Well, the first thing to say is that infertility is a particularly inexact science. No doctor would ever be able to be one hundred per cent sure that you were infertile.'

'She said that if an egg ever made it along my Fallopian tube, she'd be surprised.'

'Well, we've just had snow in Cornwall.' He gave a wry smile. 'So life is full of surprises, Amy.'

'I know that miracles happen. I know all that, Nick.' She was touched by his kindness. Often with his colleagues Nick was brusque and sometimes even sharp-tongued. But there was no doubting his concern for her at that moment. 'But I couldn't risk our marriage and Marco's happiness on a hope. The chances are that I will never be able to get pregnant.'

'And that was enough for you to decide to end your marriage?'

'It was enough for me.' *More than enough.*

'Let's assume for the sake of argument that your Fallopian tubes are blocked—there are still other options. IVF? Adoption?'

Amy stilled. 'Those aren't options for me.'

'Why not?'

'I have my reasons.' And she wasn't going to share those reasons with anyone. She'd already said more than enough. 'So now you see why I had to leave.'

'Well, not really, no. I see why you *think* you had to leave. You managed to convince yourself that Marco would be better off without you. So you spun a story about choosing a career over a family and about not loving him enough.'

'I had to give him a reason.'

'Why not give him the truth?'

'Because then he would have felt an obligation towards me. I was already his wife. I decided that the easiest way was just to end the relationship. It would have ended at some point anyway, so I didn't do anything except bring forward the inevitable.'

'That's a very negative attitude. Why would it have ended anyway?'

'Because infertility wrecks marriages. It tears them apart.' She stared out of the window, her expression bleak. 'Even strong marriages, and ours wasn't that strong. We hadn't known each other long. He didn't love me enough.'

'Didn't he? That's interesting,' Nick said calmly. 'So why did he go completely off the rails when you left?'

Startled, Amy turned to him. 'What do you mean, "off the rails"?'

'I'll spare you the details but let's just say that he wasn't a happy man.' Nick's eyes narrowed. 'I've known Marco for years, as you know. I can honestly say that you were the first woman he ever really loved.'

'He didn't love me. He couldn't have done.'

'Why not?'

'Because we were together such a short time.'

'But you loved him in that same short time,' Nick pointed out calmly, and she gave a reluctant nod.

'Yes, but…he didn't love me.' Amy frowned and shook her head. 'He never said.'

'Ah. Didn't he?' Nick gave a wry smile. 'Well, we men are terrible at saying what women want to hear, you should know that. But just because the words aren't there doesn't mean that the emotions aren't.'

'He didn't love me, Nick.' She clasped her hands in front of her. 'He didn't try and stop me going.'

'He was in shock. You'd just bought a house to move into together and then suddenly you changed overnight. He assumed you'd met someone else and were just throwing excuses at him.'

Amy felt the colour drain from her face. 'There was no one else. There's never been anyone else.'

'I'm just telling you what he assumed. He couldn't think of anything else that would explain the sudden shift in your behaviour.'

'Is that why he didn't come after me?'

'He's a proud man, Amy. He assumed that you wanted to get away from him so he wasn't about to follow you. And after he calmed down—well, that was when things fell apart here.' Nick's face was expressionless as he referred obliquely to the death of his wife. 'I expect he felt he couldn't leave.'

'Of course he couldn't. I understand. It must have been a horrendous time for you. And I didn't want, or expect, Marco to follow me.' She closed her eyes for a moment. 'I'm so, so sorry about your wife, Nick.'

'We're talking about you, not me.'

'I think we've said all there is to say. I can't have a child, Nick. I can't give Marco the family he wants so badly. And he *does* want it badly—you of all people should know that. He's Italian. He wants a big, noisy, busy family with at least four children as beautiful as he is, fighting over the large bowl of spaghetti in the middle of the table.'

'I don't understand why you're so black and white about this.' Nick stood up and rubbed his forehead with the tips of his fingers. 'There are other options, Amy. If it's so important to you both, you could look for a solution.'

The past clawed at her and she gave a little shake of her head, trying to dispel the memories. *It was always there in the background.*

'I'm not interested in any of those options. I've seen

what—' She broke off but Nick's questioning gaze was enough to tell her that she'd already said too much.

'What have you seen, Amy?'

'Nothing.' Her voice was hoarse. 'Nothing. I just know that those aren't options.'

Nick studied her face for a moment but he didn't push her for more information. 'Well, at least now I understand why you didn't want to do the antenatal clinic.'

'It was difficult,' she said honestly, 'but you don't come to terms with something by ignoring it, so I'm sure that taking that clinic will do me good in the long term.'

'Some things are more difficult to come to terms with than others. Marco can do that clinic from now on, Amy. Or I will. You can do child health or minor surgery.'

'If we swap things around then he'll ask questions that I don't want to answer, and anyway he should do child health—he's a paediatrician. I'll be fine, Nick. I can do the clinic.' Amy walked back to her desk and picked up her coat and bag. 'I'm sorry to dump all over you like this. I can't think what came over me.'

'If a problem is big enough then it eventually finds its way out,' Nick said softly, and Amy slipped on her wool coat and belted it.

'Maybe.'

'My guess is that you've bottled this up for two years. You should talk to someone about it. Talking can help.'

She picked up her bag. 'Do you talk to anyone, Nick?'

His gaze held hers for a moment and then he gave a humourless laugh. 'I'm not sure if you win that point or not. It's different. I'm a man.'

'And you know as well as I do that talking doesn't always help anything. Sometimes it makes things worse. I'd be grateful if you didn't say anything to Marco.'

'He'd want to know, Amy.'

'It would make everything a thousand times more complicated and painful and it wouldn't change the outcome.'

'He loves you.'

Amy felt as though her heart was being squeezed by a vice. 'Even if that were true, it wouldn't change the outcome either,' she said quietly, walking towards the door. 'Thanks, Nick, for listening. Actually, it *was* good to tell someone. I feel better now. More in control. I can do this. I can work as a locum and then walk away and pursue a career.'

'And is that what you want?'

She paused with her hand on the door. 'No. But life doesn't always give you what you want, does it?'

'No. It doesn't.'

She left the room and immediately bumped into Marco in the corridor. Knowing that the evidence of her distress would still show on her face, she kept walking. 'I've finished the clinic. I'll see you at home.' She kept her head down but he caught her arm.

'You're always in such a hurry! I just spoke to the hospital. Eddie doesn't have a skull fracture and they're happy with him. He's coming home tomorrow.'

'That's good. Really good. His mother must be relieved.' She glanced at her watch. 'I've got to dash.'

'Why?' He slid a hand under her chin, lifted her face and then swore softly. 'You've been crying.'

'No, of course I haven't.' She tried to ease her arm away from his grip but he held her firmly.

'Your eyes are red.'

'I think I'm getting a cold.' She sniffed to prove the point. 'It's that time of year. Germs everywhere.'

'Germs don't give you swollen eyes. You've been crying, Amy. Why?'

Given the determined pressure of his fingers, she had no choice but to look into his eyes and this time there was no trace of anger. Just concern. And the concern brought the lump back to her throat.

Oh, for goodness' sake, what was the matter with her? Why did her body have to pick this particular moment to release all the tension that had been building inside her? She'd had two years to break down and she'd chosen the most inappropriate moment possible and the most public place.

With a determined effort she freed herself from his grasp and stepped away from him. 'Honestly, I'm fine. I'm really, really pleased about little Eddie. I'll see you at home.' And she turned and hurried away from him.

CHAPTER SEVEN

'SHE was crying.' Marco followed Nick back into his consulting room, anger shaking his powerful frame. 'Amy has been crying and you were with her! What did you say to her?'

'I can't discuss it.'

'You *will* discuss it!' Marco slammed the door shut with the flat of his hand and gave a low growl. 'This is my wife we're talking about.'

'You're separated.'

'She's *my wife*.'

'Why would you care if she's upset?' Nick's tone was even. 'You've been angry enough with her for the past two years.'

'She left me. I'm human. Yes, I was angry. But that doesn't stop me caring about her.'

Nick sat down in his chair. 'How much do you care about her?'

'What sort of a question is that? So now you are—what do they call it?' His English momentarily abandoning him, Marco switched to Italian and then back again. 'A marriage counsellor?'

'Do you still love her?'

Thrown by the intimacy of the question, Marco prowled across the consulting room and stared blankly at the wall displaying a poster on the dangers of smoking. 'Yes. I still love her.' He turned sharply. 'So now will you tell me why she was crying?'

'I can't do that. Our talk was confidential.'

'So you *do* know what's wrong.' Exasperated, Marco spread his hands in question. 'Tell me what she said! How could it be confidential?'

'Because she spoke to me as a doctor.'

'It was a consultation?'

'Yes.'

'She's ill?' Anxiety replaced anger, but the emotion was just as sharp. 'Is something the matter with her?' He'd wondered. It might explain why she'd lost weight and why she was looking so pale.

'She isn't ill.'

Marco let out a long breath. For a moment he'd been afraid that— 'Well, if she wasn't ill, why did she need to talk to a doctor?'

Nick was silent for a moment. 'How well do you know Amy?'

Marco frowned and rubbed a hand over his face. 'Well enough to love her. I know the sort of person she is. She's shy with people she doesn't know, she finds it quite hard to talk about her feelings but underneath she's very loving and giving. She loves children, or at least I always thought she did.' Marco broke off, wondering why he was revealing so much to his partner. 'I don't understand what you're getting at.'

'How much do you know about her past? Her background? Before she met you?'

'I don't know. Not much. I never really worried about it. It's not that relevant, is it?' His gaze sharpened. 'You think it's relevant?'

'I don't know.' Nick's voice was thoughtful. 'I think it

could be. If you want my advice, and frankly I wouldn't blame you if you didn't take it because advice on the matters of the heart isn't exactly my strong suit, I'd get to know her better. I mean the Amy underneath. What makes her tick? What made her believe the things she believes? Find that out and you might find the answers you're looking for.'

'You can't tell me more than that?'

'No. I can't.' Nick leaned forward and switched on his computer. 'That's already far more than I should have said.'

Amy took a hot shower but it didn't stop the shivering. Desperate for warmth, she dressed in a pair of jeans and a warm jumper, her hair hanging damp and loose to her shoulders.

Her head throbbed from crying and outside the wind had picked up. The sky was grey and threatening and the word among the villagers was that there was more snow on the way.

Still shivering, she walked down to the kitchen to make herself a hot drink. The conversation with Nick had left her feeling raw and vulnerable. She felt slightly odd, having exposed so much of herself to another person. And yet, despite that, telling Nick had made her feel better. He was the first person she'd confided in and she felt lighter.

Or did she feel lighter because he'd told her that Marco had been so badly affected by her departure?

He'd cared.

And she'd so badly wanted him to care. Not that it changed anything, she reminded herself miserably. It didn't change anything at all. No relationship was strong enough to withstand such a bitter blow—she knew that better than anyone.

Thoughts flew into her head and clashed, a cacophony of childhood memories that unsettled and disturbed her.

Not now. *She wasn't going to think about any of that now.*

Hearing the unmistakable sound of the Maserati, Amy tensed.

Marco was home.

Which meant more questions.

She was just debating whether to go up to the spare room and close the door when she heard his key in the door and moments later he walked into the kitchen.

'It's freezing out there and as for the wind…' He gave a shudder that more eloquently described his views on the weather than his words did. 'They were planning fireworks on New Year's Eve but they won't be able to do them if this wind keeps up. It will be too dangerous. We will be treating burn victims.'

Amy found herself looking at the curve of his mouth and then at the dark shadow of stubble on his hard jaw. She turned away quickly. 'It will be a shame if we have to cancel. The fireworks are always a highlight of New Year in Penhally. I used to love them when I was a child.' *Why did she still have to feel like this?* It was so unfair!

Marco reached for a bottle of wine. 'You stayed with your grandmother?'

'That's right.'

'In the cottage? I've often wondered why you sold it.'

'It would have been too small for us.'

'*Sì*, but I would have thought it had sentimental value.' He jerked the cork out of the bottle and reached for a glass. 'Wine?'

'No, thanks.'

'You look tired.' His eyes lingered on hers for a moment and then he turned away and poured wine into his own glass.

Her heart pumping hard, Amy closed her eyes briefly, hoping that he couldn't sense her body's response to him. Everything suddenly felt confused. She'd arrived with one clear objective and an iron resolve, but now everything was clouded. Suddenly what she had to do and what she wanted to do seemed a million miles apart.

It was just because she was living and working with him, she thought helplessly. Marco didn't exactly melt into the background. He was a very confident, very physical man. Even now, with his powerful shoulders and long, strong legs, he seemed to fill the room, and suddenly the large, beautiful kitchen seemed claustrophobically small.

'So, your grandmother's house—was it full of memories?'

Full of memories, many of them not good. 'I didn't want to keep it.' Why was he watching her so closely? *Had Nick said something to him?*

'You're very tense,' he said softly. 'Is something wrong?'

Of course she was tense. She was so aware of him that it was almost impossible to breathe.

'Amy?' He stepped towards her and lifted a hand, stroking her hair away from her forehead with the tips of his fingers. 'Do you have a headache?'

This was insane. She had to move away now. The brush of his fingers set her body on fire, even though she knew that his touch hadn't been sexual in nature.

Her gaze lifted to his and she saw the hot burn in his eyes, the look they exchanged an intimate meshing of their thoughts.

Terrified that he'd see too much, Amy moved away from him, ignoring the instinct that was telling her to move closer. 'I do have a slight headache. Do you have any paracetamol in the house?'

His eyes didn't leave hers. 'Go and lie on the sofa. I'll bring you something.'

Relieved to put some space between them, she did as he suggested and moments later he reappeared with a glass of water and the tablets.

'Thank you.' She took them gratefully and then leaned her aching head against the back of the sofa, hoping that the tablets wouldn't take long to work. 'Sorry. Long day.'

'I can imagine.' He took the water from her, put it on the table and then moved behind the sofa.

The next thing she felt was the touch of his hands in her hair. 'Marco—'

'This will ease the pain of your headache far more effectively than medication,' he murmured softly, sliding his fingers into her hair and gently massaging her scalp. 'I remember that you often had headaches when we first met.'

'Like little Harry. Poor thing. I wouldn't wish this on anyone.' She knew she ought to move but she couldn't. His fingers were firm and rhythmic as they moved over her scalp. 'That feels good.'

'Tell me about the Penhally fireworks. Tell me about your grandmother.' His voice was deep and soothing and her eyes drifted shut.

'I stayed with my grandmother every Christmas and New Year, right through the holidays. There was a window-seat in my bedroom and on New Year's Eve I'd kneel there and watch the fireworks—they were fantastic. Then we'd have hot chocolate together. When I was older, I was allowed to go along and watch.'

'And that was fun?'

'Yes. Everyone was very friendly.' For a short time she'd felt as though she'd belonged somewhere.

'You spent every holiday with your grandmother?'

'Because my mother was working right through and she couldn't look after me.'

'And your father?'

The question disturbed the calm flow of her thoughts. 'My father spent every Christmas with his twenty-four-year-old secretary.'

'Ah…' Marco's fingers stopped moving. 'He had an affair?'

'It started as an affair, but then he married her and at the last count they had four beautiful children, two boys and two girls.' The tension flowed back into her veins and she sat up. 'Why are we talking about my father?'

'Why not?' He walked over to the table and picked up his wine. 'You said that we didn't know each other well enough and I'm starting to think that perhaps you were right. I want to know more about your life before I met you. It must have been tough, spending every holiday with your grandmother.'

'I loved it,' she said honestly. 'She was a wonderful woman.'

'You didn't miss your home? Your mother?'

Her heart beating rapidly, Amy rose to her feet. 'No, not really. What is this? The Spanish Inquisition?'

'*Calmo, tesoro.*' His voice was soft. 'Suddenly your voice is rising and you're very tense. Why does a simple question feel like an inquisition? Is the subject matter that painful?'

'Painful? I didn't say it was painful,' she said quickly. 'I just don't see how my past is in any way relevant to our current situation. You don't *need* to know any more about me, Marco. It's irrelevant. Our marriage is over, we both know that.' She regretted the words instantly, knowing that such a declaration simply invited the very response on his part that she was trying to avoid.

'It is over? Ah, yes.' His tone was deceptively casual as he strolled across the room towards her. 'I remember now. It is over because you feel nothing for me, isn't that right?'

She didn't dare look at him and she didn't need to because his slightly husky, lazy drawl revealed his feelings all too clearly. Amy ceased to breathe. 'I think I'll go upstairs and—'

'You're not going anywhere.' Without allowing her time to move, he curved an arm around her waist in an unmistakably possessive gesture and pulled her against him, ignoring her soft gasp of protest.

'What are you doing?'

'What I should have done two years ago. When you talk, nothing makes sense so the obvious solution is to try a different method of communication.' She was breathlessly aware of the dangerous glint in his eyes and then his mouth came down on hers and they were kissing, their mouths hungry, the pleasure hot and instantaneous.

It was like a storm breaking and Amy sank her fingers into the hard muscle of his shoulders to stop herself sliding to the floor. Her legs shook, her whole body trembled and the heat of his mouth coaxed a response from her, even though she was dimly aware that what they were doing now was going to make everything much more complicated later.

She didn't care about later. She only cared about *now*, and anyway it was impossible to think or concentrate when his skilful hands were reacquainting themselves with her body. They slid under her jumper and stroked the warm skin of her back and then they moved back to her waist and one thumb circled her navel. And all the time he kissed her, his mouth and hands creating sensations that threatened to consume her.

She'd missed him so much.

The hot, desperate kiss was briefly interrupted as he pulled her jumper over her head and then her shirt followed and her bra until she stood only in her jeans, shaking and shivering in his arms.

'You are cold?' He muttered the question against her mouth and she shook her head, wondering how she was expected to answer when she could barely stand.

'No. Not cold.'

Hot. *Dangerously, deliciously hot.*

Marco kissed her again and she clung to him as he pulled her gently off balance and lowered her onto the thick rug. Next to them the fire flickered but neither of them noticed or cared.

Amy could hardly breathe and she gave a low moan as his

mouth moved to her breast, his tongue teasing her nipple to hardness. He seduced and tormented until the sensation that shot through her body was almost agonising in its intensity. And then he shifted his attention to her other breast and Amy writhed and gasped, her body arching against his as he used all his skill and experience to drag a response from her.

Oblivious to everything except her own need for him, she reached down to touch him and only then realised that he was still fully clothed. With a whimper of frustration she tugged at the belt of his trousers and he covered her hand with his and swiftly helped her.

Amy felt her mouth dry as Marco dragged off his own clothes, revealing a body that was hard and fit. Had she really thought she'd ever be indifferent to this man? He had an amazing physique, the muscles of his shoulders and arms curved, his stomach flat and the movement of his body fluid.

Then he turned back to her and lowered his head, his mouth hot and hard and the touch of his fingers skilled and impossibly intimate. He wasn't slow or gentle but she didn't care because this wasn't about seduction—it was about wild, desperate need. And when he finally parted her thighs she gave a whimper of assent and wrapped her legs around him. Nothing mattered any more. Nothing except this. *Nothing except him.*

She felt the thickness of his arousal and then he paused for a moment and looked straight into her eyes, strands of inky black hair falling over his forehead, his breathing uneven. 'Amy?'

'Don't stop, Marco.' She virtually sobbed the words, her hands sliding over his warm skin, urging him forward. 'Please…'

He hesitated for just a moment and then moved his hips and entered her in a single, smooth thrust that joined them completely.

It had been so long.

The sudden intimacy overwhelmed her and then he started to move and each powerful stroke felt shockingly delicious. All she was aware of was him, the intoxicating scent of him, the skilled touch of his fingers, *the hard male pulse of his body*. He didn't take it slowly and she didn't care. Frantic, desperate, she urged him faster and he drove his body into hers with ruthless, reckless hunger until the tingle and burn inside her grew into something that couldn't be contained and her body exploded.

Her climax was shockingly intense and she heard his harsh groan and knew that her body had driven through his control and tipped him over the edge. He exploded inside her and her fingers dug hard into the slick muscle of his shoulders, clinging as they rode the storm, oblivious to everything around them.

Eventually the wildness eased and they lay for a moment, their bodies still joined and their minds still numb.

And then Marco rolled onto his back, drawing her against him. 'That was incredible. *You* are incredible.'

Amy closed her eyes tightly, waiting for the aftershocks to pass.

What had they done? What had *she* done?

For a moment she lay there, her body still weak and drugged from the after-effects of his love-making. 'We shouldn't have done that.'

'Why not? We're still married, *tesoro*. Sex is part of a relationship.'

'We don't have a relationship, Marco, not any more.' More than a little confused, she sat up and immediately felt the hot burn of his gaze on her body. Horribly self-conscious, she reached for her jumper and pulled it over her head. 'Nothing has changed.'

It took him a moment to answer and he rubbed a hand over his face, as if forcing himself to concentrate. 'You can't truly believe that.' His voice was soft and when he finally looked at her, his gaze was dark. '*Everything* has changed, *amore*.'

'No, it hasn't.' She reached for her jeans and wriggled into them. 'I— The sex was great, Marco, you know that. But it doesn't change the fact that we no longer have a relationship.'

He lifted a brow in silent mockery. 'A moment ago, when I was inside you, did that not feel as though we had a relationship?'

She felt her face turn scarlet. 'Don't talk like that.'

He gave a soft laugh. 'How can you still be shy with me? You are the most complex, confusing woman I've ever met. You don't mind indulging in hot, mindless sex but you don't want to talk about it. Don't pretend that nothing has changed between us, Amy. That would be foolish. And a waste of time. I'm not stupid and neither are you.'

She rose to her feet, unable to resist a sideways glance at his naked body. He was magnificent—his body lean and muscular, his stomach taut and flat, his olive skin liberally dusted with a pattern of dark hair that emphasised his virility and masculinity.

'Marco, don't do this. Please, don't do this.'

He rose to his feet, completely unselfconscious. 'You've lost weight.' Ignoring her plea, he slid a hand around her waist and drew her against him. 'But you're still beautiful.'

Amy put a hand on his chest. 'No.'

'Yes,' Marco purred softly, sliding his hands inside her jumper and smoothing her spine. 'Let's go upstairs to bed. This time we take more time. *Lentamente. Gentilmente.*'

Slow. Gentle.

Amy felt the smooth masculine tones connect with her insides. 'That would just confuse things even more and I'm confused enough already.'

'I am not at all confused.' He brushed her hair away from her neck, lowered his head and delivered a lingering kiss to the base of her throat. 'I am entirely clear about everything. And now we have the whole weekend ahead of us to make up for lost time.'

'No!' Dizzy from his touch, Amy gave him a push and forced herself to step backwards. 'No, Marco! I meant what I said—nothing has changed. You're not listening to me! I'm talking and you're *just not listening*!' Not trusting herself to be so close to him and not touch him, she walked over to the window and stared out into the darkness. Beyond the glass came the faint sound of the sea crashing onto the rocks below the house. 'All right, so we had sex—good sex—but it doesn't change the facts. We want different things. You still want a family and I still want a career.'

'Ah, yes.' He sounded unperturbed. 'A career. You don't love me enough, isn't that right?'

'That's right.' After what they'd just shared, she couldn't look at him. 'I don't.'

'And you always have sex with men that you have no feeling for, no? That is so typical of you, isn't it, *tesoro*?'

How did he know so much about her when they'd spent so little time together? She forced herself to turn, noticing in a glance that he'd pulled on his trousers but his torso was still bare. 'I can understand why you might read more into what just happened but, please, don't. It really was just sex, Marco. And it wasn't that surprising. The chemistry between us always led us into trouble.'

His gaze was brooding. 'Talking of trouble—since you are still so set on following this career path and not having a family, we probably ought to talk about contraception.'

'There's no need. It won't happen again.'

'I wasn't talking about the future,' he said gently, reaching for his jumper, 'I was talking about the past. We just had unprotected sex, *amore*. Do you want the morning-after pill? I have some in my bag.'

She froze. 'No.' Her mouth was so dry she could barely answer the question. 'No, that won't be necessary.'

'Why not?' He moved towards her, his eyes intent on her face. 'You have decided that you will take your chances? If you become pregnant, you will have a family and abandon your ideas of a career? You are leaving the choice to fate perhaps?'

'None of those things. There just isn't any way I could get pregnant.' She kept her tone casual, assuming that he'd take her comment to mean that it was the wrong time of the month, but he swore softly in Italian and his eyes darkened with anger.

Amy watched him, confused by his reaction. Only a moment ago he'd offered her contraception. Surely he wouldn't want her to get pregnant, given the mess that their marriage was in?

So why did he look as though he wanted to put his fist through the window?

Marco ran out of the back door and onto the coast road. It was dark but he didn't care because he knew the road as well as he knew his own kitchen and he needed to burn off his anger.

She'd turned down the morning-after pill.

There was no way she could get pregnant. Wasn't that what she'd said?

So what did that mean? That she was already taking contraception?

They'd been apart for two years so there was only one reason why she would be using contraception.

Jealousy dug its claws in deep and he increased his speed, pounding along the road, ignoring the punch of the wind and the bite of the cold as he tried to outrun his demons.

Obviously it was as he'd first suspected.

She'd found someone else.

Was that why she'd been crying? Was that why Nick had encouraged him to find out more about her past? Was this man an ex-lover? Someone she'd known before she'd met him?

Marco pounded along the road, his mind full of questions.

Was this mystery man the reason she'd been so intent on ending their marriage?

He ran until the breath tore through his lungs and then he stopped, breathing heavily, forcing his mind to work.

This was Amy. *Amy.* Not any other woman. She wasn't a woman to take a string of lovers. Despite the evidence, it didn't fit with what he knew of her.

Amy would only indulge in a physical relationship with a man if she cared deeply.

But if she didn't have another man, why was she using contraception?

Marco ran a hand over the back of his neck, remembering the way she'd clung to him and urged him on, *remembering the sort of woman he knew her to be*, and knew that he wasn't mistaken in her feelings for him.

She cared deeply. For him. After what they'd shared that afternoon, he knew that she was still in love with him. So why was she so intent on denying it?

Why did she want to end their marriage?

Amy lay on the bed with her eyes wide open, staring at the ceiling, full of regrets. She should have kept her distance from Marco. She should have known that she wouldn't be able to resist him.

If only she'd walked away from him the moment she'd felt the tension sizzling between them.

If only she had more self-control.

If only—the two most useless words in the human language. The slam of the door downstairs announced that Marco was back from his run, but judging from the violence of the sound his temper hadn't improved.

Hardly surprising perhaps, running in the freezing wind in the darkness.

Amy closed her eyes, feeling nothing but sympathy for him. Their impulsive love-making session had left her feeling equally confused and frustrated. That was what happened when you gave in to chemistry.

It produced complications.

It was some consolation that he had no more self-control than she did.

The door to her bedroom opened and she turned her head and saw him standing in the doorway, broad-shouldered and powerful. There was a sheen of sweat on his forehead and he'd clearly pushed himself to the limit physically.

His eyes glittered darkly and his mouth was set in a grim line. 'Is there someone else?'

'I'm sorry?' The question was so surprising that she sat up instantly, her eyes wide. 'What do you mean, someone else?'

'It's a plausible reason for you to end our marriage.'

'Marco, I've told you why I ended our marriage. There isn't anyone else in my life.' And there never would be. She had nothing to offer any man.

'So why are you taking contraception?'

'I never said that I was—' She broke off, realising too late that she'd revealed far too much yet again. How did people ever lie and cheat? She was hopeless, absolutely hopeless.

'You said that there was absolutely no chance that you could possibly become pregnant.'

Her heart pounded against her chest. 'It's just not the right time of the month.'

'Nature isn't that predictable, as you and I both know. If you are truly this career person now, why would you want to risk having a baby?' He strode into the room, his eyes fixed on her face. 'I've been thinking about this, going through the facts, sifting through the options, and I've only come up with one possible explanation for the way you're behaving. You don't think you *can* become pregnant, is that right?'

She felt the colour drain from her face. 'Marco…'

He watched her and nodded slowly. 'That's it, isn't it? You can't have a baby.'

Amy shrank back on the bed, her arms around her knees like a child. 'Go away, Marco.' She was shivering again and the headache was back. 'I want to be on my own.'

'Well, that's tough, because when you're married there are two people involved.' His voice soft, he sat down on the edge of the bed. 'An honest woman makes a hopeless liar, Amy, and you are an honest woman. Since the day you told me you were leaving, nothing you have said has made sense.'

'Marco, please—'

'You are a mass of inconsistencies. You keep telling me that you want a career and although you are undoubtedly an excellent doctor, it's always been clear to me that what you really long for is a family. You say you don't want children and yet I see you with them and you are warm and kind. And you say that you don't love me but when we are together…' he reached out and slid a hand under her jaw, gently insisting that she look at him '…you give everything, *tesoro*. What we shared earlier—that wasn't sex, it was love.'

She sucked in a juddering breath. 'Don't do this. The truth is that none of the reasons matter. The end is the same. I can't be with you.'

His thumb gently stroked her jaw. 'We both know that is nonsense. We were meant to be together.'

'No.' Tears welled up and spilled onto her cheeks. 'Don't let's have this conversation! I've already cried more today than in my whole life!'

'Emotion is a good thing. Only the English treat emotion

as if it were a dangerous animal.' His faintly humourous analysis of her countrymen would have made her smile at any other time.

But she was a long way from smiling.

She wiped one cheek with the back of her hand. 'Emotion gives you a headache.'

'*Cucciola mia.*'

She sniffed and tried to ignore the insistent brush of his fingers on her face. 'That's what you called Michelle. I don't even know what it means.'

'Literally?' He slid his hand behind her neck, leaned forward and kissed her gently on the mouth. Then he lifted his head and gave a slow smile. 'It is a puppy.'

'So now you're calling me a dog?'

He laughed softly. 'So now I finally see the Amy I used to know. For a long time she was afraid to come out, but I knew she was tucked away in there somewhere. I want to ask you something and I want an honest answer—probably the first one you've given me for a long time.'

'I don't want to talk about this.'

'Shh…' Amusement in his eyes, he pressed his fingers to her lips. 'You need to stop arguing with me. It's bad for you, *amore*, and it gives me indigestion. A good Italian wife should agree with everything her husband says.'

Her heart aching, she gave a wobbly smile. 'I don't think I'm a good Italian wife, that's what I've been trying to tell you.' Her smile faded. 'I can't do any of the things that a good Italian wife is supposed to do. For a start, I don't even speak the language.'

'This could be good! Most Italian men would kill to have a wife who couldn't answer back!' His eyes gleamed but this time she didn't manage a smile in response. How could he be so good about it all? Did he understand what she was telling him?

'You're refusing to take me seriously.'

'*Sì*, that's right, I am.' Suddenly his voice was deadly serious. 'Because you are talking nonsense. What is this about? Who is this "good Italian wife"? I didn't pick an Italian for my wife—I picked you.'

It was time to spell it out. 'But I can't have children, Marco. You're right about that. I'm infertile.' There. She'd said it. Finally, after two long years of anguish and misery, she'd said it. Such a small word for something so big.

There was a moment of silence and she saw a muscle flicker in his lean cheek but when he spoke his voice was calm and even. 'I understand that. What I *don't* understand is why this made you leave. Why would this have an impact on our marriage? Why didn't you share it with me?'

'Because I was afraid you'd say that it wouldn't make a difference.' She pulled away from him and hugged her knees tighter.

'It doesn't make a difference. A relationship starts with two people, *amore*. Later on more may be added but always it starts just with two.'

'I know how much you want children.'

'Look at me, Amy.' His voice was firm and he nodded when she lifted her head. 'That's better. Yes, I would like children but I am not a child myself. I know that life doesn't always give us what we want or plan for and being an adult is about making choices. When I asked you to marry me I made a choice, *tesoro*. You were my choice.'

She struggled with the tears again. 'Pretty lousy choice.'

'Certainly it's true I would have preferred to have a wife who didn't run away to a different continent for two years,' he said mildly, 'but you are back now and everything is sorted. That's all that matters.'

'How can you say that? Nothing is sorted.'

'*Belissima...*' His voice infinitely gentle, he cupped her

face in his hands and forced her to look at him. 'You are determined to make life so complicated.'

'You can't pretend that this is nothing, Marco!'

'No, I'm not going to do that. But neither am I going to sacrifice our relationship for it. And neither should you isolate yourself.' He said something in Italian and she looked at him expectantly.

'In English?'

He slid his fingers through her hair in an unmistakable gesture of affection. 'I said that this didn't happen to you, it happened to us. And now we will deal with it. There are lots of options.'

Unable to help herself, Amy leaned against his chest and felt his arms close around her. She felt his warmth, his strength and she closed her eyes for a moment, greedy for the comfort even though she knew it could only be temporary.

For her there were no options. None.

Marco locked the bathroom door securely and then crossed to the washbasin, his breathing unsteady as he struggled with the emotion that he'd been holding back.

Two years.

They'd wasted two years.

His jaw tensed and he gripped the edge of the basin so hard that his knuckles whitened.

When he'd finally realised the truth, it had taken all his self-control not to erupt with anger. But then he'd seen the torment in her eyes and realised that she'd made the decision to leave him based on a set of beliefs of which he had absolutely no understanding.

Was that what Nick had meant when he'd hinted that he should find out more about her past?

And what exactly was it in her past that made Amy so sure that their marriage couldn't survive the blow of infertility? Why did she think there were no options?

Inhaling deeply, Marco turned on the taps and splashed his face with cold water.

'Marco?' Amy's voice came from outside the bathroom, tentative and unsure. 'Are you all right?'

Marco reached for a towel and stared at his reflection in the mirror. *Was he all right?* He was angry, frustrated and disappointed, but he knew that displaying those emotions wouldn't help his cause.

What he needed to do was prove to Amy that their marriage had a future. And to do that he needed to understand why she was of the opposite opinion.

And she didn't need his anger. She needed his patience.

'I'm fine.' He kept his voice even. 'I'll be out in a moment, *amore*.'

And they were going to do some talking.

CHAPTER EIGHT

THE following morning Marco was no closer to answers despite having spent a long and sleepless night examining that question in detail.

He'd *known* she wasn't a career woman.

He'd *known* she'd loved him.

Why hadn't he managed to unravel the problem sooner?

Since when had he been so obtuse?

All he had to do now was convince her that it didn't make a difference to their marriage.

He heard a noise behind him and turned to find her standing in the doorway to the bathroom. She'd borrowed one of his T-shirts to sleep in and she looked impossibly young and slender, her face free of make-up and worryingly pale.

'*Buongiorno, tesoro.* I'm sorry if I woke you. I have surgery this morning.'

'So do I. I agreed it with Nick.' Her eyes slid from his and she gave an awkward smile. 'I'll go and use the other bathroom, shall I?'

'Go back to bed.' He splashed his face and reached for a towel. 'You're not in a fit state to do surgery. Yesterday was a huge trauma for you and you've had no sleep. I'll take your patients and I'll explain to Nick.'

'I'll be fine when I've had a shower.' After a moment's

hesitation she reached into the shower cubicle and turned on the water. 'You're not doing the surgery on your own, Dr Avanti. Who do you think you are? Superman?'

'Superdoctor, actually.' He watched hungrily as she pulled the T-shirt over her head and stepped naked into the shower. Her breasts were high and firm, her waist tiny and her hips gently curved. Gripped by a vicious attack of lust, Marco stood for a moment, feeling himself grow hard. Then he gave a soft curse and stepped into the shower with her.

She gave a gasp of shock and turned, clearing the water from her eyes. 'What are you doing? You've had your shower.'

'I decided I needed another one.' He stroked a hand down her smooth, silky skin and gave a groan of masculine appreciation. 'I've been deprived of your body for too long.'

'I thought you said I was too thin.'

He smiled and curved her body against his, ignoring the relentless sting of the water. 'My beautiful Amy, so much a woman. Always insecure and with no reason.'

'Marco…' She sounded breathless. 'We don't have time for this.'

'I can always make time for something important.'

'Things are complicated enough already—'

'If life isn't complicated, I become bored.' He buried his head in her neck and slid his hands over the soft curve of her bottom. Then he gave up on English and spoke only Italian.

'Marco, no…' But her words were insincere and her head fell back and her eyes closed. 'We really can't—*non posso*—' Then she gasped as she felt the intimate stroke of his fingers.

'You have been learning Italian for me?'

'Marco…' She stroked a hand over her face to remove the water. Her hair was dark and sleek under the jet of the shower, her eyelashes spiky. *And she'd never looked more beautiful.*

Unable to hold himself back a moment longer, Marco

brought his mouth down on hers. He felt her arms come round his neck, felt the tantalising brush of her firm breasts against his chest hair, and then he was pressing her back against the wall of the shower, his need for her so great that it bordered on the primitive.

With no preliminaries he slid his hands over her thighs and lifted her, winding her legs around his body and sinking inside her in a series of hard, determined thrusts.

'Marco…' She cried out his name and he felt the scrape of her fingernails on his shoulders, and then they were moving together, the pleasure so wild and intense that there was no holding back.

He felt her tighten around him, the involuntary spasms of her body driving him forward to his own savage release. As he tumbled over the edge into paradise he gave an agonised groan and thrust hard, his fingers biting into her soft flesh, his mouth locked on hers as he swallowed her cries.

It took him several moments to realise that he was probably hurting her and that water was still thundering down his back. He lowered her carefully and then stroked her soaking hair away from her face.

'Did I hurt you, *amore*?'

'No.' Her voice was a whisper and drops of water clung to her lashes and to her lips. 'You've never hurt me. But I've hurt you, I know I have. I'm sorry for everything, Marco.'

He held her face gently. 'Pain is part of every relationship.'

'I'm sorry,' she whispered again. 'Really sorry that it turned out this way for us.'

'Hush.' He pulled her against him, feeling her tremble, acutely aware of her fragility and vulnerability. 'Everything will be all right, I promise. You will trust me, *tesoro*.'

She stayed like that for a moment, her head against his chest, and then she pulled away. 'We have less than ten minutes before surgery starts.'

He flashed her a smile and reached for a towel. 'Then it is fortunate for both of us that I have an Italian sports car.'

Throughout the whole of Saturday surgery, Amy couldn't stop thinking about Marco. Her body ached from their encounter in the shower and she knew that even though he now understood the real reason for her departure, nothing had changed.

Her last patient of the morning was a mother with a young baby.

'Helen?' Amy smiled and forced herself to concentrate. 'What can I do for you?'

'It's Freddie. I'm so worried about him. He's always been a really sicky baby, but it's getting worse and worse.'

'And how old is he now?' Amy quickly checked the records. 'Six weeks?'

'Yes. He always has brought up milk at the end of his feed.'

'Lots of babies do that.'

'I know but—' Helen broke off and bit her lip. 'I just feel as though something is wrong. He just isn't right, I know he isn't.'

'Let me examine him and see whether I can find anything.' Knowing better than to dismiss a mother's worries, Amy washed her hands and gently lifted the baby out of the car seat. 'I'm sorry to wake you, sweetheart,' she crooned, 'but I want to have a good look at you.'

The baby yawned and stretched then closed his eyes again.

'Is he always this lethargic?' Amy gently undid the poppers on the sleepsuit and undressed the baby down to his nappy.

'Yes. He sleeps all the time.'

Amy examined the baby's abdomen. 'When did you last have him weighed?'

'Last week. He'd lost some weight. The health visitor told

me to increase the feeds, but if I increase the feeds then I just increase the sick. It's got to the point where he's barely keeping anything down.'

Amy slid her hand over the baby's scalp, examining his fontanelle and finding it slightly sunken. 'He seems a bit dehydrated, Helen. Has he been having plenty of wet nappies?'

'Actually, now you mention it, no.' Helen frowned. 'They used to be quite heavy, but now I sometimes don't even bother changing it because it seems dry. What does that mean?'

'It could mean that he isn't getting enough fluid.'

'Because he's bringing it all up?'

Amy finished the examination, popped him back into his sleepsuit and handed the baby back to Helen. 'You're still breastfeeding?'

'Yes.'

'Wait there just a moment, Helen. I'm going to ask my colleague to have a look at him.'

She tapped on Marco's door and found that he had already finished surgery. 'Can I grab you for a minute?'

'*Sì.*' He leaned back in his chair and gave her a slow, sexy smile. 'Do you want to grab me here or wait until we are home?'

Remembering his performance in the shower, she felt the colour ooze into her cheeks and clearly he read her mind because he raised an eyebrow and his eyes mocked her gently.

'Any time you are ready for a repeat performance, you just have to say the word. Or don't even speak—just switch on the shower and strip naked.'

'Marco!' She glared at him, flustered by the sudden intimacy in his gaze. 'I—I wanted to talk about a patient.'

'I know, but I love to tease you because you always blush. You are the only woman I've ever met who can be hot and shy at the same time.' He leaned back in his chair. 'I am listening, *tesoro*. You need the advice of the master? Superdoctor?'

She looked at him. 'Has a woman ever hit you really, really hard?'

'Such passion.' His smile widened. 'My little English Amy is becoming *al*most Italian.'

'Marco—be serious.'

'I'm serious.' He leaned forward. 'What is your problem, *amore*? Tell me and I will solve it.'

'I have this little baby in my consulting room.'

His smile vanished and he rose to his feet. 'And seeing the baby has upset you? It is too difficult for you emotionally? You want me to handle it?'

Touched by his protectiveness, she shook her head swiftly. 'No, it's nothing like that. It's just that I'm worried about him and I wondered if you'd look at him. He's dehydrated, vomiting after every feed and very, very lethargic. I think he has pyloric stenosis.'

Marco frowned. 'Unlikely. It isn't that common.'

'That's why I wanted you to check him. And you're the one who always taught me to remember the uncommon, particularly when faced by a worried mother.'

'True enough.' He shrugged. 'Have you examined the baby feeding?'

'No.' She shook her head and frowned. 'I didn't think to do that.'

'So—we will do it together.'

They walked back to her consulting room and Marco smiled at Helen. 'You had a good, relaxing Christmas? Plenty of food and wine?'

'I was cooking for twelve so it wasn't exactly relaxing.' Helen gave a wry smile. 'I must admit I'm pretty exhausted. I wondered if that was why Freddie had lost weight. I can't believe my milk is much good at the moment.'

Marco washed his hands. 'You shouldn't have been cooking. Your family should have been pampering you with a little one this age.' He leaned forward and stroked a gentle hand over the baby's head. 'Can I take him?'

Helen nodded and Marco scooped the baby up confidently. 'Are you giving your mother worries?' He gazed down at the baby and gave a faint smile. 'Amazing that something so small can be so much trouble.'

Amy swallowed hard, wishing it wasn't quite so hard watching him with babies.

His gaze shifted from the baby to her and she knew instinctively that he'd followed the direction of her thoughts. He gave her a warm, reassuring smile and her stomach shifted.

What was he thinking?

His eyes searched hers for a moment and then he handed the baby back to Helen. 'Amy is right that the baby is a little dehydrated. You say that he is vomiting after every feed. Is he ready for a feed now?'

'He's a bit sleepy.'

'That might be because he hasn't had enough fluid. Dehydration can make him sleepy. We will undress him a bit—make him a bit less comfortable.' Marco's fingers moved over the baby, undressing, tickling, waking him up, and eventually Freddie yawned. 'So—now try and feed him. He is a man after all, so his stomach is probably a priority for him.'

Helen smiled and put the baby to her breast. Freddie played with the nipple doubtfully and Marco curved a strong hand over the back of the baby's head and guided him gently.

'You are starving hungry, you know you are.'

The baby latched on and Helen looked at Marco. 'He's feeding. Now what?'

'Now I want to look at his tummy.' Marco crouched down and looked at the baby's abdomen. Then he gently felt the stomach. 'Amy? Can you see?' He trailed a finger over the stomach. 'The muscles are straining. They're moving from left to right as they try and push milk through the pylorus. And on the right side I can feel a small, hard lump. You're right, I think. Clever girl.' He rose to his feet and washed his hands.

Helen looked between the two of them. 'So what's wrong with him?'

Amy reached for a piece of paper and a pen. 'We think he has something called pyloric stenosis. Basically it means that the passage between the stomach and the small bowel is narrowed and that stops milk passing into the bowel.' She drew a simple picture to illustrate what she was saying and Helen stared at it.

'But why would that happen?'

'No one really knows. It tends to affect more boys than girls. Has anyone else in your family had the same problem?'

Helen shook her head and Freddie let go of the breast and vomited violently. It cleared Helen's lap and landed on Amy's feet. 'Oh!' Mortified, Helen lifted the baby and reached for a cloth. 'I'm so, so sorry.'

'It's fine, really.' Amy smiled and mopped up the mess with paper towels. 'But I think our diagnosis has just been confirmed.' She looked at Marco. 'Projectile vomiting?'

Helen cuddled Freddie tightly. 'So what happens now?'

'We refer him to the hospital,' Marco said. 'They may want to do more tests—an ultrasound scan, possibly, to get a picture of the muscle.'

'Will that hurt him?'

Marco shook his head. 'It is like the scan they give you in pregnancy.'

'And then what?'

'He will need a small operation to cut through the thickened muscle so that food can then pass into the bowel.'

'An operation?' Helen looked horrified. 'Is it a big one? How long will it take?'

'Probably about half an hour, no more than that. And afterwards he will be given painkillers.'

'I can't bear the thought of him having an operation.' Helen's eyes filled. 'He's so little.'

'But at the moment he can't digest his food,' Amy said gently. 'He needs help, Helen.'

'What a Christmas this has been.' Helen brushed away the tears and sniffed. 'All right. Well, if that's what he needs—when will he have to have it done?'

'Soon, because he is dehydrated.' Marco walked over to Amy's computer. 'We will call the hospital now and talk to the doctors. You should take him straight to the paediatric ward.'

'But it's Saturday!'

'And they will probably put up a drip and give him some fluid.' Marco swiftly completed a referral letter. 'That way they can correct the dehydration before they operate.'

'And when is that likely to be?'

'They will need to check that his blood has the right balance of minerals and salts and then they will operate as soon as possible.'

Helen strapped Freddie back into the car seat and lifted it. 'All right. I'll take him up to the hospital right away. Thank you, both of you.'

'Try not to worry,' Marco said gently, his eyes warm and kind. 'It will be all fine in the end.'

Helen gave a wobbly smile. 'I hope so. Thanks again.'

She left the room, clutching the letter in her hand and Amy sighed. 'Poor thing. What a worry.'

'Yes. Having children also comes with an ocean of worries,' Marco said quietly, walking towards the door. 'Call Paeds. I'll be waiting in the car park for you.'

She sat down at her desk and reached for the phone. 'Why?'

'I need to give you a lift home. We have the rest of the weekend off.'

'And?' *What did he have in mind?*

He smiled. 'First I am going to take you home and wash the vomit off you, then we are going for a bracing walk and finally we are having dinner at the Smugglers' Inn.'

She opened her mouth and closed it again. 'Has anyone ever told you that you're controlling?'

His smile widened. 'I'm a man who knows what he wants, that's true. Don't forget it, *amore*. Now, ring the hospital.'

'I always loved this part of the North Cornish coast.' Amy stared ahead of her, the wind whipping her hair across her face. 'It's wild, isn't it? You can so easily imagine wrecks and smugglers.' She tensed as she felt Marco's arms slide round her.

'It is wild yes, but—' He broke off and gave a shrug that betrayed his Mediterranean heritage. 'Truly? I prefer the beauty of the Amalfi coast. I like to admire the coastline without risking frostbite. One day I will take you to Positano and you will understand what I mean. Positano is a little town that clings to the cliff like a jewel in a necklace. You would love it. And it's very romantic.'

'Positano.' She turned, a smile on her face. 'You sounded so Italian when you said that.'

'*Sì*, because I *am* Italian. So, of course, I sound Italian.' He lowered his mouth to hers and she felt her body melt under the pressure of his kiss. 'Are you ready to go back?'

Still in the circle of his arms, she glanced out to sea again. 'I suppose so.'

'You came here with your grandmother?'

'No. On my own. I used to sit and stare at the waves for hours.'

'That sounds lonely.'

Her whole childhood had been lonely. 'I was used to it.'

'Tell me what made you think you might be infertile.'

Surprised by the sudden change of subject, she looked up at him. 'I had tests.'

'Without telling me?' His eyes darkened ominously and she sighed.

'At the time I didn't think there was anything to tell. To be honest, I didn't really think anything would be wrong.' She wriggled out of his arms, finding it impossible to talk about such a difficult subject when they were so closely entwined. 'We hadn't used any contraception for months—'

'No time at all.'

'I know that.' She took a deep breath. 'But I just had…a bad feeling. It was always a worry of mine.'

'Why would you worry about it? Had you ever tried for a baby before?'

'No.' She threw him a puzzled glance, surprised by the question. 'You know I hadn't.'

'I don't know that. I know very little about your past before you met me.' He reached out, caught a strand of hair that was blowing in front of her face and tucked it behind her ear. 'If I'm honest, I wasn't very interested in your past.'

And she wasn't interested in talking about it.

The touch of his fingers made her stomach tumble and Amy had to force herself to concentrate on the conversation. 'I bumped into a friend of mine who runs an infertility clinic. She suggested I have some tests, so I did.'

'And you didn't think it worth mentioning to me?' Some of the warmth had left his voice and she turned to him.

'You have every right to be angry with me but you have to try and see it from my point of view. If I'd told you, you would have said that it was too soon to worry.'

'It was.'

'No! As it turns out, it wasn't! And I was able to end our marriage quickly.'

'And I'm supposed to be grateful for that?'

'No. Yes.' She wrapped her arms around herself to keep out the cold. 'I don't know. I just know that I ended something that would have ended anyway.'

'You think I would have divorced you for being infertile?' His tone was incredulous. 'Is that truly what you think of me?'

'No, actually.' She turned to him, her voice flat. 'I think you probably would have stayed with me because for all your arrogance and self-confidence you're a decent man and I think you would have felt an obligation. I didn't want that. Only one of us can't have children in this relationship, so there was no need for both of us to suffer.'

His hands closed over her arms and he jerked her against him. 'You think I didn't suffer, *tesoro*?' His eyes blazed into hers. *'You think I didn't suffer when you walked away from me?'*

'I'm sure you did.' The wind howled angrily around them but she ignored it. 'I'm sure you suffered. But nowhere near as much as we both would have suffered if we'd limped along in our marriage.'

He stared down into her face for a moment, as if trying to work something out. Then he released her and his voice was flat. 'It's cold. Let's go home.'

He didn't understand.

And she couldn't expect him to.

Because she hadn't told him who she was or where she'd come from.

Their marriage was doomed, she knew that.

But she'd promised to help out in the practice so she'd work these few weeks and then end it properly. By then she would have been able to convince Marco that it was the right thing for both of them.

They returned from their walk and Marco dragged her into his arms and kissed her, his mouth demanding and passionate. Then he released her suddenly and took a step backwards. 'Let's go to the Smugglers' Inn.'

'Now?' Still dizzy from his kiss, she looked at him, trying to focus. 'You want to go out?'

'I think it's a good idea. We need to talk. And if we stay here...' he smiled the smile of a red-blooded male '...we won't talk. Even I won't be tempted to make love to you in front of the locals so we'll talk on neutral territory.'

'There's really nothing left to say, Marco. We don't have to go out. I could cook something.'

'Out of what?' He gave a humourless laugh. 'Have you checked in the fridge, Amy? Housekeeping isn't exactly my strong point at the best of times and these certainly aren't the best of times. Unless you nipped out between patients, I'm guessing that you haven't been to the supermarket either?'

His accent was more than usually pronounced and she gave a soft smile. 'No, I haven't. And you don't have to tell me that housekeeping isn't your strong point. You've always been a very traditional Italian male. You want your woman in the kitchen.'

And she'd loved that.

She'd loved the fact that she had finally been able to create a home.

She glanced around her, at the house she'd chosen, *the place she'd wanted to raise their children.*

His eyes trapped hers and he inhaled deeply. 'Not *that* traditional,' he said huskily. 'I was more than happy for you to pursue a career if that was truly what you wanted. But it wasn't, was it?'

She shifted. 'Do you want to argue about this now or shall we go to the pub?'

'Subject avoidance appears to be your favourite activity at the moment.' He gave a shake of his head. 'Let's go to the pub. Give me five minutes to change.'

Deciding that jeans were perfectly acceptable for a casual supper at the Smugglers' Inn, Amy didn't bother changing but went into her bathroom, splashed her face with cold water and applied some make-up. Remembering everyone's comments on how pale she was, she gave her cheeks an extra swipe with the blusher brush and then decided that she looked like a clown and rubbed it off again.

She was pale, yes. But apart from that she looked quite normal. Nothing like a woman whose insides were in turmoil and whose heart was breaking.

'Ready?' Marco stood in the doorway, a black jumper brushing the hard lines of his jaw, his eyes glittering dangerously. There was fire and confrontation in his eyes and Amy swallowed, remembering the passion that had exploded between them that morning. *And the previous evening.*

Perhaps they were right to go out.

They couldn't just carry on making love, could they? What did that solve? Nothing. If anything, it made things worse. They were becoming more and more entwined in the emotional web they were spinning and before long it would be almost impossible to extricate themselves.

Realising that the evening wasn't going to be easy, Amy gave a sigh as she followed him out of the room and waited while he locked the front door.

It was dark and cold and she snuggled deeper into her coat.

'Do you think it's going to snow again?' She slid into the Maserati, enjoying the warmth and the smell of leather.

'I have no idea.' Marco waited while she closed the door. 'I hope not. The car hates it. I hate it. The only place I want snow is when I'm skiing and there isn't much of that on the North Cornish coast.'

Amy smiled at the thought of skiing in Penhally. 'The car is still working, then, despite the cold?'

'*Sì*, occasionally.' Humour in his voice, Marco leaned across and fastened her seat belt then slid his hands over the steering-wheel in a gesture of affection. 'Except when she wants to make my life difficult. Which, of course, she does quite often.' The engine gave a throat roar and Marco steered the car onto the coast road.

'Why is it a "she"? Why does it have to be a woman?'

'Of course she is a woman.' Smoothly he changed gear, his eyes fixed on the road. 'You only have to look at her temperament. She's moody sometimes. Unpredictable. Determined to frustrate. And then other times—she is a dream.' He spoke with such affection that she looked at him with disbelief.

'Marco Avanti, you're a qualified doctor, not a little boy with a toy. You're just a little bit crazy, do you know that?'

He turned his head quickly and gave her a sexy smile. 'Crazy is good, no? Sensible is…' He removed one hand from the wheel and slid it over her knee. 'English? No passion. No emotion.'

Feeling the sudden rush of heat inside her body, Amy coloured, relieved that it was dark. Everything she knew about passion and emotion she'd learned from him. Her response to him had always astonished her. It was as if he drew out a part of her that she hadn't known existed.

'We're so different. How did we ever end up together?'

'Because what we have is powerful.' He increased speed and she gripped the edge of the seat and gasped.

'Marco! Are you planning to end the year with a speeding ticket?'

'Calm down. This car spends so long in the garage that she needs a run occasionally. And, anyway, the police have better things to do than check my speed.' Marco swooped into the car park and turned off the engine.

Feeling relieved that they were still alive, Amy undid her seat belt. *If he were less macho, would it be easier to resist him?*

Or was it his blatant, unashamed masculinity that was so attractive?

Marco was red-blooded male, through and through. Women sensed it within moments of meeting him. *She'd* sensed it.

She shivered as she slammed the car door and felt the wind whip round her body. 'It's cold.' She felt his arm slide round her and then he was urging her across the car park and into the welcoming warmth of the pub.

'*Buenas noches*, Marco,' Tony called out from the bar, and Marco sighed.

'You just wished me goodnight in Spanish, my friend. *Buona sera* is Italian. Don't you ever listen to anything I tell you?'

'Depends what it is.' Tony reached for a glass, a smile on his face. 'If you're telling me to eat less fat, no, I don't listen. If you're ordering a drink, my hearing improves.'

Marco glanced around the pub. 'It's quiet.'

'Early yet. Most folks are still tucked up indoors, away from the weather. It'll be crowded later. Always is. What will it be? Amy?'

'I'll have fizzy water.'

Tony lifted an eyebrow at Marco. 'Is she going to be decent company on fizzy water?'

Marco gave a slow, masculine smile. 'Unlike most of you Englishmen, I don't need to get my women drunk in order to seduce them. My company alone is enough.'

His comment was so outrageously arrogant that Amy couldn't hold back her laughter and he turned towards her, his attention caught, his expression curious. 'What is funny?'

'*You're* funny. You make me laugh. You always did.' Realising that paying him compliments wasn't going to help create distance between them, she turned away quickly and settled herself at the table by the fire. 'Nice fire, Tony.'

'Are you two eating? Specials are up on the board.'

Amy stared at the scrawl on the blackboard, wondering if she dared admit she wasn't hungry. There was something about being in love with Marco that just drove her appetite away.

'I'll have the goat's cheese salad,' she muttered, and Marco frowned.

'She'll have lamb hotpot. And I will, too.' He sat down opposite her and Amy gaped at him.

'I don't want lamb hotpot!'

'Amy.' His voice was patient. 'You look as though you've eaten nothing for the past two years. This morning you missed breakfast. The sandwich that Kate gave you at lunchtime came back uneaten. You are eating less than that baby we referred to the hospital. Tonight you're having lamb hotpot and you're eating it, even if I have to fork it into your mouth myself.'

'But I'm not—'

'Not hungry?' He finished the sentence for her and gave a nod of understanding. 'So—something is the matter? You are off your food because you are so in love with me you can't see straight, no?'

'Don't start, Marco. I don't love you. And you don't love me. Not enough.'

He studied her face in silence. 'All right. Because I need you to recover your appetite, we'll play a different game for the time being.' He leaned back, his dark eyes glittering in the light of the fire. 'I tell you one thing you don't know about me and you tell me one thing I don't know about you.'

'I don't like lamb hotpot. There.' She smiled innocently. 'That's my one thing. Now it's your turn.'

'I don't like really skinny women?'

She laughed. 'You should do an article for the local paper. It would help soothe all those poor women sobbing over the extra pounds they gained over Christmas.'

'Only women think that thin is attractive. All men prefer curves.'

Tony delivered the hotpot to the table and Amy sighed as she picked up her fork and looked at it without enthusiasm. 'Why is it that you always get your own way, Marco?'

'Because I'm always right?' His expression grew serious. 'I didn't get my own way when you left, Amy. That wasn't what I wanted.'

She stilled, the fork balanced in her fingers, her heart in her throat. 'I thought we weren't going to talk about this now.'

'You made the decision for both of us, just as I did with the hotpot.' His eyes challenged her. 'You didn't like it when I chose your food.'

'That's not the same thing at all.'

'You're right, it isn't. To select someone's meal for them…' he waved a hand dismissively '…that is nothing, I agree. But to choose someone's whole future—now, that's entirely different, *amore*.'

'That's not fair, Marco. A relationship can't work if one of the people involved doesn't want it to work. And I didn't—it wasn't what I wanted.'

'You're lying. You wanted it but you were afraid.' He leaned forward. 'My beautiful, cowardly Amy. You were afraid that infertility would wreck our marriage. So you wrecked it anyway. That is woman logic.'

'Woman logic?'

'*Sì*.' He dug into the hot pot. 'A man would not wreck something just in case.'

She inhaled deeply. 'It wasn't "just in case."'

'Eat.'

'But—'

'Eat, Amy, or I will have to force-feed you.'

She sighed and stabbed a small amount of food with her fork.

Marco sighed. 'Now put it in your mouth—yes, like that. Good. And now another mouthful. These tests you had done—I want to know what they told you.'

Amy stopped chewing and put down her fork. 'I had the usual done. The laparoscopy—'

'You had a laparoscopy?' He interrupted her, his tone rough. 'When? How? Where was I?'

'Busy. Working.' She shrugged. 'I don't know.'

The breath hissed through his teeth. 'All right—carry on. You had a laparoscopy. And then?'

'I had mild endometriosis. Nothing that needed treating. Just enough to have completely blocked my Fallopian tubes.' Her hand shaking, Amy picked up her fork again.

'So the laparoscopy suggested that your Fallopian tubes were not patent, is that right?'

'That's right.'

'Eat.'

Amy stared at the food on her fork. 'I really don't think I—'

'Eat.'

Aware that the pub was filling up and that a few people were glancing towards them, Amy dutifully took another mouthful of food. 'I'm not hungry.'

'Then you need to do more vigorous exercise, *amore*, increase that appetite of yours,' Marco purred softly, and her eyes flew to his.

'No, we mustn't. We mustn't do that again,' she whispered softly, and he lifted an eyebrow.

'And why not?'

'Because it is just confusing things.'

'I'm not confused.' He gave a slow, sexy smile and reached across the table and took her fork from her hand. 'I know exactly what I want. And I know exactly what you want, too, *tesoro*.'

'I want a divorce.' She heard his sigh and bit her lip. 'Marco, I know that we have fun together and I know that the sex is good.' She glanced swiftly towards the crowd at the bar but no one was paying them any attention. 'But our relationship can't carry on. It's over.'

The humour was gone from his eyes. 'It isn't over. We met and the chemistry was so powerful that for three days we didn't get out of bed. We made love almost continuously. Do you remember that, *amore*?'

Of course she remembered that. 'Perhaps that was the problem. We let the sex cloud our judgement. Sharing a bed is very different from sharing a life.'

'So you're still pretending that there is no emotional connection between us and never was?'

Trying to ignore the faint sarcasm in his tone, she straightened her back and didn't look at him. 'I like you, of course—'

'Amy, a woman doesn't lose her appetite over a serious case of "like". You were in love with me and you are still in love with me. Please, at least admit that.'

Her stomach churned. 'Answer me one question, Marco.' She pushed her plate away from her. 'How many times has a woman ended a relationship with you?'

'Never.'

Finally she looked at him. 'That's what I thought. So perhaps it's just very difficult for you to accept that I want to end the relationship.'

'You're implying that this is all about my ego?' He let out a long breath and shook his head in blatant disbelief. 'Sometimes, Amy, you are more trouble than the Maserati and that, as you say in English, is really saying something. Now, eat and forget our problems.'

Reluctantly Amy took a few more forkfuls of food. 'It's quite good,' she conceded, 'for hotpot.'

'*Sì*. And you are going to eat all of it. You're a good cook. Who taught you? Your mother?'

'No, my grandmother. She loved cooking, especially baking. Her cakes were amazing. She was quite a homely, domestic person. My mother wasn't.' Discovering that she was hungrier than she'd thought, Amy slowly ate her way through the bowl of food.

'Why did you stay with her on your own? Did your mother never join you?'

'She was always working and she needed somewhere for me to go during the holidays. And, anyway, they didn't get on. They had a difference of opinion.'

'About what?'

'About me. My mother never really wanted children.' Talking about herself felt uncomfortable and with a flash of panic she swiftly she changed the subject. 'How's Michelle Watson? Is she home from hospital?'

'Yes, and they have changed her asthma medication.' He gave a twisted smile. 'Poor Carol worries so much about her. I'm planning to call and see her tomorrow.'

'It's Sunday.'

'Sunday is the only day I have time to fit in that sort of visit. I need to check on her. She needs the support. And I also want to check on Lizzie.'

'They certainly didn't seem like a perfectly harmonious family.' Amy glanced around to check that no one was listening to them and then lowered her voice. 'I wondered whether Lizzie might be suffering from more than teenage tantrums.'

'Me, too. But it wasn't right to tackle the subject when the focus was on her sister.'

'Half-sister.'

'You think that might be the root of the problem?'

'I don't know. I suppose I'd start there.'

He nodded agreement. 'I will find a way of spending time with her tomorrow.'

Amy felt a warm rush of pride. 'You're a good doctor, Marco Avanti,' she said softly. 'You care about the children so much, I know.'

'And with that comment you have brought us back to our own problems. You are imagining that my life would be empty without my own children and that I'd therefore be better with a different woman.' He finished his food and put down his fork. 'Despite the fact you are an intelligent woman, you are putting two and two together and coming up with the wrong answer.'

She knew it wasn't the wrong answer.

She knew that from personal experience just how child-lessness could affect a marriage, but she wasn't ready to share that with him.

She'd never shared it with anyone. 'Do you miss paediatrics?'

'Sometimes. But I see a great number of the children in the practice and it is nice to have that long-term relationship so…' he shrugged '…in many ways I am very happy as a family doctor.'

'You've done a good job with the practice, you and Nick. It must have been awful after Annabel died.' She bit her lip. 'I—I didn't know or I would have written sooner.'

'He managed. I managed.' Marco shrugged again. 'The surgery carried on.'

'Kate's such a good practice manager.'

'Yes.' Marco finished his drink. 'Although I'm not sure how long she'll stay.'

'Really? She's thinking of leaving? Why?'

'I don't know that she's thinking of leaving. It is just a suspicion and I might be wrong. I just sense that things aren't altogether good for her at the moment.'

'Well, being a single mother must be hard,' Amy said quietly, and Marco nodded, his eyes on hers.

'And losing someone you love is even harder. All the more reason not to throw it away when you find it. Let's go home, *amore*. It is more comfortable to argue at home.'

But they didn't argue.

They made love and then talked long into the night. And Marco didn't mention loving or leaving. He just seduced and possessed her until she was no longer capable of rational thought.

Until she'd forgotten why it was that she had to leave.

CHAPTER NINE

ON MONDAY Amy worked her way through a steady flow of patients, but couldn't stop thinking about the visit she and Marco had made to see little Michelle the day before. There had been no sign of Lizzie and Carol had told them in an embarrassed voice that the teenager had come in drunk the night before and was sleeping it off. So Marco had merely checked on Michelle and reassured Carol, but Amy knew that he was still determined to spend some time with Lizzie.

'Amy?' The door opened and Nick walked into her consulting room. 'I've been thinking about the conversation we had on Friday afternoon. I think you need to tell Marco the truth.'

Still wondering about Lizzie, Amy pulled her mind back to the present. 'I've told him.'

'Ah.' He looked at her expectantly. 'And?'

'And nothing. It doesn't change anything just because he knows. Our marriage is still over.' She almost laughed as she listened to herself and recalled the passion of the weekend. For a marriage that was over, the relationship was intensely passionate.

And she was making trouble for herself, she knew she was. The web was tightening.

Nick looked startled. 'That's what Marco wants?'

'Well, no, not exactly.' Amy fiddled with her pen, 'He doesn't think he wants it, but I know it's the best thing for both of us.'

'You're deciding for both of you again? On what basis?'

On the basis of her past. On the basis that she had first-hand experience in this area.

Dark memories oozed into her brain and she pushed them away resolutely. 'Yes,' she croaked, 'I am deciding for both of us. Once Kate finds a locum, I'll be off.'

'Does Marco know you still feel like this?'

'I keep telling him. He doesn't seem to be listening.'

Nick grimaced. 'That sounds like Marco. He has a way of ploughing through obstacles that get in the way of what he wants. He did it when we were setting up this place. You might find he changes your mind yet.'

'That isn't going to happen.' *She couldn't let it happen.* 'In the meantime, I'll do the job you're paying me to do.'

Nick stood for a moment. 'This must be very hard for you, Amy. If you need a shoulder…' He gave a wry smile and raked a hand through his hair. 'I'm not sure that relationship counselling is my forte, but—'

'I'm fine, Nick,' she said quietly, 'but thank you. I'll manage on my own.'

The way she'd always managed. It was what she did. The way she lived her life.

The whole of Penhally came to life on New Year's Eve.

Despite another small flurry of snow and the drop in temperature, the shops were crowded as people rushed around, preparing for the celebrations. The off licence did a steady trade as people bought bottles of champagne and then picked their way home along the snowy pavements, bottles clanking in plastic bags, their breath clouding the freezing air.

The surgery was also busy and it was almost the end of the

day before Amy managed to find time to nip to the staffroom for a cup of tea.

'You, too?' Kate followed her into the staffroom and filled the kettle. 'If I don't have a cup of tea this minute, my throat is going to collapse in protest. The pavements are icy and we've had several people in after falls, but at least the wind has dropped, which is good news. The firework display should be able to go ahead. They've brought it forward to six o'clock so that the children can enjoy it. Everyone will have time to go home and get changed before the party at the Penhally Arms. What are you wearing?'

Amy hesitated. 'I'm not going.'

Kate gaped at her. 'Not going? Amy, you *have* to go. It's *the* event of the year. Well, maybe not quite the year, but it's certainly the event of the winter.' She gave a rueful smile. 'Not that that's saying much around here. We're a bit short of entertainment on the long, dark nights, as you well know.'

'I can't go, Kate.' Amy took two mugs from the cupboard and Kate dropped a tea bag in each. 'It would just be too awkward.'

'Why? What's awkward about it?' Kate poured water into the mugs. 'You're working here, aren't you? You're living with Marco. Everyone knows you're together—'

'We're not together. Not in the way you mean.'

'Oh. I hoped…' Kate finished making the tea and took it with her to the nearest chair. 'Well, anyway, it's just a party, Amy. I don't understand the problem. Do you have a dress?'

'No.' Amy thought about the contents of the wardrobe. *The wardrobe she'd abandoned along with that whole part of her life.* 'Well, yes, I suppose I do have a dress, but it isn't really suitable. I mean, it isn't me any more.'

Kate sipped her tea. 'Was it you once upon a time?'

Without thinking she answered. 'Oh, yes. It was Marco's favourite. Whenever I wore it we never actually managed to—' She broke off, suddenly embarrassed by how much she'd revealed, but Kate simply chuckled.

'You never actually managed to leave the house in it? If it was that good, you should definitely wear it to the party tonight. In fact, I insist on it. If you don't turn up wearing it I'm going to drive you home myself and force you to change.'

Amy sighed and shook her head. 'I don't think the dress sends out the right message.'

'What does that matter?' Kate's tone was dry. 'Since when did men take any notice of the messages we give them, anyway? Especially men like Marco. Whatever the dress is saying, Marco will hear what he wants to hear, take it from me. He's that kind of guy.'

Amy's stomach lurched alarmingly and she wondered fleetingly just how well Kate knew Marco. *Kate was an attractive woman.*

And then she pushed the thought away. Kate and Marco had been colleagues for two years. It was natural that they'd know each other quite well.

And she had no right to be possessive. She was letting him go. 'I honestly don't think a party is the right way to spend an evening.'

'Are things that bad?' Kate's voice was gentle. 'I was really hoping that the two of you might have patched up your marriage.'

'We haven't.'

'I'm sorry. And surprised. You're so good together and you've been laughing and you make a great team. I thought you were getting on well.'

'We *are* getting on well.' Amy thought of their passionate love-making and blushed. 'But we haven't patched up our marriage.'

Kate studied her. 'Why not? You're so in love with him, anyone can see that. And he's in love with you!'

Amy frowned. 'Nick said the same thing—'

Kate tensed slightly, her eyes suddenly wary. 'Did he?' Her tone was suddenly cool. 'You've discussed this with Nick?'

'He's surprisingly intuitive, don't you think?'

'Sometimes. With patients.' Kate stood up so suddenly that her coffee sloshed over the table. 'Oh, now look what I've done.' She walked across to the sink and picked up a cloth and Amy watched, mystified by the sudden tension in the air. Everything had been fine until she'd mentioned the senior partner's name.

'Has something happened between you and Nick?' *Had they had a row?* Or was it something more than that?

'Nothing. You know what this place is like. We're in each other's pockets all the time.' She wiped the table. 'So, if Marco *was* in love with you, would you stay?'

'No. I'd be leaving even if he was in love with me.' Amy paused. 'I can't have children. That's why I left and it's why I'll be leaving again. I can't give Marco the family he needs.' Swiftly, removing as much of the emotion as possible, she told Kate the facts and the older woman sank back onto the chair, her expression sympathetic.

'Oh, Amy, I'm so sorry. Why didn't you tell me any of this before? You must have gone through so much and all on your own!'

'I couldn't talk to anyone about it,' Amy murmured. 'I—I'm not really used to talking about problems and this, well, this was just too big.'

'But there are so many options these days and even if none of them worked, there's always adoption.'

Amy tightened her grip on her mug.

Why did people always say that?

Why did they throw it in like some sort of consolation prize with no emotional value?

'That wouldn't be a solution. It's hard to understand, I

know.' She rose to her feet quickly. 'I'd better get back. Surgery was very busy. I have some notes to tie up and some referral letters to write.'

'If I've upset you, I'm sorry.' Kate's voice was soft. 'I probably understand more than you think, Amy. Not about the infertility, no. I don't pretend to know what that must be like. But I know all about finding the man you truly love and then not being able to be with him. Life has a warped sense of humour. Whoever said that it was better to have loved and lost than never to have loved at all, had obviously never loved. Either that or he was on drugs when he wrote that. Love is agony.'

Amy stood for a moment, unsure what to say. Was Kate referring to the tragic loss of her husband years earlier? Or something else entirely?

She opened her mouth to ask a probing question but then the door opened and Alison walked in.

'Is that kettle hot? My tongue is sticking to the roof of my mouth.'

Amy looked at Kate for a moment longer and the practice manager gave a tired smile.

'Go and finish your paperwork, Amy, or I'll be forced to nag you.'

In other words, this wasn't the right time for a deep conversation. Knowing that Kate was right, Amy smiled at Alison.

'Kettle is hot.'

'Aren't you getting ready to go out? The party started half an hour ago.' Marco paused in the doorway, looking at Amy who was curled up on the sofa with a book that she wasn't reading.

She couldn't concentrate on anything. When she wasn't working, all she did was think about Marco. 'You go.'

'We're both going.' He reached out a hand and pulled her to her feet.

'I'm tired, Marco.'

He gave a slow smile and stroked a hand over her cheek. 'Too much sex perhaps. Tonight, *tesoro*, I will let you sleep. I promise.'

She blushed. 'Marco, I just don't want to go to the Penhally Arms! Everyone will be there.'

'*Sì.*' He pulled her towards the stairs. 'That is why we are going. We're part of this community.'

'You are. I'm not.'

He jerked her against him. 'You're my wife,' he breathed, his eyes holding hers. 'Remember that.'

'Marco—' She broke off and sighed. This wasn't the time to start that argument again. 'All right, I'll come to the party if it means so much to you.'

'Good.' He lowered his head and delivered a lingering kiss to her mouth. 'We leave in ten minutes.'

Amy waited for him to walk into the shower and then opened the wardrobe and took out the dress. It was scarlet, daring, and didn't match her mood at all.

If she were dressing for her mood then it would have been black, she thought gloomily, looking in the wardrobe to see what else there was.

But there was nothing.

Only the vivid red dress.

With a little shrug she slipped it on, wondering if it would even still fit.

'*Molto belissima,*' Marco breathed from behind her, sliding his hands slowly over her hips and then drawing her zip upwards in a smooth movement. 'I always *loved* you in this dress.'

'It isn't— I don't—'

'It is and you should.' He turned her to face him. 'Tonight

let's just go out and have a good time. Forget everything. No mention of problems. Agreed?'

She hesitated and then nodded. It sounded good to her. She was exhausted. 'All right.'

The Penhally Arms was decorated with clusters of balloons and rows of twinkling lights and the dining room had been cleared to accommodate a dance floor. Although it was still relatively early, the place was already crowded.

'So now you will see all my moves and be unable to resist me.' Smiling wickedly, Marco hauled her straight onto the dance floor and spun her round.

'What are you doing?' Half laughing, half embarrassed, she moved closer to him and he shrugged.

'Dancing. Your dress has a very sexy split at the side. When I spin you round I get a better view of your legs.'

'Marco, that's dreadful!'

'Not from where I'm standing.' He pulled her against him and ran a possessive hand over the curve of her bottom, leaving everyone in no doubt that their marriage was alive and well.

'People are watching everything you do.'

'Let them watch. The only way to survive in a small community is not to fight it. Don't be so English.' He smiled down at her, his eyes glittering dark and dangerous in the dim light. 'Relax and let go. All the people here wish us well.'

And, indeed, everyone seemed happy and contented, mingling, drinking and eating. Amy joined Marco as he weaved his way through them, exchanging a few words of greeting here and there, stopping to have a longer conversation with some people.

And then she saw Kate standing in the doorway, a look of such utter yearning on her face that Amy stopped dead. Puzzled, she followed the direction of Kate's gaze and gave a soft gasp of enlightenment.

Marco turned from his argument about Italian wines. 'What?'

'I just— I didn't…' She drew him to one side, her voice soft. 'Kate. Did you see the way she looked at Nick?'

'No, but I can imagine.'

Amy looked up at him. 'I think she's in love with him.'

'I *know* she's in love with him.'

'You *know*?'

'I have worked with both of them for over two years,' Marco said wearily. 'I may be a man, but even I can pick up on tension and atmosphere if it surrounds me for long enough.'

'Well, but— That's great.' Amy smiled, genuinely delighted for Kate. 'I mean, they're both widowed and—'

Marco pressed a finger over her lips. 'I think the situation is perhaps more complicated than it might first appear to be,' he drawled softly, removing his finger and giving her a gentle kiss instead. 'Say nothing to either of them.'

'But Kate is my friend—'

'All right, then say nothing to Nick,' Marco said quietly, his gaze resting on his colleague who was standing at the bar, talking to several other locals. 'Nick is a man with a lot of issues.'

'You mean he still hasn't got over Annabel's death?'

Marco was silent for a moment. 'That, yes. And more, I suspect. Come on, let's eat.'

They helped themselves to food, chatted to some of the villagers and then everyone started the countdown to midnight.

'Ten, nine eight…' everyone chanted in unison, and then the church bells started to chime and they all let out an enormous cheer.

Amy smiled and suddenly she was glad she'd come. Just because you knew that tomorrow was going to be difficult, it didn't mean that you couldn't grab hold of today and enjoy it.

'*Felice Anno Nuovo.*' Marco took her in his arms and kissed her. 'Happy New Year, *amore.*'

Amy closed her eyes, her happiness bitter-sweet. '*Felice Anno Nuovo*, Marco.'

She didn't have any reason to believe that the new year would be any happier than the last two, but Marco had insisted that tonight wasn't about their relationship and she had to admit that it had been nice to get away from the subject for a while.

All around her people were hugging and kissing and letting off party poppers, and then she saw Kate and Nick. And there was something about the way they stood—*so close but neither touching nor talking*—that made Amy catch her breath.

Across the lively crowd, she could almost feel their agony. *Couldn't anyone else feel it, too?*

She glanced around her to see if anyone else had noticed but everyone was dancing and singing and whooping.

And suddenly, Nick finished his drink, picked up his coat and strode out of the bar, his handsome face strained and his mouth grim. He had his car keys in his hand and one glance at the misery in Kate's eyes told Amy that he was going home alone.

Moments later Kate picked up her bag and followed, clearly too distressed to stay at the party.

Amy watched the door of the pub close behind her and hesitated.

Should she follow? Or should she stay out of it?

She'd seen the tears in Kate's eyes and knew that she was close to breaking down. Who did she have to turn to?

Around her everyone was celebrating noisily and Marco was in conversation with a group of people, so Amy quietly slipped away, intending to offer Kate some support.

Outside, the winter wind bit through her thin dress and suddenly she wished she'd stopped to pick up her coat.

Then she saw Kate, hurrying across the car park towards Nick. 'Nick! Wait.' Her voice carried and Amy watched as Nick paused, his hand on the door of his car, the collar of his coat turned up against the bitter chill of the wind.

Laughter burst from inside the pub but the two of them didn't even look round.

Were they talking?

What were they saying?

Amy knew she should go back into the pub but she just couldn't look away and she gave a soft intake of breath as she saw Nick's hand lift towards Kate's shoulder as if he was going to pull her against him. For a moment his hand hovered, and then his fingers curled into a fist and his hand dropped to his side.

Without saying another word to Kate, he slid into his car and slammed the door.

Nick drove off with an ominous squeal of tyres and Kate stood for a long, tortured moment, her back to Amy.

And then finally she turned and Amy saw tears glistening on her face.

'Why did you go outside?' Marco slid his coat over Amy and turned up the heater in the car. 'Were you hoping for hypothermia?'

'I was worried about Kate.' Her teeth chattering, Amy snuggled under his coat. 'She looked…desperate. Do you think we should call on her?'

'We can't solve everyone's problems, Amy.' He drove carefully on the icy roads. 'We don't even seem to be managing to solve our own.'

'There's nothing to solve.'

'We have a major difference of opinion. You love me, Amy. Admit that at least.'

Exhausted with lying, Amy looked at him. 'All right, I love

you. There, I said it. Are you satisfied?' She turned her head away from him. 'I said it and it still doesn't change a thing. We can't be together.'

'Because you think you can't have children? We're not the first couple to face this and it doesn't have to be the death of our relationship.'

The conversation continued all the way home and followed them into the house.

'If the whole children thing bothers you that much, let's talk about it.' Marco dropped his keys on the table and strode through to the kitchen. 'There are any number of options. IVF. Adoption.'

'That isn't an option.'

'Why not?'

She hesitated. 'Because it still wouldn't be your child.'

'I want you, Amy. You. I take you as you are.' Marco jammed his fingers into his hair and let out a stream of Italian that was completely incomprehensible, but the gist of it was clear even to her. He was frustrated and exasperated. 'What do I have to do to convince you?'

'Nothing. You'll never convince me. That's why I left, Marco.' Her voice was soft. 'There was really nothing left to say.'

CHAPTER TEN

THE first two weeks of the new year were flat and bleak. Children scurried along the pavements wearing hats and scarves on their way back to school, everyone removed the Christmas decorations and all that was left of the festive period was icy cold weather and frosty streets.

In the Penhally Bay Surgery, the atmosphere was tense. Amy woke up feeling exhausted every day and was beginning to wonder whether she'd contracted a virus in Africa. Marco refused to listen to her reminders that she was leaving in just two more weeks. Nick seemed more aloof than ever and although Kate was her usual efficient self, her face was pale and she hardly ever seemed to smile.

Unable to forget the scene she'd witnessed on New Year's Eve, Amy tried to talk to her, but they were so busy that it wasn't until the third week of January that Amy finally caught her on her own as they were leaving work.

'Do you fancy a coffee?'

'Now?' Kate glanced at her watch. 'I suppose I could. My babysitter doesn't leave for another hour. All right. Why not?'

They went to the nearest coffee-shop and found a small table in the window. 'You're sure you're leaving at the end of the month?' Kate unwound her scarf and picked at the foam on her cappuccino. 'I had a call from Adam Donnelly today, confirming his arrival date.'

Amy felt her stomach drop. It was one thing to know that she was leaving, quite another to actually do it. 'Yes. I have no choice.'

'For what it's worth, I think you're wrong. What you have with Marco is strong enough to withstand everything.'

Amy shook her head. 'I don't want to talk about me. I want to talk about you. Kate…' she leaned forward, her eyes gentle '…how long have you been in love with Nick?'

Pain flickered in Kate's eyes. 'Is it worth me uttering a denial?'

'No. Because I saw the two of you together on New Year's Eve.'

'Ah…' Kate gave a twisted smile. 'That was a particularly bad evening. Nick at his least communicative. Believe me, that's saying something.'

'He doesn't communicate? But you're always talking. You and he.' Amy frowned, confused. 'You're *always* planning and laughing.'

'That's business. Never personal.'

'But you'd like it to be personal.'

Kate stared down at her coffee. 'It's complicated, Amy. I can't tell you all of it. But…' She hesitated. 'I will tell you that I've decided to leave. I can't do this any more. I just can't work alongside him, it hurts too much. There. You're the only person I've said that to. I'd be grateful if you didn't repeat it until I've decided for sure what I want to do.'

'You want to leave? No! You can't do that!' Amy reached across the table and took her hand. 'You love your job. You love working with Nick. You're a great team.'

Kate pulled her hand away. 'There's only so much torture a woman can stand, Amy. I've reached my limit.'

'Are you quite sure he doesn't feel the same way about you?'

Kate stared blindly into her coffee. 'Does Nick feel anything for me? Yes, I think he probably does. Is he going to do anything about it? No, definitely not. He isn't that sort of man.'

'Has he dated anyone since Annabel died?'

'Oh, yes.' Kate gave a bitter laugh. 'Quite a few women, actually. Just no one who is remotely interested in creating an emotional connection. That isn't Nick.'

'Does he know you're thinking of leaving?'

'No.' Kate picked up her coffee. 'I'm going to tell him soon, though. I need to do something different. Goodness knows what. Get a life, as my son would say. Stop brooding. Nick's only a man after all.'

'But some men are harder to get out of your system than others.'

Kate looked at her and gave a sad smile. 'Yes. And you'd understand that, wouldn't you, Amy?'

'Kate tells me that Adam Donnelly is starting in a week.' Wondering why she was always so exhausted, Amy slid her bag onto her shoulder. 'Finally you'll have a proper replacement for Lucy.'

'You're still intent on leaving, then? Despite everything?' Marco's glance burned a hole in her conscience and she forced herself to carry on walking towards the car.

'Yes. Of course. I've told you that all along.'

His phone buzzed and Marco gave a tired sigh and answered it. 'Marco Avanti.' He listened for a moment and then his jaw tightened. 'We'll come over now.'

'What?' Amy looked at him as he dropped the phone back into his pocket and strode towards his car.

'That was Carol. Lizzie is screaming with a headache and she has spots. She's worried that she has meningitis.'

'Meningitis?'

Marco shrugged and unlocked the car. 'We will see. Are you coming?'

'Of course! Why wouldn't I?'

'Because you're leaving, Amy, remember? In another week the inhabitants of Penhally will no longer be your responsibility.'

They sat in silence, Marco's hands gripping the steering-wheel tightly as he drove the short distance to the terraced cottage that Carol shared with her husband and the two girls.

'Thank you so much for coming.' Carol's voice was thick with tears as she let them into the house. 'I always seem to be ringing you. My phone is programmed to ring your number.'

'How long has she had the headache?'

'Well, she was out with her friends last night and they were obviously drinking. Again.' Carol's mouth tightened. 'She's grounded, but that's another story. Last night when she came in she was really drunk—slurring her words and really, really stroppy. Worse than ever. I left her to sleep it off and, of course, she woke up with a headache. Nothing surprising there. I assumed it was a hangover but it's just got worse and worse and about an hour ago she started complaining that the light hurt her eyes. That's when I noticed this rash on her face and I panicked.'

'She is in the bedroom?' Marco was already on the stairs and Amy was right behind him.

'She can't get out of bed because her head is so bad. Her bedroom is the second door on the right.'

The teenager was lying on her side, crying softly, and little Michelle was curled up on the bed next to her sister.

''Izzie sick,' she muttered, and Carol hastily scooped the child off the bed.

'You shouldn't be there. You might catch something. Go downstairs to Daddy, sweetheart. Pete? Can you come and take the baby?'

Reluctant to be parted from her sister, Michelle reached out her arms. ''Izzie sick.'

Marco slid a hand over her cheek. ''Izzie is going to be fine, *cucciola mia*. Go with your mama.'

'I'll be right back,' Carol said, but Marco shook his head. 'I'd like to examine Lizzie and talk to her on my own first. Amy will help me.'

Carol hesitated and then gave a nod. 'All right. I'll be downstairs with Michelle if you need me.'

'Where she always is,' Lizzie sniffed, her forearm across her eyes as she rolled onto her back. 'If you ever want to find Mum, just look for Michelle.' Her face was red and blotchy from crying and Amy noticed the spots on her face. 'My head is killing me. It's like a bomb is exploding in it every minute. Am I dying?'

Marco sat down on the edge of the bed. 'You're not dying,' he said gently, 'but I'll take a look at you and then we'll talk.'

'Oh, don't you start,' Lizzie groaned, rolling onto her side again. 'When adults say "talk" they mean "nag". Don't drink, don't stay out late, don't spend time with those friends because they're not suitable—who the hell does she think she is, anyway, picking my friends? Life is just a load of bloody "don'ts".'

'Is that how it seems?'

'It's how it is.' Lizzie screwed up her face and started to cry. 'God, my head hurts. Mum said I might have meningitis. That's why she got Michelle out of here. She doesn't care about me, but she doesn't want her baby hurt.' The teenager put her hands over her face but Amy saw tears find their way through her fingers.

'You're her baby, too.' Marco opened his bag and took out a stethoscope and an ophthalmoscope.

'No, I'm just a reminder of Dad. They got divorced, remember? Mum can't stand him and she can't stand me either because I'm exactly like him.' Lizzie let her hands drop. 'If she'd had her way I would have gone and lived with him. Neither of them wanted me.'

Amy felt her heart twist. 'Lizzie, I'm sure that isn't true.' She dropped onto her knees beside the bed and took the girl's hand. 'You and I are going to talk about that, but first we need to check you over to see why you've got this headache. When we've got the physical check out of the way, we'll deal with the rest of it.'

Lizzie rolled onto her back, her eyes closed. 'Go on, then. Get it over with. If I'm going to die, I might as well know.'

'You're not going to die, *angelo mia*.' As kind and gentle as he always was with little Michelle, Marco examined her thoroughly and closely checked the rash around her mouth. 'Amy, what exactly were you doing out with your friends last night?' His tone was casual as he put the stethoscope back into his bag and swiftly checked her blood pressure.

'I dunno.' Lizzie didn't open her eyes. 'We were just hanging out. Having fun. Drinking. You heard Mum.'

'What were you drinking?'

'Stuff.'

'Have you or your friends tried sniffing glue?'

Lizzie's eyes flew open and colour flooded into her face. 'No.'

'Lizzie.' Marco gently unwound the blood-pressure cuff and put it away, 'I'm your doctor, not your mother. You need to be honest with me.'

'Why? So that you can lecture me?'

'So that I can help you.'

Lizzie looked at him for a moment and then covered her face with her hands and started to cry again. 'They were doing it and I didn't want to be different. They're always saying I'm posh and stuck up. So I tried it. And I felt really happy and part of everything. And then afterwards I felt totally crap. Dizzy and sick. How did you guess?'

'I'm a doctor. And I suspected it when you came to the surgery last week. You were short-tempered, your mother mentioned that your school work had gone downhill and I noticed that you had an oil stain on your jumper.'

Lizzie gaped at him. 'What are you, a detective?'

'Sometimes, yes.' Marco gave a wry smile. 'That's exactly what my job is.'

'What about the spots on my face?'

'Same thing.'

Lizzie swallowed. 'Not meningitis?'

'Not meningitis,' Marco said gently. 'Glue sniffing.'

Lizzie groaned and closed her eyes. 'It's no big deal,' she muttered. 'I mean, I've only done it occasionally.'

'It *is* a big deal. Sometimes it can kill, sometimes it causes organ damage.' He talked to the teenager, dishing out cold, hard facts until Lizzie sat up and covered her ears with her hands.

'All right, stop! I've messed up, I know I have, but—you have no idea what it's like. Mum just *hates* me.' She started to cry again and Amy gave a murmur of sympathy and slid a hand over the girl's shaking shoulders.

'I don't think your mum hates you, Lizzie.'

'What would you know, anyway?' Lizzie wriggled away from her moodily. 'You, with your perfect life.'

'Actually, I know quite a lot about how it feels to be unloved,' Amy said calmly, 'because my mother didn't want me at all.'

Lizzie looked at her. So did Marco.

'Family life is complicated, Lizzie, but I know your mum loves you.' Amy's voice was firm. 'She's worried about you and she doesn't know how to handle you, but she loves you. All the signs are there.'

'What? She spends all her time with Michelle.'

Amy nodded. 'Yes, that must be hard. Michelle is a toddler

and toddlers are always time-consuming, and on top of that she has asthma. I can quite see how it might seem that your mum doesn't have time for you.'

'She doesn't even notice me except when it's to nag about something.'

'If she's nagging, then she's noticing,' Amy said quietly. 'My mother didn't care where I was or who I was with. When I was seven she sent me to boarding school. I would have given a great deal for her to nag me about something because at least it would have showed that she minded about something.'

Lizzie was silent. 'I hadn't thought of it like that.' She looked at Amy. 'We never talk or anything.'

'Do you talk to her?'

Lizzie's gaze slipped from hers. 'No.' She plucked at the duvet. 'I don't suppose I do. Not any more.'

'Then perhaps you should try. She might surprise you.'

Lizzie pulled a face. 'She's going to kill me when she finds out I've been sniffing glue. Are you going to tell her?'

'*You're* going to tell her,' Marco said gently, closing his bag, 'along with all these other things that you've been telling us. I think she needs to know how you feel, don't you?'

'It won't make a difference.'

'Why don't you tell her and we will find out?'

Lizzie curled her arms round her knees, suddenly looking very young and lost. 'Will you stay while I talk to her?'

Amy nodded immediately. 'I will.'

'I didn't really want to do it, you know? The glue stuff.' Lizzie's eyes filled. 'But those girls were like so cool and kind of superior and they look at you like you're *nothing* if you don't go along with what they say. I just wanted to fit in but at the same time I always knew that I didn't.'

'If they don't respect your right to make your own choices, maybe they're not good friends,' Amy said quietly, and Lizzie nodded.

'I know.' She wiped her nose on her sleeve. 'I think I just wanted Mum to notice me and when I hung out with them, Mum noticed. She hates them. So what happens now?'

'To start with, you talk to your mother. Hopefully she can give you the support you need.' Marco rose to his feet. 'If necessary I can refer you to the hospital for some help but I don't think you'll need it. Eat healthily, get plenty of sleep and let's see how you go. I'll go and call your mum.'

'Poor Lizzie. And poor Carol.' Marco drove towards home, a frown on his face.

'They'll be all right. They love each other and they'll work it out.' Amy glanced out of the window. 'Where are we going? This isn't the way home.'

'I want to talk to you.' He pulled up in a small car park that overlooked the jagged coastline. 'Here, we shouldn't be disturbed.'

Amy felt her heart sink. 'Marco, we're not going over this again.'

'No. We're exploring something entirely different. You are going to tell me about your childhood.'

'That's irrelevant. And it's not my favourite subject.'

'But you mentioned it just now to help a very confused, sad teenager. Doesn't our marriage deserve the same consideration?'

'Talking about the past won't make any difference to the future, Marco.'

'At least let me understand why you're walking away.' His voice was rough and his eyes were tired. 'At least give me that much, Amy. None of this makes sense to me. I'm sure that all your beliefs about marriage and children come from your own experiences. Clearly your mother didn't want children, but why does that affect your own perception of parenthood?'

'My mother *did* want children. But she wanted her own children.'

Marco was silent for a moment. 'This I don't understand.'

'I'm not her child,' Amy said wearily. 'I'm adopted, Marco. She adopted me because she was infertile and she couldn't have children. I was supposed to be the solution to her problem. Instead, I made the problem a thousand times worse.'

The only noise in the car was the sound of Marco breathing. 'You are adopted?'

'That's right. And now can we move on? There's really nothing else to say and it makes no difference to our relationship.'

'It makes a difference to me.' His voice was a low growl and he slid a hand behind her neck and forced her to look at him. '*Ti amo.* I love you. You love me.'

Amy swallowed and spoke with difficulty. 'That doesn't make a difference either.'

'How can you say that!' Visibly frustrated, his mouth tightened. 'Of course it's relevant. Our love is strong enough to survive anything.'

'No.' She shook her head. 'That isn't true. You want children. I can't give you children. I've seen firsthand what that can do to a relationship.'

'So tell me.' His voice was soft but the pressure of his hand prevented her from looking away. 'Tell me what it can do, I want to know. I want to know what you have seen that I am so blind to.'

'My father wanted children. My mother couldn't have them. So she adopted me, thinking that that would solve the problem. It didn't. My father never saw me as his and my mother blamed me for that. She believed that had I been different, he would have loved me.' Amy kept her voice level as she recited the basic facts. 'If I'd been prettier, cleverer, more outgoing—the list was endless. By the time she finally sent me to boarding school, I was so afraid of doing and saying the wrong thing, I barely spoke.'

'Amy.' Marco breathed her name and then gave a groan and pulled her against him. 'I had no idea. Why did you never tell me this before?'

'Because I try and forget it. I have a different life now. It isn't relevant.'

'If it's destroying our relationship, it's relevant. And your father paid you no attention either?'

'My father's ego was badly damaged by the lack of children. He thought it made him less of a man. He had an affair with his secretary and she became pregnant almost immediately. There was no question of keeping it a secret because my father wanted everyone to know that he'd fathered a child, as if it were somehow confirmation of his masculinity. So he divorced my mother and married the secretary. They had four children in quick succession, each one another bitter blow to my mother. I rarely ever saw her. During term time I was at school and in the holidays I stayed with my grandmother in Penhally.'

'I can't believe that she never tried to build a relationship with you.'

'You don't understand.' Amy gave a faint smile. 'She didn't really want me, Marco. I was just a solution to her problem. She needed to produce a child and she couldn't. So as a last resort she produced me. I'm sure the authorities would have thought that they were a perfect couple to qualify for adoption. Nice home, good income and my mother was very, very excited about having me. But not because she wanted me. Because she thought I'd save her marriage.'

'And when you didn't, she sent you away.'

'That's right.'

'So now I begin to understand you.' Marco stroked a hand

down her cheek. 'You think that perhaps I am like your father and I need children to prove my manhood, no?'

'I know you're nothing like my father.' She felt exhausted. And sick again, really, really sick. 'But I also know that you want a family and you deserve one.'

'Did your parents love each other?'

'Why is that relevant?'

'It's totally relevant.' His eyes held hers. 'You see, you are the one I want to spend my life with. And maybe our life together will come with problems, because life always does. Perhaps for us it will be infertility. But we will still be together and that is what I want. That is what I choose. A life with you.'

'Marco—'

'No, it is your turn to listen to me. All this time you have focused only on the fact you can't have children, not on our relationship.'

'Because it matters!'

'Of course it matters, I'm not pretending that it doesn't matter. I'm just saying that it can't be allowed to destroy what we have.'

'You don't understand—'

'No, *you* are the one who doesn't understand,' he said firmly. 'You don't understand how much I love you. If you understood that, you wouldn't ever think of leaving me again.'

'You really love me? Why?' Amy's eyes filled. 'I can't give you want you want.'

'Amy, *tesoro*.' He gave a gentle smile and lowered his mouth to hers. '*You* are what I want. How can I make you see that? I want my life to be with you and I will take whatever problems come along with that.'

She stared at him, her heart beating hard against her chest. 'We got married in a hurry.'

He gave a wry smile. 'Amy, I had successfully avoided

commitment for thirty-nine years until I met you. Are you seriously suggesting that I didn't know my own mind? I married you because you were the woman I wanted to spend the rest of my life with, and it took me very little time to work that out.'

'You said that you wanted me to be the mother of your children.'

He grimaced. '*Sì*. In the circumstances I can see how you would have arrived at your totally false belief that our marriage couldn't work. But what I was trying to say was that you were the only woman for me. The only woman I wanted to marry. The only woman I wanted to have children with.' His voice softened. 'Or not have children with, if that is what fate dictates for us. I love you.'

Amy stared at him, not daring to believe that he meant it. Then she felt her eyes fill. 'I didn't believe that you loved me.'

'I married you,' Marco said softly. 'Wasn't that proof enough of my love?'

'You didn't come after me when I left.'

He breathed out heavily. 'To begin with I was in shock. I couldn't believe what had happened because we went from being happy to you leaving in the blink of an eye. I would have come but then Annabel died and Nick needed me here. Time passed—'

'And I didn't come back because I just couldn't see how our relationship could survive. After everything I saw at home. Even now, I can't really believe that we can be different from my parents.'

'We *are* different. No two people are the same, remember that. And no relationship is the same. Have a little faith.' He brushed away her tears. 'If we weren't already married, this is the moment when I would propose. And you would say yes.'

'Would I?' She felt hope unfold inside her like the petals of a flower. 'What if—?'

'Life is full of what ifs. Let's deal just with what is. I love you. You love me. We stay together. And don't even think of arguing because I'm not going to listen. And don't think of leaving because I'll come after you.'

'Oh, Marco.' She flung her arms round his neck and felt his hand smooth her back.

'You are tired, *tesoro*. I need to take you home.'

'I love you.'

'I know. And I love you, too. And now you are going to rest because this has all been very traumatic for you. You are looking so, so tired at the moment.'

'It's probably just the worry. I've been dreading the thought of leaving you again.'

'You're not leaving. Not ever.'

'Do you mean it? You think everything can work?'

'I know it can.'

Amy leaned against him, feeling truly loved for the first time in her life. The feeling warmed her and she gave a soft smile.

If only she didn't feel so completely exhausted, everything about her life would be perfect.

The following morning Amy woke up with a churning stomach and only just made it to the bathroom before being violently sick.

'Amy?' Marco followed her into the bathroom, stroked her hair away from her face and then sat down on a chair and lifted her from the cold tiles onto his lap. 'Are you hot? Have you eaten something?'

'Obviously. Or maybe this is why I was so tired yesterday,' she murmured, sinking against his chest. 'I must have picked up a bug.'

'You weren't just tired yesterday,' Marco said gently. 'You are always tired.'

Amy felt a sudden flicker of unease. It was true. She *was* always tired.

What was the matter with her?

Was this another of life's cruel tricks? Had she finally found someone who truly loved her, only to become seriously ill?

'It's just a bug,' she said firmly. 'I feel better now I've been sick. I'll get dressed in a minute. We don't want to be late for surgery.'

'Don't be ridiculous. You can't take a surgery, feeling like this.'

She closed her eyes, wishing her stomach would settle. 'I'll be fine.'

'Amy.' Marco slid a hand over her forehead, checked her temperature and then gave her a smile. 'Spend the morning in bed. I'll be back to see you at lunchtime.'

She knew she ought to argue, but she just felt too tired to utter a protest so she allowed him to tuck her into bed and lay there, sleeping all morning until he reappeared.

'Do you feel any better?' He sat down on the bed next to her and stroked her face, his fingers cold from his short walk from the car. 'Have you been sick again?'

'No, just the once this morning.' She sat up. 'How was surgery?'

'Fine.' He hesitated. 'Amy, I'm going to say something and I hope you won't be upset.'

Her stomach dropped. 'You've changed your mind?'

'About what?' He looked baffled and she blushed.

'About spending your life with someone who can't have babies.'

His mouth tightened. 'I'm spending my life with you, that's what I want. But what I have to say does have to do with babies and I'm afraid you may misinterpret—' He broke off and let out a long breath. 'Amy, I want you to do a pregnancy test.'

'What?' She stared at him. 'Are you mad? Haven't you listened to a single thing I've said to you?'

'Look at your symptoms. Every day you're exhausted—'

'We're working hard!'

'You were sick this morning.'

'So? I've picked up a bug!' She pushed her hair away from her face and glared at him, her insides churning again. 'You're imagining it, Marco, just because you want it to happen. Wishful thinking. This is just what I was afraid of! You say it doesn't matter, *but it matters, Marco.* I can see that it matters to you.'

'No!' His voice was sharp. 'I knew this was going to be difficult because I knew you would make that association, but it isn't true. This isn't about our relationship. I'm a doctor, Amy, and I'm looking at your symptoms.'

'Well, you obviously haven't looked very closely because there's no way I…' Her voice tailed off and she looked at him. 'I can't be. You *know* I can't be.'

'I don't know that. I do know that fertility is an unpredictable thing. I know that we've been making love for almost a month now with no contraception.'

'I can't be pregnant!'

'Then do the test and we will know. Don't cry, please, don't cry.' He cursed softly and pulled her into his arms. '*Mi dispiace, tesoro.* Don't cry.'

Amy pulled away from him and wiped her hand over her face, furious with herself for being so emotional. What was happening to her? She'd never been the hysterical, weepy type. 'All right. I'll do it. Of course I'll do it if that's what you want me to do.' She sniffed and held out her hand. 'Do you have it?'

He hesitated and then reached into his jacket and pulled out the test. 'I'll come with you.'

She stared at the test in her hand. 'Would you mind if I did it on my own?' Her voice shook and he gave a sigh.

'Don't push me away, Amy. Don't push me away, *tesoro*. Not now when we are just learning how to share.'

Amy hesitated. She wasn't sure that she could actually do a pregnancy test in company, even when that company was Marco. 'The thing is,' she said honestly, 'even though I know it can't be positive, I want it to be, so badly. I—I just need a few moments…'

'I understand that.' Marco hugged her tightly. 'We'll compromise. Do the test and then call me.'

So that he could offer comfort.

And she was going to need comfort, she knew she was.

Amy closed the bathroom door and sat on the edge of the bath, the packet in her hand unopened. Why was she even hesitating? It wasn't as if she didn't know the answer, because she did. So why was she treating the test as if it were a bomb that was going to blow her life apart?

She didn't really think she was going to be pregnant, did she? Surely she wasn't really that stupid? *That delusional?* Had she really, somehow, allowed a tiny flicker of hope to creep in and contaminate her common sense?

With an impatient sound she stood up and unwrapped the test.

A few minutes later she was still staring at the stick, tears trickling unnoticed down her cheeks. The tiled bathroom floor was cold under her bare feet but she didn't notice that either.

'Amy?' His tone impatient and concerned by equal degrees, Marco pushed open the door without waiting for an invitation. 'Talk to me, *amore*. I'm sorry. I shouldn't have even suggested that you do that test. It was thoughtless of me and—'

'I'm pregnant.' Her voice was a hoarse whisper and she felt suddenly dizzy. 'Marco, I'm pregnant. I'm having our baby.'

She heard him swear softly and then felt his arms slide around her and support her as her legs gave way.

* * *

'So now I believe in happy endings.' Nick glanced between them and smiled. 'I'm pleased for you both. Really.'

Marco laughed in disbelief. 'I just told you that I want to leave the practice and return to Italy. It's not exactly a happy ending for you.'

Nick looked at him for a long moment and Amy saw something pass between the two men. An understanding. They'd shared so much. Loss. Pain. Pride at the way the practice had developed.

'Life moves on. Things change and we have to change with them.' Nick shrugged. 'We set this place up together and a lot of the success is down to you, Marco. The practice will go on without you. Grow. Change. I can understand that you and Amy want to go back to Italy.'

'Penhally will always remind Amy of her past.' Marco slid a protective arm around her and Amy looked up at him.

'And you miss Italy.'

'Sì. That is true.' He smiled at her. 'I miss Italy. I feel like the Maserati. In this weather, my engine suffers.'

'Well.' Nick cleared his throat. 'On a practical note, Adam Donnelly is due to start tomorrow, as you know, so we won't be left high and dry.'

'We can stay for a few months if that would help.'

Nick shook his head. 'I don't want you to do that. You've managed to sort things out and I'm pleased about that. You've no idea how pleased. Now I want you to go and get on with your lives. Get ready for that baby.'

'You're very generous.' Marco's voice was gruff. 'Thank you.'

'Prego. Isn't that what I'm supposed to say?'

'And what about you, my friend?'

A shadow flickered in Nick's eyes. 'I carry on building the practice. Supporting the community. Kate's resigned.'

'Oh, no!' Despite the conversation they'd had, Amy

couldn't help feeling shocked. She hadn't actually believed that Kate would do it.

'And you accepted her resignation?' Marco's gaze was steady and Amy held her breath. It was the nearest any of them had come to asking Nick directly about his relationship with Kate.

'It's disappointing for the practice but she wants to take a new direction in her career. It would be wrong of me to talk her out of it.'

Work. He only talked about work. Nothing personal. *Nothing about missing Kate or feeling anything for Kate.*

For a moment Amy was tempted to step forward and shake him. Didn't he know how Kate felt about him? And was he really pretending that he felt nothing for Kate? She knew that wasn't true. Not after the scene she'd witnessed on New Year's Eve.

'Nick—'

'People are complicated,' Marco said quietly, closing his hand over Amy's to silence her. 'Relationships are complicated. And not all the obstacles to happiness come from outside and can be solved. Sometimes they are inside us and only time can shift them.'

For a moment Nick didn't respond. 'And sometimes time just isn't enough. Good luck, the two of you. Stay in touch. I look forward to holidays in Italy.'

They walked away from the surgery and Marco turned to look back.

'You're going to miss it, aren't you?' Amy slid her hand into his and he turned and smiled at her.

'I'm ready to move on. Do something else. I suppose I feel a little guilty about leaving Nick, especially as Kate is leaving, too. Whatever is going on between them, she has been a big part of the Penhally Bay Surgery for a long time.'

'She would have stayed if he'd told her that he loved her.'

'Nick has far too many issues after Annabel's death. He isn't ready to think about another relationship. Perhaps he never will be.'

Amy sighed. 'Why didn't you make him admit that he is in love with Kate?'

'I'm not sure that he knows it himself. And I'm not a doctor of relationships.'

Amy slipped her arm into his. 'I think you are. You cured ours. I can't believe this has happened. I arrived in Penhally a month ago to ask you to give me a divorce and now here I am back with you and pregnant. It's like a dream.'

'But a good dream.'

'Of course.' She reached up and kissed him. 'It's like being given a second chance. When I first met you I was so in love and then it all went so wrong. I didn't believe our relationship could work if I was infertile because I'd seen what it did to my parents.'

'It isn't about fertility, it's about love. Your parents didn't share the love that we have for each other.'

'No. I think you're right about that.'

'You know I'm right.' He slid his arms around her waist. 'I'm always right.'

'And so modest. So what happens now?'

'We make our home in Italy. The sun will put some colour in your cheeks and you will grow so accustomed to being loved that there will be no room for doubt in your mind. And you will speak Italian and learn how to make pasta from scratch.'

Amy laughed. 'And Penhally?'

He glanced around him, his eyes warm. 'This place has been a part of our lives. But it's time to move on.' His gaze moved back to hers. 'Will you move on with me, *tesoro*? Build a new life? Do you trust me enough to give up everything you know?'

'Yes.' She answered without hesitation. 'The only thing I don't want to give up is you. You're all that matters.'

Marco gave a slow smile of satisfaction. 'Finally, we agree on something.'

And he bent his head and kissed her.

* * * *

The Doctor's Bride
By Sunrise

JOSIE METCALFE

Josie Metcalfe lives in Cornwall with her long-suffering husband. They have four children. When she was an army brat, frequently on the move, books became the only friends that came with her wherever she went. Now that she writes them herself she is making new friends and hates saying goodbye at the end of a book—but there are always more characters in her head, clamouring for attention until she can't wait to tell their stories.

CHAPTER ONE

'PULL over, Mike...fast! I've lost him,' Maggie said tersely as the monitor shrilled a warning.

Automatically, she braced herself as the ambulance veered off the road and onto a rutted verge then jerked to a halt, but her concentration was focused entirely on Walter Dinnis and the fact that he no longer had a pulse.

With the ease of too much practice she delivered a precordial thump to the centre of his chest and began the compressions that would keep oxygenated blood circulating around his brain and vital organs, knowing that Mike would be joining her at any moment.

The back doors swung open and her fellow ambulance officer leapt in to join her, positioning himself to take over cardiac thrusts on their elderly patient without needing to be asked. That left her free to peel the gel off the backing strips and position them on the retired fisherman's skinny chest, ready for the electrodes.

'Prepare to shock,' bleated the automated voice, and Mike held both hands clear while the machine discharged 200 joules through the uselessly quivering heart.

'Damn! Back into v-fib. No viable rhythm,' Maggie

muttered under her breath. 'Come on, Walter. You can do it,' she said encouragingly as the machine charged up again, the high-pitched whine still audible over the sound of Mike's rhythmic counting as he performed the lifesaving thrusts. 'Two hundred again, Mike. Clear!'

The jagged trace returned again without any semblance of order, telling them both that there was no blood being pumped into any of the elderly man's vital organs.

'No! Don't *do* this!' she said fiercely, an image in her head of the white face of his terror-stricken wife watching them take her husband away. Betty would be following them at any moment in their daughter's car and the last thing she needed was to come up the hill out of Penhally and find the ambulance pulled up at the side of the road. The man had survived working his whole life in one of the most dangerous professions in the world...he'd been a familiar figure around Penhally all her life...and it all came down to this moment.

'You're *not* going to die on me!' she told him fiercely. 'Charging to 360 and...clear!'

The wiry body arched up alarmingly as the jolt of electricity was discharged into his heart, but this time, after several seconds of ominous silence, the blessed sound of sinus rhythm was restored.

'And make sure it stays that way, Walter, or Betty will never forgive me,' Maggie muttered sternly to her patient as Mike closed the doors again and made his way back to the driving seat. She folded the printout strip detailing the successful attempt at cardioversion into Walter's file. 'Let's get him to St Piran's...asap!' she suggested with a swift glance towards her colleague.

Out of the corner of the windscreen she caught sight of a jumble of bright colours behind some gorse bushes and turned her focus on them with a frown. It wasn't until Mike was pulling back onto the road that she suddenly realised what it was she'd been looking at.

'A kid's bicycle…that's what it was,' she whispered under her breath, then smiled when she turned back to check Walter's oxygen perfusion, glad to see that it was once more above ninety per cent and he was conscious again.

The expression in his eyes was dazed and confused and she quickly set about reassuring him, but at the same time the image of that brightly painted bike against the sere winter grass stayed with her.

In fact, now that she thought about it, there had been more than one of them in the field behind the high stone wall, and she wondered idly what they were doing this far out of Penhally. The road was steep and winding and the riders would definitely have had to walk their bikes for most of the distance—no mean feat for a youngster.

By the size of the bikes, the children they belonged to weren't very old but, then, this was half-term week for all the local schools and the whole group of them was probably exploring or building some sort of den in the corner of one of the fields or under one of the familiar trees that had been permanently deformed by the sharp bite of winter gales and the prevailing winds.

At that age, the youngsters were unlikely to be up to anything dangerous, but they could definitely be up to mischief if the traditional holiday-time rise in callouts was anything to go by. In spite of the fact that it was still mid-February, they'd already had to transport one lad injured in a fall on the rocks below the lighthouse and another rescued from an unplanned swim off the harbour wall at half-tide.

Walter's heart behaved itself for the rest of their journey and as they did a speedy handover at St Piran's A and E, Maggie marvelled at the way a brain could function on so many levels at once. Especially a female brain, they'd been told during one set of lectures during her paramedic training. The males in the room had jeered, but she'd proved it time and again when a male colleague had been concentrating on monitoring one set of injuries, only to completely lose track of other emerging symptoms.

She had certainly tried to make sure that she kept her standards up, trying not to miss anything significant, no matter how small, but that didn't stop her brain from cataloguing something extraneous...such as those bicycles...and filing it away.

Now they were on the return journey, providing un-official transport back to Penhally for Maureen, another ambulance service worker, who'd been released after day-case surgery for the repair of an inguinal hernia.

And there were those bikes again, still there behind the gorse bushes, even though it was getting dark.

'Some kids are going to be in trouble with their mums when they get back late tonight,' she murmured under her breath, while Mike and Maureen chatted with the ease of long-time colleagues.

She could easily understand how the time could get away from the youngsters while they were enjoying themselves, with the February nights still drawing in far too fast, but she could all too easily sympathise with the mothers who would be worrying about them. These narrow roads weren't ideal for cycling at any time of the day, but after dark they could be lethal, few of them having any street lighting once you left the town itself.

'Door to door, ladies,' Mike announced as he drew up in a parking space outside the surgery and hopped out to unlock the double doors at the back of the ambulance with a flourish before dropping the steps. 'Come on, gorgeous. Time to get home and put your feet up while the old man makes you some tea.' He leant a little closer and added, 'And you tell him the surgeon said he's not allowed to get fruity until you've had your check-up.'

'You watch it, Mike Barber, or I'll tell Brian what you said,' Maureen warned, but there was a gleam of humour in her eyes. Her years in the service, first as a technician, like Mike, then as office staff, when the children had started arriving, had obviously taught her not to take any nonsense. 'My Brian'll soon sort your cheek out.'

'You know he would, too,' Maggie commented, when the older woman had walked gingerly across the car park to where her husband was waiting next door outside the front of Althorp's with a car full of children. 'And you wouldn't want to be messing with someone Brian's size. Have you seen the muscles on him? It must be something to do with all that physical labour in the boatyard.'

'I've got plenty of muscles of my own,' Mike

pointed out, flexing his biceps inside his grass-green uniform, stung by what he obviously saw as a slight on his manhood.

'Yeah.' She hid her grin when he rose to the bait, the way he always did, 'But you buy *those* sorts of muscles with a few months of gym membership. *His* are the real thing, built up over a lifetime of use.'

She continued tidying the last few items away before they locked up and set off back to the depot for the end of their shift. With any luck they wouldn't have another callout before it was time to clean out their vehicle and hand over for the night.

'Hey, Maggie! Mike!' called a voice just as the two of them were walking forward to the cab.

'Mrs Furse…hello,' Maggie called back, then walked towards the motherly figure when she beckoned, pleased to see someone who had been one of her own mother's dearest friends.

'How many times do I have to tell you to call me Hazel now that you're all grown up?' she chided, giving Maggie a swift hug. 'I haven't seen the two of you for weeks, except for fleeting glimpses as you've been on the road somewhere, so I'm glad I caught you. Have you got to leave straight away or have you got time to come in for a drink? You really ought to meet our new locum. He's—'

'A drink, Hazel?' Mike interrupted gleefully. 'You wicked woman. What are you suggesting?'

'Tea, coffee or water, Mike Barber, as you very well know,' the practice's head receptionist said quellingly. 'And you behave yourself or I'll be having a word with your mother.'

He pulled a face. 'That's put me properly in my place…one of the penalties of living in the same town all your life.'

'But it can't be too bad a place if so many people want to come back here to live. Dr Nick, for example,' Maggie pointed out, as they followed Hazel up the stairs to the staffroom, trying to take her mind off what was about to happen. It wasn't an accident that they hadn't called in at the practice over the last two and a half weeks. It had been a deliberate ploy on her part to put off as long as possible the meeting that would bring back one of the most distressing days of her life.

'Nick's far from the only one to come back—there's also our newest recruit to the practice. He's an old Penhally boy, too,' Hazel said with a broad smile for someone who had just followed them into the room. 'Maggie, I don't know whether you'll remember him from when you were both at school here. He would have been several years above you. It's—'

'Adam Donnelly,' she whispered with her heart in her throat when she met those serious dark eyes for the first time in more than a year.

He was wearing a smart charcoal-grey suit that made him look every inch the respectable GP, but the shirt wasn't commonplace white but a clear blue that drew attention to the almost navy blue of his eyes. Had he remembered that she'd been the one to tell him that would happen?

At least she'd never been silly enough to tell him just how much those deep blue eyes had always affected her. That had been one of her secrets, as was the fact that she'd been head over heels in love with him long before he'd disappeared off to medical school.

Unfortunately, even though she tried to force herself not to react, those dark eyes still elicited the same response they always had…for all the good it would do her.

'Maggie,' he said with a nod of acknowledgement, but that single word in that unforgettable husky voice was enough to rip all the scars wide open again. The last time she'd heard it she'd been wrapped in his arms, believing…

'My goodness, you've got good memories!' Hazel exclaimed. 'You can't have seen each other since Adam went away to medical school, because his mother moved away from Penhally after… Oh, it must be ten years or so ago,' she finished hastily, clearly uncomfortable that she'd all but brought up the storm when Adam's father had been one of those who had died.

'We have met since then, Hazel,' Maggie said, taking pity on the poor woman's embarrassment. She held Adam's gaze deliberately as she continued lightly, 'We happened to bump into each other one day about a year ago when I went up to London to do one of my courses.' Nonchalant, that was what she'd been aiming for, but however it sounded it was better if everything was out in the open. After all, if she had known then that he…

'And then we got involved when there was an accident on the underground,' Adam added, but his casual tone sounded far more genuine than her own. 'We were on the spot and were able to provide some assistance until the people with the proper equipment could arrive.'

Maggie marvelled that he could make the whole incident sound so inconsequential. It had given her nightmares for months as she'd relived every second of…

'So, people, is it tea or coffee today?' Hazel asked as she bustled across to the kitchenette to fill the kettle. 'And there might even be some biscuits left in the tin as Nick's been out on patient visits all afternoon.'

Maggie had been waiting for her chance to refuse, but the mention of Hazel's biscuits changed her mind in a hurry.

'What sort of biscuits? Your special Cornish fairings?' she asked, eager for a taste so reminiscent of the happier days of her childhood. 'I'd love one.'

'If you've got some spare, I wouldn't mind having one, too, Hazel,' said the elegant older man on the other side of the room as he looked up from scanning a handful of envelopes by the practice mail rack. 'Your famous biscuits are one reason why I agreed to come out of retirement to help young Nick when the Avantis went back to Italy and he didn't have enough staff to run the practice properly.'

'It's very kind of you to say so, Dr Fletcher,' Hazel said with an extra wash of pink to her cheeks. 'The Cornish fairings *are* Nick's favourites,' she added with a happy smile as she gave the tin an experimental shake then opened it.

'They're fast becoming my favourites, too,' Adam said with a grin as he managed to take two at once, and the mouthful Maggie had just taken turned to dust in her mouth at the unexpected glimpse of the grin that had captivated her right from the first time she'd seen it.

Then she'd been a lowly fifteen-year-old and Adam had been one of the seniors, heading into his last year at school. He'd been so far out of her orbit that he shouldn't have even noticed the skinny little girl staring at him while her heart had tried to beat its way out of her flat chest.

But he *had* noticed her and had sent her a grin exactly like the one he'd just sent to Hazel, and she'd been utterly captivated.

The whole of that year she'd spent haunting the corridors, hoping for a glimpse of him, and gradually from an easygoing grin their relationship had graduated through breathless pleasantries to actual conversations while they'd waited for the bus to take them to and from school.

By the time her sixteenth birthday had come around they'd confided so many secrets and ambitions to each other—including the fact that he was aiming for a career in medicine—but one thing she would always remember was the fact that it had been the day when Adam had kissed her for the first time.

Then he'd gone away to begin his training and, apart from that dreadful week when he'd returned to support his mother through the wait until his father's body had been found, then the heart-breaking memorial service that the whole of Penhally seemed to have attended, this was the first time Adam had ever returned to the town of his birth.

So, why now? she wondered as he and Mike discovered a mutual interest in the mining history of Cornwall. She couldn't imagine that the beautiful willowy blonde in their wedding photo would appreciate burying herself in a rural place like this. She was definitely a London person and would probably only feel at home in the more pretentiously exclusive corners of the county.

Well, at least I won't be called on to socialise with her, she thought, stifling the pang that her lack of choices over her career brought. She would have loved to have become a doctor, too—would have loved nothing more than to have followed Adam through medical school. But it wasn't to be. In her final year at school her mother had been diagnosed with cancer and there had been no way that she could have countenanced the idea of leaving the last beloved member of her family without support while she underwent the gruelling rounds of chemotherapy, surgery and then more chemotherapy.

Still, Maggie couldn't imagine that a GP's wife would be terribly keen to socialise with a mere paramedic. Not that *she* saw her profession as inferior, just different. Paramedics were often the first people to see a patient and it was in their hands that patients' lives rested while they were stabilised for transportation to hospital. Far fewer accident victims would survive were it not for the existence of paramedics. But even though she was proud of what they were able to do for accident victims and of the green uniform she wore, she had to admit that they were still definitely from different echelons in the medical hierarchy.

She managed to keep herself on the edge of the conversation so that she didn't draw Hazel's attention. She certainly didn't want to make it obvious that she was avoiding speaking to Adam, but just when she was trying to find a way to edge towards the door unnoticed, there was a disturbance somewhere out in the street.

'*Nick!*' screamed a woman's voice. '*Somebody! Help!*'

'That sounds almost like Kate Althorp,' Hazel said, her eyes wide. 'Oh, no! There must have been an accident in the boatyard.'

Adam and Mike were already heading for the stairs, their longer legs outstripping Maggie's so that she was playing catch-up by the time they reached the reception area.

'What's the matter, Kate?' Adam demanded, his eyes already beginning a primary survey of the white, shaking woman in front of him. 'Where are you hurt? Was it the machinery in the boatyard?'

'It's not me. It's Jem…' She held up her clenched fist and they saw the mobile phone for the first time. 'He rang me and said that there's been an accident and they're hurt.'

'What accident and who's hurt?' demanded Nick Tremayne, as he appeared from the direction of his consulting room, a bewildered patient following him into the hallway.

'Jem phoned me,' Kate said through chattering teeth, her whole body vibrating with the onset of shock. 'He's with some other boys. They went exploring and there's been a rockfall in a mine. They're hurt.'

'*Which* mine, Kate?' Nick had shouldered Adam aside and was gripping her shoulders in both hands now, as though he thought he could force her to hold herself together and concentrate. 'There are hundreds of the things all over Cornwall.'

'I *know* that, but I don't know which one!' she wailed. Maggie automatically stepped forward when she saw that the woman's knees were about to fail her, but Nick had the situation in hand, wrapping an arm around Kate and swiftly lowering her onto the nearest chair.

'You're wasting time, Kate. Stop yowling and *think*!' he said sharply, and they all heard her draw in a shocked breath, her dark eyes wide with hurt at his apparently brutal treatment. But his curtness obviously had the desired effect because she was no longer out of control.

'He didn't tell me *which* mine,' she said, tears still streaming down her pale cheeks. 'And I tried to ring him back but the signal was too weak. You know how poor reception can be around here.'

'Well, what *did* he say?' Nick demanded.

'That they were exploring in the mine and…and something…or some*one*…fell and they're hurt. Oh, God, Nick, he's hurt. My baby's hurt and I don't know where he is or—?'

'*They?*' Nick snapped. 'Who are *they*…his friends? *Who* are his friends? And where were they going to play?'

'They're…I don't know…' She shook her head. 'Some boys from the school, I think. He just waved goodbye to me and said he'd be back for tea and…and…' She nearly lost it again but there must have been something in Nick's face that forced her to hang onto her control. 'They looked a bit older than him, but he's so tall for his age… He only got his bike for Christmas and he's already starting to grow out of it and—'

'They were on bikes?' Maggie interrupted as an image suddenly leapt into her head, the one she'd spotted through the windscreen of the ambulance of a tangle of brightly coloured bicycle frames half-hidden behind some gorse bushes. 'Did you say there were four or five of them, all on bikes?'

'Yes! You saw them? Oh, Maggie, where were they? You could have brought them down to the surgery in the ambulance. Surely, if they were hurt, you could have—'

'Kate,' she interrupted gently, 'I didn't actually see any of the boys, but I'm almost certain that I know where their bikes are.' She turned towards her colleague. 'Mike, you remember where you had to stop the ambulance when Mr Dinnis…when I had to take care of Mr Dinnis?' Sometimes patient confidentiality could be a nuisance when you had to be so careful to watch every word. 'Well, I could see some gorse over the stone wall and there were several bikes there. I couldn't see how many but there were anything up to half a dozen.'

'Take me there, please!' Kate demanded, surging to her feet wild-eyed. 'I've got to find my son. He's all I've got left of…of…'

'You're not going anywhere until we've contacted the emergency services,' Nick said firmly, pressing her back into her seat. 'We need to—'

'I already dialled 999 and told them Jem was stuck down a mine.' It was Kate's turn to interrupt. 'They said they were going to send emergency services to Penhally…to meet up here, at the surgery…'

'That's because all our staff have done emergency rescue training…as you know well because you were the one to arrange it when you were practice manager,' Nick reminded her.

'In the meantime, I could go up the hill with Maggie and Mike and see if we can find out if we've got the right mine,' Adam suggested, and even as Maggie's brain registered that he'd had a good idea, her heart sank at the thought of being any closer to him than absolutely necessary.

She was still coming to terms with the fact that he was just as heart-breakingly handsome as ever and that he was for ever out of reach. The prospect of having to work with him on a regular basis wasn't something she wanted to contemplate.

In fact, it might be the only thing that could persuade her to move away from her beloved Penhally.

'Good idea, Adam,' Nick agreed, even though it was obvious that he would rather be the one in the thick of any activity. 'We'll wait to hear from you and lead the rescue teams up to you if Maggie's right.'

Maggie saw Mike beckoning her to the ambulance and realised that he'd gone out to take details from despatch of their next callout. If it was another heart-attack victim, like Walter Dinnis, she would have no option but to give Adam directions to the place she'd seen the bikes and leave him to find his own way. She was not in charge of determining priorities when the emergency calls came through and would have to go where she was told.

'That was Dispatch,' Mike confirmed. 'They know we're almost at the end of our shift but they're telling us to stay on duty here and do whatever we can until they can send out a replacement crew to relieve us.'

'Shall I come with you?' Adam asked. 'Or would it be better if I followed you in my own vehicle?'

'It's your choice,' Maggie said briskly, grateful that if he were to come with them, he'd have to travel in the back of the vehicle. She didn't feel as if she was ready for any closer contact until she'd got her emotions a little better under control around him. It would be nice to know something simple…such as whether she loved him or loathed him after the way they'd parted a year ago.

'If you're coming with us you'll have to hop in the back and hang on—tight!' Mike called out. 'That twisting hill out of Penhally isn't comfortable at the best of times, and it's downright evil in an ambulance.'

'I'll follow you in my car, then,' he said as Maggie double-checked that the back doors were firmly closed and raced towards the passenger door to climb into the cab.

Mike was already reversing the ungainly vehicle out of the surgery car park as Adam put the key in the ignition of his car, and when the ambulance driver gunned the powerful engine along the road edging the harbour, with blue lights and siren both going, Adam was surprised to see just how fast he was having to travel to keep up with them.

A middle-aged car driver tried to dispute priority as they approached the narrow bottleneck of Harbour Bridge but rapidly changed his mind when Mike flipped the headlights up full and drove straight at him. Adam had no difficulty following in his wake but at Higher Bridge they both had to slow down just long enough to negotiate the tight corner onto the narrow bridge with the massive granite parapets—they wouldn't be going anywhere if they sideswiped one of those—and then he could hear the full-throated roar of the engine that told him that Mike was using every ounce of power to pull up the winding road out of the steep-sided valley as quickly as possible.

Even though it had been years since he'd lived in Penhally, the road was familiar enough that Adam could almost switch to automatic pilot to drive it, his thoughts centred on the woman travelling in the vehicle up ahead rather than on where they were going and why.

A major part of the reason why he'd signed on as a locum at Penhally Bay Surgery had been because Maggie still lived and worked in the area, but he'd been completely bowled over when he'd come into the staff-room a little while ago and found her standing there, the ultimate professional in her paramedic's uniform.

Her new hairstyle had been a bit of a shock, too. A year ago she'd still been wearing it in the same shoulder-length bob that he'd always known, tied back into a shiny dark ponytail for practicality, but he had to admit that the shorter style suited her elfin beauty even better, and highlighted all the colours that went to make her unusual hazel eyes.

He pulled a face when he replayed the expression on her face when she'd caught sight of him. It certainly hadn't been warmly welcoming but, then, what had he expected? He'd made a complete mess of things the last time he'd seen her and even though it had been un-intentional, he knew he'd hurt her.

That was another reason why he was back in Penhally…to see if he could persuade her to listen while he explained exactly what had been going on in his chaotic life a year ago, to tell her that he hadn't delib-

erately set out to make her go against everything she
believed in…that there had been extenuating circumstances that…

'Forget it for now,' he growled aloud when he saw
the indicator signal that the vehicle ahead was going to
pull off the road and slowed his own car ready to follow.
'There's nothing you can do about it until we find out
where these kids are and what kind of help they need.'

Talking to Maggie, making her understand and,
hopefully, getting her to forgive him and let him back
into her life was why he was here, but that would all
have to wait until he could persuade her to meet up with
him after work.

For now he was going to have to switch his brain into
rescue mode and, as hard as it would be, he'd have to
force himself to forget that the slender woman up ahead
was anything other than a professional colleague.

CHAPTER TWO

'SLOW down a bit, Mike. I saw the bikes just up here on the left,' Maggie said, peering through the gathering gloom in attempt to spot the right clump of gorse bushes over the top of the stone wall, glad that they were nearly there.

Every second of the journey she'd been overwhelmingly aware that the car following in their wake was being driven by Adam Donnelly, the first man she'd ever loved and the one who'd broken her heart a year ago when they'd met up at that course in London.

He was absolutely the last person she'd expected to see walking into the staffroom at Penhally Bay Surgery at that time of day. She'd been certain that it would be safe…that he would still have been out doing home visits…and her instant reaction to those deep blue eyes had been as visceral as ever.

She still didn't know whether she was horrified that she might have to deal with him on occasion while he was a locum in the practice, if she was called out to help one of his patients, or whether she was delighted that he had reappeared in her life again.

What she did know was that every breath she'd taken

in his vicinity had drawn in the unique mixture of soap and man that she'd never been able to forget, and what was worse, when he'd leaned towards her she'd been able to feel his breath on her cheek and even ruffling the hairs of her new, much shorter hairstyle.

'There's a gateway just a bit further on. I take it that's the one we're looking for?' Mike said as he indicated and swung the vehicle to a stop just beyond where they'd halted a short while ago. 'Can you—?' he began, but Maggie had anticipated his request and was already out of her seat, racing to open the gate.

'Are there any beasts in the field?' he called. 'Anything that could get out on the road and cause even more problems?'

'Nothing that I can see,' Maggie replied as she swung the gate wide and found the loose rock that the farmer had obviously left ready for use as a prop. 'But if you swing wide, we can use the headlights to make certain. Then I can leave this open.'

The wide swathe of light not only confirmed that the field was empty of any sheep or cows but also flashed across the jumble of bikes behind a sturdy growth of gorse.

'Yes! They're still there!' Maggie called. 'Did you see them?' She hurried across the short-cropped turf, pausing just long enough to count how many bikes there were.

'How many are there?' Adam asked, his deep voice startling her as she hadn't heard him following her across the grass.

'Five, all about the same size so, as Kate said, they're probably all around the same age. But where's the mine?' she demanded, turning in a complete circle.

'That end of the field is a complete jumble of hills and rocks, a bit like a mini-tor, but there's no ruined building with a tall chimney anywhere near here.'

'Well, if it isn't in this field then it must be in one near here, or they wouldn't have left their bikes,' Adam pointed out, and swiftly set off up the steep slope of the field towards the rough ground, his long legs making short work of the distance as he called back, 'I'll climb up there and see if there's anything visible over the next wall.'

'Here,' Mike said as he caught up with them. 'I brought torches and emergency packs, just in case.'

Maggie grabbed a torch and one of the bags, cross with herself that she'd completely forgotten about their equipment. She'd only jumped out of the cab to open the gate, then had got carried away with the hunt for evidence of the children.

She was hurrying to keep up with the men's far longer legs when she tripped over something near a stray gorse bush.

With a muttered imprecation she bent to see what it was. Probably a broken branch from the last storm, or perhaps from hungry cattle taking advantage of the fact that gorse was one of the few native plants that grew and flowered right through the year. But it wasn't gorse. It was a piece of a weathered old sawn plank with a very fresh break at one end.

Maggie swung her torch around, wondering where the other piece had gone, and what a stray plank was doing up here in the first place. There certainly weren't any buildings that she could see, only the rocky formation in front of her, with the sprawl of dense gorse growing at its foot.

The beam caught a glimpse of the colour change on several branches that had been scuffed. One had been recently broken, as though some animal had tried to force a way into the bush.

'Not a very hospitable place to want to go,' she muttered as she peered through the density of the plant's prickly canopy, but there was definitely nothing there but a big dark shadow. The bushes were thick and vigorous but certainly weren't anywhere near big enough to hide five youngsters, let alone the ruin of an engine house for a mine.

'Can you see anything?' she called up to Mike and Adam, marvelling that she had no difficulty discerning which was which even though it was now nearly dark. Mike had the broader, more muscular shoulders, thanks to his regular attendance at a gym, but was several inches shorter than Adam's leaner, more naturally athletic body.

'Can't see anything that looks like a mine,' Mike called back down. 'We must have the wrong bikes for a different set of kids. Perhaps someone's been stealing them and stockpiling them up here, and is going to collect their stash at some time.'

'Where do you think we should look next?' Adam said as he leapt lightly from one rock to another until he landed almost at her feet, apparently unhampered by the second awkward bag of equipment he'd taken from Mike.

'I have absolutely no...' Maggie paused and turned her head from side to side. 'Shh! Did you hear that?'

'What?' Mike's footwear was clattering on the granite as he completed his descent to join them by the gorse bushes. 'I didn't hear anything.'

'There it is again,' Maggie insisted, and turned the beam of her torch towards the bush. 'It sounded almost as if a kitten's caught in that gorse.'

Except it hadn't sounded exactly like that, because the noise was fainter and seemed much further away. Perhaps it was nothing more than the weak bleat of an early lamb in a nearby field. Perhaps…

'Perhaps it's the kids?' Mike suggested. 'Perhaps they're somewhere nearby and they can see the light from our torches and the flashes on our uniforms. Hey!' he shouted loudly, startling Maggie for a second. 'Is there anybody there?'

This time there was no mistaking the sound they heard because it was louder, as though someone was shouting with renewed energy now that there was someone listening.

'We're here!' called a distant childish voice that definitely came from the middle of the gorse bush.

'But I looked there and couldn't see anything,' Maggie protested as Adam dropped to his knees beside her.

'Neither can I,' she heard him mutter, then stifle a curse when there was the unmistakable sound of ripping cloth as he tried to force a path through the sturdy stems and branches. 'Unless…Got it!' he exclaimed, and she and Mike heard the sound of splintering timber.

'What have you found?' Maggie demanded as she dropped to her knees behind him, grateful for the sturdy fabric of her uniform.

'I think it's the entrance to an adit,' Adam said tersely, then there was the sound of more splintering timber and a muttered, 'Ouch!'

'What's an adit?' Maggie demanded, even as she wondered what he'd done to hurt himself.

'It's a mining term for a horizontal—or nearly horizontal—shaft into a mine,' Mike explained distractedly as he took the broken pieces of wood Adam was passing back to him and stacked them aside. 'It was used for access or drainage, if I remember what my grandfather told me. He was a born and bred tin miner before the bottom dropped out of the international price of tin.'

'Yes! It *is* an adit!' Adam exclaimed over the screeching sound of rusty nails being dragged out of wood. 'It was obviously boarded up some time ago, either when the yield became uneconomic for the man hours needed to extract it or when the price of tin took that tumble. *I* certainly don't remember it ever being worked.'

'Is there anybody there?' called a young voice from the depths of the entrance Adam had uncovered.

'Yes!' Adam called back, his head stuck into the hole he'd enlarged by tearing the board away. 'I'm a doctor. *Who* are you and *where* are you?'

There was the sound of other voices far in the distance, but the one closest to them shouted back to his companions with a swift, 'Shut up, you lot! I won't be able to hear what they're saying with you making that racket!'

'One at a time, please,' Adam roared, and everything went quiet.

'There are five of us,' the young voice came again, and Maggie was impressed by how calm and controlled he sounded. If she'd been in the same situation…well, there was no chance of that. Her claustrophobia was a very good reason to steer clear of anything in the least bit mine-like. 'We're mostly all right,' continued the young voice, 'except Tel. He fell on the stope and then some rocks fell down and he's stuck under them… And there's wet on the floor under him, so we think he's bleeding, but we dropped our torch and the bulb broke so we can't see.'

'And who are you?' Adam asked, while Maggie itched to get the talking over and get those kids out of there. They'd been missing for over an hour now and…

'My name's Jem…Jeremiah Althorp, and my mum's… She used to work at the doctors surgery.'

'Kate!' Maggie exclaimed, suddenly remembering that the poor woman was waiting for news of her son.

Well, she thought as she speed-dialled the surgery, the number still in her phone from when her mother had been so ill, they might not know the full extent of everybody's injuries yet but, apart from an understandable tremor in his voice, Kate's son at least seemed to be relatively safe.

'Penhally Bay Surgery,' said the familiar reassuring voice of Hazel Furse. 'Can I help—?'

'Hazel, it's Maggie…Maggie Pascoe. Will you tell Kate that we've found the boys and that we've been talking to her son?'

'Oh, thank God!' Hazel exclaimed, then obviously pulled the receiver away from her ear to call across the reception area, 'They've found them!'

Maggie smiled when she heard the sudden hubbub and cheering at the other end, then Hazel was back on the line.

'Kate wants to know if you're coming straight back to Penhally with them…well, with Jem,' she added in a quieter voice.

'We won't be back for a bit, Hazel,' Maggie confessed. 'I wanted you all to know as soon as possible that we've located the lads, but we haven't got them out yet. I didn't want everyone to think that we were still looking for the right mine.'

'OK.' Hazel's tone was more subdued this time. 'So where are you and how difficult is it going to be to get them out? Are you going to need other emergency services to help? How many of the kids are injured and how badly?'

'We're on the road out of the valley, past the junction between Bridge Street and Dunheved Road, on the way to St Piran Hospital,' Maggie explained, trying to make the directions as simple and as clear as possible. 'There's a field on the left, just past a little lay-by, with the gate propped wide open. The ambulance is parked just inside the field facing towards some piles of rocks, with Dr Donnelly's car beside it. We're probably going to need a fire crew with ropes and ladders—oh, and another ambulance in case any of the lads need to travel on backboards. Apart from that, we won't really know until we can get close enough to them to see what we're dealing with.'

She shuddered at the thought of getting any closer to that mine entrance than she was now. Just the idea of going into that dark, dank opening was enough to make her claustrophobia send her pulse sky high and double her respiration rate.

'I'll pass all that on,' Hazel promised. 'Keep in touch, Maggie.'

'Will do,' she promised.

'Hey, Maggie, we need you here,' Mike called over his shoulder before she'd even cut the call.

'OK. Which set of equipment do you need?' she said as she squatted beside the prickly bushes that looked as if they were devouring the two men whole. All she could see of Mike was his legs and Adam was nothing more than two obviously male feet clad in a totally inappropriate pair of polished leather shoes.

Even as she watched, that pair of feet started to squirm backwards out of the gorse bush towards her and she could see that his smart suit trousers were already stained and snagged and probably damaged beyond any hope of repair.

'We're not ready for our boxes of tricks yet,' Mike was saying as Adam straightened up and walked the two paces that put him right in front of her.

Pride made her stand her ground, even though the man's presence had a disastrous effect on her nervous system, and she forced herself to look him straight in the eye.

'Maggie…' he began, then it seemed as if he couldn't hold her gaze any more and he paused so long that she just knew she wasn't going to like what came next. 'Look, I know what I'm asking will be…very hard for you but… The thing is, the entrance to the mine is almost completely blocked by debris—loose rocks and suchlike—and neither Mike nor I will fit through it until it's been excavated.'

'Well, I've just been in contact with Hazel at the surgery,' she told him hastily, not liking the direction that her vivid imagination was taking her. 'She's going to let the emergency services know exactly where we are so they shouldn't be long. Then we'll have all the equipment and manpower we need to—'

'Maggie,' he interrupted gently. 'I managed to shine a torch far enough along the adit for Jem to be able to see it reflected off the walls, so he's absolutely certain that we're here. Didn't you hear him tell me that there's a puddle of blood under one of the lads…the one trapped by the rockfall? From what he said, I don't think that boy can afford to wait for anyone else to turn up because we don't know whether he's bleeding out, or heading for crush syndrome, or what. It's entirely probable that his only chance of staying alive is for one of us to go down there and take care of him. Mike and I are just too bulky to get through that gap, so that just leaves you.'

'*Me?* But I *can't*!' she squeaked as panic tightened its grip around her throat. 'Adam, you *know* I can't. Y-you know that I'm—'

'Maggie, stop! You're hyperventilating. Take a breath!' he ordered, his voice sharp even though it was barely above a whisper in the quiet of the Cornish countryside. He held both her shoulders in warm, firm hands, his thumbs stroking her soothingly through the sturdy fabric of her uniform and sending a shower of shivers through her body. 'You *can* do it.'

'*No!* I—'

'Shh!' he soothed. 'I know the whole idea freaks you out, but you've done it before. Remember?'

'Remember? Of *course* I remember!' she snapped. 'I didn't sleep properly for months after that nightmare of an afternoon. You *can't* ask me to go in there when you know how bad—'

'Maggie, I'm not asking you to do it for *me*,' he reminded her, with a little shake of her shoulders. 'I've got a bad feeling about that lad trapped by the rocks.'

That stopped her in her tracks.

She'd been part of the medical profession long enough to respect her colleagues' intuition about a situation. Often it flew in the face of logic, but it was uncanny how often it was right, so if Adam had a bad feeling about Tel's condition…

'How bad do you think it is?'

'Well, we all know that youngsters like to exaggerate the gorier things in life but, from what Jem said, I'm almost certain that his friend's leg has been badly broken by the rocks, and you know as well as I do that he's likely to lose the leg altogether if he isn't released soon. But it's the blood loss that I'm most concerned about,' he stressed, knowing she would understand the significance of such a situation. 'There's far too much of it, if Jem's description is accurate, and I'm wondering if the bone was splintered by the impact and has done some major venous or arterial damage.'

'So you think there's a serious chance that he might be bleeding out?' she whispered, suddenly understanding that there *was* something worse than being asked to face one of her worst fears. Being claustrophobic and having to go underground was nothing compared with the prospect of bleeding to death trapped under a pile of rocks. Then there was the prospect of the youngster developing crush syndrome, which could be equally fatal when the pressure was finally removed.

For just a second, as she pictured herself crawling through into that awful darkness, she was certain that she couldn't do it, but then she realised something more important. If she *didn't* do it, and the lad died, she would never be able to forgive herself. The fact that the young woman she'd tended under the underground train had survived and was slowly getting on with her life had been one of the few things that had made all the nightmares worthwhile.

'Adam, promise me you'll stay close,' she begged, the words already hovering in the chilly air between them before she'd realised she was going to say anything, her breath swirling around them like tortured wraiths.

'Of course I'll be here for you, Maggie. Like I was last time,' he promised, and she knew that whatever else had gone wrong between them, he wouldn't break his word to her.

'So,' she said, trying desperately to sound brisk but very conscious that her teeth were starting to chatter at the imminent prospect of climbing into the mine, 'how are we going to do this? What do you want me to do?'

'To put it at its most basic, you need to get in far enough to find out what's happened to those kids. Start with basic triage, the way you would with every callout. Find out how many are injured and how badly and prioritise how you need to deal with them.'

'Until I'm in there I'm not going to know how much kit I can take with me,' Maggie pointed out, concerned that she might not have the right equipment to hand when she reached the boys. 'A lot of our stuff is in portable boxes or bags because we often have to start work on a patient away from the ambulance. But if I'm the only one going in and I'm going to be climbing or…or squeezing through small spaces…' She swallowed hard, her imagination already far too vivid for peace of mind.

'Prioritise,' he repeated firmly. 'Most of all, we need to find out what we can do for the one who's trapped. See if it's possible to release him or will he just have to be stabilised as best you can until we can get some muscle or some serious machinery in there to free him and get him out?'

'And in my spare time…' she said ironically.

Adam gave a short huff of laughter and she caught a brief glimpse of that grin again. 'In your spare time, Maggie, you could keep up a running commentary so that I can be certain that you're all right.'

Then there was no more time to delay, not if that lad was bleeding as badly as Jem thought he was.

'Coming through,' she said to Mike as she threaded her way through the gorse. It wasn't until she was almost at the dreaded black hole, framed now by the last remnants of the broken and rotted boards, that she realised that he'd spent his time while she and Adam had been speaking in ripping the jagged timber away so that she could see better to climb over the rubble blocking the entrance to the adit.

'Maggie, just think about this for a minute,' her colleague cautioned quietly when she reached out a shaky hand towards the rough rocks. 'The first rule of rescue work is never to endanger yourself, and this definitely comes under the heading of—'

'Don't, Mike,' she said with a single shake of her head, knowing he was right but also knowing that she had to be able to live with her own conscience.

'Maggie, I know those lads need help,' he tried again, holding onto her arm to prevent her moving any further forward. 'But you could lose your job for going in there without the proper—'

'Mike, you know how much I love my job, but I don't think I'd *want* it any more if I let any of those kids die when I could have done something to prevent it,' she said with an unexpected feeling of determination. 'I'm not going in there because I want to but because I have to, and the best way you can help is to stand by with the bags of equipment ready to pass me the supplies I need when I get in there.'

'Ready to go, Maggie?' Adam prompted from close behind her, but she'd already known he was there, silently supporting her as she argued her case. 'Take my torch,' he offered as she nodded and took a deep breath. 'It's not as heavy-duty as yours but I think it gives out just as much light.'

'Thank you,' she whispered, gazing back for one last second into those shadowy midnight-blue eyes. Then she forced herself to begin squeezing though the awkward opening at the top of the rockfall that was blocking most of the entrance and preventing the two men from taking her place in there.

Once inside, she put her hand back out again to be

passed her emergency pack of basic equipment and then it was time to crawl into the blackness.

For several paces she concentrated so hard on controlling her breathing and putting one hand and knee in front of the other that she didn't pay much attention to her surroundings. It wasn't until the heel of the hand holding Adam's torch landed on a painfully sharp piece of rock that she paused for a second to rub it and caught sight of something that surprised her.

'Hey! Adam…Mike, it's not just a tiny tunnel in here!' she exclaimed with a definite feeling of relief. 'I can actually stand up in it once I'm past the rockfall at the entrance!' She suited her actions to her words and swung briefly back towards the entrance, suddenly uneasily aware that if she hadn't been looking directly at it, she wouldn't have known where it was. It was now so dark outside that the only light visible was from her own torch and the one held by whoever was immediately outside the entrance. The rough pile of rocks that were blocking the entrance made that part of the mine look no different from any other part.

'Can you pass the other equipment packs through?' she suggested. 'It looks as if there'll be plenty of room, and I might be able to carry them all the way to where the boys are. That would save time.'

'Stick to plan A,' Adam advised, his voice sounding strangely hollow as it echoed around her. 'Just take your lightweight emergency pack with the basics. It's better to locate the boys and find out what you're dealing with before you start loading yourself down unnecessarily.

Then you can decide what's the best way to proceed. You can always come back for more.'

'Anyway,' Mike's disembodied voice added his twopenn'orth, 'while you're doing that, we're going to be clearing as much of this rock away as we can, so we can get in there to help.'

'OK,' she agreed, and turned back to the tunnel with a shudder.

Adam was right, of course, but, then, he'd already worked as an emergency specialist in a big London hospital and had gained enough experience to be able to take over teaching the course she'd gone up to attend when the original lecturer had been taken ill.

She could feel herself smiling when she remembered her delight at seeing him walk into that lecture room. It had been so many years since the last time she'd seen him but one look at that lean athletic body and the familiar planes and angles of his face had been enough to know this really was the man who'd been haunting her dreams since she'd been an impressionable teenager.

The answering flash of recognition in those beautiful deep blue eyes had made her grateful that she'd been sitting down. The last thing she'd needed in front of a roomful of colleagues had been to make a fool of herself by falling at his feet.

'Ouch!' she yelped as her head hit an obstruction and she dropped to one knee to give it a rub.

'What's the matter?' Adam demanded instantly. 'Maggie, are you all right?'

'I hit my head on something,' she complained crossly, and shone her torch upwards to see if she could find the obstruction. Was the roof dropping that much lower already? How long would it be before she was reduced to crawling again?

When she saw the dangling balk of wood thicker than her thigh that should have been supporting the ceiling, she wished that she hadn't bothered looking.

Suddenly she was overwhelmingly conscious of just how many tons of rock were sitting just inches above her head, and she found herself fighting to draw in enough air.

'Maggie?' Adam called. 'You're supposed to be talking to me, remember?'

She was so panic-stricken that she could barely remember her own name, and as for breathing…

'Maggie!' he called again with worry clear in his voice. 'Can you hear me? Are you all right?'

'Yes,' she croaked, and had to clear her throat, but his concern had helped her to regain control. 'Yes, Adam, I can hear you.'

'What's happening, then? I heard you cry out. Did you injure yourself?'

'I hit my head,' she said shortly, giving the spot another rub once she'd made certain that she hadn't done enough damage to make it bleed.

'What did you hit your head on? Does the roof slope down that sharply?'

'It wasn't the roof,' she said, forcing herself to say the words without thinking about the significance of them. 'It was one of those wood thingies that holds up the roof. It's come off the upright one and was hanging down low enough for me to walk into it.'

She thought she heard Adam swear but his voice when he spoke was calmness personified. 'Mike says he thinks those are called sprags or gibs, depending where you are,' he told her...as if she was interested in the name of the thing she'd hit. All she was worried about was whether the fact that only one end of the wretched thing was where it was supposed to be meant that the roof wasn't being held up properly.

No! She wasn't going to think about that. There were five young lads waiting for her to get to them...relying on her to sort out their injuries before they could be helped out of the mine.

'Jem!' she called when her next few careful steps brought her to an apparent choice of directions. 'Where are you?'

'I'm here, straight ahead of you,' said a boyish voice, so unexpectedly close that he made her jump. His face was nearly at floor level a dozen or more yards ahead of her and, apart from smears of dirt, was almost totally devoid of colour when she caught him in her torchlight.

There was no mistaking that he was Kate's son, she thought with an internal grin, not with that dark hair and brown eyes set off in that bone structure.

She began to hurry forward, wondering if he was lying there because he was injured or trapped, but he quickly called out, 'Don't come too close. I'm on the top of a stope.'

Maggie paused uncertainly, her need to check that he wasn't too badly injured barely kept in check. 'What's a stope?' she asked.

'It's where the miners were following a vein of ore

and the excavation leaves steps in the rock. I found out all about it on the internet for a school project.'

'Steps? But that's great!' Maggie exclaimed as she started forward again, more cautiously this time. 'That'll make it much easier to get you all out.' Much easier than if the boys had fallen down a narrow shaft, for example.

'No. You don't understand,' he said urgently, clearly wanting her to stop. 'They're not solid steps. They're all broken and crumbly in places. That's how Tel fell.'

'Tell me what happened,' she prompted as she slowly crept forward on hands and knees again, to peer over the edge and down the precipitous stepped slope. Was this the moment when she was going to discover that she had a fear of heights, too?

'He didn't fall very far but some rocks came down and landed on him. The rest of us climbed down the rest of the way to help him get out again,' he continued, the words pouring out in an urgent, jerky stream. 'We were trying to move the rocks and Chris got hurt, then we dropped the torch and the bulb broke and we couldn't see what we were doing any more, and then I said I'd come back up to get help but I couldn't get up this last bit because I'm not tall enough, and the signal was too weak on my mobile so I couldn't tell Mum where we were. Then it got too dark and I didn't dare climb down again, so I was stuck here till you came.'

'So, where is Tel now?' she asked when she'd finally eased forward enough to see down the stope and beyond, shining the torchlight against the jumble of rocks at the bottom of the jagged steps and shuddering at the size of them. If something that size had landed on one of the boys, there would be little likelihood that they'd survived. 'Your message said that one of the boys is bleeding. That's Tel, is it?'

'Uh-huh.' He nodded. 'And he's unconscious.'

'Can you see where the blood is coming from? His head, his body…?'

'I think it's his leg,' he said with a frown, 'but there's a load of rocks in the way so I can't see properly. And I can't move them either—they're too heavy.'

'Well, it won't be too long before we can get some big strong men down here to get them shifted,' she reassured him, even as her fears about crush syndrome increased, then took a deep breath to bolster herself for what she knew she had to do next. It might still be within the so-called golden hour for his young friend and she needed to start minimising the trauma he'd suffered as soon as possible.

'Jem, I need you to help me. I need you to show me how to get down the…the stope…to have a look at Tel.'

'But…but you're a *girl*,' he said, screwing up his face in disbelief, and Maggie made a mental note to have a word with Kate about her son's gender stereotyping once this was all over.

'Yes, I am, but I'm a girl who used to do climbing ropes and gymnastics at school, and climbing over the rocks under the lighthouse every holiday.'

He still didn't look as if he believed her and she was aware of his reluctance as he guided her through every shaky step she took as she lowered herself feet first over that first enormous drop then edged backwards down the rest of the ragged steps of the stope.

'They're behind here,' he said, hurrying forward towards another pile of rock that looked as if it had been there for centuries…the pile of boulders she'd been looking at from the top just a few minutes ago looking even more enormous now she was close to them. 'Tel fell down the last bit of the stope, then some of the rocks started to fall and he tried to get out of the way so he was running into this other tunnel, but there were too many rocks coming and they were falling too fast and he couldn't get out of the way in time and they hit him and knocked him down. Some of them landed on him.'

He started climbing round the edge of the enormous pile of loose rocks and she suddenly caught sight of another tunnel entrance that had been almost completely hidden from view. Her heart began to pound with renewed panic when she saw how small it was. It was narrower than the one at the top of the stope. Much narrower and not nearly as high.

I can't do this, said a panicky voice in her head, and her feet froze to the dank, gritty ground. *I won't be able to breathe in there; there won't be enough air, especially if I have to share it with all these other people.*

CHAPTER THREE

'MAGGIE?' Jem turned back to her before he joined his friends in the second tunnel, his eyes very dark in the gloom, and she had the feeling that he was deliberately keeping his voice low so that they couldn't hear him. 'I'm…I'm really glad you came to find us. It was scary being down here all by ourselves…without any light.'

Suddenly she was ashamed of herself. She had a light—Adam's torch—and the certainty that, by now, there were probably dozens of people arriving in the field around the entrance to the adit, and all of them would be working out the best way to get them all out safely. All she had to do was the job she was trained for…to assess the injuries this group of lads had sustained and to stabilise them as far as possible until further help arrived.

The fact that she would rather be a million miles away was *her* problem, not theirs, and she couldn't let it affect the care she gave them.

'Hey! It's a girl! I thought you said it was someone coming to help us!' said another disgusted young voice, dragging her back to the whole reason she was putting herself through this misery. Maggie added a fresh mental note to suggest a visit to their school to tell them all about the wide variety of job possibilities for *girls* in the twenty-first century.

'I'm a paramedic,' she corrected him gently as she caught him in the bright light of Adam's torch, 'and I need to know what injuries you've all got.'

'Dwayne, me and Jonno haven't got any injuries,' Jem said swiftly, acting as spokesman. 'Chris got his hand hurt when it was squished by a rock, but Tel's the one who's hurt the worst.'

While he'd been giving her the details, he'd been pointing to the other lads and she quickly threaded her way through rocks and boys to bend over the silent youngster trapped by the fallen rocks.

'Is he still alive?' Jem demanded uncertainly as her gloved fingertips probed for the carotid artery in the dust-caked neck. 'I thought he was when I tried before, but I wasn't sure I was looking in the right place...'

'Yes. He's still alive. His heart's still beating, Jem,' she confirmed, remembering to smile her reassurance in spite of the fact that the pulse was weaker and faster than she would have wanted. And it was hardly any wonder that his breathing was laboured with that amount of rock inhibiting the movement of his ribcage.

He was obviously going to need fluids and a far more detailed examination, but there just wasn't room in these cramped conditions, not with so many heads leaning over her shoulder to see what she was doing.

There was only one alternative so, much as every-thing in her was telling her that she needed to attend to the most seriously injured child first, she beckoned forward the one that Jem had called Chris.

'Come here, Chris. Show me your hand,' she said, a quick flash of her torch across his face reassuring her that his pupils were equal and reactive. The fact that it had also revealed the tell-tale tracks of hastily smeared tears was something she wouldn't be mentioning to anyone.

'You won't hurt it, will you?' he asked, as he held his other hand protectively over it.

'I promise I'll be gentle, but I need to know what sort of injury you've got or I can't do anything for it,' she explained, and hid a smile at his reluctant acquiescence.

'Ouch!' she said in sympathy when she saw his bruised and swollen hand. 'It looks like the rock caught you right on the back of your hand. Can you move your fingers?'

'Don't know. It'll hurt too much if I do.'

'Can you try…just once?' she appealed, then realised she might be missing out on the youngster's need for drama. 'I need to see if your tendons, muscles and nerves are still working.'

His eyes widened, so obviously she'd made her request seem important enough to impress. 'OK,' he said grudgingly. 'But I only have to do it once, right?'

'Right,' she agreed, then held her hand out flat towards him. 'And if you put your hand on mine, you'll only need to move your fingers a tiny bit and I'll be able to feel it.'

He gingerly lowered the purple swollen mass onto her palm, drawing a sharp hiss of breath in through his teeth at one point before looking up at her.

'Ready?' she prompted gently, wishing there was

such a thing as a miniature portable X-ray to help her make a diagnosis. As it was, she didn't even dare to give him any analgesia in case his only way out was to climb up that deadly stope.

'Brilliant!' she praised when she felt him carefully move each finger one by one, his face screwed up against the pain. 'I felt each of them move,' she confirmed, and when she saw the relief on his face she was glad he didn't know that it wasn't the whole story. His nerves and tendons might have escaped major injury, but she'd definitely detected the crepitation of at least one broken metacarpal and wouldn't be surprised if there was more than one.

'Right, Chris,' she said briskly as she reached into her backpack and drew out a folded square of fabric. She was all too aware that time was passing and she still had to see Tel. 'I need to immobilise your hand so that you don't do it any further damage.'

Years of practice meant that it took mere seconds to fashion an impressive sling to support his hand up against his opposite shoulder. Not knowing how seriously Tel was hurt meant she daren't take the time to apply a splint.

'Is that more comfortable?' she asked, and received a grateful nod. 'Well, if your friends give you a hand, do you think you could climb out over the pile in front of the tunnel to give me a bit more room? I need to be able to get closer to Tel to see what the rocks have done to him. Has he been talking to you at all since they fell on him?'

'He's moaned a couple of times,' said one of the lads.

'And Jem felt his neck a couple of times to see if he's

still got a pulse, and you said he has, so that means he's still alive, doesn't it?' said another, as the two of them scrambled over the rocks to get out of the confining space, almost forgetting to take their injured friend with them in their eagerness. At the last moment, each of them held out a hand towards Chris and took his arms to help him to keep his balance without disturbing his injured hand.

Once they were out of the confining space, all three of them were obviously keen to move away from it and Maggie knew how they felt. She wasn't in the least bit keen to stay in there either, even though she knew she had to.

For just a second she flicked the torch beam out of the narrow tunnel and up the stope towards the darker shadow of the adit at the top…the tunnel that led to the opening into the outside world where Adam was waiting to hear what was happening… And the one thing she wanted most in the whole world was to get out of there as fast as she could and throw herself into his arms.

'And that just shows how being down here is messing with your mind,' she muttered under her breath. Adam may have been her hero when she'd been looking up to the handsome senior at school and weaving for-ever-after fantasies around him, but he'd developed feet of clay since. He certainly wasn't a person she could trust with her heart, but she didn't have any option but to trust him with her safety.

'Stay close, lads,' Maggie warned as the three of them disappeared out of sight behind the pile of rocks. This was no time for losing concentration, she reminded herself sternly as she banished Adam from her mind. She had an injured child who was relying on her to stabilise him, ready for the moment when the rescue team arrived. 'I wouldn't be able to cope if there were any more injuries, so don't go wandering off.'

She turned the torch back to focus on the last able-bodied youngster. 'Jem, it's your turn to climb out of here,' she said encouragingly, but he shook his head, the pale face topped with that dark shock of hair set in determination.

'I'm staying in here with Tel,' he said stubbornly. 'He knows me…and anyway you might need my help.'

Maggie was torn between wanting to hug the boy for providing her with company in this awful place and fearing that she would let herself down in front of him with a major panic attack.

'Well, a second pair of hands could come in useful so we'd better see what we can do for him,' she said, and bent to clear a small space among the smaller rocks so she could kneel as close as possible to the unconscious youngster, then dipped her shoulder and slid the all-important rucksack to the ground.

'Is his heart still beating?' Jem demanded, clearly concerned as her gloved fingertips probed once more for the too-rapid beat of his carotid artery. 'I was checking it before I climbed up the stope but then the torch got bust and it got dark outside so there wasn't any light coming in any more, and the others didn't know where to look…'

Maggie didn't need to be reminded just how dark it was or how far away the entrance was from where she was kneeling, and the only way to banish it from her mind was to concentrate on the messages her fingers were sending her mind and her conversation with this bright youngster.

'Yes. His heart's still beating, Jem,' she said, remembering once more to smile her reassurance.

As for the dark pool seeping out from under him, all she could hope was that there was a fair amount of water mixed in with it. If it was only blood, the youngster must be close to critical with that amount of loss.

Either way, it was imperative that she put a collar on him to immobilise his neck. If the lad woke up and tried to move, it could be too late to protect his spinal cord. Then she needed to get some replacement fluids into him to give his heart some volume to pump around.

'Right, Jem, if you want to make yourself useful, can you hold the torch for me, please? If you point it this way, I'll be able to find what I need to protect his neck. Then I want to put up a drip to get some fluids flowing into him,' she explained as she unzipped the relevant compartment and tilted it towards the light to find and pull out a cervical collar, then locate a giving set and a unit of saline. 'That way, everything will be ready to give him any drugs he needs.'

'It's a good job he doesn't know you're going to stick a needle in him,' Jem commented with glee as he watched her swab his friend's grubby arm then slide the needle in, hitting the vein she was looking for first time in spite of the limited lighting. 'Tel doesn't like needles. He says just looking at them makes him feel sick, but I think he's scared they'll hurt.'

'You don't mind them, though?' she asked, quite taken

with this self-possessed young boy. He was certainly far braver than she would have been in a similar situation.

'Nah,' he said dismissively. 'I watch all the medical programmes on TV...not just the fiction ones but the real ones in real hospitals, too...so needles don't bother me. Do you want me to hold that bag of water up, too?'

'That would be great,' she confirmed. 'And it's not just water in there—it's called saline because it's had a small amount of salt added to it.'

'Salt?' he exclaimed. 'Why?'

'Because our bodies don't work very well if they don't have the right amount of salt. It causes problems if we eat too much of it, but we also need to have it replaced if we've been losing fluids.'

'Otherwise you can get cramp?' he suggested brightly. 'Like I did after last sports day when we were running and got very sweaty when the sun was so hot?'

'Exactly!' Maggie exclaimed, keeping up the conversation while her fingers covered as much of Tel's body as she could reach, searching for any obvious injuries. 'It's very similar to that.'

She paused to sit back on her heels, delighted to confirm that, apart from a large goose egg on the back of his head, her young patient didn't have any obvious cranial injuries. As far as she could tell, the swelling was nothing more than a surface haematoma. If he was lucky, he would wake up with nothing worse than a mammoth headache and suffer from the effects of concussion.

But none of that was as daunting as the enormity of the next task she faced before she could complete her survey of Tel's injuries. There were an awful lot of rocks that had spilled into the mouth of this cramped tunnel and she was going to have to find out exactly how many of them were pressing down on him to know what the likelihood was that he was in danger of developing crush syndrome. Only then would she dare remove the pressure from Tel's ribs and legs.

And none of it was going to happen if she just sat here looking at it, she prompted herself. It seemed highly unlikely that Adam and Mike would have cleared enough from the heap by the entrance yet to be joining her any time soon. So that meant it was her job.

'Jem, are you OK, holding that for a while?' she asked with a shiver as the dank cold seemed to seep into her bones, suddenly realising that having to shift those rocks might have a good side to it. At least the physical activity would help to warm her up. 'I need to try to shift a few of these rocks so I can see where this blood's coming from.'

'Otherwise all the…the *saline* will be leaking out again?' he suggested cheerfully.

'You've got it.' She smiled across at him, strangely proud that he'd remembered the word she'd taught him, and wondered if that was what life would be like if she had a son of her own.

Unfortunately, the image that flashed into her head was a child with Adam's dark sapphire eyes and mischievous grin, and she knew *that* prospect was a complete impossibility. It wouldn't matter how much she still loved him or how attracted he was to her, she would never break her own code of ethics and sleep with a married man…not unless he was married to *her*. And that could certainly never be the case with Adam because he was already married to the elegant long-limbed beauty with the curtain of blonde hair that she'd seen in the wedding photo beside his bed.

She gave herself a shake and a silent talking-to for wasting time with painful memories and pointless day-dreaming, and reached for the first rock, surprised as ever how very heavy even a relatively small piece of granite could be.

It was fairly easy to shift the smaller stuff that had rolled away from the pile and she quickly cleared a space right down one side of Tel's body. Unfortunately, that only told her that, battered and bruised as it was, *that* leg wasn't the one that was bleeding. It did, however, tell her that the position of the rocks made crush syndrome unlikely, so that was one good point at least.

'We're getting there,' she reassured Jem, conscious that he was following her every move as she reached for one of the larger rocks poised atop the whole heap piled against the wall of the tunnel.

'Careful!' Jem called, as she set off a minor avalanche as soon as she gave the rock a tug.

It seemed to take for ever before everything stopped moving and even then there were odd creaks and groans as the debris settled into its new position.

'What happened?'

'Are you guys all right?' demanded an instant chorus at the opening to the tunnel.

'We're OK,' Maggie said when she could draw breath in the dusty atmosphere, knowing they needed reassurance from the only adult in the vicinity. For several very long seconds all she'd been able to imagine was that she was about to be buried alive, and her throat had closed up completely.

'Jem, can you shine the torch over a bit?' she asked, hoping they couldn't hear how much her voice was trembling with gratitude that it had only been a rearrangement of the rocks that were already there and not a fresh fall. It was bad enough that she was down here, having to cope with a lifelong phobia—at least she had the mental reassurance that at any time she had the option of climbing back up the stope to get out. She definitely couldn't cope if she knew she was trapped down there, like Tel.

Her thoughts suddenly flashed back to that awful afternoon in the London underground when a man and a woman had fallen—or jumped—off the platform into the path of an approaching train.

Maggie had been certain that she wouldn't be able to deal with squeezing herself between the rails, with the dark smelly bulk of the train just inches above her head, while she tried to staunch the bleeding from the girl's partially severed arm. Only the fact that Adam had been there, calmly talking her through the whole ordeal, had kept her rational enough to do what had to be done.

Even having Adam with her wouldn't be able to keep her sane if she were trapped deep underground, so she would just have to get moving and get everyone out as fast as possible. And that meant starting all over again, laboriously clearing the little stones and rocks first, and then tackling the bigger ones until she could find and deal with the injury that was causing Tel's blood loss.

'None of the rocks hit you, did they, Jem?' she asked as she settled into a rhythm for grabbing the next rock and stacking it out of the way against the opposite wall of the tunnel.

'Nah!' he said dismissively. 'But I bet you got a few bruises on your legs. I saw some of them hit you. Are you all right?'

'I might be all the colours of the rainbow in a day or two,' she conceded, her breathing becoming slightly laboured with the repetitive effort. *Or was it the start of air hunger?* a little voice inside her head suggested insidiously. *Were they running out of air? Would all of them pass out because there wasn't enough oxygen to support…?*

Enough! she admonished herself silently. Adam and Mike were widening the entrance. There was plenty of air coming in. Concentrate on talking to Jem and moving the rocks to find out where his friend was injured. There wasn't time to think about anything else. 'But bruises are quick to heal,' she continued lightly, 'especially if you're reasonably healthy, so it's not really a problem unless it causes a major bleed.'

'Anyway, you're a girl, so you wouldn't be a haemophiliac, would you?' he said knowledgeably. 'We learned about haemophilia when we had a boy in our class who had to be careful that he didn't fall in the playground and Miss Venning was telling us about the Russian king whose children had it. They got it from our Queen Victoria, didn't they?'

'She was a carrier of the condition, I believe,' Maggie agreed.

'It always seems odd,' he said thoughtfully, 'that a

woman can give her children a blood disease or...or colour-blindness, without knowing about it because it doesn't affect her.' He switched the bag of saline from one hand to the other, and the way he was bracing it against the wall told her that although his arms were obviously beginning to ache, he wouldn't be complaining. 'And eye colour is another thing,' he went on. 'There's someone in Mr Tolliver's class who's got one blue eye and one brown one. It's really cool. Mine are just brown, 'cos both my mum and dad's were.'

'Well, mine turned out a mixture of green and brown,' Maggie volunteered, and found herself wondering pointlessly what colour her children's eyes would have been if she'd married Adam. She knew that brown was dominant over blue, but would her hazel eye colour have been dominant over his dark sapphire blue or vice versa?

'Maggie...?' called a voice in the distance, and even though it was distorted by echoes, her heart recognised it and gave an extra thump.

Adam!

Had he and Mike cleared enough of the entrance already?

Was he on his way down to join her?

Her knees complained when she straightened up enough from her cramped position to call over the mound of rocks that still blocked the entrance to the tunnel.

'Adam,' she called back, suddenly guiltily remembering that she'd been going to keep up a running commentary for those left outside. 'We're OK.' Well, that was true up to a point, and it would be even better once she'd finished shifting these rocks and could see where Tel's injury was.

'How many injured?' he shouted—at least, that's what it sounded like when she'd unscrambled the echoes.

'Two,' she yelled back, horrified to find that her exertions had left her panting. She'd honestly thought she was fitter than this. She certainly wouldn't allow herself to think about her disappointment that he obviously wasn't on his way down to help her yet. 'One minor and one major.'

Suddenly, the fact that he was a married man didn't matter. She was just so grateful that he was there and that he was checking up on her safety that, had he been close enough, she could have thrown herself into his arms without a qualm.

'Coming out?' he asked, and she had to take a guess at the first part of the question.

For a second she contemplated the order that things should be done and balanced them against what was possible. She had another bag of saline, but the rate that the first one was emptying meant that it wouldn't last very long. Then there were the three boys waiting at the bottom of the stope. She certainly couldn't guarantee how much longer their patience would last, and if they tried to climb that treacherous stepped wall without adequate lighting, there was no knowing how many injuries they could end up with.

'Five minutes,' she shouted back, and from the muted cheer from the other lads she knew they had been following the exchange.

'You're never going to be able to shift all those rocks

in five minutes,' Jem said a minute later, after she'd resumed her efforts with the slowly diminishing heap. 'And we can't just go and leave Tel down here. We *can't*!'

'Jem, I've got no intention of leaving Tel down here,' she said quickly, stricken that he'd been left thinking that it was even a possibility. 'I'm hoping that I can clear enough rocks away to find out where the blood's coming from, and stop it. But I'm going to need to fetch some more saline and I'll need to bring a backboard down to put him on before he can be carried out, so I may as well get the rest of you out of here at the same time. Your parents are probably all waiting up at the mouth of the stope, terrified that they're never going to see you again.'

'Oh.' He subsided, and she saw his grubby forehead pleat in a thoughtful frown before she turned to choose the next rock to pit her puny muscles against. There was just one last big one that, thankfully, had landed between Tel's legs and had prevented several others from hitting him, but if she tried to move it, she risked setting off another avalanche. But if she could just remove some of the smaller ones and slide her hand in underneath, she might be able to discover whether the bleeding was in the upper or lower half of his leg.

It was closer to ten minutes before she'd achieved her aim and was able to explore the wet proof that the injury was in his lower leg before she realised that her gloves had been totally shredded by her exertions with the rough granite.

'Damn,' she muttered under her breath as she quickly pulled her hand out and stared at the evidence. Hopefully, Tel was too young to have any of the more serious blood-borne infections, because the blood coating her scratched and grazed fingers couldn't help but find plenty of ways into her own system.

Well, she certainly didn't have any water to spare to wash her hand off and there wasn't enough time or sterile wipes to do the job, or light enough to see how thorough a job she was doing, so she was just going to have to get on with it and hope for the best.

The fact that his foot was facing in the wrong direction told her that there had been some sort of serious damage to his leg, but until she completed her examination she wouldn't know whether it was a dislocation of one of the joints—with all the concomitant dangers of impingement of nerve or blood supply, a femoral break—with the danger of life-threatening blood loss, or damage to the tibia or fibula, or both.

She gritted her teeth and slid her hand back between the rocks, only to have to stifle another groan when she felt the obvious evidence that both Tel's tibia and fibula *were* broken. At least she could feel that he still had circulation in his foot and his reflexes appeared to be intact. Added to that, it seemed as if the bones were only marginally displaced, so perhaps the bleeding was from the gash on his skin where the rock had impacted to cause the fractures.

Still, his pulse had become steadier and stronger since she'd set up the IV, and with the rocks moved away from his chest his breathing wasn't being impeded any more, although there were definitely several cracked ribs to worry about when the time came to move him onto a stretcher. The last thing he needed was a punctured lung or, worse yet, damage to his heart.

For now, she'd done everything she could until he either regained consciousness or the rescue team was able to join her down here to shift the rest of the rocks.

'Right, Jem,' she said as she straightened up from checking the IV site and showed him how the new pile of rocks she'd been building as she took them away from Tel could just about be used as a temporary support for the second bag of saline. 'It's time I got the rest of you out of here. Let's go.'

'I'm not going,' Jem announced with a stubborn expression on his pale face.

'Jem…' she began, but he shook his head.

'I'm not leaving Tel down here all by himself,' he said firmly. 'If he wakes up and there's no one here…no one to tell him that someone knows he's here and that they're just making the hole bigger so they can get him out…'

Maggie shuddered at the very thought of waking up to utter darkness with the weight of millions of tons of granite looming over her head, but she could see that there was going to be no changing the youngster's mind.

It took her a moment to rearrange her thoughts. She wouldn't dream of leaving Jem in the dark. It had been bad enough thinking about leaving Tel without any light, and he was unconscious.

'Ok, if that's what you want…' She took the torch Adam had lent her and propped it carefully on the heap of stones still partially blocking the entrance to the tunnel. If she positioned it just right, it should light their way up the stope while she and the other three boys were climbing. 'I'm leaving the torch here with you,' she said, only just remembering boyish pride in time to add hastily, 'It would get in my way while I'm helping Chris keep his balance—he can't use his hand to hold on to anything. I'll need you to be in charge of it to show me where I'm going on the way back down, too.'

'I can do that,' he said, his voice far steadier than her own as he moved forward a little bit so that he could keep an eye on the torch and the drip at the same time. 'Just tell me where you want me to point it.'

'I will,' she agreed, before clambering over the rocks to join the lads waiting impatiently at the foot of the stope.

'Maggie…?' Adam's voice echoed, the strange reverberations making it seem as if it was coming from several directions at once.

'Coming,' she called back, and gestured for the two able-bodied lads to start climbing. 'Don't go too fast,' she cautioned when they began to race up the potentially deadly wall. 'I might need your help with Chris.'

'I'll be all right,' the injured youngster said bravely, but the expression on his face as he craned his neck to eye the climb he was going to have to make said something else entirely.

'You probably will, but I'm worried about your hand. I don't want you to do it any further damage before we can get an X-ray taken,' she explained as she steadied his elbow for the first, relatively easy step.

By the time they reached the last climb—the step that nearly came up to her shoulder—Maggie was shaking with exhaustion and desperately glad that Jonno and Dwayne were there to help her get Chris up the last hurdle between them and freedom.

'Don't run on ahead,' she warned when they were all on relatively level ground again. 'There's a big piece of wood hanging down from the roof and I don't want any of you to knock yourselves out.'

She might as well have saved her breath as far as Dwayne and Jonno were concerned. They could see light at the end of the tunnel…literally…and all they could think of was to get there as soon as possible.

'Hang on, lads. One at a time,' said a firm masculine voice up ahead as she matched the slower pace that Chris was forced to adopt so that he didn't jar his injured hand. 'It's taken us a long time to get this entrance shored up. We don't want you spoiling all our good work in your rush to get out.'

'Your turn, Chris,' she said when they finally reached the mouth of the adit, surprised that so little seemed to have been achieved in the time she'd been down below with the boys. She'd been expecting to see the entrance nearly clear by now, with equipment being readied for getting Tel out. All that seemed to have been achieved was that the gorse bushes had been cleared away and a series of steel props had been set up to hold fresh pieces of timber up against the roof of the entrance.

'Be careful of his hand,' she called to the unseen helpers outside. 'I've put a sling on him but he's going to need X-rays of those metacarpals.'

'Any more?' asked the same deep voice, and she could see the silhouette of a head wearing a safety helmet against the bright lights that had been set up outside.

'Just me this time,' she said as she began to climb, only remembering as it caught against the roughness of the

hewn rocks that she hadn't been wearing her emergency
pack when she'd come the other way—it had been passed
through to her once she'd climbed through the hole.

It seemed as though a forest of hands was reaching
towards her to help her to her feet and even though the
lights were bright enough to sear her eyes after the
pitch black of the mine, the first face she focused on
was Adam's.

'Well done,' she saw him say, although the sound of
his praise was completely lost under the cacophony of
a generator and voices that surrounded her, the area apparently filled with people in bulky, high-visibility gear.

She straightened up and filled her lungs with sweet,
fresh air, relishing the ever-present tang of salt and wondering how she was ever going to be able to force herself
do go back down that dank hole again.

CHAPTER FOUR

'*No!*'

One piercing shriek cut through everything else, silencing everything other than the steady all-pervading throb of the generator.

'Where's my son?' the shrill voice demanded. 'What's happened to my boy?'

'Kate...' someone said, and Maggie blinked. Was that dishevelled figure really Kate Althorp?

As Maggie watched, the normally smart former practice manager flung aside the restraining hand that Nick Tremayne tried to put around her shoulders and pushed her way through the knot of helmeted rescuers at the entrance to the adit towards Maggie.

'What have you done with my son?' she demanded, glaring up at Maggie where she still stood on the heap of rocks. 'They said there were only two boys hurt and—'

'Kate,' Nick began again, having caught up with her, and Maggie saw him wrap a supporting arm around her shoulders. 'Take it easy. Give the girl a chance to catch her breath.'

'What do you mean, give her a chance to catch her

breath?' Kate said, rounding on him furiously. 'I want to know why she hasn't brought my son up with the others. Is he the one that fell? Is he the one that's badly injured? Nick, you *know* what it was like when I lost James. You were there with me. I can't lose Jem, too. I couldn't *bear* it…'

'Kate!' Maggie called over her tirade, easily able to empathise with her terror. 'Jem *isn't* hurt.'

'He's not…' Relief warred with incomprehension, but it was anger that won. 'If he's *not* hurt, *why* didn't you bring him up with the others?' she demanded furiously. 'Why did you leave *my* son down there?'

'Because he refused to come up,' Maggie said, knowing that the simple truth would give Kate pause. She reached out a hand towards the tormented woman, even though she was too far away for any physical contact. 'Kate, Jem is the most amazing young lad I've ever met, and you should be proud of him. He didn't want to leave his friend in case he woke up alone in the dark.'

'Oh, God, help me…' Kate sobbed, but when she turned towards Nick, obviously needing his support, he wasn't there.

'That's the most ridiculous thing I've ever heard,' he said, striding towards Maggie with an accusing glare. 'He's only eight years old, for heaven's sake! I'm going down to bring him up,' he announced, intent on pushing his way through the rescue team already working systematically to clear the mouth of the adit.

'I can't let you do that, Dr Tremayne,' said a man with a similar air of authority, but *he* was wearing the appropriate safety gear and in spite of his youth was obviously the leader of the rescue team.

'You can't stop me,' the GP said belligerently, trying to stare him down. 'I've been on more rescue missions than you've had hot dinners.'

'That may well be true, Doctor,' the younger man conceded graciously, 'but in this case we're going to need special equipment appropriate to the situation, and we know you haven't had training in that. When we're ready to bring the lads out, it will have to be my team that does the job. No one else here has the authority to go down.'

Maggie could tell that the middle-aged GP was frustrated by his failure to get his own way. It had probably been years since anyone had gone against his authority, especially since he'd become the senior partner at the Penhally surgery.

Idly, she noted that while he was leaner than either Adam or Mike—almost thin enough to squirm through the narrow entrance to the adit. That was probably because he had lost muscle tone since his age had stopped him being an active member of a rescue team. Even so, it wouldn't be easy for him to get into the adit until the entrance had been cleared, to say nothing of the problem he would have once he got to the bottom of the stope and had to clamber over the rockfall and squeeze his long legs into the narrow tunnel where Tel was trapped.

'Well, I hope you don't think you're going to be stopping me going down again,' Maggie interrupted before Nick could draw breath to argue, suddenly aware with every fibre of her body that Adam had come to stand behind her. She hadn't seen him move but somehow she just knew that he was there, silently supporting her in her fight to do what she knew had to be done. 'Until you get that entrance cleared, I'm the only one small enough to get through who's got the training to take care of Tel.'

Not that she wanted to go back into the darkness again, feeling as if all that rock was pressing down on her and squeezing the breath out of her so that she had to fight for the oxygen her body needed to survive.

'I'm afraid I *will* have to stop you,' the team leader said firmly. 'The last thing we need is amateurs bumbling about when everything is so unstable. Because time is of the essence, we've only done a make-shift job of shoring up the entrance to the adit. We've made a start on clearing the access and it won't be long before the entrance is safely open again. Then we'll be able to take our equipment down and—'

'So while you're running about up here doing everything by the book to satisfy health and safety requirements, you're quite happy to leave an eight-year-old boy down there in the dark, taking care of his injured friend who's bleeding heavily and in danger of developing crush syndrome?' Maggie demanded, so disgusted that he was even considering the idea, let alone trying to insist on it, that she didn't think twice about exaggerating Tel's condition if it made her point. 'I think not!'

'Well, I'm sorry, but I can't allow you to go back down,' he insisted. 'I know you're a qualified paramedic, but this is way beyond what you're trained for…it could even lose you your job if you go down there again against my advice.'

'In that case, I'll be looking for another job,' she said with scarcely a pang for the potential loss of a job that meant so much to her. She straightened her shoulders and tried to stand tall, knowing it was a futile gesture when everyone around her was at least a head taller but still hoping he would recognise how seriously she took her decision. 'There's no way I can twiddle my thumbs up here while the last of that unit of saline runs out and Jem is left alone and terrified because he doesn't know what to do for his friend if he develops an air embolus.'

She whirled back towards the entrance of the adit and there was Adam, exactly where she'd known he would be. 'Adam, I need to take some more saline down with me, and a backboard in case I manage to get Tel free before you can get down there. Perhaps there's some sort of crowbar I could borrow to shift the last couple of rocks. I'll also need a blanket to keep Jem warm…oh, and something for him to eat. He didn't make it home in time for his tea and must be starving.'

She paused to take stock, wondering what else she needed that she'd be able to negotiate down that treacherous stope single-handed, and saw Adam exchange glances with Mike who then nodded and hurried out of the circle of floodlights towards their ambulance to get the things she needed.

'Maggie, are you sure about this?' Adam asked softly when he turned back to her, careful to keep his voice below the sound of the generator so that it only carried as far as her ears. 'I know how much you hate going into enclosed spaces and I virtually blackmailed you into going down in the first place, so don't feel that you have to— What?' he demanded when she winced as he took her hands in his and squeezed her fingers.

'Dammit, Maggie! What's happened to you?' he exclaimed when he saw the ragged, blood-stained fingers of her protective gloves. 'What have you done to your hands?'

'It's not *my* blood, Adam,' Maggie reassured him as he stared down in horror at the state of her hands, and she knew that she was largely telling the truth.

Of course, there was no way she could have shifted all that granite without collecting a few scrapes and scratches, but she was touched that he should care that she might have been hurt. 'It's Tel's blood. Because he's trapped, I was having to use the Braille method of finding out where he was injured. I needed to find out where the blood was coming from…how serious the injury was.'

'How badly *is* he injured?' Adam asked as he helped her to strip off the shredded gloves, sidetracked into throwing her a furious glare when he saw just how many scrapes and bruises there were on her hands. She clenched her teeth in preparation for the pain as she doused them in antiseptic gel then struggled to pull on a fresh pair of gloves over the fierce stinging.

Silently, he handed her some more gloves to stuff into the appropriate pocket of her pack. 'Did the lad fall a long way?'

'He didn't just fall—he brought down some rocks with him,' she explained, strangely warmed by his anger on her behalf. It had been a while since anyone had really noticed when she was hurt and showed that they cared. Even Mike tended to shrug off work-related injuries as part and parcel of the job they did.

'He's got a goose egg from hitting his head and I'm hoping that's the reason why he's unconscious, because I couldn't find any obvious evidence of cranial fractures. I've put a collar on him and he's on his second unit of saline. So far, it doesn't look as if he's in danger of bleeding out. Several ribs were broken when the rocks landed on him. He was having difficulty breathing when I got to him, but once I shifted the weight off his chest, that improved, and there's no evidence of pneumothorax or flail chest. The other lads would have cleared the rocks earlier if they'd had light to see what they were doing. He's also broken the tib and fib in one leg but they don't feel massively displaced, so I think the blood loss is probably from several smaller gashes rather than anything major like an artery. There's moisture seeping down the walls of the tunnel, so it probably makes the blood loss look worse than it is.'

'Miss?' said a hesitant voice behind her, and she turned to see a woman aged before her time, her face gaunt and white under the harsh lighting as she stood there with her hands knotted together. 'They said you've been down the mine?'

'Yes, I have. I'll be going back down in a minute,' she added, suddenly not needing to ask the question to know who the woman was. 'You're Tel's mother, aren't you?'

She nodded. 'Amanda Lovelace. Mandy,' she supplied, then bit her lip before blurting, 'Please, tell me what's happened to my boy. You brought his three mates out with you. Does…does that mean he's—?'

'He's unconscious,' Maggie interrupted hastily, sparing her that dreadful final word. If she'd realised Tel's mother was here she would have made certain she hadn't been left so long thinking the worst. 'He fell and hit his head and he's cracked a couple of bones. That's why it's taking a bit of time to get him out—we need to get a stretcher down to him to carry him out safely, so we don't do him any more damage.'

'But he *is* alive? You're *sure* he's alive?' She grabbed for Maggie's hand with frantic fingers and it was difficult to control the wince as she, too, pressed on the cuts and bruises that were starting to throb mercilessly.

'He's breathing and his heart is beating,' Maggie reassured her with a smile, sticking to the basics. 'He's got a bump the size of a goose egg on his head and he'll probably have a monster headache when he wakes up, but—'

'Oh, thank you! Thank you so much!' Mandy exclaimed tearfully. 'He's always getting into scrapes with those other lads—takes after his big brothers, unfortunately, and his dad's never there when he's needed—but Tel's not a bad boy, not really.'

'Miss Pascoe?' interrupted the incident commander, clearly ready for the next round in the battle. 'I know you mean well, but I really must insist that you don't put yourself in any further danger. You must realise what the consequences could be for your employment.'

Maggie took a moment to promise Mandy that she would be told as soon as there was any more news about her son, then she turned to face the man who was rapidly becoming her number-one adversary.

She knew he was only doing his job, but it wasn't making things any easier for her. It was taking everything she had to stop herself thinking about the danger she was returning to. She would be only too delighted to stay up here and keep the man happy, but she knew she didn't really have a choice but to go against his advice. There were two young lads down there, one of whom might still be bleeding from a wound she still hadn't found, and the other was probably counting every second and every eerie creak and groan while he was waiting for her to return.

'If losing my job is what it takes, so be it,' she said stubbornly, her conviction that she was doing the right thing strengthened immeasurably by the thumbs-up signal Mike gave her as he delivered the supplies she needed, and the fact that Adam was once more standing right behind her.

In fact, he was so close that she could feel the heat of his body radiating towards her and his breath teasing the vulnerable skin left exposed on the back of her neck by her eminently practical haircut. For one mad second she even contemplated leaning back against him, desperately needing to borrow just a little of his strength. Then she remembered, barely in time, that he was a married man and that she had no right to take anything from him, even on loan.

That realisation was enough to stiffen her spine and her resolve to do what was right.

'Feel free to report me for going against your advice

if you must, but at the moment I'm not even on duty,' she explained, almost ashamed how smug she felt. 'My shift ended several hours ago, so now I'm just a member of the public who has a bit more training than most and just happens to be small enough to squeeze through very small spaces.'

The man sighed heavily, reluctantly conceding that he wasn't going to win the argument, especially with Adam and Mike backing her. 'Well, if you're that determined, you should be wearing one of these…' he handed her a bright yellow safety helmet and checked that it fitted her head properly '…and you might as well have one of these, too,' he said, and offered her a radio. 'It's the latest issue communication system—the new one that actually works for some distance underground—so hopefully you'll be able to keep us updated on how the lad's doing.'

'And you'll be able to let me know when your lot's on the way down to get us out,' she said, and tightened her grip on the neat piece of equipment as though it were a lifeline, realising that this one high-tech gadget might actually make what she was about to do just a little more bearable.

'By the way…' A sudden thought struck her as she was about to thread herself through the rough-edged gap in the rocks. 'Make sure you tell your team to take it slowly as they come along the adit. Part way along, one of the roof supports is hanging down. I hit it on my way in the first time, but I'm short enough not to have knocked myself out on it. Your team mightn't be so lucky. Then, just a bit further along, the ground drops away completely into a series of steep, ragged-edged steps. Apparently, it's called a stope, and if you're not expecting it...'

'Thanks for the warning,' he said with a wintry smile. 'We've actually got a contact from the Camborne School of Mines tracking down underground maps of the area. We were worried that we might have to find another way in if the entrance kept crumbling, but we've got the temporary shoring in place now, and it seems to be holding. In fact, we're hoping to have you all out before anyone at Camborne has the time come up with the goods.' He paused a moment and gave his head a single shake. 'I still don't approve of what you're doing, but...good luck.'

'Thank you...and thanks for this, too,' she said holding up the radio, then threw him a distracted smile, suddenly aware how quickly time was passing. It was totally dark now, and she had absolutely no idea how long ago it had been since she and Mike had driven into the field in their ambulance.

More to the point, how long had it been since she'd left Jem down there with Tel? However long it was, she knew it would feel a thousand times longer to a young boy, no matter how brave he was.

Adam was waiting patiently to help her climb back into the awful blackness and the fact that his was going to be the last face she saw was the only thing that gave her courage when her claustrophobia once more tightened its grip on her throat.

'Be careful, Maggie,' he murmured as he held her with rock-steady hands. 'Don't take any risks.'

'As if climbing down a mine isn't risky,' she retorted wryly. 'And you're the one who persuaded me to go in the first place.'

'Well, don't do anything to make me regret it,' he demanded, his voice suddenly fierce. 'It was different when you were under the train. I was there with you, close enough to pull you out in a hurry if it became necessary. If anything happens to you this time…' He shook his head.

'Then you'll have to get hold of one of these gadgets so you can keep tabs on me,' she said as she waved the new communication link at him, not wanting to think about how much distance she would be putting between them as soon as she entered the adit. Anything beyond arm's length might as well be a million miles because he wouldn't be able to reach her; he wasn't as bulky as Mike, but his shoulders were still far too broad and muscular to fit through the entrance yet. 'That way you'll be able to talk me through it, like you did before.'

'I'll do that…even if I have to mug someone to get it,' he promised with a grin, then his smile faded and his dark blue gaze became suddenly intent. 'Maggie, we need to talk,' he said, his voice heavy with unexpected meaning that made her heart give an extra beat.

'Not now,' he added hastily when she stared up at him in surprise and caught a glimpse of secret-filled shadows she hadn't noticed before. Were they something new or had she been so focused on her hurt over the way he'd treated her a year ago that she just hadn't seen them?

'There isn't time now,' he continued. 'I know you need to get back down to those boys, but promise me that as soon as this is all over…There are things I should have told you a year ago…about Caroline…'

'Caroline?' she frowned, not recognising the name immediately and resenting the intrusion of another woman into a moment that somehow felt as if it had been exclusively theirs despite the noise that surrounded them.

'My wife,' he said quietly, and the illusion of intimacy was shattered with the reminder that, apart from the imaginings of a teenager's rose-tinted summer fantasies, Adam had always belonged to someone else.

Adam watched Maggie's petite form disappear into the darkness and had to curl his hands into tight fists to stop himself grabbing hold of her to prevent her from going through that torture all over again.

That last glance she'd thrown at him over her shoulder had been enough to break his heart.

He knew just how terrified she was of going back into the mine—knew how hard it was for her to fight the irrational fear of being trapped in a confined space. The fact that she had been willing to jeopardise her job to return to the two boys she'd left down there was a prime example of the woman she was, and he couldn't be any more proud of her.

'Bloody woman,' muttered the incident commander, the two of them standing to one side while a serious start was made on clearing the blockage from the entrance. 'Give them a bit of training and they think they can take on the world.'

'So you think she'd be better off sitting at home, darning someone's socks and cooking his tea?' Adam asked blandly when he'd rather be ripping the man's throat out. How could he *not* respect what she was doing when it was so much a part of who she was?

'Well, you know as well as I do that there are proper ways of doing things,' the man agreed. 'Proper protocols that women seem want to ignore just for the sake of it…probably because their brains aren't built to see the logic of rules and regulations.'

'You think so?' Adam was seething now and it was a real effort to keep the lid on his temper. The man didn't sound as if his ideas had progressed beyond the nineteenth century, let alone the twentieth and into the twenty-first. 'So you're incapable of admitting that without Maggie's guts and determination you'd still have five kids down there? Are you so hidebound by your rules and regulations that you can't see that one of those kids could have been well on the way to bleeding out if she'd tamely waited while you worked out the proper way to gain access?'

He turned on his heel and positioned himself as close to the entrance of the adit as he could without getting in anyone's way in the hope that it would help with the reception of the radio signal when he spoke to the brave woman already forcing herself to confront her greatest fear for the second time that day.

He'd probably already said far too much, but the thought that such an arrogant idiot was casting aspersions on Maggie's courage was enough to make him see red. She deserved praise, not condemnation for bending a few rules, and if the man thought he would win any points by criticising her for doing what she thought was right, he certainly didn't know how much that pint-sized paramedic meant to him.

Maggie's spirits were low as she forced herself to squeeze through the entrance without disturbing the temporary supports, and she'd barely set foot inside the adit when she was seized by the almost unbearable need to get out as fast as possible.

It didn't seem to matter that she'd already spent time in there, finding and taking care of the trapped young-sters, and had climbed out again virtually unscathed with three of them. This feeling was something differ-ent—a gut-deep conviction that something dreadful was going to happen if she went back down the rough slope ahead of her into the depths of the mine.

There was another torch in her hand to replace the one she'd left with Jem, but she knew just how puny the beam would seem once she left the light at the mine entrance behind and was surrounded by utter blackness.

'Hey, Maggie. How are you doing?' Adam's voice echoed strangely around her from the radio in her hand and she gave an involuntary sob of relief. She'd had her reminder that he belonged to somebody else, but she was so very grateful that he was there for her at the moment.

'You know that expression, "It's just a walk in the park"?' she asked as she ducked under the timber hanging down in her way. 'Well, this is more a walk in the dark, and it's not nearly as pretty down here.'

'So, just imagine the flowers,' he suggested, and she could actually hear a smile in his voice, could picture the way it always accentuated the lean planes of his face and made his dark eyes gleam.

There was a teasing, light-hearted edge to his voice as he continued. 'Don't tell me you do all that driving around and hadn't noticed that there are already daffo-dils out in most of the gardens around Penhally? Don't you just love living in Cornwall?'

'I'd love it better if they went round and filled all these holes up,' she muttered as she reached the top of the stope and her heart contracted with renewed fear as she contemplated the fact that this time she'd be making her way down hampered by the extra equipment she'd brought with her. She really didn't want to have to make the climb twice if she didn't have to—it would waste so much time and energy—but was it too risky to make it in one journey, laden as she was?

'Maggie?' Adam prompted, but his voice surround-ing her was suddenly a distraction she couldn't cope with, not for the next few minutes. It was such a comfort knowing that he was close enough to be able to speak to her, but now she needed every ounce of concentra-tion focused on getting back down to Jem and Tel.

'Adam, I'll need my hands free for the next part,' she told him, loath to cut the connection between them. While he was talking to her she could almost imagine that he was down there with her. 'I'll speak to you again when I reach the bottom of the stope and find out how the boys are,' she promised, then cut the signal and stowed the radio safely in her pack.

It was every bit as awkward as she'd expected and felt as if it took twice as long, but with Jem watching from the mouth of the other tunnel and carefully shining the torch at each step of the stope to help her on her way, anything other than continuing until she reached him wasn't an option.

CHAPTER FIVE

'How's Tel?' asked as soon as she reached the pile of rocks almost obscuring the tunnel mouth, her legs shaking so much that she had to pause a moment before she could attempt to clamber over the mound.

'He groaned a couple of times just after you took the others up,' Jem reported, sounding worried, 'but he hasn't woken up yet. Oh, and the saline's nearly all gone.'

'Hey, Jem, it's probably a good thing he hasn't woken up yet, otherwise he'd be in a fair amount of pain,' she reassured him, as she deposited the more cumbersome items of her load outside the tunnel, hoping that she wouldn't have to make any decisions about administering analgesia to a patient in severe pain before his head injury had been properly analysed. As it was, her initial conviction that he didn't have a significant brain injury was being tested the longer he stayed unconscious, but until they could get him out of there, there was absolutely nothing she could do about it.

Her first job when she joined the two of them in the cramped space again was to wrap an arm around Jem's shoulders and give him a hug. He'd looked so utterly relieved to see her again that she'd known just how terrified he must have been to be left down here alone with his unconscious friend. And it wouldn't have made any difference to his level of fear that staying had been at his own insistence. It had still been an amazingly courageous thing for an eight-year-old to volunteer to do.

'You've been brilliant,' she said simply. 'I wouldn't have wanted to be down here by myself, so I think you thoroughly deserve these.' And she handed him a couple of the energy bars someone had given her up at the mouth of the adit.

She smiled when she saw the way his eyes lit up, suddenly seeing him for the little boy he was. 'At least those should keep the wolf from the door until we can get to some proper food.'

'Great! Thanks! I should have been home for my tea hours ago,' he said, already tearing at the first wrapper, then sat out of the way with his back against the rough wall of the tunnel while she checked Tel over again and decided that she didn't yet need to replace the bag of saline with a fresh one.

Once reassured that his condition hadn't deteriorated in her absence, it was time to decide exactly how she was going to accomplish the next stage of her task—to get him clear from the rockfall and safely strapped onto the backboard.

Really, there was only one way…she was going to have to use the borrowed crowbar to lever the last of the big rocks aside—preferably without doing any further damage to his legs—then log roll him and slide the two halves of the backboard under him from either side before he could regain consciousness and start trying to move.

'Right, Jem, if you've finished fuelling up your engines, I'm going to need a bit of help here,' she announced. 'I'd like you to take the bag of saline as far away up the back end of the tunnel as you can without pulling the needle, and then keep an eye on the tubing so it doesn't get knocked about.'

'And I've got to make sure it's still high up enough so that the stuff runs down into Tel, right?'

'Exactly right,' she agreed, and saw him settled safely out of the way before she began to attack the remaining rocks, frustrated that she was going to have to leave the largest till last, when she'd have the least energy.

It was hard, dirty, painful work, especially as she laboured to shift the final boulder away from between Tel's legs, and she was close to tears by the time she hit her shoulder on the same rocky outcrop for the dozenth time without apparently shifting the lump of granite more than an inch or two.

'Would it be safe for you to move Tel's leg a bit that way?' Jem suggested, gesturing with his hands after a moment's pause in which she tried to control the urge to scream her frustration. 'The rock looks a bit of a weird shape and that's stopping it moving the way you want it to go, but if you could shift his good leg over to the side a bit, you'd be able to tip the rock over like that, and…what do you think?'

Maggie rested her hands on her knees while she weighed up the pros and cons of Jem's suggestion. She would dearly have loved to ask Adam's opinion—the way she had when the two of them had been battling to staunch the bleeding of the young woman under the train—but this time the decisions were all hers. She would have to balance the possibility of doing further damage by moving Tel against the probability that she'd finally be able to release him and get him safely immobilised on the backboard.

'Let's try it,' she said and, suiting her actions to her words, angled Tel's uninjured leg out into the limited space in the tunnel, hopefully without moving his injured leg or his pelvis, to give herself the chance to attack the boulder from a different angle.

'Yay!' Jem cheered when her renewed effort with the crowbar finally sent the stubborn rock flipping over in the new direction as easily as though it were one of the fake polystyrene rocks seen on children's television programmes. Not content with rolling over once, the granite rolled a second time, only stopping when it cannoned into the opposite wall with a resounding crunch.

Maggie barely stopped herself from shrieking when the impact sent a shower of dust and rock clattering down onto the three of them, but luckily there weren't many pieces and the ones that hit them weren't particularly large.

'Now we've just got to move those little bits and you can fix his leg,' Jem pointed out cheerfully, and Maggie wished it was going to be so easy.

'How about you clear away these rocks while I get my stuff in here to deal with Tel?' she suggested. 'Now that I've finished shifting rocks with it, I can stick the crowbar in this gap here and, hey presto, it's a hook for the saline.' She suited her actions to her words, jamming the sharp point of the metal bar into the space between the rock wall and one of the ancient timber uprights, leaving the hooked end at exactly the right height to suspend the unit of saline. A quick check to make certain that the tubing wasn't kinked anywhere and that the needle was still positioned correctly in Tel's vein then it was time to deal with stabilising his broken leg.

'How are you going to fix it?' Jem demanded as he scurried backwards and forwards, collecting the scattering of loose rocks and stacking them against the side of the tunnel. 'When I broke my arm, I had to have a cast on, but you can't do that down here, can you?'

'First I'm going to find out where all this blood's been coming from. Depending how badly it's still bleeding, I might need to put a pressure bandage on it to stop it bleeding any more, then I'm going to splint his leg to keep everything straight and safe while we move him. They won't put him in a cast until they get him to hospital.' *If they don't have to take him to Theatre first*, she added silently, still not entirely convinced that the youngster didn't have other undiagnosed injuries. Her biggest fear was that the blow to his head had caused an intracranial bleed; that the reason why he hadn't started to regain consciousness was because the blood was collecting inside his skull and building up potentially fatal pressure.

'So, where are you going to get a splint from?' he asked. 'If we were outside, I could probably find you a piece of wood or a straight piece of branch from the gorse bushes at the entrance to the adit. Down here there's only rocks or those great big treetrunks holding up the roof.'

'That's why we're going to use his other leg as a splint,' she explained as she positioned Tel's legs side by side, checking again that he had good circulation in both ankles before she began to bandage them together at knee and ankle. Another quick touch reassured her that the binding hadn't compromised blood flow and then it was time to manoeuvre the two halves of the backboard into position.

'Hey, I saw them using one of these on TV!' he exclaimed when she brought it over the mound of rock into the tunnel. 'There was a programme with a helicopter crew flying all over the place, doing seaside rescues and then flying the injured people to hospital.'

'Well, I hope you were watching carefully, because I'm going to need your help to get Tel positioned properly,' Maggie told him, and wondered if he'd ever realise just how much easier this whole nightmare had been for her with such an amazing youngster down here with her. It would have been better still if it could have been Adam by her side, but...

'What do you want me to do?' Jem demanded eagerly. 'Do you need me to help you roll him over to slide it underneath?'

'Good guess,' she said with a smile. 'But, actually, we're taught a special way of rolling him that we can do with just one person, because you're going to need both hands to get the board in exactly the right place. OK?'

'OK,' he said, and the little frown of concentration

drew his dark brows together the whole time she was explaining what she wanted, first log rolling Tel onto one side while concentrating on keeping the whole length of his spine perfectly aligned in case there were any hidden injuries, then reversing the procedure for the other side…the more difficult side as he'd landed far too close to the wall of the tunnel for her to position herself easily.

'Can you see how to clip the two halves of the backboard together?' she asked, wishing she could sprout another pair of arms to help him align them.

'Got it!' he crowed as they slotted perfectly into position and she lowered Tel carefully onto his back again. 'Now we have to strap him down so he can't move about, don't we?'

'That's right. Tight enough so he can't slip about but not so tight that we stop his circulation or his breathing,' Maggie agreed as she positioned the all-important wedges either side of Tel's head and secured them with a strap across his forehead. 'Then we can let the others know that we're ready for them as soon as— Oh, good grief!' she exclaimed scrambling for her pack and dragging the radio out. 'I forgot to turn this on again.'

'…you there, Maggie?' Adam's voice suddenly flooded the tiny space, in spite of the fact that it wasn't a perfect signal and there was a great deal of background noise. 'Are you all right, Maggie? Answer me, please,' he said in the tone of someone who'd been saying the same thing over and over again.

'Adam! Can you hear me?' she demanded, her fingers

fumbling in her rush to speak. 'I'm *so* sorry, but I forgot to switch this thing back on when I got to the bottom.'

'You *forgot*?' he repeated, the disbelief so clear in his voice that she felt a guilty blush flood her cheeks.

'Jem was waiting for me and he's helped me to shift rocks, splint Tel's legs together and get him strapped to the backboard. Everything's ready down here, so as soon as the team can get in, we're ready to go.'

'That's good, because we're just about ready now,' he said. 'They'll be bringing down the stretcher with them. Is there anything else you need? Anything for Jem?'

'Just to get him out of here as soon as possible and let him tuck into his tea,' she suggested, and Jem nodded furiously.

'OK. See you soon,' Adam said. 'And, Maggie, this time don't switch the radio off completely, so we can contact you if we need to.'

She heard the little click that told her he'd cut the call and missed him immediately…wished there was a good reason to speak to him again, just to hear his voice. Instead, she retrieved another couple of energy bars and sat down beside Jem while they ate them in companionable silence.

'What sort of cast will Tel have?' Jem asked after a while. 'Mine was a green one. It was made of fibreglass, but one of the girls in the top class had a big hard white one.'

'That will depend on exactly what damage they find when they take the X-rays. He might just have broken the two bones in his lower leg, but if he's injured his knee as well, he might have to have a cast right up his leg.'

'Wow! Mine was only part way up my arm, like a

long glove, and my thumb and fingers were sticking out
at this end.'

'How did you break your arm?' she asked, and there
was a brief pause before he answered.

'I fell,' he said briefly, hurrying on to add, 'And they
said I'd broken a bone that sounded like a dog. A spaniel
or a collie or something?'

She chuckled. 'You mean a Colles' fracture—in
this bone right here?' She touched his radius, just
above the wrist.

'A Colles' fracture,' he repeated with a nod, and she
was certain that this time he wouldn't forget the term.
'And I had to keep the cast on for ages and ages. Weeks!'

'Well, your friend will have to keep his on even longer
because the leg is weight-bearing, so we have to be certain
that it's properly mended before he can use it again.'

'How long will that take?' he asked.

'Well, it varies a bit from person to person because
some heal faster than others, but it's usually anywhere
from about six weeks.'

'Six weeks!' He was wide-eyed at the thought and
added with dawning delight, 'Does that mean he won't
be able to go to school?'

'Oh, I doubt he'll miss much school.' She laughed.
'As soon as the doctors are sure that he's on the mend,
he'll be back in class with you again.'

She'd been watching his face while she'd been
speaking or she'd probably have missed the look of
misery that replaced his former delight. As it was, she
was forced to make a rapid reassessment of the relationship
between the two lads sharing the cramped tunnel with her.

'Jem?' she began, then didn't know how to continue. She had absolutely no experience of dealing with children of any age, except those she was called to care for in the line of duty. What if she made a complete mess of the next couple of minutes? 'How long have you and Tel been friends?' she asked in the end, settling for something non-confrontational.

There was a pause that only gave her suspicions time to grow and it was obvious that there was a fierce inner debate going on. Would he tell her what he was worried about or would he put her off with vague half-truths?

'Tel's *not* my friend.' Jem interrupted her thoughts in a low voice, glancing across at him as though afraid that the unconscious boy might hear what he was saying.

'He's not?' It was what she'd been expecting after his reactions during their recent conversation, but it certainly went against what she'd assumed, especially as Jem had been so insistent about staying down the mine while she'd taken the other three boys out.

'He's been bullying me…him and his friends,' Jem admitted, then looked as if he wished he hadn't said anything.

As an adult, Maggie knew that any form of bullying was unacceptable, but she could still remember how strong the code of 'don't tell' could be in the playground. She'd been a teenager when she'd been a victim, rather than Jem's eight years, and the girls who had targeted her had used far subtler means of torture than physical violence, but the scars had probably been every bit as long-lasting.

She wrapped an arm around his shoulders to give him

a swift hug and the space blanket she'd tucked around him made its familiar rustling sound. 'Well, I think they're idiots because you've been absolutely brilliant today. In fact, as soon as we're out of here, I'm going to find out how to put your name forward for a bravery award.'

'You can't do that,' he said miserably.

'Why not? I think you deserve it. I don't think many grown-ups would be brave enough to stay down here with one of their friends and they certainly wouldn't want to be here for someone who was bullying them.'

'No...you don't understand. I don't deserve an award because it was *my* idea to come down here in the first place. It's *my* fault that all this has happened...Tel getting unconscious and bleeding and Chris getting hurt and everybody having to do the rescue.'

This wasn't making any sense.

'If Tel and his gang were bullying you, why would you come down here with them? Did they force you to take them?'

Now that she thought about it, the other four boys were at least a year older than Jem. He was obviously a bright lad, so was *that* why the others had picked on him? Or was it something to do with the fact that he didn't have a father around to fight his corner for him?

'They didn't force me but...' He threw an agonised look in her direction. 'Promise you won't tell anyone...not even my mum. You can't tell, or it'll only get worse. That's what happens when you tell on bullies.'

There was that unwritten code of silence that allowed bullying to continue, just as it had in her own childhood, and Maggie found herself reverting to the similarly childish ruse of crossing her fingers behind her back as she nodded, knowing that she had no intention of keeping her word.

At the same time as she was persuading the youngster to tell her what had happened and why, she was making a mental note to have a word with the headmaster to let him know what was going on…that was another note to go with all the others she'd been making, such as the talk she was going to volunteer to give the pupils about women's changing roles in society.

'Tel and the others were going to take my bike…and it's nearly new because I only got it for Christmas. And I said I'd found this mine all shut up and empty and…and I told them it might have treasure in it and…and if I showed it to them, they couldn't take my bike.'

'And then Tel fell and got trapped and your torch broke and you couldn't get out again,' she finished for him.

He nodded, his misery obvious. 'But you won't tell, will you? You promised!'

Before she could compound her lie, the radio crackled to life.

'Maggie?' No matter how bad the reception was, she could tell it was Adam's voice. 'Can you hear me?'

'Loud and clear, Adam,' she replied, her heart doing the same crazy little jig it had when she'd been a teenager.

'The entrance is clear enough for the team to come down. They're bringing a stretcher down with them for Tel. Are you all OK?'

'Looking forward to getting out of here and having

'something hot to eat,' she said, sharing a grin with Jem. 'Remind the team to take it slowly. We don't want any more injuries.'

'Will do. See you soon.'

For several seconds after the end of the call she and Jem sat there, straining their ears for the sound of their approaching rescuers, but all they could hear was the distant throb of the heavy generator and the closer sullen drip of seeping water, punctuated by the intermittent creaks and groans of the old mine workings.

Maggie didn't say anything, but she would be absolutely delighted if she never heard any of those sounds again, and as for the sensation of being trapped in an enclosed space, she had a feeling that, after this experience, she wouldn't even be wanting to put her head inside her kitchen cupboard.

'I can hear them!' Jem exclaimed, his head sticking out from their tunnel entrance. 'And I can see light coming towards the top of the stope.'

Maggie could hear them, too, as she performed a quick check of Tel's vital signs. It looked as if the bleeding had stopped, externally at least. They wouldn't know if he was bleeding internally until they had some proper diagnostic equipment available once he reached St Piran's A and E. His pulse and respirations were still within normal ranges and his circulation was still patent beyond the broken bones in his leg, so there shouldn't be any danger that he'd lose his foot.

'They're coming!' Jem announced, almost hopping from foot to foot in one of the first displays of eight-year-old excitement she'd seen from him. 'They're coming down the stope much faster than we did, but that's probably because their legs are longer than ours.'

'As long as they can go up again just as fast, we'll all be happy,' Maggie said, but her thoughts weren't really on what she was saying, not once she spotted Adam among the team members approaching the heap of rocks at the entrance to their tunnel.

'Welcome to our humble abode,' she said wryly, as she moved aside as far as she could so that there was room for both of them to kneel beside Tel's unconscious figure.

It was strange to be working with him again. The only other time they'd been involved in caring for a patient together had been that awful afternoon under the train, and even though these circumstances were equally stressful, it was almost as if they could read each other's minds.

She watched as Adam performed his own survey of Tel's situation while she passed on the details of his condition since she'd reached him and what treatment she'd given.

'He hasn't regained consciousness,' she pointed out with a significant glance in Jem's direction, and Adam took the hint, his concerned expression telling her that he was questioning the possibility of a bleed inside the youngster's skull, too.

The next few minutes were busy as Tel's backboard was loaded onto the high-sided stretcher and strapped firmly in position, the whole arrangement designed to provide virtually all-round protection for a patient while he was extricated from the mine.

The only thing that broke Maggie's concentration was the fact that every time Adam touched her—even something as accidental and simple as the nudge of his shoulder against hers or the brush of his hand—it was like an electric current racing through her body that was able to recharge her batteries in spite of the hours of tension that had drained them.

She was almost giddy with relief that their ordeal was nearly over and desperately needed to think about something else or she might make a complete fool of herself.

A quick glance around reminded her that Jem was still there, silently watching everything that was going on and patiently waiting for his turn to leave the cramped confines and start his journey up to his waiting mother.

'How's Kate been coping?' she asked Adam under cover of the instructions being fired backwards and forwards between the various members of the team.

Adam rolled his eyes. 'I think she'd have coped far better if Nick hadn't kept trying to throw his weight around. As soon as the entrance was cleared, he was trying to insist that he should be the one to come down to lead the rescue. He didn't seem to realise that he would be far more use if he stayed up on top and took care of Kate.'

'Until you pointed it out?' she finished for him, and knew she was right when she caught sight of a brief flash of white teeth as he grinned at her briefly.

'I reminded him that I'd lost my father in the same tragedy as Kate had lost her husband, and that having Jem in danger was probably bringing everything back for her. For heaven's sake, Nick's known the woman for years!' he muttered impatiently, barely remembering to keep his voice low enough so that Jem couldn't hear.

'He was probably at school with her. Who better to lend her some support?'

'Right, folks, we're ready to move,' announced a commanding voice at the mouth of the tunnel, and any chatter died away. 'Let's get that stretcher out of there.'

'Excuse me,' Maggie interrupted, and was hardly surprised at the long-suffering expression on the man's face as he turned impatiently towards her. 'I just wanted to ask that Jem be taken out first. He's been down here virtually alone for some of the time, and needs to get up to reassure his mother that he's well. I also think,' she added as the man beckoned the youngster out of the tunnel, 'that he's one of the most courageous lads I've ever met and I'll definitely be putting his name forward for a bravery award.' She gave his shoulder a pat as he slid past her in the cramped space and he smiled back at her, his eyes suspiciously bright.

'Hear, hear!' said Adam as Jem sidled past him, climbing over his feet, and patted the embarrassed lad on the shoulder before he climbed out over the pile of loose rocks at the entrance.

'*Gwir kolonneckter, mebyon,*' said one of the older members of the team, obviously praising the eight-year-old as he emerged at the bottom of the stope. Seth Tregonning had been a tin miner in his youth and was one of the few people Maggie knew who could speak the Cornish language that sounded just right in this most Cornish of places.

'What does that mean?' Jem asked, beaming from ear to ear as a member of the team adjusted a safety helmet to fit him for the journey to the surface.

'True courage, my boy,' Seth translated in the slightly sing-song accent of the region, and there was a general murmur of heartfelt agreement.

The team leader cleared his throat and Maggie was amazed to see that he'd been as affected by his team's response to the youngster as any of them.

'Right, then, Seth, I want you to go up first with Jem because you'll be able to move faster than the two with the stretcher, and we don't want any hold-ups,' he said with a swift return to his former briskness, and Maggie dropped to her knees again to finish putting the last of her equipment away in her pack, determined that she wasn't going to be the cause of any delay in the evacuation.

'The rest of you,' he continued, 'follow the stretcher up and be ready to help to smooth the ride up that wretched stope. Remember that everything is rough and has the potential to crumble under your feet. Adam, I'll leave you in charge of making sure that Maggie gets out safely as soon as she's picked up her stuff. OK?'

Out of the corner of her eye Maggie saw Adam's long legs make short work of climbing over the mound at the entrance to the tunnel as he moved out of the way for the appointed team members to take opposite ends of the stretcher to start the journey back up to the surface.

In just a few more minutes…a quarter of an hour at the most…they would all be safely up in the fresh air again, with the wide night sky spread over their heads and a sharp February breeze bringing the scent of the sea in from the bay.

Then…what?

Adam had said that they needed to talk once this was

all over. Did he mean tonight? Her heart gave an extra thump at the idea that he might suggest that she go back to his home. She had absolutely no idea where he was living. The local grapevine hadn't passed that piece of information around yet.

Unfortunately, everyone in the town knew where *she* lived—in the same cottage she'd shared with her mother—and most of them would know by breakfast-time if his car was parked outside her place overnight.

Except the whole idea that the two of them would be spending any more time together tonight was complete nonsense. Adam was a married man and would obviously be going back to his wife. Any conversation between the two of them would have to wait until he found time in his busy life.

'Ouch! Mind your knuckles, Pete,' called the stretcher carrier at the front. 'It's bad enough that we have to hunch over so we don't hit our heads, but this rough-hewn granite is evil stuff and your gloves won't stop you making a mess of your hands if you hit the walls on the way through.'

Maggie glanced up with a wry smile, her own aching hands testament to that fact, and was just in time to see the last man out of the tunnel—was he the one called Pete?—step awkwardly on a rock that Jem had missed, twisting his ankle and throwing him off balance.

'Careful, man!' warned his colleague, as he fought to keep the stretcher stable. 'Watch what you're doing with those big feet of yours.'

The poor man muttered a curse and lurched forward a couple of ungainly steps before he got his balance back, but in those few seconds his shoulder had cannoned into the abandoned crowbar that she'd set up to support the bag of saline.

As if it was happening in slow motion she saw the moment when the length of hexagonal steel pivoted against the ancient timber bracing the roof of the tunnel, wrenching it out of the position it had held for more than a hundred years and sending it crashing to the floor with a hollow thud, narrowly missing the edge of the stretcher on its way down.

Somebody swore ripely into the brief silence after the echoes had died away, but what happened next was something out of Maggie's worst nightmares as first one rock, barely the size of her fist, fell onto the dank floor, before tons of boulders followed it, cascading down in an avalanche that nearly deafened her in the enclosed space of the tunnel.

'No-o-o!' she shrieked, forced to scramble back into the depths of the tunnel as it began to fill with granite, shutting out the light of the torches at the bottom of the stope.

In pitch darkness and terrified that she was going to be trapped and injured just like Tel had been, she forced herself to retreat as fast as she could, her pack still miraculously clenched in her fist as she stumbled and ricocheted against the ever-narrowing walls.

Then, suddenly, the ground fell away underneath her and her head hit something totally unforgiving and the darkness became absolute.

CHAPTER SIX

MAGGIE groaned, wondering groggily why she'd woken in the dark and why she felt so awful.

Her head hurt…in fact, everything hurt.

And she was feeling so disorientated…as if her brain had been scrambled.

Had the ambulance been involved in an accident, or had she been injured by one of their patients? She'd escaped anything major so far, but attacks on ambulance staff by the very people they were trying to help were happening more and more, especially when the behaviour was fuelled by alcohol.

Or was she coming down with flu in spite of the jab she'd had in the autumn?

She reached out in the darkness to switch on the bedside light…and encountered a rough granite wall.

'Maggie?' Adam's frantic voice crackled nearby and suddenly she knew exactly where she was and what had happened.

'I fell,' she croaked, terror stealing her voice as she remembered those last few seconds as the ground had seemed to disappear under her.

She didn't remember landing, but the heavy throbbing of her head and the sensation of wetness in her hair was enough to tell her that she'd hit her head at some stage in the fall. 'So much for the safety helmet,' she muttered in disgust, although she supposed that it had hardly been designed with falling down a mine in mind.

What other damage had she done? Serious damage? Head injury? Broken bones? Internal bleeding?

It was so hard to do an examination of her own body when she couldn't see a thing. It didn't matter whether her eyes were open or shut, the blackness was absolute so she would have to rely entirely on her sense of touch…and knowing which bits hurt more than the rest.

How long ago had it happened? How long had she been unconscious? Minutes? Hours?

It wouldn't really matter either way, she realised with a crushing sense of despair. It had taken several hours to find the boys and effect their rescue, and that had only been a matter of shoring up the entrance to the adit and clearing the fallen granite that had been blocking it. The rockfall blocking this tunnel was enormous, and the chances that the rescue team would be able to clear it quickly…well, there was no chance at all, she admitted grimly as the full horror of her situation flooded over her.

'Maggie, please…!' Adam's voice crackled again and only then did it dawn on her that wherever it was, the radio had also survived the fall. Did the torch still work, too? She'd put it in her pack with the radio to leave her hands free, ready to climb up the stope for the last time.

Suddenly she was desperate to find that radio—her one link with the outside world. At least with the radio working she'd be able to speak to Adam and the dreadful all-encompassing blackness wouldn't feel so suffocating.

She nearly rolled over to begin her search. Only her years of training made her pause, fear of the possibility of permanent paralysis making her stay completely still for just a little longer.

She had no idea how far she'd fallen, would never have moved an inch further back into that claustrophobic tunnel unless she'd been forced to by the rockfall, so would never have known that the ground dropped away not far from where Tel had been trapped.

So it was a case of moving just one limb at a time while she did a terrified check to find out how badly she'd been injured, and with each limb cleared with little more than bruising to report, it was time to focus on her head and neck.

Her hair did feel wet, and there was a bruise forming…perhaps she and Tel would be able to compare matching his-and-hers goose eggs…but whether the wetness was from blood or the water continuously seeping down the tunnel walls, she had no idea.

Her neck felt a little stiff, so she could be suffering the after-effects of whiplash from the blow to her head, but the vertebrae weren't making any nasty crunching sounds and didn't feel any different from when she'd rinsed her hair under the shower so many hours ago that morning.

Just the thought of a steaming hot shower was enough to make her whimper. It felt like for ever since she'd last been clean and warm. Every inch of her body felt cold and wet and covered in dust and grit.

'But, dirty or clean, at least it feels as if everything is in working order…more or less,' she whispered into the darkness. There was no echo to bounce back at her, but she refused to think the logical next step…that there wouldn't be an echo in a space too small to bounce sounds back at her. The darkness was bad, but at least it was allowing her to fool herself that she wasn't trapped in a space little bigger than a coffin.

'Maggie? Can you hear me?' Adam called again; and the note of utter misery in his voice sent her scrambling to follow it, using the sound to direct her search.

In the background she heard another voice speaking behind Adam's, warning him that the radio had probably been damaged beyond use or buried under the rockfall, preventing her from using it. She could almost hear the implication that she was probably similarly damaged or buried, and suddenly knew that she had to get to that lifeline before Adam gave up trying to speak to her and she was left completely alone.

'There!' she muttered eagerly as her fingers encountered the familiar fabric of her pack. 'Got it!'

In spite of the fact that it was pitch dark, she found herself closing her eyes as she concentrated on the pack, running her fingers over it as she pictured what was inside each of the compartments until she came to the fastening she'd last closed when she'd pushed the torch and radio in for safekeeping.

The radio was silent now, and her hands were shaking uncontrollably as she tried to remember which of the many buttons was the one she needed to press before she could speak to Adam. It was imperative that she let everybody out there know that she was still alive...*before* they all gave up hope and went home.

'Maggie, *keresik*,' Adam called, his voice hoarse and unutterably weary, and her heart leapt at the sound of that old endearment. She could remember telling him that it had been her father's pet name for her mother, handed down through generations of their family from the days when they had all been Cornish speakers.

She'd teased him about his claim to be Cornish when his name was definitely Irish, as was the combination of deep sapphire blue eyes and dark hair. He'd told her the family tale that, instead of fleeing from certain starvation in the other direction, to America, the original Donnelly had come across the water at the time of the potato famine and married a beautiful Cornish girl who had taught him to speak Kernewek instead of Gaelic.

Maggie could also remember the first time he'd called her *keresik*, the very first time he'd kissed her on her sixteenth birthday, and the way her heart had soared that he'd thought of her as his darling.

'Adam?' she croaked, her throat thick with dust and emotion. 'Adam, can you hear me?'

There were several seconds of utter silence that left her terrified that she'd left it too late...that everyone had given up all hope of finding her alive...and then the darkness around her was filled with a crackly cacophony of voices whooping and cheering in delight.

'Quiet! Please!' Adam ordered before demanding, 'Maggie? Are you all right?'

She was just so glad to be able to hear his voice that

she was fighting tears. It was several seconds before she could speak.

'It's dark, it's dirty and I've just been deafened,' she complained when she could finally control her trembling chin.

'Just like a woman—always complaining,' teased one of the men, and she couldn't help joining in with the laughter at the other end.

'Joking aside, what injuries have you got, Maggie?' Adam asked, his tone telling her that he had switched into professional mode. 'Can you start at the top and work your way down?'

'I've got a bump on my head from when I fell,' she replied obediently. 'It's painful and it might be bleeding because my hair's wet, but there's no apparent underlying fracture. I was unconscious for a while but I have no idea how long.'

'About five minutes,' he supplied, but there was an edge to his voice that told her that it had felt a lot longer than that. Was Adam suffering from the same guilt as Jem, convinced that it was his fault that she was injured because he'd persuaded her to go down there in the first place? Had he forgotten that it had been her own decision to go back into the mine to finish the job she'd started?

'Apart from that,' she continued, knowing that this wasn't the right time to hold such a discussion, especially when there were so many other ears listening in, 'I've got various assorted bruises and scrapes but, as far as I can tell, no broken bones.'

'None? Are you sure?' he persisted.

'My X-ray eyes don't seem to be working very well

in the dark,' she quipped, almost light-headed with relief. 'I promise to let you take some as soon as you can get me out of here, if you think it's necessary.'

'I'll bear that offer in mind,' he said dryly. 'Now, tell me, how much of the rock actually came into that tunnel?' Suddenly all levity was gone. She was right back in the middle of a situation that couldn't possibly have a happy outcome.

'I don't know,' she admitted, belatedly feeling for the torch she'd tucked in her pack. Somehow, not being able to see how dire things were had stopped her thinking about them, but if she was going to have a hope of getting out of this mine, she was going to have to turn some light on her situation.

Her throat was already tightening again as she pulled the cold, smooth cylinder out of her pack and felt for the switch, dreading to find out just how confined the space was around her. She wasn't certain whether the fact that Adam could speak to her on the radio would be enough to keep her claustrophobia under control if she was truly on her own.

She moaned and closed her eyes when she took her first look around her, her breathing instantly harsher and her pulse racing. It was infinitely worse than she'd imagined.

'Maggie?' Adam prompted, but she couldn't speak. There were no words to tell him.

'How far back are you in the tunnel?' he persisted, then switched to coaxing. 'Come on, Maggie, you said you're not even badly hurt. All you've got to do is tell us where you are so we can get you out.'

'You can't...' she whispered in despair, hardly

caring that he might not be able to hear her. 'No one can get me out.'

He muttered a word that she'd last heard when the two of them had been trying to wriggle their way under the underground train. That time he'd just caught sight of the pulsing spray of bright arterial blood telling them that the young woman was mortally wounded. They'd both known that they'd had just moments to stop her bleeding before her heart stopped for lack of blood to pump around her body.

Well, she *wasn't* mortally wounded, but it would have been infinitely easier if she had been. The death she was facing could take many days before she finally succumbed to dehydration and starvation.

'Maggie Pascoe, where's your backbone?' he demanded sharply, surprising her with implied criticism and igniting a spark of anger.

'My backbone is in the same place as the rest of me, in a hole about the same diameter as I am tall with no visible exits except the one near the roof that I must have fallen down.' She drew in a sobbing breath but was determined that none of them would know how close she was to losing it. 'It looks as if that last fall sealed me in here as neatly as a pharaoh in a pyramid.'

Her words were received with utter silence, almost as if they'd all stopped breathing while they'd taken in the significance of what she'd been telling them…that, like a pyramid, this mine had just effectively become her tomb.

Then, because she knew she was going to cry for all the things she was never going to achieve in her life, she deliberately switched the radio off.

* * *

Dammit, Maggie! No! Don't do this! Don't give up!
Adam railed inside his head.

It was so hard to stand there, unable to do anything to help with what was going on around him.

Maggie had effectively shut him out by switching off the radio and, after an initial bout of frantic activity to help clear enough space to position props above the entrance where the tunnel had been, he'd realised that he had to step aside and let the professionals do their job.

All around him the rescue effort had redoubled in pace, the space at the foot of the stope teeming with men whose single objective was to find a way of getting to the woman trapped inside the hillside.

She shouldn't have been down there at all, Adam reminded himself as his guilt mounted by the minute. If he hadn't persuaded her to go—virtually blackmailed her into it, using her sense of duty against her in the worst way—then she would have been safe now, up on the hill behind Penhally, trying to stay warm in the biting chill of a February night.

And at least one of those five boys would have died by the time the rescue team had reached them, he reminded himself, the latest report from St Piran Hospital fresh in his mind. Terrence Loveday's injuries had been minimised by Maggie's expert attention, his breathing eased by her physical exertions to remove the rocks against his chest and the danger of major blood loss and permanent injury to his leg averted by the fact she'd correctly stabilised the fractures and administered replacement fluids. She'd even accurately diagnosed the fact that his persisting loss of consciousness wasn't just a symptom of concussion but of a slow bleed inside his skull from a damaged blood vessel.

The message relayed down to him just a few minutes ago was that Tel was in Theatre, already undergoing cranial surgery for the removal of a blood clot and, hopefully, the repair of the injury that had cause it.

Previous experience of similar cases told Adam that the boy would probably spend several days in Intensive Care in an induced coma while they waited for the swelling to go down. Only when his condition stabilised would they withdraw the drugs and wait to see if he regained consciousness; only then would anyone be able to judge how much permanent damage had been done by his fall.

The other injured youngster—Adam thought Maggie had called him Chris—would require some delicate jigsaw work to realign the broken bones in the back of his hand, but while his rehab would probably be long and painful if he was to regain his full range of motion, it was a far from life-threatening injury.

As for the rest of them, apart from a few nightmares to come about being stuck underground in the dark, they seemed to have escaped scot-free.

And, of course, the thought of the boys suffering from nightmares took him right back to Maggie and the terrible price she was having to pay, and the only thing he could do was play the whole situation over and over inside his head, wishing he could go back and do just one thing differently.

The trouble was, how far back would that train of thought take him? To the conversation at the entrance of the adit, when he'd coerced her into going into the mine against all her instincts? To a year earlier and the events of that meeting in London and the first time he'd persuaded her to put herself in danger? Or should he go all the way back nearly a decade to his failure to return to Penhally when he had been drawn back so strongly?

He needed to talk to her about all those things, to explain the what, the why and the wherefore of each of them, but most of all he needed to take away the look of distrust in her eyes that had been there ever since she'd seen the photo on his bedside cabinet.

He sighed heavily at that memory and hoped that he would have a chance to tell Maggie about Caroline, cool, beautiful, elegant Caroline who, like every other woman he'd dated after he'd left Penhally, had been as unlike dark-haired elfin Maggie Pascoe as it was possible to be.

Except he hadn't realised that was what he'd been doing until he'd seen her again, sitting at the front of the lecture theatre when he'd walked in to substitute for his sick colleague.

He hadn't been able to believe his eyes when he'd realised who she was, and from the wide-eyed expression on her face, she'd been equally surprised...and delighted?

It had been hard to concentrate on that first lecture when all he'd been able to think about had been that there would be a coffee-break coming up in an hour and a half and he would be able to speak to her for the first time since she'd been sixteen.

Oh, he'd seen her in the interim, briefly when he'd returned to be at his mother's side while they'd waited to hear news of his father. It had been small consolation to either of them to learn that he had died a hero, helping to save the lives of the group of children who had been cut off by the tide that summer evening.

And so, after the memorial service in the church over-looking a deceptively tranquil sea, he'd helped his mother to pack up their lives and move across the country to be near the rest of her family while he'd returned to medical school—returned with an image of the commiseration he'd seen in Maggie's beautiful hazel eyes to console him and a determination that one day he would return to Penhally to find the woman she'd become.

'Adam?' said a hesitant voice, and all the hairs went up on the back of his neck.

'Maggie?' he said, horribly aware that almost every-body around him had frozen in position at the knowl-edge that the woman they were toiling to rescue had chosen to contact him again.

'I'm sorry,' she said in a voice that was far huskier than usual, probably as a result of the tears she'd been shedding in the silence of her isolation. She might think that she'd hidden the fact that she had been close to breaking point and had needed time to herself, but he'd known. The only thing he hadn't been certain of had been whether she would turn the radio on again or whether she had seen her withdrawal as permanent.

'You've got nothing to be sorry for,' he reassured her, the guilt that was warring with his relief that she was speaking to him again suddenly overwhelming him. 'It's *my* fault that you're in this position at all. If I hadn't twisted your arm—'

'Adam, *don't*,' she said wearily. 'I really don't want to spend the next…however long playing the blame game. *I* shouldn't have stuck that crowbar there. I should have made certain that I'd cleared the passage better so Pete couldn't trip, and so on, and so on. I just want…' There was a wobble in her voice that made a tight fist clench around his heart. He didn't trust that his own voice would be any steadier so he simply waited for her to continue in her own time.

'I'm sitting here in the dark,' she said when she finally broke the endless pause.

Horrified, he broke in, 'Dammit, Maggie, you didn't tell me the torch broke when you fell.' How much worse could her situation get?

'No, Adam. The torch is OK,' she reassured him quickly. 'I decided to switch it off.'

'Why?' He couldn't imagine anything worse than sitting in the dark, deep underground.

'Partly I did it to save the batteries in the torch, but mostly it's because that way I can fool my mind a bit…pretend that I'm not surrounded by millions of tons of rock and I… Oh, please, Adam, would you talk to me?' she asked in a small voice that nearly broke his heart.

'What do you want me to talk about?' he offered, willing to promise her anything. Heaven only knew how long it would be before she wouldn't be able to hear him any more. Every cell in his body rejected the idea of a world without Maggie in it…her courage, her empathy, her sweetness…but logic told him that there was very little chance that they would be able to move such an enormous quantity of rock in the short time available to them. It could take weeks in such an unstable environment, with every bit of excavation needing extensive use of props to stop it collapsing again. Was that why the mine had been abandoned in the first place?

'Anything,' she said, sounding so like the young girl he'd first got to know all those years ago that his own eyes burned with the threat of tears. Why had he wasted so much time before he'd come back to see her? If he'd returned before he'd met Caroline, the whole course of both their lives would have been so different.

'Tell me about your wife,' she suggested, almost as if she was picking up on his thoughts. 'Tell me about Caroline.'

His ears burned at the thought that all the rescuers would be listening in to such a personal conversation, but if that was what Maggie wanted, who was he to deny her? She deserved that and more.

'Where did you meet? Is she a doctor, too?' Maggie prompted, just as someone tapped Adam on the shoulder.

'Hang on a second,' he said, and turned to face the slightly bashful-looking man standing behind him.

'Doc, I just wanted to tell you that the rest of us have switched our radios off to give you some privacy. The only interruptions will be if someone's contacting us on this frequency from outside. OK?'

'Thank you,' Adam said, hoping he was far enough into the shadows for the heat of his blush to be indistinguishable. 'I'll let you know if there are any messages.'

'Oh, Lord, I'm sorry, Adam,' Maggie groaned. 'I honestly hadn't realised that the whole world was listening in. I'll just—'

'They're not listening any more,' he broke in quickly, afraid that she might withdraw again. 'It's just you and me, the way it was in the library on a Friday afternoon, remember?'

The sudden gurgle of laughter at the other end was exactly how he remembered Maggie…*his* Maggie…the one who was full of laughter, not the serious, studious one that everybody else had seen.

'Until the headmaster came in and caught us,' she reminded him. 'If you hadn't lit the candles, he'd never have known we were up there.'

'We couldn't celebrate your birthday without lighting the candles on your cake,' he objected, remembering the sudden stab of fear when he'd seen the expression on the joyless man's face. He'd been so certain that he was going to be thrown out of school before he could take his final exams.

Then Maggie, his indomitable Maggie had piped up, 'Would you like a piece of my birthday cake, sir? It's chocolate with real chocolate icing.'

The voice coming out of the radio was repeating the words verbatim, and he burst out laughing. 'Only *you* would have dared to offer the old dragon a piece of cake when he was ready to breathe fire.'

'Ah, but, then, I was one of the few people who knew that Mr Pendragon had a seriously sweet tooth and couldn't resist chocolate,' she said smugly, her Saturday job, when she served the older man with his newspaper and a large bar of chocolate each week having given her the idea.

'Well, he certainly proved it that afternoon,' Adam

grumbled, still sore that the treat he'd organised for Maggie had been so thoroughly hijacked by their head-master. 'He ate nearly half of it and it was supposed to be for you.'

'It was the thought that counted more than the cake,' she said softly, her voice almost lost in the crackles. 'I knew Mum was upset about working late on my birthday, but I never dreamed that when I told you, you'd go out to the bakery in your lunch-break and bring a cake up to the library.'

He hadn't been able to believe it either. Buying a birthday cake for a sixteen-year-old certainly hadn't been the sort of thing most other seniors would have done, and if his classmates had known about it…or about the fact that, instead of taking advantage of an af-ternoon without lessons to start the weekend early, he'd been meeting Maggie up in the library for several hours of study…

About the only part of it that his hormone-ridden classmates would have applauded was the fact that on her sixteenth birthday, in the shadows behind the furthest library stacks, he'd finally found out what it was like to kiss Maggie Pascoe.

'That was my first kiss,' she said, proving that her thoughts had been following the same inevitable path.

She'd been so very young when he'd met her, capti-vated at first by her quicksilver mind and shy sense of fun. He'd thought it would be little more than a quick peck…a token to celebrate the fact that she had offi-cially become a woman. What he hadn't expected had been that her lips would be so sweet, or that they'd cling softly to his as her arms had come up to twine about his neck, pressing her slender elfin body against his and setting off an unexpected firestorm inside him. It had taken all his self-control not to let things get out of hand and it had almost been a relief when the bell for the end of the school day had sounded stridently right above their heads.

He'd needed a long cold shower when he returned home that night, but he'd made a promise to himself that, however their relationship went, he wasn't going to rush Maggie. He was the older of the two of them and it was his responsibility not to rush her through the wonderment of growing up.

He was determined that, even if he had to suffer frostbite under the shower on a daily basis, he would keep his libido under control, limiting their sexual experimentation to the kisses and cuddles appropriate for someone who had never run with the fast crowd. Just because he was older and ready to take things to a more intimate level, it didn't mean that he had the right to rush her before *she* was ready to take that step.

Neither of them could have known what that year was to bring. At the time that the two of them were laughing, teasing, talking and kissing their way through a glorious Cornish summer they had no idea that the next time they saw each other would be at his father's funeral and the memorial service for all those who had lost their lives that day.

'I missed you when we moved away,' he said, only now realising just how deep that emotion had gone. It had been as if an essential part of him had been torn away inside and hadn't been put back until he'd walked into the staffroom at Penhally Bay Surgery and seen Maggie standing there.

CHAPTER SEVEN

I MISSED you when we moved away,' he said in the darkness, and Maggie's heart swelled inside her, sending warmth to every part of her.

She'd never known that before, thinking that when they'd moved away he'd instantly forgotten the skinny bookworm he'd given her first kiss to on her sixteenth birthday.

For months after he and his mother had moved away she'd waited and hoped that he would write to her, but when nothing had come all she had been left with had been the determination to work hard enough to be accepted at the same medical school he attended. In her teenage mind she'd pictured the day when she would be able to meet him on even ground at least, both of them medical students working towards the same goal. Perhaps then he'd finally realise that she was ready for more than kisses.

Except while she was making her plans, the one thing she hadn't counted on was that her mother would become ill.

'Mum had cancer,' she said, and the stark words still had the power to wound.

'Ah, Maggie, *keresik*, I'm sorry. Once Mum moved back to be near her family we lost touch with what was going on in Penhally. How long…?'

'She was diagnosed just before I took my last school exams—breast cancer—so even though I got the grades I needed, I couldn't take up my place at medical school.' Even this much later she could remember the bitter turmoil inside her as she'd railed against fate.

Her mother had been the only relative she'd had in the world and because she'd loved her, there had been no way she could have left her to go through the misery of cancer treatment by herself. But that didn't mean that she hadn't mourned the destruction of all the plans she'd made for her future, not least the fact that she would once again be able to see Adam on a daily basis.

'What treatment did she have?' he prompted, and after years of reticence it was almost a relief to be able to talk about it with him. He'd actually met her mother and he was also someone who would understand what she was talking about without having to go into long and involved explanations.

'She had a radical mastectomy and they excised the lymph nodes, too.' She could still remember her shock when she'd seen her mother for the first time after the surgery. 'She looked as if she'd aged twenty years overnight,' she murmured, reliving her terror that her mother wouldn't survive the night, that she'd be left completely on her own to make her way in the world. 'The primary tumour was the size of a pigeon's egg and highly vascularised and every lymph node they took out seemed to be affected. She was an absolute mess by the time they'd finished.'

'Chemo?' he asked.

'By the time she called it quits she'd had everything they could throw at her,' Maggie said through a throat that ached with tears. 'The surgeon seemed so sure that they'd got it all, but somehow they'd missed a tiny tumour in the other breast, and it was one that didn't respond to the chemo she was on for the other one. By the time they found it and realised what it was…' She swallowed, recalling the day when her mother had sat her down in their tiny kitchen and told her what the oncologist had found, and what the prognosis was.

'It was very fast growing, very aggressive, and he couldn't be certain that there weren't others elsewhere in her body so he…' She dragged in a quick breath so that she could get the telling over with. 'He told her that they could hit it with everything they'd got, but the treatment would probably be worse than the disease and there was very little chance that it would be successful. So she'd decided that she would like to spend the time she had left with me rather than in a hospital ward with a load of strangers.'

It had been a strange time, full of memories recalled and memories made. A time when she'd delighted in driving her mother to all the places that had been special in her life and listening as she'd told the tales of people and incidents that had made her who she was. It had been a time when she had been very aware that her mother had been saying good bye to her life and all the things that had made it so rich, and it had obviously given her so much joy and such an air of peace that Maggie had decided that it was what she would want to do when her time came.

Except now she wasn't going to have that option, not since half a hillside had come cascading down and buried her before she was even dead.

Maggie shook her head and firmly pushed that thought into the darkest corner of her mind. She didn't know whether she had just a few hours left or several days…but, then, was that really any different to anyone else? To Walter Dinnis, for example? One minute he'd been living his life, happily retired and spending the afternoon with his wife, and then the next Betty had been frantically phoning for an ambulance to take him to hospital and Maggie had needed to use the defibrillator to shock his heart back into its proper rhythm.

So she wasn't going to sit down here getting more and more maudlin by the minute. She may not have the option of doing it in person, but she was going to do her best to revisit all the events and places that had meant the most to her in her mind. And along the way perhaps she could get the answers to all those questions that had been plaguing her for so long.

'So *that* explains why you didn't go to medical school,' Adam said with the air of someone who had discovered the secrets of the universe. 'When we met up in London, I couldn't believe that you'd qualified as a paramedic instead. You'd been so determined to do well in your exams that I was sure you'd be tapping me on the shoulder one day to show me that you'd made it.'

Maggie burst out laughing. 'That's *exactly* what I'd intended doing,' she admitted. 'I had it all planned in my head.'

'And after your mum was gone?'

'I couldn't afford to do it,' she said simply. 'Medical training was just going to take to long and be too expensive without any finances behind me. I even thought about selling the cottage, but…'

'But it was all you had left of your family,' he finished for her, knowing how she felt without her having to say it. 'I think that was one of the things that stopped me coming back to visit Penhally—the fact that I would have to see our old home and know it wasn't ours any more, that someone else was living there in the place that held all my childhood memories.'

'And now you'll be going past it on almost a daily basis when you're out doing house calls. Is it still a problem for you?'

'Not going past it, no. It looks so completely different because someone's painted the old stone walls white and stuck fake shutters either side of the windows.'

'Don't forget the fact that the windows are now plastic and the new front door is studded with fake iron nails,' Maggie said, and was rewarded with a chuckle.

'What on earth makes people think that sort of thing is an "improvement"? There was nothing wrong with it the way it was—an honest-to-goodness fisherman's cottage built of local stone, roofed in Delabole slate and with the original sash windows.'

'Well,' she said, deliberately broadening her accent, 'you know what us locals say about they incomers…

all thur taste is in thur mouth,' she teased, and he laughed aloud.

'You're not wrong there. It seems to be happening wherever there's a pretty sleepy place with tiny cottages. Before you can turn around, there's a crop of multi-million pound mansions squeezed between them— second, third and even fourth homes, meaning the locals haven't a hope of buying a home within twenty miles of their families or their jobs.'

'Well, at least the outsiders are only there for the summer,' she consoled him. 'Most of those new houses are probably only used for a fortnight every year, and long before the autumn gales come, the population's back to just locals, and life returns to normal.'

'I take it you've seen it at its worst, as a paramedic?'

'And then some,' she groaned. 'There's been an annual influx of Society types when the big public schools break up for summer. For a couple of weeks there can be several thousand teenagers congregating on the sand at one venue or another, fighting with their enemies from a rival school, or with pupils from some of the local schools. And when you factor in underage binge-drinking and the fact that some bring drugs down with them, it can be an explosive mix.

'I presume the authorities have been taking steps to minimise the damage, in human terms, at least?'

'You mean, apart from drafting in almost every available policeman in the area to police the alcohol and drugs and imposing a curfew on the beaches?' Maggie laughed wryly. 'They risk life and limb trying to separate the warring tribes while we paramedics are playing piggy-in-the-middle taking care of the injuries and overdoses. Thank goodness for places like Padstow. There's more for people to do there; more entertainment and come very good cafés and restaurants, as well as a lot of more affordable accomodation.'

'So, when we get you out of here, would you like to go to Padstow for our celebratory meal?' he asked, and her heart gave a sudden leap.

'At least in February you'd be certain of finding something open in Padstow,' she said wryly, while she tried to find the words to clarify the situation. In the end, all she could do was ask point blank. 'Adam, did you just ask me out for a meal?'

'I must be more out of practice than I thought if you couldn't tell that was an invitation,' he complained. 'Perhaps I need to give it another go. So, have you got a favourite place, Maggie? Will you come out with me?'

It was such a tempting thought and would be the fulfilment of a dream she'd had since she'd been fifteen, but there was one enormous obstacle.

'Won't your wife mind you asking me out, or will she be joining us?' she asked pointedly, knowing she wouldn't be able to live with herself if she went against her personal convictions, and that included an absolute ban on having a relationship with a married man.

'Dammit, Maggie, I should have told you about Caroline—' he began, only to break off when there was the sound of a shout from somewhere behind him. 'Just a minute,' he said distractedly, his voice fading, and she could picture him turning away from the radio to speak to the man who'd hailed him.

She tried to listen in on their conversation but the reception wasn't clear enough. She couldn't even tell from the tone of their voices whether the news was good, bad or indifferent, and had to wait impatiently until he came back to her.

In the meantime, she was left wondering just what he would have said about his wife if he hadn't been interrupted. Were he and Caroline divorced? She felt a pang of guilt that she should feel the remotest bit happy that he should have gone through that sort of misery. But it *would* mean that he was no longer married, a small voice inside her head pointed out.

Or perhaps they were merely separated, each resigned to the other's peccadilloes, uncaring that they were breaking their sacred vows. Unfortunately, that wouldn't change the situation as far as she was concerned. She believed that married was married, and only death—or divorce for those who believed in it—would change that.

'Maggie?' Adam's voice brought her out of the realms of speculation and the new energy that flowed out of the radio was almost visible. 'Someone's unearthed a map.'

'A map?' She couldn't see quite what the excitement was about. Most people might have completely forgotten that this mine had ever existed, but it was bound to have been marked on old maps.

'Young George used a few of his contacts,' Adam continued, and Maggie smiled the way she always did when she heard the old man's title, knowing it had been bestowed on him when his father and grandfather had both been alive.

'So how does that help anything?' she asked, frustrated that their conversation had been interrupted for something so unimportant. 'We already know where the mine is.'

'Ah, but this isn't the sort of map you're thinking about, with roads and railways marked on it,' he explained. 'This is a map that shows all the tunnels and whether they were adits, drifts, winzes and so on, and what level they all are in relation to each other.'

Suddenly she felt a spark of excitement, too. Did this mean that there was a chance they could find another way in to her living tomb?

'So, what have they found out?' she demanded eagerly.

'Not a lot, yet,' he admitted. 'But I didn't want to keep you in the…um…I just wanted to let you know that even though it might not seem like it at the moment, things *are* happening.'

'You nearly said you didn't want to keep me in the dark,' she pointed out with a quiver in her voice, not certain whether she wanted to laugh or cry.

For just a moment she'd thought it was all going to be easy, that with this old map they'd found there was another way to get her safely out of there, another adit coming into the mine from the other side of the hill perhaps.

Adam's narrowly averted slip of the tongue would have been funny under any other circumstances. It was only now, when she was so close to the edge, that it had nearly been enough to break her control, and that was the last thing she wanted.

If…when…the inevitable happened, he was bound to feel guilty for having persuaded her to go into the mine in the first place. He would probably ignore the fact that she'd willingly gone back down after she'd brought the three boys out, and take all the blame on his own conscience. He certainly didn't need to hear her fall apart, too. The least she could do was show the world some composure in the face of adversity.

'So…' She had to pause to clear her throat and pray for some inspiration. The one thing she *did* need was to have Adam close to her, because hearing his voice was enough to make her feel a little less alone. All she had to do was think of a topic.

'Did you ever hear what happened to the girl under the train? Joanna?' she asked, her brain instantly connecting the present situation with the first time she'd been in a cramped and dangerous situation with him. Then it had been his deep voice washing over her, instructing, calming, encouraging, that had helped her to cope with the whole thing on a minute-by-minute basis.

'I went to visit her a few days later on Orthopaedics, after she'd had some reconstruction work done,' he said, and as soon as she heard the smile in his voice she knew that there had been a successful outcome even before he told her. 'They'd managed to pin and plate her arm and done some microsurgery on blood, tendons and nerves, but she knew she was going to be looking at several more procedures to maximise function before plastics would make it look prettier. *But* she still had her arm and they were very optimistic about the outcome.'

'Did she tell you what had happened?' she demanded. 'All I heard was the rumour on the platform—that she'd screamed and jumped, and he was a good-Samaritan bystander that she dragged off with her—but while we were under the train, she didn't sound in the least bit suicidal. She was begging us to save her life.'

'Apparently, the man was an ex-boyfriend who wasn't taking the "ex" part very well,' Adam said. 'She said she'd realised just in time that he was a complete control freak who was systematically taking over her life, cutting her off from all her friends and family. She'd told him it was all over, but he didn't want to let her go.'

'So he decided that if he couldn't have her then no one could, and he pushed her under the train?' Maggie couldn't believe it. 'And to think I felt sorry for him!'

'She was just amazingly lucky that she landed between the rails without touching the live one. He had wrapped his arms around her before he jumped so even though she was struggling, he actually kept her fairly safe.'

'Except for her arm,' she said with a shudder, re-membering the extent of that injury. When she'd first seen it, she'd been convinced that the wheels had gone completely over the arm and severed it. It had only been when she'd been trying to staunch the arterial bleeding that she'd realised that it had only been a particularly bad open fracture.

'As near as they could make out, the back of his head was hit by something under the train. The blow destroyed the dens on C2—you probably know that's called the hangman's fracture—and he was dead almost instanta-neously. Her arm was caught by part of the machinery underneath, too, but it wasn't a total traumatic amputa-tion so the surgeons were able to salvage the hand.'

'So it was all worthwhile, being shoved under the train when I just wanted to run screaming into the distance,' she said wryly. 'The London underground system was hard enough to cope with, especially at that time of day with so many commuters packed onto the platform, but climbing down onto the track and seeing the tiny space I was going to have to squeeze into...' She shuddered at the memory.

'But you did it, because there was no one else small enough with the right knowledge to be able to save her life in the few minutes there was left to make a difference,' he said quietly. 'And I don't know whether I ever told you but I was so proud of you for being able to make yourself do it.'

'The way *I* remember it, you didn't really give me much option,' she grumbled, to cover up the delight flooding through her at his words. She'd been delighted that Joanna had still been alive by the time the air ambulance staff had arrived with replacement fluids and the pain relief that she'd needed. At least she could console herself that her efforts had kept the young woman going until her care had been placed in other hands.

Once their help was no longer needed, Adam had suggested that she might like to avail herself of his bathroom to clean herself up a bit and that had been the moment when she'd realised that she had been covered in so much of Joanna's blood that she'd looked like a victim herself.

Of course, that wasn't the only reason why she accepted his offer so readily. If she was being honest, a large part of her eagerness was due to the incredible attraction that had been drawing the two of them together all day.

From the first moment that she saw him walk into the lecture room Maggie knew that Adam was still the only man for her. It may have been years since he'd left Penhally but she'd never forgotten him, measuring every man she met against his impossible standard.

It was hard to concentrate on the lectures while she watched him pace backwards and forwards at the front of the room, his body more heavily muscled than when he'd left as a teenager so that his shoulders looked broader than ever, his stride long and smooth. And those stunning eyes! She'd never seen another pair such a deep sapphire colour, or any eyes that held the sparkle that his did when he smiled at her.

Looking back on it, there had probably been several disgruntled women on the course, upset that he'd made it obvious that he'd wanted to spend his break times only with her. At the time all she'd been aware of had been the fact that she had actually been there, sitting next to Adam Donnelly, and that he'd seemed every bit as pleased to see her.

So when he suggested that she come home with him, there was no thought in her head that she would turn the offer down. In fact, it was quite possible that her brain ceased working altogether, handing over control of the evening to her heart.

The maisonette was bigger than she'd expected, bearing in mind the cost of housing in London, but other than that, inside it seemed like a typical bachelor's abode, with that morning's dishes washed but left on the drainer and a pile of opened mail on the table. The bathroom was no better, with the towel he'd used slung over the shower door rather than hung on the rail and the toothpaste and brush left on the back of the basin.

'At least I put my dirty laundry away,' he muttered defensively as he did a lightning tour, picking things up and putting them away before he found a clean towel for her and left the bathroom.

Her clothes had disappeared by the time she finally turned the shower off and she shivered at the knowledge that he might have seen her through the screen while she had been under the shower, hoping that he'd liked what he'd seen. Her only regret was that she hadn't known he was looking so that she could have invited him to join her.

Just the thought of being so wanton made her blush and she groaned at the fact that she'd had so little experience, afraid that it might turn Adam off. The trouble was, she'd never been so attracted to another man that she'd wanted to share her body with him. It had always been Adam for her, first, last and always.

The pale grey sweats he'd left just inside the door were far too long for her, but that was the perennial problem for her when she bought clothes, too. Anyway, she thought as she picked her shoes up while her heart tried to pound its way out of her chest, she was hoping that she wouldn't be wearing them for very long. If the expression in his eyes was anything to go by, Adam was every bit as excited as she was to be there together at last.

Perhaps it had something to do with the life-or-death events on the underground, making the two of them feel that they had to celebrate the fact that they were alive and well in the most basic way possible, but she'd barely stepped out into the hallway when he appeared from the tiny kitchen.

'Can I get you anything while your clothes are in the washing machine? Tea? Coffee? Something stronger? Or would you rather have something to eat?' he offered, but she barely heard him, her eyes feasting on the naked chest displayed to perfection above jeans worn white in prominent places.

She was struck dumb by his sheer masculine beauty and all she could think was that she only wanted to feast on him.

'Maggie...!' he groaned, and she knew that he was every bit as desperate for her as she was for him.

Suddenly it was so easy and so blissfully simple as she walked into his arms and offered her mouth for his kiss.

Within seconds he'd swept her off her feet and into his arms but she had no idea where he was taking her, only that his kisses were even better than she'd remembered, sweeter, deeper, more exciting, stirring her to her depths and reverberating with all the emotions she'd been storing up for just this moment.

She'd thought that she would be shy the first time a man explored her body with love-making in mind, knowing that her slenderness was far from most men's ideal, but this was *Adam* touching her, stroking all the way up her shower-warmed belly as he pushed the borrowed sweat top up until her naked breasts were revealed.

'At last,' he breathed as he lavished attention on them, stroking and kissing and suckling them the way she'd longed for him to do that far-off summer. 'I've been wanting to do this for so long. You've no idea how hard it was for me to resist you back then.'

'So why did you bother resisting?' she demanded, while her brain was still in command of her mouth. 'You must have known that it was what I wanted, too, and once I was sixteen…'

'That's far too young to start a sexual relationship,' he growled, momentarily distracted from feasting on her. 'I was already eighteen and my hormones were driving me crazy, but even then I knew that it was too soon. You were too young to know…much too young for me to tie you down.'

She knew that he was right. Logically, sixteen *was* far too young, but in her heart she knew that if you met the right person at that age, there was no point in looking any further. All those years ago she'd been absolutely certain that he was the right person as soon as she'd got to know him, and now, finally, they were going to be together the way they always should have been.

He groaned as she arched her body up against him and tilted her hips, pure instinct telling her that he would find the pressure and friction against his aroused body impossible to resist.

She was right.

It took him only seconds to strip those jeans away and her eyes widened at her first look at his aroused masculine perfection before he returned to her and drew her into his arms.

She offered her mouth for his kiss but he hadn't finished speaking and touched a gentle fingertip to her lips while he met her gaze. She was disappointed for a moment, but the tension she felt thrumming through his body told her that this was just a brief delay. Well, she'd waited for years to experience his possession for the first time, so a few more minutes wouldn't make any difference, not when every inch of his body was silently shouting its intentions.

'Maggie, you do understand, don't you? I had to give you the chance to see something of the world...' he said with a concerned frown drawing his brows together, but she was far more interested in the fact that his dark eyes were slumberous with arousal and that the pulse at his throat was racing while he tried to continue their conversation. 'You deserved to have the opportunity to achieve the goals you'd set for yourself before you were tied down to a permanent relationship. I didn't want you to resent me for taking that away from you.'

'Stupid man,' she whispered lovingly as she rubbed her naked breasts against the dark silky hair across his chest. 'We could have done it all together, helping each other through it. Just think of all the years we've wasted because you didn't think I was old enough to know my own mind.'

'You're sure you know it now?' he challenged as he plucked at the sleeves of her borrowed top, helping her to slide her arms out one at a time. 'No doubts about what you're doing?'

'None!' she declared triumphantly, and flung the sweat top aside.

A sudden clatter told her that she'd knocked something over on the bedside cabinet and, afraid that it might have been broken, she craned her head to look as he reached out to pluck the garment now draped over the bedside light.

'Did I damage anything?' she asked, mortified that she'd been so clumsy. Had she completely ruined the mood with her awkwardness?

'Nothing's broken and nothing's touching the light to be set on fire,' he confirmed, setting a silver picture frame on the surface again.

From the corner of her eye she caught sight of the two sets of images frozen in time. One was obviously a photo of Adam and his mother taken on his graduation day, both of them smiling widely, but the other… She gasped in shock when she'd realised what she was looking at.

'W-who is that?' she demanded through suddenly chattering teeth, all thoughts of seduction gone as she focused on the bride and groom cutting the cake in the photo, each of them smiling widely for the camera.

The groom was undeniably Adam, impossibly handsome in his dark suit and white shirt with a blood-red rosebud in his lapel, and the tall elegant blonde beauty with the wealth of tumbling blonde hair…?

'That's Caroline,' he said heavily. 'My wife.'

Maggie didn't remember much of the next few minutes.

She knew that Adam had pleaded with her to stay, just long enough for him to explain…but he should have known that no explanations would excuse what he'd nearly enticed her into doing.

Yes, she'd been only too willing to go to bed with him, but that had been when she'd believed that he was as free as she was to give her love—she hadn't known that he was married and that she was about to commit adultery.

The next thing she remembered was slamming the

door of his house behind her with her handbag in one hand and her shoes in the other, dressed in nothing more than borrowed sweats.

Maggie never knew whether he'd tried to come after her that night once he'd put some clothes on, but presumed that he couldn't be bothered when there was no further contact from him, even though he knew she was going to be returning to Penhally.

That had been the last time she'd seen him until that afternoon, when she'd had to turn to face her nemesis.

The Penhally grapevine being what it was, she'd heard that he was returning to work as a locum and had been dreading their first meeting, expecting to hate him or, if not that, to at least despise him for the fiasco a year ago.

Instead, she'd found that her body and her heart didn't care what he had done, they still loved him as much as ever and desired him more than any other man.

She stifled a sob at the realisation that it was all too late.

Even if she'd been able to overcome her scruples, she was never going to know what it felt like to be possessed by him in that ultimate pleasure. The chances that she would be able to escape from the mine were so slim as to be negligible and the chances that she would ever fulfil the dream that had haunted her for half her lifetime were non-existent.

CHAPTER EIGHT

TELL me about your wife...your blonde, beautiful, elegant wife...

The words hovered on her tongue yet again, but this time she wasn't so sure that she wanted to ask them.

She'd spent a whole year alternately congratulating herself for escaping from his house with her scruples intact—*their* house, she corrected herself with a grimace—and the other half wondering if she'd made the most enormous mistake.

What if she asked him now, when there was absolutely nothing she could do about it whatever he told her? What difference would it make to anything?

If he was still married she would die knowing that Adam had never loved her the way she'd loved him, but if she discovered that his marriage had already been over that night a year ago, she would leave this life knowing that she had wasted the last year of it alone when the two of them could have been together.

'Adam...?' The voice in the background at Adam's end of the line called across to him again, and when Maggie realised that her chance for asking that question had disappeared again, this time she wasn't sure whether she was disappointed or relieved.

Then the voice drew closer...not close enough for her to follow their conversation but enough for her to realise that it was some sort of update about Tel.

'I don't know if you heard any of that,' Adam said when he returned to her. 'But that was a message from Neurosurgery at St Piran's. Tel's out of Theatre and is being transferred to ICU as we speak.'

'So he did have to go to Theatre,' she said with sudden feeling of dread. 'How much did I miss? Have they been able to rectify it?' At first she'd been quite certain that Tel didn't have a major cranial injury, but when he'd shown little sign of regaining consciousness her concern had steadily grown. 'How is he?'

'You were right to be worried,' he said. 'I passed your suspicions on so that the neurosurgeon was waiting for him when he arrived at St Piran's. Apparently, Tel did have a small bleed at the site of the cranial trauma that they only picked up when they did a scan. They went in to remove the clot to relieve the pressure on his brain and to make sure that the injury wasn't still bleeding, and then orthopods did a swift job on his leg.'

'And? What's his prognosis?' For Jem's sake she didn't want Tel to suffer any lasting damage. She could imagine the youngster taking it hard, even though it hadn't been his fault.

'With the usual proviso that the next few hours are crucial, they're pleased with the way it all went. Everything's looking good, and the chances are that he won't have suffered any permanent damage,' he reassured her, and she breathed a sigh of relief as he added. 'They also sent their compliments for a job well done to whoever patched him up and stabilised him.'

'Well, this is definitely my day for collecting pats on the back,' she joked, touched that the staff at St Piran's would send such a message. All too often in their job, the paramedic's contribution was forgotten almost as soon as the patient was handed over in A and E. It was gratifying that her work had warranted a special mention, especially considering the conditions she'd been working under.

She was also delighted to hear that Tel was expected to make a full recovery. Of course, there was always the usual caveat about the initial hours after surgery, in case there were any unforeseen setbacks, but he was an otherwise fit and healthy boy, which had to augur well for his recuperation.

She'd been lost in her thoughts for a while and only realised that Adam hadn't spoken for some time when she heard the indistinct sounds of a heated discussion going on in the background at his end of the radio. She even thought she heard him shouting at someone, although he'd always been the most easygoing of men, far more likely to walk away from an argument than get into a pointless fight.

'Adam? Are you there?' she called. 'What's going on out there?'

'I'm here, Maggie,' he replied immediately, but sounded slightly distracted, as though a large part of his attention was elsewhere. That impression was confirmed when he added, 'Hang on, *keresik*. I'll get back to you in a minute.' And to her horror he broke the connection between them with an audible click.

The next few minutes seemed to stretch into infinity while she waited for him to come back, and she'd even resorted to watching the illuminated seconds ticking away on her watch to prove to herself that time hadn't stood still.

'Gone midnight,' she whispered to the surrounding rock walls, and tried to imagine just how many millions of midnights had passed since this hillside had been formed. As far as she could remember from her geography lessons, granite was an igneous rock formed in conditions of intense heat during volcanic activity.

She smiled at the thought. Cornwall, land of volcanoes? Not!

Except…now that she thought about it, hadn't someone once told her that St Michael's Mount was an ancient volcanic plug isolated out in Mounts Bay, and what about Launceston Castle? That high motte could easily have the remains of another volcano at its heart. How many more could there be that she'd never really thought about before, and how could she find out about them?

Penhally Library might have the information, just a few doors along from Nick Tremayne's house. Or, failing that, there was always the internet…

Her excitement died a sudden death when she remembered that visiting the library and surfing the net probably weren't on her agenda any more, so she'd probably never know whether there really were any volcanoes in Cornwall.

'No!' A sudden surge of anger seized her. She might

be stuck down here until…for the foreseeable future, but there was no reason why she couldn't ask someone else to find out for her. Even if they didn't have immediate access to a computer, someone among the large rescue squad assembled such a short distance away must know someone who did… Or perhaps Young George knew the answer without having to consult reference books? His schooling might have been short and basic and he'd gone into mining immediately after that, but his knowledge of the industry was encyclopædic, as was his familiarity with Cornwall and all things Cornish.

'So, that's what I'll do,' she said aloud, her new determination filling the little man-made cave around her. 'As soon as Adam comes back to me, I'll ask him to speak to Young George about the volcanoes in Cornwall.'

As if her words had brought it about, there was a sudden click and crackle and her heart leapt with the knowledge that Adam had switched the radio on again.

'Maggie?' His voice sounded husky with weariness and, instead of leaping in with her planned question, she found herself wondering just how many hours he'd been working that day. Had he been on call last night, too, or did the surgery use an out-of-hours service to prevent the GPs burning out?

'*Keresik*, are you there?' he called urgently, and she realised she'd been so wrapped up in her concern for him that she hadn't replied.

'Where else would I be?' she said wryly. 'I tried to do "Beam me up, Scotty," but the Star Trek transporter-thing that came free with my breakfast cereal the other morning doesn't seem to be working.'

His chuckle emerged close to her ear, almost as though they were sharing a pillow, and wrapped itself warmly around her.

'That's one of the things that I loved about you all those years ago,' he said reminiscently. 'It didn't matter what happened, you always managed to bounce back and find a joke to lighten the atmosphere.'

'Well, I'm struggling a bit this time,' she admitted. 'Now, what was all that about a few minutes ago? Tell me you've got some good news.'

'I don't know what sort of news it is,' he confessed, serious again in an instant. 'All sorts of experts have been looking at this old map—by the way, the mine was apparently called Wheal Owl at one time. Unfortunately, there seem to be as many opinions as there are experts.'

'Not unlike a medical conference, then,' she cut in wryly. 'So is there a general consensus?'

'Unfortunately, no,' he admitted. 'Because we don't know exactly where you ended up when you fell, so there are at least two possibilities.'

'And?' she prompted when he paused, knowing there was more to come and dreading the premonition that the bad news was about to get worse.

'And both of them are under a layer of particularly dense granite that would take for ever to break through, and as it's sandwiched between softer strata, there's a danger that—'

'A danger that the softer layer would collapse before you could get me out and I'd have the whole lot land on top of me,' she finished for him, able to visualise that happening all too easily after seeing what had gone on at the mouth of the tunnel.

'*Keresik?*' he said when the silence had begun to feel as if it would stretch for ever. 'Are you still speaking to me?'

'Oh, Adam…' She sighed despondently, suddenly aware just how hopeless this all was. 'Are you all wasting your time out there, trying to find a way to do the impossible? Would it have been better if—?'

'No!' he snapped fiercely, not even giving her a chance to finish the sentence. 'We *are* going to get you out of there. It's taking longer than any of us wants, but we're going to find a way.'

Once again there was an interruption from somebody talking to him, just when she needed his undivided attention to bolster her flagging spirits. Without the torch on she felt, strangely, as if she had her claustrophobia under control—up to a point—but it wouldn't take much for the whole situation to overwhelm her and send her into a full-blown panic attack.

She swallowed down her fear, wondering just how much further she could keep it under control. She was tired and thirsty and it wouldn't be much longer before hunger kicked in with a vengeance, too, and all she had to look forward to was the last remaining unit of saline and one more energy bar. If ever there was a time when she wished she carried some extra weight, this was it—her body could have lived off its own stores for a while.

'So, what are the possibilities?' she forced herself to ask. 'Where do they think I am?'

'Well, it can't be a winze but it could have been an exploratory tunnel…along a rider that didn't go any further.'

'A winze? A rider?' she repeated, not having a clue what he was talking about. Jem would probably have known.

'I'm sorry. I'll say it in English,' he said and began again. 'It can't be a winze—a shaft between levels for ventilation—because the map shows that this mine never went below one level. But it could be a passage that was cut to follow a mineral vein that they thought was a rider—a thin seam of ore lying above a larger seam. You might be in a vertical cut that they were dropping down in the hope that they'd hit a big seam somewhere below.'

'How would they know?' She briefly flicked the torch on, squinting against the sudden brightness as she played it over the closest rock walls. She certainly couldn't see anything that looked like a seam of ore— it was all the same rough blotchy indeterminate grey with rusty-looking streaks where water had constantly seeped through over the years.

She switched the light off again, shutting out the image of the walls surrounding her so closely, preferring to try not to think about them.

'Tin occurs naturally as tin dioxide in rock called cassiterite, and the miners would have recognised the tinstone, as they called it, and brought samples up for assay to determine the percentage yield. That way they would know whether it was economically profitable to extract, and therefore worth following the seam any further.'

It made sense. Unless the whole mine had suddenly ceased operation for some unexplained reason, this could easily be the end of a failed exploration…of a failed mine. It certainly didn't go any further than where she was sitting. 'And the other option?'

'That it could be a sump or sink.'

'And they are?' she prompted when the explanation wasn't immediately forthcoming, wondering at his sudden reticence when he'd been only too keen to explain mining terms a moment ago. His strange reluctance was still clear when he began speaking again.

'Some mines were plagued with underground springs or surface water that would drain down through the workings. So, to make sure that the area where the miners were digging wouldn't flood—which would stop them working a full shift when it rained—there would sometimes be a drainage pit or pool excavated to draw the water away.'

'So I could be sitting in something that was part of the underground drainage system?' It was fascinating, but it would all be so much more interesting if she were watching it on television rather than viewing it in person. It would be nice to have some colourful diagrams to look at, illustrating the terms he'd been telling her.

Either way, she did remember learning that it was an important part of Cornish history that stretched back through the years when Cornwall had produced half of the world's tin plate and boasted the world's largest copper mine, all the way back to Phoenician traders who had come to barter and the prehistoric settlers who had first discovered and extracted the minerals.

'So this hole could actually be full of water sometimes?'

'Exactly,' he said shortly, and the unexpectedly clipped tone sent all the hairs up on the back of her neck.

'Adam, what *aren't* you telling me?' she demanded uneasily.

He was silent for so long that if she couldn't hear the slight crackle on her handset she would have thought he'd cut the connection again.

'Adam, *please*,' she said quietly. 'I need to be able to trust you to tell me the truth...now of all times.'

'I'm sorry, *keresik*, you're right,' he admitted soberly. 'I just didn't want to put any more stress on you.'

'You may as well get it over with,' she said. 'Once I know the worst...'

'Maggie, the weather report is forecasting a band of rain moving across Cornwall later on today. Heavy rain, and it'll probably arrive by midday.'

'Oh...damn!' she choked. 'And I was going to do some washing today.'

'Ah, Maggie, don't...'

'I know. It was a poor excuse for a joke,' she said, but it was better than breaking down while he was listening.

She drew in several deep breaths and blew them out slowly while she fought down panic. She'd thought things were as bad as they could be, living right in the middle of her worst nightmare, but they had just got much worse. Until now she'd had hope to cling to. There had been a chance that one of the mining engineers could come up with some way to get her out of there if she was just able to survive long enough on saline and an energy bar, but if she drowned in the meantime...

'Adam, can we talk about something else? I really don't want to—'

'Anything you like,' he offered quickly, apparently every bit as eager to change the subject as she was. Well, she couldn't blame him. Talking about her imminent death wasn't exactly a cheerful topic of conversation.

'You never told me how you and Caroline met,' she said, and was almost certain that she heard him groan.

She nearly took the question back, wondering if this was the sort of conversation that would be of interest to a woman but would bore a man to tears. Then the stubbornness that had got her through her mother's illness, without once breaking down, kicked in.

Adam had started to make love to her a year ago, before she'd caught sight of the photo taken at his wedding to Caroline and had run barefoot into the street. The least he owed her was a conversation about the woman she'd nearly had a part in dishonouring.

'Was she a doctor, too? Did you meet during your training? Or was she completely unconnected with medicine?' she prompted, then leant back against the dank support of the rough granite and made herself as comfortable as she could, totally prepared to wait him out until he spoke.

Adam stifled a sigh at her determination. Maggie was nothing if not persistent, always had been, but he hadn't been looking forward to this conversation.

If, God forbid, Maggie didn't survive this disaster, nothing would have been gained by raking over that whole miserable episode in his life, but if she came out of it in one piece, his marriage to Caroline was something that she needed to know about if there was any possibility that he and Maggie were to have a life together.

Ha! It had all seemed so easy when he'd been planning it, once he'd got his head around the fact that Maggie had stormed out like that, unwilling to stay long enough to listen to him.

He hadn't been able to leave London straight away but, then, he'd decided it was probably wiser to give her time to cool down. First there had been the situation with Caroline to resolve, and that had taken all his determination and concentration for several months and had left him utterly drained.

Then he'd seen the advertisements for a locum post at Penhally Bay Surgery and everything had suddenly come together in his head. He'd still had his contract to finish in London, but he'd decided that if he applied for a job in Penhally and got it, even though it was only supposed to be temporary...

If everything went wrong, it would only be a matter of weeks before he would be leaving Penhally for good, but hopefully it would give him enough time to mend his fences with the only woman he'd ever loved.

Then what? He'd propose, they'd get married and live happily ever after?

As if anything was ever that easy! Look at where they were now, and he'd only met her again that afternoon.

Well, he'd wanted to tell her about Caroline a year ago, when she'd first seen the photograph, so even though he knew that some parts of the story didn't show him in a very good light, there really wasn't any reason not to tell her now.

'I met Caroline just before I qualified,' he told her. 'She was a trainee midwife in Obs and Gyn when I was doing my rotation there as part of my GP training.'

'And?' she encouraged, and he briefly thought that this felt far worse than when he'd had an impacted wisdom tooth removed.

'And she got pregnant, and we got married,' he added bluntly, not proud of the fact that he'd probably just shocked her, but they were the basic facts.

'But…but you *were* in love with her?'

He could almost hear her pleading with him to agree, but he couldn't lie to Maggie just to keep her belief in happily-ever-after intact. If she wanted him to tell the miserable tale, she was going to get the whole of it, warts and all.

'I was in lust with her, certainly,' he admitted, still shamefaced about his shallowness. 'You saw her in that photo. She was a beautiful woman.'

'Was?'

He stifled a smile as he leant his head against the rough stone wall, his body curved around the radio to give their conversation a semblance of privacy in the noise and chaos surrounding him. Any other woman would have been ranting at him for being so superficial, but not his Maggie. She'd homed in on the one really important word in the whole sentence.

'We weren't really in a relationship at that point. It was just one of those things…a party and too much to drink…' And every day such a deep unrelenting feeling of loneliness, an emptiness inside that had never been filled in spite of the fact that he had been surrounded by people enjoying themselves in one of most sophisticated cities in the world. 'And a few weeks later she was standing there, telling me that she was pregnant.'

For a short while he'd hoped that marriage to Caroline and the fact that they'd had a child on the way would finally banish the loneliness, but before he'd been able to find out…

'We bought the maisonette at auction—a decent-enough sized place for that part of London—but the only reason we were able to afford it was because it was in such a dreadful state. The elderly gentleman hadn't been able to take care of it for years so it needed absolutely everything done to it…ceilings, walls, plumbing, electrics, new bathroom, new kitchen…the lot. And the last thing on the list, after all the really dirty jobs were finished, was to put a new carpet on the stairs.'

He could still picture that frayed old carpet, an indeterminate grey with all the dirt and dust that had been trodden into it during the weeks that the work had been going on, and with ugly threadbare patches at the front edge of every step.

'I was going to take the carpet up that weekend and we were going to have a ceremony to celebrate replacing it with a brand-new one, only somehow she tripped on one of the threadbare patches.' He dragged in a quick half-breath, needing to get to the end of the tale. 'I watched her fall down the stairs and saw her hit her head on the newel post.'

He heard Maggie's gasp of shock. 'Oh, Adam! How badly was she hurt? And the baby?'

'She lost the baby that night.' His tiny daughter had barely been as long as his hand, her lungs far too premature for her to survive. 'Caroline was in a coma. The scan showed a subarachnoid haemorrhage from an aneurysm. They discovered that she'd had an arteriovenous malformation in her brain that had probably been there from birth. Totally asymptomatic, so no one had known it was there. The bleed was large and catastrophic…there was massive irreversible damage to her brain.'

He would for ever blame himself that he hadn't sorted the carpet out sooner, but working on Obs and Gyn in a busy London hospital had meant long days and feeling permanently exhausted.

'If she'd been born with that malformation of the blood vessels in her head, the bleed could have come at any time,' Maggie pointed out, entirely logically. 'It could have been as a result of a car crash—even a relatively minor shunt if it whiplashed her brain inside her skull— or if she'd been mugged, it could have had exactly the same outcome. It could even have happened while she was in labour if her blood pressure had risen. Adam, you can't blame yourself. It was a disaster waiting to happen.'

'I know that in my head,' he agreed. 'My medical knowledge tells me that the chances that she'd survive into old age were extremely slim, given the fragility of those veins and arteries and the stresses that everyday living was putting on them. But that doesn't stop me from feeling guilty, from feeling that if only I'd taken the carpet up just one minute earlier…'

'I know all about those "if only" thoughts, the ones that go round and round inside your head interminably,' she said, and when he heard the sadness in her voice he knew that she was thinking about her mother. 'If only Mum hadn't got cancer,' she continued, and the connection between them felt almost as if he'd read her mind. 'If only she'd gone to the doctor sooner. If only the doctor had seen the second tumour before it had a chance to metastasise, and so on and so on. But if you go down that road…'

'But you can't just forget it, as if it never happened,' he objected.

'No, but you can gradually put it in perspective by remembering all the good things that happened before that.'

'Has it worked for you?' he challenged, marvelling that they'd slipped almost seamlessly into the same sort of relationship that they'd had so many years ago. Once she'd got over her painful shyness around him she'd become the one person in the whole of Penhally with whom he'd felt able to discuss absolutely anything without worrying how she would react.

'For the most part,' she said thoughtfully and, as ever, honestly. 'Some days are worse than others, of course. When something fantastic happens—a good save on a shout, for instance—and she's not there when I arrive home, bursting to tell someone about it.'

Now he felt guiltier still, because he and Caroline hadn't even had *that* sort of relationship, even though they'd been married. They'd been more like two small planets each confined to their own separate orbits.

'So, when we met up last year, when you were substituting for the other lecturer?' Maggie began again, clearly determined to have everything straight in her head.

'Caroline was still on life support then,' he admitted, 'but only because her mother couldn't bear to let her go. The woman I married was dead—she'd probably died within minutes of her head hitting that post—and that was several months before I saw you sitting at the front of that lecture hall.'

He was almost holding his breath as he waited for her verdict but knew better than to try to rush her. Maggie would take her time to assimilate everything he'd told her and then she'd make up her mind whether she was going to forgive him...forgive the two of them. He couldn't bear it if all he was to have of her was the memory of the only time he'd held her in his arms, kissing her without having to hold back, knowing that she'd wanted him as much as he'd always wanted her.

'I was a fool,' she announced flatly, clearly angry with herself, but all he felt like doing was letting out a cheer. 'If I hadn't leapt to conclusions...'

'Maggie, legally I was still married until the machines were switched off and she was pronounced dead,' he pointed out, acting as devil's advocate but needing her to address all the facts, not least the truth that they would, technically, have been committing adultery.

'But you would have told me that if I'd given you a chance, wouldn't you?' she said with a depth of trust in her voice that humbled him. 'If I hadn't leapt out of bed full of self-righteous indignation and raced out of your place like a lunatic, you would have told me all of this then.'

CHAPTER NINE

'MAGGIE?' Adam called, and she was surprised to discover that she'd actually been dozing.

Was she actually becoming accustomed to being in such a claustrophobic place with the rumble of excavation work going on non-stop somewhere not too far away? Or had it been it a combination of the utter darkness surrounding her combined with sheer exhaustion that had allowed her to shut out the world for a little while?

She gave a sharp laugh of disbelief that she could actually have slept away some of the precious time left to her. It was now…gone two o'clock in the morning, she noted from her watch, and the rain was due to arrive before midday. That meant that she had, at most, just—

'Maggie, are you awake?' he called again a little louder, and something in his voice told her that he didn't just want to chat to her to pass the time away.

'I'm awake,' she confirmed as her stomach rumbled loudly, reminding her just how many hours it had been since she'd last eaten. Still, there was one good thing about not having enough to eat or drink…she didn't need to go looking for a bathroom—at least, not just yet.

'What's been going on up there? Have the experts come up with a workable plan between them?'

'No. Not yet,' he admitted. 'But they were hoping you could tell them about the rocks that make up the walls where you are, to see if they can pinpoint it more accurately.'

'OK,' she said dubiously. 'But I don't really know what I'll be looking for. The last time I did any geography was at school, and the amount of geology I remember would fit on a postage stamp. Granite just looks like granite to me, but I'll give it a go.'

It took several minutes before her eyes were accustomed to the light and she had to deliberately switch her mind off to the fact that the walls she was inspecting were within arm's reach in any direction, but she still couldn't see anything remarkable anywhere around her.

'I'm sorry,' she said. 'Some of it's stained brown where the water's been running down it and there are those glittery metallic flecks all through it, but I can't see anything that looks like a band of anything different. In fact, some of the loose rocks on the floor are more interesting—there are some lovely examples of iron pyrites.'

'And you said you didn't know any geology.' He laughed.

'Well, everyone's heard of fool's gold, haven't they?' she said.

She ran her fingers over a particularly pretty chunk while Adam was reporting her lack of success to someone in the background while she mourned the fact that she wouldn't be able to give Jem a piece of it as a souvenir of his heroism.

'Maggie, exactly how much loose rock is there? Enough to pile up and see if you can look back along the tunnel?'

'I can only see the entrance to the tunnel from here because it's up at roof height…above my head. I think you're forgetting that I'm one of the shorter people of the world,' she complained.

She heard him repeat her words and was startled when instead of laughter she heard someone seeming to get very excited at what she'd said. There was another heated discussion going on as she started collecting the larger chunks of rock to pile them directly below the aperture she could see above her head. It was galling to think that Adam would probably be able to reach it without even going up on tiptoe, but if she was going to be able to have a look along it, she was going to have to do some hard work first.

'Maggie?' called Adam.

'Hang on!' she panted. 'I'm still building the Great Wall of China.'

'Well, let me know when you've got it high enough for you to be able to pull yourself up into it. Are there enough rocks for that?'

'There should be…some of them were pretty huge, and damn hard to land on,' she complained. 'It's a good job my head was harder.' She had no idea why everyone was suddenly so keen that she stick her head into this tunnel, but if there was the slightest chance that it would help them to get her out of here, she'd use every little scrap of granite to build as high as they wanted her to.

'OK,' she said, and briefly crossed her fingers that the

whole shaky edifice wasn't going to collapse as soon as she tried to put any weight on it. 'It's time to go mountain climbing.'

'Be careful, *keresik*,' he said softly. 'Don't break anything.'

It wasn't until she was perched precariously on the top of the little cairn she'd constructed that she could see that there were actually two tunnel entrances opening into her little prison. One of them had been completely out of sight behind an overhang.

She climbed down to report her findings and an even more animated discussion erupted at Adam's end.

'Is there any way you can talk to us while you're looking into each of the tunnels, to describe what you're seeing.'

'Yes, if I grow another arm,' she joked, trying to work out the logistics of holding onto a torch, the radio and having a hand free to steady herself against the wall so that she didn't overbalance. 'Hang on a minute. I've got an idea.'

She reached for her pack and found a roll of tape, pulling a length off to strap the torch to one wrist and the radio to the other. Now, if she could only point each in the right direction to be of any use…

'Right, one tunnel is bigger than the other and the floor of it is more gently sloping. I'm almost certain that it's the one that Tel was trapped in because there are an awful lot of loose rocks in it, as though they're the ones that rolled the furthest when the roof came down, and I can hear a lot of intermittent crashing and banging sounds coming from further along it, so that's probably where you lot are.'

It was such a relief to find out that she hadn't really fallen all that far and to know that *that* was the direction her rescuers would be coming from. Whether they would have a chance to move that much rock before the rain came was another matter, so she needed to give them all the information she could to see whether there was a quicker way to get to her.

She turned carefully, holding onto anything she could to steady herself one-handed as she shone the torch into the other aperture…and shuddered at what she saw.

'The other one is much narrower, not much wider than my shoulders, and probably too low to do anything more than crawl. That one slopes up and out of sight. It certainly wasn't the one I came down to get here.' And it definitely wasn't something she was comfortable looking at. She'd thought climbing under the train in the underground had been bad, but that tunnel was a sight to stop the breath in her throat completely…a living nightmare.

'Maggie, you've cracked it!' Adam exulted, exhaustion apparently a thing of the past. 'The boffins were looking at the map while you were describing what you could see, and they've pinpointed exactly where you are!'

'And?' Maggie held her breath, hardly daring to believe that there might be a happy ending to this whole disaster.

'And it looks as if you've just found your own way out,' he said, his words almost falling over each other in his hurry to get them out. 'What you've just described is an upcast…a ventilation shaft that was needed to bring fresh air into the area where the men were working and to dissipate some of the heat, so it led all the way from the mine out to the surface.'

'A ventilation shaft?' She looked from one tunnel entrance to the other. 'They both look a bit big for that.'

'That's because you're accustomed to modern ventilation,' he said with a smile in his voice. 'It's the same with modern mining. They could now drill a narrow shaft and put forced ventilation in, but the fact is, instead of the whole job being done with pick and shovel, much of the work is done by machinery run on compressed air, so that's being pumped underground at high pressure, and helps with regulating the air quality and temperature better.'

'But…' Her eyes widened as she looked back at that narrow shaft with the first awful presentiment of what was coming.

'In a mine as old as this,' he continued eagerly, 'the ventilation shaft would have needed to be bigger and would have been cut by hand by a man with a short-handled pick…or it could even have been a young lad all those years ago. You did say that it was just a bit wider than your own shoulders?'

'Yes, but…' She was having to fight so hard to breathe that she could barely form the words, her eyes mesmerised by the opening that seemed to be shrinking as she looked at it.

'Then *that's* the answer!' he exclaimed, clearly delighted with the solution they'd come up with. *'That's* your way out of the mine.'

Her throat closed up completely, leaving her standing there, shaking her head wildly. She almost fell in her hurry to get as far away from it as possible, but even with her back pressed against the unyielding stone she was too close.

It had been bad enough making herself climb into the adit and knowing that five boys had already made their way through it recently. There had also been the spur to the professional side of her, knowing that at least one of them had been injured, possibly dying.

But this? It was totally impossible! She'd never be able to—

'Maggie?'

His call snapped her out of her blind panic, the tone of his voice telling her that it wasn't the first time he'd said her name.

'I couldn't,' she croaked, not caring that there was a shrill note of terror in her voice. Adam, of all people, knew how much trouble she had with enclosed spaces. He would understand that a tiny space like that would be a challenge too far.

'Maggie…it's the only way,' he said gently, persuasively. 'You're so slight that you'd easily be able to wriggle your way—'

'*No*, Adam, I *can't*!' She dragged in a shuddering breath. 'I'll just have to wait here until the rescue team can excavate the tunnel out again and…and pray that it doesn't rain too hard.'

'That's not an option any more, Maggie.' His voice was deadly serious. 'I couldn't tell you before, but they've failed every time they've tried to shore up the roof of the tunnel. That rock layer is so unstable that they'd be putting their own lives in danger if they were to continue. You can't expect them to do that if there's a viable option. Most of them are married men with families. It wouldn't be fair.'

'But…' Her eyes flew towards the larger tunnel, hidden behind that deceptive overhang, and she was close to tears.

She'd heard the sounds of excavation going on and had been so certain that it was only a matter of time before they broke through the blockage and helped her out. To learn that the tunnel was now permanently blocked was a disaster, especially if her only alternative was to force herself to climb into *that*.

'Maggie, I know I blotted my copybook a year ago, but will you trust me one more time? I promise you, I'll be here for you every inch of the way and I'll be the one waiting at the surface when you come out at the other end.'

The thought of emerging into the freedom of a grassy hillside with nothing but the wide night sky over her head was so seductive, especially with the prospect of Adam waiting for her when she got there, but first she would have to go in there and…

'I can't do it,' she whispered as helpless tears began to stream down her gritty cheeks. 'Oh, Adam, I wish—'

'You *can* do it,' he argued fiercely. 'Trust me, you *can*. You're the strongest, most courageous woman I've ever known, and I love you.'

'You…' That was a completely different feeling of breathlessness. 'You *love* me?'

'Of course I love you,' he confirmed, with the simplicity of complete conviction. 'I've always loved you, right from when you were a shy little fifteen-year-old gazing up at me with those enormous hazel eyes and that incredibly generous heart. I wasn't in the least surprised when you told me you'd given up your chance at medical school to be with your mother, but I need you to do something for me now.'

'Something for you?' She was still reeling from his declaration. All these years she'd never known exactly what he'd felt for her; had believed that the love had all been one-sided.

'Yes, *keresik*.' There was a strange hoarseness to his voice that made her ache inside with the need to comfort him, but he was far too far away. 'I need you to trust me enough to at least give it a try, because I couldn't bear to lose you, not when we're so close to having everything we could ever want.'

'What if it's blocked?' she blurted, putting one of her greatest fears into words. 'What if I were to get part way along it and there was no way out?'

'Then we'd start excavating from the other end until we got to you,' he said with utter sincerity. 'Some of the mining engineers are already on their way up to the surface to get to the other end of the ventilation pipe, to make certain it's not hidden in the middle of a gorse bush.'

This was so hard.

Well, in one way it wasn't hard at all. She desperately wanted to be out of the mine and wrapped in Adam's arms, but... It looked as if the only way she was going to get there was to thread herself into that horribly small ventilation shaft and inch her way up however far it was to the surface, praying all the way that there weren't any obstructions to stop her getting there.

'Can…can I think about it for a minute?' she asked hesitantly, all too aware that there was a large group out there who'd been up all night working to get first the boys and then her out of this old Cornish mine.

Then there was Adam, who'd been there for her right from the moment this whole mess had started.

'Of course you can, *keresik*, but, please, don't take too long,' he warned gently. 'We're all exhausted, you included, and there's that rain band getting closer with every hour.'

She hadn't really needed the reminder. She could hardly forget that she was facing the choice between battling against a phobia that could paralyse rational thought and even compromise sanity, and the alternative of drowning.

Her abject terror was so great that she knew she wasn't going to be able to stop herself sobbing out loud for much longer. There was only one way she could prevent everyone hearing her loss of control, so she deliberately broke the connection that had been her lifeline throughout the night and then switched off the torch.

She wasn't absolutely certain how long she wept, but one thing she did know by the time she'd blown her nose was that it hadn't done anything to help her make her decision.

That was purely down to one question—did she love Adam enough to want to spend the rest of her life with him, enough to trust him to do everything he could to take care of her and keep her safe?

'Of course I do,' she said aloud into the darkness, even as she quailed at the thought of what she still had to do to get to the security of his arms.

But the decision was made, and now she only needed to prepare herself for the task ahead.

Taking her pack with her on her back would be impossible…unless she could use a length of bandage to tether it to her somehow and drag it along the tunnel behind her. She'd already made certain that she wasn't going to lose the torch or the radio by taping them to her but…

'Oh, Adam,' she whispered into what had become a very eerie silence now that all work had stopped on trying to excavate the tunnel mouth. 'I do trust you, but how can anyone know whether this ventilation shaft will be clear all the way up?'

And if she were to get stuck part way? What then?

There would be no point in shuffling her way back down the shaft only to drown, but even though Adam had said that they would dig her out if necessary, the chances of that being successful—that she wouldn't be crushed by a rock-fall in the process—were pretty remote.

She buried her face in her hands, not liking where her thoughts were going but knowing that, if the worst came to the worst, it might be her only option.

She switched the torch back on and reached for the pack, knowing that there weren't any powerful opiates in it that would ease her way into the hereafter, but there was something else that might do the job just as effectively.

'Left side down, head down and legs up,' she murmured, voicing aloud the imperatives for preventing death by air embolism, knowing that positioning a patient's body that way would force the air accidentally introduced into the circulatory system to rise into the right atrium of the heart and stay trapped there, preventing it from entering into the pulmonary arteries.

She'd drummed the facts into herself during her training, knowing that as little as ten millilitres of air could be fatal for a frail patient. So far, she hadn't needed to use the information in practice and it was an awful thought that she was even contemplating reversing it as her fail-safe plan if everything went horribly wrong.

The prospect of lying there, trapped every bit as much as a body buried in a coffin, was too much to think about now, especially when she still had to bring herself to start that journey.

Even so, she grabbed what she would need and slid it into the top pocket of her uniform, knowing that once she was in the shaft it would be too late to second-guess herself.

Then, before she finally switched on the radio again and had the possibility of dozens of people listening in, she shuffled to the far side of her little prison and relieved herself with a wry grin.

'*That's* what I think of mines!' she muttered as she pulled herself together again, disgusted with the state of her once-smart uniform. Then she reached for the radio to let Adam know that she was ready to give it a go.

'Maggie! Dammit!' he exploded, sounding half-demented by the time she spoke to him. 'Don't do that to me again! I've been going mad, not being able to talk to you…hear your voice… Lord! Let's get this over with! I need to hold you and I don't think I'm going to be letting go any time soon.'

'That sounds all right with me,' she said with a smile

as she imagined how good that would feel—to be in Adam's arms, knowing that it was where she belonged. 'I shall hold you to it, but first I've got to pile up a few more rocks. I made the heap tall enough to look into the shaft, but not high enough to climb into it.'

It didn't take long to place a few more rocks on top because there weren't many more that she could manage, not without the crowbar that had triggered this whole situation.

There was another small piece of that same glittery rock she'd found earlier and she tucked it into her pack, actually looking forward to the time when she could give it to Jem as a souvenir.

'OK. I'm as ready as I'm ever going to be,' she announced, but suddenly she was shaking so badly that she couldn't even climb onto her little construction.

'Maggie?' Adam called, sounding far calmer than she ever could. 'Did you know that the children's corner in the surgery has got a book called *The Adventures of Molly the Mole*?'

'A children's book? In the surgery?' she repeated, nonplussed.

'That's right. But I think they're going to have to change the name soon. How do you think *The Adventures of Maggie the Mole* sounds?'

'Awful,' she said, but he'd made her chuckle and released her from the shakes.

This time when she went to climb up, it was as easy as if she were stepping up into the cab of the ambulance, ready to set off to the next casualty, knowing only the bare bones of the situation she was about to face.

Climbing into the shaft was every bit as bad as she'd thought it would be and she had to focus on the basic mechanics of what she was doing rather than where she was doing it.

The second her feet finally left the floor she froze for several long seconds, overwhelmed by what was ahead of her.

Her face was just inches from the rock. In fact, all of her that wasn't directly in contact with the granite was just inches away from it, and that situation wasn't going to change until she finally reached the surface…if she ever reached the surface.

She touched the contents of that top pocket through the fabric, almost as though touching a talisman. She didn't know whether she would be able to bring herself to use it, even if her situation became dire, but there was a grim sort of comfort just in knowing that it was there.

'How's it going, *keresik*?' Adam asked, his voice sounding strangely intimate in the confines of the shaft, reminding her all too clearly of his husky endearments when he'd taken her to his bed a year ago.

'Well, I've started,' she reported, not certain whether she should concentrate on what she was doing or whether allowing her mind to wander would make the time pass more quickly.

'And I'm up here waiting for you,' he said. 'We've found the top of the shaft.'

'And removed the gorse bushes around it?' she said, inching forward and upward, using her elbows, knees and feet to propel herself along, sometimes crawling, at other times forced to drop to her belly and conscious with every tug at her waist that her pack was following along behind her like a reluctant dog.

'No gorse,' he said. 'This time it was brambles with vicious thorns. I think the plant must have been here since the ventilation shaft was excavated because we nearly needed the jaws of life to cut through the stems.'

Maggie knew that he was keeping up the inconsequential chatter to help keep her mind off where she was and what she was doing, but the one thing that was keeping her going was the fact that he was there, waiting for her, and that he'd told her that he loved her.

She refused to contemplate the possibility that he'd only said that to give her the courage to climb this narrow shaft. He'd asked her directly whether she trusted him, and she'd known without a question that she did.

So, if he'd said that he loved her, then he did. The only thing she didn't know was what part he wanted them to play in each other's lives.

It was probably too soon to know. After all, they'd only met up again this afternoon—or rather yesterday afternoon, as it was now somewhere near five o'clock in the morning—for the first time since their event-filled meeting a year ago. Before that, it had been nearly ten years since they'd seen each other.

What if it was nothing more than the adrenaline overload that was making the two of them feel such an emotional connection…each of them apparently equally drawn to the person they'd known at a time when life had seemed so much safer and more settled and so full of endless possibilities?

Her internal debate seemed to have been going on

interminably without any hope of getting any answers. How could she ask Adam what he thought when he was probably surrounded by members of the rescue squad standing by in case they had to start digging her out?

'Hey, Maggie the Mole, how are you doing?' Adam asked, and she couldn't help smiling at his nonsense. If nothing else, she was going to have to hug him just for keeping her spirits up.

'I feel a bit like a hamster or a gerbil, doomed to keep running for ever on a little exercise wheel, only in my case it's a rock-hard slope that's doing dreadful things to the knees and elbows of my uniform and— Ow!' she exclaimed when she didn't watch what she was doing and accidentally hit her head on a protruding knob of granite.

'What's wrong, Maggie? What happened?'

'Just hit my head,' she grumbled as she paused in her seemingly endless trek. 'It wouldn't have been so bad if it hadn't been the same place as it got hit before.'

'On your goose egg?' he asked sympathetically. 'Ouch! I'll have to give it a kiss better when you get here.'

The kiss sounded a wonderful idea but she was beginning to wonder if she'd ever collect it.

'It's probably bigger than a goose egg now,' she told him as she rested her forehead on her hands for a moment, suddenly realising just how exhausted she was. 'You'll be able to see it on all the maps. "Maggie's Tor"—and it'll be twinned with Mount Everest.'

She heard him chuckle and it gave her the impetus to push onward the next few inches and the next until suddenly there was nowhere to go because she was confronted by a pile of rocks.

'Adam…?' she quavered, feeling sick. She'd come so far that she'd begun to believe that he was right, that she would be able to do this and come out safely at the other end. 'It's no good. There's a blockage in the way.'

She was almost certain that she heard him swear at the other end and realised that she must actually have been nearing the end of her journey before she'd come to her enforced halt because radio reception was becoming much clearer.

Was this where it was all going to end? Was she finally going to have to find out whether she had the courage to end things cleanly, or would she chicken out and force Adam to listen to her deteriorate as dehydration took its fatal toll? One thing she knew was that she wouldn't be able to make herself switch the radio off. She would want to be able to hear his voice until the last possible moment. Or would the battery die before then?

'Maggie, how big are the rocks and how many of them are there?' Adam demanded, dragging her out of her spiralling thoughts and sending her off in another direction.

'Does it matter?' she said, unable to care that she sounded utterly defeated. 'I can hardly go around them.'

She'd managed to stay upbeat all the way through her mother's treatment without once cracking, knowing she needed to borrow her strength. Now she just didn't seem to be able to find anything left to dredge up for herself.

'Of course it matters!' he snapped. 'You might not be able to go around them, but they might be able to go around you.'

'What?' Her brain was too tired to work out what he'd just said.

'*Keresik*, listen to me,' he said patiently. 'If the blockage is a small one, with relatively small rocks, you should be able to pass them past your body one by one until your way is clear again. Now, have another look and tell me what you see.'

'Some of them are quite big,' she said when she'd had a closer look. 'But the ones they're holding up look relatively small.'

Even so, the sheer quantity of them was daunting. It would take so long to move them all, one at a time, dragging, rolling, pushing and sliding to pass them through the tiny space between the softness of her body and the immovability of the granite surrounding her.

She hardly dared to allow herself to hope that this wasn't the disaster it had looked at first sight. The prospect nearly had her sobbing with frustration, but the only way she would know if the job was possible was if she did what she'd had to do ever since this whole incident had begun…take everything one step at a time, one rock at a time, until she discovered what she could achieve.

And with Adam waiting for her, bullying her into continuing the fight, even as he encouraged her, how could she *not* give it her best effort?

CHAPTER TEN

'I've done it!' Maggie exulted as she finally pushed the last rock past her hip and forced herself forward, ignoring the fact that she'd just gathered a few new bruises.

'Good girl,' Adam praised softly, but she was beyond telling him off. 'I *knew* you could do it,' he added, and suddenly she was sure he meant it because he'd *always* believed in her, right from when they'd been teenagers.

What she didn't know was why—after all, he'd been nearly three years older when their friendship had first started, and to teenagers that could be a gap as vast as an ocean, especially when the older one was about to leave to begin professional training.

Well, if—*when*—she got out of there, she thought with new determination, she was going to make sure that she asked him exactly what he'd seen in the skinny little girl she'd been, but that sort of conversation was going to have to wait until she'd had about a gallon of water to drink, something hot to eat and the longest, deepest, hottest bath she could find, with about a yard of scented bubbles on the top, because otherwise she was going to be so stiff and sore in the morning and…

As she reached her hand forward again she caught sight of the time and groaned aloud when she realised that it already *was* morning.

In fact, in about half an hour it was going to be sunrise and time she would normally be getting up to get ready to go to work to start her next shift.

'Maggie? *Keresik?*' Adam called, and it took a moment for her to realise why his voice sounded different.

'Adam! I can hear you!' she exclaimed. 'I can hear you without the radio. How far away are you?' Her hands were suddenly shaking so much that it was almost impossible for her to find the switch on the torch to turn it off.

And there it was—not just the vague glimmer of light at the end of the tunnel that there should have been this early in the morning but the biggest, brightest most beautiful glare that she'd ever seen that told her that the generator had been moved and there were people up there, waiting to help her.

That was the moment that told her that the end of her ordeal was in sight, and the sense of relief that hit her was so powerful that for several long moments she was totally unable to move a muscle.

'Come on, Maggie the Mole. Don't be frightened of the lights,' he murmured softly into the radio, rather than calling down to her for everyone to hear, almost as though he was trying to coax a shy animal into the open. 'Come on up so I can collect the hug I've been waiting for all night.'

'You might not want to hug me when you see how dirty I am,' she warned as she started moving again, her arms and legs feeling strangely leaden so that she had to force them into dragging her body over those last few remaining yards.

'I'll take my chances,' he promised with a smile in his voice that she couldn't wait to see in person.

And then, suddenly, she was emerging from the top of the ventilation shaft and there were hands reaching for her from every direction, grabbing her sore elbows and making her squeak with pain until Adam growled at them to let her go. And then he wrapped his arms tightly around her, surrounding her with his own warmth, and was lifting her completely off her feet and whirling her round and round in a kaleidoscope of light and laughter and applause.

She was totally unable to hear a single word he was saying because of the voices around them and she had no idea why the lights seemed to be flashing until Adam finally lowered her to her feet and she realised that there must have been a dozen people pressing towards them with what looked like a forest of cameras and microphones all pointing in her direction.

'Maggie!'

'Miss Pascoe!'

'Over here, Maggie!'

It was a good job that he had his arm wrapped around her shoulders to steady her or she would have fallen over with shock.

'What are all these people doing here?' she asked, then didn't care what his answer was when he smiled at her like that.

'Do you want me to get rid of them?' he asked with a devilish glint in his eye.

'Please!' She glanced down at herself and could have cried when she saw the state of her uniform, the smart green she'd always worn with pride now dusty, stained and torn. 'I look disgusting, and they're all taking photos!' she wailed, burying her face against the shoulder of his borrowed jacket. He laughed aloud before he held up a commanding hand.

As if by magic, the cacophony died away until there was only the steady thrum of the generator powering the lights and a few indignant calls from the birds that had been woken too soon by the artificial dawn.

'As you can all see,' Adam said, his strong voice carrying easily right to the back of the crowd laying siege to them, 'Maggie's out and she's safe and well. We'll be saying a special thank you to all the rescue crew in the Penhally Arms this evening, but for now she just needs a little time to catch her breath.'

He started to turn away, wrapping the blanket he was handed around her shoulders to shelter her from the sharp breeze blowing in from the ocean below, before tucking her against his side with what felt like an extremely possessive arm.

Behind them there was a renewed storm of shouting when the media circus realised that they'd just neatly been balked of an immediate interview with her, but there was an impressive wall of rescue squad personnel wearing high-visibility clothing standing guard, preventing them from getting any closer.

Not that Maggie felt she had anything much to say.

She'd only been doing what a paramedic was trained to do when she'd stabilised Tel and prepared him for transport to St Piran's, and it had just been common sense to escort the other lads out to the surface when she'd had to collect more supplies.

As for her journey up the ventilation shaft…the only remarkable thing about that was the fact that Adam had been able to persuade her to attempt it in the first place.

'Maggie?' The young voice was accompanied by the feeling of someone tugging on her tattered sleeve, and she turned to find Jem Althorp standing there with his mother.

'Jem! And Kate!' she exclaimed in surprise. 'I thought you'd both be back home by now, tucked up in bed.'

'I couldn't go to sleep,' Jem said earnestly. 'Not until I knew they'd got you out of the mine safely.'

'I took him home to feed him and get him clean and warm, but we couldn't stay there, knowing you were still down the mine. We both wanted to be here,' Kate said. 'I *had* to be here to thank you for looking after him for me, and…and to apologise for shouting at you earlier. I—'

'Kate, don't worry about it. Just take him home and put it all behind you,' she advised. 'You've got a remarkably brave boy there, and he deserves a medal for staying down there with Tel.'

All the while they had been talking, Adam had been edging her gently away from the noise and the people until they'd said their goodbyes. Then he quickened his pace, leading her along the grassy slope and through the gate at the far side of the field until the lights and the people were left behind, the intrusive cameras kept firmly at bay by the determined efforts of the rescue squad, who had been there almost from the beginning of her ordeal.

In the shelter of a solid Cornish stone hedge he finally drew her down to sit beside him on the short-cropped grass and a tiny corner of her mind reasoned that there must have been a flock of sheep there until recently. Had they been taken to a field closer to the farmhouse ready for lambing?

'Here,' Adam said. 'You're probably ready for this.' He held out a bottle of water.

'Oh, yes!' she said, suddenly realising just how dry her throat was, and reached for it, only to realise that her battered and bruised fingers were too sore to unscrew the top.

'Ah, *keresik*, let me do that for you,' he offered with a catch in his voice as he took the top off and handed it to her.

'Oh, that tastes so good,' she said when the cool liquid had slid down her throat. 'I don't think I've ever been so thirsty.'

'Is there anything in your pack that I can put on your hands for you?'

'My pack!' She'd completely forgotten that she'd been dragging that up the shaft with her, attached by what was now a very dirty length of bandage.

She suddenly started to laugh as a ridiculous image leapt into her mind.

'What's so funny?' he asked with a frown, clearly wondering if she'd finally cracked under the strain.

'I'd completely forgotten about my pack…that I'd tied it to me… And if you hadn't seen it before you swung me round…' She laughed helplessly.

'We wouldn't have had any difficulty getting rid of

the press because I'd have flattened the lot of them with it.' His deeper laughter joined hers in joyous early-morning harmony as the day brightened steadily around them. 'I couldn't believe how heavy it was. What do you paramedics keep in there? Bricks?'

Suddenly Maggie remembered putting the souvenir pieces of rock in the pack before she'd started that last climb and reached for the appropriate pocket.

Adam had to take over when her fingers were too clumsy to open it but then she burrowed down inside until she felt the rough texture of the two rocks and pulled the bigger one out into the strengthening light.

'Not bricks exactly,' she said. 'But just before I started climbing that awful ventilation shaft I saw this and thought it would be a pretty memento. Do you recognise what it is? Isn't that what they call Fool's gold because so many people mistake it for the real thing?'

Adam examined it, turning the heavily streaked rock over and over in his hands.

'It might be an idea to show it Young George,' he suggested with a strange little smile.

'Well, he does know more than most about the mines around here,' she agreed easily. 'He'll enjoy a chuckle when he realises that the only bit of treasure I salvaged from my time down there was a bit of iron pyrites.'

'It could be.' But he was still smiling mysteriously as he continued. 'Young George and I were talking when you were asleep. He'd had a chance to look at the old map and it reminded him that the mine's original name was Wheal Owr. That was corrupted over the years and ended up being anglicised to Wheal Owl.'

'So, does *owr* mean owl?' She was always interested in anything to do with the history of the region.

'No. Apparently owl is *kowann* in Cornish.'

'So *owr* is…?'

'Gold,' he said with a significant glance at the rock in his hand. 'The mine was originally called Wheal Gold and it looks as if you brought up a piece of the evidence as to why it got its name.'

'You're kidding!' she exclaimed, and traced a bright vein with a tentative fingertip.

'I wonder,' Adam said reflectively as he turned it over in his hand. 'Do you think there would be enough in here for a wedding ring…or two?'

'A wedding ring?' Maggie wasn't sure what she was hearing. It had been a very long night and she could easily be hallucinating or…

'Is it such a hard question, *keresik*?'

She wouldn't have believed that he could sound so uncertain. When he'd been eighteen he had seemed to have all the answers and a year ago…

'While I was…down there…you said Caroline was in a coma. So how long was it before…?'

'She'd already been comatose for months by then, but her mother just couldn't let go, couldn't bear to lose her only daughter when she looked as if there was absolutely nothing wrong with her…as if she'd just wake up at any moment.'

Now she could see that the shadows she'd glimpsed in his eyes were sadness and regret for a wasted life.

'I suppose I felt guilty because I'd never really loved her, so I just let her mother go on hoping but…' He shook his head. 'I couldn't let it go on any longer, not after I'd seen you again and realised just what had been missing in my life all that time.'

He took one of her grubby, scraped hands in his and held it gently against his face, a full day's growth of prickly dark beard making him look like the perfect illustration of a pirate.

'It took me a while to persuade Caroline's mother that it was time to let go, and then there was my contract to work out, but I knew what I wanted—to come back to Penhally and persuade you that you still loved me enough to give me a second chance. What I didn't know was whether you'd allow me to get close enough to explain where everything had gone wrong.'

'And within minutes of setting eyes on you, I'm trapped down a mine and a captive audience,' she said wryly, loving the way his eyes gleamed in the light of the new day. 'Did you really mean it? That you wanted to move back to Penhally? I thought you were only here as a locum?'

'They're desperately short of staff, with two of them disappearing off to Italy last month. I'm here as a short-term locum and there's a retired GP from another practice who's been helping out. So there's a permanent position for me at Penhally Bay Surgery if I want it, but I wasn't going to commit myself to it in case you didn't want to have anything more to do with me. It would have been too painful to see you and not—'

'You mean, you wouldn't have tried to change my mind?' she teased.

'Of course I would,' he said very seriously. 'I meant

what I said when you were down there—that you had to get out of there safely because I need you in my life as much as I need air to breathe. And I would love to settle in Penhally permanently with you…unless you'd rather go somewhere else?'

'It might seem rather unadventurous, but I like living here,' she said, while the realisation was slowly dawning that he might really have meant that comment about the wedding rings to be the forerunner of a proposal. Or had he?

'That's not to say that I wouldn't like to travel abroad at some stage,' she added uncertainly, not really knowing where this conversation was going. Was he just asking if she'd mind if he moved back to Penhally, that it wouldn't matter to her if she saw him around the place on a daily basis? 'Um, the furthest I've been from home was that course in London.'

'In which case, I'll accept the permanent position,' he said with a new sense of purpose in his voice, 'but I'll work to the end of my present contract first—that will take me to the end of March. Then I'll start the new one at the beginning of May. That means I'll be giving the practice nearly a month and a half's notice that I'm going to be away on my honeymoon for the whole of April. Well, at least they'll know that I'm going to be back full time before the summer visitors start flooding into Cornwall and the practice goes manic. But perhaps you'd rather wait?' he added hastily, so he must have seen the frown of puzzlement on her face.

'Wait for what?' she asked. 'I'm sorry, Adam, but my

mind must be fuzzy with lack of sleep. What would I be waiting for?'

'Oh, *keresik*, have I done everything wrong?' he demanded, looking quite stricken. 'Here I am asking whether you'd rather wait a few more months and be a June bride when I haven't even proposed properly.'

'Proposed?' she whispered, wide-eyed as he suddenly shifted to his knees on the grass in front of her.

He was still wearing his ruined trousers and the borrowed jacket from one of the rescue team but he'd never looked more handsome to her.

The pale February sun was just creeping over the field behind her to outline the face of the man she'd loved ever since she'd been fifteen, and the wide expanse of the ocean beyond the safe harbour of Penhally Bay was spread out behind him as he carefully took both her hands in his.

'*Keresik*, I can't remember a time when I didn't love you, and I know I'll love you for the rest of my life, so will you do me the honour of marrying me?'

'Oh, Adam, yes, please. I love you, too,' she whispered, and had to swallow hard to stop the happy tears spoiling the moment. Besides, she had something important to add. 'And I don't want to be a June bride because that's too far away. I've been waiting to marry you since my sixteenth birthday.'

'So let's not wait at all,' he suggested, drawing her up to her knees so that they were facing each other before he said solemnly, 'I, Adam Donnelly, take you, Margaret Pascoe, to be my lawful wedded wife, to have and to hold from this day forward as long as we both shall live.'

Maggie knew that they would have the formal legalisation of their vows in the presence of their friends later, but she also knew that nothing could be more solemn or binding than becoming his bride in the soft grey sunrise of a Cornish February morning.

She smiled into those beautiful dark blue eyes and her heart swelled with happiness as she said, 'I, Margaret Pascoe, take you, Adam Donnelly to be my lawful wedded husband, to have and to hold from this day forward as long as we both shall live.'

'May I kiss my bride?' he asked softly, but before she could answer a sudden gust of wind buffeted them and brought the first sharp needles of rain with them.

'Your bride would love a kiss, but wonders if she could have it somewhere just a little bit warmer,' she said, as the blanket was flipped off her shoulders by the next gust and her teeth started to chatter. 'It seems as if that rain might be arriving a bit sooner than forecast.'

'Going somewhere warmer—and more private— sounds like a wonderful idea, especially for what I've got in mind,' he agreed, as he rescued the blanket and helped her to her feet, then grinned. 'Your place is closer. I hope your shower is big enough for two.' And he swung her up into his arms, travel-stained pack and all.

She squealed in surprise at his unexpected move, then laughed as she flung her arms around those broad shoulders and tucked her head where it had always belonged—beside his.

She'd thought he would stride swiftly back to the field that had been the scene of so much drama during the night, to the car he'd left there when he'd come to help find the boys, but instead he paused to gaze down at her for a long moment.

'Ah, Maggie, *keresik*, I can't tell you how glad I am to have you safely in my arms again,' he said, tightening them around her and pressing his cheek against hers. '*And* how impossible it is to wait before I have at least one kiss,' he growled in her ear, before he pressed hungry lips to hers.

And suddenly it didn't matter that the wind was getting stronger, colder and wetter. All that mattered was that she was in his arms and that this was the start of the rest of their lives…together.

* * * *

The Surgeon's Fatherhood Surprise

JENNIFER TAYLOR

Jennifer Taylor lives in the north-west of England, in a small village surrounded by some really beautiful countryside. She has written for several different Mills & Boon® series in the past, but it wasn't until she read her first Medical Romance™ that she truly found her niche. She was so captivated by these heart-warming stories that she set out to write them herself! When she's not writing or doing research for her latest book, Jennifer's hobbies include reading, gardening. travel and chatting to friends both on- and off-line. She is always delighted to hear from readers, so do visit her website at www.jennifer-taylor.com

CHAPTER ONE

HAD it been a mistake to come back?

Jack Tremayne parked his car and switched off the engine. He sighed as he stared across the bay. The view was all too familiar. He had grown up in the small Cornish town of Penhally Bay and had lived here until he had gone away to med school. He had sworn that he would never return either, yet here he was, about to start a new life right back in the very place he had escaped from.

It had been two years since he had last visited the town and he hadn't missed it one little bit. There had been nothing here for him since his mother had died. His relationship with his father, Nick Tremayne, had always been a stormy one. Nothing Jack had done had ever been good enough for his father.

It had been almost as bad for his twin sister, Lucy, and his brother, Ed: they had never lived up to their father's overly high expectations for them either. However, it had been Jack who had borne the brunt of Nick Tremayne's displeasure, Jack who had rebelled against Nick's suffocating need to control his children's lives.

Leaving Penhally Bay had been the best thing Jack had ever done. Living and working in London had suited him perfectly. He had loved the buzz he'd got from working in the city as well as the opportunities it had afforded him to pursue a hectic social life. He would have happily remained there if life hadn't thrown up an unexpected obstacle.

Jack's gaze moved away from the view and he felt panic well up inside him as he glanced into the rear-view mirror. Little Freddie was fast asleep in his seat so that was a blessing. Jack had been dreading the long drive to Cornwall and it had been every bit as bad as he'd feared. Freddie had cried, non-stop, for hours before he had finally fallen asleep as they had been passing through Exeter.

Jack had felt so helpless as he had listened to him, but there again he'd felt helpless from the moment he had been told about Freddie. Finding out that he was a father had been a big enough shock, but to suddenly discover that he was solely responsible for the child's future had thrown him into a complete spin. How on earth was he going to manage to raise a child on his own?

He took a deep breath and opened the car door before he drowned in his own fear. Hunting the key out of his pocket, he unlocked the cottage door. The first thing on the agenda was to get Freddie inside and make him something to eat. Lucy had promised to stock the fridge, and a quick check of the kitchen showed that his sister had been as good as her word. There was even a casserole all ready and waiting for him to heat up. Brilliant! At least he wouldn't have to test out his decidedly shaky culinary skills.

Jack quickly unloaded the cases out of the boot and stacked them in the hallway. The cottage had been used as a holiday let for the past few years, and the furniture was pretty basic, but it would do for now. Once he got settled then he could think about furnishing the place properly—if he stayed, of course.

He groaned. He had to stop giving himself an escape

clause. The only way he was going to be able to cope with fatherhood was if he had a lot of support, and the best person he could think of to help him was Lucy. Lucy would know what to do when Freddie woke up screaming in the night. She would know how to calm Freddie down when he started rocking backwards and forwards, locked into some terrifying world of his own. The psychiatrist Jack had consulted had explained that it would take time for the little boy to recover from the trauma he had suffered, and that was exactly what Jack intended to give him: time and a lot of love—if Freddie would let him.

His heart ached as he lifted the little boy out of the car and carried him indoors. Maybe he was hoping for too much, but he was desperate to forge some kind of a relationship with his son. At the moment Freddie tolerated him and that was all. If Jack hugged him or kissed him, Freddie didn't respond. He never laughed or smiled, only cried. It was as though the child's emotions had been switched off by the trauma of losing his mother in such terrible circumstances and, quite frankly, Jack had no idea how to switch them back on again.

After lying Freddie on the sitting-room sofa, Jack went into the kitchen and put the casserole in the oven. Lucy had left a note on the worktop to tell him what setting to switch the oven to and he grinned as he followed her instructions. Lucy was certainly under no illusions as to his culinary expertise!

He filled the kettle, then hunted a bag of coffee out of the cupboard and ripped it open, grimacing when a shower of grounds spilled onto the worktop. He was just looking for a cloth to wipe them up when there was a knock on the door and he smiled in delight. Lucy had promised to call round and he couldn't wait to see her and his new little niece.

'Hi! That was good timing,' he began as he opened the front

door. He stopped abruptly when he saw the pretty blonde-haired woman who was standing on the pavement, smiling politely at him. He had no idea who she was but she definitely wasn't his sister.

'Sorry,' he apologised ruefully when he saw her smile waver. 'I thought you were someone else.'

'Lucy asked me to give you this.' She handed him a plastic container of milk. 'She's been held up at the surgery so she said to tell you that she won't be able to call round to see you until this evening.'

'Oh, right. Well, thanks for telling me. And thanks for this, too,' he added, holding up the milk.

'You're welcome,' she replied, and turned to leave.

Jack frowned as he stared after her retreating figure. He wasn't sure if it was something he'd said, but she had seemed in rather a hurry to get away. He'd had the distinct impression, in fact, that she had been eager not to engage him in conversation. How odd.

He was still puzzling it over as he went back inside. Freddie had woken up now so Jack hurried into the kitchen and poured him a beaker of milk. He took it back to the sitting room and crouched down in front of the sofa.

'Hey, tiger, how're you doing? Are you thirsty? Here you go.'

He handed the little boy the beaker, sighing as he saw how Freddie drew back into the corner of the sofa, as far away from him as possible. Still, at least he had stopped crying, and that was a definite improvement.

He went and checked on the casserole, which was hot enough by then to eat. He spooned it onto a couple of plates, found some cutlery and placed everything on the table, then went to fetch Freddie. However, as he helped the little boy onto a chair Jack felt the same sense of helplessness over-

whelm him again. He was afraid that he wasn't equipped to
be a father—afraid of making a mistake, afraid that he would
make his son's life worse instead of better. All he could do
was his best, but he was very aware that it might not be enough
at the end of the day.

Just for a second his thoughts flickered back to the woman
who had brought him the milk and he frowned. Obviously,
she'd been less than impressed by him, too.

Stupid, stupid woman!

Alison Myers could feel her face flaming as she hurried
along the road. She couldn't believe she had reacted that way
when Jack Tremayne had opened the door. She'd had it all
planned out, too—she would introduce herself, hand over the
milk and pass on Lucy's message. Instead of which she'd ended
up behaving like some sort of…of gauche teenager! What on
earth had got into her? Was it the fact that the sight of Jack in
the flesh had left her feeling so tongue-tied that it had been impossible to trot out all the usual pleasantries? Oh, please!

Alison was still berating herself when she let herself into
the tiny cottage where she lived with her three-year-old son,
Sam. It was ten minutes before five and she had a few minutes
to spare before she needed to collect Sam from the child-
minder's house. Hurrying into the kitchen, she switched on
the kettle and dropped a teabag into a mug. A cup of tea
should help to settle her nerves, although it would take more
than a cup of tea to rid of her of this embarrassment. Jack
Tremayne must think she was the rudest person he had ever
met!

Alison's hazel eyes darkened with mortification as she
drank the tea. She knew that she was making far too much of
what had happened but she couldn't help it. Jack Tremayne had
become an almost legendary figure in her life. When she'd

been going through the dark days following her divorce she had read a lot of magazines—the gossipy sort which ran stories about all the celebrities. Immersing herself in the tales of other people's lives had helped to take her mind off what had been happening in hers, and Jack had featured prominently in many of the stories. Pictures of him and his girlfriend, India Whitethorn—heiress to the multi-billion-pound Whitethorn Holidays empire—had been plastered over all the magazines.

Alison wasn't sure what it was about Jack that had appealed to her most—apart from the obvious, of course. Tall, dark, wickedly handsome and incredibly sexy, she couldn't have been the only woman who had made a point of looking out for him. However, it had been more than just his looks that had attracted her. Although he'd always seemed to be smiling in the photographs, there'd been a vulnerability about his expression that had touched a chord. She'd had a feeling that, despite all the glitz and the glamour that had surrounded his life, Jack had been far from happy. To her mind, at least, it had seemed as if there'd been a bond between them.

Alison groaned as she realised how ridiculous that was. She and Jack were poles apart! So maybe he had come back to Penhally Bay, but that had been out of necessity rather than choice, as Lucy had explained. Now that he had a son to care for—a child he had known absolutely nothing about, to boot—he'd decided that he needed his family around him. If it weren't for little Freddie, in fact, Jack would probably never have set foot in Cornwall again.

The thought was unsettling for some reason, but a quick glance at the clock soon drove it from her mind. Draining the last of her tea, Alison headed off to fetch Sam. There was nothing like a lively three-year-old to keep one's thoughts on track.

* * *

Jack had just settled Freddie down for the night when Lucy arrived. She grinned at him as he let her into the cottage.

'I never thought I'd see the day when you swopped the high life for domesticity, Jack,' she teased him, looking pointedly at the small T-shirt that was draped over his shoulder.

'Needs must, kiddo,' he drawled, giving her a bear hug.

Lucy hugged him back, then regarded him sternly. 'You are looking after yourself properly? I know how hard it is to look after a child, and fatherhood has never been exactly top of your agenda, has it? It would be all too easy to forget that you need to take care of yourself as well as Freddie.'

'Nag, nag, nag,' Jack muttered, grinning at her. 'You haven't taken your coat off yet and here you are, giving me a lecture.'

Lucy aimed a playful cuff at his ear. 'Just be thankful that someone cares about you, you ungrateful wretch!'

'I am. Honestly,' Jack said, with more feeling than he realised. He cleared his throat when he saw Lucy look at him. His sister was the only person alive who could get him to open up, but he wasn't sure if it was what he wanted to do. Apart from the fact that Lucy had her own family to think about now, he needed to take charge of his life.

He'd led a charmed existence in London. The parties, the premières, the dinners—as an eligible bachelor Jack had been inundated with invitations to all the top events, but now he had to move on, take responsibility for his son. The one thing he didn't intend to do was have the same kind of distant relationship with Freddie that his own father had with him.

It felt odd to realise how important that was to him. Jack summoned a smile, not wanting to share the thought even with Lucy. 'So how come you're on your own? I was hoping to get a look at my new little niece.'

'That was the plan, but then I ended up going into the

surgery to help out.' Lucy took off her coat and dumped it over the back of the sofa. 'Dad got stuck at a call, and Dragan was called out too, so I offered to take the minor surgery clinic this afternoon.'

'Keeping your hand in?' Jack suggested, holding up the bottle of wine he'd opened. 'Fancy a glass?'

'I'd love one but I don't think Annabel will appreciate it. One of the drawbacks of breastfeeding. She gets to taste everything I do!'

Lucy grinned at him, her face alight with such happiness that Jack couldn't help feeling envious. It was obvious that his sister had taken to her new role as a mother like the proverbial duck to water, and he couldn't help comparing her attitude to India's. From what he had gathered, India had played at being a mother to Freddie as and when it had suited her. She had been more than happy to relinquish her responsibilities when she had grown tired of the role.

He pushed the thought aside because he didn't want to dwell on it. It upset him when he thought about what Freddie had been through, and it was pointless wishing that he had done something to prevent it. He had known nothing about the baby because India hadn't told him. She had simply used him to get pregnant. The only point in her favour was that she had left instructions with her solicitor that he should be told the truth in the event of her death.

A shudder ran through him at the thought that he might never have found out about Freddie if it weren't for that and he took a gulp of his wine. His emotions had been all upside down in the past few months, and it was scary to feel like this when he had always been in control of himself in the past.

'I don't know about keeping my hand in, but I did enjoy this afternoon,' Lucy admitted. 'I know Ben doesn't want me to rush back to work, but it was great to be back in the hustle and bustle for a couple of hours.'

'Maybe you could work part time?' Jack suggested. 'A couple of afternoons a month or something.'

'Hmm, that's what Alison suggested. Oh, she did remember the milk, I hope? I meant to get you some this morning but I forgot about it. Alison said she would drop some in on her way home.'

'Ah, so that's her name, is it? Alison.'

Jack swirled the wine around his glass as he tested out the name of the blonde-haired stranger. It suited her, he decided. She looked exactly how an Alison should look—sweet and feminine—even though she obviously hadn't judged him quite so favourably.

The thought stung a little, although he had no idea why it should have done, and he hurried on. 'I take it that she works at the surgery?'

'Yes. Didn't she say?' Lucy frowned when he shook his head. 'That's strange. Alison is usually very friendly. She's the practice nurse and all the patients adore her.'

'That's good,' Jack observed lightly, wondering what he'd done to get himself into Alison's bad books.

'We're really lucky to have her. She's a single mum—she has a little boy about the same age as your Freddie, in fact—so we try to tailor her hours to fit in with his needs.'

'What's her surname?' Jack asked, although it was a bit like poking at a sore tooth, trying to find out about this paragon who had taken such a dislike to him. He shrugged when Lucy looked at him in surprise. 'I was just wondering if I'd met her before. Is she local?'

'Yes, although she's not from Penhally Bay. Her surname is Myers. Her parents lived in Rock, I believe, although they're both dead now.' She sighed. 'She and her husband divorced not long after Sam was born so she's on her own. I don't envy her. It can't be easy being a single parent.'

'No, it isn't,' Jack agreed flatly.

Lucy grimaced. 'Sorry. I wasn't thinking. Anyway, you and Alison are completely different. After all, you have your family here to help you.'

'I have you,' Jack corrected her. 'I can't see Dad wanting to help out, can you?'

'You could be surprised,' Lucy assured him. 'He just adores Annabel. In fact, he's turning into a real doting grandfather!'

'I'm really glad about that, Lucy. I know that you and Ben had a tough time when you first got together again, so it's great that everything has turned out so well for you.'

'But you don't think Dad will feel the same about Freddie?'

He shrugged. 'I'll just have to wait and see.'

'I suppose so, but it could work out better than you think, Jack, especially now that you've moved back here. When do you start at the hospital?'

'Monday morning, bright and early.'

Jack dredged up a smile. There was no point getting cold feet at this point. He'd considered the drawbacks before he'd moved back to Penhally Bay and had decided they were out-weighed by the pluses. Having Lucy around would help to get him through this really difficult period. And once Freddie had adapted to the changes in his life, then Jack could get himself back on track.

'I'm really looking forward to it, actually. My new boss has an excellent reputation and I'm hoping to learn a lot from her.'

'Great! At least one of us will end up as a top surgeon.' Lucy glanced at her watch and groaned. 'I'll have to go. Annabel will need feeding soon, and as she refuses to take a bottle I will have to be there otherwise Ben will be pulling his hair out.'

'It's been great to see you,' Jack said, helping her on with her coat.

'It has.' She hugged him tight, then grinned at him. 'See you very soon, big brother.'

'Good to hear you acknowledging my status,' Jack teased her. He was the older twin by ten minutes, a fact that he had reminded her about many times when they'd been growing up.

Lucy laughed. 'My big brother, the surgeon. Who could overlook your position in life, Jack?'

'Out before you say something you'll regret,' he retorted, shooing her out of the door.

Lucy paused on the step. 'I'll try to call round on Sunday with Ben and Annabel. In the meantime, if you need anything phone me. You have my number?'

'Yep.'

'And if there's anything really urgent that crops up, Alison lives just round the corner.' She pointed along the road. 'Number 2, Polkerris Road. Just knock on her door and I'm sure she'll do her very best to help you.'

'Fine,' Jack said, thinking that it would need a real, live emergency before he knocked on Alison's door. One rebuff was more than enough for any man if he hoped to salvage a scrap of his ego.

Lucy kissed him again, then ran to her car, waving out of the window as she drove away. Jack stood on the pavement after she'd left, listening to the sound of the waves crashing against the harbour wall. It was the very beginning of March and the air was cold and crisp, laden with salt and the smell of the sea. The scent was as heady as wine and he felt almost drunk on it after a couple of minutes.

He glanced along the road, his gaze lingering on the turning to Polkerris Road. Was Alison standing outside, taking in the view, or was she tucked up by the fire? He wasn't sure why he was interested in what she was doing, yet he was. For some reason he found it comforting to know that she was close by.

CHAPTER TWO

ALISON was on her way to bed when there was a knock on the front door. She hurried to answer it before Sam woke up. One of her neighbours had offered to lend her a DVD, and she assumed it was her, so it was a shock when she found Jack Tremayne standing outside. He was carrying a child all wrapped up in a blanket, and Alison frowned. What on earth was he doing, dragging his son out at this time of the night?

'I'm sorry to bother you, but you don't happen to have any analgesics suitable for a three-year-old, do you? I meant to stock up before I left London, but with one thing and another I completely forgot. The only thing I have to hand is aspirin and they're not at all suitable.'

'They most certainly aren't,' Alison replied. 'It's extremely dangerous to give a young child aspirin.'

'Yes, I know.'

Jack gave her a quick smile to show that he appreciated her advice, but she flushed. He was a doctor, for heaven's sake, and he didn't need her pointing out the dangers of dosing a child with the incorrect drugs. Opening the door wide, she stepped back.

'I've got some stuff which should help. Come in.'

'Oh, I didn't mean to disturb you…'

'You can hardly stand out there if your son is ill,' she said, then immediately wished she hadn't said it in such a bossy tone of voice.

'Thanks.'

Jack's smile faded as he stepped inside the hallway. He paused politely, waiting for her to lead the way. Alison took him straight to the sitting room, because it was either that or the kitchen, and it didn't feel right to entertain Jack Tremayne in her cramped little kitchen.

'Sit down,' she invited, going over to the fireplace and poking at the embers. She added another log from the basket, replaced the guard and went to the door. 'I'll just fetch that bottle for you.'

'Thank you.'

Jack sank onto her sofa with a weary sigh. Alison paused when she realised how exhausted he looked. 'Are you OK?'

'Just about.' He gave her a tight smile as he glanced down at his son. 'I'll feel a lot better once this little chap is all right, though.'

Alison's heart immediately went out to him. She understood only too well how stressful it was when a child was ill. She smiled reassuringly at him. 'I'm sure Freddie will be fine. Let me get that medicine for you, then we can see if we can make him a bit more comfortable.'

Jack just nodded. He seemed too worn out to reply. Alison frowned as she made her way to the kitchen, because his response to Freddie being ill wasn't what she would have expected. The Jack Tremayne who had featured in all those magazine articles would have shrugged off the child's illness as something inconsequential, yet he appeared to be genuinely worried—*overly* worried, in fact.

She found the bottle of liquid analgesic, then took a measuring cup from the drawer and went back to the sitting room.

Freddie was whimpering when she got back and Jack looked more worried than ever. Alison experienced a sudden urge to reassure him.

'Here you are. Shall I pour it while you hold him?' she offered, sitting down beside them.

'If you wouldn't mind.' Jack turned Freddie round so that he was facing her. 'Alison is going to give you some lovely medicine to make you feel better, tiger,' he crooned. 'Can you be a really brave boy and swallow it all down?'

Alison poured the correct dosage into the cup and offered it to the little boy, but he turned his head away. She smiled at him. 'It's really nice, Freddie. It tastes of strawberries—just try a little sip.'

She held the cup to his lips but he immediately flung back his head, catching Jack a glancing blow on the chin.

'Ouch!' Jack waggled his jaw from side to side, then grinned at his son. 'Good shot, tiger. That was nearly a knockout, and in the first round, too!'

Alison stood up, not wanting him to see how surprised she was by his reaction. She would have expected him to be annoyed by what had happened, but there'd been no trace of it in his voice. She hurried to the door, feeling guilty for having misjudged him.

'I'll make him a drink and pop this into it. Sam is never keen on taking medicine either, and I find it's easier to disguise it in some fruit juice.'

'We seem to be putting you to an awful lot of trouble,' Jack said ruefully.

'It's not a problem,' she assured him as she beat a hasty retreat. She went back to the kitchen and took a beaker out of the cupboard, realising that she should have asked if Freddie preferred orange juice or blackcurrant. She really didn't want to go back and ask, so she made up a drink of orange squash and added the medicine to it. She headed to the door, then paused and glanced at the kettle, wondering if she should make some tea while she was at it. It seemed very inhospitable not to offer Jack a drink.

She made a pot of tea and loaded everything onto a tray, then went back to the sitting room. Jack looked round when he heard her footsteps and grinned when he spotted the teapot.

'Don't tell me you're a mind-reader as well. I am absolutely dying for a cuppa.'

'Good.' Alison placed the tray on the coffee-table, then picked up the beaker and handed it to him. 'It's orange juice—I hope that's all right.'

'Fine. It's Freddie's favourite.' Jack handed the little boy the plastic cup, nodding in satisfaction when Freddie immediately began to gulp down the drink. 'Looks as though your plan has worked. I must remember it for future reference.'

'It's a lot easier than everyone getting stressed,' she assured him, kneeling down while she poured the tea.

'So it isn't just me who gets all worked up when his child is sick?'

Alison shook her head. 'No. Every parent is the same. It doesn't matter if you're a doctor or a dustman. You still worry yourself to death.'

'That's good to hear.' Jack reached for the mug and took a long swallow of the tea. 'Ah, that's better.'

Alison smiled as she picked up her own mug and sat down in the armchair. 'The cup that cheers, or so they say.'

'Well, whoever "they" are, they're quite correct. It's definitely cheering me up.' Jack took another drink from the mug, then put it down and laid his hand on Freddie's forehead. 'He seems to be cooling down a bit now, thank heavens.'

'Good. When did it all start?'

'I'm not sure. He was fine when I put him to bed, or as fine as he ever is.' He sighed as he settled the little boy, now sound asleep, more comfortably in his lap. 'He still hasn't adjusted properly. He misses his mother, and everything is so new and strange—even me. Especially me,' he added wistfully.

'Lucy said that you knew nothing about Freddie,' Alison said quietly.

'That's right. I didn't have a clue until India's solicitor phoned and asked me to go and see him.' Jack rested his head against the cushions and there was a look on his face that tugged at her heartstrings. 'I hadn't seen India since we'd split up. Oh, I'd heard on the grapevine that she'd had a baby, but it had never occurred to me the child might be mine.'

'Why do you think she didn't tell you?' Alison asked as she digested that.

'I don't know. I've racked my brain about it ever since I found out about Freddie, but I still don't know for sure why she didn't say anything to me. I can only assume that she wanted a baby but she didn't want all the rest.'

'The rest?'

'Marriage, commitment, the whole happily-ever-after scene.' Jack shrugged. 'A lot of India's friends were having children at the time, and I think she decided that she wanted a baby as well. I just happened to be around and able to fulfil her wish.'

'There must have been more to it than that!' Alison exclaimed.

'I doubt it. What India wanted, India got, and to hell with everyone else.'

Alison shivered when she heard the bitterness in his voice. Was Jack angry because India had taken the decision to have a child without consulting him? Or was he angry because of the position he now found himself in? It must have been a shock for him to have to take responsibility for his son. Looking after a child didn't exactly fit with the kind of hectic lifestyle Jack was used to. She could understand why he might be less than pleased by the change in his circumstances, even though her heart ached at the thought of his son suffering because of it.

'It isn't Freddie's fault,' she said defensively. 'You can't blame him for what his mother did.'

'I don't.' Jack looked at her in surprise. 'Freddie is the innocent victim of all this. When I think about what he must have been through…'

He stopped abruptly, his blue eyes clouding as he gently stroked the sleeping little boy's dark curls, and Alison felt something warm and tender well up inside when she saw the anguish on his face. Maybe it had been a shock for Jack when he had found out that he was a father, but he obviously cared about Freddie and that was something she admired. As she knew from her own experiences, not every man felt the same way.

She hurriedly pushed all thoughts of what had happened between her and Sam's father out of her mind. She had promised herself that she wouldn't allow herself to grow bitter and she intended to stick to that. 'Freddie's been through an awful lot. Losing his mother must have been very traumatic for him.'

'It was.' Jack glanced up and she saw the anger in his eyes. 'I don't know how much Lucy told you about what happened. I mean, it wasn't exactly a secret when all the papers carried the story.'

'Lucy hasn't said very much, but I read the reports. India died from a drug overdose, I believe?'

'That's right. She'd been dabbling in so-called recreational drugs for years. And before you ask, no, I never joined in. I'm not that stupid. She was clean when we were going out together so it was never an issue.'

Alison flushed when she heard the reprimand in his voice. 'I never thought you *had* taken them.'

'Oh, right. Sorry. So many people seem to assume that I was part of that scene as well, and it always gets to me.'

'Well, no one around here thinks that,' Alison assured him.

'Good.' He treated her to a smile, then carried on. 'According to the coroner's report, India suffered a massive heart attack after using cocaine. Maybe something could have been done to save her if there'd been anyone with her, but she was on her own when it happened. She'd given her housekeeper the weekend off so nobody found her until the Monday morning, in fact.'

'Where was Freddie when it happened?'

'In the house with her.' Jack's expression was grim. 'The police think that India died on the Saturday afternoon, so Freddie was there on his own until the housekeeper returned.' His voice caught and she could tell how hard he found it to rein in his emotions. 'When they found India, she was surrounded by bits of biscuit and pieces of fruit. They think that Freddie had been trying to feed her.'

'Oh, how awful!' Alison's eyes filled with tears as she pictured the scene. 'The poor little mite must have been terrified.'

'He still is. He hasn't said a word since it happened. Apparently, he used to chat away before, but he's totally withdrawn into his own little world now.' Jack kissed the top of the child's head. 'I've tried everything I can think of to get through to him but nothing seems to work. It's no wonder when you think what he's been through. His whole world has been torn apart. Despite India's faults, she genuinely loved him, and it's going to be hard to make up for the loss he's suffered.'

'I wish I could think of something to make it easier for you—for you and Freddie, I mean,' she added hurriedly, before he got the wrong idea. It was concern for the child which had moved her most, she told herself firmly. Jack was capable of looking after himself, surely?

The doubt crept in on the coattails of her determination to be sensible and she cleared her throat. 'How is he now? Does he seem any better?'

'A bit. He's definitely not as feverish as he was, but I think I'll get him checked out at the surgery tomorrow just to make sure.'

'Really?' Alison's brows rose. 'You don't trust your own judgement?'

'Nope. Not when it comes to Freddie, anyway.' He smiled at her, a lazily seductive curl of his lips that did horrendous things to her blood pressure. 'I'd prefer him to see someone who knows a bit more about paediatrics. I couldn't find any sign of a rash or anything like that when I examined him, but I'm no expert when it comes to childhood ailments. I would hate to have missed something vital.'

Alison was surprised by his honesty and said so. 'Not many doctors would admit that.'

'No?' He shrugged, his broad shoulders moving lightly under the battered old leather jacket he was wearing. 'I can't see the point of boosting my ego at Freddie's expense. I know my own strengths and my weaknesses. Put me in an operating theatre and I'll give it everything I've got, but I'm nowhere near as confident when it comes to measles and mumps!'

'That's one way of looking at it.' Alison laughed.

Jack laughed as well. 'It's the only way I know,' he agreed, smiling at her.

Alison looked away when she felt her heart flutter. Maybe

Jack did seem to appreciate her help, but it would be foolish to get too carried away by the idea. In the glamorous, high-society world in which he moved, she wouldn't register as the tiniest blip on the social scale.

'I'd better go.' Jack announced. He wrapped Freddie up in the blanket and stood up. 'I've taken up far too much of your time as it is. Thanks for all your help tonight, Alison. I really appreciate it.'

'It was nothing.' Alison followed him to the door. 'I know what it's like when you have sick child to worry about.'

'Lucy mentioned something about you having a little boy?'

'That's right. Sam's three—the same age as Freddie, in fact.'

Jack paused beside the front door. 'How do you manage when you're working? Does your little chap go to a nursery?'

'He goes to nursery every morning, then to a childminder in the afternoon.'

Jack frowned. 'Do you think that's a better system than leaving him in nursery all day?'

'Not really. I can't afford the nursery fees for a full day's care. This way is cheaper.'

'Oh, I see. Right.'

He sounded embarrassed and Alison hurried to reassure him, wondering why it mattered how he felt. It wasn't as though she and Jack were going to become close friends. She didn't move in his circle and he most certainly wouldn't be interested in moving in hers.

The thought was dispiriting and she chased it away. 'I'm happy with the arrangement. Sam loves Carol, the child-minder. She also looks after a couple of the other children from the nursery in the afternoons and he has lots of fun when he's with her.'

'It sounds great. I might consider that kind of arrangement

myself once I get sorted out.' He grimaced. 'I'm afraid I took the easy option and booked Freddie into the nursery full time, although I'm not convinced it's the best thing for him at the moment.'

'You can't look after him and go to work,' she pointed out, and he sighed.

'I suppose so. It's the old rock and hard place scenario, isn't it? I want to be there for him, but I also need to provide for him. Being a parent isn't easy.'

'It isn't, but the rewards are huge,' she assured him.

'I know. Even though Freddie only tolerates me, I can't imagine being without him now.'

He gave her a quick smile, then opened the door. Alison followed him out to the step, shivering as a blast of cold air roared across from the bay. Jack turned to her.

'Thanks again, Alison. You've been great.'

He leant forward and kissed her lightly on her cheek, then strode off down the road. Alison went back inside, her hands shaking as she closed the door. She went back to the sitting room and loaded the cups onto the tray, then carried it into the kitchen, and all the time she was doing so her heart was bouncing up and down like a yo-yo on a string.

Heat flowed through her as she recalled the feel of Jack's lips on her skin. The kiss must have lasted no longer than a second yet she knew it would be imprinted in her memory for an awful lot longer. It wasn't just the fact that it had been a long time since a man had kissed her either—she could have dealt with that. It was the fact that it was Jack who had kissed her, *Jack's* lips which had left this imprint on her cheek.

Lifting her hand to her face, she touched the spot and shuddered. It was going to take a long time before the memory faded.

CHAPTER THREE

SATURDAY dawned bright and clear. When Jack opened the front door, he detected a definite hint of spring in the air. Scooping Freddie into his arms, he carried him to the car and strapped him in. Although the child seemed a lot better that morning, he still intended to have him checked over. As he'd told Alison last night, he wasn't taking any chances with his son's health.

Jack frowned as he slid behind the wheel. It was strange how he had found himself opening up to Alison. Normally, he shied away from discussing his private life with anyone else, yet he'd had no hesitation about telling her all about India and Freddie. Was it the fact that she had the rare ability to combine practicality with sympathy that had made him reveal so much? he wondered as he started the engine. True, there'd been a couple of occasions when he had first arrived at her house when she'd seemed a little prickly, but he had put that down to the fact that she hadn't had time to get to know him then. However, it appeared that his initial assessment, that she had taken a dislike to him, might have been wide of the mark, and he found that an incredibly comforting thought. For some reason he couldn't explain, he wanted Alison on his side.

There was just one other car parked in the surgery's car

park when he arrived. Saturday morning surgery was for urgent cases only and the townsfolk understood that. Although most general practices had cancelled Saturday surgeries, Jack knew that his father had decided against such a step. Nick Tremayne preferred a more traditional approach, so the doctors working at Penhally Bay Surgery did their own night calls as well. While Jack admired his father's dedication, he also resented it. He had never been able to rid himself of the thought that if Nick had been less committed to his job, he might have had more time for his own family.

Jack lifted Freddie out of his seat and carried him inside. Hazel Furse, the surgery's newly appointed practice manager, smiled broadly when he went in.

'Jack! How lovely to see you.'

'Hi, Hazel, how are you doing?' Jack replied, walking over to the desk. 'I believe congratulations are in order following your promotion.'

'Thank you. I was thrilled to be offered the job when Kate left.' Hazel smiled at Freddie. 'Is this your little boy?'

'Yes, this is Freddie. He's been running a bit of a temperature and I wondered if someone would have a look at him for me. Who's on duty this morning?'

'Your father,' Hazel replied cheerfully. Reaching into a drawer, she took out a new patient form, mercifully missing Jack's grimace. He'd been hoping to avoid his father until he was settled in, but obviously it wasn't to be.

'You can drop this in any time you like,' Hazel explained, handing him the form. 'You're in luck because we're really quiet this morning, so you can go straight in. It's such a lovely day that nobody wants to waste it by seeing the doctor.'

'Great. Thanks.'

Jack tried to summon up some enthusiasm as he knocked on the consulting-room door. He went in when Nick bade him enter, forcing himself to smile when his father looked up. 'Morning, Dad. I thought I'd bring Freddie in for a check-up. He was running a temperature last night and although I couldn't find anything obviously wrong with him, I wanted to make sure there was nothing nasty brewing.'

'Bring him over here.'

Nick's expression was difficult to read as he got up and walked around the desk. Jack couldn't tell if his father was pleased to see him or totally indifferent as he made his way to the couch. He placed his son on the bed and stood beside him. 'There's no need to be scared, Freddie,' he said softly, when the little boy began to whimper.

'Hello, Freddie.' Nick bent down and smiled at the child. 'I'm just going to feel your tummy and then listen to your chest. Do you think you can do me a really big favour and hold this for me?'

Nick offered the child his stethoscope, and to Jack's amazement Freddie accepted it. He shook his head as he watched his son clutching it in his chubby little hands.

'He's usually terrified of strangers. I've never known him accept anything before.'

'I'm not exactly a stranger, though, am I?' Nick said flatly, bending over the child.

Jack bit back his sharp retort. This was neither the time nor the place to start one of their infamous arguments. He watched as his father examined Freddie, reluctantly admiring the fact that Nick was able to perform the task without causing the child any distress. He mentally ticked off the procedures as his father performed them: a visual examination of Freddie's ears, eyes, nose and throat; a careful inspection of his skin to check for a rash; palpating his abdomen; and feeling his armpits for any signs of tenderness or swelling.

'Has he had a cold recently?' Nick asked, glancing up.

'No, nothing at all. Physically, he's been quite well.'

Nick's gaze sharpened. 'How is he mentally? Lucy said that he has stopped talking—is that right?'

'Yes. That's why it was so difficult to work out what was wrong with him last night—he wouldn't tell me.' Jack sighed. 'I've tried everything I can think of to encourage him to speak, but he still won't talk to me or anyone else.'

'He needs time to get over the trauma,' Nick said bluntly. 'It's not going to happen overnight and you need to be patient.'

He turned and smiled at the little boy, not giving Jack a chance to explain that he already knew that. 'Can I have that back now, Freddie? Thank you. That's a good boy.'

Jack gritted his teeth while Nick listened to Freddie's chest. He wasn't going to snap back, and certainly wasn't going to appear as though he was on the defensive. 'So what do you think?' he asked mildly after his father had finished.

'I'd say it was his teeth. The second molar on the right of his lower jaw has recently erupted, and I'd lay good money on that being what has been causing the problem. A lot of children feel very out of sorts when they're teething.'

'A new tooth? I never thought of that!' Jack exclaimed, feeling incredibly foolish for having overlooked something so simple.

Nick shrugged. 'It's an easy mistake to make. After all, Freddie is three and you probably assumed he was past the teething stage by now.'

'I did.'

Jack grimaced as he lifted his son down from the couch. Although he was relieved that Freddie wasn't sickening for something serious, it was galling to wonder if his father now believed he was incompetent.

He pushed the thought aside, because he wasn't going down that route again. He had spent far too much of his life trying to gain Nick's approval, and he had made up his mind a long time ago that he wasn't going to carry on beating his head against the proverbial brick wall. Nick could think whatever he liked. *He* knew that he was a damned good surgeon and he didn't need anyone's approbation to prove that to him.

'Well, thanks for that,' Jack said stiffly, taking hold of Freddie's hand.

'It's what I'm here for.' Nick sat down behind his desk. 'Just keep giving him junior paracetamol and it should settle down in a day or so.'

'Right. Thanks. I will.' Jack headed for the door, then paused when his father carried on.

'Have you seen Lucy yet?'

'Yes, she called round late yesterday afternoon after she'd finished here.'

'Good. It will be a big help to you, having Lucy on hand,' Nick said quietly.

Jack felt a shaft of pain run through him. Had that been a subtle hint that Nick himself wasn't going to offer a helping hand if he needed it? His expression hardened as he opened the door. 'It will. At least there's one member of my family who's willing to help out.'

'That wasn't what I meant,' Nick began, but Jack didn't wait to hear what he had to say. He wasn't interested.

He shook his head as he stepped out into the corridor. There was no point wishing that his father gave a damn about him *or* his son. He knew what Nick thought of him because he had made it perfectly clear that he disliked the way Jack had chosen to live his life. OK, so maybe he *had* gone a bit wild a few years ago—he was willing to admit that. He had spent a lot of time on the London party scene, although in his own defence he had never let it interfere with his work. However, in the past couple of years—ever since his mother had died—he had cut out the socialising and concentrated on his career.

He was no longer the playboy Nick imagined him to be, although his father would never accept that. Nick seemed to prefer to think the worst of him, and if that was how he felt then Jack wasn't going to try to change his mind. As for him and Freddie, they would manage perfectly well without Nick's help. He had Lucy to help him if he got really stuck, and if she was busy he would sort things out himself. Just for a moment his mind flashed back to the empathy he'd seen in Alison's eyes the previous night before he blanked out the memory. Alison had enough to contend with without taking on his problems as well.

Nick got up after the door closed and went to the window. He sighed as he watched Jack lift little Freddie into the car. He should have gone after him and made him listen, instead of letting him rush off like that. Now Jack believed that he wasn't interested in his grandson, and that couldn't be further from the truth.

Of course he cared about the little boy, just as he cared about Jack, too. The trouble was that every time he and Jack were together they ended up arguing. Annabel had said it was because he and Jack were so alike—they were both strong-minded and passionate about issues they cared deeply about.

Maybe it was true, but it didn't help to resolve this issue. Jack needed his help more than ever at the moment, and he wanted to be there for him and Freddie. It was how to convince Jack of that fact which was going to be the hardest thing to do.

Alison was on her way back to Penhally Bay when the accident happened. She'd been to the local farmers' market to buy some fresh fruit and veg. Sam had been invited to a birthday party at his childminder's home so she had taken advantage of the fact that she'd had a couple of hours to herself. She was driving back along the narrow winding lanes when a car overtook her, travelling far too fast. It reached the bend and she saw its brake lights flash on as the driver tried to slow down, but it was too late by then. It careered across the road and she gasped in horror when she saw a tractor suddenly appear, travelling in the opposite direction. There was a sickening crunch of metal as the two vehicles collided.

Alison braked to a stop and reached for her mobile phone to call the emergency services. Once she was sure the ambulances were on their way, she jumped out of her car and ran over to the vehicles. The car had rolled over onto its roof; its windows were shattered and most of its bodywork had been stoved in by the force of the impact. The tractor had fared rather better—it was still upright but the driver looked dazed as he staggered down from the cab.

'There was nothing I could do,' he said when Alison hurried over to him. 'I tried to stop but it all happened so fast…'

He swayed and she grabbed hold of his arm and led him to the grass verge. 'Sit down there,' she instructed, crouching in front of him. 'Did you hurt yourself?'

'I think I must have hit my head,' he said vaguely, touching the side of his head.

Alison gently explored the area, sucking in her breath when

she felt a definite depression in the skull above his right ear. 'You've had quite a bump,' she said, trying to hide her alarm. An injury like this could cause untold problems if it wasn't attended to promptly.

'Aye. It feels like it, too,' the man replied gruffly. He suddenly started to shiver, as reaction set in, so she took off her coat and wrapped it around him.

'I'm going to have a look at the people in the car,' she explained. 'Just stay there until I come back.'

He nodded, and she frowned when she realised that he was definitely less responsive than he had been initially. She propped him against the wall, desperately wishing there was something more she could do for him. However, it would need more than first aid to sort out his injuries.

She ran over to the car and knelt down so she could peer through the rear window. The driver was dangling upside down from his seat belt. He was cursing loudly and didn't appear to be badly injured, from what she could see. She left him there and went to check on the passenger, a teenage girl who hadn't fared nearly as well. She obviously hadn't been wearing a seat belt because she had gone straight through the windscreen when the car had overturned. Alison found her lying in the road and could barely conceal her horror when she saw the injuries to the girl's face. She was conscious, though, and responded when Alison asked her name.

'Becca.' She raised a trembling hand to her face but Alison stopped her.

'No, you mustn't touch your face, my love. We need to make sure that it stays as clean as possible.'

'It hurts,' Becca whimpered.

'I know it does, but the ambulance will be here soon and the doctors will sort it all out at the hospital for you,' she explained, mentally crossing her fingers. From what she could see, the damage was so extensive that it would need major surgery to put everything back together, although she had no intention of telling the poor girl that.

She stood up and smiled at her. 'I'm going to fetch some dressings from my car. We need to keep the germs out of those cuts.'

'Are you a doctor?' Becca whispered.

'No, I'm a nurse,' Alison explained. She patted Becca's arm. 'I'll only be a moment—stay there and don't worry.'

She left Becca sitting on the ground and checked on the driver again. He had managed to unfasten his seat belt and had crawled out through the rear window. He was holding his head in his hands when Alison reached him.

'How are you?' she asked, crouching down.

'How do you think?' He rubbed his hands over his face and groaned. 'I'm going to have a king-sized headache in the morning!'

Alison frowned. She couldn't be sure, but she thought she could smell alcohol on his breath. 'Have you been drinking?'

'Why? What's it got to do with you?' he shot back, glaring at her.

She stood up, having neither the time nor the patience to argue with him. 'Not a lot, but I'm sure the police will be interested if you have.'

He swore loudly, but she ignored him as she went to check on the tractor driver again. He was unconscious now, so she placed him in the recovery position, frowning when she heard how noisy his breathing was. His face was very flushed as well, and when she checked his pulse, it was heavy and bounding but extremely slow. He was exhibiting all the signs of compression, in fact, so Alison took out her phone and called Ambulance Control so they could alert the hospital. If blood was collecting inside the man's skull and putting pressure on his brain, it would need to be drained away as soon as possible.

Although she hated leaving him on his own, she had to go back to Becca. She found some lint-free, sterile cloths in her case and took them with her. She snipped holes for the girl's eyes, nose and mouth, then gently covered her face to minimise the risk of infection getting into the tissue, but didn't do anything else in case she caused more damage. Becca was trembling with shock after Alison finished, and she put her arm around her.

'It won't be long now, sweetheart. The ambulance is on its way.'

'Is Toby all right?' Becca whispered through the dressings.

'If Toby is the driver of the car, he's fine.'

Becca hesitated for a moment before the words came rushing out. 'He'd been drinking last night. I had no idea until we set off or I would never have got in the car with him. I was really scared, because he kept weaving in and out of the traffic when we were on the motorway. And when we got into the country he just put his foot down. When we came to a junction, I took off my seat belt and begged him to let me out of the car, but he just laughed and drove even faster.'

Alison sighed. 'He did a very reckless and stupid thing. Alcohol stays in the body for hours, and nobody who's been drinking heavily at night should get in a car and drive the following morning.'

'I know that,' Becca said miserably. 'But Toby never listens to what anyone says.'

'What were you doing here in the first place? You're obviously not local.'

'No, we're from London. We're boarders at the same school.

Toby's parents have a holiday home in Rock and he invited everyone down there tonight for a party. I was going to travel on the coach with some of our friends but Toby said he would give me a lift.' Tears welled to her eyes. 'My mum and dad are away and they have no idea that I got a weekend pass from school. They'll go mad when they find out what's happened!'

'Don't worry about that now,' Alison said softly.

There wasn't time to say anything else because the ambulances arrived just then, quickly followed by the police. Alison handed Becca over to the paramedics and went back to the tractor driver, even though there was very little she could do for him. She gave the paramedics a full report, then the police took a statement from her and she was free to leave. However, she couldn't help thinking about what Becca had told her. She couldn't bear to think of the poor girl being on her own until her parents arrived.

She got back into her car and followed the ambulances to St Piran Hospital. She found a parking space, then hurried through to the A and E department. It was extremely busy, and she had to wait her turn before she could explain to the receptionist why she was there.

By the time she got through to the treatment area Becca had been seen by the duty doctor. He took Alison aside and explained that the girl needed specialist care for her injuries and that they were waiting for one of the surgeons to see her. Alison went into the cubicle and sat with her, doing her best to keep Becca calm while they waited for the surgeon to arrive. It seemed to take for ever before the curtain swished back, and she gasped when Jack appeared.

'What are you doing here?'

'They had a rush on—a major pile-up just outside Boscastle—so I got called in,' he explained, with a smile that immediately set her heart off on its yo-yo tactics again. 'What's your excuse?'

'I happened to be driving along the road when this accident happened,' Alison replied primly, in case he thought she had dreamt up an excuse to see him. 'I stopped and helped.'

'Thank heavens you did. At least you knew what to do and didn't make my job more difficult by trying to patch things up,' he said warmly as he walked over to the bed.

Alison felt a little glow erupt inside her at the praise. She moved aside, not wanting to crowd him while he examined his patient. He smiled at the girl as he sat down on the edge of the bed.

'Hi, it's Rebecca, isn't it?'

'Everyone calls me Becca,' she shyly corrected him.

'Hmm, pretty name. It suits you. I'm Jack Tremayne, one of the surgical staff here. Now, let's take a look and see what's happened to you.'

He pulled on a fresh pair of gloves, then examined the girl's injuries, taking his time as he studied every part of her face. Peeling off the gloves, he rolled them into a ball and tossed them into the bin.

'Right, Becca, I'm not going to lie to you. You have some really nasty cuts there. There's bits of gravel and other muck in them, too, and that will need to be cleaned away before I do anything else, otherwise the dirt will be tattooed into your skin—and we don't want that happening, do we?'

'No.' Tears began to leak from Becca's eyes again. 'Am I going to look like a freak?'

'No way!' Jack grinned as he held out his hands and waggled them under her nose. 'These hands don't know how to do freaky. I give you my word that I'll have you looking almost as good as new, but it will take time. There isn't going to be a quick fix, sweetheart. It's going to take time and patience, but we have loads of both to spare, don't we?'

'I guess so,' Becca agreed, obviously reassured by his upbeat manner.

Alison smiled when she heard how much more positive the girl sounded. Jack had struck exactly the right note—not too formal, not too scary, but truthful, too—and she was impressed. Mind you, she was impressed by a lot of things he did. She hurriedly cleared her mind of such nonsense as he continued.

'The worst injury is to your left cheek. A flap of skin has been pulled away and that will need to be reattached. Hopefully, the blood supply can be restored, but it might need a skin graft as well as some fancy needlework to put it back together.'

'You mean that you will have to take bits of skin from somewhere else?' Becca said, sounding a little unsure about the idea.

'Yes, although it sounds far worse than it is. Basically, what it means is that I will find an area where the skin tone matches the colour of your face—behind the ear is usually the best place. I'll remove just enough skin to cover the injury and transplant it to your cheek. Hey presto—problem solved.' He patted Becca's hand. 'It's not certain that it will have to happen yet, so we'll worry about it if and when, shall we?'

He stood up when Becca nodded. 'Right. I'm going to take you to Theatre and make a start. I believe your parents are away and that your aunt and uncle are trying to contact them?'

'Yes. Mum will go mad when she sees the state of me…'

Jack leant over and squeezed her hand. 'No, she won't. She'll just be so glad that you're all right that she won't think about anything else.'

'Do you honestly think so?' Becca said wistfully. 'Is that what your mum would do?'

An expression of pain crossed Jack's face before he turned away. 'Yep. That's exactly what my mum would do, so trust me, Becca. You have nothing to worry about on that score.'

Alison's heart went out to him. Everyone in Penhally Bay had been shocked and saddened when Jack's mother, Annabel Tremayne, had died, so how much worse must it be for Jack? She followed him out of the cubicle, wanting in some way to make him feel better about the loss he had suffered.

'Are you all right?'

'Yes. It still gets to me at times, though.' He gave her a sad smile. 'Daft, isn't it? It's two years since Mum died and I should have come to terms with it by now.'

'Not at all. It's only natural that you should miss Annabel. She was your mother and you loved her—it's understandable that you should feel sad because she isn't here any longer.'

'I think the hardest thing is knowing that Freddie will never meet her. Mum would have been thrilled about having a grandson as well as a granddaughter.'

'At least Freddie will be able to get to know his granddad,' Alison pointed out.

'Hmm. If his granddad is interested in getting to know *him*.'

Alison looked at him in astonishment. 'But Nick was over the moon when he found out about Freddie. He told everyone about him.'

'Really?'

Jack didn't attempt to hide his scepticism and she laughed. 'Yes, really. I doubt there's anyone left in Penhally Bay who doesn't know about the doctor's little grandson.'

Jack shook his head in amazement. 'I'd never have believed it, to be honest. I thought Dad would have kept it very quiet. I mean, the fact that your son has found out he has a child he knew nothing about isn't really something to brag about.'

'That may be your take on the situation but it's definitely not Nick's,' Alison said firmly. She glanced round when she heard someone coming along the corridor. 'Anyway, I'd better not keep you. Good luck with the op. I hope everything goes smoothly.'

'Thanks.' Jack started to walk away, then suddenly turned back. 'And thanks for what you told me just now about my dad. It meant a lot to me, Alison. Really it did.'

He gave her a quick smile and left, but Alison was in no doubt that he'd meant what he'd said. There was a warm feeling inside her as she went back into the cubicle, a sense of satisfaction that in some small way she had made Jack happy.

She sighed. She could get addicted to the feeling if she weren't careful and, like any addiction, it could prove to be extremely dangerous.

CHAPTER FOUR

'ANGIE, Dave, Mel, Parkash... Oh, and that's Lilian in the corner.'

'Hi, nice to meet you all.'

Jack nodded hello to his new workmates as he approached the table. Becca had been prepped and was fully anaesthetised now. Although Jack could have done some of the work under local anaesthetic—some of the scrubbing and debriding—he'd decided it would be less stressful for the girl if she wasn't aware of what was happening.

'You're quite happy about this, Jack? I know it was an imposition to drag you in here today...'

'But you had no choice.'

Jack smiled at his new boss. Although he had met Alexandra Ross only briefly at his interview, he had taken an immediate liking to her. In her late thirties, Alex had a reputation for being a first-rate surgeon, and Jack felt privileged to be working with her. She had been head of surgery at one of the major London teaching hospitals before she had moved to Cornwall the previous year. Jack wasn't sure why she had made the move but he was glad that she had. It was good to know that he had someone of her calibre to supervise him while he finished his training.

'I was glad to help, Alex, so don't give it another thought. My contract started on Friday anyway, so it's not as though I'm breaking any rules by being here.'

'Definitely not, although I have to admit that breaking rules wasn't my first concern.' Alex returned his smile. 'I hope you managed to sort out some child care without too much hassle?'

'It wasn't a problem,' Jack assured her, trying not to think about how Freddie had cried when he had left him with Lucy. He had to forget about his personal problems and concentrate on the task ahead.

Pulling the mask over his nose and mouth, he bent over the table. As he'd told Becca, his first job was to remove all the muck from the various cuts and then see what he was left with. It wasn't a job he could rush, and he didn't intend to do so either. Becca's future happiness was in his hands, and he was very aware of that fact as he set to work.

Using a tiny metal scrubber, he carefully cleaned away all the grit. He was so absorbed that he merely nodded when Alex told him that she would leave him to get on with it. Although it was a compliment to his skills not to be supervised at every step, he wouldn't have expected anything less. He was good at his job, and the people he worked with soon realised that.

'Can I have some more saline over here?' he asked, glancing at the circulating nurse. He nodded when she washed away the minute particles of grime that he had removed from a cut on Becca's forehead. 'Thanks.'

'You're welcome.'

Jack saw her eyes crinkle above her mask and smiled back. He believed in fostering a good working relationship with the other members of the team and was pleased that they seemed so willing to accept him. 'I hope you still feel like that in a couple of hours' time,' he joked, and everyone laughed.

'Don't worry, Mel will soon let you know if you're in her bad books,' the anaesthetist, Parkash Patel, informed him. 'Take it from me, Mel has her own highly effective way of making her displeasure felt!'

'That sounds ominous. I must try really hard not upset her.' Jack chuckled when Mel grunted loudly to indicate her displeasure at being so unjustly criticised. 'Whoops! Looks like I've just earned my first black mark.'

He bent over the table again, feeling himself relax as he carried on. Surgery was the only thing he had ever wanted to do. However, when he had discovered the difference he could make to people's lives through plastic surgery, he'd known he had found his true calling.

Plastic surgery improved both the function and the appearance of a patient's body. Although some surgeons were sniffy about the value of cosmetic plastic surgery, Jack believed in that too, especially when it was used to rectify the devastating effects caused by an illness or an accident. His long-term goal was to have his own clinic, where he could help people regain their lives by restoring their looks as well as the functionality of their bodies. It was very much in the future at the moment, but it was what he was aiming for.

Fired up by his belief in what he was doing, Jack lost himself in his work. Once he was sure all the dirt had been removed he began the delicate task of stitching the cuts. Lilian, the SHO, watched entranced as he used the tiniest stitches to bring the skin together.

'I don't know how you know where it all fits!' she exclaimed. 'It looks such a mess that I wouldn't know the best place to start.'

'It's really quite simple,' Jack said, easing a tiny flap of torn skin back into its rightful place. 'You find the places where the skin seems to fit the most easily and join them together first. After that, the rest should fall into place. The one thing you must be careful about, though, is that you don't cut away too much tissue when you are debriding an area or you'll never be able to match things up.'

'Why are you using interrupted sutures? Continuous ones would be a lot quicker.'

'Yes, but they don't give as good a result. It's not speed but the quality of your work that will determine the outcome for this patient for the rest of her life. Cut conservatively, match with care and use the smallest stitches, and there's a very good chance she will thank you for it in later life and not blame you.'

'I don't think my suturing will ever be that neat,' Lilian said wistfully, and Jack laughed.

'Then practise! It's like everything else—you need to do as much as you can before you get the hang of it.'

It took another two hours before he was satisfied that he had done all he could for now. The large tear on Becca's left cheek was the thing that worried him most. There'd been too much tissue damage to match the edges successfully. It would need a skin graft, and that was something he'd have to do at a later date. He sighed as he straightened up.

'That's about all we can do for now. Thanks for all your help. It's been really great working with you.' He moved away from the table, then stopped when he heard everyone applauding. Glancing back, he shook his head. 'What's that for?'

'Well, we definitely don't want you getting too big for your boots,' Mel informed him tartly, 'but I think we all agree that was an excellent performance, don't we, folks?'

Jack chuckled when everyone chorused their agreement. 'I don't know what to say, guys.'

'How about "the drinks are on me"?' Dave, the theatre orderly, chirped up.

Jack grimaced. 'Nothing would give me greater pleasure, but I'll have to take a rain-check for now. I've left my sister baby-sitting my little boy and I need to get back before chaos breaks out. Can we make it next week? I promise I'll get myself organised by then,' he said, crossing his fingers behind his back.

He left Theatre and headed to the changing room, wondering if he would be able to keep his promise. He was loath to leave Freddie, apart from when he had to go to work, and he wasn't sure if it would be right to take an hour or so off to get to know his new colleagues better.

He sighed as he stepped into the shower. Adapting to life as a single father took some getting used to, but he would manage. He had to. He definitely wasn't going to let Freddie down, no matter what sacrifices he had to make. If he had no social life, so what? He'd done more than his share of partying and he was happy to leave all that behind him now. Basically, there was nothing he needed apart from Freddie and his work.

Scooping a handful of soap out of the dispenser, Jack lathered his chest, then paused. There was one issue he hadn't considered—mainly because it had never been an issue before. He had never had a serious relationship with a woman. Even his relationship with India had been a casual affair. But what if he met someone and fell in love with her—how would he juggle that with being a dad? If it was hard to get away for a quick drink with his colleagues, how would he find the time to spend with her? And, on the flip side, how would *she* feel about the fact that he had a ready-made family?

Jack frowned as he rinsed off the lather. He couldn't answer any of those questions. It was a case of having to wait and see what happened. He wasn't even sure what had put the idea into his head in the first place. After all, it wasn't as though he had spent much time thinking about the woman he would eventually marry. He'd been far too busy working and enjoying himself. But now he found himself giving it serious thought.

What would she be like, this woman who pressed all the right buttons? He had always fancied sultry, elegant brunettes in the past, but for some reason he found it difficult to summon up a picture of his ideal woman. Perhaps he should start with her character rather than her looks, he decided. He wanted someone who was intelligent and kind, someone who would share his interests but have interests of her own as well. He definitely didn't want a woman who hung onto his every word—that would be too boring!

He grabbed a towel off the rack, wrapped it around his waist and stepped out of the cubicle. So he wanted a woman with a mind of her own, who was independent enough to have her own opinions and yet not be at odds with him over really important issues. She would have to be understanding, too, because his job was so demanding that it took up a lot of his time and he would hate it if it caused friction between them. She would also have to like children, and he would need to be sure that she would accept Freddie as her own.

That just about summed up her personality so maybe he would have better luck with the matter of her appearance?

Jack tossed the wet towel into the hamper and started to get dressed. Underwear, jeans, T-shirt… He paused. A picture was forming in his mind's eye and he frowned as he tried to bring it into focus—soft fair hair, hazel eyes, a curvy figure… He gasped when he realised it was Alison Myers he was picturing. Why on earth had he conjured *her* up as his ideal woman? Because she was pretty and kind, and ticked all the other boxes on his list?

He dragged a T-shirt over his head and grabbed his jacket.

He must be in a worse state than he'd realised if he was dredging up such rubbish. There was no chance of him and Alison becoming an item. No chance at all.

Monday morning rolled around and Alison found herself rushing to get ready. Mornings were always hectic, what with Sam needing to be taken to nursery and her having to get to work on time. As soon as Sam had finished his breakfast, she popped on his coat and walked him to the nursery. There were a lot of parents there, most of them in cars, too, and she kept tight hold of Sam's hand as they crossed the road. She had just reached the pavement when a car pulled up beside her and Jack got out.

'Hi. It's chaos, isn't it? Is it always like this?' he asked, opening the rear door.

'Mornings are usually very busy,' Alison agreed as she paused. She cleared her throat when she heard how husky her voice sounded, but the sight of Jack bundled up in a navy ski jacket with his dark hair all mussed seemed to have stolen her breath. 'What time did you get back from the hospital on Saturday?' she said, striving for normality.

'Just after seven.' He lifted Freddie out of the car and smiled at her. 'How about you?'

'Oh, I was back home by four.' She started walking towards the nursery gates, unsure whether she should wait for Jack, but he solved the problem by catching up with her.

'At least it wasn't too late.' He glanced at the other parents and grimaced. 'What's the routine? Do you take the kids straight into their classrooms?'

'Yes. They have to be signed in first, though, so that the staff know they're here.' Alison led the way through the main door then glanced back. 'Has Freddie been to nursery before?'

'Yes. He was enrolled at a nursery school in London, so

I'm hoping that will help him settle down here. If he gets back into some sort of familiar routine, it might make him feel more secure.'

'Don't be surprised if he's upset when it's time for you to leave him,' Alison warned him. 'Sam used to be really clingy—although he soon got over it,' she added when she saw the worry on Jack's face.

'Freddie isn't so much clingy as terrified.' Jack sighed as he ran his hand over his son's dark curls. 'I don't think he cares one way or the other if I'm around, to be honest, but he's scared of being left in strange places.'

'Have you spoken to the staff about his problems?' Alison asked quietly so none of the other parents could overhear.

'Yes. I've had several long conversations with Mrs Galloway, who owns the nursery. She promised to alert the staff to the problem and I'm hoping she's done so.'

'Christine won't have forgotten,' Alison assured him. 'She's completely devoted to the children. That's why this school has such a wonderful reputation—and why there's a waiting list for places, too.'

'Really?' Jack frowned. 'I hadn't realised that. I mean, I had no problems about getting Freddie a place here.'

'I think your father had a word with Christine,' Alison explained, then wondered if she should have mentioned it when Jack frowned.

There was no time to say anything else. They had reached the head of the queue and she busied herself signing Sam in. She took him to the cloakroom and helped him hang his coat on his hook—the one with the bright green frog on it—then took him into the playroom.

'I'll see you at lunchtime, sweetheart,' she said, giving him a hug.

'Bye, Mummy,' he replied dutifully, before he raced away to join his friends. Alison smiled as she headed to the door. There was no sign of clinginess now, thank heavens!

Jack was talking to Trish Atkins, who was in charge of the three-year-olds, and Alison didn't interrupt them. She simply waved as she passed and hurried out of the door. Glancing at her watch, she realised that she would have to get a move on if she wasn't going to be late for her first appointment.

She made it to the surgery with five minutes to spare. Sue was on duty at the reception desk that morning, and she grinned when Alison rushed in.

'You look as though you've run the three-minute mile.'

'It feels like it, too,' Alison gasped. She glanced around the waiting room and discovered that her first patient had beaten her to it. 'Just give me a minute to take off my coat, then you can send Mrs Baxter up. Oh, and tell her to use the lift, would you? I don't want her climbing the stairs.'

Alison hurried up the stairs, turning right when she reached the top. The nurse's room was at the end of the corridor, next to the lift, and she left the door open so she could hear her patient arrive. She hung her coat on a peg, then booted up her computer and brought up Audrey Baxter's notes.

Mrs Baxter had been diagnosed recently with angina, a condition whereby insufficient oxygen was carried via the blood to the heart. Although there were a number of causes for the condition, the most usual one was atherosclerosis—a build-up of fatty deposits within the arteries which caused them to narrow. Dr Donnelly had requested a cholesterol test, which was why Audrey had an appointment with her that morning.

Alison got up and popped her head round the door when she heard the lift arrive. 'This way, Mrs Baxter. Come straight through.'

'Right you are, my lovely,' Audrey Baxter replied cheerfully. In her early sixties, Audrey had worked at the post office until she had retired the previous year. She now helped out at the church, and was always cheerful and always abreast of all the local gossip. She smiled as she plonked herself down onto a chair.

'I was glad to take the lift, I can tell you. I've been feeling a bit breathless this morning.'

'Are you having pains in your chest?' Alison asked in concern.

'Not really pains, as such. It just feels a bit tight, as though something's pressing on it.'

'I'll give Dr Donnelly a call and ask him to take a look at you,' Alison said immediately. She dialled Adam's extension but there was no reply, so she phoned the reception desk. 'Has Adam arrived yet?'

'No. He just phoned to say that he'll be late because he had an early callout,' Sue explained. 'Nick's here, if you need him.'

'Thanks, Sue. I'll give him a call.'

Alison phoned Nick's extension and explained that she would like him to see a patient. He arrived a few minutes later and she quickly explained the situation before he examined Audrey.

'Have you been taking the low-dose aspirin that Dr Donnelly prescribed for you?' Nick asked after he'd finished listening to Audrey's heart.

'Well, no, not really.' Audrey looked sheepish. 'It seemed a bit daft to take tablets when I was feeling fine, so I've only been taking them whenever I have a pain in my chest.'

'I see. How about the glycerol trinitrate spray? I assume that Dr Donnelly advised you to use it if you had any pains or constriction in your chest?'

'Um…well, yes, he did,' Audrey admitted.

Nick shook his head. 'You need to follow Dr Donnelly's

advice. If you don't, the situation will only deteriorate. Aspirin thins the blood and helps avoid the danger of clots forming, but it won't work if the tablets are left in the packet. And you must carry your spray with you wherever you go, in case you need it.'

'I shall, Dr Tremayne,' Audrey promised, looking suitably repentant.

'Make sure you do,' Nick said firmly. 'You're not helping yourself by not taking the medication. You could, in fact, be putting yourself at greater risk of having a heart attack.' He waited to see if that had sunk in then nodded to Alison. 'I'll leave you to get on with the blood test. Call me if you need me again.'

'Thank you.'

Alison picked up the dish containing the syringe and plastic vials and took it over to her desk. She smiled at Audrey. 'I hope you've taken heed of all that.'

'Oh, I have.' Audrey raised an eyebrow. 'He can be a bit stern, can Dr Tremayne, when he chooses, can't he?'

'Only because he has your best interests at heart,' she assured her. She took the samples and sealed them into a plastic envelope bearing both the patient's and the surgery's details. 'We should have the results back by the end of the week, so make an appointment to see Dr Donnelly on your way out.'

Alison cleared everything away, then buzzed for her next patient. However, as she waited for him to arrive she found herself comparing Nick's approach to that of his son. Jack had exhibited none of the brusqueness that Nick occasionally showed towards a patient. In fact, he'd gone out of his way to put Becca at her ease on Saturday. It had been a surprise at the time, and Alison had found herself thinking about it more than once over the weekend. After reading all those articles in the magazines, she'd expected Jack to be full of his own importance, but he wasn't like that at all.

It was exactly the same when it came to his son, too. It was obvious how much he cared about little Freddie, and that wasn't what she had expected either. So which was the real Jack Tremayne? The handsome playboy surgeon who devoted his free time to partying, or the dedicated doctor and father?

She wished she knew, because it might help her decide how she felt about him. If she could slip Jack into one category or the other, it would make her life so much simpler.

Nick decided to walk down to the harbour after he finished surgery. It had been a busy morning and they'd been hard pushed to keep on top of all the work. It was a good job that Adam Donnelly had decided to take a permanent position with the practice, he thought, otherwise they would never have coped now that Marco had left. Although he was glad that Lucy didn't intend to rush back to full-time work, they definitely missed her.

He walked along Harbour Road until he came to the lifeboat station and stopped. It was a cold, crisp day, the sun sparkling off the water. Shading his eyes, he peered out to sea, feeling the ache of loneliness nagging at him harder than ever that day. He missed Annabel, and still felt guilty about the way she had died. He should have paid more attention to what had been happening at home, instead of focusing all his energy on his job. If he'd done that then maybe his children would want to spend more time with him now, too, and he wouldn't feel so alone.

He was glad that he had made his peace with Lucy, but the situation between him and Jack was no better. He needed to find a way to get through to him, but after what had happened on Saturday he was even more wary of putting his foot in it. Maybe he and Jack were destined to remain at loggerheads. The thought was dispiriting.

'Penny for them?'

Nick swung round when he heard a familiar voice, summoning a smile when he saw Kate Althorp. He had missed Kate since she'd left the practice, missed their chats and missed seeing her around the place. However, he knew in his heart that it was better that she'd left. There was no chance of them ever being more than friends, and he didn't like to think that he was holding her back. He wanted Kate to be happy because she certainly deserved to be.

'Hello, Kate. How are you?'

'Fine, thanks. How about you?' She gave him a gentle smile. 'You looked deep in thought when I spotted you just now.'

'I was.' Nick sighed. 'I was thinking about Jack.'

Kate's pretty face clouded. 'Don't tell me that you two still haven't sorted out your differences.'

'I'm afraid not.'

'You need to make your peace with him, Nick. I know that you two have had problems in the past, but surely it's time you put all that behind you. Jack needs your help now more than ever.'

'He brought Freddie into the surgery on Saturday,' Nick said wistfully.

'To see you?' Kate said hopefully.

'No. The poor little mite had been running a temperature and was feeling very out of sorts. Jack brought him in to be checked over. He had no idea I'd be there. In fact, I got the distinct impression that he wished one of the others had been on duty.'

'But at least he asked you to see Freddie,' Kate pointed out. 'That has to be a step in the right direction.'

'Maybe.'

Kate laid her hand on his arm. 'I hate to see you tearing yourself apart like this, Nick. It isn't right.'

'It isn't what I want, believe me.' He put his hand over Kate's. 'I want to be friends with my children, not feel that I'm their worst enemy.'

'Then do something about it!' Kate removed her hand and stepped back. 'All right, so it won't be easy, and it won't happen overnight either, but if it's what you really want then you will find a way, Nick. Right, that's the end of my pep-talk. I'd better get on and do my shopping.'

She gave him a quick smile, then headed along the road. Nick watched until she disappeared from view, then turned and stared out to sea. Could he and Jack resolve their differences? He wanted to believe they could, but he couldn't do it on his own—Jack would have to meet him halfway. And he wasn't sure if his son was willing to make the effort.

CHAPTER FIVE

'RIGHT, Becca, I want to check how those cuts I stitched on Saturday are doing. If you can swing your feet over the side of the bed so that you're facing me…that's great.'

Jack smiled at the teenager as he pulled up a chair. It was Monday afternoon and he had just finished a ward round. Alex had been called away to see a patient and Jack had been left in charge of the team. He had deliberately omitted Becca from the round because he understood how traumatic she would find it to have so many people gathered around her. Now he grinned conspiratorially at her.

'The rest of the guys wanted to meet you, but I decided to keep you to myself for a while longer. Is that OK?'

'Yes.' The girl gave him a wobbly smile. 'I was dreading having everyone staring at me.'

'No way is that going to happen, sweetheart,' Jack said firmly.

He leant forward and carefully examined her face, using a magnifying lens so that he could see the more severely injured areas better. The cut on her forehead was healing well, although it might not appear so to the untutored eye. However, Jack had spent the last five years of his life—two as a senior house officer, doing his basic surgical training, followed by three of the allotted six years needed to gain his certificate of completion of training—looking at injuries such as this, and it didn't faze him. The skin wasn't inflamed, there was no puckering, and no sign of necrosis in the surrounding tissue either. He was confident that it would leave only the smallest of scars in time, and told Becca that.

'Are you sure? You're not just saying that because it's what you think I want to hear?'

'It doesn't work like that, Becca. I shall always tell you the truth, so if I say there won't be much scarring, it's because I know that for a fact.'

'Oh. I see.' Becca gulped. 'What about the rest of the cuts? Will they leave a lot of scars?'

'They're healing well. This one here on the edge of your jaw might leave a bit more of a scar, but even that shouldn't be too bad.' Jack smiled at her. 'It takes time for the scar tissue to settle down and fade, but I'm confident that your face will look fine eventually. And any areas you aren't happy with can be covered up with make-up—you'll be shown how to do that after your treatment has finished.'

'What about the big cut on my left cheek? Is it going to need a skin graft?'

'Yes, it is.' Jack sat back in the chair, knowing that he needed to explain exactly what would happen without frightening her. 'Do you know what happens when skin is grafted?'

'Not really.' Becca pulled a face. 'I've never thought about it.'

'Of course you haven't. Nobody does until they need to have one done,' Jack assured her. 'Basically, there are two types of graft—split thickness and full thickness. I will need to use a full-thickness graft on your cheek because the match will be better, and that's very important.'

'You said you would take the skin from behind my ear,' Becca reminded him, and he laughed.

'Go to the top of the class for remembering that! Most people don't remember a word they're told after an accident, and no wonder either.'

He carried on when Becca laughed, pleased to see that she was looking a little more relaxed. It would be an ordeal for anyone to have to face this type of surgery and it must be doubly difficult for a teenage girl.

'I shall remove a small section of skin from behind your ear, slightly larger than the area it needs to cover to allow for shrinkage. I'll have to put a couple of stitches into the site from where I take the graft, but it will heal pretty quickly and shouldn't cause any problems. Once I have the graft, I will fit it precisely over the area on your cheek and make sure it's securely attached. You'll need to wear a pressure bandage on it for a while afterwards to keep it flat, but that's basically it.'

'And will everyone be able to tell that it's a graft? I mean, will it look different to the rest of my face?'

'There's bound to be some scarring,' Jack explained gently. 'But the results are usually excellent. In a year or so, you will hardly notice it at all.'

'A year!' Becca sounded stricken. 'It will take that long to heal?'

'It could do.' Jack leant forward and looked her straight in the eyes. 'I know it's going to be hard, sweetheart, but I promise you that you will hardly notice any difference in time.'

'But I'll still look like a freak when I start university this October,' she wailed.

Jack tried to console her, but nothing he said calmed her down. In the end, he wrote her up for a mild sedative and went to have a word with her parents who had arrived back from holiday that morning. They too were distraught when he explained the situation to them, and that made him feel worse. He wished with all his heart that there was something more he could do, but he couldn't perform miracles. All he had was his skill as a surgeon, and in some cases it simply wasn't enough.

A cloud of gloom seemed to hang over him for the rest of the day. He checked on Becca before he left, but she was very subdued and barely responded when he spoke to her. He drove back to Penhally Bay and collected Freddie from the nursery, and it seemed fitting that his son was in an equally downbeat mood.

He took Freddie home and made his tea, then phoned Lucy for a chat, but he could tell that he'd caught her at a bad moment so he didn't stay on the phone very long. Freddie was playing with some of his toys, but he turned away when Jack knelt down beside him. He sighed. It seemed that he was persona non grata wherever he went today.

He was heading to the kitchen to make himself a cup of coffee in the hope it would chase away the blues when the doorbell rang, so he veered off to answer it and was surprised when he found Alison standing outside. She had Sam with her and she looked unusually serious.

'I'm sorry to disturb you but I've just discovered that Sam has nits.'

'Nits?' Jack repeated blankly.

'Yes. One of the other mums told me that she'd found some in her little girl's hair when I collected Sam from the nursery at lunchtime, so I made a point of checking.' She grimaced. 'Apparently, he and Freddie were playing together this morning so I thought I'd better warn you. Once one child gets them, they spread like wildfire.'

'Oh, I see. Well, thanks for telling me.'

'That's all right.' She turned to leave, but all of a sudden Jack knew that he couldn't bear to spend the evening with only his thoughts for company.

'What do you recommend to get rid of them?' he said hurriedly. He shrugged when she glanced back. 'I'm not very clued up on head lice, so is it best to buy something from the chemist? Malathion is used in most of the patented lotions, I believe'

'It is, although I'm not too keen on using such strong chemicals. Whenever I've come across a case at work, I've always recommended conditioner.'

'Hair conditioner, you mean?' Jack's brows drew together. 'Does that really work?'

'Oh, yes. If you apply a thick layer of conditioner to Freddie's hair after you wash it then you can comb any lice or nits out with a fine-toothed comb.'

'That sounds a better option than dousing his head in chemicals. Thanks for the tip. As you've probably guessed, this is all very new to me,' he added wryly.

Alison raised her eyebrows. 'I'll bet it is. Checking your son's hair for nits isn't how you would usually spend your evenings.'

'What do you mean?' Jack asked, somewhat puzzled by the comment.

'Nothing. Forget I said anything.'

She turned to leave again, but he had no intention of letting her go without an explanation. He opened the door wider and stepped back.

'I can't forget it now that you've said it, can I? Why don't you come in and tell me over a cup of coffee exactly how I should be spending my evenings. I was just about to put the kettle on when you rang the bell,' he added when she hesitated.

'I really can't see the point,' she began, but Jack was having none of it. If she had something to say then he wanted to hear it. For some reason he didn't understand, he didn't want her getting the wrong idea about him.

'Then do it as a favour. I was sitting here feeling very sorry for myself when you rang the bell, and I could do with cheering up.'

'Has something happened with Freddie?' she asked anxiously as she stepped into the hall.

'Yes and no.' He shrugged, wondering how to explain that he was feeling rejected because his son hadn't wanted to play with him.

'Hmm, that sounds ambiguous enough to be intriguing,' Alison said lightly. She unzipped Sam's coat, then ushered him into the sitting room. 'Go and play with Freddie while Jack and I make some coffee, darling. I'll be in the kitchen if you need me.'

Jack headed to the kitchen and filled the kettle as the two boys settled down to play with some building blocks. Alison followed him in, grimacing as she took stock of the tired units and chipped worktops.

'I thought my kitchen was bad, but this is a mess. It looks as though it could do with a complete make-over.'

'Tell me about it.' Jack scooped coffee into the cafetière. 'The whole place needs refurbishing. It's having the time to get it sorted out that's the biggest problem.'

'Are you going to do it? I thought you'd only rented the cottage?'

'Yes and no.' He grinned at her. 'That's becoming my favourite answer, isn't it? Sorry. I don't mean to be so vague. It's just that everything about my life seems to be up in the air at the moment. It's hard to give you a definite answer.'

'It can't have been easy for you, uprooting your life and moving down here,' she said, sitting down. 'I mean, you've left your home and all your friends—no wonder it feels as though your life is in turmoil when you've had to make so many changes.'

'It's not that, exactly.'

He sat down opposite her, feeling his heart give the strangest little flutter when she looked at him with her hazel eyes full of sympathy. Few people had felt the need to sympathise with him. He wouldn't have thanked them if they had. He prided himself on the fact that he could take care of himself and didn't need anyone to prop him up, yet it was different when he was with Alison; he felt differently around her.

He chased away that thought and smiled at her, falling back on the charm that had got him through so many tricky situations in the past. 'I enjoyed living in London, and I doubt I'd have moved away if it hadn't been for Freddie. But as for missing my friends—well, that really isn't a major factor.'

'Are you sure? After all, you led a very hectic social life when you lived in the capital. It's understandable if you feel bored and restless now that you've moved out here.'

'Ah! Obviously you read all the rubbish that was written about me a few years ago,' Jack said ruefully. He held out his hands, palms up. 'What can I say? I had a great time and I enjoyed all the parties, et cetera, but it was only ever one small part of my life. I grew out of that whole scene some time ago, and I don't miss it either.'

'No?'

'No,' he said firmly when he realised that she didn't believe him. 'There's only so much partying a person can do before it becomes boring. You see the same old faces wherever you go, have the same pointless conversations. It might appear like a fabulous way to live to anyone watching but it's not really like that, believe me.'

'Then why did you do it if you didn't enjoy it?'

'Oh, I enjoyed it well enough in the beginning,' he admitted. 'Going to all those exciting new places and meeting people you've only ever seen on television or at the cinema gives you a tremendous buzz at first. Most people find themselves swept away by the glamour of it all.'

'As you were?'

'Yes.' He sighed. 'I went a bit mad when I first moved to London—fell in with a crowd whose main aim in life was to enjoy themselves. If I hadn't had my work then heaven knows what would have happened. It's what stopped me going off the rails. Especially after I met India.'

'That's when most of the articles appeared,' Alison said softly. She blushed when he looked at her in surprise. 'I used to buy a lot of the gossip magazines, and you and India featured prominently in them.'

'You don't strike me as the sort of person who reads stuff like that,' Jack said, getting up to pour the coffee. He took the mugs back to the table then fetched the milk and sat down again.

'Normally I wouldn't read them, but I was going through a difficult time. They seemed to fill a gap in my life, if that doesn't sound too silly.'

'Of course it doesn't sound silly!' He put his hand over hers and gently squeezed it, felt his breath catch in the most alarming fashion, and hastily released her. 'If they helped, great. Don't feel guilty about it.'

He picked up his mug and took a sip of the scalding-hot brew. He wasn't going to ask her why her life had been particularly difficult at that point, not if he hoped to keep a grip on his wayward emotions. He was already stressed because of what had happened with Becca and Freddie, and he didn't think he could cope with anything else—like getting upset on Alison's behalf.

'I don't.'

She lifted the mug to her lips and blew on the coffee to cool it, and Jack felt his insides bunch themselves into knots as he watched her lips purse. From what he could tell, she wasn't wearing a scrap of lipstick, but she didn't need it to enhance the pouty fullness of her mouth.

Tingles suddenly started to shoot through his body, flashes of electricity that charged every cell, and he buried his face in the steaming mug. He had slept with a number of women in his time, kissed a hell of a lot more and flirted with probably triple that number, but at no time could he recall feeling as keyed-up as he felt right now. The sight of Alison's lush bare mouth was playing havoc with his senses, stirring them into a bubbling cauldron of desire. He wanted to lean across the table and kiss her, run the tip of his tongue over those soft, delicious lips and taste them, then gently—ever so gently—nibble the lower one. And that was just for starters!

Jack shot to his feet, mumbling something about checking on the boys because it was the first excuse his overloaded brain dredged up. He almost ran out of the kitchen, praying that Alison didn't suspect what was going on. He couldn't imagine that she would, not when he was having such difficulty accepting the concept.

He leant against the wall and groaned. This *couldn't* be happening. He couldn't be having lustful thoughts about a woman he barely knew, a woman, to boot, who apparently believed he was some kind of…of dissolute *playboy*. It was mad, senseless, stupid, ridiculous and every other adjective in between. It simply couldn't happen. He wouldn't allow it to!

He took a deep breath and turned to go back into the kitchen, then felt the floor ripple beneath his feet when he caught sight of Alison. She was drinking her coffee, and all the feelings he'd experienced before seemed to multiply tenfold as he watched her. He couldn't drag his eyes away from her mouth as it neared the cup—a small purse of her lips, a tiny puff of cool air, followed by a tentative sip. It was like poetry in motion and he would have been happy to recite the verse for the rest of his life—purse, puff, sip.

Jack quickly closed his eyes. He had no idea what was going on but he had enough to contend with: a child who was so traumatised he wouldn't speak; problems with his father; a demanding job. He didn't need or *want* to add anything else to the equation. He had to stop watching Alison and lusting after her, and get a grip!

Alison put down the cup and looked around the kitchen. It really was a mess, she decided, and if she'd had to live here she would have had to do something about it.

Her gaze skimmed over the cabinets, which had been painted in a particularly vile shade of green, and she shuddered. No wonder Jack was finding it hard to settle into his new life when he had to live in a place like this. Compared to what he had left behind in London—all that glitz and glamour—it must be a shock. Maybe he claimed that he was over the party scene, but she couldn't believe he didn't miss all the rest.

It made her wonder how long he would stay in Penhally Bay. She couldn't see him spending the rest of his life in this quiet little backwater—it was simply a stopgap. At the moment he needed his family's help to look after Freddie, but once he got used to being a father he would move on, probably return to London and jump right back into the social scene.

It was what Sam's father, Gareth, had done. He had been brought up in London and had missed city life when he had moved to Cornwall to work. Although Alison had realised when she'd met him that he'd found country living boring, she'd hoped he would adapt in time. When she'd discovered she was pregnant, she'd thought it would help Gareth to put down roots, but it hadn't worked out that way.

After Sam had been born the situation had grown worse. Gareth hadn't coped with either the responsibility of being a father or the restrictions of having a new baby to look after. He had left her for another woman when Sam had been six months old and returned to his former life in the city. She'd had no contact with him since. It was upsetting to compare Jack with Gareth and realise they had so much in common.

'More coffee?'

Jack came back into the kitchen and she started nervously. She shook her head, hoping he couldn't tell how unsettled she felt. It shouldn't make a scrap of difference whether Jack stayed in Cornwall or left, but it did.

'Sure?' He picked up the cafetière and held it, poised, over her cup.

'No, this is fine. Thank you,' she added belatedly.

Jack topped up his mug and sat down, stretching his long legs under the table and accidentally kicking her foot. 'Sorry,' he murmured as he lifted the cup to his mouth.

'It's OK,' Alison replied, tucking her feet safely out of the way.

She picked up her own mug, feeling very ill at ease all of a sudden. It had been some time since she'd thought about her ex-husband, and it was worrying to wonder why she had thought about him now. She'd steered clear of relationships since the divorce. It hadn't been difficult when she'd been so busy looking after Sam and earning enough money to keep them, but there'd been a couple of occasions when she'd been asked out on a date. Each time she had refused.

Although she hadn't ruled out the idea of meeting someone else, she was wary of making another mistake. If she ever got involved again with a man, she would need a cast-iron guarantee that he wasn't going to let her down. And a man like Jack Tremayne definitely didn't come with a warranty. Any woman who got involved with him wouldn't know what to expect—in or out of bed.

The thought made her blush and she rushed into speech. 'How are the boys—?'

'The boys are fine—'

They both spoke at once and both stopped. Jack grinned at her. 'Ladies first.'

'I was just going to ask if Sam and Freddie were all right.'

'They're fine. They're playing some sort of complicated game involving lots of cars and building blocks.' Jack put his mug on the table and sighed. 'At least Freddie seems to enjoy playing with Sam. He completely blanked me when I offered to play with him earlier. He didn't want anything to do with me, in fact.'

'He's probably still feeling very unsettled,' Alison said quietly, thinking that the son took after his father in that respect. It was obvious how unsettled Jack was feeling, and the thought simply compounded all her fears about the dangers of getting involved with him.

'That's what I keep telling myself.' Jack gave her a quick smile, then changed the subject. 'So what would you do with this place if you lived here?'

'It would depend how long I was planning on staying,' Alison said cautiously. 'It isn't worth spending a huge amount of money if it's only a temporary arrangement, is it?'

'Bearing in mind how hard it is to find somewhere to live around here, I can't see myself moving in the foreseeable future.'

'No?' She shrugged, clamping down on the bubble of happiness that had popped up inside her because Jack wasn't planning on leaving.

'No. The whole point of coming back here was so that Freddie would have his family around him. I'm certainly not thinking about uprooting him again for a very long time.'

'In that case, I suppose it depends what you're allowed to do. The cottage is a holiday let, isn't it? There must be restrictions on what tenants can do to the property.'

'It was a holiday let, but it's been taken off the market now.' Jack shrugged. 'It's owned by a subsidiary company of Whitethorn Holidays.'

'India's family business?' Alison exclaimed.

'It was. Now it all belongs to Freddie.'

'You mean that Freddie inherited the company after India died?'

'Yep. The whole kit and caboodle.' Jack waved a hand around the kitchen. 'Including this place. India was an only child, and she left everything in trust to Freddie. He'll come into his inheritance when he's twenty-five, although there's money set aside for his use before then—for school fees, university, that kind of thing.'

'I had no idea,' Alison admitted.

'That's because I don't want people making a song and dance about it.' Jack's expression was sombre. 'I want Freddie to grow up like any normal kid and not be burdened by the fact that he's so wealthy. I firmly believe it was that which led to India going off the rails, and there is no way that I'm going to let the same thing happen to Freddie.'

Alison nodded. 'I agree. I know that everyone thinks it must be great to be really, really rich, but it must be a huge liability at times.'

'I'm sure it is. Don't get me wrong—money is important and I'm not decrying the fact. You need enough to live comfortably, but after that…' He shrugged. 'It can cause an awful lot of problems, from what I've seen. That's why I don't intend to touch any of Freddie's money. I earn enough to keep us and that's it.'

Alison admired the stance he'd taken and said so. 'Not many people would feel that way, Jack.'

'Maybe not, but it's how I feel. My only concession is this cottage. We needed a place to live, so I decided to rent it with a view to buying it in the future if it proves suitable for our needs.'

'Which is why you don't mind refurbishing the place?' she suggested, and he grinned at her.

'Got it one! So, come along, let's hear your ideas for turning this place into a proper home.'

The next hour flew past as Alison did exactly that. It was only when Sam came to find her because he was thirsty that she realised how late it was. She jumped to her feet, groaning as she glanced at her watch.

'I got so carried away that I didn't realise the time. You should have stopped me.'

'No way. I need someone to set me on the right track.' Jack stood up and smiled at her, a lazy, boyish smile that made her bones melt. 'I'm not really strong on the homemaking scene, and it's good to be able to crib your ideas.'

Alison chuckled as she took Sam into the sitting room and put on his coat. 'I'm no expert when it comes to interior design, so don't go by me. I'm sure you can find someone better qualified to advise you.'

'You mean a *real* interior designer?' Jack said, making imaginary speech marks with his fingers. He shuddered. 'No, thanks. I don't want the place looking like something out o a trendy magazine. I want it to be proper home, a place wher Freddie can play and not have to worry about making a mess.

'Well, you should get that all right. There's a lot of mes when you have a three-year-old,' she said, looking pointedl at the sitting-room floor, which was littered with toys.

Jack laughed. 'I don't care so long as he's happy.' H looked at his son and an expression of sadness crossed hi face. 'That's all I want for him—to be happy.'

'And he will be, Jack,' Alison said quietly, moved by th sadness in his voice.

'Let's hope so.'

He didn't say anything else as he showed them out, bu Alison knew that he was wondering if he would ever fulfil hi wish to make his son's life better. She wished she could hel him but there was very little she could do.

It would have been different if she and Jack had bee seeing each other, she thought as she and Sam walked home then inwardly recoiled. She could never get romanticall involved with Jack. Apart from the fact that he wouldn't b interested in someone like her, she wouldn't risk her hear being broken a second time. She and Sam were better off o their own. And as for Jack—well, he would manage perfectl well without her help.

CHAPTER SIX

JACK had just dropped off to sleep when he heard the phone ringing. Rolling over, he grabbed hold of the receiver before the noise woke Freddie. 'Jack Tremayne.'

'Jack, it's Alex Ross. I'm sorry to wake you but we have a full-scale alert on so we're having to call in every available member of staff.'

'What's happened?' Jack demanded, dragging himself out from under the duvet.

'A light plane has crashed on Bodmin moor. The pilot declared an emergency and Air Traffic Control advised him to set down on the A30. Apparently the police were trying to clear the road when it happened.'

Jack's heart sank. 'Do I take it the plane hit a car?'

'A minibus bringing a group of sixth-formers back from a geography field trip.' Alex said. 'It was absolute carnage, from what I can gather. Incident Control has asked us to take the burns cases, which is why I need you in here, pronto.'

'I'll be there just as soon as I can.'

Jack hung up and leapt out of bed, wondering what he was going to do about Freddie. He could take him with him, but then what? He couldn't just dump the child in the hospital and go merrily about his business.

He dragged on a shirt and a sweater, finger-combed his hair, and headed for the stairs, still mulling over his options. He could phone Lucy and ask her to have Freddie, but it was gone midnight and he hated to wake her up when she had the baby to look after. Alison was another possibility, but he was even warier about taking that option after what had happened that evening.

His brain made a lightning-fast detour to that moment when he had watched Alison drinking her coffee and he sucked in his breath. This is neither the time nor the place for that, Jack, my lad, he told himself sternly.

He reached the bottom of the stairs and paused as he stared at the phone sitting on the table beside the front door. If he wasn't prepared to ask either Lucy or Alison for help, then who could he phone?

He groaned softly. There was really only one other option—one he wouldn't have considered if he hadn't been desperate. Picking up the receiver, Jack punched in the number, steeling himself when he heard the person on the other end pick up.

'Dad, it's me—Jack. Look, I'm sorry to bother you at this time of the night but I need a favour.'

'Jack, good to see you.'

Jack grinned at his brother-in-law, Ben Carter. 'So you got roped in as well?'

'I was already here when it all kicked off so I stayed on to help.' Ben grimaced. 'It's a bad one. There's a lot of kids injured, as well as the people on the plane.'

'I thought we were only getting the burns injuries?' Jack said quietly, following Ben to the resuscitation room, where the very worst cases were being treated.

'So did I. However, it appears there was another major accident tonight outside Launceston, involving a coach and a lorry. Every A and E unit for miles around is chock-a-block. Incident Control decided that we would take the most seriously injured from the plane crash and the rest would be ferried round to anywhere that has room for them.'

'What a mess!' Jack exclaimed.

He followed Ben into Resus, feeling the adrenaline start pumping around his body at the scene that greeted him. Every available bed was being used and the place was buzzing. He swung round when he heard the high-pitched whine of a monitor going off.

'He's arrested,' somebody shouted, and Ben groaned.

'That's the pilot. It doesn't look good, I'm afraid.' He pointed over to where screens had been placed around one of the beds. 'Alex is over there. OK?'

'Fine.'

Jack made his way across the room and slipped behind the screens, smiling when Alex looked up. 'Looks like a fun time is being had by all.'

'You could say that,' she agreed dryly.

Jack's expression sobered as he looked down at the teenage boy who was lying on the bed. The left side of his face had been burned, although it was difficult to tell how badly damaged the skin was without a closer examination. However, it was obvious that there was severe burning to his upper left arm, and Jack knew without having to check that it would need a lot of work to sort it out. He glanced at Alex and raised his brows.

'Ryan Lovelace, aged eighteen, a passenger in the minibus,' she explained crisply, leaning over to adjust the drip attached to Ryan's uninjured arm. One of the major factors in burns cases was shock caused by the rapid loss of large

quantities of fluid from the affected areas, so Jack appre
ciated why Alex was so keen to ensure that the boy's fluid
levels were restored as quickly as possible.

'Apparently he got out of the minibus, but he went back to
help some of the others, and that's how he got burned.'

'I see.' Jack smiled at the boy. 'That was a brave thing
to do, Ryan.'

'Naw, anyone would have done the same,' Ryan said
dismissively.

Jack doubted it, but he didn't argue with him—he was
more concerned about the severity of his injuries. Bending
down, he examined Ryan's face first. There was some blis
tering, but most of the dermis—the deeper layer of the skin—
appeared to be unscathed. That was good news because it
meant there should be less scarring once the area healed.

It was very different with the boy's upper arm, however.
The burns to this area were third-degree burns. The full thick
ness of the skin had been destroyed and there was a section
of muscle exposed. Although the worst damage was confined
to a relatively small area, that didn't mean it wasn't a signifi
cant injury. Skin acted as a barrier to prevent airborne infec
tion getting into the body, and once it was breached bacteria
could rapidly infiltrate the tissues.

'I take it he's on broad-spec antibiotics?' he said
glancing at Alex.

'Yes. I got him started on them immediately.'

'Good.' Jack frowned. 'I'd like to get him to Theatre as
soon as possible. What's the schedule like?'

'Chaotic,' Alex said. 'I'm waiting for a slot for one of the pas
sengers in the plane—he's got third-degree burns to both hands
Ben has a girl who needs her leg amputated—she's being
prepped at the moment, and he'll be going back to her as soon

as he's finished with the pilot. Then there's another three who need glass removed from their faces. I'm not sure if they need theatre time as I haven't had a chance to assess them yet.'

'That's quite a queue, even without them,' Jack said wryly. He arched a brow. 'What do you suggest we do—toss a coin to see who gets theatre space?'

'It might come to that,' Alex warned him, smiling. 'We're still waiting for another couple of casualties to arrive, too. The helicopter is bringing them in, and we won't really know what we're dealing with until it gets here.'

Jack shook his head. 'I thought it was bad in London, but it's no better here.'

'No. Sadly enough, accidents happen in even the quietest places—'

Alex broke off when one of the nurses came over to her. She turned to Jack. 'Theatre two is free, so that's me sorted. Are you happy to deal with this case on your own?'

'Yes, so long as you're happy to leave it to me,' Jack confirmed.

'Oh, I have no worries on that score. Right, I'll see you later. You know where I am if you need me.'

Jack returned his attention to his patient once Alex left. Pulling on some gloves, he carefully examined the boy's face. He liked to have an overall picture of the problems before he actually did anything. He checked Ryan's arm as well, and knew that his initial assessment had been correct: it would need reconstructive work to ensure the muscle wasn't adversely affected, and skin grafts to help it heal.

There was still no sign of a slot in Theatre becoming vacant after he had finished assessing Ryan's injuries so, rather than waste time, he took one of the teenagers who'd got glass in his face into the treatment room and sorted him out in there.

Using a high-powered magnifying glass, and working unde local anaesthetic, he was able to remove the slivers of glass. A couple of tiny sutures, a light dressing and the boy was free to leave. Jack took him through to the waiting room and had a word with his parents, explaining that the stitches could be removed at their GP's surgery rather than at the hospital. He hadn't realised until the parents told him they were patients o his father that some of the school kids came from Penhally Bay The accident would have a big impact on the town.

It was his turn for Theatre then, so Jack didn't have time to dwell on it. However, as he made his way to the changing room, he couldn't help wondering what Nick would think o his work when he saw the youngster.

He sighed. Alex was confident enough about his abilities to leave him to get on with the job, so his father's opinion shouldn't matter, but it would be good to have his approva for once. Still, at least Nick had agreed to look after Freddie for him, and that had to be a step in the right direction.

Maybe it was the fact that he was a father himself now, bu Jack suddenly found himself hoping that he and Nick would be able to resolve their differences in time. All it needed was fo Nick to meet him halfway and they could start being a prope family again—Dad, Lucy, Ben, Annabel, Ed, Freddie and him

Just for a moment another name flashed into his head, bu he blanked it out. Alison wasn't part of this equation and there was no point hoping that she ever would be.

Alison heard about the accident when she took Sam into nursery the following morning. Several of the mums were talking about it as it appeared there'd been a number o children from Penhally Bay involved.

By the time she arrived at the surgery, she knew that at leas three of the injured teenagers were patients there. Sue, the receptionist, greeted her with a sigh when she walked in.

'I suppose you've heard the news?'

'About the crash? Yes, I have. From what I can gather, several of the kids are from here, too.'

'That's right.' Sue reeled off their names. 'Ryan Lovelace is the most badly injured. I met Mandy Lovelace on my way here—she's Ryan's aunt, you know—and she told me that he's got burns on his face and his arm. Apparently he got them dragging some of the other kids out of the bus.'

'Really? That was very brave of him!' Alison exclaimed.

'Wasn't it? It just goes to show there must be good in some branches of that family after all.'

Alison didn't say anything. Some members of the Lovelace family were patients at the surgery. Although it was widely known that they had their problems, she didn't feel happy about discussing them and diplomatically changed the subject. 'Are the children being treated at St Piran's?'

'Oh, yes. They took all the casualties there, so it must have been bedlam. Mandy told me that Jack operated on Ryan so he must have been called in.' Sue reached for the phone when it began to ring. 'I wonder what he did about his little boy?'

'I've no idea.'

Alison left Sue to deal with the call. Picking up the stack of notes that had been left in her tray, she made her way to the nurse's room, thinking about what Sue had told her. Had Jack asked Lucy to look after Freddie for him? She could only assume he must have done.

That was one of the drawbacks of him working at the hospital, of course. He would be on call any time the situation warranted it. It must make it very difficult for him to organise child care. Just for a moment she wondered if she should tell him that he could call on her if he was stuck before she thought better of it. While she would be happy to help, she wouldn't want Jack to think there was an ulterior motive to her offer. He was so handsome and so charismatic that a lot of women must have pursued him over the years, and she would hate it if he thought that was what she was doing.

She frowned because that wasn't the only reason, of course. Normally she would have dismissed her qualms and made the offer anyway. However, she was too aware of the dangers of getting involved with him. She knew it would take very little for her to fall for Jack, and fall hard, too. And that was a risk she wasn't prepared to take.

It was lunchtime before Jack left the hospital. He had spent most of his time in Theatre, first of all sorting out Ryan's problems as much as he could, and then assisting Alex. Two of the passengers as well as the pilot from the plane had died, but the third man had survived. His hands had been badly burned, though, and Jack knew that, despite everything he and Alex had achieved, it was only the tip of a very big iceberg. It would need a lot more work to restore full use of the man's hands.

The injured teenagers had fared rather better. All except two had been discharged. Ryan would need skin grafts once Jack had a better idea what was going on in the underlying tissue, while Ben's patient—the girl who'd needed an amputation—would be kept in the orthopaedic ward. It could have been much worse, he decided as he got into his car to drive back to Penhally Bay, but it would also have been much better if the crash had never happened.

He drove home and took a shower, then headed to the nursery to check on Freddie. His father had left a message with the theatre staff to say that he was taking Freddie to nursery as usual that day, but Jack wanted to make sure his son was all right. He parked across the road and got out of the car, stepping back as a motorcycle whizzed past with its horn blaring. It was his fault for not looking what he was doing and it gave him a shock. He was just catching his breath when Alison hurried over to him.

'Are you all right?'

'Just.' Jack grimaced. 'I'm a bit spaced out after pulling an all-nighter, but that's no excuse. It was a stupid thing to do.'

'You should be more careful,' she admonished, and he grinned.

'Yes, miss.'

Alison chuckled. 'Sorry. I seem to have my bossy hat on today.'

'Don't worry about it. I could do with someone bossing me around at the moment. I'm completely pooped.'

He unlocked the gate and held it open for her to precede him, feeling his muscles clench when she brushed against him as she passed through the narrow opening. Maybe he was tired, he thought ruefully, but certain bits of him were in fine fettle.

'Did Lucy have Freddie for you last night?'

Thankfully, Alison seemed oblivious to his response, so Jack pulled himself together. 'No. I didn't like to phone her, seeing as it was so late. I asked my dad if he'd babysit for me. He came over to mine and stayed the night, then brought Freddie into nursery this morning.'

'Oh, that was kind of him. Mind you, he probably enjoyed it. It gave him a chance to spend some time with his grandson.'

'I imagine so,' Jack said, feeling guilty about the fact that he hadn't made any effort to invite Nick round before. OK, so his father had met Freddie at the surgery, but that hadn't been a social call. Apart from that, his son had had no contact with his grandfather until last night, and it really wasn't good enough.

'Did I say something to upset you?' Alison said anxiously.

Jack shook his head. 'It wasn't you. I just realised how remiss I've been by not getting Dad and Freddie together.' He shrugged. 'It's no secret that we have a rather rocky relationship, but I should have made more of an effort.'

'You haven't had much free time since you came back,' she pointed out.

'That's no excuse. I should have sorted something out.'

She touched his arm briefly. 'You're not Superman, Jack. You can only be in one place at any one time. Anyway, I'm sure Nick understands how difficult it is to juggle work and everything else.'

'I hope so.'

Jack smiled, because he didn't want her to worry any more about his problems. He rang the bell and waited for a member of staff to admit them. Most of the children stayed all day at the nursery, so there were only a couple of other parents there. He and Alison signed in, then went to the room where the three-year-olds were playing. Trish Atkins, the nursery nurse in charge of the children, came hurrying over to him.

'I'm glad you're here, Dr Tremayne. Did you get my message?'

'What message?' Jack asked, his stomach sinking as he looked around the room. There was no sign of Freddie, and he felt panic well up inside him as he wondered what had happened to him.

'I left a message on your home phone,' Trish informed him. 'Freddie has been very upset this morning and I thought I should let you know.'

'Upset? About what?' Jack demanded.

'I've no idea because he won't tell me,' Trish explained, looking worried.

'Was he upset when my father brought him in?' Jack demanded. Waking up to find a virtual stranger in the house must have been scary for the child, and he should have thought about that, although he had no idea what he could have done about it in the circumstances.

'He seemed a little subdued, but he's usually very quiet so it wasn't unusual. He wasn't crying, though,' Trish added.

'Where is he now?' Jack said.

'One of the staff is sitting in the quiet room with him. We thought it was best if we kept him away from the others in case he upset them, too.'

Jack followed her through a door at the far end of the room, his heart aching when he saw his son curled up on a mat in the corner, sobbing his little heart out. He hurried across the room and scooped him into his arms. 'Hey, tiger, what's wrong?'

Freddie took a gulping breath as he wrapped his arms tightly around Jack's neck. Jack could feel him shuddering as he lifted him up. 'It's OK,' he crooned, kissing the top of his head. 'Daddy's here and he won't let anything hurt you.'

Freddie was inconsolable as he clung to him, and Jack was at a loss to know what to do. He desperately wanted to comfort him, but he didn't know where to start. His gaze went to Alison, who had followed him into the room, and his heart caught again when he saw the expression on her face. Alison understood how powerless he felt, and realising it seemed to unleash all his fears.

Up till now he had been putting on a brave face, but he needed help if he was to get through to Freddie. Although he did his best, he didn't have any experience of dealing with such a young child. He had been thrown in at the deep end when he had taken custody of Freddie. He hadn't had time to learn how to be a good father to him, but if he didn't get it right he would *never* build a proper relationship with his son. The thought scared him to death.

Jack took a deep breath as panic gripped him. He needed help and he needed it now. Although he could ask Lucy's advice, she was in much the same boat as him. She was a new parent, too, and she was just learning what having a child was all about. His father was the next best option but, bearing in mind their already strained relationship, Jack didn't want to go down that route. That left him with just one other choice— one he wasn't sure if he should consider.

His gaze rested on Alison as he felt a sudden tightening in his chest. Could he ask Alison for help? *Should* he ask her when he was experiencing all these strange ideas about her? He would hate to think that he might solve one problem only to find himself with an even bigger one on his hands.

CHAPTER SEVEN

ALISON could have wept when she saw the anguish on Jack's face as he cradled Freddie in his arms. Hurrying forward, she put her hand on his arm. 'Let's take him home. He's far too upset to stay here for the rest of the day.'

'You're right.'

Jack tried to smile, but she could tell the effort it cost him and her heart went out to him. She squeezed his arm, wanting him to know that she understood how he felt. 'I'll just fetch Sam and then we'll leave.'

She went back to the playroom and found Sam. He skipped along beside her as they left the nursery, and his joyful attitude was such a contrast to Freddie's obvious unhappiness that it made her see something had to be done. When they reached the road she turned to Jack.

'Would you like to come home with us? It might help to take Freddie's mind off whatever is bothering him if he plays with Sam for a while.'

'Are you sure you don't mind?' Jack said hesitantly. 'It seems like such an imposition…'

'Rubbish! Of course it isn't an imposition. In fact, I insist you come back and have some lunch. It's my half-day off because I'm working on Saturday morning, so I don't need to go back to the surgery, if that's what you're worried about. To be frank, you're in no fit state to cope on your own.'

'It's that obvious?' Jack gave her the ghost of his usual multi-megawatt smile. 'I don't think I could punch my way out of a paper bag at this precise moment, to be honest.'

'No wonder, after the night you've had,' she said sympathetically.

Jack sighed as they crossed the road. 'If it was just tiredness, I could cope. It's seeing Freddie like this which is so hard to deal with. I don't know what to do for the best to help him.'

'I understand how difficult it is, Jack, but you have to hang in there.' She glanced at the little boy and lowered her voice. 'Freddie needs you. That's obvious from the way he's clinging to you.'

'It is, isn't it?' Jack said wonderingly. He turned to her and she saw tears welling in his eyes. 'It's the first time he's ever shown any sign of affection towards me.'

'Then it's a real breakthrough. Just hold onto that thought.'

She waited while Jack unlocked his car. Fortunately, there was a built-in child seat in the rear armrest so there was no question of Sam not being safely strapped in. Jack got Freddie settled, then slid into the driving seat. He started the engine, then glanced in the rear-view mirror.

'Freddie seems a bit calmer now, doesn't he?'

'He does. He just needs time to get over whatever it was that upset him and he'll be fine.'

'I just wish I knew what started it all off,' Jack said flatly. 'I feel as though I'm stumbling about in the dark all the time because he won't talk to me.'

'He will eventually,' she said encouragingly. 'He just needs time and a lot of love.'

Jack didn't say anything, but she could tell he wasn't convinced the solution was so simple. Maybe it wasn't that simple, but she was sure that what Freddie needed most of all was love, and Jack seemed to have an abundance of that when it came to his son. Whether he had enough love to spare for a woman as well was another matter. From what she had gleaned from all those press reports, he seemed to be commitment-phobic. He fell in love, and fell out of it again even faster.

She sighed. Jack's love life had nothing to do with her. Although she was happy to help him with Freddie, she wasn't going to make the mistake of getting involved with him on a personal level.

By the time they arrived at Alison's house Freddie seemed much calmer. Jack carried him inside and took off his coat. He frowned as he watched his son run over and kneel down beside Sam. 'He looks much happier now, doesn't he?'

'Yes, he does. And he'll look even better after he's had something to eat. You, too,' she added, heading for the kitchen.

'Are you sure you don't mind feeding us?' Jack followed her, but the kitchen was only big enough to accommodate one person comfortably so he propped himself against the door rather than crowd her.

'Of course I don't mind!' She opened a cupboard and took out a couple of tins. 'Beans on toast all right?'

'Lovely,' he said fervently, then grinned when she looked at him in surprise. 'I've had nothing to eat since last night, so beans on toast sounds like manna from heaven to my poor empty stomach.'

'First time I've heard them described as that,' she said lightly.

Jack watched as she found a pan to heat the beans, then cut some bread for the toast. He had never mastered the art of cooking, and he admired the way she seemed so at home in the kitchen. 'I never seem to get the timing right. Either the toast is cold by the time the beans are ready or vice versa.'

'It's just practice.' She buttered the toast and piled the beans on top, then handed him two of the plates. 'These are for the boys, if you could take them through.'

'Right you are.'

Jack took the plates in and put them on the table, then went back for the cutlery. Alison handed him the knives and forks, then picked up the other two plates.

'I'll bring these in.'

Jack laid the table, then called the boys over. Sam immediately climbed onto a chair, but Freddie didn't look too sure about the arrangements. Pulling out a chair, Jack bent down so that he was at eye level with him.

'You can sit on this chair or on my knee, Freddie. It's up to you.'

The little boy glanced at Sam, then scrambled onto the chair. Jack smiled at him as he pushed him closer to the table. 'Good boy.'

Jack sat down and tucked into his own meal, wolfing down the food as though his life depended on it. He was so hungry that he couldn't remember a meal ever tasting so good, and said so.

Alison laughed. 'What about all those wonderful meals you had in London?'

'Vastly overrated. Forget the champagne and caviar. I prefer good old baked beans on toast any day of the week!'

'If you expect me to believe that, you must think I'm really gullible.' She started to gather up the plates, but Jack took them from her.

'I'll do that. You cooked, so it's only fair that I do the washing-up.'

'There's no need,' she protested, following him to the kitchen.

'Of course there is.' He put the plates in the sink and turned on the taps. 'Where do you keep the washing-up liquid?'

'In here.'

She reached around him to open the cupboard door at the same moment as Jack turned. His body brushed up hard against hers and every cell suddenly went on the alert. He could feel the softness of her breasts pressing against the wall of his chest and froze.

'Sorry.'

There was a breathy quality to her voice that sent the blood rushing to his head and he bit back a moan. Another second of this torture and he wouldn't be held responsible for his actions!

'Here you are.'

Alison shoved a bottle of detergent into his hands and hastily retreated. Jack's head cleared as though by magic. He added a squirt of detergent to the water and plunged his hands in, yelping when he discovered how hot it was.

'Have you scalded yourself? Let me see.'

Suddenly Alison was behind him, her breasts nudging his shoulderblade as she tried to peer around him, and Jack gulped in air like a drowning man. There was only so much temptation a man could stand and he was well past his limit.

'I'm fine,' he said gruffly.

'Are you sure?' She leant forward, unconsciously piling on the agony as her breasts flattened themselves against his back.

'Quite sure,' he said, hoping she couldn't hear the panic in his voice. 'Would you mind checking on Freddie for me? I don't want him thinking he's been abandoned again.'

'Oh, yes, of course.'

She hurried from the kitchen and Jack was left on his own. Picking up a plate, he sluiced it in the hot water, wishing he could wash away the feelings that were rioting around inside him. He couldn't recall feeling so aroused before in his life, and couldn't understand why he felt this way. Was it the fact that he hadn't had sex for months that was causing the problem? he wondered suddenly.

Since Freddie had appeared on the scene he hadn't had time to think about his sex life. It hadn't been a priority before that either, because he'd been devoting every waking minute to his career. In fact, thinking back, it must be over six months since he'd been out with a woman, and closer to a year since he'd slept with anyone.

It was a shock to realise that, although it did help to explain why he was so responsive when he was around Alison. Jack breathed a sigh of relief as he finished washing the dishes. It had been scary to think there was something special about Alison when the answer was actually so mundane.

He dried his hands and went back to the sitting room. Alison was kneeling on the floor, playing with the boys. She laughed when Sam crashed his toy car into a tower of plastic blocks and sent them skittering across the floor, but Jack didn't join in. The blood was pounding inside his head again, and pounding through other parts of his body as well. Maybe the lack of sex was a contributing factor, but it was hard to believe it was the only reason he felt this way. What if it *was* Alison who was making him feel like this? What if he was falling in love with her?

A couple of months ago Jack would have scoffed at the idea of him falling in love, but he would have scoffed at the idea of him being a father, too. As he had discovered to his cost, life didn't follow a plan—it kept throwing up obstacles, and the trick was not to trip over them. He had avoided love in the past, but who said he could continue doing so?

The only guaranteed way he could avoid falling in love

with Alison was to move away, and he couldn't do that because of Freddie. Freddie needed stability in his life; he needed people around him whom he could learn to trust. Jack couldn't uproot the child again. He had to stay here, and if that meant dealing with his feelings, that was what he would do. Freddie's needs would always come first.

'That's cheating!'

Alison grabbed hold of Sam and tickled him until he squealed with laughter. Glancing up, she felt her heart lurch when she saw Jack watching them. She had no idea what he was thinking at that moment, but he looked desperately unhappy. She gave Sam a final hug and stood up.

'How about you and Freddie doing some drawing for a change? If you clear away the cars, I'll find you some paper.' She headed to the door, nodding her thanks when Jack moved out of her way. 'I'll just get them settled down and then put some coffee on.'

'That would be great. Thanks.'

He gave her a quick smile, but she could see how strained he looked and it worried her. Jack was one of the most confident people she'd ever met, so why did he appear so ill at ease all of a sudden?

Alison mulled it over as she went into the kitchen for some paper and the felt-tipped pens. She had no idea why Jack was so on edge. She certainly couldn't think of anything she'd done to make him feel that way. In the end she decided that she was imagining things, so she got the boys settled and went to make the coffee.

Jack was slumped on the sofa when she got back. He looked so worn out that her heart ached for him. He glanced round when he heard her come into the room and smiled.

'I was just about to nod off,' he explained, sitting up. He moved the coffee-table closer to the sofa, then took the tray from her.

'Power naps are the latest craze, I believe,' Alison told him lightly, kneeling down on the rug so she could pour the coffee.

'Power naps, eh? I must remember that if I'm caught on the hop in work,' he said, his blue eyes filling with laughter. 'It sounds much more professional than admitting that you're having forty winks!'

Alison chuckled. 'It certainly does. I believe all the City bankers are using the phrase to explain why they're asleep at their desks.'

'I don't blame them. If I had to spend my days poring over a lot of dusty old figures, I'd probably be taking power naps, too.'

The muscles in his arm flexed as he reached for the sugar, and she felt her heart bounce up and down a couple of times. She hurriedly stood up, refusing to allow herself too much leeway where Jack was concerned. Picking up her cup, she took it over to the chair and sat down, kicking off her shoes and tucking her feet beneath her. Jack murmured contentedly as he sipped some of his coffee, then leant back against the cushions.

'I think I'm just about coming back down to earth. It was a really busy night.'

'I believe Ryan Lovelace was one of the kids who were injured?' Alison said, cradling her cup in her hands.

'That's right. Apparently he went back into the bus to help his friends and that's how he got burned.'

'How bad is he?'

'The burn to his face should heal without leaving much of a scar, but his left arm is a different story. There's some damage to the muscle as well as to the skin and the subcutaneous tissue. Muscle damage is extremely difficult to repair and it's going to take time to sort it all out.'

'What a shame! And after he was so brave, too.'

'I know. It doesn't seem fair, does it?' he said. 'Anyway, I've done some of the preliminary work, so that's a start, and I'm hoping to get another shot at it later this week. I need to see how much more tissue needs excising first. I've removed any that was obviously burned but there could be deterioration in the coming days and I might need to remove some more.'

'Will he regain full use of his arm?' Alison asked worriedly.

'If I don't need to remove too much more of the muscle. He'll need good physio, though, plus a lot of determination.'

'There's no problem on the physiotherapy score,' she assured him. 'Lauren Nightingale will soon get him sorted out.'

'Lauren's still here? Great! She's the best person I know when it comes to motivating a patient.'

Alison felt a little stab of jealousy assail her when she heard the warmth in his voice. She took a sip of her coffee, not wanting Jack to suspect that she harboured such feelings. Lauren was a first-rate physiotherapist, and the fact that she just happened to be extremely beautiful was of no consequence. She had no right to censor the people whom Jack liked.

The thought was so ridiculous that she gasped, and some of her coffee shot down the wrong way.

Jack looked at her in concern when she coughed. 'Are you all right?'

'Some coffee went down the wrong way,' she spluttered, trying to catch her breath.

Jack stood up and came over to her. 'I'll pat you on the back. It might help.'

Before Alison could protest, he started patting her back, and the rest of the air suddenly whooshed from her lungs. The feel of his strong hand between her shoulderblades was doing horrendous things to her, making her feel both hot and dizzy, and she choked.

'You really *are* in a bad way.'

There was real concern on Jack's face now as he bent over her. This close she could see the laughter lines fanning from the corners of his eyes, smell the clean scent of his skin and taste the coffee-scented warmth of his breath on her lips. It felt as though she was being immersed in sensations and she shuddered deeply.

'Here—let's give it another go.'

He started rubbing her back then, his strong hand caressing the length of her spine in a way that made Alison want to purr with pleasure, if only she'd had enough breath to spare. She could feel the heat of his palm seeping into her flesh, and for the first time in ages she felt desire rise up inside her. She stared up at him without saying a word and saw the exact moment when concern changed to something else, something hotter and wilder that couldn't be contained any longer.

When his head dipped, she closed her eyes, anticipating the moment when his mouth would claim hers. She could feel the feather-light brush of his lips as they hovered over hers and her heart overflowed with need. She wanted this kiss so much, needed it more than she had needed anything in such a long time…

He drew back abruptly, and her eyes flew open as she stared at him in confusion. He gave her a tight little smile as he straightened up.

'That seems to have done the trick. Now I think it's time we left. Thank you for everything you've done today, Alison. I really appreciate it.'

'It was my pleasure,' she said stiffly, standing up.

She went over to the boys and quietly explained that it was time for Freddie to go home, and all the time she was doing so her heart was racing. Jack had been going to kiss her. She had no idea why he had changed his mind, but she knew it was what he had been going to do.

That fact should have been shocking enough, but what made it worse was knowing that she wouldn't have stopped him. Panic gripped her. If Jack had kissed her then she would have kissed him back, and to hell with the consequences.

CHAPTER EIGHT

WHAT on earth was wrong with him? He'd not only embarrassed himself by making a pass at Alison, but he'd embarrassed her as well.

Jack could barely contain his chagrin as he helped Freddie into his coat. He fixed a smile to his mouth as he turned to Alison, desperate to salvage some shred of his dignity. 'Thanks again for everything.'

'You're welcome.'

She saw him to the door, her own smile fixed just as firmly into place, but Jack could tell that she was upset. Although he was terrified of making the situation worse, he knew that he had to say something. He certainly didn't want her to think that he might come on to her again at the slightest excuse.

'About what happened just now—well, I'm sorry.' He shrugged, doing his best to hide how mortified he felt. He had always prided himself on being in control of his actions, yet he had come within a hair's breadth of ruining everything. 'I don't know what came over me. Put it down to the long night I had—obviously I'm not thinking clearly.'

'Don't worry about it. I shan't.'

Her smile held fast but the chill in her eyes cut him to the quick. Bearing in mind the rather unflattering picture she had formed of him initially, she probably thought he was a serial philanderer now, someone who couldn't keep his hands off a woman if she came within a ten-mile radius of him.

The thought stung because it wasn't true. It wasn't the fact that Alison was a woman that had affected him…Well, not *only* that, he amended truthfully. It was Alison herself, the person she was, that had made him want to kiss her.

It was impossible to explain that to her without digging himself an even deeper hole. Jack took the line of least resistance and beat a hasty retreat.

He took Freddie home and spent the rest of the day worrying about what he'd done. Whichever way he looked at it, it hadn't been a wise move at the moment. In a year or so's time it might have been a different story, of course. Once Freddie was more settled, and his own life had taken on some kind of proper structure, maybe he would have time for a spot of romance.

He frowned, because the thought of a little light romance didn't appeal to him. It might have been enough for him in the past, but it wasn't enough for him now. Not with Alison. He wanted to do more than just sleep with her. He wanted to sleep with her *and* wake up with her lying beside him in the morning. He wanted to know that he could do the same thing the next day and the day after that, too. In fact, there was a word for what he wanted, one he had steadfastly avoided: commitment.

Jack groaned as he got up and switched on the stereo, hoping the music would drown out any more dangerous ideas. He couldn't afford to waver at this point. He had to concentrate on Freddie and how he was going to help him. No matter how he felt about Alison, his son was his number-one concern.

* * *

Alison found it difficult to sleep that night. Every time she closed her eyes, she kept having flashbacks to the moment when Jack had been on the verge of kissing her. Consequently, she felt completely drained when she got up the next day, and it was an effort to get herself and Sam ready.

She dropped Sam off at the nursery earlier than usual so she wouldn't run into Jack, and went into work. Dragan Lovak, one of the doctors in the practice, was in the office when she arrived and he greeted her with a smile. Dragan had moved to England as a teenager to escape the war in Croatia. Alison had always found him to be very sympathetic towards his patients, and suspected that his past experiences had given him an insight into other people's suffering.

'Ah, Alison, just the person I wanted to see. I have a patient who has been diagnosed with diabetes. At the moment she's very unsure about giving herself daily injections of insulin and I feel that she needs some reassurance if she is going to be able to cope. I was wondering if you could teach her the best way to administer the injections.'

'Of course. Who is it?'

'Sophie Banks.' Dragan handed her the patient's file. 'She's just fifteen and it's a lot for her to deal with. I know it's short notice, but could you see her today? The sooner she accepts what has to be done, the better.'

'Let me check my list.' Alison brought up her list of appointments on the computer. 'I could squeeze her in at four o'clock, after the antenatal clinic finishes. Shall I get Sue to set up an appointment for her?'

'That would be wonderful. Thank you.'

Alison went through to Reception and had a word with Sue, who promised to phone Sophie's mother and make the arrangements. 'Are you going on Maggie's hen night?' Sue asked after she'd logged the appointment into the computer.

'I'm not sure.' Alison frowned. 'When is it?'

'Two weeks on Friday. Maggie says there is no way that she's having a hen party the night before her wedding, so she's booked it early.'

'I don't blame her!' Alison agreed with a laugh.

There'd been a lot of excitement when Adam Donnelly and Maggie Pascoe had announced that they were getting married at the end of the month. All the surgery staff had been invited to the wedding, as well as Maggie's friends and colleagues from St Piran Hospital. Would Jack be going? Alison wondered, then quickly erased the thought. She wasn't going to spend the whole day thinking about Jack!

'I'll have to wait and see if I can get a babysitter,' she explained, then glanced round when Gemma Johnson, the young nurse who had recently joined the practice, came in. 'How about you, Gemma? Are you going to Maggie's hen night?'

'I most certainly am! In fact, I have something special planned to make the night go with a bit of a buzz,' the irrepressible Gemma confessed.

Alison groaned. 'I don't think I want to hear this. I'll wait until the night and worry about it then!'

She left Gemma and Sue discussing the arrangements and went upstairs. The morning flew past with the usual mix of people who needed to be seen. She was just about to put on her coat to fetch Sam from the nursery when she heard a commotion downstairs and hurried down to see what had happened.

Hazel was sitting on the floor outside the office, looking very shaken, and there was blood pouring from a cut on her right thigh. Alison was about to kneel down beside her when Nick arrived. He took one look at Hazel and turned to Alison.

'Fetch some bandages. We need to stop this bleeding.'

Alison flew into the supply room and grabbed a handful of bandages out of a box. Ripping open one of the packets, she ran back and handed it to Nick, who was trying to stem the bleeding.

'Thanks. Let's lie her down first, and then I want you to continue applying pressure to the wound.'

They helped Hazel lie down on the floor, then Alison grasped her thigh, pressing firmly either side of the wound. Direct pressure flattened the blood vessels and slowed the rate of bleeding so that clots could form. However, continuous pressure needed to be maintained for up to fifteen minutes for it to be effective.

She also raised Hazel's leg and supported it on her knees, knowing it would help to control the flow of blood if she raised the limb above heart level, but the wound continued bleeding heavily. Nick shook his head as he wound a second bandage over the first one and bound it in place.

'It's going to need stitching and we can't do it here. It's far too deep.' He raised his voice and shouted to Sue. 'Can you phone for an ambulance, please? Hazel needs to go to St Piran.'

It took just ten minutes for the ambulance to arrive, and in the meantime they had to add another couple of bandages as the original ones became soaked through with blood. They also put a drip into Hazel's arm to compensate for the loss of fluid, because she was complaining of feeling cold and dizzy. However, Alison was relieved when the paramedics lifted her onto a stretcher. She turned to Nick as the crew wheeled Hazel to the door.

'I'd like to go with her, if it's OK with you. Gemma can cover the antenatal clinic this afternoon. She's sat in with me a couple of times so she knows what to do. It will be good practice for her.'

'Fine,' Nick agreed. 'I'd go myself but I have to stay here in case anything else crops up. Take a taxi back when you've finished and charge it to the surgery.'

Alison hurriedly asked Sue to phone Carol, the child-minder, and ask her to collect Sam from nursery, then grabbed her coat. She climbed into the back of the ambulance and held Hazel's hand as they drove to the hospital.

'I feel such a fool,' Hazel said weakly. 'I was only opening a new carton of stationery and the knife slipped…' She gulped back a sob. 'Dr Tremayne must think I'm useless for causing such a fuss.'

'Don't be silly. It could have happened to anyone,' Alison assured her.

They drew up outside A and E and she followed as Hazel was wheeled through to the treatment area. Fortunately, she was deemed a priority case, so it didn't take very long before she was seen. It was the same registrar Alison had met when she'd accompanied Becca, and he grinned when he recognised her.

'Doing another good deed, I see.'

Alison laughed. 'Something like that.'

He let her stay while he examined Hazel. As Nick had said, the cut was deep, and Alison could tell the registrar wasn't happy with it. He got one of the nurses to clean it up, frowning when he took another look at it through a high-powered mag-nifying lens.

'The vein's been nicked—that's why there's so much blood. I'll have to get one of the surgical team down here because it's too fiddly for us to repair.'

Alison nodded, too busy trying to control the lump that was rapidly forming in her throat to reply. She had a horrible feeling that she knew who would respond to the call, and her heart sank as she considered how it might look. Would Jack think that she had offered to accompany Hazel so she could see him?

It was immaterial what he thought, of course. She couldn't abandon Hazel now. However, her heart started racing when she heard footsteps in the corridor. Was it anticipation or fear that made it pound so hard? she wondered. Or a bit of both? She wanted to see Jack again, and there was no point pretending otherwise, yet she knew that she was getting in way over her head. All she could hope was that her natural caution would stand her in good stead. But when the curtain swished back she knew that all the caution in the world wasn't going to protect her. Just seeing Jack again made all thoughts of being sensible fly right out of her head.

Jack was surprised when he saw Alison sitting beside the bed, but he was determined that he wasn't going to let her know how he felt. He smiled at her as he drew the curtain shut behind him.

'Been drumming up more business for us, have you?'

'It's all my fault,' Hazel said before Alison could reply. 'I'm really sorry, Jack. You have enough to do without me being so stupid.'

'There's nothing to apologise for, Hazel,' he said firmly. 'These things happen, so don't beat yourself up about it. Now, let's have a look and see what you've done.'

He took a fresh pair of gloves out of the box, nodding his thanks when Alison moved out of his way. Bending down, he carefully examined the wound on Hazel's thigh, determined to blot out everything else so he could focus on what needed to be done. He wasn't going to let the fact that he could smell the fresh apple scent of Alison's shampoo affect him. No, siree! Neither was he going to pay any heed to the fact that he could hear her breathing. And as for the fact that her face seemed to be dancing before his eyes, well, he would sort that out PDQ! He'd spent the night torturing himself for his sins and he deserved a reprieve.

Jack made himself breathe slowly, in and out, and gradually his concentration returned. On closer examination he could see that the iliac vein—the large vein in the leg which ran parallel to the femoral artery—had been nicked. It would need to be repaired by microsurgery or it would continue to bleed. Peeling off the gloves, he set about explaining it all to Hazel.

'I'm going to whiz you up to Theatre, Hazel. The vein's been nicked, and although it's not been completely severed it needs sewing up to stop it bleeding. I'll also need to put a few stitches in your leg—roughly ten should suffice, but don't hold me to that, will you?'

'Will I have to have an anaesthetic?' Hazel asked, obviously shocked by the thought of having an operation.

'Yes. You'll be given a general anaesthetic so you won't know what's going on.' He grinned at her. 'It also means you'll be spared the headache if I decide to sing.'

'Sing?' Hazel repeated blankly.

'Oh, yes. There's nothing like the acoustics in an operating theatre to bring out the performer in me.' Jack winked at her and she laughed.

'Get away with you! You always were a torment, even when you were a little boy.'

'Don't tell anyone or you'll ruin my image,' he implored her, hamming it up for all he was worth. It seemed his efforts to cheer her up had worked, however. She looked a lot more relaxed and that was what he'd been aiming for. He smiled at her again as he opened the curtain. 'I'll just go and check if there's a theatre free.'

He left the cubicle, feeling rather pleased with himself. Not only had he cheered up Hazel but he'd more or less managed to ignore Alison after that initial hiccup. If he could keep it up, he would soon be back on track.

A quick phone call soon elicited the information that Theatre two would be available in approximately twenty minutes' time. Jack booked Hazel in, then went back and explained what was happening. Once he'd arranged for a porter to take her to be prepped, he was free until he was needed in Theatre.

He decided that he had time to grab a cup of coffee so long as he was quick about it. He headed for the coffee-shop in the foyer, because it was quicker than trailing all the way to the staff canteen, and bought himself a large cappuccino complete with chocolate sprinkles on the top and a biscotti on the side.

He had just sat down to drink it when he spotted Alison coming into the café and he groaned because it left him in rather a quandary. If he ignored her, it could send out the completely wrong signals. He didn't want there to be an atmosphere whenever they ran into each other, as they were bound to do. However, neither did he want her to think that he was coming onto her after yesterday. The question now was should he or shouldn't he invite her to sit with him?

Alison would never have gone into the coffee-shop if she'd had any idea that Jack would be there. When she spotted him sitting at a table in the corner her first instinct was to leave, only it appeared he had seen her. Her heart sank when she saw him beckon to her. She really didn't want to sit with him, but neither did she want him to know how much that near kiss had affected her.

In the end pride won. There was simply no way that she was going to let him think that she was bothered by what had happened. She bought herself a cup of coffee, then crossed the room. Jack greeted her with a smile as she approached his table, but she could see the wariness in his eyes and realised that he was as jumpy as she was. Why? Did he think that she was in hot pursuit of him, perhaps?

The thought set light to her temper. Pulling out a chair, she sat down. If Jack had got it into his head that she found him irresistible, then it was time she set him straight!

'I see you had the same idea as me.'

'Really?' Alison glowered at him. 'And what idea would that be?'

'Coffee, of course.' He frowned. 'Why? What did you think I meant?'

'Nothing.' Alison felt her face suffuse with heat and hurriedly picked up her cup.

'Why do I get the feeling that I'm missing something?' Jack said softly. He leant forward so that she was forced to look at him, and she felt her heart lurch when she saw how serious he looked. 'If there's something you want to say, Alison, then tell me. I hate it when there's an atmosphere brewing.'

'Of course there isn't an atmosphere. You're imagining things.'

Jack sighed. 'No, I'm not. I can tell that you're very uptight about something. If it's what happened yesterday, then I can only apologise again. I don't want us falling out over something so stupid as that.'

Alison bit her lip. She knew that she should deny it was that nearly-kiss that was bothering her, but she couldn't bring herself to lie to him. 'It's partly that. But it's mainly the fact that I don't want you thinking that I'm…well, *chasing* you.'

'Chasing me?' He looked at her in bewilderment. 'It never crossed my mind. Why on earth did you think it would?'

'Oh, I don't know. The fact that I accompanied Hazel here this morning…' She tailed off, wishing she hadn't said anything. It was obvious that Jack had never imagined she might be interested in him. Why should he have done when he clearly wasn't interested in her, as he'd been at pains to point out? What was it he'd said yesterday? That he'd been tired after the busy night he'd had and hadn't been thinking clearly? He couldn't have made his feelings any plainer than that.

Alison pushed back her chair. She couldn't bear to sit there a second longer and know what a fool she'd been. 'I have to go. I've just remembered there's an antenatal clinic this afternoon and I need to get back to the surgery.'

She knew she was gabbling, but it was preferable to admitting that she was disappointed because Jack hadn't really wanted her. She had just fulfilled a few basic criteria—young, female, available.

Pain lanced through her as she hurried to the door. She heard Jack call her name but she ignored him. She certainly wasn't going to let Jack know how devastated she felt because he would have responded the same way to any woman.

There was a taxi dropping off a fare so she asked the driver to take her back to the surgery. And all the way there she could feel the weight of her own stupidity pressing down on her. What made it doubly painful was that she'd made the same mistake once before, thought that she was someone worth loving, someone special.

Sam's father had shown her how wrong she'd been. He had found another woman to replace her and it would be exactly the same with Jack. He might enjoy the odd kiss, but he would soon grow tired of her, as Gareth had done.

A single tear trickled down her cheek and she wiped it away. There would be no tears and no wishing that things might have been different. She would accept that she'd made a mistake and put it behind her. Jack meant nothing to her. And she most definitely meant nothing to him.

CHAPTER NINE

JACK hurried to the door, but by the time he got there Alison was getting into a cab. He could only stand and watch as it drove away. He couldn't go after her when he was due in Theatre, and anyway what could he have said? That not even for a second had he imagined that she might be interested in him?

He made his way back inside, struggling to get to grips with the idea. She'd done nothing to make him think that she was attracted to him—apart from not pushing him away when he had almost kissed her, of course.

Jack stopped dead. Up till then he had blamed himself for what had happened, but was he solely at fault? Alison could have stopped him any time she'd wanted, but it had been he who had stopped, he who had realised the dangers of what they'd been doing. If he hadn't called a halt she would have let him kiss her and probably kissed him back.

The thought hit him with all the force of a bomb exploding. When his bleeper chirruped, he couldn't think what was happening at first. He hurriedly checked the display and discovered it was Theatre, calling to tell him they were ready for him. He headed for the lift, knowing that he didn't have time to think about the situation with Alison any more right then.

But later, after he had finished work, he would need to decide what he was going to do.

The antenatal clinic was under way by the time Alison arrived back at the surgery. She popped her head round the door to let Nick know she was back and he quickly excused himself.

'How's Hazel?' he demanded, following her into the corridor.

'She needs surgery. Apparently the iliac vein had been nicked, and that's why we couldn't stop the bleeding. Jack said that he would keep her in overnight, but that she should be fine by the morning.'

'So Jack's doing the op, is he?' Nick asked.

'Yes.' Alison shrugged, desperately trying to keep a rein on her emotions. 'He responded to the call from A and E. I think Hazel was pleased he was going to do the op.'

'I'm sure she was. She's always had a soft spot for Jack. Like all the women around here,' Nick added wryly.

Alison couldn't think of anything to say. She knew it was true, and that was part of the trouble. Most women would be delighted to have Jack as their doctor, or as anything else for that matter. Fortunately, Nick didn't appear to expect a reply.

'I'd better get back. Gemma's coping extremely well, so we may as well let her carry on. You take a break now. You've earned it after all the rushing around you've done.'

'Thanks.'

Alison made her way to the staffroom and switched on the kettle. Normally she had her lunch at home, after collecting Sam from the nursery, and she didn't have anything with her to eat. She poked around in the cupboard and came up with half a packet of chocolate biscuits that had got shoved to the back. She had just made herself a cup of tea when Sue poked her head round the door.

'I'm sorry to disturb you, but Louise Appleton's in Reception. She's got Chloe with her and she wants to know if the poor little mite has chickenpox. Everyone's out on house calls except Nick, and I didn't know if I should disturb him.'

'I'll take a look at her,' Alison offered immediately.

She followed Sue back to the waiting room, smiling sympathetically when she saw Louise struggling to calm her fractious four-year-old daughter. 'Hello, Louise. I'm afraid all the doctors are out on calls at the moment, so shall I take a look at Chloe for you?'

'Please. I couldn't believe it when I saw the state of her. Her tummy is absolutely covered in spots!'

Louise looked harassed as she bounced the little girl on her knee. She was a single mother and had had Chloe while she had still been at school. Fortunately, once her parents had got over their shock, they had rallied round. With their support Louise had continued her studies after the baby had been born, and had earned herself a place at the local college where she'd studied floristry. Now she had her own shop on the outskirts of the town, and was doing extremely well, by all accounts.

Alison crouched down in front of them. 'Can I take a look at your tummy, Chloe? I promise I'll be quick.'

'No!' Chloe shrieked, pushing her hands away.

Louise apologised but Alison shook her head. 'Don't worry about it. She doesn't feel well, so it's understandable if she doesn't want people poking and prodding her. However, I think it might be better if we took her up to my room in case anyone comes in. I wouldn't like folk to think that we torture our patients in here!'

Louise laughed as she picked up her daughter and followed

Alison up the stairs. It took a lot of cajoling, but in the end Chloe agreed to be examined. Alison nodded when she saw the small red spots that covered the child's torso.

'Yes, that's chickenpox. You'll probably find that the spots appear in crops—on her tummy, behind her ears, under her arms, maybe even in her mouth. They'll turn into blisters soon, and then dry up and form scabs.'

'What should I do about them?' Louise asked anxiously. 'I don't want her to be scarred, so is there anything I can use to help them heal?'

'The main thing is to stop Chloe scratching them. That's easier said than done because they can be very itchy. You need to cut her nails and keep dabbing the spots with calamine lotion—that usually helps. And do make sure that she doesn't pick at the scabs once they form. It can set off a secondary infection, and that's what causes the worst scarring.'

'Is there anything I can give her to make her more comfortable?'

'Just junior paracetamol if she's running a temperature,' Alison advised her. 'Most kids are a bit out of sorts for a couple of days, but they're not really ill. It's far worse for adults who get chickenpox, so I hope you've had it.'

'I'm not sure. My mum will know though. She kept a record of everything me and my sister Sarah had when we were children.' Louise grinned. 'I'm sure I'll never be that organised!'

'Me neither. Anyway, see how Chloe is tomorrow, and if you're at all worried about her, phone for an appointment.'

'I shall.' Louise stood up. 'How long will it take before it goes? I have to do the flowers for a couple of weddings next week, and it's going to make it difficult if Chloe can't go to the nursery.'

'It's roughly ten days before chickenpox runs its course, I'm afraid, and you'll have to keep her off school for at least that length of time.'

Louise grimaced. 'Oh, dear. Maybe my sister can look after her if I'm stuck. Mum and Dad are going on a cruise at the weekend, and they won't be back until the middle of April.'

Alison frowned. 'Sarah's pregnant, isn't she?'

'Yes, she's just coming up to eight months. Why? Is that a problem?'

'It could be. Chickenpox can be quite dangerous to an unborn child if the mother is in the latter stages of pregnancy. Unless you're sure that Sarah has had it, I think you should keep Chloe away from her.'

'Oh, I will. What a good job you told me.' Louise picked up her daughter. 'Thanks, Alison. I really appreciate all the advice you've given me.'

'It's my pleasure.'

Alison saw them out, then went back to her tea, but it had gone cold by then. She emptied it down the drain and switched on the kettle again. Talking to Louise had given her a breathing space and helped her to get back on track after what had happened at the hospital. She felt a bit of a fool, in fact, for having run off like that, but there was no point dwelling on it. Anyway, she doubted if Jack cared one way or the other. He wasn't interested in her, and so long as she kept reminding herself of that fact, she wouldn't have a problem.

Jack went straight from Theatre to the afternoon ward round. Alex had made a start by the time he arrived, and she nodded when he explained where he'd been. They worked their way through the list until they came to Becca and Alex handed over to him.

Jack ran through the girl's case notes, so that everyone was up to speed, then knocked on the door of the side room and went in. He wasn't sure what kind of reception he would receive. Becca had been very cool with him since he'd told her how long it would take before her face healed, so it was a nice surprise when she greeted him with a cheery smile.

'Hi, Dr Tremayne. How are you today?'

'Very well, thank you, Becca.' He waved a hand towards the rest of the group. 'Is it OK if I bring the gang in to see you?'

'Of course it is!'

She seemed in remarkably high spirits as he set about examining her, and he found himself wondering what had caused such a marked improvement in her mood. 'Everything is looking great, Becca,' he told her after he'd finished. 'There's just your cheek to sort out, and I'm going to do that tomorrow morning, exactly as we discussed.'

'Great. Will you be operating on me before Ryan?' She grinned at him. 'I bet him that you'd do my op first and his second, you see.'

'Did you, now?' Jack laughed as he realised what had brought about the change in her attitude. There was nothing better than a little attention from a member of the opposite sex to cheer a person up. 'Well, I might have to think about that.' He chuckled when she groaned. 'OK. You can tell Ryan from me that you're first on my morning list.'

'Brilliant!' Becca whooped with delight and everyone laughed. They all trooped out of the room but Jack hung back.

'So what did you bet him? Something good, from the sound of it.'

'Two tickets to a concert this summer. Whoever wins gets to choose the show.' She beamed at him. 'That means I'll get to choose it now.'

'I see.'

Jack sketched her a wave and left, thinking how simple life was when you were that age. It was as you got older and took on more responsibilities that life became so complicated. That thought immediately reminded him of what had happened in the coffee-shop, and he sighed. The sensible side of him knew he should ignore it, but another side of him couldn't bear to let it go. If Alison was attracted to him then surely it was too good an opportunity to miss?

Saturday turned out to be a gloriously sunny day. Although Alison had been planning to catch up with some housework, the weather was far too nice to waste the day being stuck indoors. She decided to take Sam out for a picnic, so packed some lunch for them and set off in the car. It had been ages since she'd been to Rock, where she'd been born, and she headed in that direction.

The town was just coming back to life after the winter lull. There was quite a lot of traffic on the road, although it was nowhere near as busy as it would be once the season got under way. A lot of people had holiday homes in the town, and during July and August the place was packed. However, there were just enough people about that day to make it feel alive but not overly crowded.

Alison parked her car and headed for the harbour. Sam loved boats, and she knew he would enjoy watching the yachts. There was quite a stiff breeze blowing, and the tiny craft seemed to dance across the water, their brightly coloured sails bobbing about in the sunshine.

They sat down on the harbour wall while she unpacked a flask of coffee and a carton of squash for Sam. She helped him pierce a hole in the top of the carton with the plastic straw, then poured herself a cup of coffee, sighing in pleasure as she inhaled the fragrant aroma.

'That smells good. I don't suppose there's any to spare?'

Alison's head swivelled round and she gasped when she saw Jack standing behind her. 'What are you doing here?'

'Playing truant.' He grinned as he helped Freddie onto the wall. 'I'd made up my mind that I was going to decorate the house today. I had it all planned, too—I was going to start in the hall and work my way through all the rooms. But when I woke up and saw what a lovely day it was, I caved in. I'd *much* rather spend the day at the beach than up a ladder!'

'I know what you mean,' Alison conceded. 'I've got a stack of housework to do, but I couldn't bear to stay in when the sun was shining.'

'So you're skiving off, too? Great! It makes me feel a less guilty to know I'm not the only delinquent around here.'

He sat down beside her, his face breaking into a smile which immediately made her insides churn. He looked so handsome as he sat there with the sun bouncing sparks off his dark hair. He was dressed as casually as she was, in well-washed jeans and a navy-blue sweater over a pale blue shirt which brought out the sapphire colour of his eyes. A pair of disreputable trainers on his feet added to the picture of a man who was at ease with himself. Obviously Jack didn't feel that he had to dress up to impress. He didn't need expensive clothes to boost his ego either. He was comfortable in his own skin and it was something she admired about him.

Gareth had been very different. He'd spent a lot of time worrying about the impression he made, and the impression she made as well. He had been highly critical at times, so that she'd come to dread meeting his friends. He had continually compared her to the other women he'd met, and she had invariably come off worst, so it was little wonder her confidence had taken such a battering. However, she knew instinctively that Jack would never behave that way.

The thought was far too disturbing. Alison drove it from her mind as she reached for the flask. She topped up the cup and offered it to him.

'I'm afraid I haven't brought a spare cup with me.'

'Don't worry. I don't mind sharing.'

He lifted the cup to his mouth and her heart started to pound as she saw his lips touch the very same spot from where she had drunk a moment before. She turned away, busying herself with finding another carton of squash for Freddie. She'd made a fool of herself once before, and she didn't intend to repeat her mistakes again today.

'Here. It's your turn now.'

Jack handed her the cup and her heart started doing its yo-yo trick again. The thought of drinking from the cup after he'd used it made her feel very odd, but she could hardly refuse. She steeled herself as she raised it to her lips, wondering if it was the heat of the coffee that was making her mouth tingle this way. It was ridiculous to imagine that Jack's lips could have left an impression on the cup, although she couldn't remember experiencing such an odd sensation before.

By the time the coffee had been drunk, Alison was a bundle of nerves. Being with Jack was a strain, and there was no point pretending it wasn't. She was so aware of him that every cell in her body seemed to be humming with tension. When he stood up, she breathed a sigh of relief. He would probably thank her for the coffee and leave, no more keen to prolong this meeting than she was.

'Thanks for the coffee.'

'It was my pleasure,' she said politely, packing the flask into the picnic bag.

'Was it?' His voice was very deep all of a sudden, and her hands stilled. 'Was it really a pleasure, Alison, or are you just being polite?'

'Of course not!' She gave a tinkly little laugh that sounded false even to her ears, and Jack shook his head. Crouching down in front of her, he looked into her eyes.

'I made a complete hash of things the other day, didn't I? I upset you and, worse still, I made you feel uncomfortable around me. It was the last thing I intended to do, Alison, believe me.'

'It was my fault,' she said softly, glancing down.

'No, it wasn't.' He tipped up her chin so that she was forced to look at him. 'You told me the truth, and if anyone is at fault then it's me, not you. OK?'

She gave him a tentative smile. 'If you say so.'

'I do.' He straightened up. 'So, now that we've cleared up that misunderstanding, how about we spend the day together? It seems silly for us to go our separate ways when the boys are having such fun.'

Alison felt torn as she glanced at Sam and Freddie, who were happily playing with some of the pebbles that had been washed ashore. Although she was wary of agreeing to Jack's suggestion, she didn't want him to think that she was afraid to spend time with him. That would send out the completely wrong signals.

'Stop it.'

The quiet command made her jump, and she raised startled eyes to his face. 'What do you mean?'

'Stop worrying about what I might and might not think. I swear I don't believe that you've set your sights on me, Alison.

Cross my heart and hope to die.' He grimaced. 'After all, I'm the one who made a pass at you. It's a wonder you didn't run for the hills as soon as I showed up today!'

Alison gave a small chuckle. 'There aren't that many hills around here,' she pointed out, her tongue firmly lodged in her cheek.

Jack rolled his eyes. 'I suppose I asked for that, but give a guy a break.' He held out his hands, palms up. 'Can I help it if I find you attractive?'

'Me?' She stared at him in astonishment. 'You find *me* attractive?'

'Of course.' He frowned. 'I'd have thought that was obvious from what happened.'

'But you said that you were tired and weren't thinking clearly…' She stopped, wondering if it had been wise to quote him.

Jack's expression darkened as he crouched down in front of her.

'And you took it to mean that it wasn't really you I was interested in,' he said silkily. 'That I'd have made a pass at any woman at that precise moment, in fact?'

She nodded mutely, afraid that anything she said would be too revealing. It had hurt to know that all she'd been to him was an available female body.

He sighed heavily. 'When I mess up, I do it big time, don't I?' He didn't give her time to answer before he carried on, and Alison's breath caught when she heard the emotion in his voice. 'Well, whatever impression I gave you the other day, Alison, it wasn't true. It was you I wanted to kiss. You and nobody else. Got it?' His voice dropped, sounding so husky and deep that she shivered. 'And it's you I want to kiss right now, too.'

He leant forward, and before she knew what was happening his mouth found hers. His lips were cool from the breeze and tasted faintly of salt. They were so delicious that she moaned a little with pleasure. Closing her eyes, she allowed herself to be swept away by the magic of the kiss. She could no longer hear the flapping of the sails, the clink of the yachts' rigging, the shouts of the people. All she could hear was her own heart beating as Jack plundered her mouth, but that was enough. For the first time in ages she felt wonderfully, gloriously alive. She wasn't a nobody any more, she was someone special—the woman Jack wanted to kiss!

CHAPTER TEN

JACK could feel his heart racing as he gulped in a tiny breath of air. It felt as though he'd just had an out-of-body experience, and he couldn't believe that a kiss could have had this effect on him. He had kissed a lot of women in his time, and enjoyed kissing them too, but kissing Alison had been a revelation. Quite frankly, that kiss had been better than full-blown sex!

He groaned as he went back for a second. He knew how dangerous it was to repeat the process, but he couldn't help himself. One kiss wasn't enough. He needed another, and knew he would need another after that. In fact, it would be easier if he started claiming these kisses in dozens. One dozen now, two dozen later, and so on and so forth. Even then he might never have his fill.

His lips closed over Alison's again and he sighed. Her lips were so soft and so smooth that it was sheer heaven to kiss her. She wasn't wearing any lipstick again that day, and he realised with a shiver of delight just how delicious the natural sweetness of a woman's mouth could be. His tongue flicked out as he tasted the delicate curve of her Cupid's bow, the fullness of her lower lip. When her mouth opened and gave him access to its inner sweetness, he groaned. Maybe he should start claiming these kisses in hundreds rather than mere dozens!

'Mummy, why are you kissing Jack?'

The shrill little voice burst the bubble of euphoria that had enclosed him. Jack drew back abruptly, his face flooding with heat when he found both Sam and Freddie watching them with undisguised interest. He had no idea how long the children had been standing there, but it was too long in his view. They were far too young to witness something like this.

'I...um...Jack and I are friends, darling. And sometimes friends like to kiss each other.'

Alison sounded breathless, but Jack didn't dare look at her to check. He needed to be sure that he had his emotions firmly under control before he took such a risk.

'Oh.' Sam looked at Freddie, then suddenly looped his arm around the other child's neck and planted a noisy kiss on his cheek. 'Freddie and I are friends, so that means I can kiss him, too, doesn't it?'

'I...er...well, yes, I suppose it does,' Alison said weakly.

Jack couldn't stop himself chuckling as the two boys happily went back to their game. 'Life is all black and white at their age, isn't it? There's no grey bits.'

'No.' She turned to him, her pretty face awash with colour. 'I think I've just made the situation even more confusing for them, though. Sorry. I didn't mean to mislead Freddie that way.'

'There's nothing to apologise for.' He took her hand and raised it to his lips, feeling her shudder in response as he pressed his mouth to the centre of her palm. It was an effort to stop there and not let his lips trail up the length of her arm. 'It was a great explanation. I certainly couldn't have come up with anything as good if I'd been put on the spot like that.'

'It wasn't true, though, was it?' she said, and he could tell that she felt guilty about misleading the children.

'It wasn't a lie either,' he said firmly, squeezing her hand. 'We are friends, aren't we, Alison?'

'Yes, of course we are.'

She gave him a tight smile as she freed her hand, and Jack could have kicked himself. He'd made it sound as though being her friend was all he was interested in, and it wasn't true. He wanted to be more than just a friend to her, a lot more. A *whole* lot more.

The strength of his feelings stunned him. He knew that he shouldn't be contemplating starting a relationship at the moment. Helping Freddie recover from the trauma he'd suffered was a full-time job, and he didn't have the time right now to spare for anyone else. It wouldn't be fair to expect Alison to hang around until he was able to devote some time to her, although there was no point pretending that he would find it easy to let her go either. In the short time that he'd known her she had come to mean a lot to him, and the thought of not being able to be with her was something he didn't want to contemplate.

He sighed. It might turn out that it would have to be friend-ship or nothing, and he knew what he would choose if it came down to it. But how would Alison feel about such an arrange-ment after those kisses they'd shared? Would she be happy to be his friend now that he had overstepped the boundaries of friendship? The thought that he might lose her because of his own stupidity was very hard to bear.

Alison picked up the empty squash cartons and sandwich wrappings and took them over to the bin. Jack and Freddie had shared their picnic, and now Jack was helping the boys to build a fort. At least it had helped to take the edge off the tension, although she still hadn't fully regained her composure.

She sighed as she stared across the harbour. She should never have let Jack kiss her. All it had done had been to confuse the issue even more. There was no point pretending that she hadn't enjoyed the experience, though, when it had been a revelation to her.

She'd had little experience when she'd married Gareth, and she had blamed herself when their sexlife had turned out to be less than satisfactory. It had never occurred to her that it might have been her ex-husband's fault, but after what had happened just now she might have to reconsider. She had felt more during those few minutes while Jack had been kissing her than she'd felt the entire time she'd been married, and the thought shocked her. Surely she couldn't be falling in love with Jack?

The idea filled her with panic as she made her way back. She knew that she needed to get away from Jack and stay away from him, too. It was the only way that she would put an end to all these stupid ideas she kept having.

Jack glanced up when he heard her footsteps, and her heart sank when she saw the wariness in his eyes. Was he having second thoughts, too, wondering how he could ease himself out of a situation that wasn't to his liking? Maybe he had enjoyed kissing her, but the last thing Jack wanted was commitment. The thought spurred her on.

'I'm afraid I'm going to have to break up the party.' She smiled at the boys, avoiding looking in Jack's direction in case she weakened. She knew what she had to do and she mustn't allow herself to be sidetracked. Anyway, if Jack wanted a proper relationship with a woman, he would chose someone glamorous like Freddie's mother, not a dull little country mouse like her.

'It's time we went home, so say goodbye to Freddie, Sam. There's a good boy.'

Sam reluctantly obeyed, dragging his heels as he made his way over to her. It was obvious that he didn't want the day to end so soon, and she couldn't help feeling guilty about spoiling his fun. Just because she had problems keeping control of her emotions, it shouldn't mean that her son had to suffer.

'It's time we were going as well.' Jack stood up and rubbed his hands down his jeans to wipe away the sand. 'If I don't make a start on that decorating it will never get done. Come along, tiger, I'll give you a piggy-back.'

He lifted Freddie onto the wall, then bent down so the little boy could scramble onto his back. Once Freddie was safely settled, he turned to Alison. 'It's been really great today. Thanks for sharing your lunch with us. Next time I'll bring the picnic. OK?'

It was on the tip of her tongue to tell him there wouldn't be a next time, but she managed to hold back. Jack was only being polite; he wasn't seriously planning they should meet up again. If the truth be told, he was probably as keen as she was to avoid any complications.

They left the harbour and walked back through the town together. Jack stopped when they reached her car, his eyes very blue as he stared down at her. 'I enjoyed today, Alison. I hope you did too, and that what happened hasn't upset you.'

She gave a little shrug, and his jaw tightened. 'If I've made you feel at all uncomfortable, I can only apologise. Again!'

'You haven't…well, not really,' she amended honestly. She took a quick breath, then rushed on before her courage deserted her. 'I think it might be best if we steered clear of one another, though, don't you, Jack? Neither of us is in the market for a relationship, and I don't do affairs. I don't think I'm genetically programmed for them,' she added, to lighten the mood.

'I understand, and I think you're right, too. At the moment

I need to concentrate on Freddie. I simply don't have the time to spare for anything else.' He bent and kissed her softly on the cheek. 'I suggest we stick to being friends, if that's all right with you.'

'That's fine,' she said quickly, very much afraid that she was going to cry.

She unlocked her car and helped Sam climb into his seat. Jack gave her a crooked grin as he opened the driver's door for her to get in.

'Drive carefully. There's quite a bit of traffic on the road today, and a lot of these drivers aren't used to our narrow country lanes.'

'I'll take my time going back,' she assured him, starting the engine.

He slammed the door, then waved her out of the parking space after he'd checked for any oncoming traffic. Alison glanced in the rear-view mirror as she drove away and felt a lump come to her throat when she saw him walk over to his car. Even though he had Freddie with him, he looked so alone that it touched her heart.

In any other circumstance, she would have gone back and told him that she'd changed her mind about them avoiding each other. Jack needed all the help he could get, and she would have been more than happy to try and lighten his load. However, it was too risky to involve herself in his affairs. If she allowed Jack to become a part of her life, she would find it impossible to let him go. She couldn't bear to think that at some point her heart might get broken again.

The next week passed in a trice. Jack was so busy both in and out of work that he never seemed to have a minute to himself. He didn't complain, though, because it meant he had less time to brood about what had gone on between him and Alison.

Although he respected the decision she'd made, he couldn't pretend that he didn't miss her, especially when he dropped Freddie off at nursery each morning and she wasn't there. She'd obviously changed her routine to avoid bumping into him, and he missed their brief exchanges more than he would have believed. Several times he thought about phoning her to check that she was all right, but each time he stopped himself. As she had explained, she didn't do affairs, and he wasn't in a position to offer her anything else. It was easier for both of them if they kept their distance.

Thankfully, his working life was turning out to be a lot less stressful. Hazel had been sent home the day after her accident, but only after she had promised to rest her leg. Becca's skin graft had taken beautifully, and Jack was more than satisfied with the results. So long as there were no hitches, she would be discharged at the end of the week.

Ryan Lovelace's arm had been far more complicated, however. The muscle damage had been more extensive than Jack had hoped. Extra tissue had needed to be removed, and that had made the reconstruction process even more difficult. Ryan had been quite stoical when Jack had explained that he might never regain full movement in his arm. The boy had also accepted without a murmur that he would need intensive physiotherapy for some time to come.

Jack was so impressed by his attitude that he was more determined than ever to do everything he could for him. He contacted a former colleague in London who had a particular interest in that type of injury and arranged for Ryan to see him the following week. If there was someone better versed in this area he was willing to admit it, if it meant the boy had the best chance possible of making a good recovery. And if he worked hard, and learned all he could, one day other surgeons would refer patients to *him*.

He went into work on Friday morning and made straight for the staffroom. Freddie had had a particularly bad night and it had taken ages to settle him down. Jack felt decidedly jaded, and a shot of coffee would be a welcome pick-me-up. He filled a mug, shuddering as the caffeine hit his system. Lilian, their SHO, happened to be passing, and she grinned when she heard him groan.

'It sounds as though you needed that!'

'I did. In fact, I could do with it served intravenously—it would hit the spot even quicker that way,' Jack replied, gulping down a second mouthful.

'Heavy night, was it?' Parkash said with a wink as he reached for the pot.

'Yes, but not in the way you imagine.' Jack leant against the edge of the table so he would be on hand to top up his cup. 'It wasn't wine, women and song that kept me up into the wee small hours, but one very unhappy little boy. Freddie had a really bad night and kept waking up all the time.'

Lilian grimaced. 'I don't know how people cope when they have kids. This job is stressful enough without having to factor in a family and all the problems that entails. I certainly couldn't do it.'

Jack shrugged. 'I felt much the same way. Kids definitely weren't on my agenda, so it was a bit of a shock when I found out I was a dad.'

'It must have been awful for you,' Lilian sympathised. 'Didn't you ever think of refusing to take on the responsibility for Freddie?'

'No way. The poor kid had been through enough without

having his father abandon him as well. I couldn't have lived with myself if I'd done that,' Jack said truthfully.

'Then you must be a better person than me,' Lilian said wryly.

She let the subject drop, but the conversation stayed with Jack throughout the morning. It had never occurred to him not to take charge of Freddie. From the moment he had learned that he had a son, he'd known that he'd wanted to do everything possible to protect him.

Had Nick felt that way when he'd become a dad? he wondered suddenly. And was that why he had always seemed so demanding?

It was the first time that Jack had considered the idea, yet it seemed to fit. Nick wanted the best for his children and that was why he had been so hard on him, Lucy and Ed while they'd been growing up. It had been less a desire to rule their lives, as Jack had assumed, than a deep-seated desire to protect them from harm.

It was a revelation to see the situation through Nick's eyes. He could understand now why Nick had hounded him about his lifestyle when he'd moved to London. His father must have thought that he had been going completely off the rails when he'd read all that stuff in the press, and he, being stubborn, had done nothing to correct that impression.

He realised that he needed to speak to his father and resolve some of the issues that had sprung up over the years. It was Annabel's christening on Sunday, and that would be the perfect opportunity. It was time he made his peace with his father so they could both move on.

The decision seemed to lift his mood. Jack whizzed through the rest of the morning. He stopped for lunch, then did a stint in Theatre. It was quite a complicated case to repair damage caused when a skin cancer had been removed from an elderly woman's face. Effectively, it involved him giving the woman a face lift to avoid her face looking asymmetrical. When he had explained it to her, she'd been delighted at the thought of ending up looking several years younger.

As he worked away, Jack found himself smiling at the thought that something good had come out of a potential tragedy. It filled him with a renewed hope that he could do the same for Freddie—turn his son's life around and make him happy. If he could do that, he would feel that he had achieved something truly worthwhile.

His heart gave a sudden flip, because after that he could think about himself and what he needed. Maybe, just maybe, he wouldn't have to stay away from Alison for very long.

CHAPTER ELEVEN

ALISON studied herself in the mirror. It was Sunday morning, the day of Annabel's christening. She had got Sam ready first and left him watching a DVD, with strict instructions not to get himself dirty. Although she didn't usually spend a lot of time on her appearance, she'd wanted to make a special effort that day because Jack would be there.

She sighed. She knew how foolish it was to want to impress him. Leaving aside the fact that she'd decided to keep her distance from him, she had little hope of competing with the women he had known in the past. They certainly wouldn't have been wearing a dress that had been bought three years ago in a sale, neither would they have washed and dried their own hair. They probably had minions whose only purpose in life was to help them dazzle everyone when they went out!

She swung round, impatient with herself for behaving in such a ridiculous fashion. She was a grown woman and she should be past the age where she felt the need to impress people. As long as she looked presentable, that was the main thing.

She collected Sam and set off on foot for the church, because her car was at the garage, being serviced. Lucy had told her the christening would be held after the morning service finished, and she had timed her arrival to coincide with that. There were a lot of people milling about when she got there, so she led Sam to a quiet spot to wait for the rest of the party. Lucy and Ben arrived first with baby Annabel. They had Ben's cousin with them as she was one of the godmothers. Alison admired Annabel's christening robe, a gorgeous confection of cotton lawn and hand-made lace which, Lucy explained, had been handed down through the family.

Nick arrived next with Kate Althorp, the other godmother, hard on his heels. Kate had her son Jeremiah with her, and he immediately came over to play with Sam. There was no sign of Jack, and Alison felt her tension rising as she waited for him to appear. He was Annabel's godfather, and she couldn't imagine that he wouldn't show up. However, as the minutes ticked past, she could feel herself growing increasingly anxious. What if something had happened to him or Freddie?

The churchwarden had just asked everyone to move inside the church when he arrived. He looked grim as he hurried up the path with Freddie in his arms.

'Sorry I'm late,' he apologised, kissing Lucy on the cheek. 'We had a minor crisis and that held me up.'

'You got here and that's the main thing,' Lucy said cheerfully. She went to kiss Freddie, but the little boy immediately started screaming and she backed away.

'Sorry.' Jack apologised, his face looking very strained as he tried to quieten his son. 'He's really out of sorts today. Heaven knows what he'll be like when we go into the church. He'll probably scream the place down.'

Alison could hear the worry in his voice and knew that she had to do something to help. Leading Sam forward, she smiled at Freddie.

'Hi, Freddie. Would you like to play with Sam while your daddy helps Auntie Lucy?' She opened her bag and took out a couple of Sam's toy cars. 'You and Sam can play races with these cars if you want to.'

Freddie immediately stopped crying. The idea obviously met with his approval because he started struggling to be put down. Jack smiled at her as he placed him on his feet, and she felt something warm rush through her when she saw the gratitude in his eyes.

'Thank you so much. I've been tearing my hair out, imagining what was going to happen during the service. Are you sure you don't mind, though? It doesn't seem fair that you should be stuck outside.'

'Of course I don't mind.' She returned his smile, hoping he couldn't tell how glad she was to see him. Although it had been only a week since she'd seen him, she had missed him terribly. 'You go and do your bit. Freddie will be quite safe with me.'

'I know he will.'

Stepping forward, he dropped a kiss on her cheek, then hurried after Lucy. Alison took a deep breath when she felt ripples of heat start to spread throughout her body. It was just a token kiss stemming from gratitude, she told herself sternly. It certainly wasn't anything to get excited about.

Fortunately Sam demanded her attention at that point. He was thrilled to bits when he discovered that he wouldn't have to sit quietly in a pew. He and Freddie knelt down on the path and began a noisy game of chase with the toy cars. Alison smiled as she watched them. Although Freddie never said anything, he and Sam seemed able to communicate perfectly well.

An hour later everyone began to troop back out of the church. Ben and Lucy were having a christening party at their house, and most of the guests headed off in that direction. The church was almost empty when Jack came rushing outside, full of apologies.

'Sorry, sorry! Lucy wanted us to have our photos taken while we were all together.'

'It's fine, don't worry,' Alison assured him. 'Freddie's been fine. He hasn't cried once, in fact.'

'It must be your magic touch.' Jack sounded weary as he looked at his son. 'I've no idea what upset him today. I was upstairs getting ready when I heard him screaming, and he was inconsolable by the time I got to him. I honestly thought I'd have to phone Lucy and tell her I couldn't make it.'

'I wonder what upset him,' Alison said, frowning. 'What was he doing at the time?'

'Watching a film on the DVD player.' He shrugged. 'It was just a cartoon I bought on my way home from work on Friday. I can't see it was that which upset him.'

'Unless he'd seen it before and associated it with his mother,' she suggested, and Jack frowned.

'I never thought about that, although I know there were a stack of DVDs in the house when India died.' When he saw her surprise he elaborated. 'Her solicitor gave me an inventory of India's belongings after her house was cleared, and I remember noticing there were hundreds of DVDs on it. Everything was left to Freddie, so I had most of it put into storage. I didn't see the point of keeping things like DVDs, though, so I told the solicitor to give them to charity. Maybe I should have gone through them first.'

'You can't cover everything, Jack. Things are bound to crop up that remind Freddie of the past. You can't blame yourself because you don't know about them.'

'I suppose not.'

'There's no suppose about it. You're doing a wonderful job under very difficult circumstances and you have to remember that.'

'Yes, miss,' he replied with a grin.

Alison grimaced. 'Sorry. I didn't mean to sound so bossy.'

'Oh, I don't mind. I'm just glad that you've come up with such a sensible explanation for what happened. It stops me wondering what I've done wrong.'

'You've done nothing wrong. You're doing everything you can for Freddie.'

'Thank you.' Reaching out, he squeezed her hand. 'I really appreciate you saying that.'

'It's no more than the truth.'

Alison moved away when she felt a shimmer of heat ripple through her again. She couldn't believe how sensitive she was around him. Every time Jack touched her she reacted, and it was unsettling to know the effect he had on her. She gathered up the toy cars, then shooed the boys towards the lych gate. Jack paused under the thatched roof that covered the gateway.

'Do you need a lift to Lucy's? I can't see your car anywhere about.'

'It's at the garage, being serviced,' she admitted reluctantly, because she wasn't sure if it would be wise to accept his offer.

'I know we agreed to keep our distance, Alison, but it's only a lift,' he pointed out.

'I know,' she said quietly.

'But?'

'But one thing can lead to another if we're not careful.'

'Then we shall be extremely careful. Cross my heart and hope to die,' he added, making a cross over his heart.

She chuckled. 'That's going a bit far, don't you think?'

'Not if it puts your mind at rest.' He smiled at her. 'I've missed you this past week. Dropping Freddie off at nursery isn't nearly as much fun when you're not there to chat to.'

'Oh, get away with you,' she chided, inwardly delighted by the comment, although it was the last thing she should have been.

Fortunately, Jack let it drop as he escorted her and Sam to his car. They got the boys settled and drove the short distance to Tregorran House, where Lucy and Ben lived. The rest of the party had beaten them to it, so they decided to park in the lane to save blocking anyone in. Alison gasped as she got out of the car.

'I'd forgotten how gorgeous this place is. Just look at that view. It's stunning whichever way you look.'

She turned and drank it all in. The house had been built close to the cliff top and the view across the sea from the front garden was breathtaking. It had been a working farm originally, and the house was surrounded by fields. She could see cattle grazing in one of the fields close by—big Guernsey cows with red and white coats that gleamed in the sunshine. In another field the first spring lambs were frolicking around their mothers on spindly little legs.

'I wish I could afford a house like this,' she said wistfully. 'It's the perfect place to raise a child, isn't it?'

'It is.'

Alison frowned when she heard the roughness in Jack's voice. 'You're not still fretting about Freddie, are you? He's fine, Jack. Honestly, he is.' She laid her hand on his arm, wanting in some small way to offer him her support. She couldn't bear to think that he was worrying himself to death when there was no need.

'I'm sure you're right. Ignore me. I'm just a worry-wart.'

He gave her a quick smile before he moved away. Alison sighed softly, wondering if she'd overstepped the mark. It really wasn't her place to keep on offering him advice, was it?

She helped Sam out of the car and took him inside. They used the back door, which led straight into the kitchen. Lucy welcomed them with glasses of champagne for the adults and fruit juice for the children. Alison thanked her, then went through to the sitting room, where most of the guests had congregated close to the buffet table. She let Sam choose what he wanted to eat and got him settled on a stool in the corner out of everyone's way, then went back to fill a plate for herself.

Jack was talking to his father and a strikingly attractive auburn-haired woman whom Alison had never seen before. It was obvious from their body language that she and Jack knew one another, and Alison couldn't help wondering who she was. An old flame of Jack's perhaps? Or a new conquest?

She took a sip of her champagne, but it tasted as flat as tap water all of a sudden. Jack had claimed that he wasn't in the market for a relationship last weekend, but maybe he hadn't been entirely truthful. He might not be interested in having a relationship with *her*, but he didn't appear to have any such reservations when it came to other women.

Pain lanced through her as she turned so that she couldn't see them. She had been right to steer clear of Jack. He was nothing but trouble.

Jack could barely contain his relief when he spotted Alex Ross talking to his father. He desperately needed to get back on track after what had happened outside, and he couldn't think of a better way of doing it than by talking to Alex and Nick. Did Alison have any idea what she did to him? he wondered as he led Freddie across the room. He sincerely hoped not. If she had even the faintest inkling of what he'd been thinking just now, she probably wouldn't speak to him again!

Jack's teeth snapped together when he felt desire surge

through him once more. The sight of Alison standing in the sunlight with her blonde hair blowing gently in the breeze was one he was going to have the devil of a job to shift. What made it all the more scary was that she hadn't been trying to seduce him. She'd simply been admiring the view, oblivious to the fact that he'd been admiring *her*. It was her total lack of artifice that affected him so much. While other women he'd met had capitalised on their looks, she seemed genuinely unaware of her own beauty.

'Jack! I had no idea you were going to be here today until I saw you in church. Why didn't you tell me that you and Ben are related by marriage?'

Jack drummed up a smile as Alex greeted him in her usual forthright manner. 'It never cropped up.' He nodded to Nick. 'It was a lovely service, wasn't it, Dad?'

'It was,' Nick agreed, smiling at Freddie. 'And how are you today, Freddie? Have you been a good boy?'

Jack was amazed when Freddie nodded, and even more amazed when his father delved into his pocket and came up with a bag of chocolate buttons. He shook his head when his son eagerly accepted them. 'I never thought I'd see the day when you handed out sweets. It was Mum who always gave us any treats.'

Nick shrugged. 'It's a granddad's privilege to spoil his grandchildren.'

'Really?' Jack laughed. 'I'd better warn Lucy to be on the lookout for such subversive behaviour when Annabel gets a bit older.'

Alex smiled. 'I think it's lovely that you all live so close to each other. It must be a huge relief to you especially, Jack, having your family around to help you with Freddie.'

'It is. It's the reason I came back to Penhally Bay. Knowing that I could ask Lucy for help if I came unstuck was a big incentive.'

'And not just Lucy,' Alex said, glancing pointedly at Nick.

'No, of course not.' Jack took a deep breath, knowing this was the moment he'd been working up to. 'Having Dad around is a great help as well. I really value his support.'

Nick didn't say anything, so Jack couldn't tell how he felt about the comment. He was glad that he'd made it, though, because it was time he tried to build some bridges between them. The conversation moved on to more general topics after that, and Jack was surprised when Alex told them that she had been looking at sites to build a new clinic in the area. It appeared that she had been approached by a consortium that was keen to break into the lucrative cosmetic surgery market, and Rock had been chosen as a possible location.

Nick shook his head. 'It's not private health care we need here, but more investment in local services. St Piran Hospital struggles to balance its books year after year and it needs extra funding.'

'I'm sure that's true,' Alex said calmly. 'However, it's a completely separate issue. The clinic would offer a range of services not available on the NHS.'

'Tummy tucks and breast enlargements, you mean?' Nick said scornfully.

'Along with a host of other treatments, yes.' Alex shrugged. 'There's a huge demand nowadays because people want to look their best.'

'Even though they're placing themselves at risk by undergoing what is effectively major surgery.'

Jack could tell that his father was growing increasingly irate and hurriedly stepped in. 'So long as people are made aware of the risks, they can make an informed decision.'

'So you're in favour of this clinic, are you?' Nick snapped.

'I'm not against it. It's a question of personal choice, in my view,' Jack said.

'And no doubt you'll be happy to work in the place if it does get off the ground.' Nick smiled tightly. 'Why am I not surprised? It's only what I would have expected.'

Jack could feel his temper soar, but he didn't retaliate. 'You might not know me as well as you think, Dad. Now, if you'll both excuse me, I'll get Freddie something to eat.'

He led Freddie away, wondering why he had bothered to try to make his peace with his father when Nick seemed determined to think the worst of him. Lucy caught up with him at the buffet and shook her head.

'Don't tell me that you and Dad have had another argument.'

'I didn't argue. There's no point. Dad thinks he knows everything about me so why should I bother trying to change his mind?'

'He misses Mum and that's why he's so testy,' Lucy said softly.

'We *all* miss Mum, but we have to try and carry on as she would expect us to do,' Jack said shortly.

'I know that, but it's different for Dad. He's lost the woman he loved and expected to spend his life with.' Lucy glanced over at Ben, who was holding baby Annabel, and shivered. 'I can't imagine how awful it would be if anything happened to Ben. I don't even want to try.'

'Nothing is going to happen to Ben,' Jack said firmly, giving her a hug. The last thing he wanted to do was to spoil this special day for her. 'Anyway, if you nag Ben as much as you nag me then he will make sure he takes good care of himself just to stop you giving him earache!'

'Pig!'

She playfully punched him on the shoulder, then went to reclaim her daughter. Jack helped Freddie to some mini-sausages, relieved that Lucy's day hadn't been ruined by his remarks. He glanced up when someone jogged his elbow and found himself staring straight into Alison's eyes, and all of a sudden he understood exactly how Lucy felt. He didn't know what he would do if anything happened to Alison. He couldn't bear to think about it either.

His heart began to race as the full impact of that thought hit him. It might not be the right time for him or for Alison but it was happening anyway. He was falling in love with her and there wasn't a thing he could do about it.

CHAPTER TWELVE

THE party broke up just before five o'clock. Alison found Sam, who was playing in the kitchen with Freddie, and explained that it was time to go home. Both boys accompanied her as she went to say goodbye to Lucy and Ben.

'Thank you so much for inviting us. It's been really lovely.'

'It's you who deserves the thanks,' Lucy replied, giving her a hug. 'I'm really grateful to you for stepping in like that and taking charge of Freddie.'

'It was nothing,' Alison assured her. She ran a gentle hand over Freddie's dark curls, unaware how revealing her expression was. 'Jack needs all the help he can get at the moment, doesn't he?'

'He certainly does,' Lucy replied, nudging Ben in the ribs. 'Go and find Jack, darling. I'm sure he'd like to say goodbye to Alison.'

'Oh, um, right you are,' Ben agreed, giving Lucy a funny look as he hurried away.

'There's really no need to bother Jack,' Alison said quickly.

'Rubbish!' Lucy said robustly. 'If I know my brother, he'll be most upset if I let you leave without saying goodbye. Aha, here he is now. See, I was right.'

'I…um…yes.' Alison said softly, wishing the floor would

open up and swallow her. Jack could have spent any amount of time with her that afternoon if he'd wanted to. The fact that he'd made a point of avoiding her after she'd bumped into him at the buffet table merely proved he hadn't been interested. She was mortified to think that he might believe she was responsible for Ben dragging him away from his friends.

'Lucy insisted I should say goodbye to you,' she said quickly.

'And quite right, too.' Jack treated her to one of his most dazzling smiles. It left her feeling cold, because there wasn't a scrap of genuine emotion in it.

'Thank you again for looking after Freddie,' he continued, unaware that her heart was aching so hard she could hardly stand the pain. There was no sign of the warmth she'd seen in his eyes earlier in the day and she couldn't help wondering what had changed. Was it the fact that there was someone else he wanted to charm more than her?

As though on cue, the woman Jack had been speaking to earlier suddenly appeared. She came over to them, holding out her hand as she smiled at Lucy. 'Thank you so much for inviting me join you on such a special day.'

'Thank you for coming,' Lucy replied politely. She turned to Alison. 'Did you two get a chance to meet? There were so many people here that I didn't get round to making all the introductions. Alison, this is Alex Ross—Jack's new boss, for her sins!'

Everyone laughed. Alison did her best to join in, even though the situation seemed to be going from bad to worse. She'd had no idea the woman was Jack's boss, and the thought of them working together on a daily basis was very difficult to handle. Putting out her hand, she forced herself to smile at Alex Ross.

'It's nice to meet you. I'm Alison Myers, one of the practice nurses.'

'Delighted to meet you, Alison.'

Alex shook her hand, then said her goodbyes and left, pausing on the way out to have a final word with Jack. Alison could feel her insides churning as she watched them. What were they discussing? she wondered. The welfare of one of their patients, or when they would meet again?

Jealousy clawed at her insides, and she caught hold of Sam's hand and quickly led him out of the door. It was only when she realised that Freddie had followed them that she stopped. Crouching down, she gave the little boy a hug.

'Sam and I have to go home now, sweetheart. You must stay here with your daddy.'

Freddie's lower lip wobbled as he clutched hold of her coat sleeve, and she sighed. She didn't want to upset him, but she desperately wanted to go home.

'You seem to have made a big impression on him.'

She looked up when Jack came hurrying over to them, and saw the smile that still lingered around his mouth. It was a world away from the one he had treated her to, and the thought that Alex Ross had been the recipient of it stung.

'I don't know about that,' she said crisply, standing up. 'However, I'm afraid Sam and I really have to go now.'

'I'll give you a lift,' Jack said immediately. He swept Freddie into his arms, not giving her time to explain that she didn't want a lift as he turned to his sister and brother-in-law. 'It's been really great today. Freddie and I have both enjoyed it—haven't we, Freddie?'

'We've enjoyed having you here,' Lucy said, kissing her nephew on the cheek.

Alison didn't utter a word as they set off down the drive. Jack had just ridden roughshod over her wishes as though he didn't give a damn how she felt. She could feel anger bubbling inside her by the time they reached his car. She strapped Sam in, then opened the passenger door and climbed inside, still without uttering a word. Jack got in beside her, one dark brow rising as he caught sight of her thunderous expression.

'What's wrong?'

'You know what's wrong,' she retorted, dragging her seat belt across her. She ground her teeth when the mechanism locked before she could fasten it. No amount of pulling would release it either. When Jack leant over and took the buckle from her hands and fastened it in place, she could have screamed.

He didn't say a word as he started the engine and his silence was the most effective cure for her fit of pique. Alison felt so ashamed of herself that she could have wept. What on earth was she thinking about by behaving that way? It was hardly a good example for the children, was it?

By the time they reached her house, she felt so wretched that all she wanted to do was run inside and hide. She climbed out of the car, shaking her head when Jack went to get out as well.

'You stay there. I can manage.'

She lifted Sam out of the back, said goodbye to Freddie, then shut the door. Jack zoomed down the window and leant across the passenger seat.

'If I've done something to upset you, Alison, I'm sorry.'

'You haven't.'

One last strained smile and she was free to go. She didn't glance back as she ushered Sam up the path and into the house. She took off his coat and gave him a drink of milk, determined that she wasn't going to fall apart in front of him. However, when he went into the sitting room to play with his toys, she couldn't hold on any longer.

She sank down on a chair as tears filled her eyes. She wasn't used to feeling like this. She had never been jealous when she'd been married to Gareth. Not even when she had found out that he'd been having an affair. Oh, she'd been hurt and angry, but it had been nothing compared to how she'd felt when she'd seen Jack and Alex together. Was this what true love felt like? The sort of love she'd read about in books? She had no idea, but the thought scared her. She didn't want to fall in love with Jack if she ended up getting hurt.

Jack couldn't settle. He kept thinking about what had happened when he had dropped Alison off at her house. He knew that she'd been angry and upset but he had no idea why. He paced the sitting-room floor after Freddie had gone to bed, trying to work out what he had done, but it was impossible to make sense of it. All he knew was that he wouldn't be able to rest until he had sorted everything out.

He went out to the hall and picked up the phone, then paused. Bearing in mind what had happened at the christening party, was it right to ask his father to babysit for him? However, if he didn't ask Nick then he might never get the chance to clear up this misunderstanding. He groaned. Talk about being caught on the horns of a dilemma! Either he phoned his father and risked a rebuff, or he risked never resolving this issue with Alison. Both prospects were highly unappealing, but he knew which one was worse.

It took a half dozen rings before Nick answered the phone, and Jack had reached desperation point by then, so he didn't waste any time on non-essentials. 'Dad, it's me. Look, I hate to ask you after the way we parted earlier on today, but I desperately need a favour. Will you babysit for me?'

Half an hour later he was on his way to Alison's house. Nick had agreed immediately to look after Freddie for him and, even more surprisingly, he hadn't asked Jack where he was going either. Jack wasn't sure what he would have said if his father had questioned him. He couldn't have lied to him, neither could he have told him the truth. All he could do was thank his stars that for once Nick had given him the benefit of the doubt. He grimaced as he pulled up outside Alison's house. He had a feeling that he was going to need every scrap of luck he could get if he hoped to persuade her to open up to him.

He walked up the path, then took a deep breath before he knocked on the front door. The first few seconds were crucial if he hoped to persuade her to let him in. He needed to strike the right note—calm and friendly, not too pushy, and definitely not desperate. He hurriedly pinned a smile to his face when the door opened.

'Hi! I thought I'd pop round and see how you were.'

'I'm fine,' she said shortly. 'Why shouldn't I be?'

'Oh, no reason. You just appeared a bit uptight when I dropped you off before.'

Her brows rose. 'Uptight? Whatever gave you that idea?'

'It was just a feeling I had…' He tailed off, very much afraid that he had blown it. He hadn't even got inside the house and already he was floundering.

'A feeling? I see. Well, I can assure you that you were mistaken. I was fine then and I'm fine now, thank you, Jack.'

'That's all right, then.' He dredged up another smile, although the brightness had faded from this one. He'd been a fool to come, and a double fool to imagine that Alison cared a jot about him. He swung round, not wanting her to know how stupid he felt. 'I'm sorry I bothered you.'

'Jack, wait. Don't go.'

He'd got to the end of the path before she spoke, and even then he wasn't sure if he'd actually heard her. He paused, undecided whether he should turn round and check.

If it was his imagination playing tricks, he'd look even more foolish…

And if it wasn't, he would have lost his one and only chance to sort this out with her.

He swung round and felt his heart start to race when he saw the torment on her face. It took him just a couple of strides to reach the door, but it felt as though he'd travelled to the moon and back by the time he got there. Alison stared at him for a moment and he could tell that she was trying to decide what to do. He could barely contain his delight when she stepped back.

'You'd better come in.'

Jack followed her inside and made it safely along the hall, even though his legs felt as though they were filled with jelly. She stopped in the middle of the sitting room and turned to him, and he could see the fear in her eyes. He knew that if he'd been stronger he would have turned around and left, only he wasn't strong enough to leave her now.

One step brought him within touching distance, so he touched her—just one finger skimming across the back of her wrist. Their skin made the minimal amount of contact, yet he sucked in his breath when he felt a heat so intense he could barely stand it sear his veins.

Another step took him closer still, close enough to feel the heat that was emanating from her in waves, and he shuddered, unable to pretend that it didn't affect him in any way. She stared back at him with bewilderment on her face.

'I never knew it could feel like this.'

'Neither did I,' he ground out as he took the final step, the one that brought his body up hard against hers. Flames licked along his fingers as they closed around her arms, scorched his chest as he drew her to him and held her so that he could feel her heart beating wildly against him. When he bent his head and pressed his mouth to the hollow of her throat, he was completely consumed by the fire.

'Jack…'

Her voice was the softest whisper as she murmured his name, but it fanned the flames of his desire. He kissed her again, then let his tongue trace the delicate hollow between her neck and her collar-bone, taste the softness of her flesh, and groaned. Kissing her aroused so many emotions inside him, ones he had never experienced in his entire life.

He raised his head and looked deep into her eyes, knowing that she would see how much he wanted her. He refused to pretend that his need was less than it was, even if it was too much for her to accept. He wanted her in every way a man could want a woman, and she needed to understand that.

Colour bloomed in her face, rushed down her throat, and she trembled, but she didn't look away. She met his gaze proudly, almost defiantly, and Jack could have wept because he understood how much it must have cost her.

Pulling her back into his arms, he rained kisses on her hair, her forehead, the delicate slope of her nose. By the time he reached her mouth they were both trembling, both desperate to sate their hunger. When his mouth finally found hers, he heard her sigh and sighed as well, because it was such a relief to know that he was welcome, wanted; that he no longer scared her.

He kissed her long and hungrily as his passion soared until it reached previously undiscovered heights. The taste of her mouth, the whisper of her breath, the feel of her in his arms was even more potent than he had imagined. He could feel his body reacting to her closeness and shifted slightly, afraid that he was going too fast for her, but she put her arms around him and pressed herself against him, and it was like setting light to touch paper.

He tore his mouth away from hers. When he'd made love with a woman in the past he had deliberately held part of himself back, but he couldn't do that now and didn't want to. Not with Alison. If they made love he would give her his all, and he wanted her to welcome him without any reservations.

'I want to make love to you, but if it isn't what you want too, then say so.' His voice sounded ragged with passion, but he didn't care. He took her face between his hands, his heart overflowing with tenderness as he looked into her eyes. 'I would never do anything to hurt you, sweetheart. I swear.'

'I know you wouldn't.' Reaching up, she kissed him on the mouth, her lips parting so that her tongue could mesh with his, and Jack shuddered. He had his answer now—an answer he had hardly dared to hope he would get.

He gathered her to him and kissed her softly, but with a passion that left them both trembling when he drew back. Alison held out her hand, looking so beautiful as she stood there with her lips all rosy from his kisses that he couldn't speak. He took her hand and let her lead him from the room and up the stairs, his mind in a daze, his body in heaven. When she opened her bedroom door and turned to him, he lifted her into his arms and carried her to the bed. They didn't need words when they had this. Didn't need anything except each other.

CHAPTER THIRTEEN

ALISON closed her eyes as Jack laid her on the bed. She wanted to savour this moment, store it away for ever and always. She felt the mattress lift as he stood up, then heard a click as he turned on the lamp. Only then did she open her eyes, and she felt her heart melt when she found him staring down at her with such tenderness on his face. In that second she realised that what was happening meant as much to him as it did to her. Jack couldn't look at her that way if he didn't care.

The thought chased away any doubts she might have had. Holding out her hand, she smiled at him, faintly shocked yet secretly delighted by her own boldness. She had never initiated sex before, but she was going to take the lead now.

'Why don't you come and keep me company? It's rather lonely in this great big bed.'

Jack chuckled as he sat down on the edge of the mattress. 'I would hate you to be lonely.' He kissed her on the mouth, then drew back and looked at her. 'Feeling better now?'

'A bit.' Alison smiled up at him, loving the way the lamplight played across his face, highlighting his clean-cut features and the richness of his dark hair.

'Only a bit?' His brows arched. 'So that means you still feel a bit lonesome, does it?'

'Hmm. But I'm sure we can do something to remedy that.'

Alison let her hand glide up his arm, her fingers sliding beneath the sleeve of his jacket, and heard him suck in his breath. His response was so encouraging that it made her bolder still, her other hand moving to his chest and skimming over the hard pectoral muscles. He was wearing the shirt he'd worn to the christening—soft blue cotton that flowed beneath her palm. She could feel the heat of his skin seeping through the fabric, and shivered as she imagined how it would feel to touch him without anything in the way.

Jack captured her hand and raised it to his lips, pressing a lingering kiss to the centre of her palm. 'If it's any consolation, I don't feel the least bit lonely. In fact, I can't remember when I ever felt this content.'

'Good.' Alison smiled up at him, deeply touched by the admission. To know that she was enough for Jack was more than she could have hoped for. When he released her hand, she placed it back on his chest, memorising his body by touch as well as by sight. She wanted to *soak* herself in him, absorb everything that made him the man he was.

Jack let her explore for a few more minutes, then shook his head. 'If we carry on this way, I'll be fit for nothing. And then we'll both end up feeling extremely lonely *and* frustrated.'

Alison blushed, and he laughed as he dropped a kiss on the tip of her nose. 'I love it when you blush like that. I don't think I've met anyone who's so wonderfully innocent.'

'I'm not a complete innocent,' she protested, but he shushed her with a finger on her lips.

'Yes, you are, and it's a compliment, too. I find your lack of artifice a real turn-on.'

He kissed her again, proving to her in the most effective way possible that he was telling her the truth. Alison had always believed that her lack of experience had been a hindrance in the past, but suddenly it felt like a blessing rather than something to be ashamed of. She kissed him back as passion surged between them, long, drugging kisses that filled her with joy. It was only when he started to unbutton her blouse that the first doubts crept in and she shivered.

It had been a long time since a man had seen her naked, and she was suddenly afraid that Jack wouldn't like what he saw. Gareth had been scathing about her figure after she'd had Sam; he'd even told her that it had been one of the reasons why he'd had an affair. She was terrified that Jack would feel the same way when he saw her undressed. After all, her breasts weren't as firm as they'd been, and she had a couple of stretch marks on her hips from carrying Sam. What if Jack was repulsed by the sight of her? What would she do then...?

'It's OK, sweetheart. If you want me to stop, you only have to say so.'

The understanding in Jack's voice brought a rush of tears to her eyes and he gathered her close, murmuring to her as he stroked her hair. 'Shush, now. It's all right. There's no need to cry. I didn't mean to scare you.'

'It isn't you,' she mumbled through a mouthful of pale blue cotton.

'Then what is it?' He set her away from him, his gaze very gentle as he looked at her in concern.

'It's me. I...I'm afraid you'll think that I...I'm ugly.'

'Ugly?' he repeated, and she lowered her head because she couldn't bear to look at him while she explained.

'I've had a baby, and I'm not...well, I don't look the same as I did before I was pregnant,' she whispered.

'And you think I won't like what I see?'

'Yes. My ex-husband told me that was why he had an

affair…' She tailed off, then dredged up the very last drop of her courage. She needed to be completely honest with Jack about this. 'He said he couldn't bear to make love to me after I'd had Sam.'

Jack swore loudly, then hurriedly apologised. 'I'm sorry. That's not the kind of language I would normally use around you.' He tilted her chin and made her look at him. 'I don't know exactly what your ex said to you, and I don't want to know either. However, take it from me that it was a pack of lies. No man stops loving a woman because her body has changed. It doesn't work like that.'

Tears spilled from her eyes and trickled down her cheeks. 'But you haven't seen what I look like yet.'

'No, and that's something I intend to rectify immediately.'

He kissed her softly, then laid her down on the pillows and carried on unfastening her blouse, punctuating the process with kisses along the way. When he came to the final button, he paused to smile at her. 'It's going to be wonderful, Alison. *You* are wonderful.'

Alison wanted to believe him, but she was holding her breath as he parted the blouse and slid it off her shoulders. Her bra came next, then her skirt and her panties, and she was naked. She squeezed her eyes tight shut because she couldn't bear to watch his face.

'You are *so* beautiful.'

The awe in his voice brought her eyes open and she stared at him in amazement. 'Beautiful?'

'Yes.' He couldn't seem to drag his gaze away from her. His hands were shaking as he cupped her breasts and allowed their weight to settle in his palms. 'You look like a woman should look—all soft curves and even softer skin—'

He broke off and gulped, raising his head so that she saw

the desire that had tightened the bones of his face, and every single horrible thing Gareth had said to her was erased from her mind with one single stroke. Jack couldn't look at her this way if he didn't want her!

She sat up and put her arms around his neck, held him to her and gloried in the wonder of being able to do such a thing. When he started to unfasten his shirt she helped him, laughing when he managed to rip off a couple of the buttons in his haste.

'Shall I do it for you?' she offered with a teasing smile.

Jack sat as still as statue while she undid the rest of the buttons. He didn't move a muscle when she undid his cuff-links either. However, when she reached for the buckle on his belt, he stopped her.

'I think I'd better do the rest.'

He kissed her quickly, then stood up and stripped off his trousers and his underwear, leaving her in little doubt as to why he'd felt it necessary to take over the task. Alison felt heat pool low in her belly as he came and lay down beside her. She could feel his erection pressing against her as he drew her into the cradle of his hips, feel her own response to his nearness, and it stunned her that she should be so aroused. She had never wanted any man as much as she wanted Jack at that moment.

He kissed her long and lingeringly, then stroked her breasts until her nipples peaked. Bending his head, he drew first one nipple and then the other into his mouth and suckled her until she could barely think because of the sensations that were pouring through her. When he laid her back against the pillows again and let his mouth glide down her body, stopping to kiss her en route, she shifted restlessly, unable to satisfy the hunger that was building inside her.

His lips stopped on her belly, just above the nest of curls at the junction of her thighs, while his fingers explored the very source of her heat and she cried out. She wasn't sure what was happening to her because she'd never felt this way before. All she could think about was the tension that was building inside her and her desperate need for relief.

Jack held her close as she climaxed, feeling his heart pounding from the effort it had cost him to hold onto his control. He hadn't expected her to be so sweetly responsive to his touch, so it felt like a gift to know that he could please her like this. He held her until she stopped trembling, then smiled into her eyes, knowing at that moment how much he loved her. It had to be love, of course—real love, not just sexual attraction. It couldn't be anything less when he felt this way—all fired up, yet ready to forfeit his own pleasure to ensure hers. His gaze skimmed over her flushed face, drinking in every single emotion that was etched on it: passion, yes; satisfaction, that was a given after the way she had responded to him; shock… Shock?

He swallowed hard to ease the knot of tension that suddenly tightened his throat. The only reason he could think of to explain why Alison appeared so shocked was impossible to accept. Surely it couldn't have been the first time that she'd had an orgasm?

His heart was pounding as he pulled her back into his arms. He longed to ask her if his suspicions were correct, but it wasn't the right time to ask her now. Her confidence had obviously taken a battering during her marriage, and what she needed most of all was a chance to regain her self-esteem. His heart overflowed with love at the thought, because he intended to do everything he could to help her!

He kissed her hungrily, using every skill he had to arouse her passion once more. It was sheer heaven to feel her tremble in his arms and have her cling to him. Even though he had gone way beyond the normal limits of his control he held back, wanting to be sure that she would gain as much from their union as he did, and she did. The last thing Jack heard before the world went spinning out of control was her crying out his name, and it was the sweetest, the most precious sound he had ever heard.

Daylight crept around the edges of the curtains and Alison woke up. For a moment she couldn't understand why she felt so different that morning. Then all of a sudden everything came flooding back—her and Jack, and what had happened in her bed.

Rolling onto her side, she studied his face. He looked much softer when he was asleep, younger too, and her heart welled with tenderness when she realised it. Reaching out, she traced the elegant curve of his brows with the tip of her finger, enjoying the silky feel of the dark hair against her skin. His nose came next, and she couldn't resist letting her fingertip skate down its elegant length. The only problem was that when she reached the bottom her finger was hovering just above his mouth and that was even more tempting.

She drew the tip of her finger lightly across his lips, and gasped when she felt tingles of sensation shoot through the palm of her hand. Although she was the one doing the caressing rather than being caressed, the effect was just as stimulating. She traced a path around his lips until she'd completed a full circuit of his mouth. Even then she wasn't satisfied, so she went back for a second trip—across his Cupid's bow, into one curling corner, round to the bottom, along to the middle…

She jumped when his lips suddenly parted and he drew her finger into his mouth. Her eyes flew to his and she felt heat invade her when she realised he was watching her. Holding her gaze, he sucked the tip of her finger, then let his mouth graze across her palm until it came to her wrist, to the very spot where her pulse was beating so wildly, and licked it.

Alison closed her eyes as a wave of passion gripped her. She couldn't believe that such a seemingly simple action could arouse her this way. When Jack rolled her over onto her back and let his mouth explore the rest of her body she didn't protest. Now that she knew how desire felt, she wanted to enjoy it again and again, wanted Jack to show her how wonderful it felt to be loved.

They made love, and it was just as breathtaking that morning as it had been the night before. Alison clung to him as the world seemed to shudder to a stop, felt him cling to her and knew he felt the same way. They had aroused one another's passion and satisfied it too, and it was the most wonderful feeling to know that she could give Jack what he needed. It had restored her belief in herself as a woman. When he drew her into his arms after everything had stopped spinning, she knew that she had to tell him that. It would be her gift to him, the best way she knew to thank him.

'I've never felt like this before,' she whispered. 'I wasn't even sure if I could feel this way. You've shown me how it feels to be a real woman.'

'Thank you,' he said just as quietly, although she could tell how moved he was. He kissed her on the mouth, then looked into her eyes. 'This has been very special for me, too. I've never felt this way about anyone before.'

It was so wonderful to hear him say that that she couldn't speak, and he kissed her again. They would have continued kissing, too, if the sound of footsteps on the landing hadn't warned her that Sam was awake. Although she wasn't ashamed of what she'd done, she didn't want Sam walking in on them and wondering what was going on.

'Sam's awake,' she explained, pushing back the bedclothes. She reached for her robe and pulled it on. 'I'd better go and see to him.'

'And I'd better go home and check that Freddie's all right.' Jack got up and reached for his clothes, which were lying in a heap on the floor. He grimaced as he picked up his shirt. 'I'd better come up with a good story for Dad to explain the state of my clothes, too.'

Alison paused on her way to the door. 'Are you going to tell him where you've been?'

'I don't think so.' He finished buttoning his shirt and tucked it into his trousers. 'I think it's best if we keep quiet about what's happened. We don't want everyone gossiping about us, do we?'

'Of course not,' she said quickly, wondering why she felt so uneasy all of a sudden. She knew how quickly rumours could spread throughout the town, and she would hate to think that people were talking about them. However, as she left the bedroom she couldn't help wondering if Jack was more concerned about the people he worked with finding out, and one person in particular. How would Alex Ross feel if she discovered that Jack had spent the night with her?

The thought nagged away at her while she was seeing to Sam. Jack managed to slip away while she was getting the little boy dressed, so at least she didn't have to explain what he'd been doing there at that time of the day. She'd given no thought to the implications of what had happened last night, but there was no way that she would allow Sam to be adversely affected by it. If she and Jack continued seeing each other, they would have to be discreet.

Fear clutched her heart, because it really was a question of *if*, wasn't it? Jack hadn't arranged to see her again, and there was no guarantee that he would. One night and one morning didn't constitute a commitment on either side. This might be the beginning and the end of their relationship.

As the day wore on, Jack's doubts about what had happened gathered pace. Although he didn't deny that it had been the most moving experience of his life, he knew in his heart that he should never have allowed it to happen. At the present moment he had so much else going on in his life that he didn't have time for a relationship, at least not the sort of relationship he wanted with Alison.

It had been so simple in the past. He'd separated his life into two separate compartments—his career and his social life—and he had kept them strictly apart. That was why he had never shared his home with a woman or involved her in his working life in any way, shape or form. However, he couldn't do that with Alison.

He wanted her to be involved in every aspect of his life, and that was bound to have repercussions not only for him, but for Freddie. Although Freddie seemed to like her, it was too soon to introduce her into his son's life on a permanent basis. Freddie was only just getting used to *him* and it would confuse him if the dynamics of their relationship had to change. Bluntly, Freddie might not want to share him with someone else. The thought weighed heavily on him as he worked.

Becca had been discharged at the weekend, and Ryan had an appointment with the consultant in London the following day. Jack popped in to see him, to check that he understood what was going to happen.

'So you're quite happy with the arrangements? There's an ambulance booked to take you up to London. I'm not sure how long you'll be there—that will be up to the consultant to decide once he's seen you,' he explained. 'Are your parents going with you?'

Ryan shook his head. 'Mum can't get the time off work and Dad's no use. He'll only start drinking and make a scene, so it's best if he stays away.'

Jack sighed. 'That means you'll have nobody around to visit you.'

'Oh, it's OK. Becca has promised to come and see me every day.' Ryan grinned at him and Jack laughed.

'I see.' He shook the boy's hand. 'Good luck, then. Not that you'll need it. Take it from me that you're getting the very best possible care.'

He was still smiling as he left the ward. Alex was just coming in and she stopped to speak to him.

'You're looking a lot happier than you did this morning. Has something cheered you up?'

'I've just been speaking to Ryan Lovelace,' Jack explained, somewhat surprised by the comment because he hadn't realised he was so transparent. He hurried on, not wanting to dwell on the thought. 'He's arranged for Becca to visit him while he's in London.'

'I see. Do I detect a hint of romance in the air?'

'I think the answer to that is watch this space!'

Alex laughed as she carried on into the ward. Jack went to the office and made sure that Ryan's notes were up to date. He had just finished and was thinking about going home when there was a call from A and E. Jack responded, and decided that the patient needed to go straight to Theatre. The young man had suffered extensive tissue damage after his motorbike had skidded. He hadn't been wearing protective clothing and a large area of skin and flesh had been sheared away from his right thigh.

Jack called Theatre and arranged for everything to be set up in readiness, then phoned Lucy and asked her if she would collect Freddie from the nursery. Although he felt bad about abandoning his son again after last night, he didn't have a choice. Still, Freddie had been fine when he'd got home that morning. He'd obviously enjoyed having his grandfather there to spoil him, so Jack wasn't too worried. The sooner Freddie got used to the people who loved him, the better it would be for him.

Freddie would probably get used to Alison, too, a small voice whispered inside his head, but Jack blanked it out. Probably wasn't good enough—not for Freddie and not for Alison. Until he was sure that neither of them would get hurt, he couldn't do anything about the current situation. He intended to protect his son *and* protect the woman he loved.

CHAPTER FOURTEEN

A week passed and Alison didn't hear a word from Jack. Every time the phone rang or someone knocked on the door, she kept thinking it would be him, but it never was. She even went back to taking Sam to the nursery at the usual time, but somehow she always seemed to miss Jack. She could only conclude that he was avoiding her, and it hurt. It seemed that sleeping together hadn't been as wonderful an experience for him as he had claimed.

She tried to deal with her heartache by keeping busy. It wasn't difficult because they were inundated at the surgery. An outbreak of some sort of particularly nasty stomach bug kept the phones ringing almost non-stop. Morning and afternoon surgeries were full to overflowing, and in the end Nick decided that anyone who was complaining of gastric problems should be told to stay at home. They would receive a home visit rather than run the risk of spreading the bug any further.

The decision had a knock-on effect for everyone. With all the doctors doing house calls each day, inevitably afternoon surgeries started late. Alison had to make arrangements for Sam to stay with the childminder for an extra hour each day, and that seemed to upset his routine, so he started playing up. After a week of temper tantrums, she was longing for the time when life would get back to normal. Dealing with a fretful three-year-old *and* an aching heart was taxing her to the limit.

The day of Maggie's hen night arrived, but Alison decided to give it a miss. Sam was still being difficult, and she didn't want to leave him with a babysitter, plus she didn't feel in the mood for partying. Gemma tried to change her mind but she stuck to her decision. She'd much prefer a quiet night at home.

The day flew past, although it wasn't as busy as it had been. The bug was running its course, and there were far fewer phone calls and home visits. Consequently, it was only a little after her normal time when she collected Sam, and to her delight he seemed more like his usual sunny self. They had tea, then played a game before bedtime. Alison read him his favourite story and tucked him in, sighing in relief when he immediately closed his eyes. It seemed the crisis was over in more ways than one. If only her problems with Jack could be resolved so satisfactorily she would feel so much better. Should she phone him and ask him to call round? Or should she leave him to get in touch with her—if he ever did?

She spent ages thinking about it, but couldn't make up her mind. In the end she went to bed with the problem unresolved, and woke up the following morning still worrying about it. Part of her wanted to make the first move, but another part of her was terrified of inviting a rebuff.

Saturday was another glorious day, so she decided to forgo the usual household chores and take Sam out. Once again, she headed to Rock, trying not to think about what had happened the last time she'd been there. She intended to enjoy this day with Sam and not keep thinking about Jack all the time.

She made for a sheltered stretch of the bay that overlooked the Camel estuary. There were quite a few people already there when she and Sam arrived, mainly family groups with small children who were playing in the sand. Alison chose a spot close to the water's edge and helped Sam take off his shoes and socks so he could paddle. She had a spare set of clothes in the car so it didn't matter if he got wet. As long as he was having fun, that was the main thing.

They'd been there about an hour when she spotted two familiar figures walking along the beach. Her heart leapt into her throat when she recognised Jack and Freddie. Had Jack guessed that she would be here and come looking for her? she wondered as she scrambled to her feet. All of a sudden the doubts that had plagued her all week long seemed so stupid that she laughed out loud. The only reason Jack hadn't been in touch with her was because he'd been too busy!

She lifted her hand to wave to him, then suddenly realised that he and Freddie weren't on their own. There was a woman with them, the tall woman with auburn hair she remembered from the christening. Alison felt her stomach roll with sickness as she saw Jack turn and reply to something Alex Ross had said to him. The tilt of his head and the smile that played around his mouth were all too familiar. He was looking at Alex the same way he had looked at her the other night, and she couldn't bear it. She simply couldn't bear it!

It was far too late by then for her to run away and hide. She had to stand there and wait as they approached. Her heart ached when she saw Jack's expression alter when he spotted her. She turned away, not wanting to witness his discomfort. It wasn't difficult to imagine how awkward he felt. He may have been happy enough to sleep with her, but she wasn't the sort of woman he would normally be interested in. That honour went to someone like Alex Ross, someone who was beautiful and sophisticated and worldly-wise. What would Jack want with a little nobody like her?

'Hi! I had no idea you'd be here,' he said quietly as he and Alex stopped. Freddie spotted Sam and immediately ran over to him. Alison shrugged as she watched the two children laughing together.

'It was just a spur-of-the-moment decision.'

'Oh. Right. I see.' A frown darkened his face for a second before he turned to Alex. 'You remember Alison, don't you?'

'Of course.'

Alex gave her a brief smile, but Alison could tell that she wasn't keen to prolong their meeting. She didn't blame her. If she'd been in Alex's shoes she wouldn't have wanted to share even a second of the time she had with Jack with some other woman. The thought brought a rush of tears to her eyes, and she quickly bent and gathered up Sam's shoes and socks.

'Actually, we were about to go home. It's been nice seeing you again, Alex,' she added politely.

'You, too,' Alex replied graciously. She carried on walking, but Jack hung back.

'You're not rushing off on our account, I hope.'

'No. You may find this hard to believe, Jack, but the world doesn't revolve around you.'

His jaw tightened. 'You're angry with me because I haven't been in touch. I don't blame you. I should have called you. I almost did—several times, in fact. I just didn't know what to say.'

'Really? I wouldn't have thought it would be that difficult. All you needed to say was that you'd made a mistake. How hard is that?'

'It isn't like that!' he denied hotly. 'You don't understand.'

'Oh, I think I do.' She stared back at him, bolstering up her anger to stave off the pain that was knifing through her. 'Making love to me the other night was fine, wasn't it, Jack? But you're not interested in making a commitment to me, are you?'

'No, I'm not,' he said bluntly. 'It's not the right time, for many reasons.'

'Not the right time, or not the right woman?'

'What do you mean?'

'I'm not your usual kind of woman, am I?'

'No, you're not.'

His voice was husky, and she shivered when she felt it stroke along her nerves, but she was too hurt and too angry to stop. She laughed harshly. 'That's what I thought. At least you have the decency to be honest with me. That's something in your favour.'

She tossed back her hair as the wind whipped it across her face, knowing that she had to end this for good. She mustn't allow herself to hope that Jack might come to love her one day. 'I'm not sure why you slept with me. Maybe it was a way to thank me for looking after Freddie for you, or maybe it was just an urge that needed satisfying—who knows? But it definitely won't happen again. Understand?'

'I understand. And you're right, Alison. It would be wrong for us to start something right now.' His expression was bleak. 'I need to focus on Freddie. I can't afford to take any chances where his happiness is concerned. He's been through too much already, and I won't risk upsetting his life any more.'

'And I feel the same way about Sam. I won't allow his life to be disrupted either.'

Jack nodded. 'Then it seems we're in complete agreement, doesn't it?'

'Yes.' Alison left it at that. There was nothing else to say anyway. Jack had made his position perfectly clear, although she wasn't stupid enough to think that he wouldn't change his mind if the circumstances were right.

The thought of what might make those circumstances conducive to him reconsidering his stance was very hard to deal with, and she shut it out of her mind. She didn't want to think about him and Alex, didn't want to imagine them making plans for their future together. It was none of her business what Jack did. It never had been.

She fetched Sam and dried his feet, then popped his shoes and socks back on. He begged her to let him stay and play with Freddie, but she was adamant that they had to go home. That set off another tantrum, but she didn't back down. Sam needed consistency in his life; he needed to know that when she said no she meant it.

If only she could make herself understand that concept when it came to Jack, she thought bitterly as she took Sam back to the car. She might have told Jack that she would never sleep with him again, but she knew how hard it would be to stick to that decision if the occasion ever arose. Where Jack was concerned she was as weak as a kitten, and it worried her to think that she might end up doing the one thing she would regret.

It made her wonder if she should leave Penhally Bay and remove herself from temptation, but where would she go? All her friends were here, as well as her job, and it would mean making a completely fresh start. It would also mean uprooting Sam, and that wouldn't be good for him either.

She sighed. It wasn't going to be easy, but she had to forget about Jack and get on with her life as she had been doing before he'd arrived. The problem was that now she'd had a taste of how wonderful life could be, it would be hard to settle for second best.

Jack knew that he'd made a complete and utter hash of things with Alison. He also knew there was nothing he could do at the moment to put things right. The thought weighed heavily on him, so that he found it hard to concentrate as Alex explained about the new clinic.

She had accepted an offer to be the clinic's director, and Jack knew that she was hoping to persuade him to be her second-in-command, which was why she had invited him to meet her at Rock that day. A site had been chosen and the plans were being drawn up, so it looked as though everything was going ahead. While he was flattered by her faith in his abilities, he couldn't make a decision while his life was in such a mess.

He made all the right noises, but he knew that Alex sensed he had reservations. She cut short their meeting, declining his offer of a cup of coffee with a quick shake of her head.

'Thanks, but I'll get off home. If there's anything I haven't covered, you know where I am.' She smiled at him. 'I won't take offence if you turn me down, Jack. You have to know that it's the right decision for you. I couldn't have imagined doing this type of work a few years ago either, but I've had enough of the NHS and all its problems. That's why I've accepted this job.'

'Thanks. I know it could be a great opportunity for me, but I'm just not sure if the time is right for me to make such a move.' He glanced at Freddie. 'I need to consider the impact it will have on Freddie's life, not just on my own.'

'If it's that which is bothering you then private medicine would suit you perfectly. No more callouts at the weekend or during the night, regular hours and a top salary.' She shrugged as she unlocked her car. 'However, I get the feeling it's more complicated than that, so take your time. The offer's there if you want it.'

Jack sighed as he watched her drive away. It would make a lot of sense to take the job at the clinic, yet his gut feeling was to refuse it. He enjoyed what he did, and loved the fact that he could make such a difference to so many people's lives

He couldn't imagine giving it all up, even for the benefits of working in the private sector.

It was yet another uncertainty, and he could have done without it right now. He took Freddie home and settled down in the sitting room while they watched a cartoon together. For the first time ever Freddie climbed onto his knee, and Jack's heart overflowed with happiness. He desperately wanted to share the moment with Alison, but he couldn't phone her after what had happened that day. He had to let her get on with her life while he got on with his, and the thought took some of the shine away. He simply couldn't imagine living out the rest of his days without her.

As the end of the month drew near, Jack couldn't believe how much had happened in the weeks since he'd been back in Penhally Bay. Despite his heartache over Alison, he knew he'd made the right decision when he had moved back to Cornwall. Freddie was slowly adjusting to his new life. Although he still hadn't spoken, he seemed more content. He had fewer nightmares too, and even smiled at times. He seemed to enjoy nursery and he loved Lucy. He was also devoted to his grandfather, and Jack had to admit that he was surprised at how good Nick was with him. Nick genuinely seemed to care about Freddie, and that helped to smooth some of the rough edges off their own relationship.

When Nick phoned one night and asked if he could pop round, Jack didn't hesitate. He was happy to agree to anything that would help to build those all-essential bridges between them.

He had a pot of coffee ready when Nick arrived. He showed him into the sitting room then poured them both a cup. Nick smiled when Jack handed him his cup.

'I see you've remembered that I prefer it black.'

'With two sugars,' Jack said easily, sitting down on a chair.

'Spot on.' Nick sat on the sofa. He took a sip of the coffee and nodded. 'It's very good, too. I am impressed.'

'I'm becoming quite domesticated,' Jack said, grinning.

Nick laughed. 'Your mother would have been delighted to hear that. She used to worry herself to death when you were at university in case you weren't eating properly.'

'I probably wasn't, but I survived.'

'Indeed you did.' Nick paused for a moment, then carried on. 'I'm really impressed with how well you're coping with Freddie, too. It can't have been easy for you, giving up your life in London, but you're doing a first-rate job with him.'

'Thanks,' Jack said, deeply touched because it was rare for his father to hand out a compliment. 'I appreciate you saying that.'

'It's no more than the truth.' Nick cleared his throat, then changed the subject. 'I wanted a word with you about a patient of mine, a ten-year-old-girl called Molly Dingle. She was involved in a horrific accident last year when she was on a school skiing trip. Another skier crashed into her and Molly suffered the most horrendous facial injuries— both eye sockets were shattered and her jaw was broken in two places.'

'Sounds grim,' Jack observed quietly. He'd seen those kind of injuries before and knew how difficult they were to put right.

'It was—very grim indeed. The surgeon managed to put everything back together but the results are less than perfect. Molly desperately needs another operation, but there's a waiting list and it could be over a year until it's her turn. She's due to start secondary school in September, and she's terribly upset at the thought of the other kids making fun of her.'

'Kids can be very cruel,' Jack sympathised. 'Is there any chance of her going private?'

'No. Her father's a fisherman and her mum's a dinner lady at the junior school. It took them months to save enough to send her on the skiing trip, and private medicine is way beyond their means.' Nick pinned Jack with a look. 'That's why I was hoping you might be able to help.'

'You'd like me to take her on as a pro bono private patient?' Jack said slowly.

'Yes. It's the only way Molly will be able to get the treatment she needs in time for her to start at her new school after the summer.'

'I'm not in a position to set myself up in private practice just yet,' Jack pointed out. 'I've still got eighteen months of training to complete before I'm fully qualified.'

'I realise that,' Nick said impatiently. 'However, I know for a fact that you're more than capable of helping Molly.' He shrugged when Jack looked at him in surprise. 'I've spoken to a lot of people, and I can't count the number of folk who've told me that you're top of the league when it comes to this type of surgery. As far as I'm concerned, you'd do a better job than anyone else.'

'Thank you,' Jack said, somewhat stunned by the praise. He frowned as he considered the issues surrounding Molly's surgery. 'The main problem with this type of surgery when it involves a child is that they're still growing. Usually titanium plates and metals screws are used to hold the bones in place, but they can move as the child grows and that means further surgery is necessary. However, a technique has been developed recently which uses biodegradable implants. Over a period of time, the bone regrows and the implants disintegrate.'

'That would be marvellous!' Nick exclaimed. 'Have yo seen this type of operation done?'

'Seen it and been trained in its methods.' Jack smiled. ' managed to blag my way onto a training course in German last year where they pioneered the treatment. There were te of us there and we spent three days learning how to operat the equipment.'

'How does it work?' Nick asked eagerly.

'The implants are made from a hydrocarbon material calle poly-lactide. The plates are made to fit the patient's face an hold everything together. Holes are drilled in the bones an the plates are attached to them by means of plugs made fron the same hydrocarbon material. An ultrasound device is ther used to weld the plugs to the bone.' He shrugged. 'It's highl effective. We were able to talk to a couple of patients who' had the procedure done and the results were excellent.'

'And you think Molly could have this treatment?'

'I think so. There's a couple of hospitals in the UK tha have the equipment now. I could find out if they would let u borrow it. Of course, a lot would depend on whether the man agement of St Piran's would agree to let us use the facilitie there. It would have to be after normal working hours, o course, but I'm sure I can get Alex to back me up.'

'I'll write to the board,' Nick said immediately. 'There's few favours I can call in if they refuse.'

Jack chuckled. 'I don't think they would dare refuse if yo got involved as well.'

'There's strength in numbers,' Nick said with a wry smile He drained the last of his coffee and stood up. 'Thanks, Jack I appreciate this, especially as I know I don't have any righ to ask you for favours.'

'Of course you do!' Jack exclaimed, getting up. 'You're m

father, and if you can't ask me for a favour I don't know who can. Anyway, I owe you for all the time you've given up to look after Freddie.'

'That's been a pleasure, not a chore,' Nick said firmly as he went to the door. He turned. 'I may not have been around as much as I should have been when you were growing up, Jack, but I always cared what happened to you.'

'I know you did,' Jack said with a lump in his throat. Stepping forward, he gave Nick a hug. 'Thanks, Dad. For everything.'

'Your mother would have been so proud of you, son,' Nick said huskily.

Jack saw him out, then went back to the sitting room and thought about what had happened. It had been easier than he'd thought it would be to smooth things over with his father. It was partly the fact that Nick seemed to have mellowed, but it was mainly the fact that his own attitude had changed. Becoming a father himself had made him reassess his priorities. Although his career would always be important to him, his family came first. He wanted to do what was right for them.

He also wanted to do what was right for Alison. That was equally important. Just for a second his mind went racing off as he imagined how his life could be. It would be so wonderful to have her at his side, to live with her and watch their children growing up. They could even have more children if she wanted them—he certainly did. He smiled. He would love a little girl with soft blonde hair and hazel eyes...

He sighed as he drove the images from his mind. It wasn't going to happen and he had to accept that. Alison had her own life, and it would be wrong for him to interfere at this stage when he had so little to offer her. Unless he was one hundred per cent sure that he could give her the commitment she deserved, he had to stay away from her. There could be no half-measures. It had to be all or nothing. Alison deserved nothing less.

CHAPTER FIFTEEN

THE last few days of March brought with them a storm. Rain lashed the countryside and a driving wind made getting around the town extremely difficult. Warnings were posted along the cliff top to warn the unwary about the dangers of going too close to the edge. Everyone at the surgery held their breath and hoped that any visitors would heed the warnings but, inevitably, there were casualties.

Nick and Dragan were called out to a walker who had been blown off the steps leading down to the beach and broken his leg. The man's wife had raised the alarm, and by the time they got there she was completely hysterical. When Nick phoned the surgery and asked for someone to go and attend to the woman while he and Dragan dealt with her husband, Alison immediately volunteered. Anything that might help to take her mind off her own problems was a welcome relief.

She parked in Mevagissey Road and went to find them. The sea was a churning mass of grey-green waves as it pounded the shore and she sincerely hoped that Nick and Dragan weren't down on the beach. She finally spotted them perched halfway up the steps. They were trying to attend to the injured man but his wife kept getting in the way.

Alison firmly ushered her out of the way while the two

doctors got on with their job. She insisted that the woman should return to her car, but no sooner had they got there than the woman suffered an asthma attack. Alison found her inhaler in her pocket and got her sorted out, but she was relieved when the ambulance arrived to take the couple to hospital.

By the time the ambulance left it was lunchtime and she needed to collect Sam. She headed straight to the nursery, exclaiming in frustration when she discovered the road was blocked by an overturned lorry. Hunting her mobile phone out of her bag, she rang Carol, but there was no answer. Obviously, Carol had already left to collect her other charges from the nursery.

Alison phoned the nursery to warn them that she would be late, but the line was engaged, and it was still engaged when she tried another half a dozen times. By the time the road was clear she was over an hour late, and she could feel herself growing increasingly anxious. Sam would be terribly upset if he thought she'd forgotten him.

Trish answered the door when Alison rang the bell and she looked surprised to her. 'Did Sam forget something?'

'I don't think so,' Alison replied uncertainly, wondering what Trish meant. 'I'm sorry I'm so late, but a lorry had overturned and it held me up. Is Sam OK? He's not upset, is he?'

Trish blanched. 'Sam's not here. I thought you must have asked Carol to collect him.'

'I couldn't get hold of her,' Alison said, her heart racing. 'Why did you think he'd gone home with Carol? Did you see him leave with her?'

'No. I was in the quiet room when she arrived. Sam wasn't there when I got back, so I assumed she must have collected him, along with the other two she usually picks up.'

'Maybe she did,' Alison said, doing her best not to panic.

She took out her phone and rang Carol's number. 'Carol, it's Alison. Is Sam with you?'

Alison felt the floor tilt when the childminder told her that Sam wasn't there. Trish had gone to fetch Christine Galloway, the owner of the nursery; the pair of them looked worried to death when she told them that Sam wasn't at Carol's house either.

'We need to check that he isn't hiding somewhere,' Christine said quickly.

They searched every room, and even checked the garden, but there was no sign of him. Alison felt a wave of sickness envelop her when Christine told her that she was going to telephone the police. Where could Sam be? She glanced out of the window, feeling fear clutch her heart. It was pouring down with rain—what chance did a three-year-old have outside on his own in weather like this?

Jack heard about Sam when Lucy phoned to tell him. He had just left Theatre when the call came through, and it was like a bolt from the blue.

'What's happening now?' he demanded, his heart pounding in fear at the thought of the child going missing.

'The police have organised a search of the whole town. Dad and Ben have gone along to help,' Lucy explained. She gave a little sob. 'I can't bear to think what Alison must be going through at this moment.'

'Neither can I,' Jack said grimly. He thanked Lucy, then went to find Alex and explained that he needed to leave immediately. There was no way on earth that he could carry on working while Sam was missing.

He got changed, then drove straight to Alison's house. There was a police car parked outside, and a woman police officer answered the door when he rang the bell. Alison came rushing into the hall when she heard his voice. Jack didn't say a word as he pushed past the policewoman and took her in his arms. He rocked her to and fro as he felt the sobs that shook her.

'I'm so scared, Jack. I don't know what I'll do if anything happens to him…'

'Nothing is going to happen to him,' he said fiercely. He held her away from him and looked into her eyes. 'You have to believe that, sweetheart. Sam needs you to be strong for him.'

'I'm trying,' she whispered, her eyes brimming with tears.

'I know you are.' He kissed her gently on the mouth, then he let her go. 'I'm going to ask Lucy to look after Freddie so I can join the search party. We'll find him, Alison. Trust me. I won't let anything happen to Sam, I swear.'

He kissed her again, then left. He phoned Lucy as soon as he got home and arranged for her to have Freddie, then grabbed a waterproof jacket and went to join the search party. They'd been split into four teams so they could scour every part of the town. Jack went with his father and Ben while they searched the area around the nursery, but as the hours passed and there was still no sign of Sam he was starting to despair. He needed to find him for Alison's sake—needed to keep his promise and not let her down.

The group stopped for a break at seven p.m. The weather was atrocious and everyone was soaked to the skin. Jack shook his head when someone offered him a mug of soup. He didn't care how cold or wet he was. He just cared about Sam. He wandered a little way away from the rest of the group, heading to an area of rough land that was next on their list to be searched. There was a lot of bracken and gorse, and it tore at the legs of his jeans as he forced his way through it.

'Sam!' he shouted, cupping his hands round his mouth. 'Sam, can you hear me? It's Jack.'

He waited a moment, his ears straining against the roar of the wind, and felt his heart jerk when he heard a faint cry coming from off to his right. He plunged through the undergrowth, ripping his jeans and his skin as he raced towards the sound. When he caught sight of the small figure huddled beneath a huge gorse bush, he could have wept with relief.

Crouching down, he smiled at the little boy. 'Hi, there. How are you doing? Are you ready to go home and see your mummy?'

Sam reached out his arms and Jack lifted him up. He hugged him tight for a moment, then took off his coat and wrapped it around him. 'Over here,' he shouted, when he saw some of the others heading towards him. 'He's fine. He's just very cold and wet.'

A huge cheer erupted. Jack grinned as several people slapped him on the back. One of the police officers got straight on his radio and informed the other groups that Sam had been found, safe and sound. There was some talk of taking the child to hospital to be checked over, but Jack quashed that idea and his father backed him up. The best thing for the child was to be reunited with his mother as quickly as possible.

Alison came running out to meet them when they drew up outside the house. There was such happiness on her face that Jack couldn't help himself. He handed Sam to her, then bent and kissed her, uncaring that everyone was watching them. He didn't give a damn if the whole world knew how he felt. He loved her, and tonight had shown him that it was the only thing that really mattered.

'I love you,' he told her simply. 'Now, it's time you took Sam inside and gave him a bath.' He pressed a finger to her lips when she went to speak. 'He needs you. I can wait. My feelings for you aren't going to change, no matter how long it takes you to decide if you might be able to love me back one day.'

'I don't need time to decide that,' she said softly. Reaching up, she kissed him on the mouth. 'I love you, too, Jack. And what you've done tonight by finding Sam for me just makes me love you even more.'

There was so much that Jack wanted to say to her then but he couldn't be selfish and claim any more of her attention. He kissed her again, kissed Sam and hugged him too, then left. Ben offered to stay and check Sam over, but Nick insisted on driving him home. He smiled as he pulled up outside Jack's house.

'Don't worry about Freddie. I'll look after him tonight, and for however long you need to sort things out.'

'I love her, Dad,' Jack said simply, and Nick nodded.

'Then make sure she knows that. Life's too short to waste even a second of it. If it's Alison you want, then tell her that. OK?'

'OK,' Jack repeated, feeling a lump come to his throat because he would never have expected his father to understand.

He let himself in and took a shower, then made himself a cup of coffee, but didn't drink it. Those precious seconds were ticking away, and he didn't intend to let any more of them slip through his fingers. He was going back to Alison's house and he was going to tell her that he wanted to spend his life with her.

He took a deep breath as a feeling of certainty suddenly filled him. If there were problems that needed dealing with, they would deal with them together.

Alison took a last look at Sam, then tiptoed from the room. Ben had given the child a thorough examination and had decided that there was no reason to take him to hospital. A warm bath and plenty of cuddles were the best medicine he could prescribe, and she'd been more than happy to comply with those instructions. Although she hadn't managed to get the full story from Sam about how he had come to leave the nursery, it appeared that he had followed Carol out and then wandered off after she'd left.

She went downstairs, feeling herself trembling as the effects of the past few hours caught up with her. She'd been so scared that they might not find Sam, and it was such a relief to have him safely back home. Jack would never know how grateful she was to him for finding her precious child.

A smile softened the lines of strain around her mouth as she thought about what Jack had told her. There wasn't a doubt in her mind that he'd been sincere, and her heart overflowed with happiness at the thought. When she heard the doorbell ring, she hurried to answer it, knowing it would be him. He stepped into the hall and took her in his arms, and she sighed with pleasure. Now *everything* was right with her world.

He kissed her hungrily, then looked into her eyes. 'I love you so much. You do believe me, don't you?'

'Yes, I believe you.' She kissed him gently on the lips, then smiled at him. 'I love you, too, Jack.'

He swept her off her feet and twirled her round, laughing when she gasped. 'I'm sorry, but I'm so happy I think I might burst!'

Alison laughed with him. 'And I would hate that to happen. Apart from the fact that I like you just the way you are, think about the mess it would make.'

He chuckled as he set her back on her feet and kissed the tip of her nose. 'You're so wonderfully practical. No wonder I love you so much.'

'So long as you don't think I'm boring?'

'Boring?' He looked at her in amazement. 'You couldn't be boring if you tried! Whatever gave you that idea?'

'Well, I'm not at all like your usual girlfriends, am I? I'm not glamorous or rich, and I don't go to all sorts of exciting places,' she pointed out.

'No, thank heavens!' He steered her into the sitting room, sat down on the sofa and pulled her down onto his lap. He kissed her softly on the mouth, then smiled at her. 'You're nothing like the women I used to go out with. I wouldn't have fallen in love with you if you were.'

'Really?'

'Yes, really.' He sighed as he pulled her into his arms. 'I went out with them purely and simply because I knew I would *never* fall in love with them. It meant that I could focus on what was really important—my career.'

'So you don't hanker after those days?' she said quietly.

'Not at all. I enjoyed them at the time, but life moves on. I'm a very different person to who I was then.' He smiled ruefully. 'I doubt if you'd have fancied me if we'd met a couple of years ago.'

'Maybe not. I was still trying to come to terms with what had happened to me.'

'You mean your divorce?'

'That, and the fact that my confidence was at an all-time low.' She bit her lip, wondering if she should tell him about Sam's father, but it was important that he should know the truth.

'Sam's father left me when Sam was six months old. He'd been having an affair with a woman he worked with. I only found out about it by accident when I saw them together one day.' She shrugged. 'Gareth never tried to deny it. He said it was my fault it had happened.'

'Your fault? How did he work that out?' Jack demanded.

'Apparently I'd become boring after I'd had Sam, and let myself go.' She paused, but she needed to tell him everything. 'He said that he no longer fancied me because I was so fat and ugly.'

Jack swore under his breath as he drew her to him. 'I wish I could have five minutes alone with him. How dare he say such terrible things to you?'

'I can see now that it was just a way to excuse his own behaviour. Gareth never liked to think he was at fault, so he blamed me. It was the same throughout our marriage. He was always finding fault with what I did. Even though I no longer had any feelings for him by the time we divorced, it hit me hard. It completely eroded my self-esteem.'

'You are a beautiful woman and a very special person, too,' Jack stated emphatically. 'I've never met anyone like you before. You're so warm and giving, so capable and so gorgeous—'

'Stop!' she begged, placing her hand over his mouth. 'My head is going to be so swollen I'll not be able to get out of that door if you keep on showering me with compliments.'

Jack grinned. 'We certainly don't want that happening. I have plans that involve us both leaving this room and going upstairs to somewhere more comfortable.'

Alison shivered at the image that sprang to her mind. She could picture her and Jack walking up the stairs to her bedroom… She blanked out the rest, knowing that it would be impossible to concentrate if she got too carried away. 'As I said, it took me a long time to find myself again. That's why I was so scared when I realised the effect you had on me. I was terrified of being hurt again the way I'd been hurt before.'

'I will never hurt you, Alison.' He pressed her hand to his heart and held it there. 'I swear on my life that I shall do my best to protect you and make you happy. You and Sam, of course.'

'Thank you.' Tears welled to her eyes, because there was no doubt that he was telling her the truth. She kissed him on the mouth, then snuggled into his arms, enjoying the fact that she could do so. There were no barriers between them now, and she was free to show him her love any way she chose.

Jack brushed his mouth across her hair. 'If it's confession time then I have a confession, too. I tried desperately not to fall in love with you. Even when I realised it had happened, despite my attempts to stop it, I still couldn't tell you how I felt. That's why I stayed away. I didn't want to risk telling you that I loved you.'

'Because of Freddie?'

'Yes. He needs so much of my time and attention. It just didn't seem fair to involve you in my life at the moment.'

'I thought it was because you weren't interested in me,' she admitted. 'Especially when I saw you with Alex Ross that day.'

'Really?' He groaned. 'I wish I'd known that. Alex had asked me to meet her in Rock so we could discuss this new clinic she's involved with. There's nothing going on between us, Alison, I promise you.'

'I believe you.' She tipped back her head and looked at him. 'I would never make you choose between me and Freddie. He needs you, and I'm happy to wait for however long it takes.'

'Thank you.' He kissed her gently. 'I don't want to wait, though. I want us to be together now, not at some point in the future. I need you beside me, Alison. If there are problems, I know we can solve them if we do it together—you, me, Sam and Freddie.'

Alison wound her arms around his neck. Jack was right. There was no problem too big that they couldn't solve together. Her heart overflowed with love when he set her on her feet and led her to the stairs. This was the start of a whole new life for all of them.

EPILOGUE

It was the day of Maggie and Adam's wedding, and it appeared that the whole of Penhally Bay had turned out to wish them well. The local church was packed as the couple made their vows. Maggie looked lovely in a simple white dress and carrying a bouquet of spring flowers, and Adam looked so handsome in his dark suit. They made a perfect couple and everyone was thrilled for them.

Alison sat at the back of the church with Jack and the boys, and cried throughout the service. It was just so beautiful and so moving, especially in view of what had happened to her. Jack took her hand and held it tightly, and she knew that he felt as emotional as she did, and for the same reasons, too. They were so in tune with one another that it was hard to imagine being without him now, and she didn't try. Jack was part of her life now and she was part of his—they were inseparable.

Maggie and Adam had decided not to have a reception. As they had explained, they wanted to be on their own more than anything else, and everyone had understood. Alison followed the rest of the party outside as everyone went to wave them off. When Maggie tossed her bouquet to the crowd, Alison automatically reached for it, but missed. It wasn't until a great cheer erupted that she discovered Jack had caught it.

He grinned as he handed it to her. 'This is for you.'

'Thank you.' Alison laughed as she took it from him, then gasped when he dropped to one knee in front of her. 'What are you doing?'

'What do you think?'

He gave her a wicked grin, then called Freddie over and whispered something to him. The little boy solemnly felt in his pocket and drew out a velvet-covered box, which Jack then gave to Sam. Alison's heart was racing as her son proudly handed the box to her.

'Alison Myers, will you do me the honour of becoming my wife?' Jack said as everyone held their breath.

'I…er…um…' Alison tailed off and swallowed. Her hands were shaking so hard that she could barely open the box, and when she finally managed it, she gasped again. The ring was gorgeous, a diamond solitaire in a delicate platinum setting.

'I don't want to rush you, my love, but I'm starting to get cramp,' Jack said, sounding slightly nervous. 'Please, say you'll marry me and put me out of my misery.'

'Yes,' she whispered, then took a deep breath and repeated her answer so that everyone could hear her. 'Yes, I'll marry you, Jack!'

All the guests went wild, but Alison was barely aware of what was going on around them. Jack stood up and kissed her, then took hold of the boys' hands.

'Right, let's go and see if Granddad would mind looking after you two for a couple of hours.' He smiled at Alison, a smile that was filled with promise. 'Alison and I have things to do this afternoon.'

He led the children through the crowd, pausing to accept congratulations along the way. His father was talking to Lucy, and they both turned and smiled when they saw him approaching.

'Granddad!' Freddie suddenly shouted, catching sight of Nick. He and Sam went racing off, but Jack stopped dead. He couldn't believe that Freddie had spoken at last—yet wasn't it fitting that it should have happened today?

A wave of happiness enveloped him as he looked back at Alison. He'd had so many doubts when he had come back to Penhally Bay, but it had worked out far better than he had hoped. Not only did he have a son he adored, he had found the woman he wanted to spend the rest of his life with. He had to be the luckiest man alive!

* * * *

Special Offers
In the Village Collection

Welcome to Penhally Bay—
a Cornish coastal town with a big heart!

On sale
2nd December 2011

On sale
6th January 2012

On sale
3rd February 2012

Collect all 3 volumes!

Save 20%
on all Special Rele

Find out more at
www.millsandboon.co.uk/specialreleases